A PROMISE OF VENGEANCE

RULES OF VENGEANCE, BOOK I

GIACOMO GIAMMATTEO

INFERNO PUBLISHING COMPANY

Print ISBN 978-1-940313-69-6

Electronic ISBN 978-1-940313-68-9

 Created with Vellum

CONTENTS

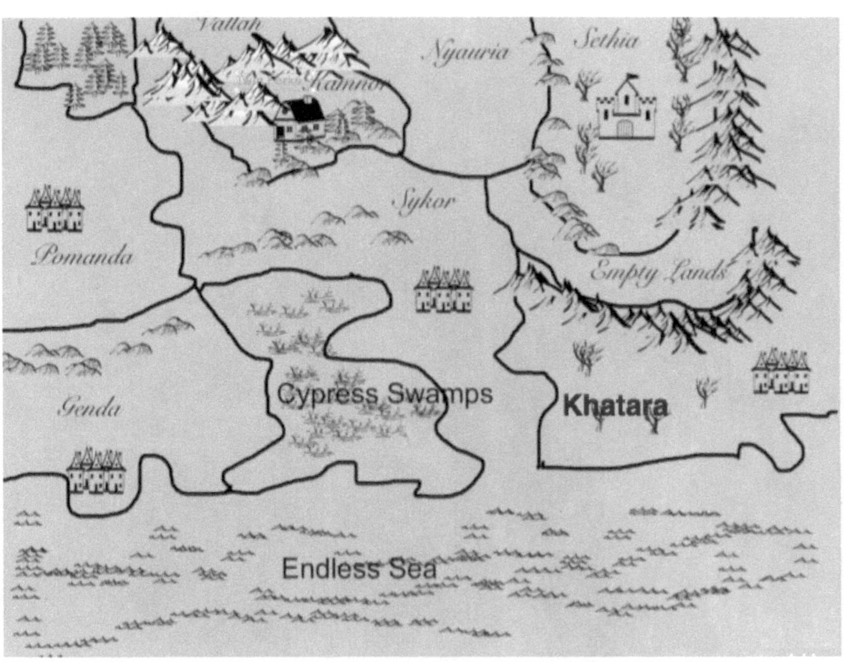

Known Map of North Forlandia

MEMORIES

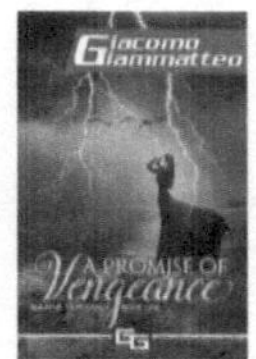

My name is Aentarra du Savarra. I don't know who should tell this story, me or my father. Probably him. He fought the Darkness Wars. He started the Wars of Light.

I cringed saying that. Technically it should have been called the War of the Lights. I hated things to be wrong or out of place. Everything should have its proper position in life. But even nature made stupid mistakes—put five legs on a frog or something ridiculous. When I found things like that, I killed them. I couldn't abide having five-legged frogs hopping around.

So anyway, yes, it should be father who tells this story, but father is dead, so I'll have to tell it after all.

~

Nobody remembers how things got started; in fact, nobody remembers anything before the time when my father and Lukaan were adults—that's the first memory anyone has of them. Despite that, life was wonderful—until the dorgans came. They appeared out of rifts, tears in the fabric of space. We fought against them in the Darkness Wars, a horrible time when millions of people died and all the worlds seemed in turmoil.

We eventually won, and father and Lukaan became heroes. Afterward the people established a new order. Each of the seven worlds designated a person to be their representative—a Light—and the seven of them formed the Council of Lights. My father held the High Seat. He was the Eternal Flame. The Light of Lights.

He had many names but after centuries, the name everyone feared the most was "He Who Drank the Darkness." That name made people remember his power. When they remembered, they grew afraid. The few who weren't afraid were jealous—especially Lukaan.

I shook my head to chase away the memories. I thought that maybe if I shook hard enough they would go away forever. They never did, though. Kept coming back.

My father was a visionary, always preparing me for the future. The most important things he taught me were the Rules of Vengeance. As a little girl, I sat on his lap and we practiced the lesson over and over.

RULES OF VENGEANCE

"When someone strikes you what is your response?" he asked me.

I remember sighing when he asked the question. It seemed like the thing to do.

"You should laugh. Laugh heartily, then walk away," I said.

"And the next day, when the insult is fresh in your mind?"

"Seek them out. Embrace them. Befriend them." I looked to him to see if it was right.

A smile lit his face. "And after your heart cools?"

"Disable them. Make them suffer. Destroy them."

He smiled and held me tightly. I remember the warmth of his hug, the pride in his voice. "You have learned well, my daughter."

So now you know how things got started, but the worst though, was when—

I looked around, thought I heard something. *A rift opening?* While I searched, thoughts popped into my head.

Perhaps I shouldn't say so much. Perhaps I should let you find out on your own.

SETHIAN PLOTS

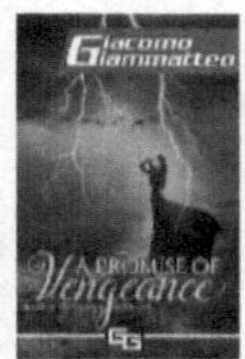

Sethian Desert
1364 AE (After Exile)
First Cycle of the Second Moon
Third Calendar of Light

*L*ukaan sought the most remote corner of Sethia, a spot where the shield might be more vulnerable, though he had yet to discover a weak spot or even a hint of how the shield got its strength.

Just like Antar's manor, he thought, stirring memories from the deepest recesses of his mind.

Memories of Antar, his trusted friend—later, his most bitter foe. Memories of the Darkness Wars, when he and Antar basked in the glory of victory—when the seven worlds of Nelstar worshiped and idolized them. Memories of the power that infused his soul whenever he used the Sacred Book. The ecstasy...

How good it would feel to be a god again.

Sethian Desert

Hot, pitiless winds tore granules of sand from the parched earth and a death–black cloak whipped about his frame, slapping the loose ends against his calves. Lukaan raised his hands to the winds and invoked a mystic call—the winds stilled.

He unleashed a barrage of forces that once razed cities and flattened mountains. Lightning shot from a clear sky and BlackFire erupted from his hands. Steaming fissures gouged wounds in the ground, spewing fire and rock, while a tempest of winds hurled brush and trees. Finally, the earth itself raised and crashed against the impregnable barrier—all to no avail.

He could see the snow on the mountains in the distance, smiling at him, taunting. Freedom so close, yet untouchable.

snow in mountains

The air rippled and the ground throbbed. He took a moment to calm himself, then Shifted to the Sethian Palace.

Lukaan's chamber grew cold, dampened with the eerie mist that haunted the palace. It oozed across the marble floor, writhed up the steps, and slunk around his boots.

He remembered a time when he had ruled; when he was worshiped; when he was not imprisoned in this forsaken land of Sethia; when the sounds of steel-against-steel rang in his ears and the feel of mind-against-mind sang to his heart.

He shuddered at the thought of freedom. It had been so long, so very long. But he would—

The prickling sensation of power interrupted his thoughts.

*M*elissara entered, bowing low. "You summoned me, Lord?"

Her words rode on a confident wave. She was one of the few who could look upon his countenance for more than a few heartbeats. But she knew that the smart dog did not show the master all its teeth, so her head remained bowed.

An aura surrounded Lukaan now, a dark, forbidding presence that threatened prying eyes.

"I can still sense the boy, Melissara. Why do we not have him?"

Images of death stole into her thoughts. Dared her to answer wrong. "It is my error, Lord. Perhaps I should have—"

"I know who is to blame. Inform the Victa commander that Twin Forks is to be destroyed. If the boy survives, bring him to me."

With her head still bowed, hair dusting the floor, Melissara backed across the cold marble. "Yes, Lord. I will see it is done."

The eerie mist climbed up Lukaan's legs, caressed him. *Soon the mortals will pay the price for siding with Mikkellana. Soon, they will all pay.*

HUNTED

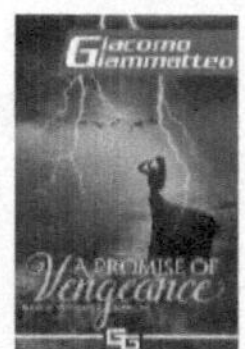

925 A.F. (After Founding)
Second Cycle of the Second Moon—Reunion

The mug of ale brushed Rhaven's lips, though he took no sip. The brew was fresh—fresher than the air in the tavern—but he would need his wits about him this night. Four men at the corner table had watched him all through the meal; he felt sure they had come to kill him—or to try.

Out of habit he reached to scratch the bottom of his right ear, most of it missing thanks to a group who had come for him years ago. Despite the time that had passed, odd sensations continued to bother him—tingling, itching, and an occasional twinge of pain.

A gentle push moved his plate to the center of the table. He closed both hands around the mug and set it close to him. His elbows brushed his dark cloak aside as he cast casual glances about the tavern. Bits of conversations bounced around the room, and stale smoke from pipe tobacco clung to candlelight and clustered in corner pockets.

tavern

The serving girl stared at his still-full mug, a scowl on her face like she'd just lost a copper. "Somethin' wrong with the ale?"

"The ale is fine. Leave me to my meal and come back when I call."

Before long, two of the men headed toward the door. They kept their eyes focused ahead of them, making sure not to look in Rhaven's direction. The third man pushed his chair back, catching it on an upturned floor plank. Rhaven suspected the last man would wait to follow Rhaven when he left. He wondered once again what they wanted him for.

He sat for a few more moments, long enough to make them anxious, then called for the serving girl, paid her, and left. *They will probably be waiting in the alley by the butcher's shop, where it is dark and cramped.*

A brisk pace carried Rhaven along the cobblestone streets, dusty from the day's business and the lack of rain. The last of the four men followed him out of the inn, though the man kept a good distance between them. Rhaven breathed the thick air, the scent of a coming rain lingering. The butcher's shop lay around the next bend. Rhaven's hands twitched; it had been a while since he'd killed a man.

He rounded the corner. Two of them hid in the shadows. *The other must be in the alley.*

cobblestone street in alley

It was a typical maneuver for an ambush—two would approach from the front, one in the alley from the right side, and the one following him from behind. When they closed to about six paces, the two in front reached for their swords. Rhaven drew a knife from a strap inside his cloak and threw it, striking one of them in the chest.

The man gasped, staggering back as he fumbled to remove the blade. Rhaven rushed forward to keep them off balance. They would have expected him to retreat, or at the least, to stop and fight. They wouldn't anticipate a charge. The second man had his sword half-drawn when Rhaven's sai pierced his throat, blood gurgling out like a gutted deer.

One man was dead and one injured, but Rhaven wasted no time. He continued his charge, dispatched the man still struggling with the knife in his chest, then spun to face the one from the alley on his right. The man attacked, swinging his blade with a great deal of vigor and inexperience. The sai in Rhaven's left hand caught the blade and twisted, snatching it from his hand. Before the man could retreat, the other sai found a channel between his ribs and into his heart.

The fourth man arrived just as the third one fell. He turned to escape. Rhaven drew a knife from his boot sheath and threw it, catching the man on the back of the leg, a hamstring shot. A scream pierced the night as the man collapsed to the pavement, then crawled to the wall and propped himself up.

Rhaven approached. "Why did you try to kill me?"

"The reward. But we wouldn't have killed you if we could have taken you alive."

"You should pay more for your information. A few extra coppers might have saved your life."

The man's eyes sparkled. "Is it money? I can get you gold."

"I'm no longer wanted, that's what I meant about the coppers." Rhaven slid a sai into the man's lungs. "Die slowly, friend."

He cleaned both sai then sheathed them, his black cloak swirling as he walked down the street.

Three horses charged past Rhaven, their hooves pounding against the stone raising a raucous clamor. Two riders dismounted and rushed toward the tavern. The last one stayed with the horses. Rhaven's long strides soon had him standing beside the man.

"Have you heard, stranger? Victas in Kamnor, heading toward Twin Forks!"

Rhaven's heart skipped a beat or two. For a moment he stood there, rigid as a tree stump, mute as a rock.

"Victas!" The man repeated himself. "We just came from Sykor and got the report from a guard post."

"Time to leave Barclaen," Rhaven said.

A puzzled look came over the rider's face. "No need, mister. They'll never get here."

"I know," Rhaven said, then went to get his mount.

He entered the stable and tossed a coin to the boy, half-asleep by the first stall. "Get up, boy, I need my horse." The stable smelled cleaner than most; in fact, straw proved the dominant odor. The boy took good care of things.

The boy bounced to his feet and stammered out a reply. "Sorry, sir, I wasn't...I mean I didn't—"

"Nothing wrong with sleeping," Rhaven said. "Get my mount ready fast and you might earn an extra copper."

Hay stuck to the boy's clothes and lay in his hair, but he didn't take time to brush it out. "I'll get him right now, sir." He raced toward the stall that held Argus.

The boy's hands worked like a rat chewing rope. He unlatched the stall door, moved the bucket out of the way, grabbed the reins, and led the horse into the main area of the barn.

"Did he give you any trouble? That horse can be stubborn."

"He wouldn't let me do nothin' but feed him. I tried to brush him and thought he'd have my arm for supper. If I'd been in there behind him..."

"You must be good for him to let you get that close. He doesn't like many people." Rhaven grabbed the blanket and saddle then walked him out of the barn, the eager stablehand trailing him like a day-old duckling.

"Anything I can get for you, sir?"

Rhaven seated himself then tossed a silver coin to the boy. "Careful where you spend this, and don't let anyone take it from you." With that, he clicked on the reins and tapped his heels. "Let's go, Argus. We head to Kamnor."

PEDNOR'S GROVE

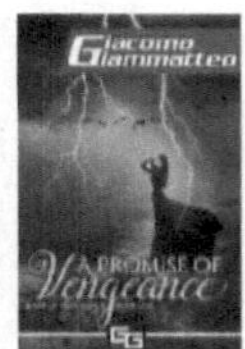

925 A.F. (After Founding)
Second Cycle of the Second Moon—Reunion

The morning sun heated the air and whisked the scent of humans up into the pass, a redolent trace of pines and mountain laurels riding along with it. Bokk savored it with a rapid flick of his tongue; it had been a long time since he had feasted on human flesh.

He removed the axe from his belt and crept behind a rock on the far side of the pass, green scales brushing the ground like a rasp scraping splintered oak. Black, beady eyes as keen as a hawk's scanned the streets and the town square. Bokk made note of the men with swords, and the women returning from the fruit vendor with children in tow. Two dogs also caught his eye, both of them at the far side of town; they would not spoil the approach.

Bokk ducked his head when three men exited the inn. Pednor's Grove counted a small population of retired Sykoran Guards, and even though the sharpest-eyed scout would find it difficult to see Bokk from this distance, he would not risk alerting the village. He had learned well his father's teachings of caution and wisdom, and how they shared the same den.

Brood Leader Trull slithered alongside Bokk, a sibilant whisper on his lips. "How many Sykorans?"

The scout's tongue flicked with each of his slow heartbeats. "Thirty to forty at most, but I count no more than seven with swords. If we take the back trail and keep to the woods, they will have no warning."

Trull nodded as he straightened his battle axe then made his way back to the patrol leaders. "Move. But slowly. Quietly."

The patrol leader stared down at the little ones playing in the square. He winced before asking the question. "And the children?"

The brood leader's black eyes bore into him. "Leave no one alive."

Bokk joined Trull as they made their way toward the village. "This won't take long."

"Not long at all," Trull said, then called to Kron. "Scout ahead at the next two villages—Treaschwig and Twin Forks. We will finish here before dusk, and I intend to march into the night." His claws scraped the edge of his axe as he spoke. "And take Jorr with you. Teach him well."

*L*ater that evening Brood Leader Trull marched the Victa army through Pednor's Grove, through the smoke and smoldering flames and stench of death. Dread filled his bones and clung to every scale. The Master had been explicit. Everyone in Twin Forks must die.

TWIN FORKS

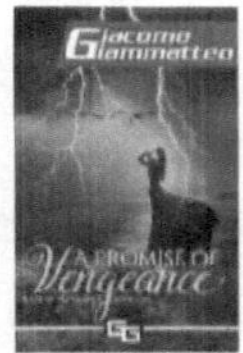

925 A.F. (After Founding)

Second Cycle of the Second Moon—Reunion

breath of cold air fresh from the long winter's romp rolled into the valley. Rahg's face chafed from the sting but he held steady the aim, sighting down the shaft of his arrow at the target twenty paces ahead. Crisp air charged his lungs, and the muscles in his forearm twitched. He blew a nagging lock of brown hair from his eyes, then let the arrow fly toward the old tree stump. Rahg's taunting began while the shaft still shook from the strike. "That's almost dead center—less than two fingers away—you can't win."

"Don't spend that money yet. You left me a clean shot." Lanky legs carried Darstan toward the target, where his black boots dusted the line scratched in the dirt. All the while, his eyes remained fixed on the target. Rahg had made a good shot, and it would take a near perfect one to get inside it. Darstan focused on the center circle until nothing else existed—like a single star in a crowded summer sky. He slowly drew the bowstring and released it with one fluid motion; there would be no wobble on this shaft.

Darstan's laughter drowned the thud of the arrow as it struck near center. "Two copper dirnars, Rahg."

"Damn, you're lucky. You'd never make that shot again."

"Maybe not, but I don't need to. Just pay what you owe."

"Next time—"

"Next time will be the same. You won't beat me until you listen to Kor Trasken." Darstan's voice was naturally as deep as a well, but he lowered it even more and slipped into his best imitation of Kor. "Hold your aim too long and that arrow will never hit the mark. You must be quick, Rahgnar. Quick!"

Laughter still had hold of both of them when they succumbed to the lure of a towering emerald and plopped down by its trunk to enjoy the morning.

"Great day," Darstan said, and stretched out on new shoots of grass.

"We should be watching the sheep."

sheep grazing

"Where we should be is fishing with Eru and Tomas. If you had done your chores we could be."

"Yeah, yeah. Did you see that both moons were full last night? They say the fish bite best during a Reunion."

Darstan grabbed a twig to chew. "Sounds like Tobias talking. He's always telling tales about Ranal and Ranalla. He once told me if I walked with a girl during a Reunion she'd be sure to kiss me."

"Well?"

"I guess you'll have to wait until a Reunion to find out—or until you get a girl." Darstan laughed to himself. *Poor little brother hadn't even had his first kiss yet.* "And don't start dreaming about Kanella again. We have sheep to tend."

"Blasted sheep can watch themselves," Rahg said, and leaned against the tree to sulk. And to dream about Kanella.

~

A column of emeralds looked down upon the crowns of spruce, pine, hickory, and even firs, all sprouting from roots planted deep in the hillside. Across the lush green valley another pair of eyes watched both the sheep and the boys. Amber eyes haunted a mask of thick gray fur as it stalked the sheep nearest the edge of the woods. A guttural growl rumbled in its throat and a long tongue licked sanguinary lips. "Play while you can, boys."

sheep near woods

The bleat of a small ewe focused the creature's attention on the prey. This ewe would feed many pups. The hunter pounced as the sheep approached the woods. Death was nearly instant, but the ewe managed to sound an alarm before giving way. The rest of the flock screamed and ran toward the village, the clamor bringing Darstan and Rahg to their feet.

~

"The sheep!" Darstan jumped to his feet, nearly tumbling down the hill as he ran, leaping over rocks and gnarled roots of old oaks, and grabbing for the ridged bark of small pines to break his descent. Rahg trailed by only a heartbeat. The bottom of the incline folded into gentle flat ground, and Darstan dashed across the valley floor, crushing new shoots of grass—standing tall like little green soldier—with each stride.

"Right behind you, Dar!"

Darstan and Rahg both nocked an arrow and let them fly, but the creature bounded into the woods. They raced to the grove where the animals huddled.

"Did you see it, Darstan?"

Darstan brushed calming hands over each of the sheep. "How many are gone?"

sheep huddled for protection

Rahg did a quick count. "Just one. Did you see what it was?"

"Calm down, Rahg, you sound like the sheep. It was a wolf, that's all." Darstan began to gather the frightened flock. "I'll get the sheep. You fetch the arrows. No sense in wasting good arrows."

Rahg shook his head, mumbling. *Wasn't any wolf. I know that.* His eyes flickered from shadow to shadow as he approached the woods. Whatever got that ewe would not catch him unaware. He nocked another arrow and held his bow ready—wolf, or whatever it was—he was taking no chances.

"Hurry up, Rahg. We need to get back."

"I've got 'em." *He sounds more like father every day.* Rahg gathered the arrows then backed away from the woods, alert for trouble.

Conversation came infrequently on the walk home, and what little did occur consisted of Rahg speculating on the punishment they would receive. "He's going to be angry, Dar."

"I'll tell him. No sense in both of us taking the blame."

*M*agmar's hand crashed on the table in the kitchen. "I thought you two were expert bowmen."

Rahg let silence cover him. He knew when not to talk, and he didn't dare tell Magmar that he thought it wasn't a wolf. *Wouldn't believe me anyway.*

"It's my fault," Darstan said. "I—"

"Nonsense! The blame's on both of you. Now get ready for supper."

~

*W*hile Rahg finished preparing supper, Darstan set plates on the bare wooden table, guilt and remorse evident on his face. It was no wonder Magmar was upset; he had the burden of raising Rahg *and* Darstan as well as tending the farm. *And we can't even watch the sheep,* Darstan thought, then let his eyes wander about the house.

The absence of a mother showed. There were no decorations on the windows, no flowers in the sills, and the boys had socks that needed mending and britches waiting for needle and thread. But despite all that, Darstan had the blessings of fortune. Magmar had taken him in when no one else would have him, and Rahg had proved to be as good a friend as a brother.

The harsh sound of Magmar's boots on the porch alerted Darstan. "Better hurry, Rahg."

The supper table was quiet, save for the hushed sounds of food being eaten, when Magmar broke the silence. "I was about your age, Darstan, when I nearly lost a whole flock of my father's sheep. Was over a girl in the village who was passing by and—"

Darstan laughed. "Sorry to interrupt, but if Rahg hadn't been daydreaming of Kanella, we might have seen that wolf."

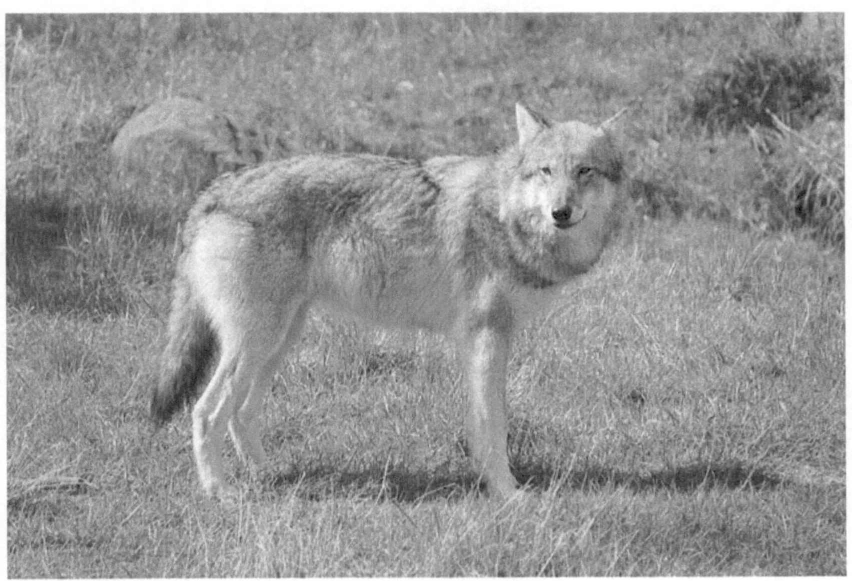

wolf

"What's done is done," Magmar said.

"I wonder why the wolves are coming in so close," Darstan said. "That's the third attack this spring. Zedd Corin lost a lamb, and wolves got a ewe from Fenn Parker."

Magmar shook his head and his brow wrinkled. "Strange."

Darstan stared at the weather-beaten skin on his father's face. *He's worried about something, but not wolves.*

~

*R*ahg had nightmares about the wolf all night, causing him to sleep late. Darstan and Magmar were already eating when he got to the table.

"About time you got up, Rahg, we have a lot of chores to do."

Rahg poked his head out the door to check on the weather. "Must have gotten cold last night, there's frost on the ground."

"I said we have chores to do, Rahg."

"I'll do mine tomorrow. Meet me later, Dar, but don't tell father about the chores."

Rahg ran to his favorite spot. He grabbed a root to chew then lay on his back and rested his head against the trunk of a towering emerald. No tree was bigger, save a blackthorn, and none held more beauty. The leaves shined like real emeralds, yet they were small and soft as cotton—almost as if they didn't belong to a giant like this. And the leaves stayed with it during the harshest winters. He reached out to scratch a piece of bark, white as lamb's fur and smooth as polished hickory. The bark smelled fresh, and it tasted tangy. He shivered when he took a bite.

He pushed himself farther up the trunk and stared into the mountains surrounding the valley. Heavy snow wrapped the shoulders of the highest peaks, like a shawl tucked around a grandmother's neck. Beyond that, in the Great Whites, blizzards raged at the summits.

It was said that nothing lived there save rock dragons. People always talked about them, repeating tales heard from bards or men with too much ale, but Rahg had never met anyone who had seen one, unless he counted old Tobias, who claimed to have fought one when he was with the Sykoran Guard.

They were chasing bandits, or so Tobias had said, and followed their trail past the northern edge of Kamnor to the foothills of the Whites.

Rahg smiled. He had heard the story so much he knew it word for word. He could picture Tobias sitting at Havril's Inn, sipping ale and telling his story. He'd been telling that story for so long it was like a legend. He would likely be at the inn tonight, cornering strangers or anyone who had heard it less than a dozen times. Rahg could almost hear him now.

"I'll tell you it was a frightful experience."

Tobias never failed to begin the story with those exact words and the same tone of voice. At this point he also wiped his brow and took a long swig of ale before continuing—as though he had just returned a short bit ago, exhaustion still with him.

"Frightful! We followed the bandits up from the Free Lands, ridin' hard. For nearly three days we drove those horses with barely no rest. They were tired. Spent. Fact is, old Erad's horse gave-out. Just plain lay down and died. We were close to Twin Forks so Erad came here while we tracked the bandits. Followed 'em all the way to the Whites, then the tracks got real confusing.

foothills of Great White Mountains

"We found two horses dead, with other tracks that went off in all directions. The two dead ones were part eaten. The tracks were all muddled and didn't make any sense. Must've been wolves, we figured, so we decided to split-up—me and three others going west, and Tadge and his four east. All of a sudden we hear this sound, like...like a...well, it was so unusual I still don't know how to describe it, but it was a terrible sound."

Rahg laughed. As often as Tobias told that story, he still left that part in. Told it the same way every time. *I'd think after so many years he'd know just how to describe it.*

"Bad as that was, what came out of the mountains was worse. A giant of a creature jumped down on us from the rocks. Was about twelve feet, head to tail, and must've weighed fifteen or twenty stone. It had gray scales all over, covering up brownish-gray skin. Now, if that wasn't enough to scare the demons out of us, the teeth were. Had a whole mouthful of 'em, like blades on a dagger. And eyes the same color as the blood drippin' off them teeth. It was a beast. Sort of half-lizard and half somethin' else—dragon, I guess."

Tobias always stopped to take several long swallows of ale right after describing the rock dragon. He wanted it to sink-in, Rahg presumed. Then he'd place both his hands on the edge of the table and lean over it, his positioning and grim expression prepping the listeners for the rest of the tale.

"It hit Tadge first."

He never failed to whisper that part, Rahg remembered, and his ploy always worked. Tobias had their undivided attention.

"Took him and Amos out before we even got our horses turned around, with them so frightened and all. I ordered the men to dismount so we could get up on the ledge—at least there we didn't have to fight the horses and that creature too. We put about six arrows into the thing but not before it got Tadge's other two men. Then it turned and came toward us.

"Only had time to hit it with one arrow apiece before it got to the rock. It started up that ledge like walkin' on flat ground—big, sharp claws finding the tiniest cracks to grab hold of. It was almost on us when Karrs put his sword right in the creature's eye. It howled so loud I nearly fell off the ledge, but I grabbed my sword with both hands and plunged hard as I could, right into its skull. That one did him in. His claws loosed-up and his head reared-back, then he fell all the way down, landin' on sharp rocks below.

"We picked up what was left of the bodies and gave 'em a good burial before comin' back to the village. It took me three to four days of solid drinkin' before I could make myself think straight again. That's when I decided I'd had enough of the soldierin' and settled down right here in Twin Forks."

Rahg smiled again. He didn't know whether rock dragons really did exist, but just in case, he'd be sure to stay clear of the Great Whites, though he did wonder what lay on the other side.

Rahg looked to where the sun sat over the mountains and realized it was almost time to meet Darstan. *He should be done with the chores by now,* Rahg thought, and quickened his pace toward the village. He was just coming to the bend in Buckhorn Trail when he heard the greeting.

"Hooo, Rahg."

Rahg ran the rest of the way to the crossing by Havril's Inn. He hopped from one rock to another, taking four stops to get across the creek, though he almost slipped on one of the rocks. The stream gurgled and splashed over stones as it made its way south to the White River. Spring thaw had not come to the mountains yet; in another month it would be too deep to cross. "Finally finished with those chores?"

"And lucky to be done so soon. Father worked the sweat out of me."

They made the turn toward Havril's and saw Tomas heading their way, a fishing pole resting on his shoulder. *It's a wonder he hasn't worn a spot in his shirts,* Rahg thought. "Didn't you catch enough yesterday?"

"Didn't catch any," Tomas said, "That's why I'm going back. Get your poles and come along."

The invitation proved enticing but they had already planned the day. "We're going to the inn," Rahg said, "but if you catch any, bring some to us."

*B*oredom soon had them wishing they accepted Tomas's invitation; the day had proved a big disappointment. They heard a few stories from Sykoran traders as they haggled over goods, and Eru's dog, Jumper, bit Havril, providing some excitement, but nothing of consequence—no tales from the great cities, no swordplay, not even anyone caught picking a purse.

Rahg tossed another stick to Jumper, trying to keep him busy lest he bite someone else. "We've wasted half the day, Darstan, and there's nothing to do." He grabbed the stick from Jumper's mouth; the dog proved to be persistent if nothing else. Rahg had his arm cocked back to throw the stick when he heard someone calling.

"Darstan, Rahg, have you heard the news?"

Eru rushed toward them, dodging a merchant's cart. His sentences fell short as he fought to catch breath. "A traveler from Sykor. Here, in Twin Forks. Mother saw him at the market, and said he'd be at Havril's tonight. She thinks the news is bad, 'cause he wouldn't say anything until he gets to Havril's."

"We'll be there." Rahg rushed the words out then turned to Darstan. "Let's go. We'll get supper and hurry back. We'll want a good seat so we have to be early."

Darstan jumped to his feet and raced toward home. "See you tonight, Eru."

~

A pair of Victa scouts crouched behind the thick brush guarding the perimeter of the town, black beady eyes taking count of each villager. Their green scales served as camouflage with the new foliage, and except for the bloodstained lips, they appeared a part of the forest itself. "This one will fall easily," the young Victa warrior hissed, unable to contain his excitement.

"They will all fall easily," Kron said. "The small villages first, but once the Master is free, even Sykor and Khatara will crumble."

Kron's thick tongue licked scaly lips. "Come, Jorr, they await our report." Kron moved slowly, careful not to snap twigs or rustle leaves.

"Step lightly, Jorr; it would not do to alert the villagers before we attack."

THE TRAVELER'S TALE

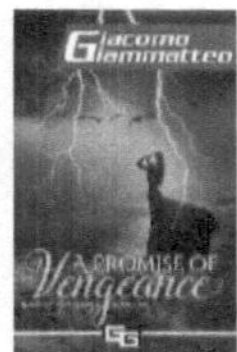

*R*ahg and Darstan raced up the steps to Havril's Inn, worried about getting a good seat. Darstan hit the landing first and shoved the door open. "Half the tables are full. Eru must have told everyone."

Darstan stood just inside the door and scanned the inn. Benches and tables crowded a big rectangular room and sat atop old oak planks held fast with iron nails. A fat candle adorned each table, and the chairs, if not easy to sit on, were sturdy and level. A huge fieldstone fireplace as big as a peddler's wagon sat near the center of the room on the outside wall. It had a hearth that could seat the whole Nester family—all eight of them.

Darstan tugged on Rahg's sleeve and pointed to a man near the center of the room. "That must be him."

The traveler stood taller than Kor Trasken by half a hand, but he was beanstalk-thin and had a long, twisted nose that hooked down toward his mouth. A dusty-brown cloak and haggard gray britches did nothing to reveal his occupation.

"Doesn't look like any bard I've seen," Rahg said.

"Eru never said he was a bard, Rahg; you're the one that thought that up. Looks more like a soldier to me." Darstan grabbed Rahg's sleeve and dragged him toward an open table. "C'mon, these seats won't last long."

Ella Havril and her younger sister, Kora, were charged with serving the ale while Ella's mother and four other girls served the food. Ella dodged old Blake Carter, already with too much ale in him and stumbling around like a cow with the fever. Then she adeptly spun to the side while holding four mugs of ale in each hand.

"Look at that, she didn't spill a drop."

"Never does," Darstan said.

～

*E*lla was serving the table next to them when she called out to Darstan, her soft voice somehow piercing the ruckus from the boisterous patrons surrounding her. "Will it be the usual tonight?"

Darstan flashed a smile. "We're here for the duration, Ella. Everyone from here to Herschwig knows about the traveler."

Ella took a deep breath. She had already stared too long at Darstan, and if she didn't leave soon she risked the sting of gossip.

"I like your dress, Ella. Is that a new one?"

Ella's younger sister, Kora, stopped on her way to the kitchen. "Don't get too flustered, sister. You might fall over."

Ella delivered a warning kick to Kora's leg, then turned and smiled at Darstan and Rahg. "I'll be right back with your drinks."

～

*E*lla grabbed Kora's sleeve and tugged her along. "Kora! He might have heard you. You'd better not do anything like that again."

When they reached the kitchen, Kora stood for a moment, ogling Darstan. "He's the catch for you, Ella. Mercy's grace but he's handsome!"

Ella wrapped her hands around two mugs of ale and turned to leave, her cheeks as red as Kairen's roses. "Who?" she asked, feigning innocence.

"Who?" Kora laughed and an exaggerated sigh ushered in her words. "He's got eyes the color of almonds, and hair as black as night, and his—"

"Shut-up, Kora, or I promise, I'll—"

"Ella! Set those mugs down before you drop them." Mrs. Havril stood with her arms folded in front of her. "As for you, Kora, if I must tell you one more time about a girl's privacy... What's said in this family stays here!" The look in her eyes demanded a response.

"Yes, Mother," Kora said, then turned to her sister. "I'm sorry, Ella. I was just teasing."

Mrs. Havril unfolded her arms, nodding all the while. "All right. That's how sisters should act." She wrapped both arms around her girls, then leaned in close to hug them. "Now tell me who's so handsome that my girls can't serve drinks."

"Either one of those Fal-Thera boys. They're both good looking, but Darstan is enough to make me weep." Kora sighed as she peeked through the door to get another glimpse of him.

Mrs. Havril cuffed the back of Kora's head. "I have a notion that a girl as young as you shouldn't be so free with her talk." The scowl on her face became a snicker then laughter. She hustled Kora out of the way and peered through the door at Rahg and Darstan. "I say Rahg is the one to go after. A girl would spend all her life chasin' other women away from Darstan. Be like tryin' to keep bees from the honey; least-wise, till he gets old and fat."

Ella chuckled. "All men get old, mother, but not all of them get fat. Look at Kor Trasken."

"He's different, daughter. He's a soldier. Besides, most men do. And no sense riskin' heartaches over a man like that. Just set your mind to findin' a good, hardworkin' soul. That'd be what you want. Someone to put food on your table and a fire in your hearth. You don't want a man to be buildin' a fire in someone else's hearth." Mrs. Havril rustled Kora's hair. "That flashy smile won't make you happy, dear, but it just might break your heart."

"Oh mother!" Ella said, then exited the swinging doors with a smile on her lips, and several ales in each hand. She negotiated through the narrow paths separating the tables, then almost bumped into Magmar and Tobias. "Excuse me, Mr. Fal-Thera, Mr. Marek. It's crowded tonight."

"I can see that, lass," Tobias said. "Where's Rahg?"

"Just past the center of the room. He and Darstan have a good table."

Tobias chuckled as Ella squeezed by them. "You know, Magmar, she's got the prettiest blue eyes I've seen since your Marna was alive. She's a bright lass, too."

Magmar nodded, then laughed. "Tobias, trying to pay attention to everything you say is like trying to count raindrops."

~

*R*ahg scanned the inn, spying Magmar. The room held about eighty people, all in various stages of sitting, rising, or shuffling their way to and from the privies out back.

Darstan stood to wave them over. "Blast it, Rahg, Tobias is with him."

Rahg let his mug set heavy on the table. "We'll be lucky to even hear what the man has to say."

Magmar crossed the room, stopping to greet friends and neighbors, and continually nodding in response to Tobias's incessant chatter. When they reached the table, Magmar sat on Rahg's left, leaving the only available seat for Tobias next to Darstan. Rahg smiled and poked Darstan under the table. He received a hard left jab to his arm as reward.

"Has the ale gotten the better of you lads already? Why, I could tell you some stories about ale, and what it does to lads and men alike."

"The traveler is ready to speak," Magmar said. "Let's listen."

"I believe I know him," Tobias said, squinting while he searched for a striker to light his pipe. "I do know him. It's Beryl."

Havril rang the large bell hanging from the rafters near the kitchen. Everyone knew the signal, and the room soon settled down.

Thank the gods, Rahg thought as the traveler began to speak. His imagination had prepared him for a smooth flowing tale, a colorful picture painted by an artist of the language, but the man spoke in short, terse statements, facts, and details. A scout in the Sykoran patrol had more spark in his report than this man.

"As I said..."

The traveler's drab, lusterless voice made it difficult to concentrate.

"There are reports from all patrols. Victas are rousing. They've been spotted far outside their territory, and the Nyaurans reported Wolfen in their lands. You need to make preparations in case they come here, though I doubt they would; Twin Forks is far off the main trade routes."

The air in Havril's stilled, then people shouted the inevitable questions from every table.

"Victas! I thought they were long dead."

"Nobody's even seen a Victa unless you count Tobias's old tales."

Beryl spoke at the first break in the clamor. "Just because you haven't seen one doesn't mean they don't exist. The people in Genda have likely never seen a bear."

"What are they doing out of Sethia?" someone shouted.

"Why would they come here?"

"We can handle the Victas," Pieter said, though his voice rang with the sound of too many ales.

Tobias pushed his chair back and stood, pipe in hand. "Stop your screeching! The whole bunch of ya sound like Netter's old hen. As for you, Pieter, I'd wager if a Victa walked through that door he wouldn't need a weapon to send the whole pack of ya scurrying home. It's a lot different fightin' Victas than it is men. Puts the fear of the demon in you." Tobias puffed repeatedly on his pipe, the smoke bursting out in great clouds. "Let Beryl finish what he's got to say."

None of the men dared speak for fear of embarrassment, but Havril's wife held no reservations. "Tobias Marek, are you to tell us these tales of Victas and Wolfen and such are true?"

Tobias lowered his head and shook it slowly. He set his pipe on the table and stared around the room. His blue eyes had gone cold and the wrinkles on his face hardened. "You all know me. Some think I'm good only for tellin' tales. Others think I'm slower than a possum with a sack full of babies. But I'll not paint a dark sky blue, not at a time like this. Truth is, if the Victas are out it can only mean trouble. The Wolfen make it worse. But we can deal with Victas and Wolfen. What worries me is *why* are they coming? Why now? Does this mean the Banished Ones have found a way out? If so, then we're—"

The mention of the Banished Ones stopped all talking. Two or three people got up and left. Tobias stared at them, puffing on his pipe until someone mustered the courage to speak.

"What about Mikkellana and the good immortals? What about Aentarra?"

"I don't know about Mikkellana," Tobias said. "And as to some of them being good, well... there's not much to support that. When two wolves fight over the same ewe it makes little difference to the ewe which wolf wins." He picked up his pipe and tapped it once, then rekindled the fire. "As to Aentarra, I'd sooner eat a toad than meet her on the street. That one makes a serpent seem as sweet as peach pudding."

"What's wrong with Aentarra?" someone yelled.

Tobias thought for a moment, then addressed the question. "Guess that depends. The stories say if you greet her on the street she might kiss you or she might kill you." At that they all stayed quiet.

With that break, Beryl continued with his report. "I've seen tracks of a small Victa party not five leagues from where we sit, though it was across the border in Nyauran territory. Could have been hunters, but I doubt it. There..." Beryl paused, as if he didn't want to finish, but when he received a nod from Tobias he continued. "There was a rock dragon with them."

Dead silence followed the crowd's gasp. Rahg's stomach burned with pangs of dread. An image of the rock dragons flared in Rahg's mind, brought to life by Tobias' stories. He could picture their teeth—like daggers—and the scales dripping blood. "Gods be dead, Darstan. Rock dragons!"

Darstan nodded.

The crowd peppered Beryl with endless questions, while other voices offered a range of solutions. Amid it all, they somehow agreed to meet at Magmar's house later that evening.

After several more rounds of questions, Magmar suggested they leave. "Let's go, lads. It's late and we'll have to finish the chores before everyone comes to the house." Magmar headed toward the door.

Rahg grabbed Darstan by the arm. "I was planning on asking Kanella's father if I could call on her."

Before Darstan could say anything, Tobias came up beside them. "Don't mean to take the snap out of your day, lad, but we've got a meeting to hold tonight. There's no time to dally. Put yourself together and get going. We'll be at your father's house after supper to discuss things."

~

*K*or Trasken walked through the kitchen and into the parlor. He plopped on the seat at the end of the sofa, across from the fireplace. Ben Corin and Jed Nester plopped down next to him.

Darstan helped Magmar bring in a few more chairs, struggling to fit them in and still leave space to walk. The room could comfortably accommodate eight—twelve with extra chairs, but today twenty-one were packed inside.

Darstan had found enough seats for the older men, with one exception—Tobias sat on the flush-hearth, his chin resting on drawn-up knees. Darstan elbowed Rahg and whispered. "Tobias looks like a lad of twelve."

Brought out of his state of euphoria, Rahg glanced over, then chuckled as Ben's father offered his seat on the bench to Tobias only to be berated.

"Young fellow, I've spent days sleeping in places so bad it would make this seem like the queen's bed chamber. One time, had to sleep for three days wedged in a crevice covered with thorn bushes—three days! Had nothin' but water and a handful of nuts with me and couldn't make a sound for fear there'd be a bandit patrol nearby." Tobias shook his head. "Sittin' on a nice warm hearth won't bother me."

Darstan elbowed Rahg and smiled. He didn't dare laugh.

Kor Trasken started out the talks, explaining his strategy for defense of the town if it came to that. Rahg didn't understand anything of what he said, and soon found himself dreaming of Kanella and planning his own strategy—how to ask her father if he could walk with her.

Darstan jabbed him again. "Pay attention."

Rahg snapped alert just as Tobias began to speak.

"We have to assume this is a raiding party. A small group we can take care of, even several patrols, but if they've got a big force with rock dragons we'll need help. We need to split up into patrols and find them."

Rahg drifted-off again, dreaming of Kanella. He couldn't help it, despite the seriousness of the matter at hand.

"Magmar, we'll take Rahg and Darstan with us." Tobias raised his voice. "We'll leave at first-light. *If* Rahg is still with us, that is."

Rahg snapped to attention. He had only caught bits and pieces of the conversation. *Darstan can tell me the rest tonight.*

~

*R*ahg lay wide awake in bed, eyes refusing to close. "You still awake, Dar?"

Darstan rolled to his side. "Hard to sleep thinking about Victas. Seems as if everything changed in two days."

"I've been thinking about that wolf ever since the traveler came. I'll bet it was one of those Wolfen the traveler talked about."

"He said the Wolfen were in Nyauran, not Kamnor, but I don't know, Rahg. I don't know about anything anymore."

"What if we have to fight them?" Rahg stared out the window at the trees swaying to the night breeze. Too many shadows kept his fear alive.

"We'll do what we can if it comes to that."

"How are you going to fight lizards? You're scared to death of little snakes, let alone lizards as big as men."

"Snakes and lizards aren't the same. If they were snake-people I'd be more scared." Darstan rested his head on both of his hands as he stared at the blank ceiling. "This is all like a dream, Rahg, it'll go away."

"I'm scared," Rahg said. "I wish it was just a dream."

"Me too, Rahg. Me too."

Darstan stared at the ceiling, listening to Rahg toss in his bed. His stomach churned, roiled with something...bad. The feeling seemed familiar, almost like the uneasiness he got as a child after he had done something wrong... but he was doing nothing wrong now. He placed both hands over his stomach, then closed his eyes again and tried to think about good things, about anything to get his mind off of this...whatever it was.

THE FIRST PATROL

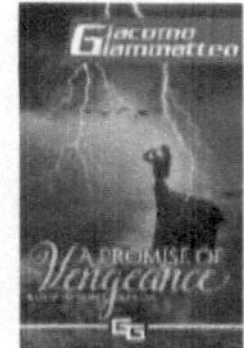

*R*ahg rose before the morning, worries from the night before tucked away in the recesses of his mind. He heated the water for khaffe and had eggs cooking when Darstan and Magmar entered. Rahg whistled as he placed mugs of khaffe on the table.

"You're up early," Darstan said.

"I was up before the birds. Ready to go on patrol."

"Better set another place, son. I invited Tobias to break fast with us." Magmar peered out the window. "Looks like he's coming now."

Rahg heard Tobias' horse, then the footsteps on the porch. The door opened with a jerk.

"Hope you lads cracked an egg or two for me." Tobias laughed as he pulled up a stout oak chair and took off his hat.

"Don't forget that hat when we leave, Tobias. You don't want your head to burn."

"I may not have much hair, lad, but at least I've got my head. I think you lost yours yesterday dreaming of Kanella."

Magmar laughed as he scraped the plate of the few potatoes that remained then scooped up his eggs with the bread. He nodded at Darstan, still with a half a plate full. "Eat up, Darstan. I need to pack the food, and you boys need to help Tobias."

Tobias gulped down the last of his meal, then stood. "Rahg, help me get the horses ready. Darstan, feed the animals."

Soon, they had the kitchen cleaned and the horses packed. "I see you lads wore your long sleeves and wool cloaks. Good thing. It'll get cold once we leave the valley." Tobias climbed in the saddle and tugged on the reins of his horse. "Let's go, lads. Got a lot of riding to do today."

Half an hour later they were riding on a knoll sprinkled with maples and emeralds. Rahg spotted Tomas and Eru tending sheep in the valley. He felt sure they had scowls painted on their faces after being forced to stay home. "Too young," Kor had said. Rahg gave a shrill whistle to grab their attention. They signaled back with a sluggish wave. Rahg couldn't blame them, even though fear had tightened his throat, the journey promised excitement.

By late morning they reached the upper rim of the valley, the foothills of the Rainbow Mountains and front door to the Great Whites. The mountains were harsh, untamed, and densely wooded. This was home to the gray wolf and mountain cat, and other things that people only whispered of. Rahg checked his sword and knife. "Did you check everything, Darstan?"

mountains, foothills to the whites

"I packed twenty-five arrows each." Darstan sat tall on his mount, black hair glistening in the morning sun. "Even as bad as you shoot, that's enough for you to hit four or five Victas."

"If we didn't need these arrows, I'd challenge you right now."

Tobias prodded his mount as they climbed to the first plateau, where a break in the tree line opened a view to the ridge. "There's Kor Trasken and his patrol."

Darstan spun in his saddle, squinting at four men on horseback far across the ridge. "You've got keen eyes, Tobias."

"Of course I got keen eyes. That's what smokin' a pipe'll do for you."

"What does smoking a pipe have to do with good eyes?"

Tobias shifted in his saddle and stared at Darstan. "When you've smoked a pipe as long as I have we can continue this discussion. Until then, you'll have to take my word for it."

"Where's Kanella?" Rahg asked. "Who's with her?"

"Not to worry, lad. She's at Havril's helping the other women with the children, but we left a score of armed men to guard them." Tobias fought back a smile. "Though with old Mrs. Ardanta, I don't think they'll need any protection."

Rahg relaxed. Twenty men with bows and swords could stand against a large force. No Victa patrol, not even a raiding party, could pose a threat to so many, not with the town offering such a solid defensive position.

"You know, lad, that Trasken girl handles a sword like a soldier. Saw her practicing with Kor one day. She's a good match for most men. If you two do wed, you better be watchin' yourself."

"Real funny, Tobias."

"Valley Falls," Magmar said. He reined in the horse but remained mounted. "Pretty sight, isn't it?"

valley falls

The roar of the falls rose toward Rahg with the spray of mist, falling just short of where they stood on the ledge. The breeze rushing up felt cool. Rahg breathed deep, filling his lungs with mountain air. The smell of pines proved stronger here, perhaps because of the falls, and he could almost taste the berries that hid in little copses where the ground flattened out.

"Let's go," Tobias said. "Can't afford to linger. Have a lot of ground to cover before nightfall."

Rahg almost fell from his saddle. "Nightfall! I thought this was a one day patrol."

"The others will be back before the moons stand tall, but we volunteered for the longest patrol. We'll be traveling to the gorge at Rainbow Falls then circle back by the high bridge. Thought you lads knew. We didn't pack that much food just to feed Rahg."

The trail steepened as they began the ascent and, as the day wore on, the emeralds and oaks disappeared, ceding to squatty pines and scrub brush that clung to rocks like a possum to tree bark. The distinctive croak of a raven brought Rahg's eyes to the sky where two of them romped on the wind, chasing each other like puppies. Rahg took a huge breath of crisp air to calm himself, but he couldn't shake the fear.

He tugged at his cloak, wrapping it around him to keep out the chill, a harsh reminder that winter had not relinquished its hold in the mountains. When the sun disappeared over the ridge, Rahg shivered, and he could not attribute it to the cold. He huddled to his mount to draw warmth, hoping to ease the trembling.

"Pay attention, Rahg. The darkness conceals danger."

Magmar's words fed the flames. Rahg found the courage to straighten, though it didn't help. Nerves jerked his head from side to side, seeking enemies, and all the while he prayed he found none.

"We're almost there," Magmar said. "Won't be long."

"No, not long," Tobias added.

Rahg's shock formed the questions. "Where? Almost where?"

"There's a big cavern a short distance away that has water," Tobias said. "That's where we'll spend the night."

Rahg got more comfortable as they neared the destination. He felt warmer, too, and though the wind increased and the temperature dropped, he no longer shivered. Rahg looked up to Ranal and Ranalla, thankful for the reunion as their bright glow rippled moonlight across the midnight–blue sky and sprinkled it over the forest.

Tobias dismounted and led his horse down a path shadowed in darkness, then signaled for them to follow. Rahg went first. Darstan fell in behind Rahg, and Magmar brought-up the rear. By the time they caught up to Tobias the trail had grown painfully narrow. A tree branch whipped back and caught Rahg's face, stinging like a whip.

"Careful," barked Tobias, an unusual sternness in his voice. "Don't break 'em. Don't want to leave any signs."

They'll be leaving signs on my face, Rahg thought. He looked back at Magmar, covering their tracks. Another branch slapped his face. "God's sake!"

"Quiet, lad. Watch where you're going and you won't get hit. Anyway, not much further now."

They twisted along several more trails, each more narrow than the previous one. A short while later Tobias took a tortuous path that led to higher elevations. Rahg fought with his mount, tugging on the reins while leaning forward to keep from falling. Tobias pulled aside a bush and exposed an entrance to a large cave.

"Calm the horses as you come through, these branches have thorns on them. Hurry, lad. Can't hold this all night."

"Hold it until I get past."

Once inside the cavern Rahg struck a torch. "This is huge!" Rahg said. "Darstan, can you believe this has been here all this time and we never knew. We'll have to bring Eru and Tomas up here."

cave entrance

"They'll never believe us if we don't show them," Darstan said. He sniffed the damp, stale air of the cave while he searched the depths. "I think half of Twin Forks could fit in here."

Magmar lit another torch and wedged it between two rocks near the center of the cave. "Darstan, you and Rahg take care of the horses. Make sure they're fed and watered, then make bed-rolls and light another torch. Tobias and I will gather firewood."

"Yes, Sir," Rahg snapped, pounding his fist to chest three times in the manner of a Sykoran soldier. He and Darstan both laughed.

"Enough!" Tobias almost leapt on top of them. He was only a breath away, and his words were sharp. Not at all like the Tobias they knew.

"I've seen Victa tracks for the last half a league or more. It looks like a small patrol, maybe five or six, but there could be more. So keep still. This is no game." Tobias started to leave, then turned back around.

"Yes, sir," Darstan said.

Rahg remained mute. Tobias' words rang in his ears like thunder.

Victas! They came on patrol to find Victas, but he never expected to see them. The laughter he shared with Darstan moments ago disappeared. "I'm sorry, Tobias."

"Don't be sorry, lad. I should have warned you earlier, but I didn't want to drop the shakes on you. Well, now you know. So let's keep quiet. We'll take turns standing watch."

"Yes, sir."

Tobias and Magmar returned, their arms loaded with scraps of deadwood. "There's more outside, Rahg, and a few rabbits and squirrels that Tobias brought for dinner. Darstan, prepare the food. Tobias and I will start the fire."

"We found plenty of wood in the cave," Rahg said.

Tobias nodded his head. "Good. We'll use the dry wood and replace it with what we gathered. Always replace what you use, lads, that way, if a storm catches someone unaware, there'll always be dry wood in the cave."

They soon had a fire going and the food cooked. Rahg didn't realize how hungry he was until the smell of rabbit hit him. He devoured the bread and cheese, and savored his piece of rabbit, but he wouldn't touch the squirrel. The memory of the first one he had ever shot still haunted him, a young one he had no business killing. He didn't know if he could ever bring himself to eat a squirrel.

"What do you think the Victas want?" The question had been tearing at Rahg's gut throughout supper.

Tobias tore a piece of meat from the rabbit's leg, chewing as he answered. "Who knows, lad? Could be they're just hungry, and this is a hunting party. Or they might feel we've wronged them somehow, something we don't even know we've done. Victas are strange like that. Or it might be that the Evil One himself has them stirred up."

"Evil One! What are you talking about? We're not to be scared with those tales." Darstan dislodged a piece of meat from between his teeth and spat. "Evil One. Come on, Tobias."

"So, you don't believe?" There wasn't any laughter in Tobias's voice. "Magmar, didn't you teach these lads anything?"

"I don't raise an alarm over a dead wolf." Despite the words, Magmar's tone hinted at regret.

Tobias spat. "Lukaan's no dead wolf, Magmar. You know that. And you can't leave these lads wandering about empty-headed like Dammie Bulta. What they need to know in Twin Forks is different from what they need travelin' in the world. If they ever take the caravan route to Khatara they better know about Sethia. They better."

"If there's something we should know, we'd just as soon know now," Rahg said.

"Didn't you pay attention to anything I said at Havril's?" Tobias asked.

"We thought you were just telling tales. I mean, we believed about the Victas and the rock dragons, but..."

"The Banished Ones? Go on and say it. They won't bite you; leastwise not here. Not now. But they're real, lads, and don't go thinkin' otherwise. They're as real as snakes and mountain cats and sangra. And they're a whole lot worse."

Magmar shook his head. "I'll take first watch, Tobias. You tell them as you see fit. You have more knowledge of these things anyway." Magmar walked to the entrance of the cave and pulled aside the blanket that Tobias had used for cover.

Tobias stretched his legs, moved close to the fire, and lit his pipe. He seldom told stories without smoke billowing from the sides of his mouth. "Don't think bad about your father, lads. He probably hoped you could live a quiet life in Twin Forks. Hoped you'd never have need to know. I know you lads want to see the world, and there's plenty to see; I won't argue that. But there are also things your eyes should never see and places you dare not go." Tobias scratched the white stubble growth on his chin while he took a deep breath. "Guess you would've found out soon enough."

Rahg put two more logs on the fire and sat as close as he could.

"There's nothin' in here with us, lad. The horses would've known by now."

"I know," Rahg said. "I just wanted it warmer. That's all."

Tobias nodded, then took three long puffs on his pipe. "Hard to say how to tell this, but I guess the best place to start is at the beginning. It's been more than a thousand winters since we came to settle these lands, and they say back then all the world was at peace. Then, Lukaan came." Tobias stopped, and his hands shook when he took a puff from his pipe. "I don't even like to say the name."

This was unlike Tobias. His stories usually flowed like the wine on Feast Day.

"The legends are old, mind you, and not always clear, but they all mention a group of immortals who possessed unimaginable powers. They controlled the winds, commanded fire and lightning, and caused the ground to shake. Some even say they determined the path of the sun and the moons. I've heard bards swear that immortals could talk without moving their lips, and others who whispered that they killed the same way."

Tobias tapped his pipe on the rock he used for a seat and took a long sip of khaffe. "But on one point all the legends agree—all was fine until Lukaan went on his rampage. They say he's the Evil One. I don't know whether he is, but if one of a hundred stories about him is true then he's got to be. If he isn't, I wouldn't want to think of what could be worse."

"This isn't true, is it, Tobias?"

"Listen close, lad. This is one story I won't tell twice." Tobias stared at Rahg and Darstan. "Lukaan wanted everyone to worship him. He tortured and killed anyone who refused until, finally, after too many years and too much suffering, Mikkellana and the other good immortals joined to oppose him; Mikkellana even got the vargels to fight alongside her. But it didn't help much. Some say it even got worse. Then Mikkellana devised a clever trap, a special kind of shield they say. She waited until Lukaan and the other Banished Ones were together in Sethia, then covered the whole land with it."

A cloud of smoke irritated Tobias's eye, and he rubbed it clean. "The stories say Lukaan's scream traveled halfway round the world when he realized what Mikkellana had done. He vowed to take revenge, break out one day and make every man and woman pay. Said he'd make us pay in ways I'm not willin' to talk about."

Tobias sat so still Rahg didn't know whether he had finished or not. "Well, that's what I know about it, lads. I can't say how much is true, but I tend to believe. I've been on the caravan route that goes past Sethia. I've seen shadows that shouldn't have been there and heard cries from the desert that sounded like the bones of the dead. I know I wouldn't wander off that caravan trail, just in case there is a shield with Lukaan behind it." Tobias wiped sweat from his brow, though the cave was anything but hot. "Anyway, the way I figure it, if he does get out he won't be fallin' for any tricks. And far as I can tell there aren't any immortals around to stop him." Tobias stood and stretched. The telling of the story appeared to have unnerved him.

"What about Mikkellana and Aentarra?"

"Mikkellana disappeared after the last wars," Tobias said. "And Aentarra... well, it's best we not see her. Just as soon meet a Banished One." Tobias paced the cavern as he talked. "Better get some sleep, lads. Tomorrow will likely be a long day."

Rahg burned with unanswered questions but he controlled the urge.

He had no desire to be frightened further. He edged closer to the fire as he pulled the blanket over himself.

Hours later, he awoke for what must have been the tenth time. The night had been one nightmare after another. Some even overlapped. Sleep finally came again and with it, more battles. He was in the midst of fighting a band of demons when something clamped over his mouth. Rahg gasped for breath then realized it was no dream. He opened his eyes and saw Magmar.

"What's the matter?" Rahg whispered, though he felt like shouting.

"Tobias went to check on a noise. It could be a Victa patrol."

Just then the blanket covering the entrance cracked opened and Tobias sneaked back inside. "It's no patrol," he whispered. "It's a whole strike force!"

Tobias took charge, barking orders like a Sykoran patrol leader. "Got to leave now! Have to get to the village and warn them, then send someone south for help. We'll put the women and children on boats to Sykor. They'll be safe there. If we get back in time to set some defenses, we might hold them until relief arrives."

"How many?" Magmar asked with cool detachment as he mounted his horse.

"I figure two hundred, but could be more. We'll have to move fast if we're to beat 'em to the village. We can't go past 'em, but they're on foot. Not a horse I know of that would let a lizard sit on its back. I figure if we go north, around this mountain, we can take the east road into town. Might cost us half a league, at worst. But if we ride hard, we might make it."

Tobias was already moving when Rahg's right leg slipped over the saddle.

"Let's ride, lads."

SUBTERFUGE

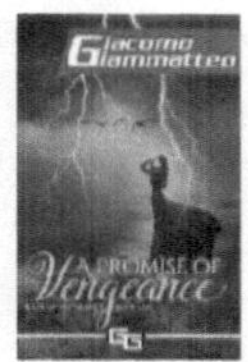

Vallah
1364 AE (After Exile)
First Cycle of the Second Moon
Third Calendar of Light

It had been more than a thousand years since the exile from Nelstar, and too much of that time had been spent in the Forbidden Lands wandering through nightmares and battling beasts never meant to live.

Aentarra du Savarra shivered with the memory and felt the all-too-familiar streak of pain that haunted her mind. She didn't know if it was the time spent in the Forbidden Lands or if it was the oath she had sworn against the Lights, but something had pushed her to the brink of madness.

A smile cracked her face then vanished with a gasp as whispers from ages past slithered along well-worn paths in her mind.

The Others! How did they get here?

She braced herself just before the strike.

A stab of pain shot through Aentarra's mind, clawing inside of her. It wracked her body. Her arm fell limp at the side and both legs collapsed. The left side of her face went numb, lips drooping, eyes sagging. Blood trickled from her ear. Something foul oozed from her nose, but she failed to stop it before it slipped past her lips and into her mouth. Rancid. Bitter. She tried to spit but had no control of her muscles. Vibrations rocked her head—like a gong calling the faithful to the temple on Lenorda. Pain prevented her from focusing, from regaining control. She remembered rocking in her father's arms, her mother's soft voice. The love of siblings and friends.

More pain. Nothing worked.

It was then that her father's words came to her, a whisper from beyond the grave.

"Avenge me!"

She forced her teeth into a grind, pried her face up, then focused again. *Du Savarras don't die like this.* She mustered her power, focused on one spot in her mind, then dispatched an unrelenting assault. Before long the battle was won. The siege ended.

A long sigh escaped her lips as she wiped clean the sweat and blood. The attacks had grown more violent of late—more frequent, too, and the pain lingered longer. When she felt it coming she fought it fiercely, albeit, to no avail; it always came, and it brought the pain with it. Bone-wracking, flesh-rending pain.

It was midday before she got to her feet, and even that proved to be a struggle. She wondered anew about the Others, and how they followed her from Nelstar. They had plagued her father, but that was worlds away.

How did they cross the Forbidden Lands?

Those thoughts stirred memories from deep within, images she fought to hide. Her mind slipped a thousand years back in time and unknown light years away to memories that lingered like yesterday's rain.

She remembered the Lights' verdict, condemning them to the Forbidden Lands, and she remembered the Oath she swore, even where she stood in the Great Hall when she had sworn it.

Great Hall

Never mind that she'd probably not live; death was but a summer itch to the loss of honor.

Once again she found herself uttering the oath on impulse. It had become her mantra since the Lights killed her father. It had become her life. For the thousandth time in as many days the words slipped past her lips. The ritual commenced.

"An oath of life I swear by Blood to be an oath of death,

And each page of the Sacred Book I whisper with each breath.

> To the Seven Lights of Nelstar—this day I swear your death."
>
> — AENTARRA'S OATH

Warmth washed Aentarra's body. Her shoulders relaxed, skin smoothed. A slight orgasmic tingle—a smile. If the Lights thought banishment would stave her vengeance they had forgotten what it meant to be a du Savarra.

She shook her head to clear the fog. This would require a day or more of pondering, but she could ill afford the time. If she were to ever get back to Nelstar she must first deal with Lukaan and the other Banished Ones. Only then could she wreak her revenge. Aentarra shuddered as tendrils of flame danced across her fingers. She forced her mind to focus then made her way toward council chambers.

Blue silk rode on a current of air and flowed with her every movement, like a spider's web fluttering in a gentle autumn breeze. Aentarra sauntered through the room, heels clicking on the white marble floor, while hair as dark as a raven's wing tickled satin-smooth shoulders. Walnut eyes flanked an Endoran nose—strong and perfectly straight—and stared at the ten inert souls filling all but four of the seats surrounding an ancient blackthorn table. The finest swords from each noble house enriched the otherwise drab walls, and on the table in front of each chair lay a dagger encrusted with priceless emeralds, their blades tainted by the Blood of ages past.

Once she had counted them among her allies, but they had lost the will to fight, and the centuries had dulled their vengeance. Now they served a different purpose, a more noble cause.

Aentarra ran a slender finger along the back of Kiris's head, tickling a neck that could no longer respond. *A shame this had to happen, though it was only a matter of time.* The thin smile returned to her face. "Only three remain." She sighed, fingering the emeralds on the dagger of

House D'Norta. *Pity their line had to end,* she thought, but her smile hid no pity.

Aentarra spun toward the door, alerted by the sound of familiar footsteps in the corridor. *Mesan,* one of the three that remained before she could pursue Lukaan.

~

The air in the corridor pulsed, a transient interval that allowed Mesan quick entry, yet limited the disturbance. He had no wish to keep a rift open with Aentarra around. The thought provoked an instinctive response that enveloped his body in a shield while he scoured the surroundings to ensure no deception awaited. It was wise to be cautious with Aentarra. He stepped toward the massive wooden doors that guarded the council chambers. Mesan's confidence grew with each successive step, as did his curiosity. *Why meet here?*

His long strides carried him into the room without hesitation. "What is it you wish, Aentarra? I have no time for your antics."

By the time he noticed, it was too late. He never saw the *slicer* hurtling toward him. Not that it would have mattered; he could muster no defenses at this point. The *slicer* pierced the shield Mesan had constructed then bore through his skull to the proper depth in his brain. Mesan's glazed stare froze in place and his body slumped to the floor.

~

Aentarra placed him in the appropriate seat, and once again let her gaze sweep the room. Eleven sets of lusterless eyes met her dark gaze. Her father's words from so long ago tickled her memory.

"Weak hearts beat in the chests of cowards, and forgiving minds dream only of redemption."

An instinctive nod displayed her approval. Another piece of her plan had fallen into place.

She had no time to gloat, though, there was much work yet to do. Dangerous work. If she wasn't careful she would wind up as dead as her father. But she knew that the road to salvation grew crowded with the aged and sick and weak. The powerful trod the road of vengeance. She had sworn an oath against the Lights, and it was one she intended to keep. It was one she *had* to keep. And Lukaan must be the first to die. *Even if I have to kill every pitiful mortal on this planet.*

VICTAS

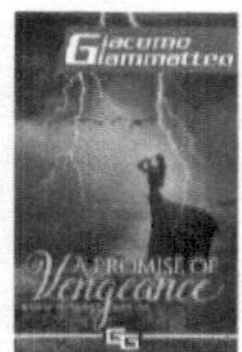

obias led the way toward town, followed closely by Rahg, Darstan and Magmar. A familiar cluster of maples sat upon the ridge, signaling a downslope of the knoll at the edge of town. *Almost there,* Rahg thought. *I just pray it's not too late.*

Exhaustion had been a companion most of the morning. Rahg's back and legs ached, and lather lay heavy on his mount's neck. He dug his heels in. "Come on, boy, just enough to top the ridge then it's downhill to town."

The challenge of the final hill fell to the strained pounding of the hooves, bringing the valley and Twin Forks into sight. Rahg's shoulders slumped and his mouth fell open. Buildings and houses were aflame and black smoke hung thick in the air. He gagged with the next breath. "Darstan, what's that stink?"

Tobias urged his mount forward. "Ride, lads. Ride hard! That's people you smell burnin'."

Fire had razed several buildings and more than a few houses. Six men crowded together on the steps of Havril's Inn, but twice as many

Victas surrounded them, each clawed hand clasping a bloody sword or axe. Bodies littered the square like autumn leaves.

Rahg panicked when he saw the Victas. They stood as tall as men, with green scales and claws shaped like hands. The cold, damp chill of fear seized him.

"Keep up, Rahg. Follow me!" Tobias charged toward town brandishing his sword. "Stay close."

Rahg, Darstan, and Magmar dug heels in and raced after Tobias. Rahg's horse responded with a lunge. Kor Trasken, Eru, and two others were fighting a group of ten Victas near the Grandel's house on the east side of the square. Tobias veered his mount in that direction.

Rahg's fear turned to anger, then rage. His body grew hot and blood boiled. Though he asked for speed, the horses moved slower as they roared through the soft, newly planted field, clumps of dirt spraying Rahg with each stride. Two Victas jumped from behind a tree, racing to intercept him.

"On the right!" Tobias yelled, and turned to attack. He dispatched the first Victa with one blow, while Magmar's first strike merely delivered a wound, though the second blow killed it. "Be prepared." Tobias reminded them.

Rahg held onto his sword like a vise in the blacksmith's shop. Soon he had to relax his grip or risk losing control. A slap on his mount's flanks had the horse moving toward Kor and Eru. As they rode through town, Rahg's mount sidestepped a corpse.

"It's the Marg boy," Rahg said. The boy had a deep gash in his face and his skull was smashed. Tears wet Rahg's cheeks. He choked down bile rising in his throat.

Mrs. Nasher's scream ripped his attention to the left, where she scrambled to escape a pursuing Victa. Rahg winced as a Victa axe dug into her back. The last meal Rahg ate threatened to surface, but he somehow forced it down, remained calm.

Havril raced from around the corner and stabbed the lizard, dropping it. They worked their way to a position between the Grandel's house and the one next to it, where Kor and Eru fought. Havril's Inn lay north of them, just across the square and a little west.

"Bows!" Tobias ordered as he dismounted.

Rahg nocked an arrow when a large Victa, painted the color of blood, leapt from the roof of the house. Two arrows struck the lizard, one in the throat, the other in the chest. Darstan nocked another arrow and claimed his second kill with a shot to the head. Four more lizards died, while three more, with wounds that would have killed a man, continued fighting with arrows protruding from their backs. "God's mercy, but they're hard to kill."

"Wattle!" Tobias yelled above the din. "Try and hit that soft skin hanging below their chins. That's the most vulnerable spot."

Tobias led the charge with steel flying. Rahg spied a large Victa about to get Eru. He stabbed his first victim in the back. The shock of the impact stopped him short, his arm aching from the jolt. This was much worse than the sacks of dirt Kor had them practice with. The feel of that blade digging through scales and muscles produced an eerie feeling—somewhat sickening but somewhat good.

The axe of another Victa just missed Rahg's head, Eru blocked the blow aimed at Rahg, then carried through with a slash that crippled the Victa's leg. Rahg killed it with a chop to the throat. This kill produced no queasy feelings.

Darstan slew the last Victa in the group, then stopped to catch his breath. He breathed slowly. Green Victa blood stained his black hair and streaked his face, and blood from his own wound stained his shirt. He shook his head and took a sip of water from a flask Kor handed him. "I hope Ben wasn't in his house when it burnt. Look at it; it's all but gone."

"I haven't seen him," Eru said, wiping sweat and grime from his face. He grabbed hold of Darstan's shoulder. "Did you see our house? God's sake, there's nothing left."

The Trasken's house had been razed to the foundation, a chimney standing tall like a towering emerald all that remained. Darstan just stared.

Darstan coughed, forcing a hand to cover his mouth, and he wiped tearing brown eyes on the sleeve of his shirt. The smoke tasted oily, rancid. "Damn, Rahg! That disgusting smell is people burning." He spat until his mouth was dry.

"I know, Darstan. Tobias told us on the way in."

Kor Trasken stood next to Tobias. "A score of Sykoran soldiers came just before the attack. They're all dead, but they took a lot of Victas with them."

"I don't need to know who's dead. Catch hold of yourself, Kor. How many people are left?"

"There are a handful of people inside of Havril's, and we sent some of the women and children to Arn Bulta's earlier. I pray they got away. Everyone else is dead." Kor's head hung low. "I don't think we can make it, Tobias. Too many of them."

"What about Kanella?" Rahg asked.

"I wish I knew, lad, but I don't." Tears formed in Kor's eyes.

"C'mon," Tobias said. "We've got to get to the inn."

"More coming!" Magmar called.

Darstan cleaned the blood off his blade and gave it a quick snap with his wrists. "Guess we better get going. That may be the last reprieve we get."

Tobias unsheathed his sword. "We need to get to Havril's now!"

They ran toward the inn, but as they crossed the square, splattering through pools of blood and leaping over corpses, a large group of Victas moved to block their path. Another band advanced from the east, poised to hit their flanks.

An anguished scream from Havril tore Rahg's eyes in that direction.

"Kora! My baby Kora!" Havril knelt and grabbed her limp body, squeezed her to his chest. Blood mixed with her tangled hair, covering the right side of her face.

Tobias grabbed hold of Havril's shoulder. "C'mon, Havril, we need you alive. Martha and Ella might still be at the inn." Havril nodded, but he refused to let go of her. Finally, with prodding from Magmar, he set Kora down, easing her head on his coat. With Kor's help he stood, a man struggling to raise himself, to even survive.

They fought their way through a small band of Victas and made it to the side wall of the inn. Victas blocked the entrance and were closing in from all sides.

Rahg felt as if he had been fighting for days, though the sun still sat high over Kenner Peak. Bodies lay all over the square. *I'll probably soon join them,* he thought, then shifted his worry to wonder about Kanella. *I hope she got away.*

A fresh patrol of Victas mounted a furious charge, forcing the battle to resume. An immense, blood-splattered Victa sliced Darstan's arm with his short sword. When Darstan's defenses dropped, another Victa poised his axe to strike. Rahg stepped in to protect him and, while he and Darstan battled, he saw something strange from the periphery—a huge black stallion raced through the square, straight toward a group of Victas.

Astride him sat a man wearing a long black cloak that whipped wildly behind him. The horse trampled two Victas who had leapt in front of it, then lashed out with its back feet, striking a Victa in the head. Four more Victas rushed the stranger as he slipped from his mount. The black–cloaked man shouted challenges while standing in the square, still as a demon in a night wind.

The man wielded a sword in one hand and a trident–shaped sword-breaker in the other. The stranger's steel cut down two more Victas with little struggle. A madman had just joined their cause.

Rahg's stomach burned with the singe of steel—only a thin cut, but instinct spurred a quick response. He raised the sword in time to block a lethal blow from the Victa, but when he did, another one pressed the attack. Rahg's racing heart lent speed to his arms, but not enough; he'd never defeat two of them. Rahg shuddered when he looked into their beady black eyes. He had never felt such coldness. *By the gods, but this is a horrible way to die.*

The first lizard came at him, scales glinting with sunlight and stained red with blood. Rahg trembled. "Help, Darstan!" He tried blocking the blow but the axe beat him down. His knees buckled and his arms were too weak to hold the blade.

Tobias rushed to stave off the killing blow. "Get a grip on yourself, lad. If not, you'll die."

Tobias' blade cut the Victa's arm then, quick as a cat, he struck its neck. Before the second Victa could react, Tobias killed it also. Rahg had never pictured Tobias as much of a fighter, not much of anything except storyteller. "Thanks, Tobias. It would've gotten me if not for you."

"Save your breath, lad." Tobias reached down and took a short sword from the Victa's belt. "Use it as a shield." He then turned to Darstan. "Get that other sword. We need to get to the back door before they come again."

"I'm having trouble enough holding onto one sword."

Tobias turned around and glared. "Pick it up! You'll wish you had it when you go to block an axe and all you've got is your arm."

"Get the sword!" Magmar said. "More coming."

"Bows," Tobias shouted. "Shoot like they're targets, lads. Forget they're lizards."

Rahg dropped both swords and nocked an arrow, but he shook so much that the arrow wobbled on the draw. The arrow flew wide of its mark and the Victas were now too close to chance another shot. Tobias dropped one on his second shot, and even though Magmar had gotten two shots off, and both hits, the lizard rumbled toward them, arrows protruding from its chest like straw from a scarecrow. Darstan's first shot missed, like Rahg's. His second shot was only a leg wound. Kor, Eru, and Havril had spent all their arrows long ago.

"Watch it, Rahg!" Darstan screamed.

A Victa sword almost caught Ragh. Fear overtook him as the Victas approached. *We shouldn't have come back. What good did we do?* He blushed, and felt as if everyone knew his thoughts, as if his face had yellowed instead of reddened.

"Don't worry, lad. We're not dead yet."

Rahg jerked toward Tobias. Shame drowned his fear. "I'm scared, Tobias."

"Right now, lad, there's nobody more scared than I am. Just hold onto those swords and kill as many Victas as you can." Tobias laughed. "You can always tell when I'm scared, lad—I talk a lot."

Tobias had gotten Rahg to laugh. Their odds had not improved, but Rahg had voiced his fear and lived through the shame. Death might be bad, but perhaps it wasn't the worst of things. Rahg stepped toward the front. Somehow the swords felt lighter. He chanced a quick glance to the stranger, who was cutting down Victas like a bear does pack dogs.

"Blasted lizards!" Darstan yelled. "Blasted, bloody lizards!"

"I'm coming, Darstan," Eru yelled.

Rahg struggled against a Victa wielding an axe and a sword. The Victa backed him up against the wall. Rahg braced his elbow in his side, then shoved against one of the Victa claws holding the axe. The claw felt like steel and he cringed at the feel of the scales, like singed leather.

"You will all die," the Victa said. Its garbled voice sounded like rocks scraping together.

Rahg's arm gave way. The axe took a bite from his side and sliced his gut. Rahg winced but managed to strike a crippling blow to the lizard's right side followed by a killing strike to the throat.

Magmar looked over. "You all right?"

"I'm all right."

"Don't let 'em get so close," Kor said. "They're too strong."

"Anyone know who the stranger is?"

Two Victas rounded the corner and focused on Rahg.

"Hang on, lad." Kor Trasken's voice infused him with hope. As Rahg dodged a Victa axe, Kor's blade caught its neck. With one gone, Rahg and Kor dispatched the second one with little trouble.

"Thanks," Rahg said, while keeping his eyes alert.

"More comin'. Keep alive."

The only ones left were Darstan and Havril—guarding the left side—Tobias, Eru, and Magmar—at the front—and Rahg and Kor holding the right. And that madman.

Six more Victas reinforced their brood members, pushing hard on the front line. Tobias and Eru met them but soon had their backs pushing toward the wall. Havril rushed to relieve Tobias and drew three Victas at once. He flailed to keep them at bay.

"I'm coming, Havril," Kor yelled. He killed the Victa he was fighting then charged to save Havril but was too late, a Victa's axe had all but beheaded him.

"Watch it!" Darstan screamed.

A Victa axe chopped a rut in Kor's side, ripping through flesh and bone. Kor turned and reached for Eru before he died.

Eru leapt into the middle of four Victas, slashing with his blade. A badger guarding honey from a bear couldn't have been more ferocious.

"Eru, no!" Darstan screamed, but the warning went unheeded. Eru's quick sword slew two of them and wounded a third, but the fourth Victa delivered Eru's inevitable fate.

Rahg choked on his fear. "Eru, dead!"

The onslaught subsided when five of the Victas rushed to engage the madman. Two Victas succumbed to his steel before another patrol shifted to converge on him. The stranger whirled to face them, blades slashing and jabbing, drawing blood with every strike. Lightning-quick, he parried two blows, and with reflexes that a wolverine would envy, ducked, jabbed and sliced two more. He carved a path through the rest of the lizards and joined Rahg by the wall.

"Stab their backs when they come to get me, boy."

"I will," Rahg said, then heard a scream from Darstan.

"Father!"

It stabbed Rahg's heart. He felt certain that it was Darstan's death song, but when he stole a glance, he saw a knife in Magmar's gut, blood gushing from the wound. Darstan had the crazed look of Ned Barker just before he attacked the mountain cat.

"Father! are you all right?" Dread filled Rahg's bones. He struggled to make his way to Magmar, but Tobias stopped him.

"You won't do your father any good if you're dead. Stay alive. That's the best you can do for him. Now take hold of yourself."

Rahg knew Tobias was right but he had to get to Magmar.

Tobias butted him with his shoulder, knocking him back three steps. Rahg felt as if he'd been nudged by a bull. "You'll be dead as Eru if you don't listen, lad. Stay put!"

A few paces away the stranger fought-on. Whenever a Victa swung an axe or sword, his trident-shaped weapon caught it and twisted it out of the Victa's clawed grasp, then he followed through with a thrust and stabbed the lizard in the wattle. The stranger was killing quite a few Victas.

A flicker of hope lightened Rahg's sword, but only for a moment. Fresh Victa troops marched across the square with two rock dragons running ahead of them. Rahg gasped. They looked worse than he had imagined from Tobias' story. Rahg couldn't take his eyes off of them. Huge feet, like a bear's paw, supported gray scaly legs as thick as the young oaks at the sawmill, and their necks were as round as Havril's belly. Three giant claws on each foot dug into the ground as they moved, each step lifting their legs like a man trying to walk with his shoulders hunched up. Their heads were triangular and funneled to a long snout that housed daggers for teeth. Rahg shuddered when he saw their eyes—red as blood and staring right at him.

When the terrifying hiss came again, fear buckled his knees. He was about to lay down his sword when the stranger shouted and pointed toward the woods.

Off in the distance a shape appeared, a blurry mass the size of a black bear that bounded across the fields, its paws tearing at the soil and hurling clumps of dirt high in the air. Rahg tried to keep watch while he struggled against the renewed blows of sword and axe.

The huge shape surged forward with ground–eating strides. At one-hundred paces, the creature took the form of a giant black dog—a brilliant, blinding, glinting black that absorbed the rays of the sun then spat them back. The fur was as black as snow was white. It had the look of a dog, but it had no tail.

"Vargel!" Tobias shouted as if he just sighted a demon.

In the span of a few heartbeats the beast was within striking distance of the rock dragons. They turned to intercept it.

The vargel leapt and landed on the nearest rock dragon with a crunch that smashed the dragon's bones. With the next lunge it seized the second dragon by the throat, large teeth ripping through the soft underside to open a gaping wound. The first dragon, hampered by its shattered bones, then suffered a similar fate.

The vargel ignited fear in the Victas and they turned to confront it.

Green blood covered its massive jaws and dripped from huge teeth, meant for the rending of flesh. For tearing tendons and cracking bones. The vargel pounced on them before the Victas organized an attack. They flailed with sword and axe, but the vargel proved so swift that none of the blades drew more than a trickle of blood. The vargel finished with them and then charged the remaining Victas.

Rahg had decided the vargel was more dangerous than the stranger but it didn't matter, both delivered death-blows to the Victas—one with whirling blades of steel—the other with teeth as hard as steel. Before long, it was over. The Victas were dead.

At first, Rahg couldn't believe it. When no more Victas rushed to attack, the realization set in. Rahg's legs wobbled. He dropped to his knees and threw up. Then he saw Tobias holding Magmar. He jumped up and ran to him. "Is he alive?"

"Barely, lad. Just barely. I'm no healer, but I don't think even the best one could save him now. The wounds are too deep."

Rahg took Tobias' place, holding Magmar's head. "Father..." Tears filled

Rahg's eyes and ran down his cheeks to mix with the dirt and dried blood. "Don't die. You can't. Not yet."

Darstan rushed over, blood dripping from wounds as bad as Rahg's. "Father, are you all right? Don't worry. We'll take care of you."

Tears traced Magmar's face, his raspy voice a whisper. "I loved both of you boys... Sorry to..."

Darstan knelt beside him. "Save your strength. You'll be all right."

"Listen to Tobias, he..." Magmar's eyes closed with his last breath.

~

*D*arstan found it difficult to swallow, and even harder to fight the tears. He pulled Rahg to his feet. "Rahg, I know how you feel but this won't do any good. Father would want us to take care of each other. He'd be glad that we're still alive."

Rahg nodded between sobs. He stood for a while, then stumbled toward the inn. He fell and lost consciousness before he hit the ground.

Darstan knelt beside his Rahg and wiped his head with a cloth. He stayed with him a few minutes, until Rahg came to, then he moved to kneel alongside of Magmar. He took Magmar's bloody hand between his own. A lone tear traced his cheek as he whispered in his father's ear. "I love you. May the gods accept you as you are."

"Help me over here, lad."

Tobias brushed water on Rahg's face. He coughed as he woke, then jumped up on shaky legs. He looked to his father on the ground, then found Darstan and hugged him. "They killed him, for god's sake. He's dead!"

Darstan held back tears while he consoled Rahg. "Come on. We need to help get things ready. We'll get some shovels from Havril's and start digging graves."

The stranger spoke for the first time since the battle had ended. His voice was cold. "No time for graves. Get food and water and gather as many arrows as you can. Pull them out of the dead, but make sure to clean off the blood or they won't fly true."

"We've got to bury them!" Darstan shook as he said it.

The stranger turned a cold stare onto Darstan. "Boy, I know this was your village. I know these people were your friends and family, but there will be more Victas coming. They'll be here to check on these, and then they'll track us down."

"That's my father! I'll bury him even if I have to do it myself." Darstan stood tall and firm, brown eyes cloudy with tears and his black hair matted with sweat and blood.

The stranger looked at Tobias.

"Talk sense into them, old man. I'll search for survivors and bury their father." The man glared at Darstan. "We don't have time for words over his grave. You help get things together and find more horses. There may be Victa scouts watching us now."

SYKORAN ROAD

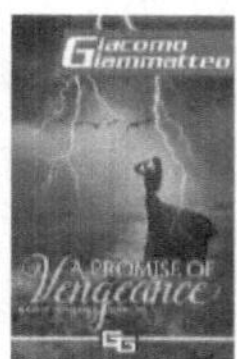

*D*arstan stared at the stranger preparing to climb atop his wild mount. The horse was black as the night and as crazy as a bear in season.

Argus

And the stranger was no better. Maybe worse. Darstan had dreamt of demons that weren't so dark. He eased his mount alongside Tobias, near the front of the line. "Who is he, Tobias?"

"There's a time and place for everything, Darstan. We can talk about it later."

"I just want—"

Tobias' raised hand told Darstan he'd get no more from him now. He joined Rahg at the back of the group." It had been two days since they left Twin Forks, and Rahg hadn't said a word.

"Rahg, you still with us?"

"Where are we?"

"Heading south is all I know."

Rahg's face sunk. His eyes closed, then clouded. "Father's dead! I can't believe he's gone. And Eru and Tomas. God's sake, what are we going to do?"

"I don't know, but we have to keep moving so we don't run into any more Victas. That stranger said we should reach a Sykoran outpost sometime tomorrow. We'll be safe there."

"But then what are we going to do? Twin Forks is gone. And father..." Tears came. "I can't believe he's gone."

Rahg's eyes opened wide at the sight of the other travelers. "What about Kanella? Did she get out? Is she here?"

Darstan held his head low. "She wasn't in Havril's. We searched all the houses but we didn't find her. Nobody except who you see here. Twelve of us; that's all." Darstan checked behind him, the sides, too. Fear had become an uninvited companion since the battle. "They even killed Jumper. I saw him when I went to get clothes. Both his back legs chopped off. Blasted, bloody Victas!"

Rahg rode in silence for a moment then spoke, though his voice was soft, hesitant. "Did you see anyone who looked like Kanella? Was she..."

"We couldn't tell who a lot of them were. You saw what they did."

Rahg wiped tears away. "Guess it's just you and me then."

Darstan reached to pat the horse's neck. "We've got Timor and Lanna. That's something. And Tobias. He might know somewhere we could find work. I've also got a cousin in the Sykoran Guard. I never met him, but he's an officer, I think."

"I see the stranger is still with us, and that beast. Scared the life out of me when I saw it."

Kella

"Tobias said it's a vargel; comes from the Whites." He said it's like half dog and half bear. Looks like it, too. And as to the stranger, I don't know any more than I did before, not even his name. He never talks except to give orders, and Tobias follows his lead like a new puppy."

"Can't blame him. Did you see the way he fought?"

Tobias rode up next to Rahg, smiling like a guard on payday. "Didn't know whether you'd be joinin' us again, lad. I've seen it before, a man goes off into his own after somethin' bad happens—like losing a loved one—goes off and never comes back. Didn't think you'd let it get the best of you, but you never can tell."

Rahg wiped away the last of his tears. "Tobias, did you... did somebody bury father?"

"He did," Tobias said, nodding toward the stranger. "Gave him a good soldier's grave. And you don't have to worry about anything gettin' to him; he made the grave deep, deeper than I could've. And the stone on top's as big as the one that marks Jed Nester's grave. No markings, but that can be done anytime. After all this is settled with the Victas we can go back and take care of that. I'll go with you."

His head drooped a little. "Like to say my own words over him. Didn't get the chance when we buried him. A man should have the words to send him off, but I figure they're just as good said later as now."

Tobias tugged on his cap and brushed a piece of tobacco from his white stubble. "Anyway, keep smilin', lad. Remember what your father always said. 'A smile cures quicker than a frown.'" Tobias's own smile was as broad as his face right now. "Think on it, lad. I believe you'll see he was right." He nodded to Rahg as he tugged on the reins and steered his mount toward the stranger.

Rahg shifted in his saddle, wincing as his hand shot to the wound on his stomach. A bandage padded his gut just above the waist. "I forgot about this," he said, and straightened his posture. "We need to thank the stranger for burying father, Dar."

"I tried. He just shrugged it off. I told you he doesn't talk much. And that vargel follows him everywhere. I know they helped us, but I don't like being around them." Darstan looked around again. "Tobias said he knows him, but—"

"Knows him! Who is he?"

"Tobias wouldn't say. Said we'd know before the crows." Darstan laughed. "I still don't know what that's supposed to mean but I guess it means he'll tell us soon enough."

Rahg laughed. "He has more sayings than father did." The laugh failed with the mention of Magmar. "I miss him, Dar. What are we going to do without him?"

"Rahg, that's the first time I laughed since we left home. First time you have, too. I feel the same way about father, but..."

"But what?"

"Let's try to move on. It's what he'd want."

"Move on?" Rahg yanked back on the reins and glared. "That's all right for you to say. He wasn't..."

"Wasn't what! Wasn't my father?" Darstan's big bony hands poked a finger at Rahg. "I may not have been his real son, but I loved him as much as you." He fought to control the tears welling in his eyes.

"Sorry, Dar. I didn't mean it."

Rahg nudged his mount forward, letting silence be his companion.

Darstan shoved the hurt aside and focused on the surroundings. The terrain had started to change, mountains softening to steep hills, and then lush valleys braced by gently rolling mounds. Huge, long-armed oaks and grandfather pines mingled with maples, sycamores, and ash, and proudly wore their new spring coats. He was interrupted by the voice of the stranger.

"We make camp on the rise," he said, and pointed to a thick copse of trees at the highest elevation. "No fire tonight. There will likely be Victa scouts searching for survivors."

Darstan moved alongside Rahg and tapped his arm. "Would you look at that horse, the way the sun is shining on him. I wish I had a horse like that."

Argus in sunset

Rahg let out a big sigh. "Don't we all?" he said.

~

Rahg didn't think he'd mind doing without a fire, but as the day faded and the night stole what warmth remained the order became more disagreeable. After a cold meal the villagers spread bedrolls on ground cushioned with spring grass and huddled together for warmth, their cloaks wrapped snugly about them. The vargel lay next to the stranger.

"What's her name?" Rahg asked.

"Doesn't belong to me."

"I thought since she came with you..."

"Coincidence," he said. "Or fate, if you believe in that." The stranger looked at Rahg. "You should name her if she stays around."

"Me, name her?" Rahg didn't wait for a response in case he had heard wrong the first time. "I'll do it." He had already begun sorting through potential names when he remembered the other business he wished to discuss. "Sir, I wanted to thank you for helping us, but also for taking care of my father. Tobias said you gave him a proper burial. That means a lot."

Rahg couldn't tell whether his eyes were steel–blue or gray, but they never flickered.

"No need to thank me." Rahg felt the man's gaze on him. "Where will you go, lad?"

The unexpected conversation surprised Rahg. "Darstan has a cousin in Sykor, an officer in the guards. I'm going to learn to fight." Rahg nodded his head, as though he had just found his path in life. "I'll learn to be a master at the sword...and then I'll kill every Victa I can find."

"Not many blademasters left in this world."

Before Rahg could respond, Tobias's words sailed past him. "You could train them, Rhaven."

By the time Tobias affixed a name to the stranger—in less than the time it takes for a word to form on his lips—a knife appeared in Rhaven's hand. Rahg figured he could stick it in any of them before their next heartbeat.

"There are men who would try to kill me if they knew who I was." Rhaven's eyes held Tobias riveted. Rahg could see now that they were blue, ice–blue. His face was a chiseled piece of granite and the arm that held the blade had been carved from the same rock.

Darstan walked up next to Rahg. Tobias stared at Rhaven. "If there are men trying to kill you, I imagine they must be young, and fools to boot. Once saw a man leap into a pit with a nest of waggers, though he never did come out."

Tobias pulled out his tobacco pouch and packed his pipe. "But an old man like me would never try such a thing. I plan on livin' for quite some time yet."

"You seem to have me at a disadvantage. I don't recall meeting you."

"Didn't expect you to remember. I fought with you in the Swamp Wars. Served with Takar at the battle of Cypress Swamps."

"You must have the gods' own luck to have survived two such hopeless battles."

Tobias laughed and turned a stump into a seat while he lit his pipe. Rhaven plopped to the ground, his back planted against a large oak. When he stretched, Rahg caught a glimpse of a thin-bladed knife sheathed under the upper part of his arm. The man had more weapons than a Sykoran patrol.

"I remember you now," Rhaven said. "You were Takar's patrol leader, the one who flanked the Krov's at Landers Bend."

Tobias nodded. "It was Takar's strategy, and I'm thankful for it. That war would've lasted a lot longer without him." Tobias leaned down and pulled his boots off. "Have you seen Takar? I recall that you and he were friends."

"He's still in the guards, but a sergeant now, demoted."

Rhaven reached to scratch his ear. Rahg noticed a piece of it was missing. He nudged Darstan and whispered. "Look at his ear."

Tobias filled his pipe two more times before the small-talk ended. Soon Rahg found himself yawning. "I'm going to sleep," Rahg said, and headed toward the bedroll.

A large oak tree served as a fitting backboard. Rahg curled up next to it, a blanket pulled over his shoulders. *Maybe I'll do what Rhaven suggested and give that vargel a name.* Before falling asleep, every girl's name he had ever known cycled through his mind, but the only one he could think of was Kanella, and his heart ached every time he did. *I can't name her Kanella,* he thought, and began thinking of more appropriate names. Soon slumber overtook him.

The aroma of morning cooking woke Rahg with recollections of his home in Twin Forks. He imagined breaking fast with Darstan and Magmar until the surroundings jarred his memory. Darstan was just coming in with an armload of wood. "Where's the vargel?"

"Went with Rhaven to scout the area. I was up before first-light and they were already gone." Darstan shook his head. "He's a strange one. Last one to sleep and first one up."

Tobias was sitting next to the fire, with a large heated rock alongside his seat to keep the biscuits warm. Mrs. Marsten had potatoes cooking on another fire. Rahg breathed deep, savoring the aroma again: biscuits, khaffe, and potatoes with wild onions! "Save some of those biscuits for me, Tobias."

Rhaven rushed them through breakfast and soon had them heading south on the Sykoran Road.

"It looks like the vargel will be staying with us," Darstan said.

"I forgot to tell you her name," Rahg shouted.

All night he had dreamed of names, but the only one he could think of was Kanella. Then it finally struck him; he would use part of Kanella's name, but different enough to not shame her. It would preserve Kanella's memory with no disgrace. Rahg announced the name proudly. "Kella," he said. "I decided to name her Kella."

Tobias jerked the reins of his horse and turned to gawk at Rahg. "What!" The shock came through as he repeated himself. "What have you named her?"

Rahg's puzzled look mirrored his confusion. Tobias seemed angry, and Rhaven, who never showed emotion, appeared disturbed. Even the vargel stopped and looked.

"Kella!" Tobias shouted louder this time. "Have you gone mad, lad?"

"What's wrong with Kella?" Rahg told them how he thought of the name.

His explanation relaxed Tobias a little, though he still seemed unnerved. He then told the tale of Kella—legend among beasts.

"Mikkellana had enlisted the aid of the vargels during the last war against Sethia." Tobias paused to collect his thoughts. "That was when Lukaan sent his armies against the other lands. The Banished Ones couldn't escape, but he sent the Victas, Wolfen, Gnakas, and Sethians. It was Mikkellana and her own vargel, Kella—leading an army of them—who turned the war against him. They say the vargel died in the last battle, and ever since then no one has dared use the name of Kella."

Embarrassment painted Rahg's face but, more than that, he felt sorry that he'd have to change what he thought was a perfect name.

"Let him keep the name," Rhaven said. "Can anyone argue her courage? You saw her fight. I doubt that Mikkellana's vargel could have been any braver."

Rahg jumped off his mount and ran to the vargel. "Kella! Kella girl, come here." To his surprise, she responded.

"Well I'll be," Tobias muttered. "May be that it was meant by the gods. I'll be."

"Looks like she's yours now, boy. She fixed herself to you, and they say vargels heed only one master."

Rhaven's words had Rahg bursting with pride. He thought nothing could take away the pain of losing both Magmar and Kanella, but the vargel seemed to help. The hurt remained, but the unbearable pain had gone.

~

*A*s they neared the Sykoran outpost a small patrol rode out to greet them, halting short at the sight of Kella. The vargel drew the patrol leader's eyes, but he managed to tear away long enough to scan the group of riders, where his glare settled on Rhaven.

"State your business."

Rhaven sat silent while Tobias told the story. The Sykorans wore a dull-gray uniform with calf-high black boots. Each had a sword sheathed over one shoulder and a quiver of arrows on the other. Next to each saddle lay a short, curved bow designed for quick access while riding, and each horse carried an extra quiver of arrows.

The patrol leader—Atil—listened to Tobias' story then barked orders in rapid succession. "Tonrak, go to the garrison at River's Bend and inform the post commander. Borsu, send two patrols to warn the other villages. Morgan, dispatch a runner to the capitol suggesting all border garrisons be reinforced."

Tonrak saluted and departed the instant Atil completed his orders. Borsu also saluted, pounding his clenched-hand to his chest, before spinning his horse around and speeding toward the garrison. After his men departed Atil led them back to the post. Rahg tried to get Kella through the gates but she wanted no part of it and stayed outside.

By the time dinner came, Rahg was starving, though all they had was bread, cheese, and a broth. During the meal, Atil probed Tobias about what happened at Twin Forks.

"Do you know the name of the patrol leader? We have several patrols not yet in."

Tobias shook his head. "By the time we got there everyone in the patrol was dead. Kor Trasken said they took a lot of Victas with 'em."

Atil and his strike leader kept a wary eye on Rhaven as Tobias talked.

"We'll provide an escort to Sykor. If the Victas took Twin Forks, they can do the same to any village."

"We don't need an escort," Rhaven said. "Just a few supplies."

Atil nodded as if relieved, then looked to Rahg and Darstan. "Where will you lads go?"

"We don't know yet, but I think we'll go where Rhaven goes, if it's all right with him."

Atil's hand raced toward the hilt of his sword, and if the strike leader moved any slower it was by little margin.

"Our good King Favian had a death sentence on a man called Rhaven." Atil's face tensed. He was shaking.

"Favian revoked that sentence." The strike leader was quick to remind his patrol leader.

Rhaven was poised to strike. "Who I am is of no concern to the Sykoran guard."

Tobias stood, his hands in clear sight, and nowhere near his sword. His eyes were rock-gray and the glare he directed at Atil was as hard as granite. "I heard your strike leader tell you about the pardon. Now if you've got a hankering to die, go poke your head in a wagger's nest. You'd stand a better chance of makin' it out alive."

When the man didn't move, Tobias shook his head in disgust. "Soldier, if that sword clears leather, the buzzards will be pickin' cheese out of your belly come tomorrow noon. I'd suggest you sit down and finish your meal."

Rahg looked to Darstan, then quickly back to Tobias, Rhaven, and the Sykorans. He had leaned forward in the chair, his feet pressed against the floor, ready to jump up and fight. He hoped no one else got killed, but he was prepared to fight if it came to that.

Tobias nodded to Rhaven. "If you're done with the meal, go on. When the time comes that I can't handle two Sykoran Guards, I'll eat my pipe."

They stood still as stone until Rhaven exited the room. Most of the tension left with the swirl of Rhaven's cloak, but Rahg was still thankful when Tobias attempted to soothe things. "It's late and we've been travelin' all day. I think everyone needs some rest. We plan on leavin' early, so there's no time for arguin'. I wish you a good night, sir. After tomorrow we'll be troubling you no more."

Rahg and Darstan stayed awake talking, too excited to sleep, though their bodies insisted they do. Tobias refused to reveal their destination, and, as a consequence, Rahg and Darstan discussed every conceivable option, fretting over some possibilities, hearts racing at the prospect of others. "Do you think Kella will be waiting for us?"

"I don't know, Rahg, but I'm going to sleep. We'll see in the morning I guess."

Rahg's hands helped pillow his head as he pondered all the paths that tomorrow might bring. Soon, sleep overtook him.

∼

The sun cast the first rays of light as Rahg woke. Thoughts of Kella quickened his pulse and he roused Darstan so they could rush to check on her. Loud curses at the gate carried the answer to their question as they saw Kella guarding the gate and refusing entry to a patrol that had been out all night. "Kella!" Rahg could not contain the excitement as the humongous vargel bounded forward, nearly knocking him over. "Kella, you waited for me." He was still busy hugging her when he heard Tobias yell.

"Better eat, lads, we'll be leaving soon."

"To where?" hollered Darstan.

Tobias smiled. "We're headed for Sykor, and we're goin' with Rhaven."

Rahg and Darstan grinned ear to ear. This was going to be a good day.

~

Atil watched from the window as they exited the gate. "Send a messenger to the Force Leader and tell him Rhaven's coming."

"I thought the strike leader said—"

"He did." Atil's look froze the guard. "At times, the strike leader is soft. Let's see what the Force Leader thinks."

A WATCHFUL EYE

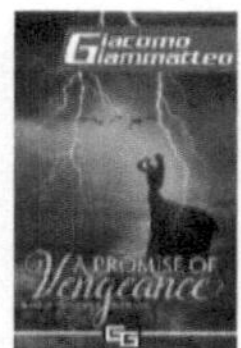

The air shimmered, cracked, and surged with power, revealing a warp in time and space. Aentarra stepped through the rift and scoured the area for trouble. Mikkellana and Xanthes were still unaccounted for, and she had not come this far only to let carelessness take her. Xanthes was strong, none would contest that, but Aentarra had no worry about him—strong as he was, he had a weakness for a woman's touch.

Mikkellana was another matter. She was far too clever with shields to be taken lightly; besides, until Aentarra could unravel the mystery of the Sethian Shield, Mikkellana must remain untouched.

The searing heat of the midday sun scorched Aentarra's bare shoulders, and the fiery sands scratched at her feet, yet neither elicited reactions. She Cloaked herself using the Powers of Stealth, then approached the Sethian shield unseen and unheard. The shield was invisible to most—another puzzling feature—but Aentarra could see it. Lukaan and the Banished Ones were inside Sethia, trapped by Mikkellana's ingenious design.

Curse the woman and her weaving. There was a time when she needed the shield up, and strong, but there would come a time when she needed it down.

If the design had not been so confusing, Aentarra might have discovered the mystery to it, but this shield was worse than the labyrinth in the Gorshan caverns, and its paths were riddled knee–deep with the bones of those who had tried to unravel those secrets. She shook her head to clear her mind then focused her attention inside the shield. *A Wolfen, a Victa, and a Sethian Guard stood not more than a few span from the shield. A perfect test for the Slicers.*

Aentarra dispatched Slicers for each of them, waited for them to get out of sight, then closed her eyes to concentrate, and Shifted.

～

*D*arstan frowned and tried to keep his mind busy. For three long, wet days Tobias had talked almost nonstop, words falling as fast as the raindrops. The bantering was like a hen clucking in Darstan's ear.

"As I was saying," Tobias continued, "when we get to Sykor you'll have to be careful. It's quite a different place than you're accustomed to. The guards control everything, and they have no qualms about puttin' country lads to work in a stockade. They'll lock you in shackles on a whim."

Darstan gave a perfunctory nod. "What did Atil mean about a death sentence on Rhaven?" The question had lingered on Darstan's lips for days and, since Rhaven had gone scouting with Kella, now seemed like a good time to ask.

Tobias let the stem of his pipe sit between clenched teeth while he smiled. "Had somethin' to do with Rhaven killing the king's nephew. Takar might be able to tell you more. We'll see him when we get to Sykor. Anyway, there's no time to talk. Rhaven and the vargel are coming now."

Darstan squinted, staring ahead at two blurry shapes. *If I didn't know better, I'd swear what he says about that pipe making his eyes better holds truth.*

Rhaven rejoined the group and dismounted to let Argus rest. "Darstan, did you see the way he slides off of his horse? He's like a snake."

"I've seen you practicing that move, Rahg. But you don't look like Rhaven. You look ridiculous."

"It might help if I had a better horse."

"I doubt it," Darstan said.

"Find a place to camp?" Tobias asked.

"Just inside the woods, there's a path that leads to a big clearing by the river."

"Are you still worried about Victas?" Darstan asked.

"Not Victas he's worried about," Tobias said. "If it were Victas he'd have chosen a spot in the woods where we could hear them coming—they're not very quiet. A clearing tells me he's concerned with Wolfen. They sneak through a forest like a whisper. Rhaven's preparing for the worst. That's how you stay alive; always prepare for the worst."

A short while later they arrived at the campsite. Darstan rubbed his sore thighs and stretched and twisted, trying to work the aches out of his back. He waited for Rahg, then they led the horses to the side of a fast-flowing creek. "This reminds me of that section of creek in the woods back home."

fast-flowing creek

Rahg stared at the creek. "I don't imagine we'll ever see that creek again. Or even Twin Forks." He picked up a stick and tossed it in the creek. "What do you think we'll do? Stay in Sykor?"

"I don't know, Rahg. We'll have to see how we like it."

Rahg and Darstan talked for a few minutes, then a whistle from Rhaven called them to eat.

Supper was unusual that night, consisting of the regular bread and cheese but, in addition, Rhaven cooked a soup made from grass and herbs. Darstan thought it tasted horrible but he wasn't going to be the first to say so. He managed to finish it all, and fortunately had saved enough cheese to rid his palate of the taste. Rhaven and Tobias scraped the remaining bits of food from the pan like pigs cleaning a trough. "They'll eat anything," he said to Rahg.

They sat and talked by the fire for a while, then Darstan stood and stretched. "I need to get some sleep."

"Me too, Dar." Rahg walked on stiff legs to his bedroll.

Rhaven and Kella checked the area one last time, then Kella padded over to sleep next to Rahg. He draped his arm over Kella's shoulder and stroked her heavy black coat.

"Thickest fur I've ever seen," Rahg said.

"I guess she needs it living up in the Whites." Darstan shifted to lay on his side. "Now quit talking, Rahg. I need sleep."

Rahg buried his head deep into Kella's thick mane and closed his eyes.

Sleep had not taken Darstan yet, and though he drifted off now and then, he was still awake enough to follow the conversation between Tobias and Rhaven.

Tobias warmed his hands by the fire and nudged Rhaven with his elbow, pointing toward Rahg lying with his arm draped over the vargel's body. "Sure has done wonders for the lad, hasn't she? I wish something could help Darstan. He keeps everything to himself."

Rhaven sharpened his sword as he listened to Tobias, the whetstone gliding up and down the steel creating a harmonious sound that proved comforting in an ironic way. "Darstan will find a way to vent his emotions. Everyone finds some way."

Everyone finds some way. Darstan almost laughed. *That's a nice thought. But what way will that be? How will I rid my mind of these horrors? How will I ever be the same again?*

He felt something foul within him, an evil seed growing in the pit of his stomach, and this feeling was happening far too often. During the daylight he suppressed it, but when he sought the comfort of sleep it wormed its way into his mind, festering like a wound gone bad.

⁓

Rahg awoke to a pounding head, recalling that Wolfen, and other creatures, had invaded the privacy of his mind. Wolfen were everywhere: waiting for him at each turn of the road, hiding in the corners of inns, and leaping onto his back from oaks and towering emeralds as he rode Timor through the forest. Strangely though, the identical woman who had rescued him in previous dreams, came again—a woman he had never seen before yet, somehow, she seemed familiar. She was the most beautiful woman he had ever seen, with long hair the color of a raven's wing, and walnut eyes so warm they called to him, like a fire in the hearth on Wish Day eve.

Tobias wore a worried look. "Another headache, lad?"

Rahg nodded and lowered his hands. "Pretty bad one. I seem to be getting a lot of them lately."

"Don't worry, lad. They'll probably go away once we get to Sykor. You'll have so much to do you won't have time for headaches. Won't be long."

"It can't be too soon for me," Rahg said. "When will we get there?"

"Sometime today. More than likely around supper time. Let's pack things so we'll be ready to go after the meal. A good meal will take the worst of it away."

Rahg and Darstan prepared everything for the journey and, after eating, they restored the campsite to its original form. Soon, they headed back through the woods, turning south on the Sykoran road. Tobias stopped at a point where the road narrowed between two large boulders that looked like sentinels guarding the gate. Another, larger rock bridged the top.

Rahg thought it was an odd place for them to be, just sitting there in the middle of nowhere. As he got closer, he could see that there were markings inscribed on the boulder to his right. It appeared to be written in Sykoran but was much too faint to decipher. Tobias began reading the sign: "Says five leagues to Sykor. We'll be there today."

"How did you know what it said?" Darstan asked. "I could barely make out a single letter."

rock monument by Sykor

"These rocks have been here since before Lyssic's time." Tobias leaned over a little in his saddle. He looked at Darstan and Rahg with an expression they both knew all-too-well—they were about to be taught another lesson. "Right there on that perch, the flat part, is where the first warning came to Lyssic during the wars. He had his scouts stationed five leagues from the gate. I knew what the words said long before we got here."

As they rode through the gap between the ancient boulders, an odd sensation came over Rahg, forcing a shiver to race the length of his body. He jerked his head, searching in every direction.

"What's the matter, Rahg?"

There was a long pause while Rahg continued looking around. "Nothing, Dar. I guess it was nothing," he said, but again checked the sides of the road. "Must be my headache. That's all."

Darstan nodded acknowledgment but continued staring at Rahg.

~

*A*entarra sat atop the largest of the two boulders. She had cloaked herself using the powers of stealth. She carved a snide look from thin lips, and dark brown eyes watched every move. *You will soon experience much more than headaches, Rahg Fal-Thera. Before I am through with you, your headaches will be a fondly recalled memory.*

She watched as they rode toward Sykor, a sly smile twisting her lips up at the corners. She closed her eyes to concentrate, the image of a palace at the top of the world forming in her mind, then Aentarra shifted, and was gone.

SECOND COUNCIL OF NELTSAR

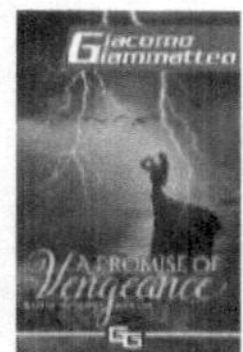

entarra's supple legs mingled with satin sheets while a gentle breeze from the balcony caressed silky skin and puffed the curtains—curtains almost as sheer as one of her opulent gowns. She stretched, arched her back, then uncoiled from the sheets, goosebumps rising with the wind's soft touch. Bare feet met the marble floor, sending a shiver all the way to her shoulders, where she shook it away.

Music drifted in from the courtyard and drew her to the balcony, her smile growing with each step. Morning doves cooed from their perches in the elms, adding their plaintive voices to the exuberant trilling of a thrush sitting next to a pink magnolia blossom. A smile stayed on her lips until the aria ended, then Aentarra went inside and dressed herself: black boots slid under charcoal pants as light as silk, and a white blouse with pearl buttons clung to creamy skin. She glimpsed a wry smile as she passed the reflector, gave a slight curl of her lip, then departed for Council.

The courtyard was alive with the sounds of birds and the soothing trickle of waterfalls slipping into obsidian pools. Even though it had been a thousand years, each breath tasted of the damp air of Asolo, and the smell induced fond images of the crystal shores of Lake Mago. Aentarra swept through the courtyard and up the stairs to a landing bedecked with sculptures, pillars, and gardens moist with mist. A discordant chirp of distress called her eye to one of the many fountain pools adorning the hall's entrance.

courtyard

Aentarra's smile vanished as she bent to pluck a newly fledged bird from the water, a baby sparrow. "What happened, pretty one? Did you jump from your nest too soon?"

She cupped the timid creature in her left hand while she bent to kiss the top of its head, fresh feathers soft as her skin tickling thin lips.

Chirps of terror affirmed her fears.

Her sweet voice and soft caresses proved comforting, and soon it lay still. "You will be fine," she whispered. Aentarra spotted the nest and stared until the image formed in her mind, then she lifted from the ground to a spot near the top. She placed the bird back in the nest, indulged it with one last caress and a soft kiss and then descended.

Aentarra continued toward her destination, stepping through a majestic archway into an enormous, corridor that constituted the perimeter of the Hall of Legends.

Great Path

The Great Path, they named the promenade, and it now reverberated with the sound of her footsteps as leather boots met the polished surface of black marble floors.

Two rows of ornate columns divided the Great Path from the lesser walkways on each side. Aentarra hesitated at each column to study the carvings that sprang to life from the marble floor. The intricate designs spiraled upward, each twist of the stone detailed by sculptures that related tales of famous battles.

The one commanding her attention told of a siege, of great legends falling, and of common soldiers consecrated heroes by acts of daring and bravery. The story culminated, as did the battle, with the destruction of one army's mightiest warrior at the hands of a young recruit. *Odd that this is so much like the battle of Syrnia with Arton,* she thought, and meticulously reconstructed the image in her mind.

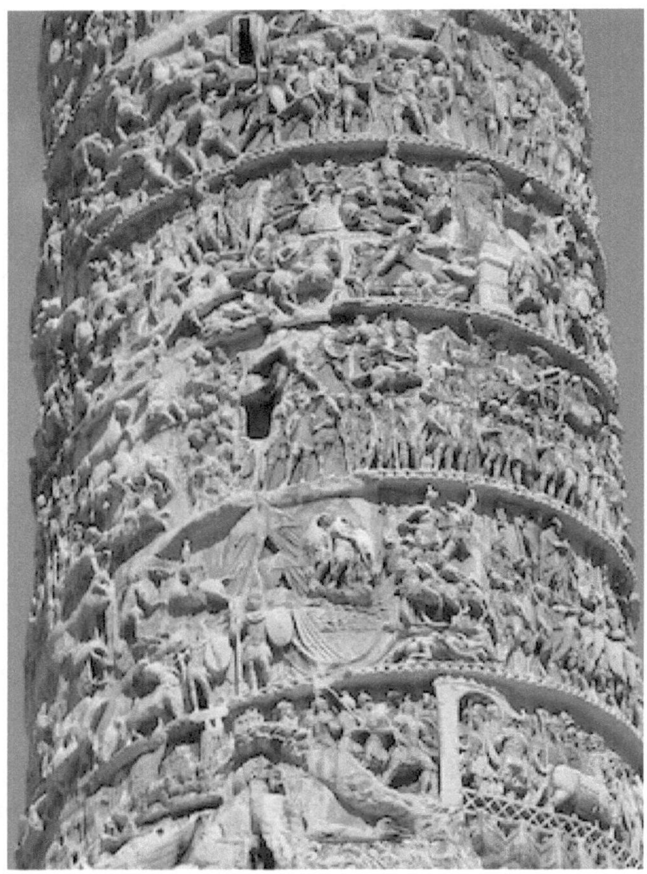

Arton's column

He was tall, she remembered, and muscular. And when his chest heaved after exertion... "Ah..." she sighed. "How magnificent he was."

Arton had fought like a man possessed that day, the vigor and stamina of a dozen warriors coursed his veins. None could stand against him as he slashed and chopped a bloody path through the ranks of

Ghruehne's forces. A man driven by fate, destined to slay the invincible warrior poised arrogantly atop the rise. News of heroes' bravery travel fast during times of war. It wasn't long before all had heard reports of Arton's exploits—the bravest of warriors during an era of endless war, when every child dreamed of being the hero, and every man dreamed of siring one.

The most perfect specimen of manhood I have ever seen. A pity what happened, she thought, recalling Arton's struggle to reach the portal. "Pity," she said, then continued her journey along the Path.

~

The Path was a book, the columns and murals its pages. Great hunts, quests, and other wonders chronicled with the care and detail of a master storyteller. The murals depicted scenes of battle, of love, of vistas never seen by mortal eyes, and of man and beast long since extinct. She ambled along the Path, intent on self-indulgence. It was not often she walked this way; normally she traveled a route that took her through the Hall of Echoes, where she sought clues to mysteries older than man. But today Aentarra had no concern with time. She stopped to stare at will, smiling as she recognized some of the characters she had dined with, plotted against, and loved in ages past.

She stopped in mid-stride, glaring at a mural picturing Xanthes and Melissara in an explicit love scene. *Xanthes, whom I once cared for. And Melissara, once my sister. Both betrayed me.*

Aentarra's eyes narrowed. Knots twisted her stomach. Muscles tightened. Lightning shot from her hands. A crack like a stonemason's hammer split the wall, ravaging the mural that ignited her anger. A strong sulphuric odor suffused the air. A heartbeat after, it was calm. Broken pieces of granite lay scattered upon the floor. A snicker replaced the scowl on Aentarra's face.

Aentarra veered down a side corridor that branched away from the

Great Path and led to the council chambers of Vallah. No columns lined the walkway. No murals hung on the walls. The only adornments were the massive sculptures of ancient warriors wielding weapons of lore. "It appears that I may be late again," she said, and slowed her pace. Laughter echoed off the walls, hot on the trail of her last spoken words. She then walked through an open courtyard with massive columns.

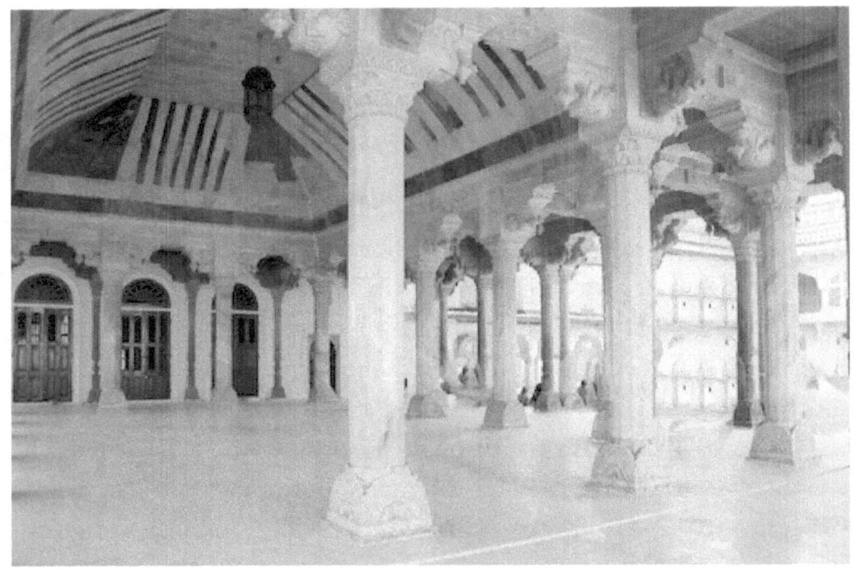

open courtyard

The final segment of the corridor secreted a pair of great wooden doors that opened at her will to reveal the council chambers beyond. A round, black table stretching four lengths in diameter filled half the room. The rings that emanated from its core revealed it to be a slice of an ancient blackthorn tree. Twenty-five chairs surrounded the table, though eleven had been turned up to lean against it. Seven of those had once been reserved for Lukaan and the Banished Ones, the other four belonging to the ones Lukaan killed. Of the remaining fourteen, bodies occupied eleven, the most recent seat filled by Mesan only yesterday.

Marble covered the floor, though not colorful as marble goes, consisting of dull-brown hues with an occasional smudge of gray—gray to match the drabness of the cold stone walls. The sole, uplifting feature of the room was a stained-glass window that showered a rainbow of muted colors throughout the chamber.

Aentarra scanned the room, thinking of all that must be done. It was then that she sensed the disturbance in the air and heard the muffled footsteps in the corridor. Recognition was instantaneous.

Xanthes! It has been a long time, my love.

~

Xanthes heard the call from Aentarra and came at once. Curiosity as much as lust drove him. He fondly recalled responding to her whims before, whims that led to amorous nights, although it struck him as odd that she would choose here to meet instead of her chambers. He Shifted to a spot he knew well, a dark corner tucked into a secluded section of the corridor. Aentarra was not to be trusted, so despite his feelings for her, he managed some semblance of caution.

The air cracked. *Too loudly*, Xanthes suspected, and spun a shield while he searched the corridor. He breathed deeply, filling his lungs, drinking the air in the corridor; it was ripe with her scent.

Memories of passion flushed his mind and drove his body to stiffen. *Control!* He chided himself for being predictable. She might have anticipated his reactions; might have come this way on purpose; might have worn that same scent, the one she wore when they had last embraced. The images drowned his concentration and, in his mind, he once again saw her naked splendor: the long lithe legs; the silky skin, so smooth to the touch; her raven hair, how it blew in the breeze like fine threads swept from a weaver's loom. *Blood's sweet glory*, she was wonderful.

From the periphery, he caught a glimpse of devastation scattered across the marble floor. He recognized the fragments as part of the mural of him and Melissara. Motes of dust danced in the stilled air of the corridor; he was not far behind. It was no puzzle as to whose work it was—hunters left smoldering campfires; Aentarra left destruction.

She's mad. Mad as any mind can be.

Xanthes cast wary glances to the alcoves and searched for shadows while peeking around each bend. She might be lurking anywhere and, though fear claimed no grip on him, prudence demanded caution. The massive doorway that guarded the council chambers opened at his will. Xanthes pushed his way through, but not before he had doubled the shield woven around his body. She would not take him unaware.

It was then that he saw the eleven seated around the table; it was then he saw the fate that had befallen them. His throat swelled as he struggled to swallow. *Too late!* Too late, he realized the trap. Too late, he saw the crystal shard of death racing toward him. The shimmering glow of the Slicer lent it an intelligence, almost an omniscience, as it eagerly sought its mark.

"How?" he managed to utter just before the Slicer struck. It penetrated Xanthes's shield as if it did not exist, as if it were not a force that had repelled the attack of a thousand armies over countless centuries.

~

*A*entarra swayed in tantalizing motions as she approached, staring into Xanthes's torpid eyes, all the while supporting him with powers to hold him erect. "Do you remember my soft skin?" Her arm brushed his cheek. "Feel it, Xanthes. Feel it, and remember. Do you yearn for the sweetness of my lips? Long to taste them one last time," she said, and pressed her lips against his, then brushed her hair across his face. "Smell the sweetness of my hair. Once you loved caressing it. Breathe deeply, Xanthes. Let me be the last thing your senses experience."

Sweet memories of Nelstar rode in on the inhalation: floral scents from the legendary gardens of Lenorda; wind whistling through the bell towers on Taragon; and the majestic, cloud-piercing peaks of Nagassa's southern range. Her own voice reverberated through the chamber, rolling with the perfect acoustics. It reminded her of the Canto Villa on Runella, the way...

The frown came so quick it stopped her. Sweet memories mutated into images of the Lights and all they had stolen from her. Aentarra's eyes closed and her head raised, the Oath forcing words through her lips. "An Oath of life..." She repeated the mantra again—it had become necessary now, like eating, breathing.

After her mind cleared, Aentarra led Xanthes's flaccid body to his normal seat and placed him gently in the chair. "No reason to change things now. Everyone should have the proper seating."

She sat and let her gaze sweep the room. One lone chair loomed like the bright southern light of Chrynal, the ever-steady beacon for mariners who dared the Gorshan Sea. *Mikkellana!* It was not yet time to trap her—those special talents were needed to maintain the Shield; besides, Aentarra had not yet determined what held that shield in place, though she felt she was growing closer to a solution.

A sigh escaped as she stood, strutting along the backs of the chairs, her fingers tracing the nape of Jorell's neck, then Mesan's. "You should have listened to me. I was right, you know. But you'll see that soon enough." Aentarra straightened the collar on Mesan's shirt, then adjusted the necklace on Sonella. She always hated when it wasn't centered. She stopped to align the chair next to Kiris, a nudge to bring it parallel to the others. Everything must be in place.

"It would have been easier with cooperation. You didn't think I would forget my oath, did you?" Laughter pushed her lips open. "No. I wouldn't forget that. Couldn't." Aentarra's smile shifted to a scowl. "Lukaan will soon learn as well. Then the Lights."

The gentle rays of the sun burst through the stained-glass window, supplementing the golden glow with hues of blue, red, and green. The brilliance almost succeeded in bringing a lifelike quality to the stilled shadows of the once-great members of Council. Bars of sunlight danced across the crystalline objects protruding from both sides of each council member's head, ricocheting off one, then another, in angles that formed an endless display of strange geometric shapes.

Aentarra spun toward the exit, the doors swinging open as she stepped onto the Path. The room remained deathly quiet as the giant twin doors closed, save for the lingering sounds of her laughter echoing in the chambers. Her footsteps faded as the great wooden gates snapped shut, like a seal on the sacred tomb of Xanethon.

Great Path, alternative route

She retraced her steps through the corridor, snickering. She had often wondered how she would deal with them, ever since they instituted the ban on entering the portals—not whether she would—just how.

Then her memory jarred and she remembered the Slicers. It had been so long she had almost forgotten.

The Council never suspected anything. She knew. She had observed them while in her Cloaked state. There would now be no more trouble. All were taken care of... "All but one," she said aloud. Aentarra's pace slowed as she considered this. Voice again shifted back to thought as she continued. *And Mikkellana is the most dangerous one of all—powerful and clever—not one to succumb to my traps. When she discovers what I have done, she... will not be pleased. I will have to be careful.* "Very careful," she whispered.

~

The drab stone that formed the walls of the chamber also served as the header for the stained-glass window. Two tiny flies hung motionless beneath the lintel, the only witnesses to this cataclysmic event—the last session of the Second Council of Nelstar. The fly on the right began to glow, weak, like a dying ember. Brighter it shined, as if being fanned with fresh air, then brighter still, increasing in magnitudes until a thousand candles would have been but a flicker in the night. Soon, the resplendence that was once a fly achieved full power and began taking form, altering to the shape of a woman.

Mikkellana felt weak from the transformation; a small form proved the most difficult to hold, the most strain on her powers. Her knees buckled, causing her to falter, but recovery came quickly. She circled the blackthorn table, the horrors of this last session too recent a memory.

"Kiris, Mesan, Sonella... I'm sorry, my friends. I should have foreseen this. Should not have let her roam free." Mikkellana smiled at the necklace on Sonella, sparkling like a sun buried beneath the sea. She had always loved Runellan diamonds. She reached to her own neck, tickling the scar where a similar necklace once lay.

Thoughts of her mother, Molina, teased her memory, but she soon shook it off, letting her eyes run across the others until they found Xanthes.

Curiosity had made her follow him, but she arrived too late to help. Mikkellana brushed his long black hair with her fingers, like wading through strands of silk. A tear fell as her lips touched his head, a lover's parting kiss. Sorrow tried to fill her but she forced it down, deep into the depths. *Time for that later,* she thought, and reached to touch the crystalline object protruding from Xanthes's head.

She yanked away, receiving a jolt that burnt her skin. *Slicers! Where did she get them?* No one had even spoken of them since the Wars of Light. Mikkellana had known little of the Slicers even then, when they were the weapon of choice for some of her father's favorites. But Aentarra had always favored them. And she was skilled with them, perhaps the best, after Antar. *Yes,* Mikkellana thought warily, *there is much to learn. But I'll not let a Slicer enter my mind. Not without a struggle.* Mikkellana paused and closed her eyes to concentrate. She created a barrier that her mind had not formed since before she left Nelstar.

She stared at Xanthes and recalled images of them walking, talking, enjoying each moment of life. "You were the only one I ever loved, Xanthes. Or trusted." Mikkellana's mind began to roam again, but she willed it to the present, shutting out the loving, yet painful, memories. There were new dangers to consider and she had no time to brood. Aentarra had grown stronger, and she had obviously gone mad, though she had never been far from it.

The fool doesn't even realize what she has done. She doesn't know how the shield works... It was then that a horrible thought struck Mikkellana. *Or does she?*

Mikkellana considered her options. She now knew that Aentarra could Cloak, an ability that no one had possessed since before the Wars. That in itself was dangerous enough, but she also had Slicers, and the gods only knew how many. *Curse you, father! You* and *your accursed Slicers!*

The blackthorn gates that constituted the seal on the council chambers opened, this time at the will of Mikkellana. Making no sound, she started down the corridor in the direction Aentarra took moments ago. Even now her bare feet changed, grew smaller and thinner. Her toes became miniature talons, and her legs altered to a reedy-thin form. The creamy-white skin of her arms darkened, and a blanket of brown feathers covered wings that had taken the place of limbs. Mikkellana's nose and lips sharpened into a beak, completing the transformation. Soon a tiny bird flew down the halls of the Great Path. She passed Aentarra, who was still walking, then turned to alight on her outstretched hand.

"Well, well. I see my little friend has learned to fly. You'll do fine if you stay away from the fountains."

Perched atop Aentarra's finger, the form that was now a sparrow screeched in a continuous barrage of chirps and peeps, but these were only reflections of Mikkellana's thoughts.

What will you do, Aentarra, when you face a Crystal Dragon? What good will your lightning and Slicers do you then? Who will you find to dampen your smoldering flesh? And who will heal your charred bones?

With a gentle flick of her wrist Aentarra hurried her friend on its way. "Go play, my baby. I have much to plan for. Much work to do before I'm ready for Lukaan. It would not do to face him ill–prepared. And I intend to savor this death, the first step toward fulfilling my Oath."

The sparrow seemed to smile as it settled on a limb. *Yes, my sister, we both have much to plan for, don't we?*

NEW FRIENDS

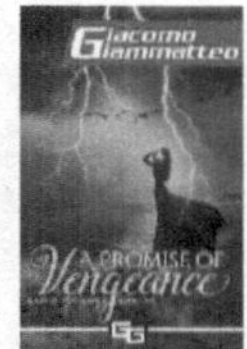

The city of Sykor sat atop three hills that loomed high above the valley. Buildings and houses crammed together on old narrow streets that twisted and wound through the city like a web from a hungry spider. Houses faced with brown and gray stone appeared to be stacked atop one another as they climbed out of the lower vales like ivy up a trellis.

"It looks like a giant fortress," Rahg said, eyes darting about, afraid to miss a new sight.

"And built like one," Tobias said. He scratched his bald head as he pointed to the guards at the gate. "Only two ways into Sykor, and everybody has to register when they go in or out. They like to keep track of things here. Fact is, they'll ask you a lot of questions when you get to the gate, so just tell 'em you came to see the city and you'll only be stayin' a few days. That should satisfy 'em. If you have any doubts about what to do, follow my lead."

Sykor

"We're not waiting in a line," Rhaven said. "Follow me."

"What about Kella?" Rahg said, but when he turned, she was gone.

"She wandered off into the woods a few minutes ago," Darstan said.

One of the guards moved to intercept them, but Rhaven stared at him and shook his head. "Not worth it, soldier. I'm just visiting."

His hand slid toward his sword, but slowly. Soon enough they were past him and under the walls at the city gates.

northern entrance

"Where are we going?" Darstan asked.

"I thought I would buy you a meal and a bath before I go my way," Rhaven said.

Rhaven set a fast pace through the merchant district, then turned south.

"Where are we staying?" Rahg asked.

"Trader's Inn. It's around the next corner."

Tobias cleared his throat and got Rhaven's attention, sounding almost apologetic. "None of us have any coin. If you'll pay until we can return the loan..."

"I told you I would pay." Rhaven pulled several pouches from his saddle bag. He tossed one to Tobias and one each to Darstan and Rahg. "There should be enough money to keep you for a while. And don't worry about returning it; I have more than I need."

Rhaven stared at Rahg and Darstan. "After tonight you will be on your own, unless Tobias intends to care for you. Either way you should learn to master weapons. There are a few teachers I could recommend, although Tobias could probably teach you as much as anyone. But we can talk of that later, for now let's take care of the horses and get something to eat."

Rhaven turned toward the stables, flinching as a bolt fired from a crossbow flew by. Rahg fell to the ground.

Darstan raced to him. Blood pouring from Rahg's shoulder. "Rahg! Are you all right? You're hit!"

Rhaven dove forward and rolled on the ground. With one fluid move he pulled a black tube from his back and brought it to his mouth, firing a dart that struck the forehead of a man perched on the roof of the building. The man tumbled forward, his body convulsing as he hit the stone pavement.

Rhaven stooped to examine the corpse, extracting the dart as he did. The dead man wore a cowled, dark-brown tunic tied with a sash. Rhaven pushed back the sleeves and found a black rose tattoo. "Assassin," he said, and proceeded to split open the man's tunic from belly to neck. A fiery red sun was carved in the man's chest. Rhaven stood in a hurry. "This is no ordinary assassin. Let's go before the guard comes." He walked briskly to the inn, threw the man standing by the door a silver piece and commanded him to care for their horses, then took a table in a deserted corner of the room.

"How's the shoulder, lad?" Tobias leaned close to inspect the wound. "Looks all right. Not too deep, but a nasty scratch."

"I'll be fine, Tobias. I've had worse when Darstan got me with the pitchfork that time. If we can just get something to eat..."

Rhaven tousled Rahg's thick brown hair. "What do you think of your brother, Darstan? He gets shot by an arrow and all he can think of is food."

"If Rahg was bleeding to death he'd be asking for a meal."

"What was that tattoo?" Rahg asked.

"The Black Rose are assassins that work for gold—bad enough that, but the red sun named him a follower of Lukaan. Not all of the Rose are. The problem is they'll have someone watching us, so you better stay here until I resolve the matter."

"We can help," Rahg said.

"You'll stay here," Rhaven said. He nodded to Tobias, tossed a few coins on the table, then left the inn.

They waited patiently for someone to take orders for food or drink. Rahg looked around at the people, checking to see if he recognized anyone, even though he knew as sure as pigs eat slop that he knew no one in Sykor.

The big center posts caught his attention as he scanned the room. They were as thick as the beams at the dock by Havril's and rested on wide-planked flooring the color of acorns. The bar was built from bricks, as was the fireplace, and both the mantel and the bar top looked to be carved from maple. "This is a beautiful inn," Rahg said. "Even the chairs are comfortable."

"I can't wait any longer, Rahg. I'm going to fetch my own ale and, if lucky, a serving-girl." As Darstan made his way to the bar, he brushed a patron's arm, spilling the man's ale. "Sorry," Darstan said, and continued toward the bar.

The man at the table wiped the ale from his arm, then nudged his companion. "Lad didn't apologize properly. Might need a lesson."

Darstan got several pitchers of ale, then began his way back to the table.

The man he had bumped into was large, with a red beard that would have covered his belly if it hadn't been so big. "Where ya goin' with so much ale, servin' boy?"

He stuck his foot into the aisle tripping Darstan, but the young man who had stabled their horses caught Darstan before the stumble became a fall. Darstan's face turned red. His eyes narrowed. He plopped the mugs on the table, glaring as he turned to face the man, who was still whooping with laughter.

Another man at the table prodded his companion. "Look, the lad's comin' to get ya."

The big man's laughter stopped before his mug slammed the table top. He stood like a bull being roused from sleep.

Darstan had worked the farm since he was six. Twelve years of clearing fields, plowing, and chopping wood toned his muscles. Aside from that, he never feared pain the way his friends did.

Red-beard stood half a head taller than Darstan, with shoulders as big as his gut. Despite the man's size, Darstan's first punch went straight to his face, like tossing a bale of hay to the loft. The man staggered back. Before he stabilized, Darstan's left hand struck—two hard jabs to his stomach followed by a powerful right that knocked the wind out of him. He grunted, nearly doubled over. Darstan raised his hands above his head and slammed down onto the back of red-beard's neck, as if he were swinging a pickaxe. The man crashed to the floor like a felled tree.

Two of the man's companions started toward Darstan, but before they came to blows the innkeeper leapt over the counter. He yanked one of them back then smashed him in the gut with a heavy wooden club. The man wailed as he leaned forward, then the innkeeper brought the club down on his back.

"That one did it," said Tobias. "Won't be any more trouble from him. Not tonight, anyway."

Rahg slapped Darstan on the back. "Can't believe you beat him so quick. He was a blasted giant!"

"Fighting's no different in the city, Rahg. Same as fighting at home." He rubbed his left arm as he spoke. "Arm feels like a tree fell on it. I thought that wound was healed. Guess not."

"Don't be thinkin' you know anything about fightin', Darstan. Back in Twin Forks the worst that might happen was somebody better than you would blacken an eye or break a bone. You were lucky tonight. Most fights I've seen end up in somebody drawin' blood with a knife or sword."

Tobias lit his pipe, adding to the smell of smoke already in the room. "You'll need to keep a watch out, too. No tellin' if they aren't out to pay you back now."

The burly innkeeper scanned the crowd, still wielding his club. He stood as tall as the man Darstan had fought, and was at least as large. Hair the color of dirty carrots and a red blotch on his face gave the appearance of an angry man. *Far cry from Havril. He'd as soon bash you as feed you.*

"For those of you who don't yet know, my name's Brock Larnigin. There'll be no brawlin' or you'll answer to me." He pointed to two men, prone on the floor, and bellowed for his companions to haul them outside. "If you come back, I'll toss ya into the alley and let the rats have a feast."

Brock plodded over to the table and hunched forward, staring at Darstan. "Laddy, you did right. If you had started the brawl, I'd have beaten you the same as I did the other." Brock beat the club against his other hand as he spoke. "She's a handy friend to have around. I've taken swords and knives away from many a man who bucked my rules."

"Broken a few heads too," the sweep-up said.

Brock eyed him through narrow slits, but laughter seemed to come even quicker than anger to Brock. He clapped the lad on the back. "You're right, laddy, I'm bein' too harsh. After all, these are new guests.

Don't want to give them a bad image of the Trader's Inn, now, do we?" He extended his large paws to shake hands. "I'm usually a friendly type. Just ask Kender, he'll tell you. He's been workin' here a long time now. Knows everything, he does."

After introductions, Tobias told Brock they would need two rooms, probably for several nights.

"We don't boast a noble's bed, but you'll find our rooms comfortable, and they're warm enough to keep the chill off. Kender will take care of you. I've got to get back."

"Thanks for helping me," Darstan said as he faced Kender. "You're the one who stabled our horses, aren't you?"

"That'd be me." A wry smile came to his face. "Also the one who saw your friend kill that man on the rooftop with whatever he had in that tube. Dangerous man, your friend." Kender's eyes darted among them. Tobias's left hand rested on the hilt of his sword. "Don't worry. I'm not one to talk. I see and hear enough around here to have collected a fortune in reward money, but I don't go in for that. Ask anyone, they'll tell you. Kender Darnell is a man to be trusted."

The door burst open admitting five Sykoran guards. They dressed the same as the ones Rahg had seen at the outpost: a dull-gray uniform, calf-high black boots, and a sword sheathed over one shoulder. The guards scanned the room, searched every face, then swaggered to the corner where Rahg, Darstan, and Tobias sat.

"New in the city?"

"Just arrived," Tobias said.

"There's a dead man outside," the guard said, then eyed each one of them.

Just when Rahg felt certain he would give them away, Kender interrupted.

"Perhaps it was Wisp, Somar? Ever think of that? Or do you try not to dwell on Wisp? Is it because he has eluded you for so long?"

"Not tonight, Kender. That blasted Wisp stole into a manor belonging to the king's niece and made off with some of her jewels. Favian's running about the palace like a madman. He issued edicts for all patrols to concentrate on finding Wisp and not to stop until we do." Somar slapped his hand into a pole supporting the ceiling. "How do we find somebody that no one has ever seen? Blasted, bloody Wisp!" Somar eyed them again, one at a time. "Fair warning, friends. Stay out of trouble. The guards are edgy."

Rahg and Darstan breathed a sigh of relief as the door slammed shut behind Somar, and both of them thanked Kender for keeping their secret. "Who is the Wisp?" Darstan asked.

"Who is the Wisp!" Kender stared. "You must be new to Sykor. The Wisp is the most famous thief to have ever worked the city. The guards have been trying to catch him for four or five years now, and they don't even know what he looks like. No one's ever seen him. He's robbed every major house in the city and most of the rich merchants' homes. One story claims he even stole into the castle of King Favian just to steal a kiss from the Princess. Why, the Wisp..."

Kender told tale after tale of the Wisp: how many times they thought they caught him; the countless descriptions of him that circulated; how he was surprised while in a noble's bed-chamber, yet still managed to steal away unseen; and his name—how he had been named by the people because he was like a wisp of smoke—couldn't hold onto him even if you grabbed him, the stories said.

"Kender Darnell!" Brock Larnigin's bellow found Kender's ears.

"Coming," Kender shouted back.

"Thanks again," Darstan said.

"Don't worry. That man you fought was trouble. He was looking to fight anyone. If it wasn't you, it would have been someone else. We don't want that kind of trouble here." Kender started toward the door then turned back. "I'll send someone to take your food order. Her name is Camissa. You'll like her."

As they waited for Camissa to show, Rahg scanned the room, marveling at the size of it. Havril's wouldn't hold a third as many, he guessed, estimating the Trader's Inn would feed about two hundred people in the main room. The rattle of dice steered his attention to one of two side rooms, where merchants and peddlers—and even a guard or two—gambled their wages. It piqued Rahg's interest, but the serving girl's arrival cut short further observations.

"Good day, gentlemen. It must be your first time to the Trader's Inn, because I surely would have remembered two such handsome young lads." Camissa's voice was as sweet as her honey–colored hair. A couple of freckles stood out against her pale neck, just below her left ear. *Silky skin would have been lost on her,* Rahg thought, entranced by her plain features. Camisssa's smile soon settled on Tobias. "Are you and your sons from Sykor, good sir?"

"We're from Kamnor," Rahg blurted out, as he stood to introduce himself. "I'm Rahg Fal-Thera, and this is my brother, Darstan. What about you? Are you from Sykor?"

A tinge of pink flushed Camissa's cheeks. "I hail from a small village to the south," she said, "though I've been in Sykor quite some time now. But you don't want to hear about me. Sykor has enough sights to keep you busy for days." She flashed a cute little smile that popped on and off her face as quick as a lightning bug. "Now what will it be for supper," she asked.

Camissa's manner seemed rushed. Rahg hoped he had not offended her, but right now all he could think of was the food. Camissa recommended the roasted lamb with mint jelly and a potato cooked with cheese. Rahg had been smelling that lamb for what seemed like days, so his mind was already made up about that. The potato sounded odd, but he'd try anything once, and he was hungry enough to eat dirt. Everyone placed the same order, then Camissa left. Rahg whirled to face Darstan. "She's pretty."

"She's pretty enough, Rahg. She's no Mary Lannis, but she is pretty. Friendly too."

"Don't neither one of you get smitten over that girl. Something strange about her," Tobias said.

"Seems nice enough to me," Rahg said.

"Me too," Darstan added.

"Nice she may be, lads, but she asks too many questions for just bein' nice. And she's not from any village south of here, and she's not from Sykor either. I know accents; she's from Khatara."

"Khatara? Why would she say she's from Sykor if she's from Khatara?"

"People do lots of things for lots of reasons, lads, and none of it is our business. I'm just sayin' keep a watch, and don't get caught up with a pretty girl just 'cause she's pretty. That's all I'm sayin'."

Camissa brought the food, which stopped the conversation. Rahg never said a word while eating. After the last bite went down, a piece of bread sopped with gravy, he leaned back in the chair and rubbed his stomach. "It was all she said it would be," he said, grunting. "I haven't had a meal this tasty since Ella's mother cooked for us when father was sick."

Tobias swallowed a mouthful of potato and took a swig of ale. "Don't know how you even tasted it, lad. You gulped it down like a wolf does a rabbit."

Rahg laughed, wondering if he had room for a piece of apple pie, when Camissa noticed the dried blood on his shoulder.

"What happened, Rahg?" She set the mugs of ale on the table then picked at his shirt where the bolt had struck. "Let me take care of that for you," she said, and proceeded to undo the top two buttons of his shirt.

"No need to undress me right here."

"Relax, Rahg. I doubt you have a chest I haven't seen before."

Darstan burst into laughter, even Tobias joined in, slapping his hands on the table. "Might as well cede, Rahg," Darstan said. "She reminds me of Maddy Corin. And you know how far an argument would go with her."

Camissa suddenly seemed to have sympathy for Rahg's discomfort, and offered to finish her mending job in the back room.

"It's not a bad wound," she said, "I'll clean it out with some of my herbs, though." She prepared a mixture of witch hazel, thyme, and rosemary, and applied it to the cut. "Just keep it clean and it will give you no trouble," she said. "How long will you be in the city? If you intend to be here for more than a few days, I'll be glad to take care of it for you. Will you be staying here at the inn?"

"I don't know yet. We came to..." Rahg remembered Tobias' concerns, about how inquisitive she was, and though he held no suspicions himself, he thought better of providing too much information. "...see the city more than anything. Darstan and I have never been here." While she bandaged the wound, she peppered Rahg with questions. When she finished, he thanked her, then made his way back to the table. After a few more ales and much conversation, they secured two rooms and retired.

~

*A*s the Trader's Inn prepared to close, Kender Darnell mopped the hardwood floor, cleaning food and drinks spilled during the night's entertainment.

Camissa strolled by and stopped next to him. "They are not what they seem," she said. A few moments afterward, she ushered the last patrons out the door and locked it shut.

Kender Darnell nodded. "That was a Black Rose their friend killed. Not many people can kill a Black Rose. They all bear watching."

THE DONGREL

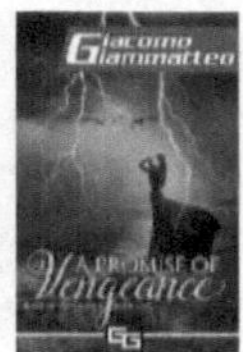

The streets of Sykor were dangerous at night, the footfalls of thieves and cutpurses as common as those of innocent citizens, but nowhere was the danger more prevalent than in the Dongrel quarter. A wagger's den was safer than the Dongrel at night, and no one ventured there alone. Even in pairs men took their lives in hand, treading narrow streets strewn with refuse, and alleys teeming with human waste.

Garbed in black, Rhaven was but a shadow on the walls, and only that by the grace of the moon's light. A pouch baited with coin hung from his belt, but the sword on his back and the two sai at his side were enough deterrent for even the most desperate of souls. Few men carried both weapons, and those that did lost even fewer fights. *When you need to catch a rat, bring some cheese,* Rhaven thought as he moved deeper into the Dongrel. The narrow alley grew tighter, more cramped, as long hushed strides carried him along.

alley in the Dongrel

Steely eyes gathered moonlight and narrowed to slits as he scanned the path ahead, noting potential traps. He hurried past the faceless wall of an empty building—it offered no promise for an ambush—but he grew attentive when he spied a corpse in the alley ahead. The sickly sweet stink of death, tainted by feces, permeated the air. Blood oozed from the remains, where rats dressed in skeletal frames picked at the flesh. "No one deserves this," he muttered, and booted the rats from their banquet.

Heavy clouds moved in to cover the moon, their trail a cloak of darkness that swept through the Dongrel. Rhaven crouched, turning quickly at the sound of water dripping. A shiver traced his veins as memories returned, memories of his own blood splashing onto a floor soaked already soaked in it. Rhaven's teeth clenched, hands balled into fists, body tensed as it did prior to battle.

Krovs! More people I have yet to kill.

Rhaven let his arms dangle, hands relaxed, fingers stretching toward the ground as he breathed in deeply, despite the putrid air. A few more breaths, then he pressed forward. Less than twenty paces ahead the remains of a cat lay unmolested in the alley—untouched, when it should have drawn scavengers. The rats should have been feasting.

Unless they were just driven off.

The hair rose on the back of his neck. Broken crates littered with garbage were stacked high against the building on the left side of the street and, across from that, scraps of rotted wood covered empty doorways. Either spot could hold them. Rhaven suspected men would be waiting at the curve in the alley ahead, though his analysis did not worry his step.

When he rounded the curve, a large, rough-hewn man greeted him with a raucous voice, the kind often heard rumbling from taverns where men consumed ale like water, and brawls served as the night's entertainment. "Fine evenin' for a stroll, 'eh, friend."

Rhaven let silence deliver his reply.

"It looks like you're havin' a bit of a time carryin' that heavy purse. How 'bout lettin' me tote it for ya, 'eh, friend?"

Rhaven took the man's mettle with a glance. His hands could wrap a three-year-old pine, and he had a frame like the trunk of an oak. They probably expected Rhaven to run. Most would from a man this size. Sheep run from wolves, but Rhaven was no sheep. If he ran it would likely be into the blades of the man's associates.

A noise from behind him confirmed his suspicion. Rhaven listened as they drew closer. Just a few more steps and they would be in perfect position. He measured the distance in his mind, picturing them as they crept along the shadows of the buildings. *Now,* he told himself, and whirled around, drawing both sword and sai before the rotation completed.

Rhaven's right hand caught the first thief. He smashed the hilt of his sword into the thief's head, dropping him instantly. The second man unsheathed a short, curved blade, good for speed and the confines of alleys braced by brick walls. The man relaxed into a fighting stance, then lunged. Rhaven easily sidestepped the attack, but realized as he did that he had no time to take the man alive. The large one had proved to be unexpectedly quick and was almost upon him. Rhaven could not chance being wrapped up in those paws the big man called hands.

A quick thrust with the sai put a gaping hole in the thief's chest, then Rhaven ducked under a brutal swing from the giant and slashed him across the back of the legs as he maneuvered into position. The big man howled. Most of the large ones were not accustomed to being hurt. He suspected that pain was a new experience to this one, which was precisely why he wanted him alive.

The big man staggered, a dazed look in his eyes. "I have been forced to kill tonight," Rhaven said. "But no need for you to die. I need information. If you provide it, I'll leave in peace. If not..." Rhaven pointed to the corpse on the street, "...you will join your friend."

The big man's eyes narrowed. "What information?"

"I seek answers about the Black Rose. Anything you can tell me—names, descriptions, their location, anything. I am willing to pay with gold."

The previously unconscious thief stirred, his voice groggy and strained. "Tell 'im nothin'. The Rose will kill us if you do."

Rhaven cast a frozen glare at the man. "And I will kill you if you don't." A brief pause let his words take hold. "What is there to lose? If the Rose never find you out, you continue your life, and if they do, at least you have a bit more time to breathe."

The thief stood and drew his sword. His eyes were narrowed and his lips pressed together into a thin line. "I'll take my chances with you, stranger. I know the Black Rose."

Rhaven swatted him with the sword, like a cat would a mouse, only quicker. The thief screamed, fell back against the wall as his severed hand dropped to the street still grasping the hilt of the sword. When he screamed again, Rhaven stepped over and drove the hilt of his sai into the man's head, knocking him unconscious. The big man moved toward Rhaven, but a warning glance held him at bay.

"Tell me what you know."

"I don't know any by name," he said, "but I know where they meet."

Rhaven nodded. This was a start. He threw a silver piece to the thief, then added another for his partner's healing. "Keep it yourself or use it on him. I don't care which." As Rhaven made his way back to the inn, he thought of the job ahead of him. This might take more time than he had planned.

GUTTER RATS

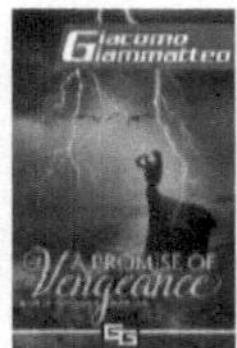

obias woke early and looked to see Rhaven stirring from sleep. "Didn't even hear you come in," he said.

Rhaven looked to Darstan. "Rahg said you had a cousin in the guard, Darstan. An officer?"

"As far as I know, but I've never met him."

"Tobias is going to take you to see him. If the assassins have someone watching, it might give them pause to see you with an officer of the guard. And I might need the extra time." He started for the door, then, almost as an afterthought, turned back. "How is the shoulder, Rahg?"

"Better. Much better. Thanks."

Darstan smiled and nudged Tobias. "He sure complained about it earlier."

"Come on, Tobias, let's go eat," Rahg said.

"Warm your backside while I shave, lad. Won't take me long."

"I don't know why you bother. By suppertime you'll have that white stubble showing again."

"It just so happens that the ladies like this stubble, lad. If you ever get a chance to grow one you might find out."

Darstan gave Rahg a light kick on the leg and winked. "Come on, Tobias. I'm hungry, and we need to get a table where Camissa is."

Tobias stopped his shaving and spun around to face them. "Darstan, you've kept people waitin' half your life. I think you can wait on me for once."

They laughed, and Tobias mumbled all the way down the stairs.

"Good morning, Rahg, Darstan, and of course, a good morning to you, Tobias." Camissa's voice was as sweet as a songbird's, and her mood seemed to match. "I hope you have an appetite."

"It smells good," Rahg said. "I'm thinking bacon, biscuits, potatoes and eggs. I'm starved."

When the meal came, Rahg dug in like he hadn't eaten in days. "This is good," he mumbled through a mouth crammed with food.

Tobias stopped eating and stared at Rahg. "Lad, if you can't slow down, then quiet down. You're makin' more noise than Timor does with a bag of oats."

Rahg paused to swallow, then took a sip of the khaffe. It went down with a shiver. "Whew, have you tasted the khaffe, Darstan?"

"It's good. Nice and strong."

"I hope Camissa comes back," Rahg said.

"I told you before, lad. Something strikes me strangely about the lass. May be that I'm wrong, but until Rhaven settles this business about the Black Rose, we'll keep a close watch on what we say, and who we say it to." Tobias finished his meal then pushed the chair away from the table. "Let's go."

As they left the inn, Rahg saw a guard posting a reward sign on the outside wall.

'Reward for the capture of the Wisp—-10,000 gold.'

"Ten thousand gold! I'd try to catch one of the Banished Ones for that much money," Darstan said, then he and Rahg hurried to catch up with Tobias.

~

The Trader's Inn grew busier as patrons eager for their morning meal crowded the common room and filled the tables. Kender stopped Camissa, rushing by with a food order. "Did you find out where they're going?"

"No. The old man is cautious," Camissa said. "He got them where they won't say anything. But if I can get the others alone, they'll talk."

"Never mind. I'll take care of it."

~

Vendors crowded the streets of Sykor as they prepared for another day of peddling wares. Rahg smelled a freshly–baked apple pie and wandered over to sample a taste.

"Go on," the chubby merchant woman encouraged, "take a taste. If ya don't like it ya don't pay. Nothin' to lose." She wore a confident smile. "I know you'll like it though; it's what I count on. People tell others about Mollie's pies. Best in town they are. Go on, take some," she said, and dished-out a small slice.

Mollie reminded Rahg of Mrs. Parker. She was shorter than Rahg by a head, and stout enough to push at the sides of a plain, brown dress that looked more like a sack—and everything covered with a dusting of flour. Dirt smudged her face, and a trickle of perspiration streaked the white on her cheeks, but her eyes sparkled with pride. Rahg took a taste. "It's good. Taste it, Dar."

Darstan took a bite, then said, "Give me a slice. That's good."

"I'll have another one, Mollie," Rahg said.

"Well, blast it," Tobias said. "Let me try it. Apple pie is apple pie. Don't know what could be so special about this one." Tobias munched doubtfully on the slice of pie as Mollie eyed him. "Is different," Tobias said, then ate some more. "What spice do you use?"

Mollie chuckled. "If I go and tell all my secrets they wouldn't be secrets long, would they? Everyone would be able to bake a pie like Mollie's. I have special recipes for all my pies. Cakes too. And nobody, not even that no good husband of mine, knows what's in 'em." The wrinkles around her eyes tightened when she smiled. "Come by tomorrow, it's my special day. I'll have a real treat for ya. And don't forget to tell others where the best pie can be got—Mollie's." Another customer came by and Mollie started her sales pitch all over.

Tobias licked his fingers as he walked up the street. "That sure was tasty," he said. "We just might have to come by here tomorrow."

"And you were the one eager to leave if I recall," Darstan said.

"Can't be stoppin' at every vendor stand in the city. Though I could make a habit out of that one."

A ruckus from down the street interrupted their chatter. They quickened their pace to investigate. Rahg squeezed his way through a crowd of angry people. A handful of guards had several people in chains.

"What's going on, Tobias?"

"Guards are rounding up people with powers," a man standing beside them said.

"Powers? What kind of powers?"

"Fire, boy. They say that one in the middle shoots fire from his hands."

"I've never heard of such things," Rahg said.

"Can't say I've seen it, but I've heard of it too many times for it not to be true."

Tobias grabbed Rahg by the arm. "Let's go. We got no time to dally."

"What was he talking about, Tobias?"

"Got no time for tales, Rahg. The soldiers' barracks are just ahead."

Four armed guards stood at the gate. Tobias approached one of the guards. "Come here to see a man," he said and turned to Darstan. "What was your last name, lad? I've only known you as Fal-Thera."

"Ludar," Darstan said. "I believe he's an officer."

The guard glared at Darstan. "That would be Force Leader Ludar," he said. His face twisted into a scowl. "And who might you be to ask?"

"I *might* be his cousin," Darstan said. "And if I am, you might want to fetch him before it brings you trouble." Darstan's eyes met the soldier's, until the guard ceded. None of them wanted trouble from a force leader.

A moment later the guard returned, trailing an officer. The man looked frightening. He stood taller than Rhaven, and broader, his upper frame a solid block and tree trunks for legs.

"I'm Force Leader Ludar," he said, his voice like the rumble of a wolf. He stared at Darstan. "My soldier tells me you claim kinship to me, a cousin, he said."

Darstan smiled and offered his hand. "My parents were Grendl and Cobb Ludar, traders from Khatara."

"Why should I believe you?"

Darstan stood back, his face blank.

Tobias nudged his way between Darstan and Ludar. His face was streaked with red, and his hackles rose like a mad dog. "You should believe him because he said so. If that's not good enough, I'm tellin' you flat out." Tobias got closer to Ludar. "We thought we'd come and introduce your cousin to you. Thought you might help out with work, or kind words. Guess we were wrong. C'mon lads. No need to waste time on a man like this. I'm beginnin' to feel foul just standin' near him." Tobias turned to leave, Darstan falling in beside him.

The force leader's face reddened, and he held himself rigid as stone. They had only gone about five paces when Ludar called them back. "Hold."

Tobias whirled around, his hand gripping the hilt of his sword.

Ludar put a smile on his face, though it looked to be a false one. "Perhaps I was hasty in my judgment. I would not wish to be wrong where relatives are concerned."

It wasn't an apology, but Darstan relented and slowly stepped toward Ludar. Rahg and Tobias followed.

Ludar's smile seemed more genuine when he shook hands with Darstan. "If you have the time, let me show you around the barracks."

Darstan smiled and Rahg beamed. "We'd like that," Darstan said.

Ludar showed them the soldiers' quarters, introduced them to officers, and explained the hierarchy of the Sykoran army, detailing how many patrols a force leader was responsible for, the number of sergeants a captain had. And he told them about the duties of the new recruits.

Rahg thought they were leaving when they crossed the center court again, but Ludar said there was one more stop to make. They soon entered a building used as a warehouse. A modest entry opened to a large storeroom brimming with weapons. Rahg gaped at rows of swords, shelves that climbed to the ceiling, and racks bursting with lances and pikes. A center row held crates crammed tight with sheathed knives and daggers. "I never dreamed so many weapons existed. There are enough weapons here to arm the whole world," Rahg said.

"Not quite so many as that," Ludar said. "But these days an army can hardly have enough. Wolfen and Victas are raiding towns, and we're finding common citizens with the powers of the dark. Bad times are upon us." Ludar's voice abruptly shifted to a lighter tone. "But let's not speak of trouble. I brought you here to offer a gift." He pointed to the racks of swords and an open crate of knives. "Darstan, you and Rahg choose any blade and dagger you wish."

"Thank you, sir," Rahg said, as he scanned a heavy curved sword.

Darstan examined dozens of swords. He quickly abandoned the large two-handed swords and the ones used for slashing. The Sykoran blade was renowned for its good steel, but Darstan had not found one he liked, then, while rummaging in a deep pile, a short rusty sword with a hilt of bone and a disk-shaped pommel caught his eye. Both sides featured a wolf's head with teeth bared viciously. The blade, a double-edged thrusting type with a spear-shaped point, showed evidence of fine workmanship underneath layers of rust. His smile told it all as he examined it. Darstan liked the idea of a short sword. Most fights were in close quarters anyway, so a short weapon was more practical. He studied the design on the hilt, a mountain covered with forests and within the forest, a pack of wolves hunted. The light in Darstan's eyes revealed his choice.

Ludar frowned at the decision. "Odd selection, Darstan. That sword appears to have outlasted many an owner. The rust is eating it, and I suspect the blood alone would have worn its edge. There are good Sykoran blades to choose from, some of them newly made."

"What kind of sword is this? Are there others like it?"

"It is called a Cergalan sword, but why, I don't know. That one has been there since I've been in the guard. No one seems to want it; it's not a blade for a soldier."

Darstan ran his hands over the sword, flakes of rust peeled off and fell to the floor. He fingered the shapes of the intricate designs on the blade, and though he couldn't yet make them all out, he felt the detailed work of a master. "A little dirt can't hide a pretty face," he said, recalling one of Magmar's favorite sayings. "This will do fine."

For his dagger, he opted for a Wolfen long-knife; it was nearly the length of his sword, though thinner.

Ludar searched through a crate of sheaths and found one to fit Darstan's sword. "If you insist on that old blade at least hide it in this sheath. It will do until you can have one made for you."

Darstan smiled. "The blade just feels right."

Rahg selected a more traditional Sykoran sword, a straight, single-edged blade with a false-edged point for stabbing. It was a slashing weapon with a thrusting point, and it was almost half again as long as Darstan's. The blade had no carvings save for the crested-helmet emblem of Sykor's royalty, which meant it once belonged to someone in the king's guard, but it did shine like the sun, and when Rahg held it in his hand, his smile rivaled the blade for brilliance.

Rahg strapped on his belt and sheathed the new sword. His face lit up like a lad with a full chest on Wish Day. "Let me see yours, Darstan."

Darstan extended his hand to show Rahg but Ludar interrupted them. "Time grows short, Rahg, and you must still select your dagger."

Rahg found a plain dagger with a sheath that fit neatly into the back of his belt. "This will do," he said, and tucked it into its sheath.

"You should give thought to joining the guard," Ludar said, as he walked them to the gate. "It will keep you out of trouble and keep your belly full."

"I'll think about it," Darstan said. "We just got here. I want to see more of Sykor first."

The guards at the gate snapped to attention as Ludar drew near. "Take your time, Darstan. You, too, Rahg. Give the guard consideration yourself. Nothing better for a young man."

They thanked Ludar again and started walking back to the Trader's Inn, a walk that shed new light on unpleasantness. Tobias grumbled the entire way. "I'm tellin' you, and I know. Somethin's not right with Ludar. Don't care if he is your cousin. Did you see the way the guards treated him? I expect a young recruit to have the look of fear in them when a force leader comes by, but the old veterans did, too. That's not natural."

Darstan's attempts to defend Ludar irritated Tobias all the more. His mumbling continued while his head shook back and forth. "Somethin's not right. Can't put my finger on it yet, but I will. Somethin's just not right."

"I'm thinking about Ludar's offer to join the guard," Darstan said. "I think we should, Rahg."

"And I think you drank too much ale last night. I'm not doing it."

Rahg and Darstan argued, while Tobias muttered, but none of them noticed the two beggar boys who had been trailing them since early morning.

~

As soon as it became apparent that the Trader's Inn was their destination, the urchins ran past them and sneaked to the side door, unobserved. They knocked three times, then twice more, but softer. Kender Darnell poked his head out, checked both ways. "What did you find out?"

"Like you guessed, Master Kender, they went to the barracks. Asked for none other than Ludar, that black-hearted son of a serpent."

Kender smiled and folded two coppers each into hands as dirty as their faces. "You've done a good job, my little gutter rats. I'll send someone when I need you again. Now go before you're seen." He booted them in the backside as they left, scurrying off down the alley and disappearing into the shadows.

A THIEF IN THE NIGHT

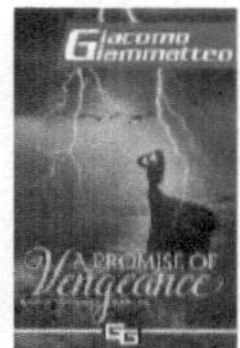

*T*he area surrounding the fisherman's warehouse reeked with pungent odors of the day's catch, the stink leaking out like smoke from a building on fire. Few places could match the rankness—perhaps the Dongrel—but the two men meeting inside seemed unaffected as they conversed in hushed tones.

Carmine's shifty green eyes scanned the shadows of the warehouse while his meaty callused hand straightened a few errant strands of silver hair that brushed the side of his head. "I just received word. Bren Bulta's prized jewels are in Sykor."

Wisp nodded. An easy smile crossed the thief's face and lit his brown eyes. "Not much would please me more than getting back at Bulta, but still, you shouldn't have called me."

"No one followed me."

A sigh, followed by a heavy breath, brought the stink of fish in through Wisp's nose—the most prominent feature on an otherwise plain face. "This will be difficult. Bulta will have those jewels protected."

Carmine nodded, his bull neck barely moving with the gesture. "They'll be well guarded, to be sure. But he won't be able to keep his eyes on them all the time. Besides, think of what the jewels will bring on the Khataran market. They might even write another poem about you."

The promise of riches no longer lured Wisp from the comforts of a warm bed, or a lady's friendly smile, but the mention of a poem had the thief's heart racing. "I'll think on it, but if I decide to do it, nobody can know. Nobody! I've been watched lately. I can feel it."

"Watched? Gregor again?"

"I don't think it's Gregor," Wisp said. "But there's a new man in the city. A dangerous man, although I'd not have guessed him a bounty man."

"I'll see if I can find out anything," Carmine said. "As for Bulta, let me know by tomorrow."

"I'll do it," Wisp said, making up his mind. "By my rules."

"Agreed," Carmine said and related the details to Wisp.

"Any news of the Black Rose looking for a man who wears two sai?"

"It's none of our business."

"I'm making it my business," Wisp said. "This is the man I mentioned earlier, the dangerous one."

"Any business he has with the Rose is no concern of ours."

"It might not be your business, but it *is* mine. The guards are already on alert. If the Rose cause trouble, there will be so many guards around that none of us will be able to work. Get word to them. If they must kill the man, see if they can wait."

"I'll find out," Carmine said. "You'll get word in the usual way."

The door of the warehouse cracked just enough for Carmine to peer out. When he was certain no one watched, they both departed.

~

The Trader's Inn had a small, raised stage along the front wall, midway between the door and the main fireplace. Rahg watched intently as a bard entered the stage. He was a short man, and his flowery-cloak and bright green clothing made him shine in the crowd. The bard sported a purple cap which clashed with the other colors and barely fit over his thick crop of blond hair. A flute and a khithara lay strapped across his back like a soldier's weapons.

The bard plucked on the strings of the khithara to quiet the crowd, then he recited a few tavern songs.

> A rich older man from Licenda
> Met a frivolous young woman from Genda
> She soon spent his gold
> Then left him, I'm told
> For a merchant who traded in Senda.

The people applauded after each song, some adding in rhymes of their own. After a moment, he strummed the khithara again, a signal to the patrons to quiet down.

"This is a story of a girl from Pomender. He purposely mispronounced Pomanda the chief rival of Sykor. The crowd hooted and hollered.

> A girl that I know from Pomender
> Wore dresses that near showed her gender
> She exposed so much thigh
> It made the men sigh
> Wishing their wives were so tender.

"I know several girls like that," one man yelled, "and right here in Sykor. Don't have to go to Pomender to see a leg or two."

"Down in the Dongrel you can see more than thigh," someone screamed hysterically.

"And for a few copper coins you can do more'n just look," his companion added, barely able to get the words out he was laughing so hard. The banter continued for several moments, rolling around the room with each table taking turns.

The bard had paused to fetch a drink of ale. When he returned to the stage he was dressed all in white, including cloak. He donned a black hat as he stepped up onto the platform. The crowd hushed. He strummed the khithara, stopped, and scanned the room. All attention focused on the short little man in white.

"For those of you who are not familiar with the next recital, this is the tale of Sykor's most beloved hero—by the common folk. And her most notorious enemy—should you ask a guard."

Several screeching drunks urged him on. One strum on the khithara brought the room to utter silence. *Mountain-cat quiet,* thought Rahg. The bard's voice was just above a whisper, forcing the patrons to pay close attention. When the bard's eyes met Rahg's, it seemed as if he were telling the story for Rahg alone.

"The night snapped crisp. The sky shone clear.
'Cross the rooftops above, a shadow appeared.
Descriptions abounded from those that would bother
One named him skinny, *fat* swore another.
His hair was black, or brown, or some shade of yellow.
Truth is, no one knows the looks of the fellow.
'Cross the tiles of the roofs he would dance, having fun.
Not a slate would he loose even at a full run.
Deftly, he crept through the night air so cool

Spying on merchants hiding their jewels.
He passed-up a bracelet with emeralds aplenty.
Would have fetched a nice price, but of those he had many.

Ah, a noble's house—a Sykoran lord.
Now there was a challenge. *They must have a horde.*
He peeked through a window. Locked. Bolted. Secure.
But that posed no problem, he'd done it before.
Saw diamonds like prisms, rings with rubies afire.
Enough gems in there for a thief to retire.
Just a moment or two, that's all it would take
And he could be gone. No noise would he make.
A short bit of time to claim a prize so great,
But he had an appointment and must not be late.
He'd vowed when he saw her, though 'twas from afar,
That a kiss he would steal from sweet Cynemar.
Her beauty was legend. Her virtues were many.
And by Favian's orders—no kiss gave she any.
"Until the right man, impress *me*," swore the king,
"Cynemar will submit to no suitor's ring."

Locked windows, barred doors, guards in the hall,
They presented no challenge to a thief with his gall.
The unspoken dare proved too much to dangle.
Into Favian's castle he must somehow wrangle.
Through defenses plenty and guards by the score.
Cynemar's kiss he would steal—this, he swore.
The virgin lay sleeping a princess's sleep.
Disturbed by no one, safe within castle's keep.
The guards itched restless. One called, "Who goes there?"
"Tis nothing," swore the others. "Tis nothing but air."
"I know I heard something," he said, kind of oddly.
While over the wall, slunk the thief's hidden body.
Each bolted chamber he checked with great care.
The guards, though they sensed him, saw nothing but air.

Relentless, he was. Giving up—not a thought.
Not till he found the treasure he sought.

If I have to search till mid-morn, or noon,
I'll kiss the sweet princess. I'll make her swoon.
Up ahead, guarded well, he spied what must hold her.
The night air, he noticed, grew suddenly colder.
Four pikes and a lance, and several with sword.
Stood fully alert, barring the door.
He observed, in addition, many locks on the portal.
This, he realized, challenged any a mortal.
Scanning alternate entry, he finally did spy,
A slit of an opening, though it sat up quite high.
Up on the wall, the very top of it though,
He saw a window of light bearing Cynemar's glow.
It's not barred, he could see. *A trap?* "No," he said.
They'd expect no one here, lest he be soldier, or dead.
The sheer wall he climbed, gripping cranny and crack,
Then slithered through the portal flat on his back.
Dropping from high, he flipped—like a cat.
No sound did he make, he listened for that.
There, on the bed royal. "Like a goddess," he sighed,
Lay sweet Princess Cynemar. His eyes had not lied.
She proved more than a vision; she had an aura; she glowed.
And over emerald cased-pillows, her golden locks flowed.

"By the gods," the thief whispered, whilst he silently crept,
To the poster-board bed where Cynemar slept.
For a moment he stood there, awe-struck with wonder.
Should he disturb so precious a slumber?
He bent low to kiss her. Her lips, sweet as honey.
This, he knew now, was better than money.
Such succulent lips—rich, full, delicious.
Nearer he closed on the treasure so precious.
Then, just afore bonding, he quickly diverted

His kiss pecked her cheek. Cynemar woke, now alerted.

She rose up in fright, bosom covered with fur.
One hand touched her cheek. Had one dared to kiss her?
Her eyes, slow adjusting. She saw him, though brief.
"Who?" she said haughtily, "are you?—a thief?"
He smiled whilst he spoke, words flowing like wine.
A professional orator could not do so fine.
"I steal women's virtue, and hearts. I do right.
"I'm just a young lover. A thief in the night."
He sat on the bed, pulled her close, kissed her tight,
Then shed the embrace and whispered real light,
"Guards could be called. At your scream, they would scurry,
"And away they would take me, in chains, in a flurry."

She looked at him warmly, again, they did kiss.
Smiling broadly, he vowed. "You, I will miss.
"But the sun is soon rising, and I must be gone.
"My work is conducted 'tween midnight and dawn."
He spun, cloak whirling. A blur he appears.
Afore leaving he turned, saw Cynemar's tears.
"Fret not my sweet princess, your secret is mine.
"And my life I entrust to you, my divine.
"If ever your lips yearn for kissing, my sweet,
"Put word to the beggars, or thieves, on the street.
"The message will reach me afore nightfall for sure.
"And into your chamber I will steal once more.
"And if Favian should query, 'Who's so bold? So brazen?'
"Search the rooftops, my dear, they are my haven."
He was gone in a flash. She wondered, did I dream this?
Once more felt her cheek, then remembered his kiss.

The sky—it shone clear. The morning snapped crisp.
And into the shadows stole a thief named—the Wisp.

The crowd clamored rebelliously, shouting and screaming their approval, banging on tables and stomping their feet on the oaken floor. Rahg turned to Darstan who had joined in the revelry, pounding his heavy mug on the table and effecting a loud, shrill whistle. "They sure like the Wisp," Rahg yelled over the clamor. "Do you think it's true?"

"What?" Darstan shouted back.

"The story about the Wisp."

"Who knows?" Darstan hollered, unconcerned. "Who cares? The people of Sykor believe it. That's good enough for me."

"I suppose you're right." Rahg said.

The bard took his bows then proceeded to make his rounds to each table, mixing light conversation while he gathered his tips. Rahg tossed a silver piece into his hat. The bard effected a gracious, sweeping bow that made the feathers on his hat touch the floor.

The bard smoothly completed his elegant gesture, then addressed Rahg as if he hailed from noble blood. "So generous, young lord. I could suffer a benefactor such as you at all my performances. I recite other tales, you know. Some proclaim them to be even more intriguing than what I rendered this eve, and whilst I would never think to advertise another's establishment—least not while performing for the honorable Brock Larnigin, a most-magnanimous sponsor, if you would but make the proper inquiries you will learn the whereabouts of my next rendition. If your pleasures border on the arcane, then most assuredly my tale a fortnight from now will enthrall you—a legendary tale of the Ancient Ones, and the Immortals; of other worlds; and of creatures so gruesome your mind would struggle to fathom them, and your sleep might leave you for nights on end. Come, hear my tale, good sir. And do not feel obliged to contribute on the next occasion; I enjoy a man who revels in my tales." The bard extended his hand in friendship. "Baldomere Testa is my name, though most use only my last."

Rahg took his hand and shook it, surprised by the firmness of the grip for one so thin. "My name is Rahg. Rahg Fal-Thera. And this is my brother, Darstan, and our friend, Tobias."

Testa heartily clasped each of their hands, then begged to leave so he could continue his rounds. "If I let much time elapse before I visit their tables they forget how enjoyable a performance it was." He laughed, then leaned toward them and whispered. "Ale makes short memories." Even Tobias chuckled at that, as Testa moved to the next table. "Baldomere Testa's the name..."

"We'll have to go," Rahg said.

"Go where?" asked Tobias.

"To hear Testa's story—the one about the Immortals."

"Rahg Fal-Thera," Tobias said, frustrated. "Does your mind ever stay on one thing for more than a moment? Do you have to let yourself be blown about by every little breeze that comes along? Can you, for once, just concentrate on what's at hand? And another thing, throwin' that silver piece in his hat—what were you thinkin', lad? The man told a good tale, I'll grant you that, but I'll tell tales for days on end to earn a piece of silver. Come next reunion you'll be wishin' you had that one back. I'm tellin' you now so you don't forget." Tobias sat at the table shaking his head back and forth, like he always did when he was angry. "Lookin' out for you, is like—"

"...sittin' on a needle," Darstan said, finishing the statement for Tobias.

A scowl formed on the old man's face. "Don't be thinkin' you're so innocent, Darstan," Tobias growled. "You're a thorn in a cat's paw yourself at times."

A large burly soldier entered the inn and headed in their direction. He carried the rank of sergeant and looked to be as big as Ludar, with a scar that covered the left side of his weathered face from chin to ear. A thick bull neck sat atop a powerful chest, and big, battered hands looked as if he could wring sweat from a bear's neck. Sharp green eyes surveyed the room with just one glance.

"Tobias Marek!"

"Takar! Sit down. Join us in some ale."

"What are you doing in Sykor?"

"You heard about what happened in Twin Forks?"

"You were there?"

"Me and these lads. Came to Sykor with Rhaven." He paused to light his pipe. "Have you seen him?"

"No, but I've been searching for him. I suspected he was in the city.

"How's that?"

The big sergeant looked around suspiciously, then related his explanation in a quiet, but clear voice. "There have been dead men found in the Dongrel, not unusual for the Dongrel, but these were hard, tough men. And there have been reports of someone new who stalks the rooftops of the city. Tales claim it to be only a shadow, but this shadow has a face I know. It has to be him."

"Does sound like Rhaven," Tobias said, then noticed Camissa working her way toward them. "Not here, Takar. Too many ears."

"I see you have noticed things are amiss in our fair city. Meet me tomorrow after breakfast at the old fort on the hill."

"Agreed," said Tobias. "It's time anyway. They're getting ready to close, and there are things the lads and I must do. Until tomorrow, Takar."

"Until then, Tobias."

~

*C*amissa swept the floor while Kender cleaned the dishes. She checked the locks on the doors, then climbed the stairs, calling good night to Kender as she did. It had been a long and busy day. At the top of the stairs she blew out the candle then stepped quietly down the hall coming to a stop outside Rahg and Darstan's room. She leaned close to the door and listened.

A moment later the door opened. She fought for balance but was yanked off her feet, heels scratching the wooden floor as she was dragged into the room.

"Keep quiet, girl."

Darstan and Rahg stared at her. Tobias glared. "I think you better tell us what is going on."

THE TRAP

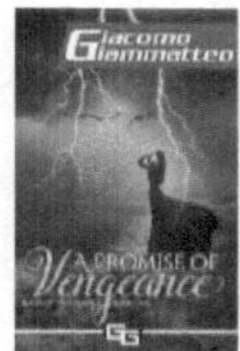

a trace of moonlight sprinkled its favor over a damp Sykoran night. Wisp embraced the darkness, slinking through the shadows of a side alley, flitting from one buttress to the next. His furtive moves appeared as little more than shadows, or the moons' reflection playing tricks in the night. Wisp scaled Bren Bulta's wall, reaching into cracks that defied all save the rats and a few other creatures of the night. Where he found no crevices, a jagged piece of stone sufficed. He could scale a wall of glass, rumors claimed. Feats such as this fed those rumors and made them ring true.

Search lanterns spread across the walls of the mansion. Wisp stilled, becoming another rock on the wall. Soot smeared his olive face and the backs of his hands, making him one with the darkness. Once they had passed him by, he scurried up the wall—just like the rats he loved.

Three floors above the street the searching lights ceased. As he passed the window of an unoccupied room, he studied. The sap used to seal the frame looked to be torn loose, the latch half closed. It would be easy to slip a wire through and undo that catch. *How strange. Do they think me the fool, going through an open window on a house guarded so well? They'll not catch this rat with such smelly cheese.* He paused at the eaves of the roof to study the situation. The overhang projected almost a length—inordinately long, and loose-fitting tiles dangled from the edge, poised to snap off and fall if he tried to use them as leverage.

He perused the area. There was no way to get to the roof—unless...yes, that should work. His bare feet searched for ledges in the stone, toes gripping small projections with the dexterity of fingers. He seldom went prowling without his soft leather boots, but he knew that Bren Bulta's house presented a special challenge.

One small step at a time, he eased around the corner and onto the chimney. When he looked down, he saw Bren's guards talking and drinking khaffe, moonlight reflecting off the top of their shiny helmets. *They should search more and drink less.*

It took little time to finish scaling the chimney. In less than a moment he was on the roof, gingerly placing his feet on the tiles to ensure they were secure. The steep pitch of the roof forced him to bend forward to maintain balance. The faint bit of moonlight cast a silvery glow on the gray slate, and as the moon of Ranalla peeked from behind the cover of a cloud, he could see the skylight ahead. A good place to enter.

As he made the final steps to his destination, he pored over everything that had transpired since he got to Bren's house. Something bothered him, stuck in his gut like a knife, but he could not pinpoint the problem. The warning signs were strong, though, and Wisp had never been a careless person.

He sat on the roof to think. Too often his instinct had saved him. Far-too-often, when all else indicated which path to follow, intuition warned him to choose another. And his intuition had always been right. He knew this would be a trap. Word of the jewels had gotten out on the streets too quickly, indicating that someone had leaked information.

So why would Bren Bulta risk his jewels to trap me? And it surely was a trap; Carmine's informant had far-too-many details, even down to the room where the jewels were kept. The answer struck Wisp with a suddenness that caused him to chastise himself. Bren Bulta would never risk his prize jewels unless Favian were behind him.

It was right under my nose. Those guards with their helmets shining were not Bren's guards. *Bren's guards wouldn't have the discipline to shine their helmets.*

Wisp quickly put the pieces together. They were the Sykoran night-watch, Favian's personal command. That meant Somar or Takar would be in charge. He thought about that window again, the one with the poor sealant and half-open latch. Bren might have expected him to enter there, but Somar, and surely Takar, would know better. They would have anticipated his reactions, expecting him to seek another entrance, an impossible one, a place no one could access—like the roof.

They almost had me. He now felt certain the skylight held the real trap, but caution fused his bones, so he crawled up to verify his suspicions. He waited for cloud-cover. Only Ranalla shone tonight. The reunion was almost gone, so he would not have long to wait.

Soon it was pitch-dark. Wisp peered over the rim of the skylight into the hall. It would ordinarily be bright with the glow from candles or lamps. It wasn't. They had all been dimmed.

Very inviting. Even with the lights dimmed he could see far down each corridor. All the doors were closed. *A thief's dream, this house.* A candle flickered, but only one, the one next to the curtain. *You breathe too-heavily, my friend,* thought Wisp, now satisfied beyond doubt he had made the correct assumption. Sitting back down on the roof, he pored over the problem from a different angle. *All I need now is a plan.*

ON THE TRAIL OF ASSASSINS

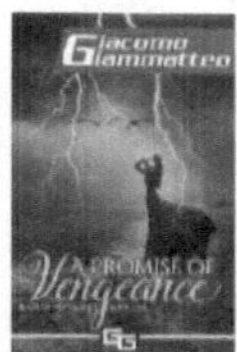

Rhaven had been waiting on the roof since before dark. He stretched continually so he wouldn't be stiff when it came time to leave. The Black Rose were in a building across the alley and they had a rooftop exit. Before long a door opened. The man exiting wore assassin's garb: brown clothing and a cowled cloak. Rhaven sat in silence. A rock made more noise.

The Black Rose looked at the adjacent rooftops, then crouched and crept toward the edge of roof. Halfway there, he whirled around, checking that no one followed. The dull garb made him difficult to trail in the dark, but Rhaven had followed man and beast alike through forests with no moonlight—tracking the Black Rose along the rooftops of Sykor would present no problem.

The assassin moved with grace, the rooftops familiar to him. Rhaven kept pace, following at a safe distance. The assassin made his way through the merchant's section, then into the noble district. Halfway up the hill to Hightown, the assassin turned and headed toward the Trader's Inn. Rhaven shadowed him silently.

A short distance from the Trader's Inn, something alerted Rhaven.

The hair bristled at the back of his neck. He had the feeling of being watched. He had been so engrossed in tracking the assassin he had paid no attention to whether he had been followed. He stared into the darkness behind him, but saw nothing. He wanted to check the rooftop behind him but the assassin was moving and the Trader's Inn lay just ahead. *Only one more building to cross.*

The assassin perched behind a small parapet with a clear view of the front door. He laid a crossbow on his lap and got into a comfortable position. Rhaven ducked behind the roof partition, the last of the obstacles separating him from the Black Rose. He took a throwing knife from his boot and crept forward, avoiding any position that might produce the snapping sound of bones creaking.

~

*A*nother figure danced on the rooftops, trailing both Rhaven and the Black Rose. He peered through the slats of an abandoned crate, watching every move. He watched as Rhaven approached the assassin. *He is good, this man in black. But I wonder why he follows a Black Rose?*

~

*R*haven advanced slowly. *Don't move. I don't want you dead.*

The assassin turned, a startled look in his eyes. He went for his blade. Rhaven threw his dagger, aiming just to the right of the man's face, then dove forward, both hands landing on the roof. He spun his legs and kicked the assassin's knife from his hand.

The assassin drew a second knife with his other hand and stabbed at Rhaven. The blade came within a hair's breadth of his stomach. Rhaven sidestepped and latched onto the man's wrist, twisting it with a hard jerk as he did. The Rose dropped the weapon but smashed his fist into Rhaven's face. Indignant, more than hurt, Rhaven landed a crushing blow to the mid section, followed by two punishing blows to the face. The assassin stumbled backward, tripped on a loose board and toppled over the parapet to the cobblestone street. Rhaven cursed as he leapt over a narrow alley and disappeared into the night.

~

The third party stepped from the shadows and descended a ladder to the street below. "A dangerous man," he whispered, "a man worthy a healthy measure of respect." He shook his head, then knelt and picked up the Black Rose, blood spilling onto his cloak as he threw the body over his broad shoulder. He whistled an odd tune while strolling toward the guards' barracks, his quarterstaff banging on the cobblestones as he jostled some drunkards, swinging the dead-man's body. "Stand aside, good men. I carry a Black Rose—an assassin."

CAMISSA

amissa dried her eyes. "I told you, I heard voices. I didn't even know it was your room."

"Girl, it's one thing to spy on us, but it's another to lie about it."

She managed to shed a few more tears. "I thought you were friends. Now...now you treat me like this."

Tobias paced. "Put the tears away. I'm certain you've got those lads near to shedding tears themselves, but it won't work on an old man. As pretty as you are, I'm past the craving stage. Your tears might work on young boys, like Rahg and Darstan, but they won't work on me."

Rahg sat on the floor brooding, and Darstan stood by the door, guarding it. Suddenly the door popped open. Rhaven walked in.

"Get rid of the girl. We need to speak."

"Can't. She's up to something. Caught her outside the door listening to us."

Rhaven reached out with his left arm, seized Camissa's throat, and yanked her off the bed.

She gasped.

Rhaven leaned close until his face almost pressed against hers. "I am not a man of patience. I will ask only once. What were you doing outside the room?"

"Don't hurt her!" Rahg said. He moved toward Rhaven.

Without releasing his hold on Camissa, Rhaven whirled around. A knife had somehow appeared in his hand. He hurled the blade, sticking it into the floor between Rahg's feet. The handle was still vibrating from the impact when Rahg halted. "Don't interfere, boy."

Rhaven focused his attention once again on Camissa. "Tell me now, girl."

She nodded, and Rhaven released his hold on her. "I was afraid."

"Of what?"

"When I tended to Rahg's wound yesterday..."

Rahg stood. "What about it?"

"I...I used a...talent I have to help it heal." She cried again. "I shouldn't have, but it looked bad. After that I got afraid, so I had you followed. When I learned you went to see Ludar...he...the guards are killing people with powers." She buried her face in her hands. "Please don't tell. Don't turn me over to him."

"Knew we were followed," Tobias said. "Knew it."

Rahg went to her, put his hand on her shoulder. "What do you mean about talent?"

"Let me see the shoulder, boy."

Rahg took his shirt off. Tobias inspected the wound. "I'll be," he said. "Can't even tell it was there."

He turned to Camissa. "You're a healer?"

She nodded. "I can't do it all the time, but sometimes it just...happens."

"Why would that bother Ludar?"

She shivered. "He's got the guards looking for anyone with powers. They put them in the dungeons and...people say he kills them."

Rhaven took a look at Rahg's shoulder then turned to Camissa. "If that is all you're hiding, you have nothing to fear from us. I don't care if you plan to kill the king, so long as it doesn't interfere with me."

She looked at each of them. "You promise you won't tell?"

"We've got our own problems, girl. No need to worry over a healer."

"You mean the assassin?" Camissa said.

Rhaven nodded. "I followed one tonight. I planned on taking him alive but didn't. With two of their men dead the Black Rose won't quit. They'll be after us."

Camissa was quiet for a moment, then whispered. "I know someone who might be able to help."

"Help how?" Rhaven asked.

"With information. He knows everything that goes on in Sykor."

"Who is it?"

"I have to ask him first," she said. "You understand."

"Do it by tomorrow."

"I will have an answer then."

"Fair enough," said Rhaven. "Now, I need to sleep." He sprawled across the bed as he spoke.

"What about Camissa?" Rahg asked.

"Let her go," Rhaven said. "I'm certain she wants sleep as badly as I do."

Camissa expressed her thanks with a smile, then left the room. "I will see you tomorrow," she said.

JEWELS

tiles on roof

isp grabbed some loose tiles and made his way back to the unlatched window. It would be dangerous, but he had not come this far to be denied. Besides, the thought of besting Bren Bulta added motivation.

Clinging to the stone like a spider, Wisp searched the darkened room with eyes trained for the night. If Somar was in charge one trap was all he could expect, but Takar would be more thorough. He would plant guards in both rooms and the corridor upstairs. As Wisp watched two shadows moved. *So, it is Takar.* He crept closer, pressing his ear to a spot where the sap they used for sealant had broken free from the stone.

"I don't know why we're stuck in here," one guard said. "He won't come in this way."

"Better than being where he will," said the other. "Can't tell what might happen."

"The Wisp never hurt a soul. Truth be known, I'm wishin' him well tonight. Hope he don't show up."

Wisp smiled. *I even have supporters in the guards.*

Wisp studied the room carefully. This plan would take a lot of luck to work, and it had to be done at just the right time, when it was dark enough. Wisp wrapped string around several tiles so that when he tugged on it they would slide off the roof and crash onto the street, identifying his location. He spaced them so that it would appear as if he were running over the roof, after the first one "gave him away." The final piece to the plan held the key to success. Once he had their attention, he would fling a slate into the pond outside Bren's house. The pond was deep and close enough to the house that he could jump if he had to. It was time to find out.

He tugged on the first string and sent it sliding down the roof.

"He's on the roof," a soldier said.

Wisp let the second tile loose, then waited a few breaths, then the third; another five seconds and he cut the fourth loose. Things inside were in a state of turmoil.

"He's running. He knows he's caught now. Hurry, get the rest of the men. We've got him trapped."

"Sergeant," a harsh voice yelled. "The Wisp, sir. He's on the roof, running to the east side."

It's time, Wisp thought, and flung the slate as hard as he could. It splashed with magnificence.

"He jumped into the pond," a guard shouted from below. "Hurry, he's in the pond. Surround it." The soldiers remaining in the house ran down the stairs.

Wisp slid the wire through the caulking, pulled the latch, then opened the window and climbed through. No guards remained in the corridor. He slithered toward the room containing the jewels, and stopped abruptly, sensing something wrong.

He quickly made his way back down the corridor and peered over the railing. There, at the entrance to the mansion, stood Bren Bulta, shouting and screaming to the soldiers to find Wisp.

Odd. He's not even worried about the jewels. He should be on his way up here to check on them. Unless, Wisp now mulled, *they are not in that room.* Wisp recalled the legendary greed of Bren. He would never leave those jewels out of his sight. He was far too greedy, and trusted no one. *They must be with Bren.* Once again Wisp altered his plans.

He searched the second level from the stairs. Bren stood at the front door, and guards were outside, everywhere. Ten paces down the corridor a door was ajar, the room dimly lit. Wisp lowered himself then dropped with a hushed thud. No one would hear with all the commotion outside. As he stole into the room, his mind raced with thoughts of anything he might have missed.

I wonder where Gregor is tonight?

Wisp could barely see in the darkened room. The light he had seen from the stairs must have been the moon shining through the clouds. Wisp shook it off. His eyes were trained to the night. He could see better than the soldiers, so if things got tight he'd rather have it dark.

He felt behind the pictures on the wall. Nothing. The chandelier hid no jewels; neither did the massive, carved bed. Bren would have a good place to hide them. But where? Time was running short. He had to find them soon or give up and leave. The guards would not search for long.

Wide strips of wood boasting ornate carvings covered the walls. Wisp ran his fingers delicately across the wood, searching for any signs: differences in texture; seams where there should not be; anything that might indicate where a small safe could be secreted. Frustration took hold, but it didn't show. He closed his eyes to concentrate, then opened them; he could now see better—the night seemed more like dusk.

After more futile searching, logic took command of the hunt. If he couldn't see it, then perhaps it was something he had to touch or turn —a handle, or button, some item that was part of the decor. He pressed on pictures, lifted vases, twisted bedposts, and tapped lightly on the wooden floor to check for a hollow space—nothing. Finally, he started over at the entrance to the room methodically feeling his way along the carved paneling. Halfway down the first wall, the eye on a mountain cat's carved head gave way, producing a slight clicking noise.

Wisp knelt on the floor to examine it. The paneling under Bren's desk had popped-open to reveal an alcove, and in that alcove lay the necklace he sought. He snatched it and exited the room, turning the opposite way into the corridor. He knew there must be another set of stairs for the servants to use, and within a few paces he found them and dashed up the steps two at a time. Only a few minutes had passed since he entered, and he was already making his getaway. As he was about to exit through the window, he stopped, listening to Bren Bulta shouting at a guard.

"Sergeant, bring three of them back to guard this corridor."

"The corridor? But, sir, the jewels—"

"Don't argue, Sergeant. Remember, you are under my command. You worry about catching Wisp. I will see to my jewels."

"Not to worry," said Wisp, completing his escape. "Your jewels are safe with me." He laughed while rapidly descending the stone wall. In the background he could hear the splashing in the pond as the frustrated soldiers prolonged their search.

street where Bren Bulta lives

"He must be here. I saw him jump in."

"Did you actually see him?" asked another.

"I'm conv—"

Wisp once again flitted down the alley, the voices of the soldiers fading, as did he, into the shadows of the night.

THE WISP

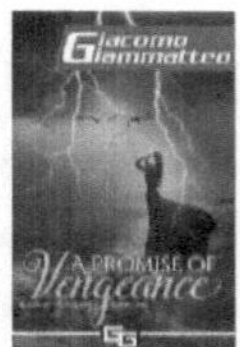

The soft light of dawn pierced the open windows, catching motes of dust as it spread warmth on the tables nearby. Customers shuffled hurriedly to set cold bottoms onto warm chairs, and basked like lizards in the morning sun. Rahg and Darstan rushed down the steps, Rhaven and Tobias following.

Camissa snuffed out the few remaining candles at the far end of the room, then made her way toward the kitchen. She waved at Rahg and Darstan, then hurried over to seat the four of them. Smiles came easy to Camissa, especially when talking with Rahg. He had an easy smile, too, and he smiled with his whole mouth and face, not just a grin. "I hope you have an appetite, Rahg."

Rahg inhaled deeply. "Smells like bacon, ham, eggs and potatoes. Makes me want one of everything." He was glad to see Camissa in a good mood. After last night he had expected a much cooler reception.

As they ate breakfast, the door exploded open, crashing against the back wall, and shaking down the one picture that adorned the walls—a small lad with a knife surrounded by rats. A patrol of guards burst through, knocking chairs and tables aside.

At the front stood Takar, looking more rugged than usual. His left eye, the scar side, drooped a little, and his hair was wild and stringy, like he just got out of bed. Coarse stubble covered his face, and his uniform was mussed, but it did not interfere with the Sykoran short sword peeking over his shoulder. A gaunt-faced soldier standing next to Takar held a scroll in his hand. Takar nudged him and the trooper unrolled it and began reading.

"By order of the king. Last night a thief, believed to be the notorious Wisp, robbed Merchant Bulta of a priceless piece of jewelry, a necklace intended as a gift for Princess Cynemar. Twelve Khataran emeralds, each chased by a sapphire from Jattan-Kir, form the circle. The heartstone is a diamond as large as the other stones combined."

A collective gasp hushed the soldier momentarily, allowing him much needed respite to catch his breath. "Anyone in possession of the necklace, or in the company of anyone caught with it, shall be subject to the sentence of death. Execution will be instant. The good king has ordered it so, and so it shall be done." His voice was weak, almost squeaky. He didn't sound like a Sykoran guard. When he finished, the squeaky-voiced man rolled up the parchment and stood at attention.

At least he knows how to stand like a soldier, Rahg thought.

Takar walked slowly around the room, pausing occasionally at a table to stare into the eyes of customers. When he reached their table he stooped, whispering to Tobias.

"Same place," he said, "but meet nearer to noon. I have more stops to make."

Tobias nodded.

Takar looked at Rhaven. "We should talk in private."

Rhaven finished a mouthful of food before looking up. "If you wish to speak with me, come when I'm not busy."

Rahg choked on a piece of bacon, then his mouth fell open as he slid his chair away from Rhaven, expecting a brawl to begin at any moment.

The scar on Takar's face reddened. His hand balled into a fist as big as a melon. He pounded the table then straightened and stormed out of the inn, pushing brusquely past patrons and his own men as he charged through the door.

"Time to leave," Tobias said, placing six copper dirnars on the table. "Let's go, lads."

Rahg and Darstan got up to follow, looking back at Rhaven as they departed, a hundred questions nagging at them.

~

While Rhaven finished eating the room came abuzz with chatter. Most involved speculation about what Wisp would do with the jewels. At the table next to Rhaven, three men whispered.

"I tell you," the one farthest from Rhaven said, "I heard from the merchant himself. There was no way that anyone should have been able to get through that many guards. He must have powers. That's what everybody's saying."

The man seated to the right of the speaker tapped the table, awaiting his chance to speak. "My source is none other than the guard on watch last eve. He told me that two full patrols guarded Bren's house, all entrances and exits. But Wisp still got in, stole the jewels then got up on the roof and jumped into the pond. After that he disappeared." The proud man wore a smug look as he sat back with his arms crossed over his chest, leaning in the chair until it rested on only two legs.

Rhaven studied them. *It didn't take much to make some people proud,* he thought, glancing at the jackass-grin on the fellow. Rhaven was about to leave but something about the way the third man told his tale caught Rhaven's attention.

The man started in a low, non-bragging tone of voice. "You can't repeat this, as I heard it from a sergeant in the guard."

"Who?" The second man asked.

"Who it was, isn't important, but what happened is." The statement silenced his friends. "This sergeant was hot on the trail of Wisp, they were sure of that. He was only about ten paces ahead of them running through the River Edge section and he turned down an alley that the sergeant knew was a dead end. He sent several of his men to the roof of each building to cover any escape and he left four to guard the entrance, while he and five others followed Wisp. They found no one. There was no way out; no doors; no ladders; and yet he was gone. The guards on the roof saw nothing. And heard nothing. What do you make of that?"

Rhaven gave consideration to the man's statement. A Sykoran patrol leader, or sergeant, would have used that same basic strategy to cover the alley. Either the man told the truth, or, he knew how to tell a good lie. Rhaven decided that he was at least telling the truth as he saw it.

He didn't see how anyone could have escaped, but, it was clear to him that there was some measure of truth behind the story. Enough to warrant further checking. He recalled the feelings he had experienced while hunting the assassins. The first time he paid it no mind, but on the second night someone had definitely been watching him; he felt those eyes on him, and yet, he saw nothing. *If those eyes are watching tonight, I'll be prepared.*

~

"*I* don't understand," Darstan said as they left the Trader's Inn. "I thought Rhaven and Takar were friends."

Tobias chuckled. "Sooner or later, you lads will learn. Sooner, I hope.

You should have suspected something. We'll ask Takar when we meet. Now, let's worry about more important things, like whether Mollie has any fresh-baked pies."

Tobias quickened his pace, and Darstan wondered if it was the pies or Mollie that put the extra spring in his step. He smelled the cinnamon in those pies from half a block away and smiled as they drew near.

Mollie looked just as Darstan remembered her. Flour dusted her hair and face, and her soft blue eyes sparkled, betraying an underlying warmth she tried to disguise with her gruff demeanor.

"Good morn to ya, gents. Come back for my special? I knew ya couldn't hold out, 'specially you," she said, nodding to Tobias. "The most reluctant ones usually come back first." Mollie went about her work, placing the pies on the shelves, mixing dough for more, and all the while talking.

"Where's this special you bragged on so much?" Tobias asked.

Mollie cut a slice and scooped it onto a plate. "It's my oldest recipe and, most say, my best."

Tobias took a bite, then another. "Not bad."

"Ha! You loved every bite and I'll fall down dead if you don't beg me for more."

He cackled and slapped his legs. "By god but you're a sassy one." He finished eating and handed her the plate. "And you were right. I'll go to my knees beggin' for more."

"Better watch it," Mollie said. "Eat too much and you'll get fat like me. I tend to pick a little too much myself."

"I'm too old to worry about bein' fat, so I guess I'll be havin' another 'fore I leave."

She put another slice on his plate.

Tobias finished his second piece "How much will you steal from me to pay for these pies, Mollie?"

"Whatever I charge won't be enough," she said, "but I guess two coppers will do."

"Not enough!" Tobias said. He handed her four coppers.

"Better watch being so kind, old feller. I'm not used to that."

As the three of them departed, Tobias hollered back over his shoulder. "I'll not ask what your recipe is, Mollie. But when I return, I expect at least a hint of the ingredients." Mollie brushed the air as if she were swatting away a fly, dismissing the group with a flashing smile and a beam in her eyes.

Tobias had more bounce in his step as they walked through the city streets.

~

The *old fort*, as it was known around Sykor, sat atop the highest rise in the city, only the castle loomed taller. The fort was in a state of disrepair. The impenetrable walls of stone that once resisted battering rams and charges of cavalry, now wobbled on crumbled mortar joints. Fire had gutted the innermost section. All that remained were the deteriorating walls and one torn and tattered replica of a banner displaying Lyssic's coat of arms—a mighty warrior astride a white stallion with a black vargel at his side.

"They used to change that flag every summer," Tobias said. "Now, Favian forbids it."

Rahg was still staring at the fort when Takar's horse topped the rise.

"Tobias, it's good to see you again. At least up here there will be no ears but ours."

"You had the lads all worried, Takar. They thought you and Rhaven were about to draw swords at any moment."

"Me, fight Rhaven! I'm no fool, lads."

"But the way you spoke to each other—" Darstan started.

"Rhaven was just letting me know he didn't want to be seen talking to a guard. When he said for me to come when he's not busy, he meant when no one else was around."

Darstan shook his head. "You had me. I thought it was real."

"Me too," said Rahg.

"Then I imagine it fooled whoever Rhaven had concerns about."

"Sergeant Takar—" Rahg said.

"Just Takar. I don't care to be reminded I once held a loftier position." He laughed. "I used to be Force Commander Takar. Now I'm just a sergeant, thanks to Rhaven."

"What happened?" Darstan asked. "I mean, why did you get demoted? What did Rhaven have to do with it?"

"Darstan! It's not your business."

"It's nothing, Tobias. Been long enough so it doesn't grate on me like it once did." Takar kicked a few rocks with his boot, then paused for moment. "I know you lads would love to hear stories about Rhaven, but we'll save them for another time. Let's just say that Rhaven forced the king to revoke his sentence, and the king blamed me."

"So are you going to train us, Takar?" Rahg drew his new sword and showed it to Takar. "Ludar gave this to me."

"So you two went to see Force Leader Ludar?"

"We did," Darstan said. "We each got a sword and a knife."

"Maybe you should join the guard, let Ludar train you."

Rahg's expression grew suddenly solemn. "You can make fun all you want, Sergeant, but I did well enough with the Victas. Not saying I can't learn, but I held my own against them."

"That he did, Takar. They both fought like veterans. Probably killed half dozen Victas each. I'd guess not many of your own men could claim as much." Tobias patted Rahg on the back. "These lads have grown up fast. They grate my nerves sometimes, and test my patience always, but put me in a tight spot and I'd be proud to have the two of 'em with me."

Tobias snapped his head toward them. "Now don't be gettin' your heads swelled up hearin' these lies I'm tellin' Takar. It's just to get you out of my hair for a spell while he trains you."

"What little hair you have," Darstan said.

Takar laughed. "Is a little thin, isn't it, lads? All right, I'll help you. But privately, not in the guards. I don't want you involved with Ludar. There's trouble in the guards right now."

"What's wrong with the guards?" Darstan asked.

"Ludar is what's wrong. There is something strange about him. I trained Ludar. He was always a good soldier, one of the best, but the higher up he got the meaner he became. And he has an obsession for finding people with powers."

"I can't blame him there," Darstan said.

"You'd blame him if you knew what he did to them."

"I imagine it's dangerous to talk about the Force Leader, so you lads make sure to keep quiet," Tobias said.

"More dangerous than you can imagine," Takar said. "Ludar has spies everywhere. I'm reluctant to trust my own men anymore."

"What does he do with them?" Rahg asked.

Takar shook his head. "Let's forget about what I said. And take my word for it and don't join the guard."

"Told 'em the same thing," Tobias said, then he filled Takar in on the Black Rose and the attempt on Rhaven's life.

"So, that's what's happening," Takar said. "I wondered why he was prowling the Dongrel. He's already killed several men, but he must have left a few alive to question because rumors are spreading everywhere about a black-cloaked demon roaming the Dongrel. We've also had two assassins turn up dead. I knew it was Rhaven." Takar paused for a moment reflecting. "Well, now I know what he's after. Guess it'll eventually help, him killing some of the Black Rose."

"So he's really that dangerous?" Rahg asked.

"Most deadly man alive," Takar said. "Only knew of two others who were even close. One was Malakai. Tobias knew him."

"Malakai, the pirate?"

"That's him," Takar said.

"Who's the other?" Darstan asked.

"The other? He was the most evil man I've ever known, also the most accomplished weapons master I ever laid eyes on. Thank the gods he's dead."

"Who was he?" Darstan asked.

"His name was Damon Pirrhar." Takar was silent for a moment then went on. "It would be difficult to compare, lads, but if I had to...I'd say Pirrhar was better than Rhaven."

"Better than Rhaven! I can't believe that." Rahg was still shaking his head when Takar stood to leave.

"Speaking of Rhaven, I've got a few stops to make before I go to meet him, so I better be on my way."

⁓

The assassin whisked over the narrow rooftop and made a smooth leap to the adjacent building. He landed with a soft thud, so faint he barely heard it himself. The Black Rose moved with extreme caution. Two assassins had died in the past few days. Someone hunted them, and he had no desire to join their company.

⁓

Rhaven's cold eyes followed the assassin's slightest movement. *This one will live to answer my questions.*

⁓

Across the alley, perched atop another roof, another set of eyes watched Rhaven. Gregor, the bounty man, had followed him for days, believing he might be the Wisp, or that he would lead him to the thief. The promise of ten thousand gold would make a man do many things. The bounty man greedily counted it as he squinted through gray-green eyes that pierced the night.

Rhaven waited until the assassin was again in midair before he effected his own leap onto the building previously occupied by the Black Rose. "Wise thinking, fellow. The assassin cannot turn to see you while he jumps." Gregor muttered to himself often.

Doubts crept into Gregor's mind. Each time he had trailed this man, the one he so desperately wanted to be Wisp, the man had been tracking an assassin, people Gregor had no love for. And once a robbery had taken place that had all the marks of Wisp, but it happened while Gregor had the man in his sight. The bounty man didn't know, but he intended to follow this one and see where the trail led. *He's good,* Gregor noted, as he watched Rhaven quickly whirl and seek cover behind a thin chimney.

It embarrassed Gregor that Wisp had managed to elude him for so long, but he meant to remedy that soon. Gregor made his leap, timing it perfectly to match the two ahead of him. He sought cover behind a crate, peering through the slats at the assassin who sat motionless on the next roof. The one in black pulled a tube from a sheath on his back with a move a serpent would have envied. In one fluid motion he grabbed something out of a belt at his side and pushed it into the tube. The man placed the shaft to his lips, then the assassin dropped to a heap within heartbeats.

Rhaven had already moved halfway across the roof when the assassin slumped to the tiles. Something made the man hesitate just before he scooped up the assassin, threw him over his shoulder, then descended to the alley below. Gregor would have to be careful when dealing with him.

He paused before continuing, a thought suddenly struck him. Just when the man hesitated, he saw something—a figure or shadow, something moved. The other one must have seen or sensed it also, as he stopped briefly at the same spot. As Gregor thought more on it, he realized it was not something he saw, but something he didn't see. There was a faint hint of moonlight shining down on the rooftops, enough to cast some shadows. What he saw was that moonlight temporarily blocked, as if someone, or something, moved across it. Whoever it was—he was also good. Very good. *Yes,* Gregor again reminded himself, *this could be a dangerous night indeed.*

~

Rhaven ran down the deserted alley into the street. He had memorized the layout in this neighborhood. The next turn was a dead-end alley, not very long and filthy with refuse. The alley was narrow, as were all in Sykor, suiting his plan perfectly. He could hear the vaguest hint of footsteps following him as he veered into the footway. *There should be just enough time.*

~

*W*isp slowed down as he approached the passage Rhaven ducked into. He stood at the front of the alley piled high with garbage. Several hauntingly thin dogs quarreled over food scraps as Wisp peered into the night. The dark turned to pitch-black only five paces deep in the alley. Wisp sensed that he shouldn't follow, but curiosity, and a need to discover the man's intent got the better of him. He carefully placed each foot, as if treading on the edge of a beam. The back street was mostly dirt; the cobblestones had long since been removed or worn away. What remained was smoothed slick and smothered with slimy moss. Wisp was not prone to splash in a puddle of stale brew, or inadvertently kick a picked-over bone. Amateurs made noises—amateurs, and old, worn-out thieves. He sidestepped some broken glass, then maneuvered his left foot onto a securely positioned piece of wood.

The two scroungy dogs gave the first indication that something was wrong as they abandoned the feast that sparked their fight. In the next instant the pile of refuse shifted. A hand shot out and latched onto the Wisp's ankle, gripping it like a vise. Wisp stomped on Rhaven's wrist then, placing all his weight on the loose foot, he yanked free with the other. Wisp tumbled, then scrambled to his feet. When Gregor entered the alley, Wisp reversed course and disappeared into the darkness.

Rhaven crawled out from under the heap and stood with sword drawn, eyes glaring.

"I'm after Wisp," Gregor said. "If that's him we'll split the reward."

"Stand next to me. There's no way out for him if we block the alley. It won't matter if we can see him or not." Rhaven advanced, his blade whirling before him.

Tightly pressed to his side, Gregor's staff became a blur. As they approached the end of the alley, Rhaven called a warning. "You can't escape, but there's no need to die. I only seek information."

"Information!" shouted Gregor. "I want the reward."

"I gave this man my word. Don't think to buck me, bounty–man—if that is what you are."

Wisp listened carefully. *There's no sense getting hurt over any of this. I can escape later.*

~

"I'm not a patient man," Rhaven said.

They had drawn to within five paces when Wisp revealed himself, stepping out of the cloud of darkness.

"You?!" Gregor said.

"What do you want with me?" Wisp asked, feigning all the innocence he could muster. "I've done nothing wrong."

"You're not an assassin," Rhaven said. "But neither are you the dove you claim to be, unless you have an explanation for the soot on your face and why you prowled the rooftops."

"You mentioned information," Wisp said.

"In due time," Rhaven said, and stared briefly at Wisp. Before leaving the alley he stooped to pick up the still-limp body of the assassin. While tossing the body over his shoulder, he wondered if it had not been something more than the darkness that concealed the thief in the alley. *I couldn't see him until he surrendered,* Rhaven thought, but then he brushed the consideration aside. "bounty man, stay close with that thief."

Gregor kept close, and maintained a firm grip on Wisp.

"You don't have to grip me so tightly," Wisp said. "When I want to escape, I'll tell you."

"What good is the word of a thief?"

"Let him go," Rhaven said. "He won't run."

"I appreciate your trust, stranger. I am familiar with Gregor, a bounty man of some repute, but I have yet to experience the pleasure of knowing your name."

"My name is not important. And the trust I hold is not in your honor. If you try to escape I'll put a dart in your back before you run ten paces. And I fear the only ones remaining are coated with a deadly poison, not like the one I used on this assassin."

"You say the Black Rose is alive?" Gregor asked.

"I need to question him," Rhaven said.

"You are free to make use of my home," Gregor said. "It is quiet and close, and no one will disturb us. Best of all, the loudest noises will go unheard."

"Lead on then."

Gregor's house sat at the end of a narrow, unusually clean alleyway. Mortar weeped from the joints of the brick facing. It was bordered by a vacant home and abutted the rear wall of a tavern.

"From your description I thought this was a remote location."

"I never said it was remote. But don't worry, I often entertain guests late at night, and more than occasionally they scream and shout curses. My neighbors don't seem to hear them."

Rhaven smiled. It was a sharp contrast to the scowl on Wisp's face.

INTERROGATION

Gregor's house

*L*oneliness hit Wisp the moment he walked in the door. Stark walls pleaded for color or adornments of any kind—even a smudge of dirt would have done. Three wooden chairs, like stout stickmen, surrounded an oval piece of oak, nudged tightly against its unfinished edge. Wisp wondered where the fourth chair went, or if there had ever been a fourth.

Does he only have two friends?

With each step he took, the walls seemed to close in, pushing him toward one of those three chairs. The candles Gregor lit when they entered cast long shadows across the bare floor. No cushions covered the chairs. No carpet on the floor. No coloring of any kind. It was clean, but doleful. The window had a dull-green drape hung over it to keep curious eyes from looking in, if they could see that high. And the floor, though it showed spots of wear from vigorous scrubbing, bore stains of blood under the table.

They strapped the Black Rose into a chair and waited for him to wake. The tempting aroma of fresh khaffe wafted in from the kitchen.

"I could use some khaffe," Wisp said. He wiped his face with a cloth he carried, then sat on the floor opposite Gregor and his companion. The man in black sat still as a statue with an expression that had been chiseled onto his face. He had eyes like a blue diamond and a forehead that a smithy could use for an anvil. Experience had taught Wisp that noses broke easily, but he suspected it would take a stone mason to break his.

Rhaven walked over to Wisp. "Empty your pockets."

"I thought you only wanted information."

"I need to know who I'm dealing with. Empty them, or I will."

Wisp scanned for a means to escape, but even as he did, Gregor returned to the room.

"I see you've finally come to understand these thieves, friend."

Wisp stood slowly and pulled three rings from a purse tucked behind his back, inside the waistband of his breeches.

"I told you he's a thief," Gregor said. "He's Wisp. I know it. And once the guards get hold of him, he will admit it. Ten thousand gold," Gregor said, and rubbed his hands together.

"Don't count that gold yet, bounty man." A sneer fixed to Wisp's face. He had come this far with them, but he'd make the break if he had to. No one would collect a reward on him. And he would tell them he was leaving, just before he left. No breaking of honor for this thief.

"Do you have any business with these assassins, thief?"

"No." He held Rhaven's gaze without blinking.

"Do you know why they wish me dead?"

"Hurry and finish," Gregor said. "I won't be denied that reward."

Rhaven shot Gregor a glare that would have cowered a mountain cat. "I'll ask the questions, bounty–man. If his answers prove unsatisfactory, you can have him."

"I don't know anything about the Rose," Wisp said. "And they must be rat-gut crazy for trying to kill you." Wisp stared at Rhaven. "He won't talk, you know. Members of the Black Rose never talk. You'll have to kill him."

Rhaven looked at Wisp, then studied the Rose. "I have ways of persuading men to talk. We shall see."

"I know someone who might be able to help," Wisp said.

Rhaven eyed him before making a quick judgment. "Gregor and I know who you are now. Don't try anything."

"I give my word."

Rhaven nodded. "I'll have your oath before you leave. Get your friend, then go to the Trader's Inn. There are three men who traveled with me. Bring them here, along with the girl named Camissa."

Wisp reached for the door.

"The oath, thief."

A rat with a pound of cheese couldn't have smiled brighter than Wisp. "My word is good."

"Then you'll have no concern about that oath," Rhaven said.

Wisp nodded, his face now a mask of stone.

> "May the rats feast on my flesh, rip out my eyes and hair,
> If I should I break this sacred vow that you now hear me swear.
> May the Goddess eat my soul, my heart and liver both,
> If I fail to do as sworn and break this sacred oath."

Rhaven brow furrowed. It looked as if he might laugh. "Is this an oath of your trade, or did you just now make this up?"

Wisp raised his brows in feigned innocence, then smiled when he saw Rhaven nod his approval. "Go, then. But I'll see you on the Chugarran Path if you fail me."

"I won't," Wisp said, and walked toward the door.

"I don't like you letting him go like that. He's worth ten thousand gold."

"He'll be back," Rhaven said. "Now, let's finish with this assassin."

≈

*P*erspiration ran down Gregor's cheeks as he delivered another punishing blow with his staff. The assassin reeled and groaned, but still he would not reveal as much as his name. Rhaven watched from the side. Gregor had worn out threats, and he had tried bribes, all to no avail. Finally, he took a brief respite, turning to Rhaven for suggestions.

The sound of footfalls in the alley caught Rhaven's attention. He pulled aside the window covering and peered down to see the thief returning with the others. The thief led with long smooth strides. Tobias tailed him closely, favoring his right leg. He was chattering and swinging his cap with his left hand, leaving his bald head exposed, a sharp contrast to Darstan's thick crop of black hair, or Rahg's longer brown mop. Camissa brought up the rear.

The door opened after a light tap, Tobias the first to barge through.

"What's the meaning of this?" Tobias asked. "Dragging us out in the middle of the night."

Rhaven stared. "Where's the friend you promised, thief?"

"It's Camissa."

"What about Camissa?" Rahg asked, eyes darting about.

"Thief?" Darstan asked. "Who's a thief?"

Rhaven continuing staring. "I see you have not introduced yourself." Rhaven turned to face them. "Kender, the sweep-up boy, is Wisp."

"What?" Rahg said.

"Kender!" Darstan said.

Tobias shook his head and muttered. "Told 'em something was wrong with those two. Told 'em."

Camissa's hands covered her gaping mouth. She stared at Kender in stunned silence before her palm reddened his face. "You didn't even trust me?" Her voice shook. "So that is where the money came from. And the gifts. If I had known, I wouldn't have taken a single copper."

Rahg stared, too, before the questions poured out of him. "Kender, what's she talking about? Are you really Wisp? What money?"

"We can discuss this later. Right now, I need answers from this assassin." Rhaven looked to Wisp. "How can Camissa help?"

"Just question the assassin."

"I have been questioning him."

"Then keep it up. She'll be able to tell if he's lying."

Bruises peppered the assassin's body and blood dripped from numerous cuts. Rhaven stepped to the table assuming the role of interrogator. "You know who I am."

The Black Rose examined his face. "No."

"No? You have an assignment to kill me and you don't know me?"

"We were never after you."

"Who was your target? If you don't answer, you'll die."

"I'll die either way. If you don't kill me, the master will. And he'll kill my family. If I hold my tongue, my wife and children will be safe."

Rhaven's tone hardened. He leaned on the table, his face a breath away from the Rose. "I killed your two henchmen. I caught Wisp." Rhaven lowered his voice. "And since you are so fond of your family—it will be me, Rhaven, who hunts down and slaughters your wife and children."

Recognition seemed to come to the assassin's face with the mention of Rhaven's name. Blood mingled with sweat on the sides of his face, where beatings had splattered it to his ears and matted his hair. Snot and blood both dripped from a dainty nose, not one to expect on an assassin's face, but a noble's daughter instead. His lips were cracked and several teeth were missing. Despite what he had endured, terror truly seemed to take hold of the man now.

"Who was your target?" Rhaven asked. "Last chance to tell me."

The Rose sat silently for a moment, then the brow of his head wrinkled and his lips began to form words.

Suddenly, Camissa shouted. "It's Rahg! They plan to kill Rahg."

The assassin stared blankly at Camissa. "How did you know?"

Rahg's knees buckled. "Gods blood! Why me?"

Rhaven swung his gaze from Camissa to the Rose. The assassin's shocked reaction convinced Rhaven that Camissa was right. "What more can you tell me?"

"I can sense no more."

Darstan stared at Camissa. "How did you know that?"

"What else?" Rhaven shouted at Camissa.

"I can't!" Camissa wrapped her arms around Rahg, and pressed her head tightly to his shoulders, letting the tears flow.

～

*D*arstan bolted forward. He cracked the assassin's swollen nose with a punishing blow. He cocked his arm back to strike again, but halted at Rhaven's signal.

"Revenge is best carried out with a cool heart. During the heated passion of anger you might kill a man too quickly. I will demonstrate for you, Darstan. This is a secret I learned from the Krovs." When Rhaven turned to face the assassin, there was a haunting grin on his face.

"The Krovs take a knife with a finely honed blade. The blade must be sharp, as this one is." Rhaven demonstrated by rubbing his finger over the end of the knife, drawing blood easily. "First they remove the eyelids, then they take the tip of the blade and cut a thin line beneath the eye. It drains all the fluids." Rhaven let the steel tease the assassin's face.

"The simplicity is genius, and the pain—pure magnificence. They say you cannot imagine the effect, when dirt, lashes, and other small items lodge themselves in the eye. And with no lubrication it is no longer capable of rinsing itself; the discomfort is continuous. Attempts to clean your eye only worsen the suffering, scratching the insides permanently. The Krovs are creative in their tortures, the primary reason they are so feared."

Rhaven touched the blade against the man's skin. "Speak now, or your family will suffer the same fate as you."

"If I talk you won't harm my family?"

"They will not be touched," Rhaven said. "But either way, you die. The only question is whether the guards do it, or I do it."

"Allow me to write a letter to my family, to warn them of the danger they face. And have a messenger, a fast one, deliver it to them at once." The Black Rose paused. He seemed to be in conflict with himself. "If you do that, I'll tell all I know."

"I'll do better than that. Name your master, and I vow to leave him no breath to issue orders against your family. Either he, or I, will die."

The assassin sighed. "Orders came from Pomanda where the master of the Black Rose lives. He's a powerful man in the city. The assignment seemed simple. 'Kill the village boy from Twin Forks. Name—Rahgnar Fal-Thera.' A description accompanied the scroll. No reason was given, but then, none ever are."

"Who is your master?" Rhaven asked.

The man hesitated. This was the worst breach of oath. "He's a deadly man. You'll find it difficult at best to even find him, let alone kill him."

"The name," Rhaven said. "I want his name."

The Black Rose looked at Rhaven. "Damon. Damon—" "Pirrhar!" Rhaven spit the name out like a curse. "Damon Pirrhar!"

Rhaven's body stiffened. His face turned red. Knuckles whitened as he squeezed the blade of the knife. He yanked the assassin from the chair.

Rhaven forced the next words through teeth ground together tight as two grist stones. "Write your letter, then make your preparations. But go to the grave knowing your family will be safe. Now that I know who the master assassin is—I vow to you on all I hold sacred—Damon Pirrhar will surely die." The Rose shook as Rhaven sat him back down at the table. He could barely hold himself still.

Darstan trembled, too. "Damon Pirrhar," he whispered.

Rhaven turned the assassin over to Gregor. "He should be worth something, bounty man."

"What about Wisp?"

"I can help in Pomanda," Wisp said. "I was born there. And I know all the thieves. There is no better way to know the city than to be in with the thieves."

"You will come with us," Rhaven said.

"Then I go also," Gregor said. "I'll not let go of ten thousand gold so easily."

Tobias straightened his cap as he stood. "Gregor, let's take that assassin to the guards and collect the reward, then we'll get some food and come back here. "We can discuss the trip to Pomanda while we eat."

Rhaven was silent for a while, then walked to where Rahg sat on the floor next to Camissa. "You once asked me to teach you swordplay. I believe your lessons should begin."

"I guess I'll need it now more than ever. If you'll teach me, I'll learn."

Rhaven nodded. "We begin tomorrow."

It was nearly noon before Tobias and Gregor returned. "They're coming back," Wisp said.

Rhaven listened to the sound of the footsteps. "And not alone," Rhaven said, drawing a knife from his sleeve.

~

obias, Gregor, and Takar approached the door. Gregor was about to open it when Takar grabbed his arm. "Rhaven," he shouted through the door. "It's Takar. I'm with Tobias and Gregor. You can put the knife down now, we're coming in." Takar turned the latch and entered to see Rhaven tucking the blade into his sleeve.

"Don't think you know me so well," Rhaven said. "But tell me, how did you follow two such stealthy men as this without being seen?"

"No accident," Takar said. "Been looking all over Sykor for Darstan. Ludar will be ordering his conscription in the morning."

"What?" Darstan shouted. "Why?"

"During the night, Force Commander Dorre died. Ludar now holds the title. He is casting blame for the death on the people with powers. Odd that Ludar's superior officers seem to die in strange fashions." Takar paused. "I said it when Dorre took over. I'd not want to be the force commander with Ludar under me."

Takar shook his head and looked around before continuing. "A massive hunt will begin soon to round up anyone even suspected of having powers, which is why he is madly trying to enlist men in the guard. He decided not to gamble on whether you would willingly join the guard. I received the information from my most trusted patrol leader. We need to get you out of the city, tonight."

"Then we'll need a few passes," Rhaven said.

"How many?"

"Six."

"Seven," said Camissa. "I'm going with you."

Rhaven stared at her. "It will be a rough journey, and I'll not be held up by anyone."

"I can keep up," Camissa said. "But I must leave Sykor." She glanced at Takar when she spoke.

Takar studied Kender a long time. "I know you, Kender Darnel."

Kender never flinched, and he offered no response.

Takar paced the room, talking. "Wisp has caused me a lot of grief. It would be a promotion if I turned him in."

Gregor grimaced. Bounty-men hated for guards to catch thieves, hated to see bounties go uncollected.

"Ludar claims Wisp has committed a number of atrocities: murder, stealing from the poor and helpless, and other crimes."

Kender interrupted. "Good sergeant, I happen to be acquainted with the habits of Wisp. A violent act has never crossed his mind, unless he found himself being unduly persecuted. And he has never once stolen from anyone who could not afford to lose more than what he took."

Takar listened, then turned to Rhaven. "I'll be back as soon as I can get seven passes. Be ready to leave when I return."

~

Takar was talking with one of the guards on duty when the party arrived at the gate. He stared at them as if he never laid eyes on any of them. "Passes," Takar barked in a voice rough enough to frighten most men. "Everyone needs a pass to leave the city."

Rhaven handed Takar the passes. He leafed through them one at a time. "This you?" he asked.

"It is."

"Who's Tobias?"

Tobias stepped up. "That'd be me, sergeant."

Each received the same treatment, Takar growling, and muttering remarks no one could hear, but it did affect the guards; they seemed comfortable letting Takar accept responsibility for allowing so many to leave the city at once. Finally, Takar gave the signal to pass them through. As they left, Takar called Kender back. "You," he yelled, then clarified. "Darnell."

Kender looked as if he might bolt, but he slowly returned. "Yes, sergeant?"

Takar signaled for Kender to lean down, then whispered. "Now that you are leaving Sykor, tell me—did you really steal a kiss from Cynemar?"

Kender smiled. "Her lips were sweet as honey, good sergeant." Kender stared at Takar, admiration shining in his eyes and sincerity suffusing his voice. "You always presented my most thrilling challenge, Sergeant. I shall miss the excitement of the chase."

Takar took his hand, shaking it heartily. "I can't say it was fun," he muttered, "but a challenge it most definitely was. Good luck to you, lad."

As Kender rode away, Takar said, "And don't come back."

Kender laughed, and rode to join the others.

"What did he want?" Darstan asked.

"I can't believe it," he said. "Takar knows who I am."

"And he just let you go?" Rahg asked.

"Who told him?" Wisp asked.

"No one told Takar," Tobias said. "Didn't have to. He already knew."

"That's impossible. No one knew, not even Camissa."

"Takar is crafty," Tobias said. "He frequented the Trader's Inn quite a bit. I'm sure you noticed."

"All the guards came by the inn," Wisp said, "but none of them suspected anything."

"Don't think you know so much about us old people, Kender. While I waited for Gregor to finish his business with the guards, Takar named you the Wisp and told me the story as he had it figured. Takar wanted to warn me since I was staying at the inn where you worked. He didn't know we'd be leaving Sykor."

"What do you mean by that?"

"Well, as I was saying." Tobias started most of his unfinished stories the same way. "Takar was puzzled by Wisp. After the first few thefts, when no one turned up any of the missing goods, he figured they were sold outside the city. Even so, he reasoned, whoever was stealing the stuff was gettin' mighty rich, so he started checking for people spending a lot of money—not nobles and merchants, but people who ordinarily didn't have any money to spend. He still couldn't find anything but he never gave up on his idea. Sooner than not, he figured, the Wisp is gonna have to start showing his hand, so he kept at it. Takar's not one to give up easily.

"I once saw him track a wounded mountain cat for near four leagues. Mind you now—four leagues. Most men would have quit after half a league, the more determined ones might have tracked him for one or possibly two, but Takar wouldn't quit. That's the kind of man Takar is." Tobias turned to Rahg and Darstan. "There's a lesson in that for you, lads—if you care to learn from it."

"Since we're speaking of tracking, Tobias," Darstan said, "would you mind getting back on track with this story. I'd like to hear the end of it before we reach Pomanda." Everyone but Tobias laughed.

"Well, as I was saying, Takar kept lookin' for a money trail. He was lookin' mostly for jewelry, houses, silk, and other luxury items. Then something caught his attention. It seemed strange to him but it was too much a coincidence to let it go. Two inns had been sold in a matter of just three months: the Trader's Inn and the Sparrow's Lodge. At first he thought he'd figured wrong 'cause they had been purchased by different men. Brock Larnigin bought one; Jargin Timms the other. Didn't seem to be any connection, but Takar kept diggin'. He discovered that both men came from poor backgrounds; Jargin from River's Edge, and Brock from the Dongrel. Now how did they get the money to buy those inns, Takar asked himself? He went and talked to the previous owners, bitter rivals, he said, and they confirmed what he already suspected, that all the negotiations had been carried out by a young lad. Kind of fit your description, Kender, or Wisp, whatever you want to be called." Tobias paused to laugh. "Wait while I light this pipe," he said. A few puffs later, he continued.

"Anyway, just to make sure, Takar began haunting the inns. Noticed you were always at the Trader's Inn, and just so happened Brock was not as good a manager as Jargin, so he assumed you stayed there to keep an eye out for your goods. He followed you on couple of occasions though, when you went to collect money from Jargin. You never even knew you were bein' trailed, did you?" Tobias threw the last in as a taunt.

"Well," Tobias sighed, "After that, Takar put everything together. I'll give you this," Tobias said in a praising voice. "Takar thought you were the most clever man he knew. Said you could have been a rich merchant if you hadn't been a thief. He admired the way you sold both your inns' goods by comparing with each other, and nobody else. Very clever."

"What do you mean?" Darstan asked.

Wisp explained. "We had two of the best locations in the city, so we wanted to take advantage of that, and of perceived competition. Instead of offering meals for less money, a terrible way to do business, we always boasted of how good our food was. Every seven days, we advertised our specials by comparing them to the other inn, and in doing so, we would state how good the other was. For example; the Trader's Inn would tell its patrons that it would have a special of Cynemar's Delight the next three days, and our servers would say, it is far better than the Pomandan Pie served at the Lodge, though they knew that was good, they'd add."

"I remember when Camissa told us about a strawberry dessert at the Sparrow's Lodge. I even thought about going there the next day."

"That's how it was supposed to work," Wisp said. "So why didn't Takar take me in?"

"Takar's a strange kind of man. You see, in doin' all this work to find you he discovered that someone was givin' food and clothes to the poor people in the Dongrel and over at River's Edge—and that description fit you as well. That hit a soft spot in him, 'cause he was raised poor himself. Now don't misunderstand the sergeant, he didn't truly believe you did this out of the goodness of your heart; fact is, he figured you did it so no one would ever turn you in. If he had caught you in the act, though, he'd have taken you in just like any other thief. He just wouldn't take advantage of his other knowledge and haul you in as Kender. He's a strange man, but a fair one."

"Did you give all your money to the people?" Darstan asked.

"I've got some saved," Wisp said, "The rest went to Camissa and her people. We were trying to get enough to send them away to Khatara."

"What do you mean, Camissa's people?" Rahg's curiosity bubbled over.

"The ones with powers," Rhaven answered, dryly. "Or have you forgotten so soon that she read the assassin's mind?"

Gregor muttered to himself. "Thieves don't give money away. Besides, I'll not let him go, no matter what he does. Ten thousand gold is a lot of money. I don't care if he raises somebody from the dead; he'll not escape me."

They arrived at a fork in the road, then took it west, toward Pomanda.

Once they passed the heavy grove of trees, Rhaven increased the pace to a canter.

Rahg struggled with his new mount as he looked around in all directions. *I wonder where Kella is?* He felt bad that he hadn't given much thought to Kella since they came to Sykor. The last he saw of her, the vargel disappeared into the woods. *I hope she went home, to the Whites. Nothing will bother her there.*

PRICE OF PLOTS

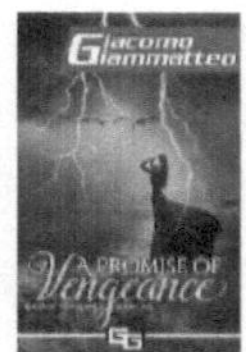

Sleep had eluded Kardel and Vennel of late—fear proved to be a worrisome bedmate—but the sight of Jar–Tal allayed their frayed nerves. "Greetings, fellow conspirators."

Kardel scanned the area while Vennel hissed his displeasure. "Caution is wisdom's partner, Jar–Tal. You would do well to pay heed. Lukaan has ears in every corner of Sethia."

The Sethian smiled. "Everything is ready for tonight. We will have access to Lukaan when he is most susceptible. Even *he* has to sleep."

Kardel's amber eyes grew murky with reluctance. "I don't know whether we should do this, Jar–Tal."

"We must! How long before he brings war to us? Our only hope is to stop him before the wars begin anew."

Kardel's ears twitched. They were all afraid. But if he wanted his pups to live a better life, then Lukaan must die. The plan was dangerous, but at least they had an edge. As Jar–Tal said, even Lukaan has to sleep. "Agreed," growled Kardel.

"So be it," hissed Vennel.

"Done," echoed Jar–Tal.

~

Construction on the Sethian Palace began shortly after the shield closed around Lukaan. The "Throne of the Sun," was known, and feared, throughout Sethia. Some referred to it mockingly, but when they did, it was only in whispers and only in the darkest of alleys. The palace owed its structural integrity to the granite which supported the stress points, granite which first had to be mined then hauled a great distance from the gorge in southern Sethia. The toll paid in lives was far greater than the distance in leagues.

The more ornamental decorations of the palace proved only slightly less demanding to acquire, but fortunately, Khataran merchant caravans traveled perilously close to the Sethian border, and it was from these that the Wolfen satisfied their consignments. Magnificent paintings embellished black marble walls; alabaster vases and urns garnished fine tables chiseled from blackthorn and emerald; and veils of gossamer silk lay draped over sculptures coaxed from raw blocks of white marble by master artisans.

palace of the sun sitting room

The three conspirators ambled through the gates of the outer hall wearing white cloaks emblazoned with the symbol of the fiery red sun. The cloaks forestalled the questions of inquisitive guards—no one questioned a Guard of the Sun. Fear grew as they strode ever-deeper into the palace, progressing toward Lukaan's chamber.

A cold shiver traced their spines when a door opened in the corridor ahead. Two palace guards ushered a pair of Nyauran horsemen down the hall, nodding as they passed them.

Jar–Tal veered right at the next corridor. It was wider than the others. Darker, too. Vennel's muscles tensed at the sight of the first door, a large silver entry marked with the seal of Iazzo, a notoriously vicious Banished One. The air of the palace suddenly acquired a wintry bite. Jar–Tal froze in midstream, his racing heart inexplicably loud. Even his breath seemed noisy, crackling in the air like shattered ice. For the longest moment they stared at each other—Kardel's glowing amber at Vennel's black slits, and those at the rusty brown of Jar–Tal; then, with the Sethian's almost imperceptible nod, they renewed the advance with increased caution.

They crept past two more of the silver doors, Tirzinitzia's and Ghruehne's, with no problem save blood roaring through veins too small to accommodate it. The next door, however, ignited a squelched tremor. It was the same silver portal but with a carving that pictured a horde of gruesome creatures attacking people huddled against a mountain of rocks.

Vennel shuddered. "Are you sure the Banished Ones will seek no revenge?"

A finger to Jar-Tal's lips silenced Vennel.

"We are near," Kardel whispered.

The entrance to Lukaan's chamber was open. They skulked past, stealing a glimpse inside. A marble bed sat on the far side of the room, with Lukaan asleep. They stole into the room and crept forward.

"Do not look at him until it is time," said Jar-Tal. "Even the sight of him breeds fear."

When they reached the foot of the bed, each one drew a knife, then lunged for his heart. Lukaan disappeared. A gut-wrenching fear seized Jar-Tal. He turned to run. Kardel and Vennel were beside him. Before reaching the door, he froze, unable to move.

"I cannot have you die so soon, mortal friends. Death is something to be enjoyed. To be savored."

~

*M*elissara entered the great chamber with a hint of trepidation. "Good day, Great One. I have come regarding the problem with Vennel and Kardel and the Sethian."

Lukaan's thoughts bored into her mind—a directive regarding the disposition of the traitors. With so little as a nod and a twist, she departed, the swish ushering her from the room. Blonde hair bounced off bare shoulders and tumbled down her naked back, while long tresses of curls dropped to cover her breasts. The tresses danced as she moved, but never enough to reveal the treasure they concealed. Melissara had found it impossible to preserve her creamy complexion in the searing heat of these stark and sterile lands, where the women had skin like scalded milk. Skin not fit for animals, but these pitiful wretches seemed not to mind.

A guard leered, but turned quickly away. It would not do to be caught stealing a glance at Melissara. She smiled at the guard's frightened look; fear was the one emotion she enjoyed propagating more than lust.

~

The midday sun in Sethia blazed inordinately hot. Bodies glistened under the sweltering heat, but it was more than heat that boiled skin, this was fear–wrought sweat. The torture had begun at dawn, but what remained of Kardel and Vennel and Jar–Tal were three unrecognizable bodies suspended in midair and writhing like gut–slitted waggers.

One of Kardel's pups wiped tears with the back of his paw. He seemed in pain watching his father be tortured.

Melissara soon assumed the role of executioner, promising a similar fate to anyone who opposed Lukaan in the future. Lukaan stayed, with front-seat attendance, until they died then he returned to the palace.

After Lukaan left, Melissara knelt to search the charred remains of the victims. *Something I saw...* Ashes and blood soiled her hands as she combed the ground, stopping at a familiar touch. Among the vestiges lay three crystalline objects. "Slicers!" The word slipped past her lips aloud.

Where did these come from?

Suspicion turned her head as she scoured the area, searching everywhere for a spy. Melissara hesitated. She searched her memory to recall the Slicers' peculiar nature and the rules that governed them before she attempted to pick them up. Finally, she smiled.

They are no danger to me now; their mission is over.

She plucked them off the ground to clean, stood, then sauntered off. *I have much to think about, now.*

A PASSING IN THE NIGHT

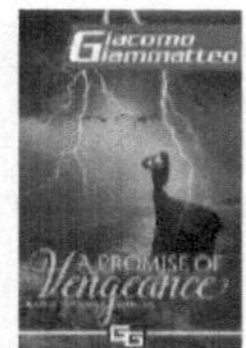

*R*ahg rode near the back of the party, taking a position just behind Camissa. The deep-throated croak of a raven perched high in a birch tree startled him, forcing out a muffled gasp. He cursed his fear. Already a bluejay's squawk and the chitter of a squirrel had nearly unseated him. He wanted nothing more than to be done with this business and find someplace to work and live.

Besides that, he was tired of riding. His thighs and calves ached, and his neck was stiff from checking behind them for Sykoran patrols. He hadn't seen the vargel since leaving Sykor, three days ago. Rhaven insisted she might show, but Rahg didn't share his confidence.

I should never have left her.

Camissa rode up beside him. "Smell the flowers, Rahg. Aren't they wonderful?"

"Haven't noticed."

"You need to get your mind off those assassins. Keep thinking about it and you'll go crazy. Take a look around. Beauty is everywhere."

rolling hills

Rahg nodded but rode along in silence. Before long Rhaven turned up a small trail. "We'll make camp up on the rise."

The trail narrowed as they climbed. "Dismount," Tobias said, and got off his horse. "Path's too steep. No sense in breakin' a horse's leg."

The underbrush encroached on the path, vines tangled with deadfall attesting to the paucity of travelers. They came to a natural clearing, cut from the forest by a circle of large boulders planted in rocky ground. Densely packed trees and undergrowth came right to the edge of the opening then stopped, but the boughs of the large trees stretched out from all sides forming a ceiling of dark green foliage. Rahg began dreaming of bed rolls, warm fires, and hot food, but Rhaven's orders shattered the dreams.

"Feed and water the horses first. No fires. Rahg, take first watch. And take Darstan with you. I want no surprise visits during the night. Be alert. Wisp, take second watch with the bounty man. Tobias and I will finish the night."

Camissa's face had the look of a child facing an empty chest on Wish Day. "What about me?"

"Join Rahg and Darstan, but if so much as a flea enters camp unreported..."

Wisp spread the bedroll on a bare spot of ground under a low-hanging branch, tucking himself in with a blanket pulled tightly over his shoulders. "Keep a sharp watch, Darstan. I'm worth a lot of gold to Gregor, and bounty–men tend to worry about gold."

Darstan laughed.

Gregor sat under the tree next to Wisp. He put a knife to work carving a piece of rock maple into a new staff. "You'll not catch me with both eyes closed, thief. Not until I collect that reward."

Camissa tugged the hood of the cloak over her head as she stood watch with Rahg and Darstan. "I'm worried about Kender. I know that bounty man will turn him in."

A slight pang of jealousy hit Rahg. "I like him, too, Camissa, even though he is a thief."

"He's done no harm that I can see," Darstan said. "No one except some nobles and a few rich merchants."

≈

Though Darstan had barely spoken above a whisper, Wisp overheard their conversation and smiled, huddling in his bedroll. *If I can only get Gregor to feel like that... but I fear the bounty man has a heart as hard as the knob on the end of his staff.*

≈

*D*arkness covered the campsite. The gray skies parted, and a small slice of one moon shone, though its reflective glow barely pierced the canopy of leaves. Rahg sprang to his feet at every call of the night birds. He jerked at every rustling bend of a wind-blown bough, and each time the crickets chirped his hand shot to the polished hilt of his sword. Soon, he learned to distinguish the sounds.

owl hunting

An owl hooted, then swooped down and grabbed a meal—a vole or fieldmouse—and some crickets chirped close by, but Rahg paid them no mind. He moved over to join Camissa and Darstan.

"Tell us about your powers," Rahg said.

Camissa squinted her eyes, staring first at Rahg, then Darstan. "I thought you were afraid of powers."

"Not afraid," Darstan said. "Maybe a little nervous. We never thought anyone really had powers, except the Banished Ones, and we didn't believe in them either." Darstan flashed a warm smile at Camissa. "What can you do?"

"When I was young, the villagers where I lived killed my mother. Stoned her. They would have killed me too, if not for an old man. He protected me from them and took me away. We settled in Sykor and he taught me control, and how to live life without using my powers. I've been trying to teach others to do the same thing, so people like Ludar don't bother them."

"What happened to him?" Darstan asked.

She cried. "Ludar killed him."

Darstan jumped to his feet. "You don't know he was killed."

"He was. When I have been close to someone I can sense them, always. I knew the moment he died."

"I'm sorry, Camissa," Darstan said.

"What else can you do?" Rahg asked.

"I can sense peoples' thoughts and feelings," she said. "Sometimes I can even read minds, like with that Black Rose assassin."

"Can you read my thoughts?"

"Perhaps I could, but I try not do that with friends. It makes for bitter relationships. I vowed never to do that."

"Tell me what I'm thinking," Rahg said.

"No."

"Come on, Camissa. Tell me."

"No! This is no game, Rahg." She stormed off. As she rolled under a blanket, her earlier experience with Darstan tossed back and forth in her mind. There was something about the feelings she sensed from him, something odd, but she couldn't quite make it out.

"I think I'll name my horse Marchall," Rahg said. "He reminds me of Kor Trasken's horse."

"That first horse Kor had?"

"Remember, Eru wanted to name his horse Marchall, but Kor wouldn't let him, even though his had been dead for a long time." Rahg's head drooped a little as he thought of Kor and Eru, and he couldn't help but think of Magmar. "Guess Kor wouldn't mind now. What do you think, Dar?"

"About Marchall?" Darstan paused for a moment. "No, Kor wouldn't mind. I think he'd be proud." Darstan seemed about to slip away, but then he spoke up. "I'm going to name mine Grayson."

"Grayson?" Rahg asked. "Where did you get that name?"

"Just thought of it," Darstan said, and smiled. "Grayson, it is."

~

*B*ehind a thick cluster of yaupons, heavy with new foliage, two Wolfen listened to the conversation. Eyelids tinged with fur shut quickly as Rahg cast an unconcerned look in their direction then, when safe, opened again to slits, revealing amber eyes that shone even in the dim light.

Pack Leader Vornyar leaned close to his Nettar. "That is the one the Master wants." Nettar stood steady as a tree, silent as a rock. His nostrils flared as he sniffed.

It was all the reply Vornyar needed; Nettar had fixed his scent. There would be nowhere the boy could hide now. Once Nettar got a scent he could track someone over leagues of rock and through the worst of storms; the village boy was as good as dead.

Darstan roused Wisp and Gregor for the second watch then he and Rahg climbed into their bedrolls.

Wisp and Gregor traded stories of long nights spent eluding bounty-men, and chasing thieves, respectively. "You provided me the most excitement of any," Wisp said. "None of the others offered such a challenge. Gregor, do you recall a night, late last summer, when the merchant's guild was robbed of their dues? You chased me almost until dawn. I thought you were going to catch me that night."

Recognition lit Gregor's eyes. "I remember. For almost two months I seemed to have your trail every time you struck. I tracked you over the rooftops and through alleys and tunnels, and although I couldn't see you, I knew which way you went. I almost had you that night. I even began counting the gold."

Wisp laughed as he scouted the bushes. "That was your undoing. It's not about gold, Gregor. Had you stayed the course and sought me only for the game... who knows, you might have caught me."

Gregor spun his staff, scoffing as he did. "What do you mean, not about gold? You steal for profit. I hunt thieves for the reward. What else is there?"

"I hope you find out someday, Gregor. I truly do," Wisp said, and walked away shaking his head.

WOLVES AND MEN

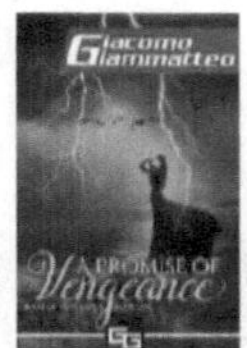

For three long and muggy days the group beat a brutally driven path toward Pomanda. The soft swales and gentle hills of Sykor grew to steep inclines with old-growth forests that no axe had touched. Sycamore, beech, maple, and a smattering of oaks danced with long-coned pines that held firm against the battering of heavy winds that spring delivered with a vengeance. During the too-few hours of daylight they drove their mounts hard, so hard that Rahg felt certain they would collapse at any moment, and at night they trudged along at a grueling, if less demanding pace.

Rahg soon learned to sleep in the saddle. Two back-aching falls had taught him the nuances far quicker, and better, than Tobias' tired explanations. He now rode in slumber like a grizzled veteran of war, able to awaken and maintain balance, yet within moments regain his drowsy state of mind.

Tobias stopped his horse in the middle of the road, staring at the storm clouds rushing toward them. "It's gonna be a big one. We'll need to find high ground, and fast."

"What's that?" Darstan asked.

"Said it's gonna rain. Bad storm comin' up." Tobias yelled over the noise of the whipping gusts of wind. "Need to get up high. I've seen floods come fast in terrain like this. Wiped out a whole patrol once, men and horses swept away like twigs."

Rahg pulled the hood of the cloak over his head; the wind was warm, but the debris it carried bit harshly when flung against soft skin.

"Hurry!" Tobias said. "We've got to make that rise before it gets much worse."

thunderstorm

Rahg patted Marchalls' neck, grateful for the solid mount he had. Close to the top of the rise, Tobias and Rhaven found a small clearing surrounded by huge white oaks, their broad arms spreading three to four spans. Smooth-barked beech and mountain pines filled the gaps.

Tobias had already started building a lean-to out of thick branches. "Get those cloaks off. We'll need 'em to tie to the boughs. It'll keep us drier."

Despite the weather, they soon had a reasonable camp built. Rhaven even relented for the first time since leaving Sykor, and allowed them to build a fire.

"Darstan, you and Rahg gather wood, but don't get white oak, it holds water like a well. Get some beech or red oak. No pine, either," Tobias yelled.

Rahg thought the fire a small concession considering their flesh had gone soggy and their clothes weighed half a stone heavier from all the water. But at least they would have a fire. That was something to be thankful for.

After supper the rain became ferocious, and though the fire had been tucked under a lean-to, the wind blew the rain so hard it doused the flames. New puddles formed as huge drops splashed like rocks thrown from the sky. Rhaven wanted to post a watch but everyone argued so strongly against it that he ceded to the majority opinion.

"I still think we should post a guard, but no matter, Argus will watch for us."

Shortly after nightfall, the entire camp had fallen asleep.

~

The rain and wind beat relentlessly against the forest, bending and snapping branches, cutting gullies into small gorges, and splattering onto the surface of the ponds that earlier in the day had been puddles, and earlier yet, dry ground. Nothing, save the roar of wind and the rumbling growls of thunder could be heard over its tumult.

Through the clamor in the woods, a pack of Wolfen stalked toward the camp. Nettar crept ahead. He would enter the camp first. Once he killed the boy, they would all attack.

It will be a slaughter, Pack Leader Vornyar thought, *even with Black Death on their side.* The Wolfen knew Rhaven. Many times Wolfen and Victa had faced him, only to bury their own dead afterward. Even when relations had been peaceful Rhaven had hunted them, slaying for no apparent reason. Vornyar did not know what drove him to do such things, but it no longer mattered; tonight, Black Death would die.

~

*N*ettar moved closer, peering through bushes drenched with rain, the water running off the thick leaves in streams instead of droplets. A glance from the Wolfen's yellow eyes separated Rahg from the others. He crept through the clearing, the Wolfen long-knife clutched in his hand. Stooping now, Nettar quickened his pace. When he got within a few paces he raised his arm to strike.

Argus neighed, raising the alarm. It startled Nettar but other sounds caused more concern: the unexpected snapping of large twigs; the cracking of branches; saplings crashing to the forest floor; but above all, the thunderous drum of heavy feet pounding the ground, driving a furious charge.

Kella in woods

A small tree tumbled, then the thick bushes surrounding the campsite were forced apart. The shadowed form of a black beast crashed through into the clearing. The darkness came alive and leapt at Nettar. In a desperate attempt to complete his mission, Nettar plunged the blade toward Rahg.

Kella roared then struck the Wolfen with full force. Her maw clamped tightly around his arm, crunching bones.

Nettar screamed. The impact sent him reeling. Kella ripped back and tore his arm off.

Pack Leader Vornyar heard the sound, and advanced.

*R*haven jumped up when he heard the alarm. "On your feet!" he shouted, as the sound of steel brushing leather whistled from his sheaths.

Rahg awoke just in time to see Kella ripping the limb from the Wolfen's body. He screamed.

Kella sprang again. Rhaven had already planted knives in two of the Wolfen. Now his sai and sword came alive—slicing, cutting, and piercing their way toward the center of the battle, drawn to the fury and the blood.

Wisp jumped from his bedroll and let out a screech as Kella hurtled over him. "Rats blood! It's a demon!"

Rahg and Darstan drew swords, even Camissa faced a Wolfen, though before she had made her first cut, Kella attacked. Gregor twirled his staff, keeping two Wolfen at bay. A quick jab to the chest of the one on his right sent it into a stumble. The bounty man followed through with a sweeping arc of the staff from his left, catching the second Wolfen on the side of the head. He brought the right end of his staff overhead in another arc, crashing down on the head of the beast, rendering it unconscious. The first Wolfen recovered, charging him. Gregor jammed the tip of the staff into the Wolfen's throat.

Wisp seemed to be everywhere, cutting and slicing with knives, while deftly eluding the blows of Wolfen like a heron dodges a moccasin's bite. Wisp darted behind a very large Wolfen, ducked to slice into the hamstring, then stood and jabbed his other blade into the Wolfen's kidney. He dodged a strike by a Wolfen to his left, but took a cut to his arm.

"Rats blood!" He moved quickly to his right, then turned and threw the knife, though it glanced off of the Wolfen's arm. Wisp pulled another knife from a sheath on the upper part of his left arm. He feigned a throw, and, when the Wolfen moved, he charged in with both blades and struck. One in the gut and the other in its thigh. Wisp took out the knife and finished him off with a stab to the throat.

A Wolfen long-knife whizzed by Rahg's head. He turned to see three Wolfen advancing. "Darstan, help!"

Darstan cast a quick glance in Rahg's direction. "Somebody help Rahg. I can't get to him." A Wolfen long-knife caught Darstan's forearm. He cursed and took a few steps back. With a dagger in his left hand and the Cergalan sword in his right, he pressed forward. He jabbed with his left hand then moved in quickly with his right, catching the Wolfen in the gut.

~

Rhaven's sword sliced through the neck of the Wolfen facing him, then he slammed the pommel of his sai into another's face, dropping it to the ground. He rushed to help Rahg. "Tobias, Gregor, keep the front line closed. Don't let them in on our backs."

Tobias fought better than men half his age, and handled a blade better than most. The bounty man, too, proved to be more than able with his staff, often keeping two or three Wolfen at bay. A master with a staff was a deadly opponent, a lesson the Wolfen were learning now.

Rahg stumbled as he tried to hold off the Wolfen.

"Black Death!" a Wolfen yelled, then fell when Rhaven's sai pierced its throat. The other two Wolfen turned toward Rhaven. When they did, Rahg pushed his attack against the one to his right, wielding sword and dagger.

~

Their numbers diminishing rapidly, the Wolfen Pack Leader retreated, howling a signal for the others to follow. Rhaven thought the battle had been far from decided, and, by his count, ten escaped. Kella charged through the woods in pursuit. Rhaven tore down the path after them. He would not leave the Wolfen to stalk their trail.

Rhaven sped through the forest, splashing through puddles and mud and swatting aside branches dripping wet. He could never hope to catch the Wolfen under normal circumstances, but if they followed the easy paths out, he might. Kella had taken off through the woods on a course that would likely intercept them.

A fierce growl followed by piercing screams confirmed his suspicion. Rhaven slowed, creeping silently. Within a moment two Wolfen came back down the path toward him. A sai in his left hand and a sword in his right, Rhaven waited alongside the path next to a broad white oak. He let them pass, checked to see the way behind them was clear, then struck. The sai found flesh in the middle of one Wolfen's back. The second one got a sweeping gash across the neck. Rhaven wiped his hands clean on some leaves, then wiped down the hilt of his weapons. Afterward he rubbed them both on the thick fur of the dead Wolfen. His hands were still sticky with blood, but they weren't as slippery as they had been.

Howling and screams marked a battle yet raging ahead. Rhaven set off at a hurried pace, yet slow enough to keep a wary eye on the woods around him. A small clearing housed the battle—Kella fighting five Wolfen. She had already killed three. The vargel had her back to a tree trunk, teeth bared, and matted gobs of blood-stained fur plastered against her neck and chest like a nobleman's vest. The Wolfen formed an arc around her but kept their distance.

Rhaven sheathed his sword and removed his other sai. Kella attacked to her left just when Rhaven reached to strike to her right, the sai pierced the Wolfen's lung. He drove the other sai into a Wolfen's neck. Blood spewed out in a great gush, spraying his face and head.

Kella had already killed the one on the left. She held the other two at bay. Rhaven came around behind them. He took the one on the right, Kella the other. Soon it was all over.

❧

Rhaven returned to camp, his face and head covered with blood. "Any injuries?"

"None to speak of," Tobias said. "Rahg's got some scratches. Darstan's got a slice on his arm."

Rhaven looked to Wisp and Gregor. "Check the Wolfen. Make sure they're all dead."

"I'll check," Gregor said.

Wisp kept his eyes fixed on Kella. "What is that?"

"That's Kella," Rahg said, reaching over to pet her. Kella shied away, teeth bared, eyes scanning the woods. A guttural growl rumbled in her throat.

Wisp took a step back, even Tobias moved to the side, but Rahg moved closer. He wrapped his arms around her massive neck and hugged her. "Thanks, Kella, you saved us again."

Her eyes lost their glow, and her lips fell down to cover the threatening teeth. She sat down on her haunches and sidled up to Rahg, but she kept her eyes on the woods.

Wisp kept a suspicious eye on the vargel. "Mother of rats! I didn't believe you when you told me about her. She's a demon."

Tobias cleaned the blood from his sword. "Any get away?"

Rhaven had just started to clean his sai. "None." He stared at Camissa, then Rahg and Darstan. "Are those wounds bad?"

"Just a scratch," Darstan said, and finished cleaning his arm.

225

"Same," Rahg said. "My neck's just a scratch, but the one on my leg hurts. It's not bad, though."

Wisp dabbed the blood oozing from his arm with meticulous care while he inspected the wound. It required no stitching, but bled at a steady flow. "Do you anticipate much of this, Rhaven? I have a strong aversion to swordplay."

"Are you all right?" Rahg asked.

"I'm sure I'll be fine, but I can ill afford to shed blood for you. I cherish the little I have."

Rahg smiled, then turned to see the bounty man examining his staff. "What's wrong, Gregor?"

"Checking for damage—cracks, or nicks that cut too deeply." Gregor showed Rahg and Darstan a few of the nicks, then moved toward Wisp. "I would think a thief to be used to bloodshed. You chose a poor trade if not."

"I avoid the gnashing of blades whenever I can; the clanging of steel disturbs my ears and the sight of blood upsets my stomach, especially my own sweet blood."

Tobias frowned. "You wield the blades well for someone who professes an adherence to the vows of the White Robes."

Wisp smiled for the first time since the battle. The bleeding had slowed to less than a trickle. "Your ears betray you, old man. I said I had an aversion to swordplay and shedding blood. That is quite different from a vow to the Whites. Presented with no alternative, I will fight, though, like the rat, I prefer to scurry off unharmed."

Rahg shook his head. "But you're so good with those knives. When I get that good with the sword I'll fight anyone."

Wisp let the smile touch his face again, like the rat who knows where the cheese is hidden. "Even a stablehand can bleed the best of blades."

"I'd still rather fight," Rahg said.

"Then you will lose blood sooner than I, my friend, and likely your life as well. As for me, I intend to grow old, like Tobias."

Gregor continued inspecting his staff, running his hands gently over every bit of it. "Do not grow so fond of the life you have, thief. When I collect that reward the guards might relieve you of it."

Wisp laughed as if he knew something the others didn't. He crawled back into the bedroll and tucked himself in. "Sleep well, friends, Wisp is standing guard."

Darstan snickered. "I wish I could stand watch in a bedroll."

"You could," he said, "if you were Wisp."

Darstan laughed as he walked to stand guard. "I don't know why, but I really like that thief."

Gregor ran his hand up and down the staff as if it were a lover. He stopped at the feel of the slightest imperfection. Grey eyes squinted, trying to see in the poor light. The rain had stopped but the clouds kept the moonlight from shining through. "Shall we break camp?" he asked Rhaven.

Rhaven continued cleaning his steel, never looking up. "No reason. It will be light soon. Get some sleep. I'll stand watch with Darstan. Rahg, you get sleep, too."

Kella huddled close to Rahg when he lay down. Her wet fur stank but he didn't mind. He felt secure with her next to him. As he lay in the bedroll hugging Kella, the sound of Rhaven's whetstone sliding up and down the blades sung him to sleep.

~

Rahg felt a boot lightly tap his back.

"Time to get up," Tobias said, moving to wake Darstan.

"You'll be learnin' some weapons today, so Rhaven wants to get an early start."

"This early?" Rahg asked, still groggy. He looked around the campsite, checking everywhere, then jumped to his feet. "Where's Kella? Anybody seen Kella?"

"She left early this morning," Rhaven said.

"Mount up," Tobias said.

"Aren't we going to eat?" Rahg asked.

"We'll eat on the road." Tobias looked at the heavy tracks the horses left in the mud. "If the guards decide to follow us, we're makin' it easy on 'em."

"They won't." Rhaven said. "I already told you, these are bandit roads. Even the guards won't come here."

Rhaven's assurances did nothing to make Rahg feel at ease. If the guards wouldn't travel the roads they must be bad.

After a few hours of riding Rhaven ordered a halt. "Need to rest the horses. The mud will wear them out if we don't."

on the way to Pomanda

Rahg dismounted and looked around at the open space. The scenery reminded him of the southern part of Kamnor, where the mountains faded into big knolls and high hills. Darstan strolled up beside Rahg, chewing on a hard piece of cheese and stale bread.

"That was close last night, Dar. I thought we would all be killed."

"We've already been through this a hundred times," Darstan said.

Rahg tore off a small piece from the end of Darstan's bread. "I know, but I can't help thinking about it. We would've been killed without Rhaven and Kella. Those Wolfen would have taken us for sure if not for them."

Darstan's mouth was full of food, but he nodded his agreement.

"Wisp and Gregor fought well, too," Rahg said. "I've never seen anybody so fast with knives. That's what I want to learn. Tobias said we'll be learning new weapons; I want to learn the knife."

Darstan finished swallowing. "Did you see Gregor use that staff? He fought off three Wolfen at the same time last night. That convinced me."

Tobias walked up behind them. "Rahg, you need to cut that hair, lad. It'll be tickling your back before we get to Pomanda. You should wear yours like your brother. Keep it neat and trim. Respectable, that's what Darstan is."

"You're just jealous, Tobias. Besides, I'm growing mine long so I can give you some."

Darstan laughed as he brushed Grayson's mane. "He might have something there, Tobias."

Tobias bit hard on the stem of his pipe. "As for you, Darstan, you'd do well to take a shaving knife to your face. Startin' to look like a Wolfen with all that hair." Tobias let a chuckle escape while they laughed. "As far as weapons go, you'll learn everything."

Rahg turned to look at him. "What for?"

"Everyone needs a sword, and since you both are fair hands already, it won't take much to get you good. I've not seen many as good with a bow and arrow; Rhaven might be able to help you more there, but you'll both learn the knife and staff, and you'll learn how to really fight with the sword. I mean fightin' to kill."

~

*D*arstan was about to protest, but thought better of it. He'd seen Tobias in moods like this; there was no sense in talking to him once his decision was made.

"First thing to learn is how to defend yourself. Won't do you any good knowin' how to kill a man if you're already dead." The old man laughed, a little cackle that sometimes proved irritating. "The key is staying alive. That might sound simple, but most people think that the key to swordplay is striking a lethal blow. They're wrong. The key is defending yourself. Learn it well enough, and sooner or later the other person will make a mistake. When they do, you strike. Swords are not like arrows; the key to arrows and knives is striking first with a lethal or crippling blow. You have no defense with a bow and not much with knives, so you need to kill your opponent before they can get to you. Balance and speed!" Tobias shouted so loud Darstan took a step back. "Balance and speed. They are the keys to swords."

"What about those weapons Rhaven carry? Those sai." Darstan had been wondering about them since he first saw Rhaven use them; now seemed like a good time to ask.

Tobias shook his head. "Hard to learn, lads. It's the kind of weapon that'll get you killed before you learn it, more often than not, which is why few use it. But, for someone who knows how to use the sai, it's the best thing there is for close-in fightin'. And Rhaven's a true master. It's like those sai have become part of his arms. But don't go gettin' your sights set on learnin' the sai, lads. You need to learn the sword first."

Rahg opened his mouth to speak but Tobias cut him short.

"And, before you learn the sword you need to be able to hold that sword for an entire fight without your arm givin' out. So you're gonna get some training."

"Tobias, you already had us doing this. Remember, in Twin Forks?"

Tobias stared at both of them until they nodded, then turned his attention to Camissa. "Come here, lass. You need to be part of this. You too, Kender. A sword will fit your hands like any other."

Wisp turned at Tobias' call. "I'll not be playing with any rusty old swords and putting calluses on my hands. I've lived this long with my wits and my knives. I suspect I'll survive a little longer."

Darstan laughed. "Somehow, Wisp, I think you'll live to be older than Tobias." Darstan carried a smile with him as he went to sit by Rahg. A large oak provided shade and dry ground to rest, not to mention a trunk big enough for everyone to lean against. The cheese Tobias passed around was tasty and satisfied the pangs of hunger that nagged at Rahg and Darstan, even though they were not far past the noon meal. Darstan rested while Rahg dreamed, but all the while he dreaded hearing Rhaven's words, which came far too soon.

"Let's go," Rhaven said. "Horses are rested enough." He mounted Argus and took the lead.

"Hold those swords straight out," Tobias ordered, "and when your arms can't take it any longer, hold it some more, then switch sides. You do that for three months and you'll have arms with enough muscles so you won't tire during a long fight. That'll give you an edge on most men, and until you get to be masters, you'll need every advantage you can get."

"We know, Tobias, you—"

"Lad, I know you've held a sword before, but when you can hold it straight out like I showed you, and hold it long enough for a man to eat dinner, then you'll be ready." He started to go, then stopped. "And I don't mean the time it takes Rahg to eat. Someone civil is what I'm talkin' about."

Camissa couldn't hold the heavy sword for long, but every time it dropped, she used all her strength to raise it again.

Tobias tugged on the reins and moved in next to Camissa. "I'll ask Gregor to lend us that staff he's workin' on, lass. When the sword gets too heavy, you can use the staff. Anything's better than nothing."

Camissa smiled, but shook her head. "I'll get it. Don't waste any worry on me. I told Rhaven I'd not hold you up, and I'll not be the weak link during a fight." She held his gaze. "Don't worry, I'll learn."

Tobias couldn't help but smile. "I believe you will, lass. I do believe you will." As he clicked to his mount to move ahead, he glanced toward Rahg and caught him letting the sword slip downward. "Pick it up, lad. Pick it up. When you're in a fight, the Wolfen and Victas aren't gonna let you stop and rest cause your arm is tired." Tobias laughed as he moved over close to Gregor. "Can you carve a staff for the lass? I think she'd do better wielding a staff than a blade."

Gregor looked at Tobias, then turned to stare at Camissa, still practicing with the heavy sword. He nodded. "I've been carving this one as a spare for myself, but I can trim it down to make it lighter. I'll teach her. Teach the lads, too, if you want. Never hurts to know the staff."

"Good, we'll start tomorrow." Tobias spurred his mount to a slightly faster pace to catch up to Rhaven, riding ahead of the group to scout the trail. When he brought his horse alongside Argus, he could see the concern on Rhaven's face.

"Riders ahead." Rhaven said it before Tobias could even ask.

Tobias leaned forward in his saddle, squinting. "Looks to be a dozen. Maybe more."

"Tell the others," Rhaven said, "and tell them to stay calm." Rhaven fell back to join them. The riders were only a short distance away now. "Fifteen of them," Rhaven said. "Tobias and I will take the front line. Gregor and Wisp between us, but slightly back. Darstan and Rahg, you guard Camissa. And keep those bows strung and arrows nocked."

The riders rode in at a fast pace, only halting at the last moment. The man in the front leaned forward, hands pressed on the pommel. He eyed Camissa, a lascivious leer planted on a handsome face. Most of the others cast their glances toward the saddlebags, or to Rhaven. Wary looks appeared on their faces when they eyed him. The man in the front spoke, the one who had been eyeing Camissa.

"Don't know what you're carryin' in those bags, but since you're concerned about avoiding the guards on the main road, must be worth somethin'." The man's glare fell on each of them in turn, finishing with Rhaven. He let his gaze linger there.

"Since the guards don't find it necessary to patrol these parts anymore, we decided to take up the service for them. It would only seem fair to pay us the tax you'd be payin' the guard." The leader's face cracked into a grin, baring strong teeth and greedy eyes. "I'd say two silvers apiece would do nicely."

A man in the second line had a Sykoran short bow draped across his lap. He had an arrow nocked, ready to fly. *He'll have to go first,* Tobias thought. "We'll pay nothin' to the likes of you," Tobias said. "Stand aside."

The one in the middle slowly raised his bow while the leader continued talking to Tobias. The instant the bow left the saddle, Rhaven reached for his knife. As he did, a blade whizzed by his head and punctured the man's shoulder. By the time Rhaven drew his own knife, another blade caught the bandit in the throat, then a third knife hit another one in the chest. Rhaven sheathed his knife and bared sai and sword. Wisp was off his horse and stood with two more knives ready.

Tobias drew his sword and moved to the left. Gregor dismounted, staff in hand. Rahg and Darstan had hit two of the thieves, while they drew swords, but one was an arm shot and the other barely nicked the man's shoulder. They now had bows raised and two more arrows nocked. The bandit leader advanced brandishing his sword.

"Put the next ones in their hearts," Tobias said.

Rahg nodded. "Yes, sir."

Rhaven's eyes never left the bandits, scanning to see who presented the most danger. The one bandit lay on the ground, gasping his last few breaths, and the other lay dead. They were down to thirteen now, and two of those with wounds. Still favorable odds. The bandits had drawn swords, but before they could advance, Kella tromped from the brush and stood between Rhaven and the bandits, teeth bared.

"You can be on your way without losing any more lives," Rhaven said. "Or, you can stay and die. But I am not a patient man."

The bandit leader cast a last glance at the party, then Kella. Finally, he sheathed his sword. Without another word, he tugged on the reins and turned his horse south. "Pick them up," he ordered, staring at the two dead bandits.

Wisp breathed a sigh of relief when it became evident there would be no confrontation. "While you're down there, pull those blades free and hand them to me. I'll not lose a good blade on a bandit."

They threw his knives on the ground, spat, then mounted and departed, casting backward glances as they rode off. Wisp grumbled while he retrieved his knives.

Rhaven stared at him a moment. "You have quick hands, lad. They fit those blades well."

Wisp smiled. "Slow hands make a poor thief—or a dead one."

Rhaven's eyes lit briefly with a smile. "I suppose you're right," he said, then turned toward Rahg and Darstan. "Keep a keen eye on the road behind you and look to the sides. I'd not be surprised to find them waiting for us somewhere ahead."

"Yes, sir," Rahg said.

"And the next time you shoot somebody, kill him."

Rahg gulped. "Yes, sir."

~

The remainder of the day passed uneventfully, but by the time they stopped for supper they were all tired. Wisp told stories all night about Pomanda, while Camissa spent her time healing wounds.

"It's different from Sykor," he said. "The streets are filled with beggars and thieves, so you need to be careful. They'll steal anything. Even steal the hair off your head." Wisp laughed. "Tobias, have you been to Pomanda lately?"

Darstan and Rahg nearly fell over, and Tobias laughed so hard his side began to ache. Rahg looked over to Gregor, putting the finishing touches on the staff, and saw that the bounty man was smiling. Wisp stirred the fire with a stick. "You know, Tobias, when we get to Pomanda, you should get a new shirt. You've been wearing that one a long time."

Tobias chomped on his pipe stem. "Lad, I'm not one to give up on a garment just 'cause it's got a few tatters. This shirt will do me fine. It's done me well for many a season, and I guess it will last a few more. Might be with me till I die."

Wisp reached over and rubbed the sleeve, frowning. "Tobias, I appreciate a frugal man, but the suggestion is worth consideration. That shirt has been wounded. When we get to Pomanda, I'll get you a new one."

Tobias had a sarcastic chuckle at times. "Lad, nothing against you, but

I'd rather not be wearin' a piece of clothing that someone else might claim to be theirs, 'specially with me not knowin' if they're tellin' the truth or not."

Another round of laughter raced through the camp, even Camissa found it difficult to control herself. Rahg shifted his attention to focus on Rhaven, sitting off to the side, next to Kella. He talked to the vargel more than people.

~

*R*haven gently rubbed his hands over Kella's massive head, smoothing the thick black fur that felt so silky to the touch. "You're a great warrior, girl. A companion to be cherished. If I could have my way, we would leave now, go hunt Victas and Wolfen."

Rhaven let his hand rest on the back of her neck. "We would make a good team. Kill a lot of them. If I survive this fight with Pirrhar, perhaps we'll do battle again." Rhaven stared into the night while he talked. A whimper from the vargel alerted him, and he realized he had squeezed her too tightly. Kella's black eyes met his and Rhaven saw the tenderness in them. "I meant no harm, brave warrior, I was... thinking."

Kella lifted her head and stared at Rhaven, her black eyes remained soft and, somehow, Rhaven seemed to know what she wanted. "So you want more petting?" He laughed. "I guess you deserve it," he said, and patted her back with a gentle stroke that soon had the vargel laying her head back down with eyes closed.

Once he saw she had fallen asleep, Rhaven joined the rest of them, still reveling in the tales Wisp was telling about Pomanda. "We'll be leaving at first—light, and there is training to complete." Rhaven's announcement stopped the mirth. "Better get some sleep. We will need rest before we face the Black Rose. Damon Pirrhar is not a man to treat lightly."

~

At the mention of his name, a cold chill passed through Rahg. He recalled what Takar had said about Damon Pirrhar being the most dangerous man he had ever seen. And the best, he had said. Perhaps better than Rhaven. Right now, Rahg wished he could be back in Twin Forks, sleeping in his own bed, in his own house. He wanted his father to greet him when he broke fast, and he wished more than anything that his biggest worries could once again be tending sheep or chopping wood.

Rahg wiped a tear from his eye before anyone noticed. Twin Forks was gone. So was his father. And all of his friends. And now... Gods blood! He wished for it all to be a dream. But all that was gone. The one cold reality was that Damon Pirrhar, the leader of the Black Rose, hunted him..

I hope Rhaven can beat him.

POMANDA

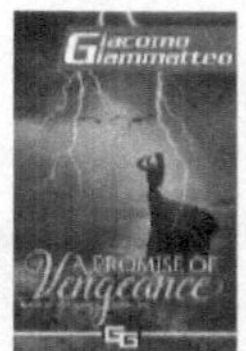

*P*omandans had an innate distrust of monarchy, of being ruled at all. They avoided rulers like a mad dog shucks a leash. There was a king there, but he wore a false crown. The council of seven leading families shared the government with the king—each family receiving one vote while he got two. Even this proved to be a tentative rule, for if the people didn't like a law, they simply disregarded it.

Sykor ruled with an iron glove, but even a silk one spurred revolt in Pomanda. At the slightest hint of an unjust law Pomandans took to the streets, swarming the Great Houses like maggots on a four-day carcass. Where the bellow of a force leader cowed the Sykorans, the people of Pomanda barely tolerated a raised voice. Guards trod lightly there.

Tobias had taken the point and waited with his mount at the crest of a large rise. The sun glistened off his scalp, and beads of sweat dotted his forehead. "Pomanda!" he shouted, just as the others neared the top of the hill.

Pomanda

Rahg could not believe what he saw: two large hills squeezed the northern edges of the city into a tight valley, and houses climbed the slopes like ivy on a trellis. The city spread far south, crawling through large, rolling hills until it erupted into an undulating plain blanketed with tall grass. Red tile roofs colored every house and basked in the burning sunlight, and a large wall ran the perimeter of the city, protecting it from invasion.

For days Rahg had imagined Pomanda, taking descriptions provided by Tobias and Wisp and assembling them like a puzzle until a complete picture had formed. When he at last caught his first glimpse of the city, he discovered his imagination put to shame. Roads ran in all directions, busy with the flutter of travelers, visitors, and merchants coming and going as they pleased. It was a pleasant sight after experiencing the rigors of getting in and out of Sykor.

~

Camissa had been nervous during the trip, uneasy about another large city and what might happen if anyone in Pomanda discovered her unnatural abilities. On more than several occasions, she asked Wisp about the laws, and the guards, and how they dealt with people like her. She wasn't dangerous, and it didn't hurt that she was attractive, and seemed to stir feelings in Rahg that he once thought he could only feel for Kanella. He did his best to justify accepting her and allay any underlying fears he might be harboring.

"Of course I'm not dangerous," Camissa said.

"What!"

"I said, of course I would never harm anyone."

Rahg's mouth fell open. "How?" he began, "Can you do that all the time?" He paused briefly, then finished the thoughts. "What else did you hear? Or whatever it is you do."

Camissa laughed, enjoying every moment of Rahg's discomfort. "I can sense peoples' feelings. Sometimes, when I am near a person, or if it is someone I am close to, I can actually *hear* their thoughts in my own head. I find it difficult to explain, but it's almost as if you were talking to me."

"Can you do it all the time? With me, I mean. Who else?"

"It's rare that I can actually read thoughts, and even then I can grasp only part of what the person is thinking, but sometimes, like when you were remembering about...Kanella? Was that her name?"

Rahg nodded.

"Well, those thoughts were so strong that I was able to read all of them." Camissa smiled, her pale face glowing with a rosy blush. "Perhaps because you included me in those thoughts."

This new twist disturbed Rahg, and he whispered, *"Now I can't even have private thoughts. Blasted Camissa. Now she's ruining my dreams."* He quickly glanced over to see if she had heard. Camissa rode on with no apparent interest; showing no signs of having read his mind that time.

~

*T*obias pulled his mount next to Argus and stopped. "What's your plan, Rhaven?"

"We'll need to find an inn, probably two, so that we can split up and gather as much information as possible. And they need to be the kind of places where we might learn of the Black Rose, even if we have to buy the information."

Rhaven turned to Wisp. "Make contact with the boss of thieves. Get him to help us no matter the cost; I have gold. Gregor, there must be bounty-men in Pomanda. See to getting them on our side. There will be rewards."

"I will find them," Gregor said. "I can always find thieves, and wherever the thieves are, we will find bounty-men."

"He'll find them, but only with my help." Wisp laughed, then rode off, the bounty man close on his heels.

The rest of them moved at a slow pace into Pomanda. "I know someone who might help us," Tobias said. "I'll take the lads and Camissa with me."

"No! Rahg and Camissa stay with me. Darstan can go with you."

~

*T*obias tugged lightly on the reins, and started down the same road Wisp had taken. "Let's get a move on, Darstan. I'm hungry as a bear."

Rhaven brought Argus to a halt and turned to face Camissa. "You seem to have attached yourself to Rahg. That might allow you to sense something useful to us, so stay alert."

Camissa's eyebrows raised. "You know about my powers?"

"I have seen many things. Powers neither surprise nor fascinate me. I knew a woman once..." he paused. "She had powers similar to yours. She could sense good in people. But she refused to recognize the bad side of anyone she felt kindness toward. Much like you, Camissa."

Rhaven's soft words and even softer tone shocked Rahg. *Does he care for her? Am I being a fool?* Rahg shook his head to clear it before Camissa heard. "How can that cause a problem?"

"The one she refused to recognize as evil eventually killed her. Tortured her. Caused her pain beyond belief." Rahg heard a cracking sound, and looked over to Rhaven. He had snapped his whittling stick in half, yet he continued to squeeze it, as if he were crushing the life out of it. White-capped knuckles squeezed harder, and Rhaven's face tensed.

"His name," Rhaven said, grinding out each word, "Is Damon Pirrhar." Another cracking sound brought Rahg's gaze back to Rhaven's hands where the remaining half of the stick snapped.

Rahg recognized the name immediately—Damon Pirrhar, the Black Rose leader. "Why, Rhaven? What did the woman do to him?"

Rhaven looked as fierce as Rahg had ever seen. "She had the misfortune to give birth to him."

"He killed his own mother!"

"He did." Rhaven spat it out, then his voice became quiet. "Also, his father." The final piece of wood produced a cry as it, too, was halved.

"Gods blood!" Rahg knew that Damon Pirrhar was deadly from what Takar had said, but he wouldn't want to be the man now, not with Rhaven like this.

Camissa gasped, her eyes wide with fright.

~

 *id she sense Rhaven's feelings?* Rahg thought. *Is she that close to him?*

A shuddering whisper escaped her lips. "Sweet Glory."

~

obias and Darstan rode through the great city's streets, slowly, so they could appreciate its glory. Darstan looked everywhere but ahead, marveling at the enormity of Pomanda and the wonders it held. They came upon a large open-air plaza with a beautiful fountain in the center. The streets converged on the circular paved road that surrounded it, merging into a bustle of traffic.

"We better get off and lead the horses, Darstan, lest someone get trampled."

Darstan slid off Grayson to join the throng of citizens who filled the plaza. He walked into a plaza crowded with people, many of them gathered about a fountain to the side of the square.

statue of the gods

As he was about to say something, Tobias pointed toward the other side and said "The Fountain of the Ancients," naming the structure as he gestured.

Darstan examined it as they passed. Three, giant sculptures of god-like beings dominated one side of the monument. Some great artisan from ages past had freed them from the prison of a huge block of white marble. Twisting strands of hair painted a beard on each of the gods, and the sinews in their arms and legs bulged with unerring accuracy. "What does it mean?" Darstan asked.

"Don't know," Tobias said. "Some ancient legend, I believe, but I don't know the story."

"I can't imagine you not knowing a story," Darstan said, then turned to study the structure again. The three gods stood with all the splendor of warriors. Their hands, gripping weapons unfamiliar to Darstan, were poised for battle and aimed at a single, female statue carved from black marble. The goddess lay on her left side, half-raised, and supported by her elbow. Her right arm was raised, as if fending off the attack of the other three gods. Despite the defeated pose she held her head in defiance. The sculptor had captured a dangerous look in her eyes.

"C'mon," Tobias said. "We can come back later."

With a final glance, Darstan noticed that the figure of the goddess cast a shadow inside the fountain pool, whereas the shadows of the gods fell outside, onto the paving. And the ripples of the pool did not affect the water where the shadow of the goddess fell. *Odd,* he thought, reaching down to touch the water. *Perhaps it's because...*

The touch of the water interrupted his thoughts. He yanked his hand back. The water was cold, death-cold, and it shouldn't have been. The sun was blazing hot. A violent shudder took hold of him. The feeling reminded him of his fall through the ice–covered pond in Twin Forks. He recalled the bone-chilling cold, and the way he trembled. It had taken half the day for him to feel warm again. Darstan shook his head to clear a foggy mind. The chill passed quickly, and he wondered what had happened.

Tobias tugged at his arm, cutting short his musing. "Let's go, Darstan. Got no time to be looking at statues."

∼

*W*isp felt comfortable now that he was back in the city; any city made him feel at home. "The first thing we need to do is stable these horses," Wisp said. "Pomanda is too crowded."

Gregor agreed, and they quickly found someone to care for their mounts.

"We should separate," Gregor said. "Though it rankles me, I doubt that your associates and mine will get along."

"Good idea, Gregor, and don't worry, I gave my word that I'll attempt no escape. Leastwise, not until we help Rahg." Wisp laughed. "The Inn of the Turtle is two blocks down this street, assuming it's still there. We'll meet back here at dinner." Gregor nodded, then they both went separate ways.

Wisp vanished into the rush of people, and in short time found the most promising section of the city—where thieves would be marking their prey. Wandering down a likely avenue, he spotted what he guessed to be three probable purse-snatchers weaving their way through the crowd, their trained eyes catching each person as they passed. They were young, about ten to twelve years old, but he knew they would be good. Wisp adjusted his purse, making it all but impossible for them to resist, though he did empty it first.

Shops lined the street on each side, merchants selling linens and jewelry mixing with those providing feed, candles and meats of all kinds. A lamp shop caught Wisp's eye, as people milled about in front and crowded the inside of it, gawking at what they couldn't afford. Wisp breathed deeply, savoring the aroma of fresh khaffe. He followed his nose to a merchant offering khaffe, te, and other spices from as far away as Jattan-Kir. He longed to stop inside, but he had thieves to catch.

Wisp turned and walked back up the street so that he would be facing them. They bumped him hard, then apologized profusely in the polite, charming manner only young lads can effect. Wisp recognized the gleam in their eyes. At first, they sauntered down the street, but once a safe distance passed, they hurried off with their haul. Anticipation would be running rampant in their minds, each one guessing how much the purse contained. And their calculating minds would be busy dividing it up, minus the cut for the boss.

Wisp fondly recalled the memories as he took inventory of what he had taken from them. The little thieves had enjoyed a prosperous morning: ten coppers, four silver, and an old Khataran coin. Wisp sat down on the side of the street to wait, observing each person who passed with suspicious eyes. The thieves would be back soon.

Moments later he spied the little urchins making their way back through the crowd, darting in and out of the heavy traffic, while arguing. The taller one was busy berating the other two, blaming them for their misfortune. Wisp chuckled as he listened. He could discern their high-pitched voices even above the din of the city.

"It's your fault, Tema. You bumped me just 'fore we hit 'im."

"I never bumped nobody in my life that wasn't s'posed to be bumped. I'm tellin' ya. I hit 'im like we always do, and next thing I know my own purse is gone."

They kept so busy arguing that they passed right by Wisp. He let them go for about half a block, then followed at a safe distance. Their path led through several side alleys lined with tall brick houses that rose and fell with the hills of Pomanda. He followed them over rooftops, separated occasionally by an alley a man could spread his arms across, and then he descended and went across the square. All the while he trailed them undetected.

The lads continued their debate, mostly verbal, but with occasional shoving and at least one half-hearted punch. Finally, they arrived at the destination Wisp sought. The lads ceased fighting and checked to make sure they had not been followed or watched. Wisp laughed. *They'll learn. Or they'll be caught and jailed.*

A series of coded raps on a battered door tucked into a brown stone frame produced a slightly cracked opening, followed by admittance for the runts. *I better get in there before their boss beats them too badly.* He had been close enough to hear the sequence of raps, and memorized the code.

Splinters riddled the old door, so Wisp, always conscious of damage to his hands, selected the smoothest section of the door and tapped out the code. Tap, tap... tap..tap,tap... tap,tap......tap. The door creaked open. A burly looking gent with a heavy gray beard peeked through.

"What's your business?"

"Came to save those lads a beating."

"And would you be takin' their place?" The burly man only half-joked.

"I think not." Wisp jammed his shoulder against the door while wedging his foot at the bottom. He placed a dagger against the man's throat. His left hand maintained a tight grip on the thief's hair, applying constant pressure to the blade while he whispered in the man's ear. "I think, my friend, that if you are not cooperative I might put you in their place." The door opened wide. The man backed–up to allow Wisp entry. From the corner, Temal was the first to scream an identification.

"That's him. He's the one that took our coin."

Wisp scanned the room in a glance. The little ones sat on empty crates, and two other thieves occupied broken chairs. There was an old table with only three legs, and a mattress tucked against a stone wall with crumbling mortar. Wisp caught the eye of the one he calculated to be the boss, a tall man with dangling arms but a broad chest. A small set of ears peeked out from behind a crop of blond hair that distinguished him from most Pomandans, though Wisp knew from his time here before that some of the nobility passed on those traits.

Rumors abounded in certain quarters of royal offspring being raised by whores. The man had a nose so small Wisp wondered if he could smell, and it made his blue eyes appear to belong to a horse. *More telltales,* Wisp thought. Blue eyes were seldom found in this part of Pomanda.

"Carmine sends his greetings," Wisp said in a confident and disinterested fashion.

Surprise covered the boss's face, but it did not replace the suspicion that lingered as he articulated his coded response. "Carmine is dead."

"If Carmine's dead, then he's been running Sykor from the grave."

"And how would that grave be marked?" asked the boss.

Wisp hesitated. This was the last response in the code, the one that required him to identify himself. There would be only a few people Carmine would trust with the code, and this man may know the others. Wisp thought long on this. He had never revealed himself to anyone but Carmine, until the group he traveled with. Now another would know.

"And how would that grave be marked?" the boss asked again, tension in his voice.

Wisp nodded. He had to risk giving his own name, despite the dangers. He had to do it for Rahg. He sheathed his dagger, then moved toward the boss. When he had come close enough to whisper without being heard by anyone else, he finished the discourse. "The grave be marked with the name of the Wisp."

The boss jerked back, staring at Wisp with eyes as big as a Gendan coin. Wisp knew what he must be thinking. He would be trying to remember what Carmine had told him of the Wisp. Did he have a large nose, like this one? Was he gaunt? Was his skin olive, like a Pomandan, or pale Sykoran gray? Wisp also knew that searching his memory only emphasized the problem—Carmine would have told him nothing. "I need more proof than that." The boss no longer spoke in code.

Wisp nodded. He knew what the man wanted, some secret of Carmine's that few would know. A quick signal with his fingers motioned the boss to a spot offering more privacy. Wisp leaned toward him and whispered. "Carmine reeks of fish."

The man ran his eyes up and down Wisp, his face now relaxed, the tenseness gone. A slight smile cracked what had been a grim facade.

"So, you are the Wisp," he said, but quietly, so no one could hear. "I am called Sengua, and you are welcome to Pomanda. Your talents will be rewarded here."

Wisp worried even while he answered. He had kept his secret from everyone but Carmine for all of these years, and in the past two moons, the truth of his identity had spread like a plague. "I have not come to ply my trade; however, I do need your help."

A puzzled look came to Sengua's face. "Come with me. We'll talk privately."

~

*R*haven's brisk pace led the way through the crowded streets of Pomanda. Most travelers had to fight their way across the plazas, but people moved aside from Rhaven's path.

The awe of Pomanda struck Rahg at every new turn. Granite and marble were everywhere, and in all colors. He had only seen gray before, like in Sykor, but here he had already seen black, white, green, gray-green, even shades of blue and brown. And the sculptures—how magnificent they were. Rahg continued walking, entering a mobbed plaza as he marveled at the statues. He saw the fountain from across the plaza and nearly fell over. *I've got to see that.* "Rhaven, I'm going to see the fountain."

Rhaven nodded. "I should return shortly. Wait for me at the fountain, and don't move."

Rahg and Camissa fought their way through the crowd and managed to find a spot to sit at on the side of the fountain. Rahg lazily swished his hand in the pool. The water was hot, offering no respite from the burning heat of Pomanda.

Camissa stared at the sculpture. "It's beautiful, isn't it?"

Rahg gave a perfunctory nod while he gawked at the statues of the gods. "It sure is," he said, and marveled at how human hands could have created such beauty. Following the gaze of the gods, his perusal fell to the almost recumbent form of the goddess. Save for her defensive posture, she appeared idyllic and at rest, and yet, her eyes held a defiant stare. Rahg sat mesmerized by her perfection, his eyes transfixed on the black marble figure until Camissa interrupted his trance.

"I wish you would look at me like that."

Her statement tore him from his spellbound state. "I didn't know you wished for that, but now that I do..." Camissa playfully hit him, as he ogled and leered at her. Soon, his mind was once again lured away by the enchantress of stone. Something had caught his eye just when Camissa distracted him. He was trying to remember what it was, when Camissa's carefree splashing in the pool prompted his memory. He followed the path created by the ripples all the way to the shadow cast on the water by the figure of the goddess. "There," he said.

"There what?"

"Look closely. When the ripples of the water reach the shadow, they stop. They just stop." Even while Rahg explained it to her, he didn't quite believe his own eyes, so he dragged Camissa over for a closer inspection.

Next to the half-prone sculpture stood an old woman, her wrinkled skin clothed in a tattered red robe. As Rahg reached down to show Camissa exactly what he meant, the old hag screeched a warning, her voice a harbinger of evil. "Don't touch the shadow."

"What do you mean?" Camissa asked.

"The Curse of Anciara," the hag explained. "Touching the shadow brings death."

Camissa grabbed Rahg's hand, just in case he decided to ignore the old woman's counsel. "Come, Rahg. Let's go wait for Rhaven, over there." Camissa pointed to the spot where they sat originally. As they left she turned to thank the old lady but the hag was gone. "Where did she go?" Camissa cried. "She was right here. She couldn't have just disappeared." Camissa stood on tiptoes and craned her neck in a vain attempt to find the old woman.

Rahg tried to logically resolve the mystery of the missing woman by insisting she blended in with the crowd, but Camissa would hear nothing of it. "It was only an instant, Rahg. Besides, I would have recognized that red robe she wore. It was very different." Camissa pointed at the crowd. "Look. Do you see any like it? You could spot that color anywhere on the plaza." They didn't have time to debate the issue longer, as Rhaven arrived and called them away.

Camissa had to almost run to keep pace as Rhaven's long strides carried them at an even faster gait than before. They passed another statue on the way across the square. This one featured an image of some god lying back and resting.

image of a god resting

Rahg wanted to stop and look at the statue, but Rhaven would have nothing of it. Camissa tugged on Rahg's sleeve. "Come on. We have to hurry."

They left the center of Pomanda and headed into the poor section of the city, the majesty and splendor of before replaced by filth and squalor. "Why are we going this way?"

"Find an inn to stay the night," Rhaven said.

"An inn, down here? We surely have enough coin to stay somewhere more pleasant."

"Too many people," Rhaven said. "An assassin could be hiding among any of them. Here, a stranger is easily recognized, and with a few well-placed coins we can buy an army of spies. We will be notified the instant someone strange comes to the Falora."

With Rhaven's mention of *assassin*, Rahg's hand instinctively went to the hilt of his sword. He scanned the surroundings, taking note that the crowds had thinned and the demeanor of the people on the streets had taken new form. Instead of mingling with other visitors or merchants, they now passed by beggars, cripples, and thieves. At the thought of thieves, his other hand reached to clutch his purse. "Still there," he said, thanking the gods.

They checked into an inn, named the Bentarina Cormal, and, by contrast, it proved to be as horrible as its name was beautiful. "What does it mean?" Camissa asked Rhaven. "The name," she added, "It's a pretty name."

"In the old tongue it means House of Good Fortune."

Rahg scoffed. *Pretty name? Girls think everything is pretty.* "Perhaps they should change it," Rahg said.

Rhaven made the arrangements, paid the man, then started up the stairs. The old wood creaked under their weight causing Rahg to wonder if they should all be climbing them at once. About halfway up he noticed one of the treads missing. "Be careful, Camissa. That could be a nasty fall."

"There used to be a railing," the innkeeper, explained, "but it got broke in the last brawl we had."

"We don't care about amenities or idle talk," Rhaven said. "Just show us to the rooms and do as you were bade, nothing more."

The innkeep's lips started to move when he turned to Rhaven, but he must have thought better of it and stopped. "Follow me," he said, and led them to the rooms.

Once inside, Rhaven outlined plans for the remainder of the day. "The others will soon be here. When they arrive, explain where we left our horses, and have Darstan and Wisp bring our gear. Also, tell them I have altered the plans. We will stay here." Rhaven stared hard at Rahg. "Don't go anywhere until I return." The shabby door slammed shut as Rhaven left.

It irked Rahg that anyone would order him to stay in a room, even though it was for his own benefit. The only consolation was that Camissa would be keeping him company. His mind began to wander about Camissa: being alone with her, holding her on a cold night, kissing her soft lips. Suddenly, he remembered her powers. *By the gods, she's probably listening to me now. Are you Camissa? Are you hearing my thoughts? I'm beginning not to like this at all. Can't even have private thoughts around her.*

Camissa had her back facing Rahg. She fell, banging her knee on the floor. "Ouch."

Rahg rushed over and bent to check her knee. "It's only a little scratch. But you did manage to get a splinter. Let me get it out for you." He did his best to gently remove the errant sliver of wood, though it was difficult with short fat fingers. Finally, he got it. "Are you all right?"

"I'm fine, Rahg. Just fine."

THE BLACK ROSE

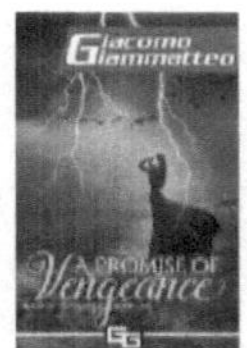

"We'll get this taken care of, Rahg. One way or another. We won't leave Pomanda before we do." Rhaven sat in a chair across from the bed, hands folded behind his head and the chair leaning against the wall. Rahg sat on the floor next to Camissa and Darstan. Gregor paced the floor, his staff continually tapping the hardwood planks.

"bounty man, my head's startin' to pound. Would you put that staff away?" Tobias lay on the bed, resting on his elbow. "I spoke to Preman. He said there'd be gold in this for everyone if we get the Black Rose leader."

"How much gold?" Gregor stopped tapping his staff and leaned it against the wall.

Wisp slipped into the room just as he finished. "If we're talking about gold, it must be Gregor leading the conversation. Ah, there is the illustrious bounty man now." Wisp smiled, then turned to Rhaven. "Got it," he said, "the head of the guild will help us, and he also told me where the Black Rose stay. It's not far from here, down by Minnaro Park."

Rhaven nodded and cracked his knuckles while his eyes narrowed to slits. "I'll pay their leader a visit tonight."

A broken twig hung from Tobias' mouth where he normally held his pipe. "Preman said the Black Rose have powerful allies in Pomanda. Many of the nobles support them and use their services. Guess they don't have to worry about hiding with connections like that."

Rhaven leaned forward in the chair, then stood. "Wisp, Gregor, while I'm gone, check with your friends. We might need someplace else to stay, and I don't want to be searching in the middle of the night."

As they prepared to leave, Rhaven turned to Tobias. "Stay with Rahg. You too, Darstan. Keep Camissa and your brother company. Even though we have spies, I'm not comfortable. Keep a close watch," he said, then followed Wisp and Gregor out the door.

～

Camissa sat at a table near the center of the room, Darstan and Rahg pulling up chairs beside her. Tobias sat close to the door.

There were only a few customers. The Bentarina Cormal offered little to draw a crowd, at least nowadays. But traces of beauty from ages past were hidden throughout: remnants of ornate carvings dotted rotting pillars that now needed braces to support them; and vague hints of inlaid wood hid beneath layers of dirt and years of scratches on a bar that stood chest high. Deep gouges marred paths on the floor and offered splinters in place of shine. Stout legs shouldered thick slabs of oak for tabletops, and the chairs stood strong and steady on crusty birch planking.

"I'm hungry," Rahg said.

Camissa's eyes sparkled. "Are you ever *not* hungry?"

Darstan searched for a serving girl. "I wonder if we have to get things ourselves here?"

"I served enough tables in Sykor," Camissa said. "You or Rahg can get this. And when you go, I'll have soup, that's all. And te."

Rahg handed four coppers to Darstan. "Ale, bread and cheese for me," he said. "Soup, too."

Darstan went to get the food, while Camissa stared at a carving on the pillar. "Look at how beautiful that is, Rahg."

Rahg brushed aside dirt with his sleeve then joined Camissa, admiring the work of an old master. They continued their scrutiny as Darstan returned with the ale. "I'll be right back with the rest."

"I wish I had talents like this. How wonderful to be able to create something with your hands." She was thinking about the carving when she felt a bump to her chair. She scooted in to make room for a man who was stumbling past. Fear swept over her as she turned to see his face. "He's one of them, Rahg. Watch out!"

~

The assassin spun toward Camissa, eyes agape, but the pause was brief. He threw a chair out of his way and drew a short sword and a dagger.

Rahg jumped to his feet. He backed up, sword and knife drawn. *One of them she said. Did she mean assassin?* Fear clutched at Rahg's throat.

Darstan raced back, upended the table, and pushed it toward the assassin, buying needed time for him and Rahg.

The short, Cergalan Sword whisked from his sheath as the Wolfen long-knife filled his other hand. "Tobias!"

Camissa stepped away from the table, her knuckles white from gripping the back of a chair. Tobias jumped from his seat at Darstan's call, racing toward them, shoving people and chairs out of his way.

A flash of steel rushed toward Rahg. He leapt aside, bumped a pillar, then moved quickly back. The assassin was fast! Rahg swung his sword, but the man brushed it away with a flick of his wrist then dug steel into Rahg's right arm. "Gods blood!" He jerked his arm aside, fumbling with his sword as he did.

Rahg fell back, struggling to defend himself. The man was too fast. Taking a firm grip on his sword, Rahg moved forward, this time jabbing at the Rose while keeping the knife poised for what little defense it afforded.

When the assassin struck at Rahg, Darstan moved in with his sword, a swift jab that caught flesh, but the assassin twirled just in time. Darstan's blade only grazed him. With his long knife, Darstan parried the other man's dagger, then positioned himself to strike again with the sword. Blood spurted to the surface of Darstan's arm, as a twisting move by the assassin caught him off guard. He cursed, falling back to recover.

Rahg pressed forward with the distraction offered by Darstan, and when he did, his knife found blood on the man's upper right arm. Before the assassin could turn, Tobias reached the fray, his blade singing as it met the assassin's steel.

Rahg kicked a chair out of his way and pressed the assault, forcing the man into a spot caught between the three of them. Darstan and Tobias moved in unison, with Darstan's blade the first to draw blood, a knife wound to the man's left side. The assassin shifted his weight to the right side. When he did, Rahg took advantage. He thrust his sword into the man's guts, the resistance like plunging a blade into loose sand. Rahg grimaced as the steel met bone.

The assassin fell to the floor, blood spilling onto the planks, oozing into the grooves and cracks.

Camissa rushed over. "Rahg, are you hurt?"

Rahg pushed her aside and stooped to the corpse. He tore open the man's sleeve, revealing the Black Rose tattoo, then shifted his gaze to the man's chest. "The Red Sun. No doubt who he was."

Darstan knelt beside Rahg, carefully avoiding the spreading pool of blood. He patted his back. "Well done, brother. An assassin is not an easy kill."

"You did as much. I have no illusions about how this would have turned out without you or Tobias."

"Fact is, it's him on the floor, lad. Not you." Tobias looked about the room. "Be best if we got out of here. Wasn't our fault, but no sense askin' for trouble with the guard. Let's go."

Rahg stared around the room as they left. Most of the people had gone; in fact, all he saw was one old man who appeared drunk and an old woman in a hooded brown cloak sitting near the back.

Tobias approached the barkeep, glaring at them from behind the counter. "Our apologies for the trouble, and for losing you business." He pulled two silver dirnars from his pocket. "One's for cleaning up the body, and the other's for keeping quiet. We don't want to have to leave the inn."

After a long pause, the man picked up the coins. "I'll take care of it."

Camissa grabbed hold of Rahg's hand as they walked. "Your skin feels cold. Are you all right?"

"I'm fine, Camissa. Don't worry about me."

Gregor came in right after Wisp, so Tobias started his story over again, telling them all that had transpired. Wisp patted Rahg on the back. "This business will soon be over. Very soon."

"I intend to go with you when you hunt Damon Pirrhar. I'm tired of hiding and being hunted. If they mean to kill me, let them do it facing me, not with a crossbow or a knife in the back."

Wisp's brown eyes stared back at Rahg. "Spoken like a warrior, Rahg, but you should let Rhaven handle this. He is eminently qualified."

"I want to do my part."

Camissa came to the room with bandages and a pail of hot water. Some herbs, too, from the smell of it. "I'm all right," Rahg said.

"There are other people in this world besides you, Rahg Fal-Thera. Darstan is hurt, and I'm certain he won't mind being bandaged."

Tobias laughed so hard he coughed and turned red. Darstan and Wisp laughed too. Even Gregor. Only Rahg remained grim faced. Finally he gave in and rolled up his sleeve. "Sorry, Camissa."

"As well you should be," she said. "But now you'll have to wait your turn."

~

Rhaven kept to the shadows, a determined gait taking him deep into Pomanda with every long stride. He felt almost naked, having shed most of his weapons for the sake of agility. He carried a minimum to face Damon Pirrhar: two sai, his kunai, a few knives, and the blackthorn darts.

Grand maples lined the banks of the Veran River, weaving its way through the city like a lover's caress. Majestic oaks sprouted massive limbs and spread their protection over gardens filled with hedges and benches built from granite. Rhaven slipped into the embracing arms of a century old oak and climbed his way up and over rows of hedges that formed a maze. He wedged between two thick branches and waited, watching for movement, anything to determine the secret entrance he knew would be nearby.

A rustle of branches north of him exposed two men exiting between parted bushes. Rhaven deftly made his way to a perch above and scanned the area. A door to a caretaker's shed looked to be the only possible egress. Rhaven lowered himself, careful to make no noise, then ducked for cover, shielding himself behind a tree as the door opened again. Another Rose emerged. *Like snakes from a den,* Rhaven thought, and clenched his teeth.

A short while later, Rhaven entered through the door. He found a small building, not much more than a few lengths each way, and, as he suspected, a tunnel at the rear. He put his ear to the opening, then moved quietly ahead, his blowgun loaded with a dart. Dank, musty air filled his senses; it stank of mildew and bore a bitter taste. Long fingers brushed lightly against the moist earthen walls. Occasionally he felt a wooden brace. Progress proved to be slow as he had to rely on smell and touch. He had walked nearly fifty paces, by his count, and still he could see no exit. After ten more steps, and a short bend, he heard a sound from above, men walking, talking. Rhaven stopped. His heart slowed though it should have raced. Two more careful steps revealed an exit, a slight shaft of light from a doorway in the ceiling of the tunnel.

Rhaven listened for a long time then he carefully opened the door. Light gushed at him. His eyes closed reflexively, then slowly opened to slits, then fully. He peeked out into a long corridor—dark, but not like the tunnel. A doorway sat at the end of the hallway. Rhaven climbed out, then let his long legs carry him silently toward his destination. He passed by several empty rooms then found the room he sought.

~

*D*amon Pirrhar sat comfortably at his desk, his back toward the door. The Black Rose stiffened when he sensed an intruder. He pressed his foot to a signaling device on the floor. Before Damon could do anything else he heard the warning.

"Move and you die."

The Black Rose recognized the threat as real; he had learned to tell what a man might do by the tone of his voice. Damon Pirrhar froze, though his voice brimmed with confidence. "May I turn?"

"Do it slowly."

Damon Pirrhar stood as he turned. He was taller than Rhaven and at least as brawny. Harsh lines marked a rugged facial contour, and two curved swords hung at his sides, bearing the polished hilts of a master swordsman. When Damon's eyes met Rhaven's, a glimmer of recognition lit his stony face. "It has been a long time. I wondered if you would ever find the courage to seek me out."

Rhaven stood still as stone. The black tube close to his mouth held the assassin at bay. "Had I known you lived, I would have found you long ago, though that is not the reason for my visit."

Questions danced in Damon's eyes.

"Why is the Black Rose concerned with Rahg Fal-Thera, a mere village boy? What has he done to warrant an assassination?"

"So," Damon nodded his understanding, "you are the cause of my troubles with this boy. I was beginning to believe the Master had finally awarded me an assignment that required my personal skills. Now I see it was merely coincidence. If you put down that tube and do battle like a warrior, we will resolve that problem as well."

"Master? You obey another's orders like a trained hound?"

Damon fumed. "I follow only one," he said. "And you would be wise not to mock him. Even on the verge of death. Especially on the verge of death." A crooked smile remained on his face.

"I intend to finish you now," Rhaven said. "I only wish I could make the pain last longer, but the blackthorn—" A slight sound came from the corridor. Rhaven leapt aside, careful to maintain his aim on Damon. A knife flew past where he just stood, landing near Damon's desk.

"Hold!" Damon called, his hand raised to the men who stood in the hallway outside his door. "It seems we have a dilemma. You have your dart trained on me, but I have my men blocking your retreat."

"I should have killed you as soon as I saw you," Rhaven said.

"That would have been your only chance."

Rhaven glanced to the side, where three assassins now stood. "You'll come with me," he said, nodding toward Damon. "I'll let you go when we reach the street. We can settle our business tomorrow."

Damon shook his head. "I'm afraid that won't do. How do I know you will let me go once you are out of harm's way?"

"My word," Rhaven said. "I give you my word, that I won't harm you until we meet tomorrow."

Damon thought for a moment, then nodded. "Agreed. Let him pass," he said to the men in the hall. "And don't follow us. For all of the trouble he has caused me, I know I can trust his word." Damon returned his gaze to Rhaven. "There is a warehouse in the Falora quarter that sits mostly empty. We will meet there tomorrow, at daybreak." Damon thought for a moment more. "And the boy, you will bring him with you? And you will ensure me that no one else will interfere?"

Rhaven nodded. "Upon my word, no man or woman shall interfere once the battle is done."

Damon stared at his opponent for a long time. "The weapons are new. What made you wear sai?"

Rhaven sneered. "There is much new about me. I'm now known as Rhaven." He slowly began moving toward the door, motioning Damon to go before him.

Damon trod carefully. The last thing he wanted was a blackthorn dart in him, but the news proved shocking. "Rhaven! So that's the name you have hidden under all of these years. It shall indeed be a memorable battle."

Rhaven continued his cautious retreat until they led him to the door exiting onto a main street.

A broad smile stayed on Damon's face the entire way back to his office. He sat down to unfinished bookwork, the outline of a meticulous trap forming in his mind. He thought of how he would torture the boy, and Rhaven. *Let's not forget I know your true name, Rhaven. Tomorrow I shall put an end to this long overdue task.* Damon dipped the quill into the ink well and laughed.

❧

*E*veryone was asleep when Rhaven returned to the inn. He woke them to give the news. "I had to make concessions, and I've agreed to fight Damon Pirrhar tomorrow morning."

"What!" Tobias stomped over to Rhaven like he was going to scold him. "Why didn't you just kill him?"

"It wasn't as simple as that," he said, then told them what happened. "Anyway, we need to prepare for tomorrow." Rhaven turned to Wisp. "You and Gregor find all the help you can and plant yourselves in the warehouse. Damon won't show up until shortly before dawn, so we have the time. Tobias, see if you can arrange for Preman to reward the men they bring. Also, take Darstan with you and find Kella. We'll need her."

Rahg looked to Rhaven. "I'll not sit by idly while everyone else risks their lives for me. Give me something to do."

"You have the most important job. You and Camissa stay here and guard me while I get sleep. I don't want any of Damon's men coming in here to keep me from my vengeance."

~

*D*amon Pirrhar approached the storeroom with confidence. Since dawn his men had watched the building and seen no one enter. Damon knew the fool would be good to his word. The master assassin entered with ten of the Black Rose close behind him. They would ensure he got the boy, just in case Rhaven's friends were not as bound by honor. Damon paced as he waited, eager to be done with something that should have been taken care of long ago.

The storeroom covered a large area scattered with remnants of unused and spoiled goods. Crates, boxes, and heaping piles of refuse filled the corners and side walls of the building, and the tightly packed dirt floor still held impressions of the stone that once covered it, stone that had been hauled away for other projects. He nodded as a messenger arrived from the outside.

"They're coming," he said. "Seven of them. One's a girl."

"Good. The boy will soon be mine. You can do what you please with the girl."

~

"*W*hy so many of your men?" Rhaven asked.

"This is my guarantee that the boy, and you, will die, in the unlikely event that I do."

Rhaven removed his cloak and handed it to Tobias. He never let his eyes leave sight of Damon. The assassin mirrored Rhaven's moves.

They both took off the black tubes on their backs, then knives. Each move was slow, calculated, both careful not to make a false start. Finally they doffed their shirts.

Rhaven ran his hand through chest hair as thick as Kella's fur, and over a stomach riddled with old wounds. He stretched his torso, a melted mass of tissue with skin fused together. He felt the scars that crisscrossed his back, reminders of blades, arrows, whips, and other devices of torture from time spent in the hands of the Krovs. Three paces away, the symbol of the Red Sun glared at him from Damon's chest.

"It's time," Damon said.

Rhaven whistled, a signal to Wisp, who echoed it with a piercing, shrill whistle of his own. Simultaneously, from every corner, box, crate, and alcove, even from under mounds of refuse—thieves and bounty-men appeared. They knifed, clubbed, pummeled, and fired bolts from cross-bows, overcoming the assassins. The Black Rose who was aiding Damon lay convulsing in the dirt, a victim of a dart fired by Tobias, using Rhaven's weapon. He used that same weapon to hold Damon at bay.

Kella charged through an open window and dispatched three assassins, their throats ripped apart. The black beast now stalked Damon Pirrhar. Her teeth gleamed red with blood.

"Halt," Rahg called to Kella. She stopped, though the fierceness never left her eyes, and her lips remained curled, baring formidable teeth.

In less than a few moments it was over; every assassin either lay dead or was captured. A search of the area by Wisp confirmed this as he nodded to Rhaven. Satisfied now, Rhaven turned to Damon Pirrhar. "Remember what I said? 'No man, or woman, would interfere with you taking the boy. When it is done.'" Rhaven paused to let that sink-in. "If you win, Kella will gladly avenge me. She appears to be hungry today."

Rhaven paused again. "I will—"

The assassin attacked with both blades drawn, covering the distance between them in less than a few heartbeats. Rhaven reacted in a flash, drawing both sai and folding them back against his arms. Damon struck down with the right, but Rhaven blocked it with his sai, then spun the sai forward with a jab. He caught the other sword with the sai in his right hand. Rhaven twisted, but not enough to wrench the blade free.

Damon's own reactions mirrored Rhaven's in speed. Rhaven circled, both sai poised to strike, although a flip of the wrist turned a sai to block a blow or to catch a blade. Damon lunged with his right, while holding the left close to him. Rhaven stepped back pushing the sword down with the catch of his sai, then trying to force it from Damon's grip. A jab or a lunge proved easy to deflect, but it was more difficult to wrench a blade free that way. When the assassin's move failed, he snapped the sword back before Rhaven could wrangle it away from him.

Rhaven watched Damon's eyes, looking for a signal of his next strike. The assassin's blade shot out like a cobra, catching the inside of Rhaven's arm. He risked a quick glance to assess the damage. There was little blood. Rhaven stayed loose, balanced on the balls of his feet while he sought an opening. Sai originated as defensive weapons, but the master who had taught him showed him the offense as well. Besides, most fights were won by being patient. Waiting for the other to make a mistake.

Two lightning jabs by Rhaven tested the assassin's reflexes. He was still fresh. Rhaven lunged, a strike from his right to Damon's gut, but when he did, Damon spun to the side and came across with a sweeping arc toward Rhaven's left. He sucked in his gut and drew back, but not in time; the Black Rose's blade cut into his stomach. Rhaven needed no glance to know this one bled badly.

Need to get this over with. Can't afford to give him this advantage.

Sweat stung his eyes, and ran in rivulets down his face, dripped off his nose. It stung the wound on his stomach. He no longer felt the pain from the cut on his arm. A few moments, he knew. That's all he had before his body refused to react like it should. If that happened, it would be all over. Damon could smell a man's weakness. He would come for the kill. Rhaven blinked to clear his vision, then scanned his opponent for any sign of weakness, anything he could use to his advantage. He attempted a few different combinations, but Damon countered them with ease and left no openings that Rhaven could see.

The assassin began a furious assault that Rhaven had trouble defending. Each time, he was able to brush the blades away, glance them to the side, but barely. Just barely. When the assassin struck again, Rhaven sidestepped, and slipped. His left shoulder hit the ground with a jarring thud that he felt through his whole body. Thoughts of death flashed in his mind, thoughts of vengeance left undone. Then instinct took charge. He rolled quickly, the assassin's steel hitting the ground just as he moved. Rhaven rolled once more then jumped to his feet. The sai against his right arm blocked the blow he knew was coming.

He moved back a step, more careful now. Aware of what was around him. Thinking of death did that sometimes. More energy came with those thoughts. Rhaven found he moved faster now. He caught Damon's sword with his left sai, and twisted with all the strength he had.

Damon screamed as the sword fell to the floor. He pushed the attack with his left hand, but Rhaven saw what he was doing and countered with a furious assault using both sai. *Got to keep him from getting that sword.*

He dragged again. Blood dripped on the floor and he felt himself slowing. He only prayed that Damon was tiring. Rhaven now had the advantage.

Damon circled. Rhaven wouldn't let him get to the sword. He moved in with his right, a short jab, and before Damon countered it, Rhaven shifted his weight and lunged with his left sai. The assassin spun, but could not avoid it. The sai caught him in the forearm. A deep gash.

He retreated, sword poised for defense. Rhaven pressed the attack. Advanced. When Damon made his strike, Rhaven caught the sword with one sai, then quickly brought the other sai over top of it, twisting it out Damon's hand. Steel clanged on a broken piece of stone still embedded in the floor. Damon tried to scramble free, but Rhaven's sai plunged into the side of his gut.

Damon gasped, both hands going to the wound. Rhaven stared into his eyes, leaned in close and whispered. "This is for Rinna." With his fist wrapped tightly around the other sai, Rhaven slammed it into Damon's lungs.

The assassin slumped to the floor, blood gushing, moaning. Rhaven knelt beside him. There was work yet to do. He pulled the sai from Damon's gut and, with his left hand, shoved it into Damon's eye. "This is for Shara."

Damon lay still, though his lips parted slightly with rasping breaths. He didn't know if he still lived. Didn't care. Rhaven plunged the sai into Damon's other eye. "This is for me."

Rhaven collapsed, blood from the assassin running across the floor and soaking into his clothes.

~

*S*ighs of relief filled the cavernous room as all who had been holding their breath released at once. "Caused the air to stir," Tobias would swear, later.

Rahg and Darstan rushed to Rhaven, grasping him by the shoulders to help him stand. "Are you all right?" Rahg asked. "By the gods, that man was nearly as good as you."

Despite being winded, Rhaven managed to sound threatening as he uttered his response. "That was the man who taught me most everything I know. Damon Pirrhar was my brother."

Rhaven almost fell as Rahg's muscles failed him. Every emotion ran through him like a chill: shock, terror, amazement, and finally, pity. The man had no friends, no family, and he had been forced to kill his own brother. *What could have happened to cause that? I could never kill Darstan.*

An odd thought just struck Rahg. Ever since he first saw Rhaven, at Twin Forks, he had always wished to be like him. *Not anymore. Not today, or any other. From now on, I'll just have to be satisfied being Rahg Fal-Thera.*

"C'mon, lads," Tobias said. "Let's get him back to the inn."

"Not that inn," Rhaven said. "Take me to a good inn, one without the bugs. And I need a hot bath."

Tobias laughed. "Not so sick we can't wish for the better things, 'eh. All right, Rhaven, I guess you've earned a bath." They walked off, Rahg and Darstan helping Rhaven, with Tobias leading the way and Camissa trailing behind.

～

*R*ahg turned to look at Camissa and noticed a frown. He left Darstan supporting Rhaven while he went to her. "What's the matter?"

It's odd," Camissa said, "for the first time since I've met Rhaven, he seems to have some of the darkness removed from him."

"What's wrong with that?"

Camissa shook her head as if clearing a foggy mind. "Oh, nothing, Rahg. Actually, I'm just happy that this is over, that's all." A forced smile came to her face but Rahg didn't notice.

"Me too," he said, and rejoined Darstan to help with Rhaven.

Camissa's frown returned. The problem was not with Rhaven. That, she was happy about. But as she had sensed Rhaven's relief, something else came to her, some change in Rahg. *I'm sure it was him.* She remembered how dreadfully dark and ominous a feeling it had been. She could not determine exactly what it was, nevertheless, it was evil. *I'll have to watch him more carefully. I can't let anything happen to him.*

A DEADLY WOUND

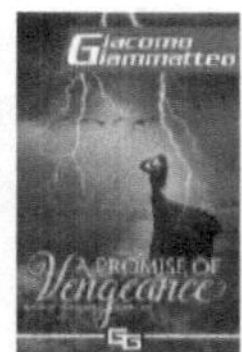

The Dead Man's Inn sat atop one of the highest elevations in Pomanda. Only one street marked the way, an ancient, cobblestone path that twisted a course around old mansions built by nobles and merchants with too much wealth. One measure of success in life was having a house built on the Corrina Tumal, the road of riches. At the peak of the street, wide steps carved from flat stone rose to the summit which offered a breathtaking view of the entire sprawl of the city. A walkway led to the inn.

"Look at these, Rahg." Camissa gawked at flowers that lined the walk on both sides: crocuses and tulips, sunbursts and moonglows, and several varieties that Rahg had never seen.

The inn rose four floors above the ground, and the stone looked as if it had been mined from the same quarry as the walkway. "Expensive looking," said Wisp, smiling like a rat watching cheese fall to the floor.

Gregor turned to the thief, his grey eyes fixed on him. "Don't even consider it, thief. Remember, you gave your word while with us."

"Habit, Gregor. Just habit."

A man hurried down the walk to intercept them at a pace just shy of a run. He was impeccably attired with the look of a gentleman. Even his fingernails were clean.

He nodded his head slightly. "I am Briston. Welcome to the Dead Man's Inn."

Briston reminded Rahg of Arn Bulta's wife, Ledelia, who looked at everyone else in Twin Forks like they were the last sheep sold at the auction. He remembered how she greeted him when he'd see her in the square. "Good morrow, Rahg. How are you boys and Magmar doing in that cozy little house?"

Rahg grimaced thinking on it. Her voice was always polite, too polite, and even though she never said it, the implication that they were bumping into each other with every movement hung on each word.

He remembered telling his father about it because it embarrassed him. Magmar said that the only reason she built a house so big was to let the guards sneak out the back door when Arn Bulta came in the front. Rahg had never understood what he meant by that until several years later, and after that he just laughed whenever he saw her. It never bothered him again, her saying that about his house.

"May I possibly be of service to your... group?" Briston's voice held no warmth. "Could I provide directions to another inn, perchance?"

"Need some rooms," Tobias said. "Likely two or three. And we want to stay here."

"I am afraid that would be impossible. This is an expensive inn."

"We have gold," Tobias said, shifting his weight from one foot to the other. He did that often when he got angry.

A scowl twisted Briston's thin face. "The inn is *very* expensive."

Tobias took the pipe from his mouth and removed his hat, a sure sign his temper was rising. "We have *lots* of gold."

Briston's voice rang with impatience. "Perhaps I could phrase it differently. A merchant, no matter how wealthy, cannot hope to marry a princess. Some things are simply beyond—"

Rhaven broke free of Darstan's grip and struggled to get at Briston. "You snit. If..."

"Enough!" a bellowing voice rang out. Rahg turned to see Lord Preman, a short, stocky man who walked with the confident air of a someone who knew his station. Rahg had seen him once before, and though the meeting was brief, Preman was a hard man to forget: hair the color of wheat stood out in Pomanda, and his barrel chest and strong nose provided quick reminders of who he was. Preman grabbed Tobias by the shoulders with short, meaty hands and greeted him with an embrace that a bear might give. "Good to see you again, Tobias." Preman looked toward Rhaven. "How is he? Not bad, I hope."

"Nothin' a meal, an ale, and a pretty lass won't fix," Tobias said with a smile, but an almost imperceptible shake of his head told Preman otherwise.

The noble nodded, as he cast a glance at Rhaven, then turned to Briston. "You will admit them to the best rooms, the ones on the fourth level." Preman glared at Briston's reaction, not allowing him the opportunity to object. "And at no charge."

Briston held his teeth clenched and his hands tightly balled. "If you would be so kind as to follow me, I will have someone escort you to your rooms."

The first thing Rahg noticed upon entering was the fresh smell. Most inns smelled of ale and whatever the innkeep happened to be cooking —beef, lamb, fowl. This inn just smelled fresh, like the bedclothes they used to hang to dry in Twin Forks. It was quiet too. No boisterous crowd or raucous drunks. No barkeep threatening to toss someone out. Rahg decided he liked this place.

They carried Rhaven the last two sets of stairs; his condition grew worse rapidly. "I don't know why he's taken so ill," Tobias said. "He hasn't lost much blood."

Rahg stared at the decor as they walked down the luxurious fourth level corridor. Lamps flickering through stained glass globes lit cool gray walls, and tapestries woven with images of ancient Sethian tombs stretched down the long corridor like the road through the Empty Lands. An ornate wooden table hugged a corner, supporting a large vase. The flowers that were inside the vase were beautiful, but the ones that were painted on it appeared withered, and the vase itself brought to mind an urn.

Rahg wondered if someone's ashes lay inside. *No wonder they call it the Dead Man's Inn,* he thought, and decided he didn't like this place after all. "Why did we come here, Tobias? There are plenty of good inns in Pomanda."

"Rhaven said he wanted someplace nice," Tobias said. "The Dead Man's Inn is the nicest in Pomanda."

"He deserves it," Preman said. "You all do."

Briston opened the door and stepped aside to let them in.

"As for the reward, Tobias, I'll be back tonight or tomorrow with that. No matter how you divide the split, there will be some wealthy men come out of this."

"We can worry about the gold later," Tobias said. "Let's worry about Rhaven for now."

The room was huge. A bed sat on the far wall, with a mahogany night-stand on each side. A pitcher of water sat on one and a bottle of wine graced the other. Rahg turned to see a chest of drawers big enough to hold his winter clothes, and yet another table stood beside it, with a stiff-backed green chair on the other side. A set of three steps led to a sitting area with a sofa and two more chairs, each with its own table. Lamps hung on three walls and adorned two of the tables, sitting tall above candles so thick their wicks looked like strands of hair.

"What a place!" Rahg said.

"He won't lack comfort here," Preman said. "As long as we can get him healed, it will be a memorable stay."

Darstan helped get Rhaven into bed, then turned toward Tobias. "What can I do? Is there anything we can get?"

"For now, you can all get out of here. Camissa and I will take care of Rhaven."

Preman took his leave. The rest of them went to the Inn of the Turtle. "There's nothing we can do for Rhaven," Wisp said. "I'm sure Camissa and Tobias will have him healthy before two days pass."

~

$\mathcal{C}$amissa trudged up the final section of stairs to their room on the fourth floor. She had made this trip countless times, lugging pails of water for Rhaven, and her calf and thigh muscles felt the strain; even the tops of her feet hurt. *I didn't know the body had so many muscles,* she thought.

"Sweet mercy," she screamed, lifting her bare foot. Blood dripped from a puncture wound, the result of a nail protruding from the stair-step. She climbed the rest of the hard wooden stairs. A slight sigh of relief pushed through nerve-bitten lips as her bare foot touched the thickly matted floor on the landing at the top of the stairs. The plush carpet felt good after scaling the steps. She would have to complain about that nail, though she wondered if they'd fix it considering it was the servant's stairway.

The corridor seemed much longer with her slow steps, but she had to be careful not to spill any of the water from the pails she lugged. Master Charn would not think kindly of her if she spilled water on his carpet. She glanced down at the flooring, staring at the thick weaves. The pattern showed a lush garden surrounding thick-trunked trees with intricate floral patterns interlacing the branches. Beautiful flowers crawled over trellises enveloping fountains made from stone. *It must be a Farizi design.*

Farizi carpeting was the finest in the world, originating from a small province of Jattan-Kir. The local women weaved it from a secret process and no one had been able to produce carpet of equal quality. Camissa scoffed at how much money they must have spent. *I could have fed and clothed fifty people in the Dongrel,* she thought, wondering anew how some of them might eat now that Kender was gone. For all his faults, he was a generous man.

Continuing along, Camissa observed the paintings hanging on the walls, and the finely detailed furniture that hugged each bend of the wide corridor displaying old pottery and sculptures from ages past. She held her breath as she tip-toed by the entrance to the next room, not wishing to disturb its occupants, or call attention to herself.

Nobles were staying there, and she had a natural aversion to them. She didn't feel right, up here on the fourth level with all the fanciness and the high-bred patrons. When she saw the place she hadn't liked it at all, but Preman had insisted, proclaiming that they would receive the best care and be able to attract the best physicians. On that account he was right, though none had been able to do anything.

Camissa moaned under her breath as a chambermaid approached. Her temper rose as she recalled how the physicians had argued with each other, and the advice they gave. "Bleed him," said the personal physician to the Duke. Another had proposed a concoction of remedies so revolting that it still made Camissa gag when she thought of it. "I believe I could do as well myself," she growled.

Rhaven's room lay at the end of the corridor. She entered quietly so as not to disturb him, though in his condition it would hardly matter. Her eyes opened slightly at the sight of the king's physician standing alongside Preman and Tobias.

"Nothing can be done for the man," he stated with an arrogant indifference, standing to re-light his long, curved, ornate pipe. One that matched his pompous personality.

"Just give him plenty of wine so he feels no pain. In a few days you can put him in the ground."

He said it like someone saying the weather was nice, or the ale was tasty. The physician paused, looking around the expensively decorated room. "No need to keep him here, unless of course the cost matters none. A less expensive room will do him as well. Pain is pain. It will hurt no less in a palace than a shed."

"How can you say such things? A wild animal does more to care for their sick than you. It's a wonder your king is still alive with you attending him. Should we bring in dirt to cover him up now? What would—"

Preman hurried the man out the door. "Thank you for coming," he said, and left with the doctor.

Camissa slammed her hand on the cluttered table top. "Imagine that man. He should be hanged. Calling himself a healer. He knows no more than any of the others. None of them know a thing about healing if you ask me."

Tobias cursed as he placed another cool cloth on Rhaven's forehead and on the wound gnawing at his stomach. "Can't get this fever down, lass."

Camissa rinsed the old cloths in the wash basin, already stained with blood, while Tobias wiped Rhaven's brow. "He can't last long with a fever like this, Tobias. We must do something."

"I'll get some more cool water. And I'll get some herbs from Briston."

"You're no healer, Tobias. How do you know—"

"Lass, I don't claim to be a healer, but right now, I'll try anything. Be back soon."

Camissa held Rhaven's hand, while she continued to dab cold cloths on his head. The mattress of the poster bed sat waist-high on Camissa, and it was as wide as two of the beds in most inns. The bed had a place for curtains and a canopy, though none adorned this one. Frescoes exploding with vibrant colors covered the walls, scenes of men falling in battle running rigid against ornate moulding around the windows.

A heavy sigh from the warrior brought a fetid odor, and Camissa's cheek twisted up in response. She grabbed a glass from the nightstand alongside the bed and poured water for him. "Try to drink," she said, though she knew he couldn't hear her.

Camissa sighed again as she looked down at his face, pallid, though not frail. Rhaven could never look frail. If he had been a rock it would have been granite, Camissa speculated. His eyes set deeply into his face, like a cave in a mountain, though when his blue eyes shined, they lit his whole face. A strong straight nose divided high cheekbones and ran like a ridge from forehead to lip. His jaw was all granite.

With a heavy sigh, she pulled aside the bandage—it told her what she feared. She had been refusing it, not daring to admit it, but the festering had grown worse. The room stank of death. Camissa recognized the scent, that foul precursor of anguish and sorrow. Gently, she laid the bandages over the wound, then put her hand to his head again. Blazing hot! Camissa lay her head next to his, her soft cheek nestling coarse hints of a beard. "Please don't die, Rhaven."

Tobias came through the door moments later, two pails of water in his hands and a package of herbs stuffed under his arms. "Any change, lass?"

"He's worse. Fever's up more."

Tobias stomped his foot and cursed. His hands rubbed a beard that wasn't there, and twice he started to light his pipe, only to put it away. "Fetch the lads, Camissa! We're not gonna sit around and watch him die. Have them and Gregor muster help and try to find a real healer.

Tell Kender to ask every cutpurse he knows about people with powers of healing."

Her stunned reaction drew an angry red face from Tobias. "This is no time to worry about the little things, lass. I'd kiss the Dark One himself if he promised to heal Rhaven. Now go on, get moving. I'll take care of things here."

Camissa rushed out the door, but before it even slammed, Tobias yanked it back open. He poked his head out and yelled down the hall. "You tell 'em, we'll pay whatever we must. Just tell 'em to hurry."

Camissa raced down the hall, down the steps, then out the door, not bothering to cover her bare feet, and ignoring the pain from where the nail had pierced her only a short while ago.

OLD TOMES

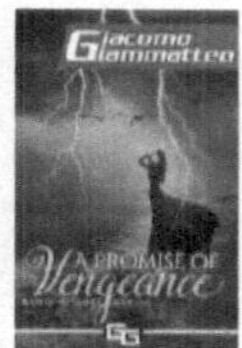

A glow came to the lamps as Aentarra entered the Great Library, her black hair brushing lightly against a gown as soft and white as the petals of an Endoran Rose. Instinct caused her to flinch as the lamps lit, a reflex from battles and wars that had lasted for ages, but she continued to wonder on the workings of the lamps. Someone had been here before them. Someone with power, and the ability to create objects that Aentarra and her kind had not been able to duplicate.

She didn't come to Vallah as often as before, but recent events in Pomanda sparked a memory, a faint image of particular importance. She felt certain it had come from the Library. The others thought her crazy, spending so much time poring over dusty old books and meticulously mending torn and charred pieces of parchment, but Aentarra knew her time was well spent. She would reap the rewards from her efforts.

Carrying stacks of books to the table, Aentarra sat to read through them. "The Spoils of War," written by the scholarly Melissara. "Hah. What did Melissara ever know about anything, other than teasing boys barely old enough to be called *men*."

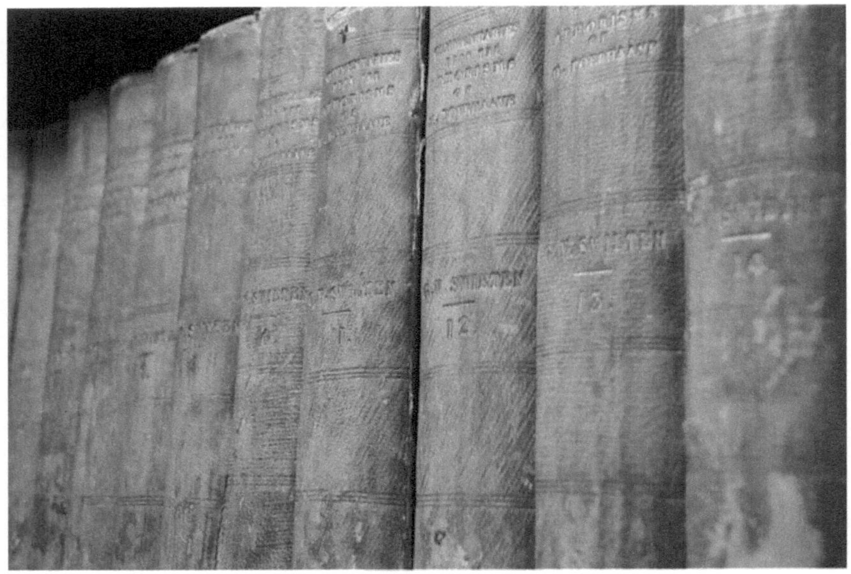

old books

Aentarra gently closed the cover shut on the book as she finished, then picked up the next volume—a discussion on battlefield strategies by Tirzinitzia, another Banished One. *Perhaps they should have stuck to writing; they did not fare so well in battle.* She searched through several more books, then returned to the bookshelves scrutinizing each one from top to bottom. *Ah, this may be the one,* she thought, and retrieved a stepping stool to reach the top shelf. An image of Antar, her father, came to mind, dragging a smile with it. He often spent time with her in his library.

Aentarra forced the image away—quickly—dreading the onslaught that the *Others* might bring. They seemed to come with memories of her father, almost as if they waited for him. She grabbed an ancient, delicately bound tome from the shelf, anything to keep her mind busy. The book had no title or listing of an author. Aentarra sat at the table and, ever-so-carefully, turned the worn and ragged-edged pages.

'...the mortal races are growing stronger, yet still they need assistance. They seem to revere her, though certainly that can be attributed to fear, not adoration...'

She turned the pages faster, though no less carefully. '...can he be so far away? Send a Messenger...Yes...do not go through... No...it must be done. Send one, now!'

.....three keys for three gods...... three keys....one tomb.....one womb...danger! .....do not.....never....

Gibberish! Aentarra grew impatient. She felt certain that what she sought lay hidden in this book. It all seemed so familiar, but then, how many times had she been through these books. Centuries of visits to the library and she seemed no closer. She flipped the pages. '...danger awaits all who enter. It is forbidden...'

raven flying

Finally, she saw it. The first image showed a raven flying alone in a blue sky, but the second image showed a great city, and hovering above it was a raven clutching in its talons the broken stem of a black rose, its petals withered and dead. Beneath it stood two young men looking up at a bright red sun—the falling petals shading their eyes from the blinding beams.

It confirmed her suspicions. She no longer held any doubt. A sigh of satisfaction escaped her lips as she closed the book. Now eager to get to the old section of the palace, she hurriedly departed but only after putting everything away. It was a quirk of hers; everything must be neat and orderly, especially in the library.

Aentarra studied the murals in the old part of the Palace at Vallah, a structure already standing when they had first found the city. Had it not been for their fortunate discovery of the portal, they might never have found the place. Vallah was situated in the extreme north, beyond the Great Whites, an almost impenetrable mountain range. On the other side of those peaks, however, something strange took place. A shield surrounded Vallah, keeping out the cold and the winds, but allowing the sunshine and rain to nurture the beautiful gardens and trees that decorated the palace like so many paintings on a wall. The temperature remained consistently mild, and the setting ever-peaceful.

It proved refreshing to come back occasionally and rest, but pleasure did not drive this day's visit. She remembered seeing something in one of the murals, a clue to a mystery she intended to solve. She reviewed the scenes once again, careful not to overlook anything.

The image depicted three beings of power. They looked down upon a mortal man, youthful and strongly built. The mortal held a finely woven shield in his hands, and a black amulet hung from a chain around his neck. And that amulet glowed with an aura. *Just like the blue sun of Nelstar.*

This aroused her curiosity, but what intrigued her the most was the object that one of the three immortals pointed to—a black doorway carved into the side of a mountain.

A Portal of Darkness. If there is another on this world, I must find it.

And most important of all—the young man in the book staring at the red sun was the same one in this mural in front of the portal. *Yes. It is all coming together now.* Excitement drove her back to the library where she began to pore over the ancient books once again.

Night turned too quickly to day, and Aentarra's tired eyelids slipped shut at more frequent intervals. Despite vast amounts of khaffe and spirited walks, she could no longer remain alert. Besides, she had discovered what she came for, some of it anyway. She gathered her writing instruments and penned a letter, the ink barely dry when she rolled it up, sealed it, then tucked it into a loose-fitting sleeve of her gown. She put away the rest of the books and the writing instruments then shuffled down the corridor.

The glow from the lamps faded as she passed, their light extinguishing with the echoes of her footsteps. Her pace quickened as she left the library and crossed the courtyard. More eager than ever now, she almost ran to the Chamber of Council.

The doors burst open ahead of her. "Ah, my friends. I see you have awaited my return." Aentarra's mocking laughter filled the room. She paused behind Kiris and reached to touch the Slicer protruding from her head. A faint shimmer extended up Aentarra's arm, all the way to her head. Aentarra repeated the procedure at each occupied chair; first, with Firzil, then Salendra, Mesan, and the others, and the glow grew successively brighter with each one. Finally, only Xanthes remained. Aentarra whirled Xanthes' seat around to face her.

"You could have shared the glory," Aentarra said. "You might have sat beside me, but for her." She spat, grabbing hold of the Slicer with a violent jerk, yanking Xanthes's rigid form toward her. The glow now fully enveloped Aentarra, the ambience strong, overpowering the bright rays of the sun that exploded through the stained glass window. She kept a firm grip, sating her desires, then let go of the Slicer. The glow remained but grew no stronger. "I will settle the score with my sister, Xanthes. But it will not be a pretty sight. Of that you can be sure."

Anger still burned in Aentarra. Jealousy roared through her bones and seized control of her emotions. Aentarra turned to Kiris, slumped over in her chair. "You always were weak, Kiris. It appears I have no further need of you." Waving her hands, a translucent layer of shield formed in the air. Aentarra slammed it into Kiris, slicing her cleanly in half.

"Not pretty at all," Aentarra crowed, as the doors shut behind her. "Not pretty at all."

HEALERS AND OLD CRONES

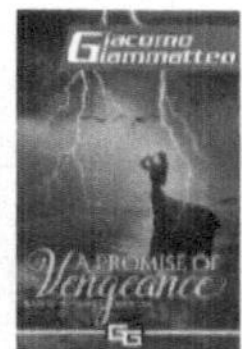

*C*amissa burst through the door to the Inn of the Turtle. She wore a scowl, like a wife tracking down an errant husband. "Get up. All of you. Rhaven needs us and you're sitting in here drinking!"

Darstan stood. "What do you want me to do? Die with him? I've lost my father, my friends—everyone I've ever known except Rahg and Tobias." Darstan stared into her eyes. "This is how I deal with it. This is my way. If I can't be happy, at least I can pretend to be."

"Don't you care?" She screamed.

Darstan gently lifted her head. "I'm sorry, Camissa. We all care for Rhaven, and we'll do anything to help. Just tell us what we need to do."

"No one has been able to help. We need a healer. A real one. Please find one. And don't come back until you do."

She was halfway back to the Dead Man's Inn before it struck her that she had no shoes on her feet. Master Charn would not like her coming in the front door of his fine inn without shoes, but he would just have to like it because she had no time to be taking extra steps, or washing her feet just to please him. She'd go up the back steps but that was the only concession she'd make.

~

*T*obias dabbed more cool cloths on Rhaven's head. He had already cleaned the wound again, but the fever wouldn't break.

Camissa opened the door and stepped into the room. "How is he?"

Tobias suspected she could not have kept the worry from her voice if she tried. "No better, lass. If truth be known, probably worse. His skin is hot as ever, and he's startin' to get delirious. I've seen it on the battlefield. I'm afraid there's not—"

"Don't say it. Just don't say it. I will not hear from one more person that there is nothing to be done. Soon we'll have healers here to look at him. Then we'll see."

Tobias nodded his head and walked away with slow steps. He wanted Rhaven to be healed as much as Camissa, perhaps more, but he was a realist. He had been in the wars, and seen men die with the fever, and he had seen many wounds, but none that refused to heal like this one. *Something strange about this wound,* Tobias thought, and sat in the chair to rest for a moment. It was the first time he had been off his feet for almost two days. Sleep came easily.

*I*t was morning before Tobias woke. The clamor of a room full with people startled him and he jumped up, embarrassed at having slept for so long. "How's Rhaven?" he asked, "and who's this?" His nod pointed out the middle-aged woman standing over Rhaven.

No smile showed on Camissa's face. "She's a healer. The third one since you fell asleep. At least the men haven't been resting; they roused every healer in the city." Camissa's face lit up, but quickly turned a sober expression. "I don't believe any will be able to help us, Tobias."

"Don't be so sure, lass. One of these fine healers will have something to cure our friend. You can heal the wound, can't you?" Tobias addressed the new healer with a sense of optimism.

The middle-aged woman turned to stare at Tobias. She was plain looking, with a pale face and yellowish hair. Slim, but not too thin. "It's not the wound that'll kill him."

"What do you mean?" Camissa asked.

"He's been poisoned. Whoever cut him used a deadly poison on the tip of that sword. It's dug in deep and festered. He'll not be getting any better."

"It can't be too late," Camissa said. "He hasn't been sick that long. What's the cure? Where can we find it?"

The woman lowered her head, then pulled Camissa close. "There now, child. It will be all right. Time cures everything, child, but nothing— nothing can cure the poison of the black rose. It just cannot be done." She continued to pat Camissa's back and rub her head for several moments before she walked her to a chair by the window and helped her sit. "Here, you rest for a while. I'll go and fetch a holy man. There's nothing more I can do."

Tobias took her gently by the arm, his warm smile thanking her for being so kind to Camissa. "How much do we owe for the healing? I'll be payin' in gold."

The woman looked at him with eyebrows raised. "I've done no healing. I'm due no pay. There may be some healers who aren't what they seem, but not me. Not Addie Mayson. I won't take gold for something I haven't done." She turned to leave, then spun to face Tobias again. Pain and sorrow glazed the pale skin of her face. "I'm sorry I couldn't help," Addie said. The door closed quietly behind her.

Wisp and Darstan tried to comfort Camissa while Gregor and Tobias stood over Rhaven. "He was the best I have ever seen," Gregor said.

"Best there ever will be," Tobias added.

"Don't talk like that!" Camissa's tears flowed freely. "He's not dead."

Gregor and Tobias hung their heads in shame. "You have the right of it, Camissa," Gregor whispered.

Tobias looked around the room like he'd lost something. "Where's Rahg?"

"He's still out looking for healers," Darstan said. "Should we go look for more?"

"I don't think we'll need any more healers," Tobias said. Nobody argued. Not even Camissa.

～

*R*ahg's body dragged. He was hot, and physically worn, exhausted from climbing hill after hill looking for healers in back alleys and taverns. He sat on a cobblestone walkway to rest his aching feet. He had walked all night, and now that the streets were busy with the morning business he would need to try harder. There would be a better chance of finding a healer in the daytime. At least one that was legitimate.

Resting made him aware of his hunger. He opened his pack and broke off a hunk of bread. A curly-haired dog with bare patches on its fur hustled up the street and sat next to him, big hungry eyes pleading to share.

"So, little friend. You wish to share my meal, do you?" Rahg laughed as he reached to pet the dog, offering it a piece of bread. "What's your name, little boy? Huh? My, you're dirty. Doesn't anyone bathe you?" Rahg continued talking to the dog as if he expected a response. He didn't realize he was being watched until he felt eyes on him. He jerked his head up, embarrassed. An old woman loomed over him, the skin of her face wrinkled and leathery. Her ragged face wore a strange look, with eyes that fixed him in place.

"Like animals, do you?" she cackled.

Rahg nodded, still staring up at the hag.

"Haven't I seen you before, young man, perhaps with a much bigger beast?"

Rahg thought for a moment, still somewhat startled by her appearance. She made Tobias look like a youngster. "You probably saw me with another dog. Actually, she's a vargel. Her name's Kella." He continued to stare blankly at the woman. "What's your name?"

When the old woman smiled the wrinkles on her face seemed to fold into cracks. "You seek a healer?" she asked through grinning teeth.

He tried to conceal his surprise. "How did you know?" Then another thought struck him. "And how did you know about Kella? You've never seen me with her. In fact, I've never seen you before today. Who are you?"

"Your friend will perish soon." The old woman said. "Do you want a healer? He doesn't have long."

Her gaze held him riveted, seemed to penetrate his soul. He didn't trust her, but she was right—Rhaven didn't have long. He *had* to trust her. "Come with me," Rahg said, and got up to leave, patting the dog on the head.

"Be patient, young man. We must first discuss my fee." The old hag appeared to straighten for a moment.

"If you heal him, we'll pay your fee—in gold. You just worry about healing him."

The old crow laughed. The taunting, agitating sound sickened Rahg. "What is it that says I want gold?"

"What do you want? But hurry, I haven't the time to dally."

"You have all the time I want you to have. There is no one to heal him except me. All I want is the dog."

"The dog?" He looked down at the pitiful little creature. "You don't have to ask me for the dog. I don't even know who it belongs to, but if it's so important, take it."

This time her laugh rang right through him. Like her gaze, it ran through to his bones. "I'm talking of your dog, Kella. I believe you call her a vargel. That is the dog I want."

The breath left Rahg's body. "No! You'll not have her for any reason. Not for anything."

The old hag turned to leave.

"Wait! Don't leave. I'll do anything else you ask, but Kella's not mine to give."

A sparkle of light emanated from her transfixing eyes. "Anything?"

"Anything."

She stepped close. "One day, I shall ask you to do something for me. I want your oath that whatever I ask, whenever I ask it, it will be done."

Rahg held her gaze for a long time. It seemed simple enough, yet he knew oaths to be binding, and she was asking him to pledge to anything she wanted. But Rhaven had no time. "Done," Rahg said. "Now, let's go see to my friend. We're staying at—"

"The Dead Man's Inn," she said. "What an appropriate name."

Before Rahg could move the old woman began up the street toward the inn, walking at an unusually brisk pace.

They walked into the inn and Rahg led her to Rhaven's room.

❧

*R*haven had become delirious by the time Rahg arrived with the healer. His fever showed no signs of breaking. Rahg's eyes widened when he looked at Rhaven.

"Had to tie 'im to the bed," Tobias said. "He got so bad, began attacking anyone who came near. We couldn't get close enough to care for him." Tobias lowered his head, almost in shame. "Doesn't look like we've done much anyway."

"Untie him," the healer said, and as Tobias removed the ropes, she walked straight to Rhaven.

He seized her arm, brought it to his nostrils and sniffed wildly, like an animal. "Who are you? I know you."

Rahg thought he saw recognition come briefly to Rhaven's eyes before he faded. The old woman soothed him, gently talking as she moved her withered hands over the wound.

Rhaven knew the old woman from somewhere. Unless he's further gone than it looks. The mystery gnawed at Rahg. "You didn't mention that you knew Rhaven." His tone was filled with suspicion.

The old woman spun faster than someone her age should be able to react. "Did I say I knew him? Strange, I do not recall." The old woman looked as if she wanted to laugh. "Your friend ranted madly. When people are taken with the fever they are apt to say anything. I can assure you, lad, your friend has never seen this old woman's face before tonight."

~

"*H*e's in bad condition," Tobias said. He looked down at Rhaven, then at the woman. "Is there anything you can do?"

The old woman pulled some herbs from a pouch that hung at her side and mixed them with wine in a goblet on the table by the bed, then bent to press the mixture to Rhaven's lips.

Tobias seized her arm and yanked her back. "What are you doing, woman? I've not seen herbs like those before. You'll tell me what you're giving this man, or out you'll go."

She turned her head slowly, then, using strength that an old woman should not possess, she forcibly removed Tobias's hand from her sleeve. Tobias reached to grab hold of her tattered garment again, but something in the old woman's eyes stopped him.

"He is dying. I see no physicians here to cure him." She glanced about the room. "I know you tried other healers. I'm all he has left." Her gaze dared Tobias to deny the logic.

"I think we should trust her," Camissa said. "What harm will it do?"

The old woman began giving orders. "I need ten candles made from beeswax, pure. I need wine, and ale also, the strongest available. Lastly, the roots of the murjora plants—the forbidden ones. I need three of those."

"We can never get those in time," Tobias said. "They only grow in the swamps—"

"Your thief-friend will know how to acquire some. I am certain he can find an ample supply right here in the city."

Then she looked to the door. In fact, I believe your friends are just arriving now.

Darstan, Wisp, and Gregor walked in, wet with perspiration.

Tobias told them what was needed, then Wisp nodded. "I'll get enough. Be back soon."

Darstan looked around the room. "I didn't even see Wisp leave," he said. "Anything for me to do?"

"You can leave the room, along with everyone else save the girl." The healer's glance pointed out Camissa. "I will need you to assist me."

The men returned with the supplies before much time had passed, then she ordered them to leave.

~

*D*arstan paced the hall like a man waiting on his firstborn. "How long will she take, Tobias? Do you think she can do anything?"

Wisp leaned against the far wall, a slender blade picking dirt from under his fingernails. "I've seen people survive some tough situations," he said, "but this..."

Gregor walked back and forth across the hall, talking to himself. "He does that a lot," Tobias said. "I've never seen anyone talk so much to themselves." Tobias lit his pipe, but even that didn't perk him up the way it normally did. "Sad to say, lads, but I'd be casting thoughts toward the gods if I were you."

"I think he'll make it." Rahg said.

Dealing with grief was not Tobias' best trait. He thought before he answered. "I was there when Kor's mare died. Got snake bit. We tried everything to save her, but that leg swelled up with poison. When we cut a slit to drain her... well, the blood and pus oozed out of there like milk gone bad. And the stink that came out with it would have snatched the appetite from a starving man."

Tobias placed a hand on each Rahg and Darstan's shoulders. "I'm not saying there's no hope, lads, it's just that... well, there's that same smell of death creeping out of that wound in Rhaven's stomach, just like Kor's mare. It's gonna take more than an herb or two to heal him."

~

*W*hen the door closed shut behind Tobias, Camissa turned to the healer. "What will you have me do?" Weariness dragged the words out.

"Rest, my dear. Rest."

"Rest! What of the candles? The ale? What about the root you asked for? Tell me what needs to be done." Camissa's voice rose with her temper. "I'll not be the cause of Rhaven's death for being tired." The more she spoke the more spirit seemed to flow into her.

The old healer stared at Camissa. "I have no need of candles, or ale, or root."

"But—"

"It is what people expect a healer to do—perform miracles with odd items and concoctions. I let them believe what they will. You, however, I wish to teach the truth." The old woman's voice sounded younger, much younger. Her eyes glowed, holding Camissa transfixed. "Behold the glory of healing, Camissa Menastha—and learn."

A humming noise sounded in the room. Soon, it filled the room. Every particle of air carried sweet, vibrant music. A glow began with the healer, spreading. The old woman's skin softened, began to smooth. Camissa cleared her eyes. That couldn't be, but...something was taking place. Something unusual.

The glow became brighter. It enveloped the healer's body then spread across the floor and ceiling like an eerie mist. It fell down the walls and crept up from the floor. The brightness increased and the humming grew louder. Soon, the glow was everywhere. Like the music, it permeated the air and filled every vacant spot in the room. All except where Rhaven lay on the bed.

Suddenly the glow condensed. From all angles, it converged on the healer and collapsed into the old woman. Camissa stared at Rhaven, her gaze drawn to him, the only dark spot in the room. Fear ran through her. She had seen people with powers before, many of them. And some of them had been very strong, but none had even come close to this.

Who is this woman?

Camissa jumped, startled by a burst of light. It shot into Rhaven. He was aglow, radiating an aura similar to that of the old woman. Camissa stretched her mind to feel the other woman's presence, but it was blank. She sensed power all around her, yet nothing from the woman. *She must be doing something to block me.*

Soon, the humming ceased and the lighting returned to normal. The glow was gone from the old healer, and from Rhaven. Camissa ran to the bed, touching Rhaven's forehead first.

"He will be fine," said the healer. "All he needs is rest. Several days will suffice, though until next seventh day would be better."

Camissa smiled. The fever was gone. She heard the pounding on the door and realized it had been going on for some time now.

"Open the door. Are you all right? Open the door, Camissa." It was Tobias' voice.

She started toward the door when the healer stopped her. "Did you learn?"

"Learn what?"

"Do not play with me, girl." The healer's tone was unnaturally harsh. Her eyes burned into Camissa's heart. "Did you learn anything of the healing?"

Camissa tried to look into her eyes, but couldn't. "No. No, I saw nothing but light. I... I did not learn anything. Why are you asking me? Why me?"

Gentle hands touched Camissa's shoulders. They pulled her up, guiding her gaze into the healer's face. The healer's voice matched her gentle touch. "Sometimes, my child, you see more than you think. Sometimes, you learn what you wish to forget. Goodbye, child."

Camissa smiled and went to unlatch the door. Tobias pushed his way through. "What happened? Is Rhaven alive?"

"She did it, Tobias." Camissa's tears were joyous ones. She wrapped her arms around Tobias. "The healer made him well."

Tobias and everyone else stared. So too, did Camissa. There was no healer. The old woman was gone.

"What happened to her?" Rahg asked.

Wisp never asked. He surveyed the room, but didn't mention the healer. "We can discuss her later," he said. "For now, let's see to Rhaven."

~

They gathered around the bed, eager as the next to see for themselves that Rhaven's fever had broken.

"I wonder where that healer went?" Darstan asked again.

"Far away, I hope." Rahg didn't realize he had said it aloud until everyone turned to stare at him. "I don't like healers," he said. A drawing on the table caught his eye. It was a picture of a woman holding an axe, acting as executioner to a young man with a large crowd observing. "What's this?" Rahg asked. "It wasn't here before."

Wisp looked at the picture. "You're right. It wasn't here before, and I don't think the rats brought it in, so my guess is that healer woman." Wisp looked around the room again. "Nothing else is different. Anyway, this drawing is of a famous incident that happened long ago in Pomanda. It's called 'Oath-Sworn.'"

A chill rushed through Rahg, buckling his knees. He felt sure his voice would crack, but he spoke regardless. "Tell me about it, Wisp."

"It's only famous because of how sad it is. As the story goes, one day a child met a god and gave him his oath, a silly oath, but sworn nonetheless. Time went by and the god asked the boy to honor the oath he made long ago. The boy was now a young man, and both he and his mother refused, excusing the boy due to his age at the time of swearing. As punishment, the god not only sentenced the young man to death, but stipulated the mother be the one to slay him."

Rahg shivered. *I wonder when I'll see her again. I wonder where?* Most of all though, he fretted terribly over just what the strange healer woman would have him do to honor his oath. *It can't be too bad. She wouldn't have healed Rhaven if she was evil.*

A SILENT MESSAGE

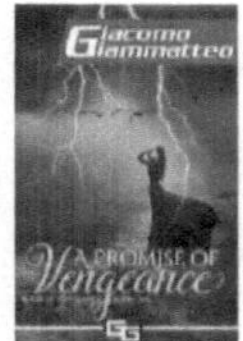

*D*arstan stood next to Rhaven's bed, taking his turn on the watch. The fever broke shortly after the healer left, and his condition improved with each notch on the candle. "Good to have you with us, Rhaven. For a while, we didn't think you'd make it."

Tobias got out of his chair and came to the bed. "Feel better?"

"Weak," Rhaven said, "and hungry." He looked at Darstan and tried to smile.

"Healer said you'd be better soon. Six or seven days rest, she said." Tobias fidgeted with his tobacco pouch, and packed his pipe. "Strangest thing..." He paused, lit a striker and put it to his pipe. "That woman healed you, then just disappeared. Just–"

"Something about that woman... She had a familiar scent to her."

Darstan laughed. "A familiar scent? She didn't smell any different to me."

Rhaven managed a smile. "Maybe it's the hunger, Darstan. I feel as if I could eat as much as Rahg." He pushed himself up on his elbows. "Where is he? And where's Camissa?"

"They went to look for Kella. It's the first time Rahg's been happy since we left Twin Forks. With Damon Pirrhar dead and you healed, he feels safe."

The scowl on Rhaven's face turned darker. "He shouldn't feel safe. We need to get him back here, at least for now."

"Why? What's the matter?"

Rhaven sat up. "Damon Pirrhar may be dead, but the Black Rose didn't do this on their own. Assassins kill for gold. Someone hired Damon Pirrhar. And with him wearing the Red Sun on his chest..."

A lump rose in Darstan's throat. "I'll find him."

Tobias grabbed his sleeve. "We don't need to alarm him. I don't think he's in danger yet. I'll send someone to fetch him."

"All right. Just make sure you get Rahg back here."

Wisp was leaning against the wall, shaking his leg and tapping with his fingers. He could sit as still as a statue if he had to, but he had no patience for boredom. "I'll get him."

Wisp leaned forward. "Tobias, if you keep Rhaven company, Darstan and I will take the bounty man out and force him to smile."

"They may not have enough ale to make Gregor smile." Rhaven said.

"Go on and get out of here," Tobias said. "I'll take care of Rhaven."

~

*G*regor led the way down the old cobblestone walkway, the tapping of his staff echoing through the narrow streets and alleys. Darstan's heels clicked noisily. "You sound like a horse, Darstan."

Darstan stared down at Wisp and Gregor's boots, almost identical to his, yet Gregor made little sound and Wisp none. "How did you learn to step so quietly?"

"Practice."

"Necessity for me," Wisp said, then pointed ahead of them. "Do you see that alleyway? Not far from here, there is another like it where they trained young thieves. Back then it was a secluded area that no one traveled. The boss of thieves sprinkled the walk with broken glass and small stones, then put three of his men in there, blindfolded. The challenge was to creep up on each man and tap him on the shoulder before he heard you. Failure meant losing half of your take for the next thirty days, and a beating as well, though the beating meant nothing; most of us got enough of that at home. Success, though, meant you got your full share of the take from then on—minus the boss's normal cut of course."

Wisp captured Darstan's interest. "How many times did you have to try it before you made it?"

Wisp smiled. "I was the only one to ever succeed on the first attempt."

Darstan's laughter spurred Wisp to continue telling tales. He told of his first theft, of the friends he made, and of the only time he was ever apprehended—when he had been eleven years old. The tales went on and didn't stop until they arrived at the Inn of the Turtle.

"Good day, Mira," Wisp said, as they entered the inn. Mira nodded while she continued serving the table she had been waiting on, dishes clanging noisily against each other. "I see you can hardly restrain yourself from greeting me."

Mira looked up and smiled. "I don't know why I even talk to you. If not for Darstan—"

"If not for Darstan you would not be able to keep yourself from me." Wisp's large nose flared when he smiled.

Mira burst into laughter, and pushed Wisp aside. "I guess that's why I like you," she said, then straightened her hair and wiped her face. "Good day, Darstan. I'm pleased to see you returned."

Darstan pulled a flower from behind his back. "And this is for you, my sweet. I picked it myself this morning and carried it all this way."

Mira cupped the rose in her hands. A sparkle lit her eyes. "Did you expect me to faint with delight?" She laughed. "I saw you just pick this from outside the inn. That might work on the other girls, but not me."

Gregor laughed as loud as he ever had. "Lead us to a table, Mira, and be glad you are done with this charming lad."

She seated them at their favorite table in the corner, then brought ale and a small meal. After the third ale, the stories began to flow, even from Gregor.

As Darstan drank more ale, he became more talkative. "Wis... I mean, Kender, what do you plan to do, now that this business with the Black Rose is through?"

The smile vanished from Wisp's face as he straightened in his chair. "That depends on our friend, the bounty man. I gave my word that I wouldn't attempt an escape..."

Wisp stared at Gregor then smiled. "All I ask for is the count of ten on a crowded street, bounty man. If you cannot grant that, I'll go with you willingly."

Gregor's frown deepened. *A thief with honor!* "I might retire."

Wisp laughed. "You couldn't convince Mira with that statement. Besides, I'm worth a fair amount of gold, a fact I feel certain has not escaped your memory."

"I could buy a tavern with the money I got for the reward on the Rose. I've always wanted to own a tavern."

Wisp leaned his head forward, almost to the center of the table. "The chase," he whispered. "Don't tell me you weren't thinking about it. I've seen the look on thieves a hundred times. You could no more give up the chase than Tobias could his pipe—or Rhaven the hunt."

Gregor waved his hand to contest the statement. "I need more ale."

Mira brought the ale and told Wisp a man was asking for him. Wisp looked to the front and saw Sengua, boss of Pomanda's thieves. He had two men with him—Pelle and Rinck.

"I need to see what he wants," Wisp said. He spoke with Sengua for a moment then returned to the table. "Sengua said there is a woman inquiring about us. And a good-looking one at that. We should look into this." Wisp smiled. "Perhaps we could even persuade the fine lass to join us for a mug of ale."

Darstan drained the ale from his mug and stood. "Let's find her."

Three stops later they stumbled into the Lucky Hawk, an inn that had not seen the smiles of fortune in many a long winter. Only the worst element of Pomanda visited the Lucky Hawk: sots, poor thieves, and desperate citizens from all walks of life. The ale cost little; the wine came from the newest batches; and the liquor burnt as it went down. But the patrons of the Lucky Hawk didn't come for the quality of the drink.

The innkeep crammed them into an airy, damp corner at a table shaded in darkness.

"It stinks in here," Darstan said. "No way I'm staying here."

"We just got here, Darstan. Might as well make a night of it. Even Gregor isn't complaining."

"I don't care about Gregor. I'm leaving. Can't stand a foul smell."

Wisp laughed. "All right we'll go. Chances are she won't come here anyway."

"Me and Rinck will stay here," Pelle said. "Might find a wench to go home with."

"If you're lucky you won't," Wisp said. "But suit yourself. And let us know if you hear anything of the mystery lady."

"We'll come see you tomorrow," Pelle said. "Unless..."

"I know. Unless you get lucky."

Pelle laughed.

Darstan, Wisp and Gregor went back to the inn. Wisp told Rhaven and Tobias about the lady and how Pelle and Rinck planned on continuing the search for her.

"I don't like the sound of it," Rhaven said. He could barely get out of bed, but he was strategizing.

"It's probably nothing," Wisp said. "Besides, Pelle will be here in the morning. We'll see what he has to say."

"And morning won't be long in coming." Darstan said, after yawning. "I'm going to bed."

"Right behind you," Rahg said. "It's been a long day."

~

*R*ahg lay down in the corner of the room, bone-tired. Within minutes he was asleep, but nightmares waited for him. He found himself in a mountain pass, peaks above him blanketed with snow. Blood covered his hands, knuckles scraped raw. He glanced skyward to a peak towering above the others like a black-thorn in a forest of pines. The clouds hung low, forming a ring around it, and an angry red cap spewed smoke above a mantel of snow.

*R*ahg's mind swirled—a twig caught in a vortex. The mountain called to him. He must move on. Sweat stung his eyes, but he had to move, get to the top. Fog had moved in, a thick blanket that clung to him like oily smoke. A huge cave lay just ahead, mist creeping out to greet him. The maw of the cave resembled a giant beast, the haze its smoke-filled breath. That calling came again, tugged at his soul, beckoned him to enter. He thought he heard his name from somewhere deep inside the cavern, an enchantress's song.

~

A shriek of terror awoke Camissa, who slept in the adjoining room. She leapt to her feet and ran to Rahg, too frightened to worry that she wore only a nightgown. She bolted through the door and ran to his side. Darstan was shaking Rahg.

Camissa knelt beside him, putting her hand on his forehead. Rahg's fists were clenched, knuckles white, his eyes shut tight. Camissa slapped him hard, across the face. When he didn't awaken, she slapped him again.

Rahg shot up to a sitting position.

"Are you all right?" Camissa asked.

Rahg stared at the wall for a moment, then turned his head to see everyone standing around, even Wisp and Gregor. "What's the matter? Why is everyone looking at me?"

"You don't remember?" Camissa asked.

"I don't remember anything except falling asleep." He started to move, then grabbed his head with both hands. "Gods blood, but I've got a headache."

Camissa wore a worried look. "Does this happen often? Dreams followed by headaches?"

Rahg massaged his head gently. "I don't know. I don't remember any dreams."

311

"Do you remember anything? Think hard."

"I've had plenty of bad dreams before. And I've had headaches more times than I'd like. If I get some sleep I'll be fine."

"Then try not to wake the rest of us up," Camissa said.

When she got back to her own room, the indifference changed to worry. She had seen this before and the outcome had not been good. She remembered how horribly her father had died. *I'll not allow that to happen to Rahg. Not him.*

JUST REWARDS

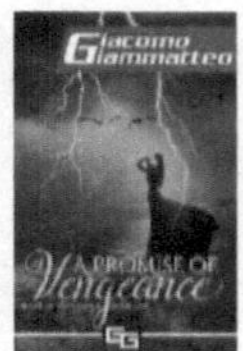

Sethian Desert

1364 AE (After Exile)

Second Cycle of the Fifth Moon—Reunion

Third Calendar of Light

irzinitzia's boots slapped against the granite floor as she rushed through the corridors toward Lukaan's chamber, lithe legs forcing a long stride. A thought could have whisked her there, but Lukaan forbade shifting inside the palace. He also forbade lights in the halls, save the flame from a few candles, like flickers of moonlight on a forest path. The black-and-gray stone that lined the floors and walls stole what little light the candles provided.

Her heart raced as fast as her feet. Why had he summoned her in the middle of the night? *Light's Blood! It could only be bad news.*

She raced down one set of stairs, then up another before traipsing down a long corridor that was one of the few places that was lit well enough to see clearly.

palace of the sun, interior stairs

A mirrored alcove, barely visible in the dim light, provided a glimpse of her image as she passed. She frowned. What she wouldn't give to wear her green gown again, the one she had made from the Victory Cloak at the battle of Katsintal. Another frown. Even that wouldn't be the same; her hair no longer bounced on her shoulders, and she couldn't chew on the ends. The thumping in her chest brought realization with it. After tonight she may not be breathing, let alone playing dress-up.

She shuddered more as she continued her walk. This corridor was almost identical to a section of the Great Path in Vallah. *Why had he done that?* she wondered.

Tendrils of pure white mist emerged from the walls and wrapped around her legs. The mist *followed* her, clung to her, as if it had been instructed to.

She wondered again about the extent of Lukaan's powers. *How much was there that she didn't know?*

corridor in Palace of the Sun

As she started on the final stretch of corridor that led to his chambers, she considered how her life had changed. She was not a beautiful woman, yet there were those who had called her beautiful—and not just her parents.

As a child, a tall forehead hinted at the height she would attain, so legends said. In her case the legends had not been wrong. Children teased her about her long legs, and though she once despised her legs due to those taunts, she had grown proud of them in the later years— years that coincided with women's envy and men's lust.

She shivered as she caught the first glimpse of the white marble entry. It seemed to rush her, like the waters of Lake Charto the time she fell from the cliff. Everything moved faster now: her heart, her blood, even her skin felt as if it moved, a vain attempt to disassociate itself with a fallen hero. Two steps before the entry, the doors slid open, a fluid silent movement, like walking through fog.

Tirzinitzia raised her head and muttered a calming mantra, forced her shoulders to relax. Her fists unclenched, stretching into long, bony fingers.

An expanse of marble covered the floor and wrapped the columns. An image of the sun from Lenorda was embedded. She was surprised it did not have an image of him as well.

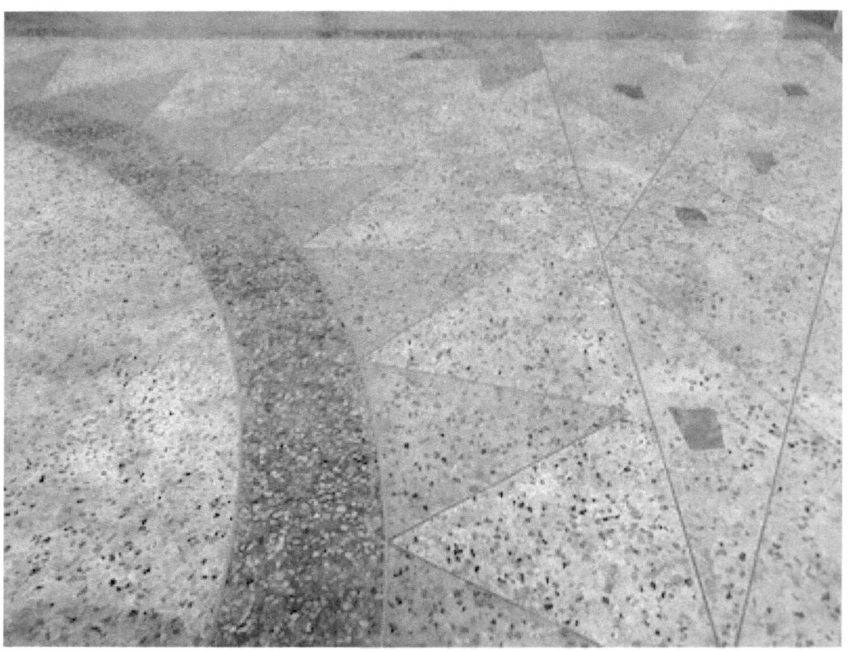

marble floor

Pockets of mist hung in the air, some knee-high, some staring back at her. Between the thickets of fog she saw Melissara's icy gaze and platinum hair. Then she saw *him*, or an image of him, mounted on his throne. The vapors that haunted this chamber surrounded him, clung to him like an aura of darkness. The pain hit her as she bowed her head.

Why is he not here?

Tirzinitzia wondered who he meant. She dared not turn her head. Such an insult would be intolerable. Death could come with her next thought.

Was Ghruehne not here? Should he have been?

It came to her as her stomach twisted—a moving, crawling, oozing feeling like a serpent sneaking in through her bowels. Muscles tightened, buttocks squeezed together, but she could not control the fear. It erupted with a terrible shudder. "I... I beg forgiveness, Great Lord. He..." A dull pain hit her, as if someone jarred her head with a club.

Silence!

Tirzinitzia lowered her head until the marble floor became a blur, fading in, then out of her vision. She heard things she might not have otherwise: footsteps in the corridor; breathing—was it her own; a chuckle—no, Melissara would not dare that, not here. Humming? She thought she heard humming, and risked raising her head the slightest bit. Out of the corner of her eyes, at the periphery, she saw them—two red disks burning like miniature suns, hovering in midair. Serpents waiting to strike. She felt the dampness in her skin. Sweat beaded on her forehead and traced her cheeks. Her shoulders hunched, and her fists and teeth clenched.

It struck before she could blink, burning into her face, worse than a branding.

"Arrgh!"

She tightened her jaws, kept them sealed. Tirzinitzia knew better than to scream in *his* presence. The orb burned through the skin, bored to the bone. "Arrgh." She groaned again, lower this time. She had at least managed that much control. If only she could heal, if only—

"Arrgh." When it had dug deep enough, a finger-width deep, it stopped, fusing to her face like a jewel set in a ring.

Tirzinitzia rocked on her heels. Every muscle ached from tensing. She brought her cries under control, knowing she should never have let them get so bad. Perhaps it had been too long since she had suffered the rigors of war.

Tears hissed as they ran over the mark on her face. Her nose ran like leaves dripping morning dew. A stab of pain slapped her when she moved her jaw. She would not try that again so soon. *Lukaan's pet.* She was now truly his pet, with her own little red sun implanted in her cheek.

Why did your charge fail you?

Tirzinitzia swallowed, though it hurt. Her throat was as dry as the Sethian desert, and it had swelled like a constrictor after a meal. "I will look into it, My Lord. He must—"

"There is no need, Tirzinitzia. The Black Rose is dead."

She turned toward the voice. Melissara's icy stare chilled her. Fear sought the marrow of her bones. *What would he do to her now?* "Dead? How did the boy—"

A scolding sound escaped Melissara's palate, the *tsk* of a mother chiding a child. "Not the boy, Tirzinitzia. He could not have killed the Rose. But the boy has help. And if they killed Damon Pirrhar they must be formidable." Melissara's eyes did the scolding this time. "Must we forever discover events for ourselves? Can no one tell the Great Lord disturbing news?"

The putrid stink of burnt flesh drifted by her nose. She gagged. Then her body registered another strike. The orb from the opposite side of her face. Now she would have two brands—two Red Suns to mark her like livestock.

An urge to resist swirled in her gut, but the love of life forced her to remain still. She dare not move. Dare not show emotion.

The second sun burned deep, ever-deeper into her smoldering flesh.

Her eyelids would no longer stay open, despite her attempts to keep them still, and her nose quavered like a hound on the hunt. Blood dripped from the palms of her hand, where clenched fists dug her nails deep into the skin. Tears ran freely, sneaking out from under closed lids, hissing steam as the rivulets channeled into the red-hot craters. She prayed for death to pay a hasty visit.

Her knees buckled. She collapsed to the marble floor, landing on her elbows with a thud. *A little longer. Just a little longer.*

Tirzinitzia shivered, though from cold or fear she couldn't tell. The chamber held both in abundance. She kept her head bowed low. Her only opportunity was to hope for a chance to serve again. A low humming permeated the room, stirring both curiosity and fear. She dare not look up, though she did risk a glance when the sound moved near. *Is there yet another...*

She gasped when she saw it, hovering less than a hand's width from her face, level with her forehead, another red orb resembling a miniature sun. Her mind registered the movement, but before the thought was complete, it struck like a whip, drilling into her head as if it sought her brain. She smelled the burnt hair.

She leaned, as if to rid herself of the pain, but she knew she toyed with death now and resisted all urges to reach for comfort or relief. Even worse, she strained to control herself from using her powers, to do that in Lukaan's presence would be suicide—worse.

She heard strange sounds within her head. Sounds that should not have been there. Tirzinitzia had never been blessed with the healing talents, so she could only wonder at what was happening to her, and if it could be repaired. *Calm. I must think of calm.*

She thought of her sister, who had been truly beautiful. Before Antar killed her. The errant thought stirred more memories. Images of all who had died in the wars raced to her mind. Calm was not working, but *vengeance* was. She ground her teeth together. Tightly. So tight she thought they might crack. *Yes, the pain is better. It is easing. Forget calm. Vengeance is what I need.*

A shuffle of footsteps drew her gaze to the side, where Melissara stood. No compassion showed in her steel-blue gaze, and none could be heard in her disinterested voice.

"Lord," Melissara said, and lowered her head, "perhaps Tirzinitzia is able to withstand the pain due to her increased ability with the shield."

The room fell deathly still—until only Tirzinitzia's racing heart could be heard.

Tirzinitzia can shield?

Melissara bowed her head, deference obvious but not overstated. "My apologies, Great Lord. I would have informed you sooner, but the news seemed so trivial. I had hoped to surprise you if we made further progress." She paused.

"Tirzinitzia has had only small successes; however, she is the only one to have done so." Melissara stood rigid to receive a thought.

"Take her, Melissara. Have her study the shield. See if we can discover a weakness. Even the faintest of hopes cannot be dismissed. Punishment must cede to hope."

Melissara acknowledged the responsibility, as if accepting a gift.

The pain clawed at Tirzinitzia, spread through her like a primordial ooze. And though the agony would persist, and the pain would resurrect itself in her memory whenever she passed a reflector, she was at least alive. Much as Tirzinitzia hated to admit it, she owed that life to Melissara, though that concerned her almost as much as the lingering pain, and the scars she would carry for eternity.

Tirzinitzia bristled with suspicion. Melissara had saved her from death but to what end? She and Melissara claimed allegiance to the same master, but Melissara was a du Savarra, and certain things ran in their blood: unnatural beauty, an unfailing memory, a keen mind—

and *vengeance*. And vengeance was the strongest trait of all. It was well known on Nelstar that a du Savarra never died from losing blood—all they required was a taste of vengeance. With that they could make their own blood.

What is her game?

Melissara had a plot in mind. Tirzinitzia knew the du Savarras too well to think otherwise, but she was so relieved at being alive that she didn't care. She had survived Lukaan's punishment. All she had to do now was survive Melissara's plot.

DESERT PLOTS

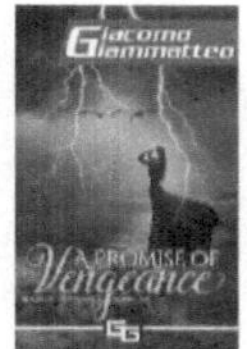

Sethian Desert
1364 AE (After Exile)
Second Cycle of the Fifth Moon—Reunion
Third Calendar of Light

*T*irzinitzia stood, head held low, eyes squinted as Ghruehne entered. It pained her to have him see her like this—scarred and, even worse, subservient to Melissara. Ghruehne was still handsome—beyond handsome—almost beautiful, for a man. Many would have killed to achieve such perfection, but Tirzinitzia knew that Ghruehne rarely found satisfaction in anything.

She recalled his first battle scar. The scar itself was nothing, but the damage to his pride nearly killed him. *Arrogant fool.* No woman was ever good enough for him but that never bothered Tirzinitzia. Men never stirred her blood, not even as a young girl. Oddly enough, she felt no feelings for women either; only her work mattered—and battle. The wonderful smell of a battlefield.

Ghruehne rushed past her in a hasty attempt to reach Lukaan. He didn't look at Tirzinitzia but he cast a quick glance at Melissara, his hungry eyes running across her body. Ages ago he had been infatuated with Melissara, but she spurned him. Soon his lust grew into an obsession. When she rejected him completely, he nearly went mad.

Ghruehne winced under Lukaan's glare.

You will find the boy, Ghruehne. I want him brought to me, or dead.

"What about the other one?"

Give him to our friends in Sykor. Do not fail me, Ghruehne. If you do, I shall make a gift of you to Melissara. She will have you for her pet.

≈

*M*elissara's face remained a stone, though inside she beamed. Laughter pushed at her lips as an image of Ghruehne on a leash danced in her mind. Ghruehne, who hated her as much as any man could hate a woman—and still want her, still lust for her. "It would disappoint me to see Ghruehne fail, Great Lord." A thin smile turned her lips up. "Though I cannot conceal my delight at the prospect of fitting a snug collar around his pretty neck."

Lukaan roared with laughter. "Go now, Ghruehne. Think of failure, and how Melissara will torture you as her pet. Imagine the humiliation you will suffer and the pain you will bear." Lukaan leaned forward, the darkness that surrounded him sliding down the stairs. "Perhaps those thoughts will be the impetus for your success. Now, go!"

≈

*G*hruehne exited the chamber at a brisk pace. He dare not go too quickly lest he offend the Great Lord. He wore a smile and an accompanying friendly facade; a demeanor deceptively calm for one who had just departed such an embarrassing audience with the Great One.

Melissara's pet! Many will die before I submit to her.

Memories fueled his burning hatred for Melissara, a fire sparked long ago by lust. His pace accelerated as he distanced himself from Lukaan, slamming his boots onto the granite floor with every thunderous step. He ripped off his gauntlet and slapped it against a column, grinding teeth as he did.

A guard moved too slowly to get out of his way. Ghruehne uncoiled, smashing him with a clenched fist. Two of the guard's teeth fell out. Ghruehne raised his hand to lick the blood from his knuckles. *Primitive,* thought Ghruehne, *but effective, in a barbaric way.* The violence temporarily eased his tension as he stormed into the streets of Sethia.

The remaining soldiers darted from his path, bowing low as he passed, and paying him the homage due an immortal. A smile replaced the scowl on his face as he focused on the task at hand. "Kill the village boy" Lukaan had said. So shall it be. Rahgnar Fal-Thera shall soon die.

~

Melissara roused Tirzinitzia with the sun. A large brown robe had been laid out for Tirzinitzia to wear. It hung on her like a sack and hid her finely toned body. Tirzinitzia followed Melissara through the house, across the tile floors, cool on her feet. Soon the scorching heat would return, as it did everyday in Sethia, and she would long for such a refreshing touch.

Melissara hurried down the hall, across the parlor and into the courtyard. Cacti and stone decorated the gardens, along with desert blooms. A brown stone walk snaked side to side like the dry riverbeds in the Empty Lands. A snort from a horse brought her gaze to the back, where servants waited with mounts just outside the gate. "Why are we riding, Melissara? It will soon be hot." Tirzinitzia questioned her because she knew there must be some reason for this barbaric mode of travel.

Melissara's glare seemed to steam in the morning heat. "My wish, Tirzinitzia. Need you know more?" She grabbed the reins from the servant, swung onto her mount, and kicked her heels into the sleek white mare.

Tirzinitzia's horse snorted and pawed the ground, but he responded perfectly to a gentle prod from her knees. For almost half the morning they rode north into the arid wastelands. Tirzinitzia tempered her curiosity with sound judgment. Soon after, Melissara spoke to her.

"We will arrive soon."

Tirzinitzia nodded, doing her best to adapt to her newfound life. It was not a life she looked forward to, but it proved better than the alternative—for now.

Forced to remain mute, Tirzinitzia's other senses worked in earnest. She meticulously scanned the surroundings, taking note of every landmark: a mound of rocks resembling the rubble at Menden Pass; a patch of sand stained rusty brown, spurring images of the copper mines on Savar; and a beautiful patch of yellow brittle-bush arranged in a pattern similar to the altars in the Temple of the Sun. She breathed deeply, cataloguing each scent that rode the air. Each breath was ripe with moonglows, though they would only show for the third and fourth cycle; and a stand of prickly pear bearing red and purple fruit stood as tall as Tirzinitzia, teasing her with their aroma. Lastly, she noted some blue scorpion-weed peeking out from behind sagebrush.

There, she thought, *this location is marked.*

Tirzinitzia's memory was her prime asset. She could look at a landscape once, then, years later, reconstruct every detail. The asset had made her invaluable during the wars. How she longed to put those talents to work again.

"Don't waste your energy, Tirzinitzia." Melissara's voice was cool and indifferent. "I'll make no attempt to hide the location from you." She smiled as she prodded her mount to a faster pace.

By midday they arrived at their destination. Melissara dismounted Tirzinitzia stared into a huge crack in the floor of the desert. She cataloged everything in her memory. Off to the right Melissara descended a set of stairs carved into the desert. Melissara didn't speak until they were far below the surface.

"You may speak, now. Lukaan cannot detect us." Melissara must have noted the astonished look on the Tirzinitzia's face. "Why wear such a foolish look, Tirzinitzia? I know you cannot shield, but I spared your life so that I might use you."

The shocked look never left her face but Tirzinitzia managed to at least control it. She had always thought Melissara was as tied to Lukaan as his arm, but now...

Or, it could be a trap, she thought. *But why go to the trouble of a trap when Lukaan was going to kill me himself?*

Something foul was brewing. "What is it that you wish, Melissara? You are not known for your kindness."

Melissara's eyes seemed threatening even when relaxed. "One day, I will require your assistance. When that day arrives, you will be there." Melissara stared into her eyes. "And always remember, if ever you lose that shielding ability that I claimed you possess, or, if your abilities do not live up to what we thought, then that would be unfortunate. Indeed, it would prove very unfortunate, as the Great Lord's death sentence would be recalled immediately. And the next time he may indulge himself with the delights of torture. I am certain that he would if prompted."

Tirzinitzia nodded, then followed Melissara through a narrow tunnel that led almost straight down. She estimated that they were two spans lower than the desert floor. A glow lit the path ahead, and she squinted to see their destination.

Many slaves toil for something. I wonder what?

The path opened to an immense chamber where hundreds of slaves worked with picks and shovels digging more tunnels, and building new roads. Others kept busy shoring up the walls as the hordes of slaves dug ever deeper, their shovels filling carts to remove the fresh diggings.

Tirzinitzia listened to the Gnakas cursing and yelling for others to get out of their way as they hurried outside with their loads of dirt and sand. The Gnakas made excellent miners. They were short, thus able to work in small places, but they also possessed an unusual level of stamina.

Her attention was drawn to a huge object in the center of the chamber. She stared at the obelisk rising from the floor. The illumination from the torches gave the appearance that the black stone glowed. Tirzinitzia moved closer, her gaze fixed on the monument. She increased her pace to keep stride with Melissara.

"I see that you are affected as well."

Tirzinitzia tried to hide her reaction, but failed.

"Do not be concerned. It draws me also. What puzzles me is that it apparently has no effect on the mortals. They can walk by it, even touch it, without emotion. I can feel the pull, Tirzinitzia. It is like the dawn of battle when the energy is flowing and the air is thick, and tense, and full with power."

Tirzinitzia opened her senses and smiled. She too, felt the power, the energy. And she yearned for more. "What is it, Melissara?" Tirzinitzia rubbed her hands over the surface of the black obelisk, then gently lay her cheek against it. It felt cold against her scars, yet a certain warmth radiated from deep within. For a moment, the briefest moment, Tirzinitzia thought her pain had eased.

"I have had a Sethian priest examine it. He believes it to be a temple from a long-lost city; one that is often mentioned in their legends. He was afraid, Tirzinitzia, though the realization that legends may be true make the bravest of mortals fearful.

It is, however, old. Look at these inscriptions. The language is an ancient form of the Sethian tongue that hasn't been spoken in thousands of turns of the sun. Only the temple priest recognized it, and even he is not able to provide a translation."

Melissara stared into Tirzinitzia's eyes. "This is what I need your assistance with. We must discover the secrets of this obelisk and whatever else might be buried here."

Tirzinitzia's interest had indeed been stirred. She smiled her most wicked smile. "It appears that the Great Lord may have acted hastily when he subjugated my will to yours." A smirk lit her face, though it hurt. "Perhaps I can help you discover something that will aid you in your... quest."

Melissara returned the smile. It seemed genuine, for once, though with Melissara one never knew.

"Perhaps, Tirzinitzia. Perhaps."

THE JOURNEY CONTINUES

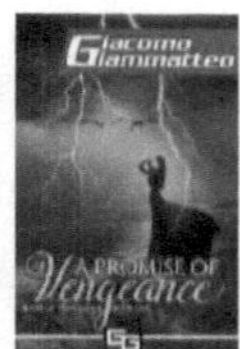

The barkeep from the Lucky Hawk walked briskly up the street. Despite the steep incline and a shortness of breath, his pace never slowed. He climbed the steps to the Dead Man's Inn, breathing a sigh of relief when he reached the door. He only hoped he wasn't too late.

A prissy man greeted him. He was small and thin, with his hair slicked back, every silver strand in place. The buttons on his shirt were fastened from belly to neck and he had eyes that looked as if he could weigh a man with little more than a glance.

"May I be of service to you, good sir?" Honey coated Briston's words, but his eyes dissected Carter like a father would his daughter's first suitor.

"Need to deliver this letter...to one of your patrons."

Briston's eyebrows nearly brushed his hairline. "What is the name?"

Carter looked down at the name on the letter, rolled tightly and with a seal to mark it. He could read, but not well. "Ra...Ragner Fal-Thera," he managed to say, though not without some difficulty.

Briston frowned. "Master Fal-Thera is not available. If you will surrender the letter to me, I will assure you of its delivery."

Beads of perspiration rolled down Carter's flushed cheeks. The sagging skin under pale blue eyes told of little sleep, and the glazed look spoke of fear. "I must deliver it to him. *Only* him."

The letter shook in Carter's unsteady hands, though he gripped it like a vise. Briston's glare fell to his callused hands, then down to torn and dirty britches perched above shoes with half the leather worn away. Pity ceded to judgment. He invited Carter inside. "Follow me, good sir. I will escort you to Master Fal-Thera."

Briston led Carter across the entry hall of the inn and onward into the dining hall. Carter's preoccupation blinded him to anything else: he never noticed the ancient sculptures that lined the corridor they walked; he did not observe the spiral stairs carved from the single trunk of a blackthorn in ages past; and if others did, Carter never paid mind to the noise he made as a pebble stuck in the sole of his boot clanged on the white marble floors. None of it mattered. He was there for one reason.

~

*S*even of them sat around a circular cherry table eating breakfast. Rahg shoveled food into his mouth as if he hadn't eaten in days, and Rhaven devoured his at an equally alarming rate.

Briston stopped short, his outstretched arm ensuring that Carter advanced no further. "We shall wait until they finish."

Rhaven reached for more potatoes. "I feel like Rahg. I'm even considering ordering more food."

"Be prepared to pay for the meal in gold," Gregor said.

"What is gold for but to spend?"

Rahg smiled. Gregor always cringed when Rhaven spoke about gold that way.

Briston came forward at the first break in the dialogue. "Good morning, gentlemen, and my lady. Forgive the interruption of your meal; however, this good man seems obsessed with delivering a letter to Master Fal-Thera."

Briston paused until Rahg acknowledged him. "I offered to deliver it myself but he would have nothing of it. Frankly, I cannot conceive of—"

Carter stepped forward. "Are you Ragner Fal-Thera?"

Rahg stood. "I am."

"Take this," Carter said, and shoved the scroll at Rahg.

"Who gave this to you?"

Carter said nothing.

Wisp took the letter from Rahg. "Must have been the lady I told you about. This is the barkeep from the Lucky Hawk."

Carter's eyes darted to Wisp, then the others. "I swear. I didn't have nothin' to do with killin' them two. Wasn't me."

"Killing who?" Wisp asked.

"I think we should go to the room," Rhaven said. "We are drawing a lot of interest."

Carter was trembling by the time they reached the room. "She's gonna kill me. Said she'd peel the skin off my body. I'm not much of a man, but every man's got a right to live and a right to die decent. I saw what she did. I'm not wantin' to die that way."

Wisp grabbed Carter by the hair, yanking his head upright while a blade dug into his throat. "Are you talking about the two men with us?"

Carter wiped his eyes as he stammered a story. "After closing I was cleanin' up the place when all of a sudden... she was there. Don't know how she got there 'cause I locked the door." He looked at Wisp as if he had to convince him of the story. "I know I had the door locked. The Lucky Hawk's in a bad spot. You saw yerself. No one forgets to lock a door down there."

"*Who* was there?" Wisp asked.

"Some woman looking for you." Carter looked around the inn warily, as if she might hear him. "'How'd you get in?' I asked her. Careful, I was. Didn't want to upset her."

The barkeep took a swig of water. "She was carryin' a sack. I hadn't even noticed at first. "Did you send these?" she asked and opened the sack. The heads of two men rolled out, bloody, but with their eyes still open. I screamed. Then I fell down. Almost landed on one of 'em. That's when I vomited," Carter said. "Those eyes just starin' at me. I couldn't take it." Carter closed his eyes, squeezing them together, as if he were seeing it all over again.

Wisp stared. "Were they—"

Carter nodded. "They were the two with you."

"I'll kill her myself," Wisp swore.

Carter wiped his face and ran a hand through his hair. "She said to tell whoever sent those men not to meddle in her affairs. Said not to bother with business that's not theirs. She said it with real fancy words, but that's what she meant, I asked her." Carter looked at Rahg. "She also said to tell you to go on alone. 'Tell him he has a message to deliver.' Those words were exact. She made me remember them."

Tobias blinked his eyes rapidly. "Give me that letter, Kender. Let me have a look at what's in there."

"I'll see for myself," Rahg said, and grabbed the letter from Wisp. He lifted the envelope to open it, but Wisp stopped him.

"Wait, Rahg. I want to inspect the seal on that letter before you break it."

The seal was two crescent moons, back to back. Imposed over the moons was the image of a wild boar, its tusks unusually long, with a decidedly fierce expression.

"Anyone see this before?" Wisp asked, handing it to Tobias for him to inspect.

"Not me," Tobias said, "but Preman would know. He's familiar with all the Houses." Tobias turned to Darstan. "Lad, go find Preman. Tell him he's needed."

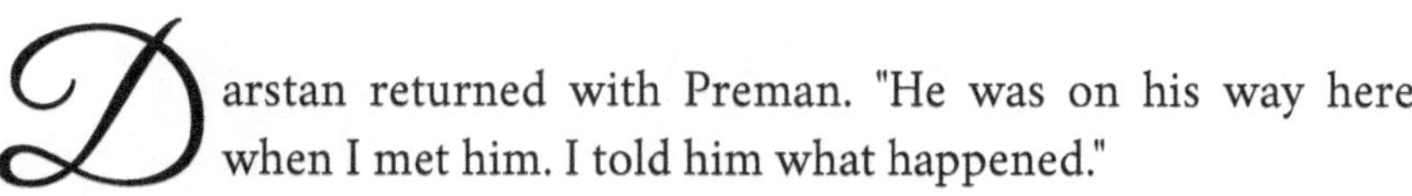

Darstan returned with Preman. "He was on his way here when I met him. I told him what happened."

A crop of wheat-colored hair sat atop Preman's head, and hung loose in the back. His face was clean shaven, and though he sat a half a head shorter than Darstan, his voice carried the sound of a giant. Preman held out a meaty hand. "Let me see the letter."

Preman scanned it. "I know all the Houses of Pomanda and Sykor; it is not from any of those."

"What about Khatara?" Rahg asked.

"Or the Lorns?" Dartan said.

"The Lorns, the Nyaurans, Gnakas. None of them have noble houses as we do. As for the Khatarans, I am not familiar with their Houses but I know enough of their beliefs to know it could not have come from there. They revere the two moons in their religion, and no one is allowed to use both moons as a symbol on anything. Not even the

Emperor." Preman handed the letter to Rahg. "Open it so we can see what it says."

Rahg broke open the letter and unrolled it. As he read, his brow wrinkled.

"What's the matter?" Camissa asked.

"I can't read it," he said.

Preman took the letter. "This is written in Ancient Sethian. No one uses that anymore, and even fewer know how to read it." Preman returned the letter to Rahg. "The priests might be able to translate it. If anyone can, it would be them."

Carter stood, still trembling. "Are you done with me?"

"Let him go," Rhaven said. "He knows nothing more."

Carter's glance dashed from one to the other. When no one objected, he hurried out of the inn.

"Looks like we need to go to the temple," Rhaven said.

"I don't like priests," Wisp said.

Rhaven smiled. "At least we agree on *something,* thief."

THE TEMPLE OF THE GODS

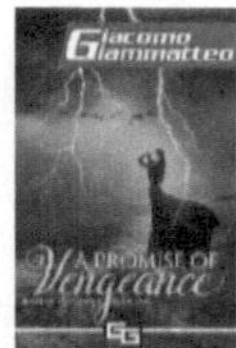

The temple sat atop a mountain on the north side of Pomanda. An ancient stone road cut a tortuous path into the mountain's side as it climbed toward the summit.

monastery

Camissa rode at the front of the party along with Tobias and Rhaven. Rahg, Darstan, Wisp, and Gregor brought up the rear.

Guards dressed in the gold-and-white colors of the temple blocked the entrance. "Here to see the shera," Tobias said.

One of the guards led them down a path to sweeping marble steps that rose to a pair of wooden doors. From the center of each door hung a large horse head cast from bronze, with a ring serving as a knocker. Tobias lifted one of the brass ornaments and knocked on the door. Soon a priest peered through a slit in the doorway.

"May I be of service to you?"

"We're here to see the shera," he said.

The doors swung open. A small man dressed in a plain brown robe with a hood that hung on his back greeted them. He had the robe tied at the waist with a worn sash made from old rope. "We have many sheras, but they are often busy in prayer. I would suggest you arrange an appointment." He spoke in a soft monotone voice that echoed the expression on his face.

Tobias pushed forward. "Tell Shera Darian that Lord Preman sent us. We have a letter that needs to be translated."

"We could have saved time if you told me that Lord Preman sent you. Please come in and rest. I will bring the shera."

monastery interior

He shuffled off down a long corridor, the strap from one of his worn sandals dragging on the floor. The entrance hall was as big as the Trader's Inn with two sets of marble steps arcing to a landing bedecked with marble columns. Ivy scrabbled up a trellis near the back of the stairs and a sweet-scented plant with white blossoms fell from a garden box on the second floor, dangling over a fountain.

Before long the priest who had greeted them returned with the shera. He wore a white robe tied at the waist with a red sash outlined in gold. Red trim adorned his collar, and on his breastplate was a broken sword woven from gold thread— the sign of peace.

The shera's haughty voice filled the hall. "I am Shera Darian, and you are all welcome to the Temple of the Gods. Please forgive my assistant for not admitting you at first. He did not realize you came on the business of Lord Preman." The shera greeted them with open arms, hugging Tobias then Wisp before stepping back. "How is my friend Preman?"

"Preman's fine," Tobias said. "He said you might be able to translate a letter for us. It's written in Old Sethian."

The shera's smile turned quickly to a frown. "Translating a letter from Old Sethian would be tedious."

"If it's money you're worried over, we can pay."

The smile returned quicker than it disappeared. But he wasn't done negotiating. "Certainly a donation would be appreciated; however, time is a factor. Many of our most loyal patrons have work for us to do: translations, copying manuscripts, tutoring of children. The list is endless."

Temples were no different than the cities when it came to the games of power. Knowledge was traded like khaffe or te, and in Pomanda, influence sat on a throne next to gold.

Tobias and the shera continued negotiating with neither one ceding ground. Rhaven fidgeted with his sai, while Gregor talked with Wisp and Darstan. Rahg stood alone, wearing a worried look. Camissa sensed his frustration. She moved between Tobias and the shera.

"Shera Darian, we are in a hurry. We'll pay gold for a literal translation of this letter. Leave nothing out. Do not embellish. One Pomandan gold piece is the pay, and you'll get no more for good news than you will for bad, so don't bother with subtleties or coatings of honey."

The holy man struggled to determine a course of action. If these people were not important, he should take the gold, translate the letter, and see them on their way. If, however, they were important enough to offer a gold piece, their gratitude could be worth much more.

From the corner of his eye he caught sight of Rhaven's menacing glare. The shera slid unconsciously to the side. Once he had seen a wild mountain cat, and this one exuded that same predator aura. Shera Darian arrived at a wise decision. Keeping one eye on Rhaven, he looked to Camissa. "Well put, fair lady. I have decided to help you by examining your letter."

Darian held out his hand to receive the paper from Tobias. He was certain he felt Rhaven's eyes burning into his back, and that prompted him to further concessions. "And there will be no charge for the translation, of course."

He bowed to Camissa, feeling comfortable with his decision. If they were as dangerous as the evil-looking one indicated, he would likely not be paid anyway. It might even save his life. And by the remote possibility that they were of noble house, then his offer would be received warmly and he would earn a favor. *Yes*, he thought, *I have made a wise choice.*

The shera studied the letter while Camissa and the others watched. At first, his eyes went slowly, then his interest was aroused, his eyes darting back and forth and up and down. Suddenly he stopped.

Camissa tensed. "What is wrong, shera? What have you found?"

"You will need to find someone else."

"You said you would help."

Darian looked about the group, eyes stopping on Rhaven. "Who is Rahgnar Fal-Thera?" he asked, voice quavering.

Rahg stepped forward. "I am."

"I..I cannot decipher it," he said. "Only a few words..I.."

"Which words?" Rahg grabbed the letter. "This. What does this mean? The words by my name." Rahg thrust the letter back into the shera's trembling hand. "I can see my name."

Darian shook. "Rahg Fal-Thera Ihra Renegalla," he said, his voice barely a whisper. "Rahg Fal-Thera is the Fate Sealer." The old priest gulped. "More precisely, it means 'One who brings the fate.'"

"What does that mean? Fate Sealer?"

"Meanings can be deceiving when translating. I am not so fluent as to be able to translate this much without a mistake. I suggest you take this letter to my teacher, Shera Kevon. He has a small temple on the far reaches of Pomanda, north of the Great Forest. He has studied all the ancient languages and, more importantly, he is familiar with the old prophecies as well. He will be better able to assist you."

"You can tell us no more?" Rhaven asked.

"I might provide the wrong information. When dealing with something so important, I presume you wish to be precise. There is no one alive that knows the Old Sethian language better than Shera Kevon. And no one who understands the prophecies as he does." The shera stared at Rhaven. "Seek him out, my friend. For the good of us all, seek him out."

～

*C*amissa packed sacks with food for the upcoming journey while Rahg and Darstan gathered other necessary items and fed the horses.

"Where are Wisp and Gregor?" Darstan asked.

"Arranging supplies for the trip. They said it's a long way to the temple."

"I still don't know why we're going," Rahg said. "This is nonsense."

"Nonsense or not, Rahg. We will get an answer from the old shera."

"It's not that important."

Camissa's soft blue eyes narrowed to angry slits and her face reddened. "It *is* important, Rahg. *Very* important."

Rahg shook his head and returned to packing. Before long he was whistling. "I can't wait to get to the Blackthorn Forest."

"Don't forget about the woman who sent that letter, Rahg. She killed Pelle and Rinck. Remember?"

"Nothing to worry about."

"Nothing?" Darstan shook his head. "Didn't you notice the priest? He was terrified."

"He was just afraid of Rhaven."

Camissa sighed. *But he feared you more,* she recalled grimly, and when she did, the unwelcome memories came back. This time, they were only memories, but when that priest read the letter and looked at Rahg, she *saw* his fear. Saw right into his soul as the demons of fear grabbed at Darian's throat and heart. She heard fear's deathly scream and felt its chilling breath. Even now it frightened her.

What am I becoming?

Camissa had no answers, but there was no one to trust with this. Already, people were uneasy with her powers. What would they think if she told them her powers were growing? Would Rahg still smile warmly at her if he knew she could read his every thought?

She reconsidered, remembering what new information she now knew about him. How did that affect him, she wondered. Camissa wondered about the fear that came upon Shera Darian today. She had never seen fear before, but she could not imagine it being any stronger.

Meanwhile, fear built a base inside of Camissa. Fear of a different nature. *I hope it is not what I suspect. Please, don't let it be that.*

A LITERAL TRANSLATION

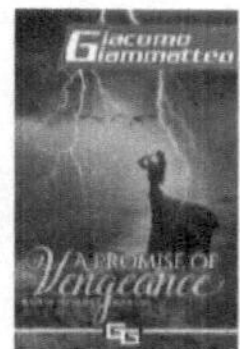

Rahg peered out the window into the darkness; sleep would not stay with him and the moon had a while to go before it ceded to the sun. He felt anxious about the trip, had mixed feelings; the prospect of seeing the Blackthorn Forest and the Lorns excited him, but he was in no hurry to discover the meaning of the letter, although, if nothing else, it would relieve the tension he felt from the rest of the party.

No one had said anything, but he noticed subtle differences in the way they treated him. Only Camissa seemed the same, and Darstan of course. He heard footsteps in the hall just before the door opened.

"Prepare for leaving," Rhaven said.

Rhaven seldom put more than two sentences together. He hung onto words like Gregor did gold. *Not like Tobias*, Rahg thought, smiling at the recollection of him in one of his storytelling moods.

Rhaven's voice roused Darstan and Wisp from their sleep. Rahg often wondered how Wisp did it. He slept less than anyone, but he didn't appear to suffer from missing sleep. "Good morning, Dar, Wisp."

"Morning? You call this morning?" Darstan asked.

Rahg smiled as Darstan rubbed his tired eyes. Unlike Wisp, Darstan grew as irritable as a mare with foal, unless he got the proper amount of sleep. He grumbled as he rose from the bed.

"We just went to sleep, and now he's waking us. Don't see why we have to be in such a hurry to get there anyway. That letter isn't going anywhere, and I doubt that the old priest is either. We could have slept longer and gotten food instead of eating on the trail."

"Much as I hate to admit it, I agree with Rhaven," Wisp said. "The longer we delay the more chance of a trap."

"Trap? No one knows where we're going. We didn't tell anyone, and I'm sure the shera wouldn't. How could there be a trap?" Rahg asked.

Wisp shook his head as he put on his shirt. "I've been thinking about it. Someone went to a lot of trouble to write that letter in Ancient Sethian. And in case you've forgotten, that woman searched half of Pomanda trying to find you, and she killed three men in the process—three that we know of. I'd be surprised if we didn't find a trap. Did you stop to think of why her message was in that language? Perhaps she knew we would have to seek out the old priest to get it translated."

Wisp stuffed a knife into each boot then stood. "Doesn't it also worry you that we have received no word from either the thieves or the bounty-men as to her whereabouts?" Wisp stared into Rahg's eyes. "You must learn to think like a thief. Suspect everyone. Trust no one."

As Wisp finished dressing, Rahg noticed for the first time how many knives he carried: one in each boot; two attached to a special sheath sewn into the back of his britches; two additional ones in a similar sheath higher up his back, just below the neck; and one on the upper part of each arm in a sheath that hung upside down. When Wisp put his belt on, Rahg noticed the two traditional knife holders attached to the belt, where one might carry a sword. "Do you always carry so many knives?"

"I prefer to be prepared, and I've never had occasion to wish differently."

Darstan had been stumbling around getting dressed while listening to their conversation. "Why not carry a sword?"

"The rooftops are hardly the place for swordplay, and there's no room in alleys. Besides, I have no desire for clanging steel to announce my presence to the guards. On a rooftop I can throw a knife with no noise. In a narrow alley, it would be difficult at best to draw a sword let alone handle one proficiently, so I have learned to use knives, and prefer their advantages."

Rahg remembered when Wisp killed two of the Wolfen with his knives. Better than most would have been able to accomplish with a sword. "Well, we had better be going." Rahg threw a sack over his shoulder and went to the stable. Darstan and Wisp followed.

~

Camissa glared at the three of them ambling toward the stable. Her hands were planted against her hips and she wore a scowl on her face. Strands of honey hair protruded like pieces of straw from her head. "It's about time you got here. We've been ready and could have eaten while waiting for you."

Wisp exaggerated his graceful bow. "My apologies, princess. Darstan and I were otherwise engaged. We shall prepare to leave at once."

Camissa tried, but could not hide the smile. "All right, Kender Darnell, just saddle your horse, and let's get going."

Rahg climbed atop Marchall and they soon left Pomanda behind, kicking dust on the road toward the Blackthorn Forest.

Darstan pulled up alongside his brother. "We'll get this straightened out, Rahg. Don't worry about it."

"It can't be soon enough, Dar."

As they traveled, Camissa reached out with her powers, studying the other members of the party. Since leaving the temple she had experimented with various methods of reading the thoughts of others and drew mixed results. At times the thoughts came through clearly, but just as often she saw only vague images. In the past she could only read the thoughts of someone close to her, or the thoughts of others that affected someone close; now, however, she experienced success in gathering information from the mind of almost anyone, even strangers.

The stable hand had been an unwitting subject. When they entered the stable, she had sensed his fear: *someone coming at this time of the night*, he had thought, and believed them to be thieves.

Before the experience at the temple, she would have been fortunate to have even detected his fear, and she would never have been able to *hear* his exact words. But this new-found power came with a share of problems. When she sensed an emotion, fear, for example, she became afraid herself, and the stronger the fear, the more difficult it proved to control. The opposite was also true, she discovered this morning. Once the stable-hand had realized who they were, she had sensed his relief, and it was like a warm bath on a frigid winter night. The relaxation was so strong, so comforting to her, that she felt as if sleep might overtake her right then.

Camissa shook her head to clear the thoughts. She must stop thinking on this. It was not good to be probing her friends' minds. She had sworn that she would never do it, yet she had never dreamt that reading of minds like this was even possible. Did that make a difference? She chided herself. Why should that affect her decision. It would be like Wisp swearing not to steal something, but only because he thought he couldn't steal it. The struggle continued as she blindly rode along.

She knew what she was doing was wrong, but her oldest oath won out in the end. It was true that she had taken an oath to not delve into peoples' private thoughts, but she had also sworn an earlier oath—a blood oath to her mother as she lay dying.

And in light of what they learned at the temple, she could not afford to be righteous. She must glean information any way she deemed necessary, and it just so happened that the members of this party possessed the knowledge she required. That blood oath took precedent over anything else—over everything else. Long ago, she had established her priorities, and she was as bound by them as a wrap of Khataran chain. Morals would have to wait for another day.

~

Gregor had asked for the scouting duty with Rhaven; tracking held more than a professional interest for him, and though anyone might be hard-pressed to match his skills inside a city's gates, the forests presented unknown territory. Rhaven could teach him much, and, as the day wore on, Gregor found him to be a patient instructor.

"What do you see here, bounty-man?" Rhaven knelt next to Gregor. Argus pawed the ground next to them.

They had arrived at a juncture in the trail where the road continued north, but another road led east toward the bandit territory of Mandar. Gregor studied the ground with care. Rhaven wouldn't have asked if there was nothing of import. "I see nothing. Perhaps I'm missing the obvious."

"What does that tell you?"

Gregor shook his head, embarrassment flushing his sallow face.

Rhaven's blue eyes seemed at ease as he stared at the bounty-man. "If you entered an alley in Sykor and saw no sign of rats wouldn't you suspect something wrong? This is a well-traveled road and yet there are no tracks, and, there's been no rain to wash them away."

Gregor smiled and nodded. His lanky frame seemed to nod with him. "Someone covered up the tracks. In the city I would have noticed."

Rhaven also smiled. "It's the same, Gregor. You have but to learn the differences and know what to look for. It takes many years to become an expert, but you can be better than most before the next reunion."

"Why are we going to Barclaen? Isn't that a little out of the way?"

"Barclaen is the last city before entering the forest, and we need supplies. Besides, I want to see if we can gather any information; I still believe we might be riding into a trap."

"I have no doubt." The bounty-man's grip on his staff firmed, long slim fingers wrapping it, clenching, then unclenching with each thought. "Three men dead that we know of, and no hint as to the whereabouts of the woman, even though we had good men looking for her."

Gregor turned to ensure that no one was close enough to hear. A deep voice prevented the softest of whispers, but his voice did not reach as low as Darstan's or Rhaven's. "I believe we face someone with extraordinary abilities."

Rhaven nodded. "It would stand to reason. Ever since I became involved with Rahg there have been strange happenings. His village being attacked could have been a coincidence, but that doesn't explain the Black Rose, nor this mystery woman who is so quick to kill. And don't forget, the Rose were followers of Lukaan."

Rhaven sighed. "Yes, Gregor, there is definitely something wrong, but I intend to see this through."

Gregor detected a curious note in Rhaven's voice. "You don't suspect Rahg?"

"Until I know the truth, I suspect everyone."

Twice more on the way to Barclaen, Rhaven asked Gregor to read the signs of the road. They saw nothing out of the ordinary, but it did help the bounty man to be able to study the tracks and learn from his mistakes. "Thank you for the help," Gregor said. He knew how much patience it took to teach someone. He had his own patience tested daily while trying to teach Rahg, Darstan, and Camissa how to use the staff.

"No thanks are necessary. It will help to have someone else who can read tracks. Tobias is good, better than most I've seen, so once you learn there will be three of us. I expect our talents will be tested."

"Rahg and Darstan have improved in all of their training, but they still have a lot to learn of the staff."

"They'll need it. They are already near the skill of archers, and before the winter comes again they'll be better than most soldiers with the sword. They have fought Victas, Wolfen and been involved with the guild of assassins. Not many can claim that experience."

They rode along silently for a while then Gregor interrupted the calm with a question. "I have heard bits and pieces of the battle you fought in Kamnor. Was it as bad as they say?"

"They shower me with credit, but we would have all been killed if not for Kella. Rahg and Darstan fought like soldiers that day. Fought-on even when their father had been killed. Never gave up when all seemed lost. That's the only reason I decided to help them. That, and the vargel. She seems to take to Rahg, and I have an itch to have her travel with me."

Rhaven brought Argus to a halt, dismounting. "Here, bounty man, tell me what you think of this. These tracks appear to have been covered recently."

Gregor got down to examine them and, after a short lesson, they were ready to go again. Argus neighed as Rhaven climbed on his back, then he reared up with a scream, an arrow catching him just below the neck. Another arrow hit Rhaven in the thigh, and he fell out of the saddle. A third one flew by his chest, a near miss. "Take cover!" he said before scurrying toward a lone tree for shelter. Camissa dismounted and ran to help him.

"They're in the woods," Tobias yelled, and he drew his sword and charged, tapping his horse on the flanks to get him moving. Gregor ran the short distance to where the attack had come from, dodging an arrow just as he found a tree to cover him.

Rahg and Darstan were close behind Tobias. Rahg had his sword drawn, and Darstan had an arrow nocked. When he reached the woods, he quickly dismounted and advanced toward the ambushers.

"Spread out," Tobias said, "There are only three of them."

Gregor moved toward the left flank, while Tobias and Rahg, now dismounted, advanced from the front. Darstan had taken the right flank, using large oaks and maples to shield him from fire. He crouched low, advancing with slow, steady moves.

Where is Wisp? he wondered, risking a glance behind him to see if he could spot the thief. A disturbance in the brush ahead froze him. He was caught in the open, a span or more from the nearest cover. Kor Trasken's lessons replayed in his memory as he drew back the bowstring with one fluid motion. Just poke your head up. All I need is one shot.

An arrow flew past, grazing his arm. Darstan dropped the bow, scrambling to pick it up and get an arrow nocked again. He heard the rush of someone charging through the bushes toward him and elected to draw his sword instead. Out of nowhere, Wisp popped up and drove a knife into the man's gut. He jammed it in hard, then pulled the blade out and stabbed him again, this time in the throat.

"You all right, Darstan?"

"I'm okay. Thanks." Darstan picked up his bow and nocked the arrow. He and Wisp made their way toward the other bandits, circling toward the rear.

~

An arrow just missed Rahg, and another came within an arm's length of hitting Tobias. "Now," Tobias whispered to Rahg, and he rushed into a small clearing that separated them from the ambushers.

Rahg was right behind Tobias. And Gregor, who must have seen them charge, was advancing from the left. There was a scramble in the woods and the two bandits ran, fleeing toward horses a short distance behind them. As they reached their mounts, Darstan and Wisp came out from behind the trees and attacked. Darstan took one down with an arrow to the chest, and Wisp hit one in the stomach with a thrown knife, then followed up with a slice to the neck.

Tobias stopped short, panting. "If you lads had told me you'd do all the hard work, I wouldn't have rushed in here. I'm getting' too old to be wastin' breath like this."

"Darstan, are you all right?"

Darstan held up his arm. "It's nothing, Rahg. Just a scratch."

"Check them for gold," the bounty man said.

"Gregor!" Camissa seemed appalled.

"He's right," Tobias said. "No sense in leavin' anything of value out here for some other bandit to get. Besides, we might get some clue as to what these fellas wanted. Take any coin you find and take their weapons. Horses, too. We'll sell them when we get to Barclaen. You can leave the bodies. I'm not goin' to waste my time burying bandits."

"This is better than stealing," Wisp said. "Maybe I'll take up killing bandits for an occupation."

Darstan laughed despite the gravity of the situation.

"Hurry up," Tobias said. "We need to get back to Rhaven."

~

*R*haven was busy tending to Argus when they returned, cleaning the wound and applying a bandage. "You'll be fine, big boy. I'll get this taken care of in Barclaen."

"Looks like we shoulda' kept that healer woman with us." Tobias said.

Rhaven turned, focusing on Darstan. "Get Camissa to clean that wound. Anyone else hurt?"

"Never got close enough," Tobias said. "Darstan and Kender took care of them."

"That was a fool thing to do, Tobias. Running off after them like that. You could have been killed."

Tobias shook his head. "Knew there were only three of them. They only fired three arrows at us, and I figured if there'd been more they all would have fired at once to get the most damage. Besides, it seems like they were after you. You're the only one they shot at."

"Any of them talk?" Rhaven asked.

"These lads killed 'em too quick. We did get their goods though and their mounts. Might tell us somethin'. I'd say for now, we better get to Barclaen. I'll feel safer in a nice inn."

Rhaven nodded. "I can't ride Argus. I'll take one of theirs."

"Help him up, lads."

Rhaven limped toward the horses. "I'll do fine by myself. Just get yourselves ready. I need to get Argus help."

~

*A*s soon as they arrived, Rhaven looked for a stable. There would be unguents and clean bandages and a place for Argus to rest.

"Rhaven, you need to get that leg looked at," Camissa said.

"Argus needs tending first. My leg can wait."

"Barclaen looks to be twice as big as Twin Forks," said Rahg, but it looks a lot different.

The trading city sat on the border between the Great Forest and Pomanda, and was the focal point for all activity from the Lorns. Mandar, the bandit territory was close by, and as always happens when gold is involved, stolen goods from there seemed to make their way into the markets of Barclaen. The streets were hard-packed dirt, like Kamnor. Rahg missed the clip-clop of the hooves that he had grown so accustomed to in Pomanda and Sykor. When he first arrived in Sykor, the sound kept him awake at night. Now it seemed strange to not hear them.

The main street housed the vendors' stands: fruit and vegetables; leather goods; khaffe and te from Khatara; and a variety of wood crafts from the Lorns, carved from emerald and blackthorn. A party of Lorns stood less than twenty paces away, negotiating with a vendor selling arrows. Most of the merchants had closed their stands for the day, though a few remained open. Curiosity drove Rahg in their direction. He had never seen a Lorn before.

The traders arranged arrows by type, each in its own compartment, feathers facing outward. He saw arrows made from ash and maple and others of cane reed—for speed—and of course there were the emeralds, the best arrows available other than blackthorns.

Blackthorns were only for the Lorns—*and Rhaven*, Rahg reminded himself. Some had pictures painted on the shaft, and others had carvings cut into the wood. They would be for decoration only; they would never fly true without a fine-turned shaft. He also noted that the prices varied depending on the type of feathers used. Rahg had been so intent on studying the arrows that he paid no attention to the Lorns, until he noticed them pointing toward Rhaven, who was just now returning.

There were three Lorns: two younger ones about Rahg's age, and an older man about the age Magmar would have been. His first reaction was shock at the size of them. None of the three were any taller than his shoulders. Sharp angles shaped their faces, and the older one's nose resembled the tip of one of his arrows. Rahg noted the serious expression on the older Lorn's face as he walked toward Rhaven. He wandered over to hear the conversation.

The Lorn stared suspiciously at Rhaven's quiver of blackthorn arrows, then at him. The worried expression left the Lorn's face as he spoke.

"I am called Rhiva Tenarma." The Lorn bowed to Rhaven, then offered a strange greeting. "May the light of the sun always touch you, Rhaven Teldren. You are ever well come to home."

Rhaven bowed and steepled his hands. "We have met before, Rhiva, at Skyebridge many years past."

Rhiva bowed lower. "You are kind to remember. I did not expect you to recall one so low as myself. May I ask your honor in greeting my sons? We have lived in Barclaen for more than a few years now, and they have listened to the tales of Rhaven. Fortune might smile upon them if they see you."

A smile came to Rhaven's face, a rare occurrence, especially of late. "Please, bring them."

Rhiva had to chide his sons to keep them from running, but pride was evident on his beaming face as he made the introductions. "This is Rheen," he said, pointing out the tallest, "And this is Rhenka. They will become traders like myself. Rheen has been quick to learn the art of negotiating, though I would not yet send him to Khatara, and Rhenka has an eye for value; together, they will make a good pair."

Rahg watched as they bowed low to Rhaven. They could hardly keep their eyes off him. It reminded him of when he first saw Sykor. "You are well come to home, Rhaven Teldren. You honor us with your presence."

Rahg almost fell over. Rhiva had called him Rhaven Teldren, too. Now his sons did. Is Teldren Rhaven's last name? But how could that be? He said Damon Pirrhar was his brother?

He continued to listen as the two Lorn boys peppered Rhaven with questions. "We heard you fought a great battle with the Victas in Kamnor; is it true? And they say you captured a vargel and it travels with you; where is it?"

Rhaven smiled. "The battle at Twin Forks was bloody, but it was the vargel who won the day." Rhaven stopped and looked to Rahg, now joined by Darstan and Wisp. He pointed to Rahg and Darstan. "Those two lads fought with me in that battle, side by side. They are brave soldiers despite their young age. You should speak to them and learn more, for I now have things to do. Perhaps some day we shall meet in Skyethorn."

The Lorns now stared at Rahg and Darstan as if they were legends in their own right. They bowed, and bid fare well to Rhaven in the traditional Lorn fashion. "May the light of the sun always touch you. You are ever well come to home."

~

*R*haven and Gregor went to replenish supplies while the others stayed to talk with the Lorns. Camissa sat on the ground by the stand of arrows. Dirt soiled her britches but she seemed not to mind; she enjoyed the brief respite. Rhaven had set a grueling pace, one she was not accustomed to as yet, but she was not about to be the slow camel in the caravan. They had all harbored doubts about her when they left Sykor. She would give them no cause to complain, especially not now, when it was so important that she learn the truth. Camissa closed her eyes to rest for a moment and dreamed of her long-dead mother.

Soon, too soon for Camissa's likes, Tobias arrived and led them to a tavern that Rhaven had selected for supper. The Music Box it was called, taking its name from the lively entertainment provided most nights by an assortment of local minstrels and traveling bards. Rhiva secured a table near the stage where the minstrel would perform.

~

*R*ahg brimmed with excitement as he recalled the few times in Kamnor when a bard had come to town and settled at Havril's Inn for the night. It was enough of an occasion to bring most of the villagers out for the eve, though it only happened once in a great while, not like here where someone took the stage often.

Rahg remembered the bard in Sykor—Baldomere Testa. The name had a wonderful ring to it, and though it was strange, it fit the odd man like a glove. Rahg wished he could have gone to the other performance that Baldomere had told him about, the one where he was going to tell of creatures, other worlds, demons, and more. *I hope the performer tonight is as good*, thought Rahg, though he felt certain that he wouldn't be. Few would be as good as Baldomere Testa, and it made the urge to see him even stronger.

As Rahg had feared, the minstrel had little to offer beyond a few common songs and tales as bland as the food they ordered for supper. It had turned into a disappointing evening. Even Wisp and Darstan, who tended to stay until the taverns closed, elected to go to bed early.

~

*C*amissa caught Rhaven by the arm as he rose to leave the table. "A moment to talk?" Camissa pretended to stay and finish a mug of ale and Rhaven volunteered to sit with her. When the others were out of earshot, Camissa began. "How long have you known Rahg? Do you know where he came from?"

Rhaven never twitched. "Why are you asking?"

"I need to know. Something is wrong for someone so young and innocent to be drawing so much trouble."

"They were after me today, not Rahg."

"Today, yes. But what about the rest? What about the Black Rose? What about this mysterious letter? There is too much surrounding him to be coincidence."

"Then use those powers of yours wisely. Perhaps you will learn something of significance."

Camissa looked to see if Rhaven was being sarcastic, but she saw only sincerity in his eyes. For a moment she started to probe with her mind, then hesitated. She fought the feeling but decided that she had to know. With that conviction, her mind reached out and entered Rhaven's head.

Pain. Agony. The feelings hammered into Camissa's mind like a smith pounding metal. She fought to release her grip on Rhaven, but the dark emotions flooded through the gates she had opened like a raging river through a broken dam. Fire. Flesh burning, searing. Charred bones.

The bile in her stomach rose, and she struggled to remain calm. Suddenly, the image of a sweet woman holding a child in her arms and singing. The wonderful smell of lilacs. The refreshing touch of a gentle breeze.

She knew she was smiling. Her heart was all joy. Camissa concentrated. She could see the doorway closing, and then, with a violent crash it blew open again. Blood. Angry red blood. Bodies ripped apart. Torsos clawed open with entrails spilled onto blood-soaked ground. Then the pain came again. Horrible pain that she could not bear. She felt her body burning and thought her mind would explode.

She screamed. Again, she screamed, and again. Rhaven slapped her face, then harder.

The owner of the tavern ran to the table, while customers looked on from a distance. "What are you doing?" He shouted at Rhaven, while grabbing his arm. "I can't be having this in my tavern."

"Stay out of my business, innkeep." Rhaven's eyes burned. "Out of respect for Rhiva, I will spare your life, but if you interfere again, Rhiva's reputation will have to suffer."

Silence marked the innkeep as he went back to his post.

"You'll be all right," Rhaven said. "Just take a moment to breathe."

Camissa knew her hair must have been thrashed about wildly. Two of her fingernails were broken and several had blood under the nails from the scratches.

She rubbed her face where Rhaven had slapped her. "That hurt," she said, then broke into tears. "I'm sorry. I'm so sorry." Over and over she repeated the phrase until Rhaven calmed her down. They sat and talked for a long time, but not about Rhaven and not about her. Soon they both went to bed.

"It is almost dawn," she thought she heard him say as they climbed the stairs. "We must leave soon, so try to get some sleep."

Sleep? I can sleep. But how can you? How can you possibly sleep with that in your mind?

~

*I*n a small room, at the Temple in Pomanda, a novice waited while Shera Darian finished writing the second of two identical documents. He rolled the parchment then placed his seal upon the joint. A gold ribbon tied in the center would further identify him to the recipient. The young priest had been standing beside him watching for the better part of the morning. "Bring two messenger birds for the temple in the north. Shera Kevon must receive these at once."

messenger bird

"Two?" The novice knew the shera was tired; he meant no disrespect.

With less impatience than the novice expected, the shera responded. "Yes, send one bird now, and one soon after but from a different location. This must get to Shera Kevon. I can afford no chance of accident or error. As instructed, we will dispatch two birds. One, we will release from here; the other will be taken to the other side of the city and then let go. If anyone is watching, at least one should arrive." The shera seemed relieved, as if being released from a heavy burden.

The curiosity of the novice prevailed. "What is so important, Shera?"

A grave appearance took over his face. "Shera Kevon must be warned. These must arrive."

"But, why?"

Shera Darian placed his hand on the young man's shoulder. His voice sounded tired, and he stared at nothing. "Because, my son, the Prophecy has begun!"

The young priest dropped the scrolls. "I...I did not know it was real.

The Prophecy, I mean." He looked up into Shera Darian's eyes, searching for a denial. The novice desperately wished for him to say it was not true, that the world would not be taken over by the Evil One.

"I am afraid it is true, my son. And, I am afraid!" He paused, staring blankly, then began walking, his arm draped over the novice's shoulder. "Come, we will send the birds. That, at least, is something."

THE PROPHECY BEGINS

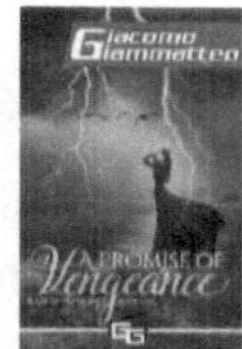

For five days they traveled through the forest. On the second day Kella rejoined them. Rahg still worried about her when she left but he now felt comfortable she would find them.

Rhaven had them practicing with weapons: Gregor teaching the staff; Tobias the sword; and Wisp instructing them in the handling of knives. When Rahg and Darstan weren't training with the sword or staff they helped Camissa learn the bow. She wasn't strong enough to be effective with the sword. Knives were good but that still involved close fighting. Rhaven insisted she learn to use a bow. Gregor suggested she learn the staff also.

Perspiration covered Rahg's brow, and the heat brought his mind back to the trip. The first two days had been fairly cool but today was hot. The forest provided some cover from the sun but it made the air sticky. Worst of all, there was no breeze. Not a leaf moved, and the rancid smell of decay rose from the forest floor.

A bead of sweat rolled into the corner of Rahg's eye, the salt stinging. He wiped it dry, then looked ahead to Rhaven sitting tall astride Argus with his black cloak hanging limply in the dead calm of the air. He never seemed to be cold, or hot, or tired.

"How long till we get there?"

"Soon, Rahg."

~

Shera Kevon scooped grain from the pail and threw it onto the dirt floor of the enclosed pen, smiling as the fowl scurried over to peck at their daily nourishment. Across the yard, pigs squealed, demanding food. From the corner of his eye he saw a young monk running in his direction. The shera assumed there was trouble when he saw the monk coming, but he never lost count of the scoops he had already used.

The monk ran until he stood in front of the shera. Out of breath and panting, he was anxious about relating his story. Shera Kevon's outstretched hand signaled that he wait and, with the obedience he was trained to observe, the monk bided the time. "Six, seven, eight," Kevon counted, "there, it is done. What is it, Fharlo? Excitement seems to have a hold on you."

"They are coming! It must be them."

Shera Kevon extended his hand to calm Fharlo. "Who is coming?"

"The ones Shera Darian warned us of. The ones from Pomanda."

A hint of surprise touched Shera Kevon's tone. "So soon? I would have expected it to take several more days." The shera stared into the forest south of them. He could see them now. "Come, Fharlo. We must prepare to greet them."

~

*R*haven led the party, riding cautiously onto the grounds of the temple. It appeared as any farm might, with a clean, plain-looking house surrounded by several animal pens and some storage bins for crops. The open field they crossed showed signs of being well tended.

As they approached the main building, a man exited the doorway. He wore a plain brown robe, dirty and worn at the bottom.

"My name is Shera Kevon. I am the keeper of this temple and tender of these farms." The shera bowed low. "You are welcome to our place of worship."

Rahg was confused. If he had heard correctly, this was the shera that Darian had spoken of, the old priest who would translate their letter, but he appeared much younger than Darian.

"You are Shera Kevon?" Rhaven's cold, dangerous eyes drilled into the priest.

"I am Kevon, though from your doubtful tone you must have been told to expect an older man." The priest held Rhaven's glare. "I have not been seen in Pomanda for more than twenty years. Perhaps I appear younger than I am."

Rhaven looked toward Camissa. The shera's eyes widened as she stared at him. Camissa moved her horse next to Argus, then nodded.

"Perhaps you should tell me the truth, holy man." Rhaven's gaze had become a glare.

For a long time Kevon held steady, then he smiled and responded. "Perhaps I should. Come inside." He made a gesture with his hand indicating friendship, then turned to enter the place of worship.

Rhaven signaled the rest of the party to dismount, just as Fharlo arrived offering to stable their horses. The house had a tiny chapel for prayers, and several rooms used for storage. There was a kitchen area and two rooms used for resting and reading and a large common room. Camissa edged close to Rhaven.

"They are afraid. I can sense fear in them all, except the shera."

"I can see it in their eyes," Rhaven said, "yet they try not to show it."

Shera Kevon clapped his hands together, bringing all the members of the temple to attention. "I wish everyone to leave us alone. Inform all the brothers." Immediately, the other monks rose and followed orders.

Like Sykoran soldiers, Rahg thought.

When they departed Kevon locked the door. "Let me see the letter," he said. Everyone but Rhaven seemed shocked. "Messenger birds." Kevon explained without being asked to.

"Not until we have some explanations from you."

"I do not have the time to banter. You have a letter in your possession given to you by a stranger. A woman, I believe." Shera Kevon let his stony gaze sweep the lot of them. "And that letter names one of you as the Messenger."

Everyone's eyes went to Rahg. "I am Rahgnar Fal-Thera. Nothing else."

Rhaven looked at Kevon. "You haven't seen the letter yet. Besides, Darian called him by a different name, the—"

"Shera Darian told me. He called you the Fate Sealer, though the names of the Messenger and Fate Sealer are thought by some to be interchangeable, even though they are not."

"I thought he couldn't translate the letter," Camissa said.

Shera Kevon's expression never changed. "Darian knew everything the letter said. What he did not know were the prophecies, and what role they played. That is why he sent you to me. I have studied the prophecies for a long time—a very long time."

Camissa's brow wrinkled, as if she detected something wrong with what the shera said.

"If you will surrender the letter, I might be able to help."

Rahg trembled.

Tobias handed the letter to Kevon, who immediately began reading. Kevon pored over every word, sometimes going back over a line two or three times. "Rahg Fal-Thera Ihra Renegalla." Kevon read it aloud. After a moment his gaze focused on Rahg. "I am sorry. This letter as much as names you the Messenger."

"What does it mean?" Rahg asked.

"According to most, the Fate Sealer is prophesied to kill the Messenger. The Messenger is prophesied to set the Evil One free."

"And you say that I'm the Messenger!"

Kevon lay his hands on Rahg's shoulder. "*I* am not saying anything. Whoever wrote this letter is the one naming you."

Rahg did not seem appeased. "But how can you think it's me? What proof is there other than this mystery woman naming me in a letter?"

"If it is who I think, be thankful it is only a letter."

"Who do you think it is?" Wisp asked.

Rhaven glared at the priest. "Answer him."

"The author of that letter was one of the immortal ones. And the seal tells me which one—Aentarra."

Silence filled the room like a thick fog. No one spoke; few even breathed after an initial gasp.

"I see you are familiar with the name. It is not one to utter lightly. I have only spoken it myself accompanied by an occasional curse."

"Why does Aentarra—Who—"

Shera Kevon held up his hands to stop them. "In due time I will answer all the questions. In due time."

"It's not me," Rahg said. "I know it."

"There is a way we can test the prophecy. It is not foolproof, but it will lend credence to the theory, or it might confuse the issue even more."

Rahg stared at him. "Let's get this over with."

Rahg's heart raced as Kevon led them down a long set of winding stairs. They came to an old bronze door with rust on the hinges. Spider webs hung near the top, and dust covered the panels in layers. Kevon reached inside his robe and extracted a necklace with a key attached to the end. The rusty metal creaked when he turned the key. It screeched its resistance, grinding metal against rusty metal. The stench of stale, musty air greeted them. Beyond was nothing but darkness.

"Follow me," Kevon said.

The room grew brighter with the lighting of a second candle. Shera Kevon lit a third, then a fourth until the darkness disappeared. The room had no windows; no doors other than the one they had entered; in fact, with the exception of the candles the shera had lit, the only thing in the room was a structure of stone the size of a burial vault.

A sword lay inside. The blade appeared to be plain steel. The hilt, wrapped in old leather, was worn and dirty. Rust had claimed the edges of the blade, in some places digging deeper than the nicks in the steel. All in all, it looked like a blade a good swordsman would cast aside at the first opportunity. Rahg recalled how many steps they had descended—thirty eight—and he remembered the locked door. Now they were in this large, empty room. Logic told him that there was more to this than what there appeared.

Kevon laid the sword on the floor and reached inside his robe to extract another key. He inserted the key into a lock inside the vault and twisted. There were no rusty squeaks to greet them this time, no sound of old metal. The shera repeated the procedure at the bottom of the vault. A table rose—and on it lay a sword.

The blade seemed dull, not unlike the other, but there the resemblance ended. The tail of a creature wrapped around the hilt and spiraled toward the guard, its scales serving as grips. Wings spread out to form the guard of the sword, the boned sections serving as a sword-catcher on either side. The body of the creature ran straight through the guard. It was there that the head opened onto the blade displaying a magnificent maw of teeth. Flames shot from the creature's mouth and were etched on a blade that held a slight curve.

"A dragon!" Rahg said.

Shera Kevon handed him the sword. "Take it, Rahg."

Rahg looked at the sword then, with trepidation, reached out to grasp the handle. His hands shook as they closed on the hilt. He rolled it over in his hand several times admiring the detailed work.

Shera Kevon appeared surprised. "Perhaps Darstan would care to see it."

Darstan reacted much the same as Rahg had, though he was a bit more bold. He swished the blade through the air once or twice to gain a feel for the balance. Gregor also laid hand to it, but simply inspected the workmanship. Rhaven was standing next to Gregor. Always interested in weaponry, and never shy, he firmly gripped the hilt.

The sword glowed, lighting up the room. Everyone stepped back. Kevon smiled.

"What happened?" Darstan asked.

Rhaven set the sword down. "An explanation seems in order, holy man. I believe it is time you told us your story."

Shera Kevon stared at Rhaven, then at Rahg. "I believe it *is* time," he said. "I have waited a thousand long winters to tell this story."

THE SWORD OF MIKKELLANA

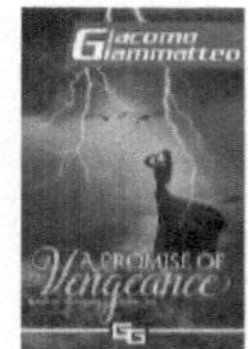

Rahg stared at the shera. "A thousand winters! How old are you?"

"Some people live longer than others. I was around when Lyssic was king of Sykor. That's when I first met Mikkellana. She's the one who gave me the sword."

"That's impossible," Rahg said.

Kevon looked at Rhaven. "I have tested this sword with many people. It wasn't until you touched it that it responded. The sword was made for you."

"I don't need another sword."

"You will have to make room. It is your destiny to wield this one."

"I don't know Mikkellana."

"The sword fits your hand, my friend. Somewhere, you met her." The shera paused for thought. "The first time she came to me was after the battle a thousand years ago. The second time she came as an old healer woman. It was—"

He stopped when he noticed the change in Rhaven's expression. "So, it was in that form she came. Did she heal you?" Kevon smiled. "Mikkellana would not allow you to die without getting the sword. Not if she could help it."

Tobias turned to Camissa. "You were in the room with that healer woman. Did you see anything?"

For a long time Camissa remained still, staring at the shera.

"You can tell them, my girl. If Mikkellana made herself known to you she would not hold it against you."

Camissa lifted her head to face Rhaven. "She used powers to heal you. It was unlike anything I have seen."

Rahg shook. If Mikkellana was the healer, she was the one who took his oath. *Gods blood, what have I done?* He folded his hands under his arms and wrapped them around his chest. Now there was another immortal involved and, as much as he wanted the truth, he was afraid of it also. "What can you tell me, Shera?"

"I don't much believe in prophecies, though when dealing with Aentarra and Mikkellana it is wise to be cautious." The shera read from a scroll. "His coming will awaken the vile and ancient evil. Peace shall be shattered. Countries shall fall, and the good shall be subjugated to evil."

"What is that supposed to mean? It doesn't say anything about me or this Fate Sealer."

"If Aentarra sent this to you, and it seems as if she did, then she knows something."

"That's not good enough for me," Rahg said.

The shera sighed. "There is a way to find out more."

"I thought you were the one who knows the most."

Kevon's expression turned grim. "There are other lands. Have you never heard of Entiria? Or Arangar?"

"Arangar! Do you expect me to believe that Arangar is real?"

"Yes, I do expect you to believe in Arangar. And you will believe in, and even swear by, much else before your journeys are completed." He stared with cold eyes at Rahg. "Seek out the Entirians. They will tell you more about the Prophecy. If they don't know, they can help you find Arangar."

The shera paused and looked around the room. He seemed concerned about something.

"So how do I get to Entiria?"

"I'm sure your friends can help you," Kevon said. He pulled a parchment from a drawer and handed it to Rhaven. "This is an ancient map. It shows where Entiria is, but you will need someone brave to lead you there." He laid a hand on Rahg's shoulder. "Go with God, my son. And may your journeys be safe."

"What do you know about this sword?" Rhaven asked.

He shook his head. "I am certain you will discover its powers when needed. Now I must hurry. There is much for me to do."

~

*A*s Rahg mounted Marchall he swore on every oath he knew that he was not going anywhere near Entiria. *We'll all die before we get there.*

Tobias rode next to Rahg. "Been thinkin' about who might take us, lad, and the only name that comes to mind is Malakai."

Rahg turned quickly. "The pirate? I thought he was dead."

Tobias laughed. "Aye, the pirate, lad. Malakai the pirate. And I'd not believe him dead unless I bled him myself."

Rahg shook his head, muttering. "Arangar, Entiria, pirates, the Sea of the Lost. What's next?"

~

*S*hera Kevon hurried back to the dining hall, leaving instructions not to be disturbed. He paused before entering, closed his eyes and concentrated. A glow surrounded him, an aura protecting his body. He entered with extreme caution, closed the door and the shutters, then threw a ball of light into each corner. He stretched his senses, seeking, probing. Finally he let go of the shield. "I suppose I am getting jittery in my old age."

A disturbance in the air caught his attention, a vaporous mass taking form in less than a heartbeat.

Aentarra wore a smirk as she became visible. "Were you searching for me?"

A fist seemed to clutch Kevon's heart. His throat tightened and his mind raced. Instinct formed a shield while his hands called the fire. By the time he recognized her, he knew he had erred—grievously erred. "Aentarra!"

The fire sped toward her. She caught it in her bare hands, spun it, played with it, then wove a shield and snuffed it out. Kevon's head sunk. He used all his concentration to maintain his shield.

"You must be a stray," she said.

Kevon did not respond.

"I should have come fully Cloaked, but I did not suspect anyone would be capable of detecting me."

A shiver crawled along Kevon's spine.

"I heard you speak of Arangar and Entiria. What do you know of them?"

Shera Kevon mustered what courage he could. "What interest do you have in the boy?"

Aentarra's smirk altered to a sneer. "More than you might guess."

Boldness crept into Kevon's heart. "I'll tell you nothing. Not about the sword, the boy, or Arangar."

Her brown eyes burned. She withdrew a long, crystalline object from a pouch on her belt. It stretched the length of her hand and was thin as a strand of hair.

"This is a Slicer."

It hurtled through the air straight at Kevon, breaching his defenses without even slowing. He screamed as it slammed through his eye and into his head. Blood ran down his face. The pain was unbearable.

"I could have made that painless. With a numbing instruction on the front end and a healing agent on the tail, no one would even know it was there."

Aentarra walked around Kevon, taunting him with her near nakedness. Even with his pain, he couldn't help but to stare. Couldn't help but to lust for her. Never had he seen such perfection on a woman. He tried to hide his embarrassment and his shame, but all he could do was follow her lithe movements and chastise himself.

"I will tell you nothing," he managed to say without stammering.

Aentarra came close to Kevon. "Why didn't you tell the boy the whole of it?" Kevon stared at her, rage in his expression. "The prophecy, I mean. Why did you only tell him half of it? He has a right to know. Or did you want him kept ignorant so he would not be afraid?" She laughed. "I can hardly blame you. Perhaps he needs to discover it on his own."

"You might as well get your madness over with. If you plan to kill me, do it. The Gods will be merciful."

"Gods, indeed. I am afraid, my good shera, that I am all that is left of the gods. Or soon will be." Aentarra closed her eyes and issued a directive to the Slicer. Soon the shera told her all he knew.

THE LORNS

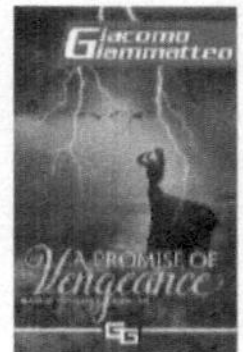

Rahg's head pounded, thoughts racing to Arangar and Entiria, places he thought were only legends a few days ago. He had hoped for comforting answers from Shera Kevon; instead, Kevon told Rahg he would be the one to set Lukaan free. He wiped sweat from his brow. The searing sun had turned the forest into a steaming cauldron.

"Dismount," Rhaven said. "We're entering the Blackthorn Forest, so you better pay attention. The Lorns are a peaceful people, but they have laws that govern these forests. Harm no tree or animal. The Lorns cherish life, but they will not hesitate to take yours if you break these laws."

blackthorns

Rhaven pointed to one of the many huge trees that loomed just ahead. "The sap of the blackthorn is a deadly poison. If you so much as scratch yourself...." He looked straight at Darstan and Rahg. "Remember the assassin in Sykor? That was a blackthorn dart." Rhaven took hold of Argus's reins and led him into the forest. "Follow me. We can't risk being scratched by a thorn."

Dampness greeted them as they left the last of the sunlight behind. It felt good to be away from the heat, and his skin tingled with a slight chill.

"Keep tight hold of your reins," Rhaven reminded them, though he didn't need to tell Rahg. The memory of that assassin convulsing on the cobblestone street was all the reminder he needed.

fallen blackthorn

Rhaven called for a rest at the first clearing, where a large blackthorn had fallen—a giant from long ago. Rhaven walked toward one of the trees with a pouch in his hand. He pulled a knife and cut into the bark just below a large thorn, drawing a thick syrupy substance that oozed from the tree into a container. Next, he mixed a white powder into the mixture. "I coat my darts with poison. This powder keeps it potent for a long time. Two years, maybe more."

He placed the container next to him, then pulled out a handful of darts. Using a small, thin brush he applied the mixture to the darts, working his way to the point but stopping short.

"Why not coat the top?" Darstan asked.

"There is no antidote for the blackthorn, and I have no wish to risk nicking my finger. If I want someone dead, the dart will penetrate enough to allow it to work. All it needs to do is touch the blood." Rhaven finished, put the darts away, then walked toward Argus. "Time to go," he said. "Skyethorn's not far now."

When they reached Skyethorn, Rahg could not help but gawk. A moment ago they were in an endless forest of giant trees, now they were in a city built into the forest—carved from the forest. Houses linked together and bridged the gaps between trunks that stood twenty feet wide in some places. Even the smaller trees were three to six feet wide. Some shops were carved right into trees, or between clusters of them. Children dangled and swung from ropes attached to branches high in the air. Some of them ran along walkways built high in the trees, treading the planks as if on solid ground.

tall trees

Children rushed to greet Rhaven and Argus. Some pretended to wield swords; others, knives. Rhaven tossed the little ones about with care or lightly knocked them down. Even Argus appeared to enjoy it, rearing in the air and neighing as if in a battle.

A young girl ran toward them waving her hands. She was short, her head barely reaching Rahg's chin. A colorful ribbon tied her long blonde hair at the back—like a horse's tail—and it bounced on her back like a fat man's laugh.

"Rhaven," she shouted, then jumped in his arms and hugged him.

Rhaven spun her around then gently set her down. "Rhiana, you've grown."

"You have been gone too long. I'm surprised you even remember me. Now introduce me to your friends."

The girl broke from the friendly embrace then turned toward them and bowed. Her soft musical voice proved inviting. "I am Rhiana Teldren, daughter to Rhalan and sister to Rhunar. You are well come to the city of Skyethorn."

Teldren! The Lorns in Barclaen had called Rhaven by that name.

"Rhiana, we need to see your father."

She led them to the center of the city, Rahg admiring her muscular build as he followed.

Camissa nudged him. "Better watch the trail, Rahgnar."

When they reached the meeting hall, Rhalan embraced Rhaven. "It has been a long time, my friend. We were not expecting you."

Rhaven grabbed Rahg by the shoulder and pulled him forward. "We have come from an old shera who claims this lad has something to do with the prophecies."

Rhalan looked at Rahg and smiled. "There are many prophecies."

"He called him the Fate Sealer."

"Perhaps we should go inside," Rhalan said.

For the next hour or so, Rhalan asked Rahg questions about his parents, where he was raised, what he dreamt about. Nothing that seemed important, but Rhalan weighed each response as if his life depended on it.

Rahg felt nervous. It made him feel as if he had done something wrong. He reached to pet Kella, lying on the floor beside him. She always made him feel more comfortable. "What do the Lorns know of the prophecy?"

Rhalan stared at Rahg, then reached to the center of the table. He grabbed a parchment, unrolled it, then read from it, his voice as solemn as an oath.

> "From darkness, from light, where day can be night,
> Comes a warrior, a savior, one who will fight.
> One hand wields a sword, BlackFire the other.
> A man alone, without friend, none to call brother.
> To the sun-sated lands, to the city of sin,
> Where an ancient evil is trapped within.
> An evil foretold that man will set free.
> A man come to these lands from across the sea."

"Why didn't the shera know about this prophecy? I thought he was the expert."

"These prophecies are old," Rhalan said. "From long before my people settled here. Perhaps from the time of the old lands. Some of the prophecies we have shared with no one."

Confusion fought with worry to get hold of Rahg. "Came from where?"

"From Arangar."

The name struck Rahg like a thunderbolt. *Arangar.*

"Fabled Arangar," Rhalan said. "Home to all the peoples except the Sethians and the immortals, though who can say where they came from."

Rhalan looked at Rahg with sorrow in his eyes. "So you see, Rahg, when the prophecy speaks of him coming 'from across the sea', it could be that the prophecy was written in Arangar, in which case you would be 'across the sea.'"

"What am I supposed to do?"

"You must do as the shera suggested. Go to Entiria. They are the guardians of the prophecy."

Rahg stood, fire shining in his deep-brown eyes. He had heard enough of prophecies, the Messenger, and people telling him what he should do. He stormed out of the meeting room.

~

*R*halan rose to go after him, but Rhaven grabbed his arm. "You have badgered the boy enough. If he's guilty of anything, he has fooled me. Tell me what can be done and what you know."

The old Lorn stared at Rhaven with a fondness normally reserved for a father. "You have softened your heart for him. It is something I had not expected to see in you, Rhaven Teldren. It stirs my pride to see you care, once again."

Rhaven met Rhalan's gaze. "Don't mistake my feelings. I'll protect the boy because I believe him innocent. But if I suspect him of any complicity I won't hesitate to kill him."

"The winters have trod harshly upon you, my great friend, but I know you better than you think. I, too, believe in the boy. He is fortunate to have you as a protector."

"What can we do?"

"I can only offer advice, and it is a journey fraught with perils. You must cross the Sea of the Lost to Entiria. The prophecies are complex and uncertain. The Entirians will know the truth."

Rhaven nodded. *The Sea of the Lost. No one had been there and returned.*

~

*R*ahg wore a dour expression when he exited the meeting hall, though the sight of Rhiana brought light to his eyes.

"Would you care to walk?" Her voice was teasingly sweet.

He still burned from the meeting with Rhalan. He stared blankly at Rhiana, then said, "Yes, I'd like that, but I have no desire to be poked by one of those thorns. I've seen what they can do."

Rhiana laughed. "These thorns won't hurt you, well, not beyond a little stick. It's the blackthorns you need to watch out for, but they stopped before the last clearing you passed, by that little creek."

bridge and river

"But these look like the blackthorns," Rahg said.

"They look like them, and they *are* them, but not the ones that have the poison. We wouldn't live and play where poison thorns are."

Rahg shook his head. "I'm glad to hear that. I was beginning to think you were all as crazy as Rhaven."

Rhiana laughed again. "Nobody is *that* crazy. Come with me and I'll teach you some of our ways," she said, and led him toward a narrow path.

"How do you know Rhaven?" Rahg asked. "And why is he called Teldren, that's your name isn't it?"

"As to the name of Teldren, he got it long ago from my father, but Rhaven's past with the Lorns is his to tell. I will not break that trust."

They walked a ways, and, as they neared the creek where the real blackthorns grew, Rahg stayed close to Rhiana, his curiosity dragging his eyes from one sight to another, but always returning to the giant trees with their poisonous thorns.

Rhiana must have sensed his curiosity. "The legends say that when the gods looked at the trees they created, they were so impressed they put the thorns there to protect them. If you notice, Rahg, the thorns go up less than half a span, after that the bark is clean."

Rhiana led him along a twisting path. "There is Rhunar's Dagger," she said, pointing to a young tree almost one span high.

It was a blackthorn, but no thorns had formed as yet. "How old is that one?"

Rhiana's giggle made Rahg smile. "As old as Rhunar, of course. When a Lorn child is born, a tree is planted in their honor. In this fashion, a person's memory is kept alive for hundreds, or thousands of years. If it is a notable person, or one of high rank, that tree is granted a second name, such as Rhunar's Dagger. Others are simply called by the name of the person."

"What about the thorns?" Rahg asked.

"The trees don't get their thorns for about thirty years, so before then, they are safe to touch."

"Where is yours?" Rahg asked, then he saw her blush. "What's wrong, Rhiana?"

She blushed even more. "A man does not ask a woman the location of her tree. That is reserved for a special occasion. I forget that you are not familiar with our customs."

They walked along the path quietly, Rahg enjoying the relaxation and the company. She pointed out trees of people he met in Skyethorn. As they came to another bend in the path, he saw several Lorns hacking away at a young, healthy tree. "What are they doing?"

Rhiana frowned. "That was Rhol's tree. He broke an oath. His tree will be cut down and his honor will be lost."

Rahg shivered at the mention of oath-breaking. Ever since that healer-woman in Pomanda, the one he now knew to be Mikkellana, he felt uneasy discussing oaths and, in particular, the punishment that breaking them might bring. Nonetheless, he forced himself to ask the question, dreading the result. "What will become of him?"

"Rhol will leave Skyethorn. He will settle in another Lorn city until they discover that his tree was cut. He will go out among the outlanders, but he will have no honor. His family will never wish him an honorary fare well, and he will never be buried on sacred ground." Rhiana took Rahg's hand. "Come this way. I'll show you some more Naming Trees."

straight blackthron

Rhiana showed him Rhalan's tree; it was so straight it looked unreal. "Rhalan's Plight, it is called."

An odd name, thought Rahg.

Soon, Rhiana stopped and pointed ahead. Rahg stared at the tree. From what Rahg had learned, he judged the tree to be about thirty-five or forty years old. The tree rose straight up for a while, perhaps a span, then it split in two and continued to rise. "That is 'Rhaven's Blade.' It is the only tree named after an outlander."

Rahg smiled. It came as no surprise that Rhaven proved to be the only exception to a tradition. "It seems strange to see a tree split like that."

The glow on Rhiana's face dimmed. "Legends say that when a Naming Tree grows like that it means the person's life has yet to be decided. The gods have not decreed what his fate will be." A frown covered her face, but only for an instant. "Come, Rahg." She grabbed his hand and walked briskly along a well-worn path.

They came to a spot where sunlight pierced the canopy, spreading its warmth across large ferns and young blackthorns fighting for height. Nearby, a meandering brook trickled over its rocky bottom. Next to a small stone bridge, stood a young blackthorn with bright green leaves. Rahg gently rubbed them. It was the place they had passed earlier, but now they were on the other side of the creek.

Site of Rhiana's Song

He was about to ask a question, when Rhiana pulled him under the lowest of the limbs. Using a rock to stand on, she reached up and kissed him. "This tree is 'Rhiana's Song,'" she said. "And this is the tradition I told you about." She stretched to kiss him again. Rahg pulled her to him and returned the kiss.

～

"Just follow me," Tobias said, "we'll be drinkin' the best ale you ever tasted and eatin' the best food, too."

Darstan and Wisp trailed along. "I'm hungry enough

that anything will taste good," Darstan said. "Gregor, are you coming?" he hollered over his shoulder.

The bounty man had worn a scowl on his face since leaving the temple. He had cracked his staff testing it against Rhaven's new sword. "I must find some wood to make a new staff."

Camissa scoffed. "With all of our troubles, you worry over a staff." She stormed past Darstan and Wisp, then joined Tobias at the lead.

Camissa had not mentioned what was bothering her, but Darstan felt certain it had something to do with Rhiana; in fact, he felt it had *every-thing* to do with Rhiana, remembering one of Tobias's old sayings.

'Put two women together in a room and they'll become best friends, but throw a man in there with 'em and they'll turn into she-cats.'

Darstan laughed at the prospect of seeing Rahg and Camissa, once they got together again. *If Rahg thinks he has a lot to worry about now, wait till Camissa gets hold of him.*

The ale proved to be as good as Tobias promised. Gregor complained about his staff, and all Wisp talked about was how great it would be to have an entire band of Lorns trained as thieves. "They climb like spiders and are small enough to squeeze through the smaller windows," he said. Darstan couldn't stop laughing at the thought of Wisp leading a band of Lorns through the streets of Sykor. Camissa didn't see the humor in it, but she hadn't seen humor in anything since they arrived in Skyethorn—more specifically, since Rahg met Rhiana.

As evening turned to night, Rhaven came into the inn. "We'll be leaving in the morning, so rest well. Darstan, you and Wisp see to the supplies. Camissa, follow me." Rhaven and Camissa started for the door, then he turned and looked at Wisp. "Kender Darnell, these people are my friends. Don't think to ply your trade here."

The smile disappeared from Wisp's face as he stood. He got face-to-face with Rhaven. "You should take more time to learn who you travel with. Have I once broken my word? Haven't I fought with you, and for

you? Haven't I stayed when I could have escaped a thousand times?"
Rhaven held firm, but so did Wisp.

"I could have relieved Preman of his gold purse and all his jewels; I
could have taken the rubies and emeralds from the temple in
Pomanda where they sat so invitingly on the tables in the entrance
hall; and I could have slipped away into the night with your own gold
pouch, without you knowing until I was long gone." The thief paused
as he shook his head. "Not all kings are noble, Rhaven. Not all soldiers
are brave. Remember that the next time you think me a thief." He then
turned and walked back to the table.

Rhaven watched his back until he was halfway there, then walked out,
the door to the tavern slamming shut behind him.

~

Camissa struggled to keep pace with Rhaven's long, hurried
strides. "Slow down, Rhaven. I can't keep up with you." He
continued the pace for a moment, then slowed to allow Camissa to
catch up. "Why didn't you offer an apology?" she managed to spit out
in shortened breaths.

"We'll arrive at the village shops soon," Rhaven said.

Camissa darted in front of Rhaven and turned to block his way, her
hands on her hips, and her face set with an intractable expression.

"I have no time for this, Camissa."

"You would have made him feel better if you apologized. He would
have known that you trusted him."

Rhaven kept silent for a moment. "I can't take away what I said, and I
can't convince him that I trust him now just by saying so. If we all live
long enough, he'll know I trust him. Let's leave it at that." Rhaven
brushed her aside and continued his brisk pace.

"Where are we going that's so important? And why did you bring me?"

"You will see when we arrive. As to why I brought you—you are making me regret my decision already."

The village shops of the Lorns resembled the activity of a beehive, people scurrying about in all directions performing one task or another. Camissa noticed the leather shop first and marveled at the work of the tiny women who did the processing. Situated next to the leather shop sat a small building housing artisans occupied with the cutting and polishing of jewelry—necklaces, rings, and other items meant for nobles or rich merchants.

Camissa eyed the pieces with envy as she passed by, careful not to fall too far behind Rhaven. He took them past the clothing shops, and the ladies who made fine threads for special garments. She could have spent a day in any one of these stores, but Rhaven had no intention of stopping. Near the back of the building that housed the fletchers, he entered a small door. She followed and Rhaven introduced her to one of the council members.

"She is the one?" he asked.

Rhaven nodded.

The Lorn looked at her. "Rhaven tells me you can read others' thoughts."

"Sometimes," she said.

"And the young one, Rahgnar, you can read his?"

She hesitated, but then acknowledged it. "Usually I can, yes."

"You are to keep a close watch on him. If you sense anything out of the ordinary, tell Rhaven at once."

Camissa kept silent.

"This is important."

She nodded. "I know it is. I'll keep watch."

The Lorn bowed to her and Rhaven and then took his leave.

As they walked back through the factories, Rhaven said, "You may select any gift you like from any of the shops."

"I couldn't do that—"

"It would be an insult to refuse a gift from the Lorns."

Camissa bowed her head. "Thank you, Rhaven. I ..."

"Don't thank me. Just be ready to leave in the morning. I sense time running short, and we have a long way to go."

DREAMS AND STRANGE BEASTS

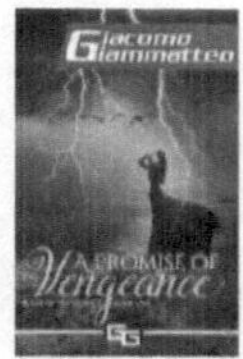

Skyethorn—Blackthorn Forest

Camissa had a scowl planted on her face. The morning seldom woke her on a sour note, but she had trouble finding smiles since they arrived in Skyethorn. Rhaven nodded a greeting to her as she passed. Camissa acknowledged it with a brisk tilt of her head and a smile that was no more than a flicker.

"I'm glad you're a male, Argus." Rhaven brushed the knots from Argus's long flowing mane, strands of black silk with a hint of silver dotting the tips. "We'll be leaving soon, boy. Going to Genda. Perhaps other new lands."

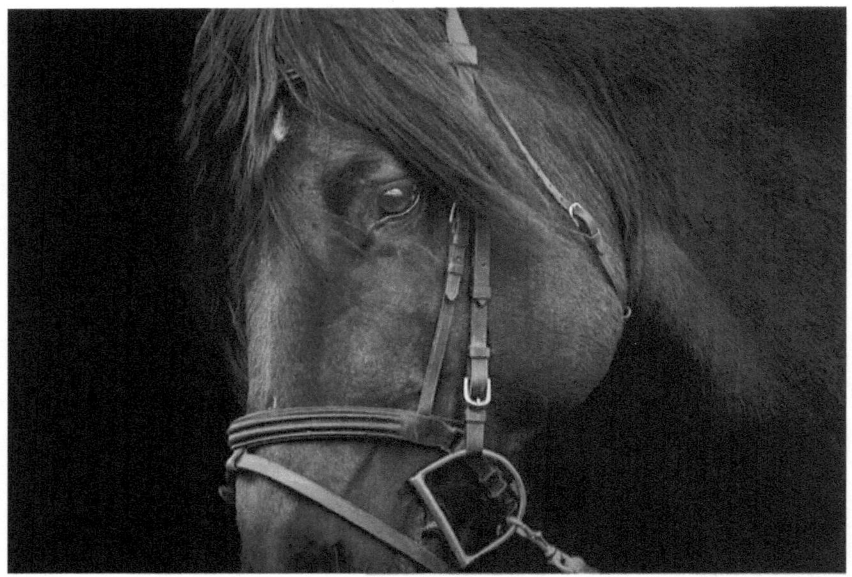

Argus

Rhalan Teldren stepped through the early morning mist. "How many winters has Argus been with you?"

"Enough to have heard all my woes. He must be tired of listening by now." A rare chuckle slipped through Rhaven's lips, and it left too soon.

"My heart would be lightened if you stayed a while; perhaps we could force a few more smiles to your face, even a laugh or two."

"We need to leave, Rhalan. Have you the gifts?"

"Time should always be spared for ceremony. I thought you had at least learned that."

"You know my heart is with you, and with all the Lorns, but this can't wait. I fear there is little time."

Rhalan nodded. "The gifts are ready. Bring our guests."

*R*hiana presented Camissa with a beautiful box carved from blackthorn; the lid, of inlaid emerald, birch, and walnut, featured a garden of roses climbing a trellis that touched the sky. When she opened it, she found twelve compartments with blackthorn dividers as thin as parchment. Tears formed in her eyes. "I have already chosen a gift."

"This is a special gift from me, Camissa. Please accept it as my friend." Camissa stared at the box; she had not yet lifted her eyes. "It is a spice box. Rahg told me how you like to cook."

Camissa wanted to be angry with the girl; she had all but chased Rahg down. But despite her emotions, she found herself smiling. "Thank you, Rhiana. This will stay in my memory forever." She hugged Rhiana, and for the first time in days, her stomach did not churn.

A bustle of activity brought her focus around to Rhunar. He held the finest sheath that she had ever seen—black leather etched with a scene depicting a giant eagle fighting a wolf. The scene depicts eagle's talons scratching at the wolf's eyes.

"It once belonged to my brother," Rhunar said, as he handed it to Darstan. "It should fit your sword; I noted it was short. The inside is processed to let a blade slide easily, but with no noise, an advantage you might need someday."

Darstan gulped, and his face flushed red. "I don't know what to say. I cannot—"

He stopped when Rhaven whistled, a warning sign they all knew.

Camissa thought that Rhunar must have known the warning also. He looked to Rhaven, then back to Darstan. "These are gifts from our heart. We are proud to share with Rhaven's friends."

Darstan smiled and bowed. "Your gift is a treasure, Rhunar. I will someday return the favor."

"Outlanders always want to return gifts for gifts." Rhunar laughed. "If it can help you stay alive, that is gift enough for me."

Rhalan presented Tobias with a pipe that looked as if it set his heart racing. It had a slight curve to the handle, and the bowl was larger than his own by half. It was pure blackthorn with tiny carved leaves to provide a firm grip. When Tobias touched it he beamed like a candle after dark.

"Don't think I've ever seen a pipe like this," he said. "Won't know what to do with such a pretty pipe. Might not even smoke it," he said, but he already had it in his mouth, chewing on it, as he searched for a striker.

Gregor stood behind Wisp, a disinterested look planted on his face, until Rhalan walked by carrying a blackthorn staff.

"I'd pay all the gold in Sykor for a blackthorn staff," Gregor said.

Rhalan offered the staff to Rhaven, who refused it with a smile. The Lorn turned and raised the staff over his head. "The gift has been offered and refused. It can now be gifted again."

The bounty man's eyes went from somber to exultation as Rhalan walked toward him. His shoulders went rigid and his boots scrunched up as if he were clenching his toes.

Everyone fell silent when Rhalan spoke. "I began carving this long ago for Rhaven, but he has insisted I give it to you. Only Rhaven would deny me the privilege of a gift." The old Lorn laughed, evoking a similar response from the others, but Gregor's laughter could be heard above everyone's. He fondled the gift as if it were gold.

"I have never seen its like."

"And you never will again," Rhalan said. "May it grant protection for you and your friends, and death for your enemies."

Camissa laughed. Wisp had to stop Gregor from offering his thanks after three times. She had never seen the bounty man so excited; even the Lorns were laughing.

Rhunar approached Wisp with no gift in his hand. "Rhaven told me of you, my friend. I struggled to find an appropriate gift, but I believe you will be pleased." Rhunar reached behind him and brought back a thin black leather sheath containing a small black tube. In his other hand were two leather pouches, one black, the other green. Rhunar paused then handed him the green pouch, "I give you life," he said, then handed him the black. "And I give you death." Rhunar's eyes held Wisp fixed while he spoke. "There are twenty in each pouch, but use them wisely. Each time you take a life it is a reflection on me."

"I will take no life that would not take mine, or those of my friends." Wisp bowed low. "It is a gift that I hope to never use, and the less I use it the more I will cherish it."

Camissa imagined that no words could have pleased Rhunar more.

Tension gripped Camissa when Rhiana stepped in front of Rahg. A smile painted her face, but it could not hide the streaks of tears. A small, round stone, like a crystal, but with a bluish tint, hung from a chord around her neck, and in her hand she held an identical one, except for size; it was twice as big as hers.

She handed the larger one to Rahg. "This is Ranal," she said, and while he put his on, she held her own up to him. "And this is Ranalla. During a reunion if we touch them together and hold them to the sky they will glow—just like the moons." Rhiana's smile disappeared as she tucked hers away again. "Someday, I hope to see them glow, Rahg. May your journey be a safe one." Her bow completed the ceremony and she stepped back to rejoin Rhalan.

Rahg's face turned red when he received the gift. Camissa hid her smile. She was certain he thought of the legends which claimed that Ranal and Ranalla always fought, but during a reunion they forgot everything and fell in love all over, which was why they glowed so brightly.

Rhalan stepped forward and bowed to each of them offering his fare well, saving the traditional Lorn custom for Rhaven alone. His bow was lower and held longer. "May the light of the sun ever touch you. You are ever well come to home."

Rhaven extended his own fare wells then took hold of Argus's reins and headed out of Skyethorn on the southern trail. "We will walk for a while," Rhaven said, "until the path widens."

∼

They walked for almost half the day before Rhaven let them ride. Rahg climbed atop Marchall, and as the day wore on he dreamt of Skyethorn, and of Rhiana. Camissa had been quiet since leaving the city. Rahg suspected trouble. She was riding at the back of the group; normally, she rode next to him. He slowed down to allow Camissa time to catch up, then moved in alongside Camissa's horse. "I've hardly seen you since we left Skyethorn. Is something wrong?"

"I didn't think you would notice if I were missing or not, Rahgnar Fal-Thera."

Rahg confirmed his suspicions when he heard her sharp words and cutting tone.

"It is a pity that Rhiana could not join us. I know you campaigned so hard to convince her father that she should come, and she would have made wonderful company for you." Rahg now knew without question the source of his problem. Camissa glared at him. Her voice sang like sweet music, but Rahg knew better. Camissa soon nudged her horse, Ranger, forward to join Tobias and Rhaven, bringing a sigh of relief from Rahg.

They made good time the rest of the afternoon, and by late evening they had made camp and eaten. Rahg kept his conversation with Darstan and Wisp most of the night. It helped to keep his mind off of things.

Late that night, Rahg lay down to sleep. All his troubles clashed together in his mind, while a splitting headache worked at rending it apart. Rahg stopped rubbing his eyes and brought his hands to the sides of his pained head. He rubbed his temples, but gently, as the slightest touch hurt.

The headaches seemed to come every other day, each one lasting longer than the one before. The throbbing continued. The pain kept pace with the beating of his heart, each pulsation a hammer pounding inside his head. With all the strange things going on he sometimes wondered if there wasn't some tiny little man inside him wielding a mallet and chisel.

Rahg had his eyes closed to ease the pain but even without seeing he knew when Kella came near. He had gotten accustomed to her smell and the sound of her heavy breathing. She always sounded like she was panting, yet, when she needed to be quiet she could not be heard. Rahg didn't bother to lift his eyelids, he just pursed his lips and whistled. When he didn't hear her moving in his direction he whistled again and called. "Kella. Come here, girl."

A smile came to his face when he felt the padding of her heavy paws as she pranced over to him. If it wouldn't have hurt, he would have laughed thinking of how Kella walked. She had a swagger like a bull in a field full of cows. She was as confident as Rhaven and as brash as Wisp.

The vargel plopped down next to him, letting her back come to rest against his. Rahg moved slightly away; her thick black fur proved no comfort on a hot sticky night. Rahg thought of the nights she had kept him warm, how he wrapped his arms around her and shivered. She always made him forget his troubles.

I hope she can take this pain away. Or stop the worries, or the dreams.

Despite the heat Rahg soon had his arms around the vargel, hugging her like a boy with a new pup. He whispered in her ear and told her of his problems. Sometimes, he felt like Kella was the only one to talk to. At least she listened without remarking. As Rahg rubbed her belly and her thick mane, he thought more of other matters and the pain in his head began to ease. Soon, his arm fell limp, his fingers stopped scratching, and he no longer whispered to his friend. Kella squeezed out from under his relaxed grip and sauntered through the camp into the woods.

Rahg's troubles ran circles through his mind, covering the perimeter of his brain like a horse race, one constantly chasing the tail of the other. When they stayed on the perimeter he was safe, but when the eddy formed, Rahg's troubles began—that was when the dreams came.

whirlpool

He could see the eddy forming. See it. Not just feel it, or sense it, and it grew in strength until it became one of epic proportions. Rahg was sucked in and dragged under. He gasped for air as the water filled his lungs. He choked and coughed, and spat to get it out. Then, as if nothing had ever occurred, he was there, standing on a rock cliff overlooking the sea.

The wind blew. Always, the wind blew. He remembered that now.

Gusts slammed wet foamy sea against the rocks, and sprayed him—stung, as it slapped his face. Soon the wind would grow worse. It always did. The waves would crash on the spot where he stood, so he moved inward like he had many times before, scrabbling toward the top, hands and feet scraping against craggy edges, and leaving blood stains on the chiseled points and knife-sharp ridges.

Cold. The cold came from somewhere above. *Must keep climbing.* Below him the winds smashed huge waves against the ledge—waves that could crush him, bash him against the sharp rocks and batter his brittle bones.

The storm painted the sky a misty gray. No clouds. No wind—at least, not now, but soon it would snow. The instant he thought it, it came. The snow whipped his body—a body clothed for summer's heat. He felt the cold all over again. Rahg finished scaling the precipice and crawled over a jagged-edged spire of stone with bloodied hands.

His eyes were drawn to the top of the mountain, looming above him like a vulture over a carcass. That had not been there a moment ago. He stared at the summit where clouds had descended to below its peak and hung about the snow-covered mount like a white collar on a wolf.

A mysterious force drove him onward until, at last, he saw the cave; it was then that he remembered. *The cave! The cave is the path to the top.* Everything stood as before—just as memorable and every bit as foreboding.

cave entrance

Rahg stood before it like he had in the past, staring into the perfect circular entrance suspended in the air, with an unnatural smoke that filled the void—a mist that had an aura of evil. Rahg stepped into the darkness. The feel of it made him cringe. It felt damp, steamy, cold, then hot, and when the blackness enveloped him—he recalled the beast.

Rahg closed his eyes. It was only a matter of time until the beast appeared. He dared not open them now. *Perhaps I can go somewhere else,* he thought. And then the voice invaded his mind.

So, you have returned.

The voice resounded throughout the cavern. It boomed. The stone walls shook and the floor moved. Rahg's bones vibrated. He cringed and his muscles gelled. Somewhere he found the strength to respond. "So I have," he heard himself say. "So I have."

And your friends? Where are they?

How does it know of my friends? He composed himself prior to responding. "They do not know of this place."

The laughter from the beast left Rahg awestruck. It was a voluminous roar that shook the cavern until he thought the walls would burst. Rocks shifted and fell. The echo of the blast hurt as it penetrated his ears, again and again. Rahg gathered all the strength he could; he dared not exhibit his discomfiture and show weakness to this creature. He clamped his jaw shut and bit teeth together. He opened his eyes and glared at the beast.

When the creature stopped laughing, it lowered its head to Rahg's level, eyes red with fire. Rahg tried to hold its gaze but found it impossible, like staring at the sun—yet somehow, in some strange way, he could not turn aside either. For a moment, however brief, he thought he saw flames dancing in the red eyes of the beast—eyes that penetrated his soul.

And you believe to know this place, young one?

The hackles rose on the back of Rahg's neck. "I've been here before." Every muscle tensed and every joint ached but, despite it all, Rahg found the courage to draw his sword. Laughter again shook the walls as the beast taunted him and lowered its head. Tendrils of smoke leaked from its mouth and crept toward him. The fiery eyes drew closer with every breath. It's scales appeared impenetrable.

"Do you intend to slay me?"

The piercing voice felt as if it gouged a hole in his head. *Do you yet know who is friend and who is foe?*

Rahg struggled with his fear while attempting to focus on the words. *What does it mean?* The beast either guessed, or read his thoughts.

Do you know which of your friends will betray you? And which you will destroy? The creature laughed yet again. *No, young one. You do not yet know this place. And you can sheathe the sword. You shall not be harmed by my doing. Not on this journey.* Giant eyes strangled with flames stared at Rahg. *Remember this, young one. Remember when you thought someone meant you harm and did not. Be wary of friends. Be wary of all who would sit at your side. Spin a web around yourself and let no one know of its existence—no one. Only that way will you succeed in catching your prey.*

Salty perspiration rolled off Rahg's forehead into the corner of his eyes. It stung. Step by step he backed toward the wall of the cavern. The creature moved one giant foot aside, the talons on it as big as Rahg's arm, and they looked as if they could pierce the rock on the ground. "I will give it thought," Rahg said as he crept by, sword held high despite the monster's vow that he would be unharmed.

This time, the creature did not laugh. *You will not. Not this time, young one. Look past the flesh. Look into their souls. That is how you will know.* Scales carved a smile on the dragon's face. Rahg hurried past, and the creature laughed as he struggled with the decision of which path to take.

Rahg pondered his dilemma. In front of him lay four possible paths, each, he guessed, hiding its own set of dangers. He craned his neck forward in an attempt to see, but blackness greeted him on each path.

~

*C*amissa remained still in her bedroll on the ground. She had been observing Rahg since dawn and the sun had risen long ago, enough to rid the grass of dew. It was obvious to her that he had been troubled again by dreams, and she was curious to discover their meaning. She tried to read his thoughts, but something was not working. Perhaps he would talk. "Good morrow, Rahg. It seems like it will be a fine day. A good day for traveling."

"It should be." He stared at nothing for a moment, then stood and walked into the dense section of the woods. Camissa's concerned gaze followed him until he was out of sight.

"His troubles are plenty, lass. If you can help, he needs it."

Camissa turned to face Tobias. She hadn't even heard him get up. "I can only offer consolation. He must do as he sees fit."

~

Rahg smelled Tobias's cooking before he reached the camp, then he heard the familiar chatter of tales being told. It was a relief to hear Tobias back in his old form.

"Well, lads, I figured you'd be gettin' tired of hearin' all my tales by now. But then, I do tell the best tales, so I should've figured better." Tobias stirred the gravy and poured himself another mug of khaffe.

Rahg took a sip of his own, which had grown lukewarm, and shivered. "This is terrible, Tobias. What did you do to the khaffe?"

Tobias laughed. "It bites, doesn't it, lad? Good to have khaffe bite ya in the morn. If you're a fisherman and you're planning to sail the sea, then you'll need a good nip from a mug of khaffe before ya sail. This is how they drink it in Genda."

Rahg smiled. Though it was good to hear Tobias talking normal, he knew he would tire of it soon. Rahg plopped next to Darstan, already stuffing a biscuit in his mouth.

Camissa sat down to eat, taking a spot next to Darstan and Rahg.

"Where's Rhaven?" Darstan asked.

"I was awake early and never heard him," Camissa said.

Tobias laughed in that knowing way, the *old man* laugh Darstan had named it, and Rahg smiled as he listened to Tobias.

"No one ever hears Rhaven," Tobias said. "He makes less noise than moonlight."

Gregor laughed aloud. "I've had him walk up on me while I stood watch and never noticed."

Since the Lorns had given Gregor the blackthorn staff, Rahg had seen more smiles and heard more laughter from the bounty man than in all the time he'd known him. Rahg had already seen him polish the staff two times and now he examined it as if it were a jewel.

"How far is it to Genda, Tobias?" The bounty man asked, but he never looked up from his staff.

Tobias munched on a biscuit and sipped khaffe. "At the pace Rhaven keeps, I'd say two days to get to Pomanda and then ten or eleven more before we reach Genda."

"I intend to get there sooner." Rhaven stepped to the fire and picked up two biscuits.

"Be pushin', won't it?"

"If the horses can take it, we can." Rhaven sat on an old stump close to the fire. "Did anyone see, or hear, anything last night?"

"No," Rahg said, and looked around to the others even as he did. The fact that Rhaven asked scared Rahg. He wouldn't ask if it wasn't important.

Tobias stopped eating and stared at Rhaven. "You asked for a reason."

Rhaven took another sip of his khaffe. "The woods can be deceiving at night, but I was certain I saw a woman watching us."

"A Lorn?" Rahg asked, perhaps with a little too much enthusiasm, as Camissa's suspicious glare burned into him. He recovered his wits after realizing his mistake. "Since we're still in the Great Forest, I thought it might be a Lorn." He hoped the explanation proved good enough.

"The woman I saw was tall. Nearly as tall as me."

Tobias had begun cleaning the encampment and covering the fire. "Since you're askin' us. I'm guessin' there were no tracks."

Rhaven smiled. "Since there were none, I must have been wrong." He let it go at that, rose from his seat and headed toward Argus. "It's time we left. We'll stop in Pomanda for supplies, then head to Genda." Argus neighed.

Rhaven and that horse are fit for each other. With one fluid motion Rahg flung himself up into the saddle, then patted Marchall on the side of the neck. "What do you think, boy? Do you think you could be like Argus?" Rahg kicked his heels into Marchall and steered him toward the trail. *No more than I could be like Rhaven.*

RETURN TO GENDA

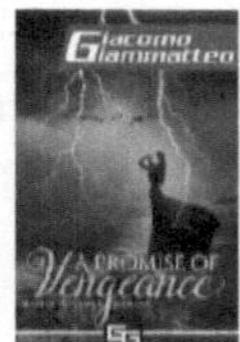

It had been a difficult twelve days since leaving Pomanda—days that Tobias would sooner forget, as would his tired bones and aching body. Rhaven pushed the mounts to their limits each day, which was far past what Tobias had grown accustomed to. It almost seemed as if his body forgot how to ride a horse. As a young man he would have ridden this distance and spent the nights in a tavern drinking vidda, but those days had passed with his wife, Shia. He thanked the gods that she wasn't here to see him return to Genda this way.

The days had grown hotter as they traveled south, another thing that Tobias' old body seemed to have forgotten. The terrain had changed too, though he didn't remember it being so barren. Thick forest had ceded to rocky ground surrounding an occasional copse of pines or cedar. He wiped sweat from his face on a rolled-up sleeve, then removed his cap and used it to fan his bald head. "Feels good, lads," he hollered to Darstan and Rahg. "Bet you wish you didn't have hair now."

Tobias took a swig of water, poured a little over his head, then nudged his mount forward. Rhaven ordered them to bring the horses to a walk, and it couldn't have pleased Tobias more. His back hurt, though it never used to when he rode. They reached the top of a long hill soon after the midday meal. Tobias stopped, pulled out his pipe and pouch, and leaned back in the saddle after he lit it. "Can you hear that, lads?"

"Hear what?" Darstan asked.

"The roar of the waves crashing against the rocks. It's like a cold ale and a warm lass rolled into one." A sigh escaped his lips and he sucked on his pipe as if it were his last time. "That could sing me to sleep at night, lads. Surely could."

Darstan stood in his stirrups, scanning the ground in front of them. He bent his head to listen. "Tobias, I can't hear anything.?"

Tobias laughed until he had to sit up straight again. "That's all right, lads, neither can I, but I've got this memory tucked away so tight in my head, it's just like I'm hearin' it now." He grabbed the reins in one hand, puffed on his pipe and kneed his mount forward. "We'll be hearin' it soon enough though. You'll not only hear those waves, but see 'em, too."

Toward late afternoon, Tobias felt his stomach churning. If memory served him well, the next crest would bring Genda into sight. His nose quavered as he sniffed the air. He prodded his mount to a trot. Tobias dismounted at the top of the rise, then leaned back and breathed in as much air as he could. "Smell that, lads," he said. "*That's* fresh air."

Genda

Darstan and Rahg gawked like the country lads they were, but Camissa and Gregor stared as well. Kender too. Mountains rolled in from the west, crashing into the sea and stood like stiff-backed soldiers. Large houses wearing red-tile roofs sprawled atop terraced streets overlooking the majesty of the Great Sea. White or beige stucco covered all the homes, and knee-high walls guarded the perimeter of gardens bearing lemon trees and grapevines. Umbrella pines perched over patios, like pillars wearing hats, and cypress trees waged a perilous game along the edges of cliffs.

Hello, Genda.

~

Camissa looked out across the city, a sense of wonder filling her with warmth. She had never seen the Great Sea. It was mesmerizing. Genda proved to be something far more than the village Tobias had named it, and while not quite as large as Sykor, it didn't miss by much. The streets were steeper than any she'd ever seen, worse even than the Corina Tumal in Pomanda, and it looked as if they all emptied into the sea. She breathed deep, tasting the tangy salt in the air and savoring the smell of the sea. The houses seemed to be clutching onto the hillside as if they were tied to it.

A woman with two small children walked by them, then three men with hoes and rakes. Camissa studied their dress with a furrowed brow. The clothes looked to be of a loose-fitting silky material, and both the women and men wore their tops tied at the waist, midriff showing. *And the children wore no shoes!*

"We should walk," Tobias said. "Should be some stables not too far from here and an inn down by the wharf." He turned to look at them, patting his thighs as he did. "Besides, it'll do us all good to walk these streets some. gonna be a painful reminder for an old man like me though."

A growling stomach reminded Camissa how hungry she was, and the aroma of fresh-baked bread drew her head to the south, toward the sea.

"Is no one hungry but me?" Wisp asked.

Tobias laughed. "We're not far from food, lad. Good food."

They walked the horses around the next corner before Tobias spotted the stables, tucked into a dead-end street near a spot at the western edge of the city. While Rhaven settled the account for the horses's care, Camissa noted the sullen expression on Tobias.

She thought she saw him go misty-eyed, so she reached out with her powers. With the first thought she pulled back. Tobias was lost in sorrows about the loss of someone named Shia. *Perhaps his wife,* she thought, but she knew that whoever it was, she was gone. Guilt gnawed at her. "That's it. Never again."

"Never again, what?" Wisp asked.

"Nothing, Kender. Mind your own business, which should be enough to keep three or four people busy." Camissa turned her attention back to Tobias, just as a smile came to his face.

"This tavern was a wild place back when I was here," Tobias said. "Many a man's blood been spilled on those floors. Some of the best blood in Genda."

"Including yours, Tobias Marek."

The voice belonged to an older man, leaning against the building with a whittling knife and a piece of wood. He appeared to be carving a fish. The man looked to be as old as Tobias, though he had a thick crop of rusty colored hair. His face was clean-shaven and his nose was as crooked as a fish hook.

Tobias stared at the man for a long time, then Camissa saw images in Tobias's mind: two small boys playing on boats; working the fisheries; those same two arguing over women and vidda, the harsh drink that the fishermen of Genda turned to at night; arguments, fights. After that, she could sense no more.

Tobias lowered his head and extended his hand. "It's been a long time, Talen. What news will you tell me of family?"

Talen shifted his feet to a balanced stance and pushed off the wall. He spat on the ground close to Tobias' boots. "You've got no family. And no friends. You're not welcome in Genda." Talen stopped his whittling and returned the knife to its sheath. "There are more than a few people waiting with knife and sword to claim their honor. I doubt you'll be leaving Genda a second time."

Two knives flashed in the air. Rhaven pressed them into Talen's throat, the pressure enough to cause the man to crane his neck. Blood trickled out, then Rhaven pushed harder. Talen stood on his toes now, and from the looks of it, he couldn't go any higher.

"I'm not knowing who you are stranger, but you have no business in affairs that aren't yours," Talen said. "You know nothin' about—"

Rhaven pressed harder. Talen gasped, stepping back until he came to rest against the wall. "I know Tobias. I know about the First of Genda. And I know of useless customs and ancient beliefs."

Talen gulped, but stayed silent.

"We'll be staying in Genda, and I don't know for how long. I know that Tobias won't cross swords with you, perhaps not with others." Rhaven leaned closer and glared. "Have no doubts about me. Should anyone harm Tobias, they'll die," he said, then sheathed his blades.

Talen seemed to relax. "And who should I tell them they'd be fighting?"

"They'll need no name," Rhaven said. "Ask any of your cutpurses or assassins, or well-traveled men. If any of them wish to test their skills, we'll be at the docks."

Tobias grabbed Rhaven's arm as Talen scurried off down an alley. "I take care of my own matters."

Rhaven leaned close and whispered. "You have been keeping things from me, Tobias. Things you should have shared. Your problems with Genda are yours, but until you tell me all you know about this prophecy, I plan to keep you alive."

"Perhaps it's time we talked," Tobias said. "By the sea there's an inn. Winds of Storm."

Rhaven nodded.

Tobias nodded also. "If we're goin' to Entiria we'll need Malakai—if he's alive, and there's no better place to find him. First we'll get some rooms though, and I'll tell you what I know."

Camissa joined Rahg and the others then they went to check into the inn. *Just what does Tobias know?*

～

"*H*ow did you know?" Tobias asked.

Rhaven took a sip of ale from the jug they brought to the room. It was a small room but it had bed, a bedroll on the floor, and a small table on the side with a candle. Tobias had asked for a pail of sand for his pipe ashes. Rhaven and Tobias talked while the rest of them waited downstairs in the common room.

"Camissa's powers are becoming stronger. When the shera told us of the prophecies, she detected no change in your emotions. No sense of surprise." Rhaven said it, then waited for Tobias to respond.

Tobias nodded. "Knew I didn't like the girl from the beginning. Nobody's business what goes on in a person's mind. She's got no right to go pokin' around in somebody's head," Tobias mumbled, then resigned himself to the fact that it was over and done with. "I didn't know she was gettin' so strong. But she's right. I knew of the prophecy." Tobias shook his head, muttering. "It has cursed me all my life, this prophecy."

The slightest roll of Rhaven's eyes showed his curiosity.

"It began when I was made First of Genda. That's when she first came to me. At first, she only came at night. I thought I was just dreamin' bad dreams. But then, one day when I was out to sea she appeared in my cabin." Tobias stuffed tobacco in his new blackthorn pipe then lit it. "If there'd a been a chance, I believe I might have jumped into the sea, but she wrapped some kind of shield around me, wrapped it so tight it came close to stranglin' me. Then she told me how I was supposed to leave the city—give up bein' the First of Genda. She said after some time another would come to me and tell me what to do."

Tobias took advantage of another pause to get the pipe going strong. Smoke leaked out of the sides of his mouth as he puffed. "I'd swear this same tobacco tastes better in a blackthorn pipe." He inhaled deeply, then continued.

"After four or five winters I figured they forgot, or couldn't find me." He laughed. "Guess that was pretty stupid to think that, but find me they did, and this time they told me to just start travelin' and when I felt real strong about a place, I was supposed to settle down. It didn't take long. After my experience with a rock dragon north of Kamnor, I decided to settle at Twin Forks."

Tobias took a deep breath. "Came to me one last time after that, and told me that the lad I was supposed to be protectin' would come from this village, and by some of the things they said, I knew it would be one of Magmar's lads." Tobias sat still, hands fiddling with an empty mug of ale and his gaze fixed to a barren spot of the floor. "I always wondered though."

Rhaven stared at him. "And that's all?"

Tobias looked straight at Rhaven. "That's all." He knew he could never tell Rhaven about the dreams of the sea. How could someone like Rhaven understand a person fearing the sea because of a dream. Especially a man from Genda.

Tobias's eyes remained glued to a blank spot on the floor. He recalled the first dream, the one with the violent storm. He was on a boat with people he had never seen and they were sailing through a heavy fog. The winds howled and the waves rose up and crashed upon the deck. Lightning flashed in the background, threatening them with every crack, and deafening thunder roared above, heard even over the screaming of the wind that tore down the sails and blew men overboard.

*T*obias saw the wave coming—a huge wave that washed him overboard, and he remembered grasping for anything to hold onto, but all he found was slippery deck. As he tumbled into the roiling sea he recalled the face staring at him from the deck. For so many years he wondered who that face belonged to, remembered seeking recognition of it in every man he met—until Twin Forks, when the features of a young man solidified into the face on the ship, the one who watched from the deck—Rahg. And now that they were here in Genda and destined to make a voyage to Entiria across the Sea of the Lost, Tobias felt sure of his fate. With an audible sigh, he rose from his seat and moved toward the door.

Rhaven rose to join him. "You know they'll not rest because of my warning."

"No," Tobias said. "They'll not quit just because of you. But it'll make them think real hard, and it might give us enough time to do our business and get out of here. I have no wish to stay in Genda."

Tobias opened the door and stepped into the hall treading lightly on rotted wood that might give in at any time. "But you know, Rhaven, I'd give all my gold to be able to stay, in peace." Tobias never turned to see Rhaven's response. He knew instinctively that he nodded his understanding. *Somewhere, there's a Genda in Rhaven's past.*

~

The skinny Gendan thief climbed down the ladder into the darkness under the wharf. "Psst. Psst," he signaled, then waited to hear the reply. His bare feet left marks in the cool damp sand. To the right, waves caressed the shore and lapped at the wooden supports for the deck above. The smell of fish was strong.

"Well?" one of them asked.

"Saw 'im," the skinny one said. "It's 'im."

"Are you certain?" a fat man asked. "Don't want to be wrong."

"Have I ever been wrong?" The skinny Gendan thief locked eyes with them. "I do what I'm told."

"What about the other one?" Talen asked, "the one I told ya about."

The skinny one's eyes shone like hot coals on a winter night. "The dangerous one? Aye, dangerous he is. I could tell without askin'. That one walks like a barracuda swims." He lowered his voice and looked about. "We'll do well to avoid 'im."

The fat man offered a suggestion. "There are six of us. We could—"

The thief grabbed him by the neck and shook him. "He's the one that killed Damon Pirrhar up in Pomanda."

Silence followed. Even the waves seemed to stop for moment. "Damon Pirrhar!"

"And hundreds more if ya listen to the tales. He looks it too. We'll just wait our chance. The other one'll come free soon enough." They all looked at him and nodded. "Soon enough," he said, then they departed.

Wisp waited until they had enough time to make their way back to the inn several times before moving. He had learned patience long ago, when he first became a thief; he could wait until dawn if need be.

A web of footprints crossed in the sand where the six men had just met; one more was added to theirs as he made his way to the ladder. The waves still lapped at the shore, and the squawks of the gulls along the sea could be heard, but that was all. Wisp made no sound, and hadn't all the while he had listened to them. As he ascended the ladder his shadow danced on the sand with the light of Ranalla.

So, they're planning harm to Rahg. We'll need to put a stop to that.

SHARKS AND WHALES AND OTHER GAMES

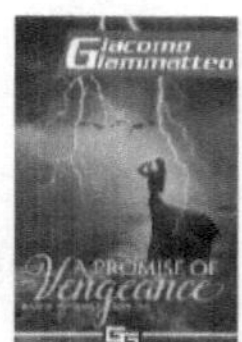

The Winds of Storm had a common room that rivaled the Trader's Inn for size, but the walls were bare and the flooring was a patchwork of new wood mixed with splintered planks. The floor had gouges in it caked with grime and muck. More than a few chairs sat on bowed legs, and the tables were old and rickety with crumbs and spilled ale on top. *The Traders Inn would have put this to shame,* Wisp thought.

The smell of fish permeated the place, as it did the whole city. Wisp coughed as a lung full of tobacco smoke caught him unaware. He brushed a strand of brown hair from his forehead and gazed out over a long crooked nose. With his olive skin he could have been mistaken for a Gendan. "We could have done with a few nights as busy as this in Sykor," he said to Camissa.

Crowds of people funneled their way through the narrow spaces between tables, all in a hurry to test their fortune at dice or cards. Wisp paused next to a large table seating six fishermen, waiting for the line to move. The one he assumed to be the captain was lighting a pipe, his head inclined toward a thin man across from him.

"Was dry as the bottom of a drunkard's mug," he was saying, relating a tale of some kind. "Hadn't rained in a full cycle and there was no drinkin' water left. The sun was blazin', makin' the plankin' so hot could barely walk. Had to keep men haulin' buckets of seawater up and sloshin' the deck down, so's we wouldn't burn our feet."

Camissa nudged Wisp from behind. "Come on, Kender. Darstan has a table for us."

"There's something odd about this bunch," said Wisp, "but I can't put my finger on it." He furrowed his brow, as if giving it more thought, then he moved forward and breathed in deeply. Camissa's hair smelled like lilacs, reminding him of how long it had been since he shared a woman's bed. He needed to rectify that before they put to sea.

They were seated close to the gaming tables. *Too close,* thought Wisp as that familiar itch prickled his skin. He only gambled when the odds favored him, but that never stopped the itch. It had been a long time since he had tempted the fates.

He took a seat with Camissa, Rahg and Gregor, while Darstan went to the games of chance. They shared several mugs of ale, but stayed away from the vidda, a strong mixture that the fishermen favored. "The more vidda they drink the more likely a fight will start," Wisp said.

They sat and talked through several more mugs of ale, and all the while Darstan played dice.

Rahg yawned, and covered his mouth. "That's the fourth time for me. I'm going back to the rooms."

"It's been a long day for all of us, Rahg. I'll get Darstan." Wisp went to the back and found Darstan heavy into the games. "Come on, Darstan."

Darstan rolled the dice again. "Two whales," the gaming man yelled, and Darstan scooped more coin into his pile.

The dice games in Genda were similar to the ones used in other cities, only the images were different. Three cubes were used, each with six pictures. Matching any two of the die paid equal the amount wagered, with two whales paying twice as much, but if a shark came up on any die, the bet was lost. It was the same in all the cities: in Pomanda they used horses and wolves; and in Sykor it was geese and fox, but the game was played the same. Darstan shook the dice in his hand and threw them.

"Two whales again," the man screamed. "This one's got the fever in his blood."

Darstan laughed at a man who had bet against him. "Have faith, my friend. These dice have no sharks." His voice grew louder with every drink he took.

Gregor held his staff in one hand and a mug of ale in the other. He leaned down and whispered to Wisp. "We might only be a word or two from trouble, Kender. We should go. Men who lose don't like to be taunted."

Darstan threw a shark on his next turn, losing the dice. "You've done well," Wisp said, "but save some of your fortune for another night. The good lady loves to dance with men who are bold, but too much she considers greed."

Darstan drank two more mugs of ale while they talked, then his attention was drawn to a large group of men standing about and yelling. "What's that?"

"A new game starting," Wisp said. "Fishermen love to play games of chance."

A glint shined in Darstan's eyes.

"No time for games, Darstan. We have information to get."

Darstan pushed his chair back, almost knocking it over. He rose, feeling at the pouch he carried under his shirt. The jingle of coin brought a new smile to his face. "Let's go, Kender. We might get our information and some gold besides."

Wisp shrugged his shoulders and followed Darstan back to the corner.

~

*A*fter a moment, Gregor got up.

"Why do you always go along with them?" Camissa asked.

"Because that thief is worth ten thousand gold, and I have not yet decided if I'll take him or not."

Camissa stared at the bounty man with her pale blue eyes. "How could you do that, now that you know him?"

Gregor stopped. "He was my nemesis and my enemy, long before I came to know him. I respect him. I might even like him. But he is worth ten thousand gold. Wisp would be the first to tell you, Camissa —gold makes a difference. And that much gold makes a lot of difference."

"I thought he was your friend."

The sadness showed in the bounty man's eyes as he stared at her. "I have no friends," he said. "Sometimes I wish I did, but..." Gregor shook his head and walked back toward the games.

Camissa reached out with her powers. She felt his pain, his sorrow, and most of all, his confusion over what to do with Wisp. *He really is in turmoil.*

She turned to Rahg, who was finishing a mug of strong Gendan ale. "Perhaps we should leave. I don't think it would be wise for just the two of us to remain. Come, we'll walk by the sea."

~

Tobias and Rhaven entered the common room and soon located Wisp and Gregor. "Where's Rahg?" Tobias asked, having spied Darstan even as he formed the question.

"At the table," Wisp said, and turned, but the table was empty. "They were there a moment ago." Panic filled his voice. He grabbed Gregor and tugged. "Come on, Gregor we need to find them."

"Why such concern?" Rhaven asked.

Wisp explained the conversation he had overheard under the docks, about how they would wait until they found him free and then get him. He relayed every detail to Rhaven though he appeared in a hurry to leave.

"You and Gregor go with Tobias. I'll search alone," Rhaven said.

"What about Darstan?" Tobias asked.

"He's too much into the cups to do us any good," Wisp said. "Come on, let's go."

~

"He's not in the room," Wisp said, and Gregor and I checked both taverns between here and there."

"You should have told us sooner," Tobias said as they left another tavern, the third one they'd searched since leaving the Winds of Storm.

"I saw no harm in waiting, not while we were all in the tavern. I was waiting until you and Rhaven returned. I didn't expect them to leave."

"And they wouldn't have if you'd have told 'em." Tobias wore a scowl on his face as he admonished Wisp. "There's another tavern on the next street. Let's go." Tobias knew most every street in Genda even though it had been more than twenty years since he had been there.

They walked through the old section of the city, the one closest to the sea where nothing had changed in many years.

Any new building took place on the outskirts of the city, to the north; it was the only area remaining that could be built on. The east and west sides of Genda were hemmed in by steep, mountainous cliffs, and existing buildings occupied all the land that bordered the sea in Genda's natural bay.

Tobias poked his head in every inn along the shore and checked all the taverns to the north. Upon exiting a tavern set high on a northern bluff, Rhaven awaited them.

"I found them. They were out walking."

Tobias shook his head and turned left on the next street.

"I thought we were going back to the rooms," Rahg said.

"We will," Tobias said, "but this tavern used to have the best food in Genda and I'm hungry."

~

*R*ahg smelled the fish as they entered and wrinkled his nose, his hunger already abating. The smell of the city irritated him, especially by the docks where the odor was overwhelming.

"You'll grow accustomed to it," Camissa said.

A serving girl arrived and offered them wine and bread. As Rahg suspected, fish was the meal. "How do we find someone to take us, Tobias?"

"Won't be easy. Men don't jump into a sinking ship."

"We've got the gold. How bad can it be to get to Entiria?"

Tobias laughed again. "Gold will buy a lot of things, lad, but it won't

424

buy back your life. This place we'll be askin' them to take us is surrounded by legends, and no one has ever come back from there."

Tobias tilted his mug and drank the last of his ale, having finished the wine before his story ended. He signaled for the serving girl to fill his mug. "But I suspect we'll find someone. Someone is always willin' to risk everything, even their life if you give 'em enough gold. Don't worry, lad."

Rahg laughed at the prospect. It was not a comforting thought that in a city full of fishermen none might be willing to take them up on their offer. Somehow, he didn't feel fortunate that some fool would.

The bounty man scraped the last crumbs of bread from his plate and chased them down with a gulp of wine. "I would like to stay and eat, Tobias, but we must be off." The chair squeaked across the floor when Gregor stood, drowning the sound of the coppers he dropped to the table.

Wisp's chair slid back as he got to his feet. "Where do we look for Malakai?"

"The Tern's Wing be a good place to start. I doubt that anyone will share what they know, but it never hurts to plant a seed. Tell enough people we're lookin' for him, and he just might show."

"I'll go with them," Rahg said, but before he even straightened, Rhaven stopped him.

"You'll stay with me until I decide it's safe."

Before they left, Tobias caught Gregor's arm. "Take enough gold to let them know you're serious, but not enough to tempt them to rob you of it while you stand there. Let them know there's a lot more waitin' when the job is complete."

Rahg scanned the room while they talked. This was a quiet inn, with only a few tables. Small sconces holding oil lamps sprayed a shower of light across the room, enough so that candles weren't necessary on the tables. Oil lamps were common in Genda, not only because of the sea, but also the olive trees that populated the hills to the east.

A decrepit old seaman sat alone in the corner, staring at blank walls. A bottle of vidda stood half empty in front of him and a partially eaten bowl of soup had been pushed to the side. The bread that accompanied the meal was gone, no trace remained save a few errant crumbs which he brushed to the floor.

The man held his left hand tucked away in the sleeve of his shirt. The hand was deformed. It appeared as if fire had marred it, curled it into a mass of flesh. It wasn't until the man turned to call the serving girl that Rahg saw his face, the entire left side had been scarred like his hand. He was missing an ear and all the hair on that side of his head. *By the gods, what could have happened to him.*

The side of his neck was a twirled mass of skin resembling the bark on a tree. And when he spoke, a raspy whisper scraped at his throat to get out. Rahg swallowed a lump of pity, yet he found himself turning away, repulsed by the sight of him. The feelings he had embarrassed him, but he couldn't help it. Just then, the owner of the inn brought the food, and Rahg changed his thoughts to concentrate on the fish that he was not excited about eating.

Tobias ate in silence, an unusual occurrence for him. There was worry in Tobias's face and disappointment in his eyes. For the first time since he'd known him, Rahg felt sorry for Tobias.

Before the meal was finished they were interrupted. "Words carry in this old tavern like a maiden's whisper on a lonely night."

The gravelly voice announced the stranger's presence. Rahg looked up to see the burnt old man. He shied away, though he nodded his head in the form of greeting.

"If I heard ya speak right, yer lookin' to go into the Sea of the Lost."

Rahg shivered when the man chuckled, a noise like someone walking on loose rocks.

"I'm the only hope ya have. Anyone else that can sail a ship good enough to get ya there is afraid to die."

"And you're not?" Tobias asked.

A strange expression came to the stranger. He bent down and shoved his gnarled old face at Tobias. "Look close. Do I look like I'm afraid to meet ol' Nappy?"

"We have none who know the sea. Can you get a crew to follow you?"

"I'll get a crew, but it'll cost ya half of my fee up front—and in gold. The other half when we get wherever it is yer goin'."

"We need to leave in two days," Rhaven said.

What Rahg thought might have been a smile formed on the old man's lips. "With enough gold, I could have a crew before dawn."

Before long they struck an arrangement. Rhaven gave a payment in gold to the sea captain, Sennar was his name, to secure the contract. Sennar got one fourth the gold now and an equal amount when he found a crew. The captain tucked the bag into his shirt and rose to leave. "At dawn, in two days' time," he said as he departed.

~

Wisp and Gregor had searched five taverns so far. Everyone swore Malakai to be dead, and no one would even talk of going into the Sea of the Lost. The next tavern was filled with seamen, as most were, but he had been told the ones who frequented this establishment were the bravest and most daring. Most daring, he knew, meant desperate and willing to do anything for gold. It didn't matter to Wisp. He was accustomed to dealing with men such as these.

Gregor nudged Wisp's arm and nodded his head to the back of the room. "In the corner. They look to be a likely group."

Wisp followed Gregor's gaze and studied the men from afar. At a table meant for four, a fifth chair had been pulled up. Occupying each were burly seamen. Wisp recognized the captain by his hat. He was the smallest of the bunch, but if a brawl ensued Wisp would go for him first. Gregor turned sideways to squeeze between two tables, even Wisp had to twist his thin frame to get past.

No space wasted in these establishments. If I had done this at the Trader's Inn we could have doubled the crowd.

"Have you a ship for hire?" Gregor interrupted them without even a greeting. The bounty man was not one for manners or beating about the bush.

Wisp's long beak twitched at the smell of fish but it didn't bother him. He had met Carmine at the fishery in Sykor enough times and, though he didn't enjoy the odor, it no longer offended him.

All the fishermen smell of the sea, he thought, as he let his gaze fall on each one in turn. Even as his thought formed, it struck him what had been puzzling him about those men at the table back at the Winds of Storm—they didn't smell like fishermen. None of them had that odor of the sea that everyone in Genda seemed to have.

He forced his thoughts back to the present. He could not afford to be careless now. Wisp moved his hands toward his knives and watched for signs of aggression. He did not wish to be caught off guard, and Gregor had proved to be no diplomat.

A large seaman had been talking, telling some tale no doubt, when Gregor interrupted. He now faced the bounty man with his lips curled in anger. The man's right hand balled into a fist, where before it had gripped the mug of ale. Gregor shifted his weight to the left foot leaving his staff free.

He's been too eager to use that new staff ever since he got it from the Lorns.

The seaman glared at Gregor like a street dog whose meal had been interrupted. The captain kept his hand tucked inside his shirt. *Grip-*

ping a knife, no doubt. Wisp decided it was time to intervene. "Aye, good sirs. It's a good ship we're needin', and a good crew. And we'll be payin' in good Gendan gold."

The captain focused on Wisp. He withdrew his hand from the shirt then stayed his large accomplice with so little as a glare. The captain owned a boastful voice. "If ya be needin' a ship, the best is mine. And there's no crew on the seas that can raise a sail to equal them."

The other men with him nodded their approval. He leaned over the table motioning Gregor and Wisp to bend down to hear. His tone had changed. Gone was the boastful crowing of a proud seaman. Replacing it was the probing and suspicious tone of a man who had seen too many twists on fate to trust anyone.

"Tell me what yer needin' a ship for, and where yer' wantin' to go. If that's all good, I'll say how much gold ya need. And there'll be no dickerin' on the price." The captain looked at Wisp. "I say that because ya look to be the type to like dickerin'. Just lettin' ya know before we start that I'll have nothin' of it. I set my price fair and I'll take no less."

Wisp smiled in recognition of a good negotiator. If it got to that, there'd be negotiating, and Wisp planned to have the best of it. "We're needin' to go into the Sea of the Lost." Wisp said it as if it were right around the corner. "Need to find a place they call Entiria."

The thin man next to the big one spit out his vidda and nearly choked. "Sea of the Lost! Have ya no brains?"

Wisp stared straight at the captain, looking at him like no one had spoken.

The man stroked his beard. "I can see ya be serious, lad, so I'll not be wastin' yer time. Not all the gold in Genda could buy ya into the Sea of the Lost. Not on my ship. Nor on any that I know. I'm curious though, why do ya wish to go and get yerself killed?"

"I've got gold."

"I told ya, lad, not all the gold in Genda would entice me. I mean that. I've never been there but I heard the tales. Sea monsters big as ships, or bigger. Storms that could make the worst I've seen seem like dancin' with a pretty woman. And fog so thick that man nor beast can see through it."

The captain laughed. "And if ya get through all that, then they say the worst begins. Straights so narrow the oars can't be turned out, and rocks that move so they can't be mapped." The captain shook his head. "No, lad. It's not me that'll be takin' ya into the Sea of the Lost. Not me."

Wisp could tell there'd be no convincing him, but he still might provide useful information. "Then tell me where I might find Malakai, the pirate."

The captain shot Wisp a look as if he had asked to see the Evil One. "Malakai be dead, lad. And if ya discover different, you'd be wise to think him dead. The Sea of the Lost is bad enough without bringin' Malakai into it."

Wisp saw a smile enter the captain's eyes. "Though you do have the right of it. If anyone could take ya there, Malakai could. He'd be the one to steer ya into the jaws of death, laughin' at its ugly bite while the wind tore the sails and whipped the sea into a frenzy. That'd be his way. But he's dead, lad. Been dead for a while now."

Wisp thanked the man and began to leave. "Hold, lad." The captain called him back. "There's one more might be willin' to take ya, an old tar named Sennar. It'd be a risk, though that shouldn't matter to ya seein' as you're goin' to the Sea of the Lost. Sennar knows as much of the sea as anyone, as much as a shark, some say; and ya might be better askin' a shark to take ya—the man's got a bitter eye and a bitter mouth. If you're still wantin' to go, find Sennar, he's the only one I know who'll think of takin' ya."

"Where will I find this Sennar?"

The captain laughed. "In one of the taverns. He'll be in his cups by dark most any night, but fear no, he'll be sober and sound in the morn'. In fact, he'll be up and ready long afore most men stir. You ask around, someone will direct ya to Sennar."

Wisp flipped a silver coin onto the center of the table. "Allow me to buy the drinks for your men. Payment for the interruption." He nodded in apology to the large man who Gregor offended. From the looks of surprise on their faces he knew it was more than enough. The big man would have been happy with a copper, but no sense in making enemies.

As they made their way across the tavern, dodging serving girls and men who had too many drinks, Gregor grabbed Wisp by the arm.

"Where did you learn to speak Gendan like that?"

"There's much you don't know of me, Gregor. But as to that, I was raised for a while by a thief in Pomanda who came from Genda. He taught me to speak it claiming that I might need it someday. I've used it on many occasions."

Wisp stopped, staring at two men who were just now taking a table. "I know them," he whispered to Gregor. "They're two of the ones who were under the wharf." Wisp nudged Gregor with his arm. "Let's see what information we can discover. The skinny one is a thief and should live by the honor of the guild." The bounty man snorted loud enough for Wisp to hear, which drew a frown but nothing more.

The thief cast wary looks at Wisp and Gregor as they approached. He was a thief, no doubt. Wisp had cast that same discriminating glance at many a stranger in his day. "I've come to claim the honor of a friend," Wisp said in the customary greeting of a member of the guild.

There was a series of questions and responses that would now follow depending on how high up in the guild a thief was positioned. The more code a person knew, the more prestige it carried. Wisp turned to Gregor and indicated he leave. He might trust the bounty man with his own life, but not with the honor of the guild.

The Gendan thief ran his eyes over Wisp, then back to Gregor. Wisp knew he'd be suspicious, but he'd go along for a while. He steered Wisp to an empty table close by. "And who might you claim as parents, friend?" The thief had not wasted time with false implications, he had put sarcastic emphasis on the *friend* part, grinning while he did.

Wisp ignored the slight. "I claim the rat as my father, and the weasel as my mother." Wisp could have prolonged the event by going through several more stages of questioning, but he cut to the chase. He felt certain that this thief was not placed high in the guild so he got into codes that would be above him. "I also claim the Lady Death as my patron." The man's eyes went wide.

"And her siblings as my victims." Wisp grinned when he said that. "Can you cite the names of her siblings?" And then Wisp waited an inordinately long time before saying, "*friend.*"

The thief bowed his acknowledgment that Wisp was his better. "How might I be of service?"

Wisp gave a nod of respect. "My name is of no import, but I bring greetings from both Sykor and Pomanda." This subtly told the man he was acquainted with the bosses of both cities. The man bowed again while Wisp continued. "I need information on a pirate named Malakai. Barring that, I require the services of one who is capable of taking us to the Sea of the Lost."

The thief wore a puzzled look. "Far as I know, Malakai's dead." He appeared to be giving thought to the other question. "And an old sot named Sennar is the only one I know who might be foolish enough to take ya on yer' journey, not the only one able mind ya, but the only one crazed enough to do it. Beware though, friend, Sennar's heart is bitter and easily swayed by gold. He's not a man to be trusted."

"Not many are these days," Wisp said as he spun to leave.

"Stay and quench your thirst," the thief invited. "What could be the rush?"

Wisp had been holding his temper as well as a deep desire to question the thief about Rahg. He had made up his mind to leave but was now losing patience with the man. He decided to see how far the honor of the guild would carry. "I might stay, if you'd tell me why you'd do harm to my friend from Kamnor."

The thief's brow furrowed. He stood and leaned closer to Wisp. "I believe yer knowin' more than ya should, friend. But out of respect for the guild I'll not hold it against ya. Now, stay and ya might be kept safe this night."

Wisp assumed his statement had something to do with Rahg and he turned to leave. Four large men with knives drawn blocked the way. He and Gregor were trapped, and if his guess was right the thief's friends would be after Rahg tonight. If it wasn't for their own desperate situation Wisp would have smiled. Whoever they sent would be in for a surprise when they had to deal with Rhaven.

As Wisp and Gregor were being forced to take a seat at the table, the captain and four crewmen that they had just been talking to approached them.

"Well, lad, are ya comin' or stayin'? I'll not be waitin' on any man." The captain stared straight into the Gendan thief's eyes. "You'll not be mindin', will ya?"

The thief and his men evaluated the burly seamen. Wisp saw in their eyes that they wouldn't challenge them. "We'll be joinin' ya," Wisp replied, and he and Gregor rose and departed with the captain. As they departed Wisp shot a look to the thief that told him they'd meet again.

FISHERMAN'S CATCH

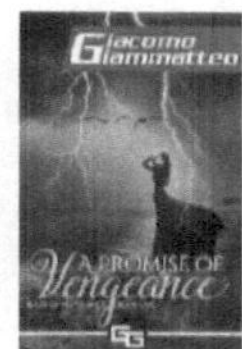

At the gaming table, Darstan gave full rein to the fates and, for now, they were being kind. Every roll of the dice brought him good fortune, and he rode his winning streak until a sizable amount of copper, silver, and even gold coin lay before him on the table. Darstan finally saw his winning streak coming to an end and quit before he lost it all. He looked around for Wisp and Gregor, but they were nowhere to be seen.

Pockets bulging with coin, Darstan kept a wary eye on all who came near. He had won enough for unscrupulous types to risk an attack. The need to be alert had a sobering effect on Darstan. When the serving girl came he requested khaffe instead of ale.

A pretty woman delivered the khaffe. She set his mug on the table and sat in the chair next to him.

"You're not the one who took my order," Darstan said.

"Should I leave?" she asked, her voice soft as powdered snow. The warning signs that should have been there melted with her first words.

"I'd prefer you stay."

~

The gnarled old man limped along the stone street hugging to the walls of the buildings. The street lamp had been snuffed out, but Sennar paid no attention. He turned up the darkened alley and made his way toward home.

The path was steep and narrow, and the walls of stone buildings rose on either side to a height of a span or more. Damp air seeped into his joints, aching. The pain slowed his pace. Midway up the hill a voice called to him from the shadows. He reached inside the lining of his shirt for the hilt of his knife, yet he didn't draw it; the voice belonged to a female.

"A moment of your time?" the gentle voice asked.

Sennar kept a firm grip on the blade of his knife. "Go on your way, bawdy woman. I'm past the temptin' age and by the looks of you, though it do be dark, I see your temptress days are long behind you."

The alley was dark but the moon provided ample light. A smile appeared then vanished from the old woman's face. She came closer.

"You should abandon your plan regarding the travelers you agreed to take-on."

Sennar squeezed his eyes and stared. "And what plans might they be old crone? What parts of a whisper did ya hear that made ya think ya could pry a copper out of ol' Sennar?"

The old hag cracked a wry smile. Something about it chipped away at Sennar's confidence.

"More than a whisper," she said. Her hushed voice forced Sennar to lean close. "And I want far more than a copper, twisted old man. I know about your plot to kill them and take their gold."

Sennar's mouth twisted into an evil grin; his eyes sharpened; and his good hand balled into a wadded fist. "Be dangerous to talk 'bout, old crow."

The old woman's eyes sparkled when he moved his hand toward the inside of his shirt. He had it tied at the waist, like most Gendans, and buttoned halfway up.

"I sense your fear, old man. I feel your pain."

The words needled Sennar yet he slowed. Something in her manner warned him to be cautious. She stared straight through him with eyes too young to belong to her. Sennar's hand rested on the hilt of the knife. In the blink of an eye he could draw it, but he wondered if it would be enough time. The more he looked, the more he didn't like something about this old hag. A faint glow came from her hands.

"If you bare a glimmer of steel, you will breathe no more."

Her words burned into him and her eyes held him fixed. Somehow he knew it was true, yet he couldn't allow himself to be pushed by a woman.

"I'll grant ya time to explain yerself—" Sennar had been about to say "old crow" but again, that strange feeling made him reconsider. "I can kill ya, or cut out your tongue. I've done both and not regretted it."

Her hands glowed brighter. Sennar took a step back. Something moved on the ground, slid across the rough stone blocks. It seemed to fade in and out of sight, like a mirage—clear, like water from a spring, yet it had form—life. A thin slice of it slid under Sennar's feet. Before he could do anything, it rose up around him like a waterspout, but slow, purposeful. It engulfed him, closing over his head to form a seal. His arms wouldn't move. The shield, or whatever it was, held him fast.

Before Sennar could scream, she slammed him against the wall, releasing the shield just in time for him to feel the full impact of the collision. He crumbled to the street, gasping for air. His gnarled hand pushed against the paving blocks in an effort to get to his feet. Sennar remained stooped, whether from fear or pain, even he wasn't certain.

"What is it you wish, My Lady?"

She smiled. "I wish nothing more than the safety of the party you have contracted with."

Sennar was eager to provide her with an assurance but his mind raced. There were problems. "Lady, I want to do your bidding, believe me. But others are involved. I planned to split the gold with the crew, and they'll not be lookin' kindly to me changin' my mind."

Her expression never altered. "Find another crew. I will...explain to the others. You have no need to worry of my well being."

That same wry smile crossed her face and gave her a mischievous look, though more sinister than that. Sennar didn't like the crew he had chosen anyway, none except Tesro, and he wouldn't miss him much. "I'll be findin' another crew tomorrow."

"Fear has hold of you now, old man. Fear gives strength to words of the moment. By tomorrow you will forget your promises, and I can't have that." The old woman held him under her gaze for a long time, as if his soul had been revealed to her. "As to the new crew you choose, tell them as little as possible of where you are going or why."

Sennar took another step backward. He had no desire for a repeat of whatever it was she did to him earlier.

"Old man, you know what I'm capable of. Be still and no harm will visit you."

She moved her hands toward his side, the side that was twisted and marred like his face and hand. A blue light crawled along her skin. He closed his eyes and pressed his head against the wall. Her touch was cold. So cold it burned.

Sennar flinched, his mind overcoming natural reflexes to pull away.

He gritted teeth, and clenched his fist. He pressed his back tighter against the wall and squeezed his eyes, cursing himself for trusting the old woman.

The cold of her touch burned through his clothes and into his skin. He felt movement, like a snake crawling inside his shirt. A low moan wriggled up his throat and out his lips then a queasy feeling turned his stomach sour. The twisting continued and the cold grew worse and deeper.

Suddenly, it was like he was afire, the flame searing his already burnt side. It was the first he had felt sensations there in many years, and it caused him to recall the night of the accident, how he had been trapped under the riggings with the whole ship afire. His skin was burning and the putrid smell assaulted his nose. When the deckhand tried pulling him out, Sennar begged to be left to die, and many nights since he still wished he had died that night.

The old man winced. Pain was such a new feeling to his old scarred tissue that he had no tolerance for it. He shivered and shook and held his back tight against the wall but he never tried to escape. When it ended she stared into his eyes with her penetrating gaze. He placed his hands to his side. The smoothness startled him.

"Look at yourself," she said.

His eyes went wide. Where there had only been burnt flesh, it was as new skin. Sennar's voice cracked. "H..how?"

"Never mind the how," the old woman said, "simply know that should I wish it, most of your body might be restored. If you assure the safety of my friends, I shall mend the remainder of your woes. That is a promise."

Sennar stared at her and nodded. He came close to shedding tears. "They'll be kept safe, Lady. I'll tear the lungs out of a gorphon with my bare hands afore I let any harm come to that group. And if you're wishin', Lady, I'll take care of that other crew myself. No sense wastin' yer good time on it, if—"

"No need. I have said what I'll do. It will be done. Believe me, you have no need to worry about that crew."

Sennar tipped his head and bowed. "My thanks go with ya, My Lady. May the gods look kindly on ya." Sennar walked away rubbing his hand along the newly healed side.

Before turning the corner, Sennar looked back, but the woman was gone. Her absence caused him to stop and look closer. There was no way out of the alley other than to pass him, or to go the long way back down the hill, and she could not have made it so far in this short a time. For a while, he stared then he spun back around and continued on his way home. He whispered a prayer in Tesro's honor. He didn't know what fate the old woman had planned for that crew, but he wouldn't want anything to do with it.

~

Wisp and Gregor hurried through the door to the Winds of Storm tavern. The bounty man exhaled a sigh of relief as he saw Rahg and Camissa at the table with Rhaven. "They're here." Gregor jostled his way through the crowd until he reached the table. "Did you have any trouble?" he asked Rhaven.

"None," Rhaven said. "Have you seen Darstan?"

Wisp and Gregor looked at each other. "Not since we left him here playing the games. He might have gone back to the room to sleep off the vidda."

"I checked," Tobias said. "Are you certain it was Rahg those men were after?"

"Exactly what did they say?" Rhaven gulped what remained of a mug of vidda.

Wisp shivered. He couldn't take a swig without gagging. Wisp thought back to the night under the wharf when he overheard the conversation between the thief and his cohorts. He had uncanny powers of recall and was able to reconstruct the exchange word for word in his head. The thief had been telling them they didn't want to deal with Rhaven. "The other'll come free soon enough," he had said. "We'll just concentrate on the boy."

Shame and embarrassment tainted Wisp's cheeks red. "I made a mistake. They only referred to him as *the boy* and I assumed it was Rahg. It never occurred to me it could have been Darstan. Ever since I've joined you, Rahg has been the target."

Rhaven shoved the chair back and pushed the table forward. "Save your apologies for Darstan—if he lives." He stormed out of the tavern.

"Where are you going?" Camissa called, but her words were absorbed by the crowd.

Wisp, red-faced now, turned to leave as well. Gregor grabbed his arm, the bounty man's face a question. "I'm going to find the thief," Wisp said. "This time, he'll not have his friends to help him, and he *will* answer my questions."

Gregor released his hold and followed Wisp, a determined prance told his attitude.

Rahg was leaving when Camissa reached for him. "I'll not sit idly by, Camissa. Darstan's my brother." The three of them rushed out the door and headed toward the inn where Gregor and Wisp had seen the thief.

~

Half the night passed before they located the thief. Wisp searched several taverns then questioned some of the local thieves to discover where he worked. "The merchant district," they said. It was a logical place for a good thief. "If he's down there, we'll find him," Wisp said. "Let's go."

Wisp surveyed the scene to determine where the thief might strike. He saw a store that dealt in fine jewels and another that offered crafts carved from rare stones. A third boasted of spices, khaffe, and foods from remote sections of Khatara. A sign in the window claimed they had red pepper leaves from Sethia, one of the most sought after spices of all.

He suggested that Gregor and Rahg remain below and wait on the streets while he went up on the roof. Wisp scaled the wall as if it were built for climbing. Once on the rooftop he blended with the shadows. Before, it would have been difficult to see him, now it was impossible. He waited for the thief to show.

The Gendan thief crept around the corner of the rooftop and approached the spot where Wisp waited. The thief gasped as Wisp's knife pressed hard against his throat.

"You!"

"Make no sound," Wisp let out two short whistles, the second of a higher pitch, a signal to Gregor and Rahg. They climbed a ladder fastened to the end of a building at the intersection of the next street. When Rahg came into view, Wisp questioned the thief. "Is he the one you sought?"

The thief shook his head. "No, the other one, though you'd be wise to forget about it now. It's a dangerous game yer playin' in. Besides, the other one's sure to be gone by now."

"What do you mean by that?" Wisp asked.

"They were to get 'im tonight, if they could."

"Who?" Rahg shouted.

Wisp held up a hand signaling Rahg to be quiet. "As my friend asks, who?"

"The stakes are too high. Even the honor of the guild is not enough. ya just don't understand—"

"I think, my friend, that you are the one who does not grasp the seriousness of the matter. If I don't discover what I need to know, your life will be forfeit."

The thief laughed. "Ya forget so soon that I offered to spare yer life earlier by keepin' ya at the inn."

Wisp got a long length of rope from Gregor and secured the thief's hands behind his back then he tied his feet to his hands so that the man's body was arced like a bow.

"There's no need to tie me, friend. If yer wishin' to get yerself killed chasin' yer friend you'll not find me blockin' yer way. But I won't tell you where they took him."

"You still fail to understand," Wisp said.

Gregor tied another line to the middle of the rope and the other end they wrapped around the chimney. The three of them hoisted the thief up and over the roof and let him dangle over the edge. The pressure of his weight caused the rope to pull and stretch him further. The thief howled. Wisp held his blade against the rope. "Make more noise and I slice."

Wisp waited for a few heartbeats. "Who is after Darstan, and where were they going with him?"

The thief gasped in short, pressure-filled breaths. "Told ya," he said. "Too much... at stake."

Wisp nodded as if he had expected that answer. He dropped the loose end of the rope that secured the man's hands and feet. It fell nearly to the ground, almost two spans below.

"Are you leaving?" Rahg asked. "We need to find out about Darstan. I'll get a response from him."

Wisp grabbed Rahg's loose sleeve. "Trust me. I will."

They walked to the end of the building and descended using the ladder. Soon after, they stood below the man suspended from the rooftop. Wisp grabbed the loose end of the rope he had dropped. Tilting his head back, he looked up. "One final time, you have the opportunity to save yourself. Mark me well, you'll die if you keep silent."

The thief looked as if his sides were cramping, legs too. "Can't... now, let me down."

"I will." Wisp removed a firestriker from his shirt and struck the two pieces together to light the end of the rope. Flames danced up the dried hemp.

"What are ya doin'?" The thief's panic-stricken voice carried far into the night.

"You have little time," Wisp said. "I'll not be able to reach the rope to extinguish it after that."

For all his bravado, the thief must have recognized the danger of the situation and knew that he had run out of time. "I don't know where the orders came from, but it wasn't through the guild. Whoever it was sent six men with a lot of gold. I think the men might be Sykoran guards." Terror filled his plea. "Now cut me loose."

Wisp feinted a gesture as if he were reaching for the rope, then smiled. "I apologize, friend, but it's too late."

The thief screamed. "Ya can't leave me! I got kids! Two boys," but Wisp was already walking away.

"You broke the honor of the guild by partaking in this. You knew the penalty." He looked back at Rahg and Gregor. "Come, we have men to track down—Sykoran guards."

"You're going to just leave him?" Rahg asked.

"And we'd better hurry before the Gendan watch comes," Wisp said, and broke into a sprint down the darkened street. Gregor and Rahg followed.

~

The thief heard their boots click on the cobblestones, but his own screams drowned the noise. He watched the fire rush toward the knot that held him safe. The flames raced toward the knot that held his life. The rope slipped a notch.

The thief stopped shouting and muttered a silent prayer, something he hadn't done since he was a little child. The next slip began his descent. He plummeted toward the paving stones. He knew the worn out old stones had no edges but they appeared sharply ridged to him, as he rushed downward to meet them. Instinctively, he turned his face sideways and closed his eyes just before he hit. He was screaming and saying prayers of forgiveness when his head cracked into the pavement.

~

Rahg heard the final wail of the man as he plummeted to his death. The silence that followed roared in Rahg's ears. He winced. They had stopped running, slowing to a brisk walk. "Why did he have to die?"

Wisp stopped and stared. Rahg had never seen such fire in his eyes before. They were as brown and shiny as a beaver's winter coat. "He was caught. He knew he might be and took the risk. If the Sykoran guard catch me, I'd be sentenced to die. I know that. He knew it, too. Now let's find Darstan."

~

*T*obias and Camissa started their questions with the women at the inn. "Darstan would draw their attention," Camissa said.

At the fourth table, someone remembered him. "I saw 'im," a woman said. "Was with a pretty lass, sittin' at that table right there." She pointed in the direction of a table only two spaces away.

"That was no pretty lass," one of the men blurted out. "That was Nirida."

"Did they leave the inn together?" Tobias asked.

"Believe so," the woman said.

Tobias was just completing his questions when Wisp, Gregor, and Rahg arrived. He offered thanks to the people for helping, then departed.

"Have you found anything?" Camissa asked.

"Sykoran guards took him," Gregor said.

"Ludar!" Tobias uttered the name like a curse.

"What?" Rahg seemed puzzled.

"Ludar," Tobias said. "I'd wager good gold he was the one behind this. Remember, he tried to stop Darstan from leaving Sykor. I told you I didn't like him the first time I saw him."

"Where should we look?" Rahg asked.

Even as he said it, Rhaven raced toward the door. "Take charge, Tobias."

Tobias bit hard on the stem of his pipe. "We're gonna hunt 'em down like eels," he said, hand squeezing the hilt of his sword. "Rahg, you and Camissa come with me. Wisp, go with Gregor." He threw a few coppers on the table and pulled his hat down on his head. "If you find 'em, one keep track while the other finds us." He was shaking his head as he left. "If they hurt that boy..."

CAPTURED

*D*arstan's head throbbed with each step the horse took. He lay strapped across a saddle, fastened like a prisoner. But the horse wasn't Grayson, and he wondered what became of his own mount. Two men were in front of him and two behind. A pair of bodies lay sprawled over another mount.

The men wore dull–gray uniforms coated with dust from the trail, and each had a quiver of arrows strapped to their backs and a sheath to hold a sword. Black, leather-wrapped hilts peeked over uniforms that Darstan recognized as belonging to Sykorans. Their polished helmets named them as members of the king's personal guard. He wondered if they were truly part of the guard or wearing the uniform for disguise. Last night they were dressed as Gendans.

Must have been a disguise.

The sight of the bodies brought the memories rushing back. He had been drinking vidda—too much if truth be known—and gambling. He had won a fair amount of gold and then met Nirida. He talked to her a lot at the tavern, then they went for a walk. He knew what kind of woman she was, but that didn't bother him. Her conversation was pleasant, and she had a smile that put a glitter in her eyes.

They walked for a long time along the old street by the sea, then turned up a steep hill toward one of the old sections of Genda. As they made their second turn, crossing a street by an old warehouse, Darstan noticed a group of men following them. He recognized them from the inn. "How far to your home?"

Nirida must have sensed the danger. "Several more streets yet. Why?" Her eyes darted about as she clutched his arm.

Darstan glanced back at the group on their trail. The gap between them had closed and they no longer made a pretense about it. Three continued to follow them while the other three appeared to be making a sweep to cut them off. Darstan realized they would not make it to Nirida's house, so he maneuvered into a defensible position. He recalled Rhaven's teachings about fighting more than one man at a time.

"When it is one against one," Rhaven explained, "each person is trying to kill the other. When there are many against one, each of your opponents is more concerned with sparing himself injury, relying on the others to do the killing."

I sure hope so, Darstan thought, just as they rounded the corner.

"Remember, we want him alive," one of the men said.

The statement was all the confirmation Darstan needed. He leapt from the doorway to attack.

His sword found its mark in the lead man's gut. He crumbled to the street, blood gushing. Darstan felt excitement, but he knew the man's shrill cry would bring the others from down the street. The two remaining men were taken unaware; they retreated, but soon regained composure and advanced. There wasn't much time before the others arrived. His opponents kept him occupied with an occasional parry or thrust, biding time until the others arrived.

Darstan couldn't afford to wait. He feigned a wild thrust toward the one on his left, hoping to draw the other one in. Without hesitation, he spun forward then around to his right and lunged at the man who had delayed his attack.

Darstan's sword found his exposed belly. He rammed the blade in. The man moaned, clutching his gut as he fell to the ground. The last of the three stepped back, fear in his eyes. "Come to me, now," Darstan said, then felt a crushing blow to the back of his head. He remembered falling to the street.

Those memories brought him all the way to the present. *Where am I? And where are they taking me? And why?*

The pain in his head continued to pound, and at this point Darstan didn't know whether to blame the vidda or the blow to the head. "Stop!" Darstan yelled.

The lead rider halted, tugging hard on the reins of his mount. He turned, focusing an angry glare on Darstan. "What do you want?"

"I need to piss. Use the woods, too."

The man glared for what seemed like an eternity, then nodded to another guard who untied him. Darstan dismounted, groaning when he touched the ground. Every movement hurt. Thick, clinging vines grabbed his britches as he fought his way through the underbrush to a secluded spot. Everything was damp, yet he was sure it hadn't rained. Even in his condition he felt certain he would have remembered it raining. He wondered where the dust on the uniforms had come from. Not here.

"Here's good enough," the guard said.

Darstan scowled, pushing low hanging cedar branches aside, while deftly avoiding long strands of demon's claws. A large hickory had carved a small clearing suitable for Darstan's purposes. The guard stuck to him like beeswax; privacy would not be an option.

Darstan kept a slow pace on his return to the horses, the guard right on his heels. The other three men had remained mounted, waiting. Now that he had the opportunity, he examined their garb for more details. One wore a simple guard uniform, the sleeves had the light-gray band of a recruit.

The one who followed him into the woods was a sergeant. He recognized it as the same insignia that Takar wore. The third one looked the meanest; he had a hawk-nose, curled-up lip, and a pock-marked face. His rank was below sergeant though he looked like he'd been in the guard for thirty years and been through a hundred battles. Darstan turned to face the leader. He had been in Sykor long enough to recognize the differences in rank of the Sykoran guard and he knew this man wore the uniform of a strike leader. "Where are you taking me?"

Darstan reeled from the impact of a hard boot against the side of his face. He staggered and fell but jumped up as soon as he hit the ground, standing defiant, ready to fight. His hand reached for a sword hilt that wasn't there. The hard-looking one had kicked him.

"Put a blade in my hand," Darstan said. "We'll see who's the better man."

"Enough," the strike leader yelled.

The man who struck Darstan obeyed with no hesitation. Darstan decided to press his luck while he had the attention of the strike leader. "What became of the girl?"

The sergeant laughed. "Why? Did you like her?"

The guard who kicked him joined in. Even his voice irritated Darstan. "Shame you never got to have your time with her—we did."

Darstan stared at each one. The young guard wasn't laughing, neither was the strike leader. It was then and there that Darstan swore vengeance. *I'll live to kill them,* he vowed.

Darstan laughed. "She was sick, fools. There's not a man in Genda that would be her bedmate. Serves you well. Just rewards, I'd guess." He began to say something else when the leader struck him from behind.

Darstan staggered.

"Are you speaking truth, boy?" He hit Darstan harder, knocking him to the ground. "Are you?"

Darstan lay prone on the ground. As he rose, he wiped dirt from his mouth. His head bled and the throbbing was worse. The leader had hit him with a guard's club. *Must be what he hit me with last night. He'll suffer double for that.*

The strike leader cursed. "Fools! Caen, I told you not to bother her. And you, Bartel. It wasn't part of the plan to bother anyone but him. Well, now you've got your rewards just like he says, and I can't be sorry for you."

One of the guards reached for a knife, the hardened one. *Caen.* Darstan committed the name to memory. Caen appeared as if he might cut Darstan with the blade, but the leader stepped in front of him.

"No harm. You know what will happen if we bring him back damaged. Remember that."

Caen glared at Darstan then sheathed his blade.

Darstan smiled. This was important information to know. If whoever ordered him abducted wanted him kept safe...he could take liberties he might not otherwise try. Darstan saw his sword strapped to Caen's belt. His eyes narrowed, and his jaw tightened like a vise. "I'll get that back when I kill you."

The strike leader turned, glaring. "Fair warning, we have orders not to harm you, but don't let that taint your judgment. I know of ways to cause a man pain without it showing. Irritate me and you'll be yelping like a lost pup."

The man never blinked while glaring at him. He was serious.

"Mark it well, lad. Now, let's ride." The strike leader's heels dug into the sides of his horse. "We have a long way to go."

Darstan was concerned, but his curiosity had now been aroused. Who had ordered him taken? And why? *I'll find out, and I'll make him pay, too.*

As they set off through the woods, Darstan plotted. Rhaven would come for him, so the best thing to do would be leave as many clues as possible. Whenever he could, he broke branches, snapped twigs, and left marks in the woods.

The sergeant approached from the rear, having remained behind to determine if they were being followed. "See anything?" the strike leader called.

"Nothing. I'll watch him now."

The strike leader spun in the saddle. "Keep checking. I don't want that other one creeping up on us."

Darstan smiled. They must have been referring to Rhaven. When the sergeant turned away, Darstan broke another branch. He knew that no matter how they tried, they could not hide their trail from Rhaven, but Darstan might as well make it easier for him. As he thought that, an image of what Rhaven would do to them flashed in his mind. Darstan smiled. *Just save Caen for me.*

IN SEARCH OF DARSTAN

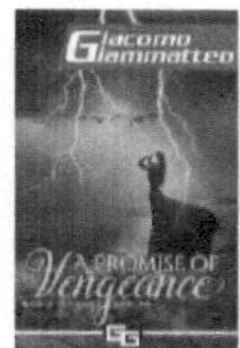

Rahg rubbed tired eyes pried open by morning sun. They had spent all night searching for Darstan, though not even Rhaven could find a trace of him. Rahg dressed and sat on the edge of the bed, despair weighing him down. *Where could he be?*

A tap on the shoulder startled him. "Come, Rahg. We'll eat, then find your brother." Gregor's words offered comfort but Rahg heard no confidence in his voice.

"We'll find him," Wisp said.

Rahg smiled. "Perhaps we will," he said, and descended the steps to the common room.

Tobias sat at a table with Rhaven and Camissa. "Morning, lad. Better hurry if you plan to catch up on the khaffe. Rhaven's already had three, and I believe I might have matched him. Food's good too."

Camissa sipped on a cup of te and wiped sleep from her eyes. She had on the green shirt that Rahg liked, the one that made her blue eyes shine.

"Good morning, Camissa. How long have you been up?"

"Long enough to have finished two cups of te," Tobias said. "Sit down, lad."

Rahg pulled his chair in close to the table, just as the serving girl placed a mug of hot khaffe in front of him. "I'd like some biscuits," Rahg said. "Nothing else. Just khaffe and biscuits."

Tobias frowned. "Need more than that if you're gonna be traipsin' all over Genda lookin' for Darstan. Not like you to skip a meal, lad. It's a hot one already, and the sun's just barely startin'. It'll get bad before the day is through. I've seen 'em like this. Gonna get real hot."

The serving girl raised her eyebrows as she looked back to Rahg.

"Just biscuits," Rahg said. "That's all I want."

"Suit yerself," Tobias mumbled.

"We've got to get going, Tobias. Darstan's in trouble and I'm not going to sit around eating when we could be looking for him."

Tobias set his mug down and looked at Rahg. "Got to eat too, lad. It's gonna be a long day. You'll need the food."

Rahg nodded. "How do we find this... Nirida? Isn't that her name?"

"I know where to find her," Rhaven said. "It's but a short walk from here."

While they ate, Sennar entered the inn and limped toward their table. Rahg grimaced. Just the sight of him caused Rahg to cringe. He knew it was wrong to feel that way but he couldn't help it.

Sennar's twisted and gnarled hand came to rest on the table right next to Rahg. Rahg leaned closer to Camissa and pretended to whisper to her.

Sennar's voice was all gravel. "I'll be needin' the rest of the gold now, and we're leavin' at first light tomorrow, so be ready." Sennar spoke to Tobias but all the while he stared at Rhaven.

"Is the weather right?" Rhaven asked.

"I've been out to look this morn'. It's right as it'll ever be, far as I can tell. That's why we need to take advantage of it. Can never tell when a storm'll come up. I've been through a lot of storms, but no need in fightin' one if it can be avoided. Especially where we're goin'. Don't need no extra troubles."

Rhaven's eyes narrowed. "Why not go now?"

Sennar's smile added to the uneasiness Rahg already felt. He was reminded of Kanella's cousin, the one who was crazed and jumped off the high bridge into the icy waters of the river just after Wish Day. He had that same kind of smile. If Sennar's smile struck Rahg as odd, his voice caused him further discomfort. A cackle seemed to lurk behind every syllable.

"The crew that sails with us is brave, not stupid. Most will know they'll never return. Some have families, though I try to limit those to only a few. Men with families have too much to care about. Might cloud their judgment. Still, most have someone they want to share their gold with should they meet the Great God of the Sea. They'll be wantin' to give 'em some of their pay in advance and spend a few moments with 'em. It's a right, and it's not up for arguin'. I did it as well, though I plan on returnin' to spend it myself."

Rahg must have been grimacing, for the old seaman turned to him with a look of sympathy. "Don't fret, lad. There are worse ways to die than to go at sea. And if we don't come back they'll spin tales about ya and tell yarns of how ya went out with old Sennar and fought great sea monsters, and rocks that move, and all the other things that can only be found in the Sea of the Lost."

Sennar took the gold from Rhaven. The cackle that seemed hidden behind his every word now surfaced like a great whale. "Who knows," Sennar bellowed, "It may be that we'll do all those things. Think of that, lad. Wouldn't ya like to die fightin' a sea monster?" The crowded room absorbed the sounds of Sennar's cackle as he walked out of the inn, but to Rahg the taunt seemed to linger, and it echoed in his mind for a long, long time.

~

Sennar walked toward the wharf, cursing the leg that caused his limp. He strained to increase the pace, but even with the cane for support he couldn't equal the comfortable gait of a normal man. Three seamen accompanied him, armed with sword and knife. Even unarmed they would be dangerous and, as anyone could tell from the looks of them, trouble would be no stranger.

Sennar reached inside his shirt to rub the spot that the old healer woman had touched. He was almost afraid to touch it; afraid it would be deformed, twisted, and burnt; afraid that the memories of the other night would disappear and he would awaken from a cruel, tormenting nightmare.

He sighed when he felt the smooth texture of the freshly healed skin. He stretched his hand further to feel the difference as it brushed against the old scars. Now he knew he wasn't dreaming, and the realization renewed his energy, filled him with confidence for the task ahead.

He was here to hire a crew, one that could take their passengers through the Sea of the Lost. Sennar stifled a laugh. It was probably impossible. Nonetheless, he would try, and he'd take many with him. He would lie and bribe and do anything else necessary to get a crew to accompany him, all the while knowing that most would never return.

Strange. In the past this wouldn't have bothered him; he wouldn't have given a second thought to lying to these men and sending them to their deaths. Odd that he should care now, when it really mattered to him; when the outcome of the journey was so important. No matter. The decision had been made. There was no turning back.

Sennar stared at the gnarled lump of flesh that was his hand. He tried to imagine it as normal. It once was, before the fire. He brought the corner of his twisted mouth up in a curl. He could feel the tightness of the scarred tissue. A memory of what he once looked like flashed before him. Handsome, women had called him, and he was well aware of it. Even if things worked out, he wondered what he would look like. It had been so long since he was a whole person. Anxiety burned in him, and like a shark with the scent of blood, he pressed on. This mission would be finished. Of that there was no doubt. How many men would return with him? He had no notion, but *he* would return.

The raucous shouts of the seamen gathered at the docks captured Sennar's attention. He would find the best of them, the most desperate and most wicked. They would be the ones who would risk all for gold.

"I have gold!" Sennar shouted above the din of the early morning crowd. "Gold for those who are brave."

"For goin' where?" a seaman shouted.

"If ya need to ask where, you'll not be goin' with me."

Sennar climbed atop an empty crate so he stood a full head above the tallest of the crowd. He scanned the gathering of hungry, desperate men, and made sure he touched each of them with his stare. "I have enough room for fifty good men—fifty, good and *brave* men. You'll be sailin' with me, 'Old Crazy.'"

A hush fell over the crowd.

Sennar smiled. "That's right. I know what's said about me. And it may be that they're right. Could be that I'm crazed." He leaned toward the front line of men and lowered his voice, knowing the ones toward the back had to strain to hear. "But it'll take a madman to get us where we have to go." Sennar sensed the anxiousness in the men.

From the middle of the crowd someone shouted. "Where are ya takin' us? And what are we lookin' for?"

The gnarled old sea captain bent over and glared at the man. "I'll not be needin' you. You'll be gettin' no share of the gold." He smiled when he saw the panic in their eyes, when they moved away from the man as if he had the fever.

"How much gold?" a man in the middle of the pack demanded to know.

"More gold than ya can all care to count. You'll be eatin' gold. And drinkin' gold. And you'll be throwin' gold in the streets for the *scugini* to fight over." He paused a long time. "Those of you that come will have it. But mind ya, I only need fifty men. And I'm tellin' it to all now —this is a *dead man's run.*"

Sennar saw the greed in their eyes, and remembered when he would have sailed for those same reasons. He noted how each one turned to count how many men were considering the trip, then judged their own chances of getting selected, and of surviving. Soon, more than three dozen voices called out, begging to be chosen. That inspired others, and more shouted to join. Sennar smiled.

"Some won't come back," he shouted again, but only so he could say that he warned them. They were committed. Each one was certain that some would die, but each one also assumed it would not be him. Sennar wished to rile them up one last time. "Some won't return. But *I* intend to. We sail tomorrow with the morning sun."

Rousing shouts and cheers echoed his enthusiasm.

~

"*I*s this it?" Rahg asked.

"This is the place," Rhaven said. "This is where they said the girl lived."

Wisp pounded on the door once again. "I can't imagine her being gone at this time of day. Most of the... uh, night-women prefer to sleep late."

Camissa smiled, but couldn't resist the chance to taunt. "And how would you know so much of the 'night-women', Kender Darnell?"

Wisp's face flushed red. "Keep a watch. I'll go through the window and unlatch the door."

"Hurry," Gregor said, "We don't wish to be seen."

Wisp scurried up the wall like a spider, popped open the window, and soon afterward they were staring at him through the opened doorway. Wisp had a grim look on his face. "Hurry," he said. "Darstan's not here, and the girl's hurt."

There was only the one room; it was adequate, no more. A table stood in the far corner that held a basin, and off to the side stood a small eating table with two chairs tucked underneath. A large bed sat against the opposite wall. Huddled in the darkest corner was the girl.

She cringed as they approached.

Camissa moved to the front. "It's all right, Nirida. My name is Camissa. I'm a friend of Darstan."

The fear left Nirida's eyes, and she unfolded her arms from their protective grip around the bedpost. Her face was battered, left eye swollen shut, and dried blood caked under a broken nose. Her knees were tucked against her chest. She wore no clothes.

Rahg grabbed a loose blanket. "Take this," he said, and threw the cover to her. She seized it like a hungry pup.

"No one will harm you," Camissa said. "We came to find Darstan." She stroked Nirida's hair while the girl released her emotions. "Come, I'll help you wash, then we'll clean these wounds and have a meal. Some hot food will do you good."

Camissa turned toward the men, gathered about looking helpless. "Tobias, you and the others get something for her to eat. Gregor, find a healer with herbs to fight the fever. Kender and Rahg, get hot water and bandages." Camissa looked at Nirida again. "What drink do you take?"

"Khaffe."

"Bring khaffe, Tobias, and I'll take some more te. Hurry. You men be off and let us be."

isp and Rahg returned soon with the hot water. "I brought a clean cloth for Nirida to use," Rahg said. "Is Gregor back with the herbs?"

A light rap sounded on the door then it opened, admitting Tobias and Rhaven with the food. Nirida had dressed, and though her face still showed signs of a rough beating, she looked much better. Cleaning the dried blood off of her face made a biggest difference.

"You look a lot better." Rahg said.

"Thank you." Nirida's voice was sultry, even when being shy and reserved. "And thank you for the blanket."

Rahg lowered his head. He didn't know how she felt about him seeing her unclothed.

Gregor's entrance proved timely, shifting the focus of Nirida's attention away from Rahg. "I have the herbs, Camissa, though at the price the old hag demanded I would hope the girl to be healed by nightfall."

Wisp grinned. "Gregor is ever thinking of gold, Nirida. Don't be offended by his remarks."

Nirida's face formed a gentle smile.

"I have no wish to be harsh, lass, but you must tell us what happened. Where is Darstan?" Wisp had a way of impressing a sense of urgency on people without seeming offensive.

A frown returned to Nirida's face along with sad eyes. She lowered her head and told her story. She told of how Darstan began talking to her at the inn, and how they shared many stories together. "We talked for a long time before deciding to come here. I liked him."

She started crying again. "They followed us. Six of them. I begged," Nirida said, "But they seemed to get worse when I did."

Rahg gritted his teeth as she described the horrors they inflicted upon her. He noted, too, the whitened knuckles on Rhaven's hand, his fist clenched tight enough to crush a stone.

"...and I think they said they'd be taking him to Khatara. I heard the mean one say it to the other."

"Why would six Gendan fishermen take Darstan? And why to Khatara?" Tobias wondered aloud.

"Did they mention anything else?" Wisp asked. "What happened to the two that Darstan killed?"

"They took the bodies with them. I saw them pick the dead ones up when they went. Left me here to die, I guess." Nirida cried. "I hope they didn't kill Darstan."

Wisp waited until she calmed down somewhat. "Did you hear them say anything else? Anything at all?"

She thought for a moment, then shook her head. "No. Nothing else."

Rhaven rubbed her back. "Don't fear, girl. We'll find these men, and then we'll kill them."

"Not the young one!" Nirida looked up to Rhaven. "He didn't...hurt me. Not like the other two." Nirida's sobbing started again. "The leader didn't bother me either," she added almost as an afterthought. "It was just those two."

Rhaven nodded, then handed her a pouch with copper and silver coins, even gold. "Take this." He started toward the door, then turned back to Nirida. "Perhaps you might use this to begin anew. There's enough gold to take you anywhere you wish. You could go where no one knows you."

Before she said anything, Rhaven added. "But do as you wish. I'm not one to preach." He headed for the door.

Camissa stayed for a few moments after the others left. When she joined them in the street they were arguing over which way to begin the search for Darstan.

"I know who they are," Wisp said. "When I heard Nirida's description I recalled seeing them at the inn. Fact is, I was standing right next to their table. Something struck me as odd about them. I didn't know what at the time, but now I do. They were from Sykor. I'm certain of that now."

"How can you be sure?" Gregor asked. "Just because that thief said so? He lied!"

"One of them was telling a story about sailing on a ship, and he kept referring to 'buckets' of water. Someone from Genda wouldn't say *bucket*, they'd say *pail*. It didn't strike me as odd at first because I'm accustomed to hearing it in Sykor, but when Nirida was telling her story it just occurred to me. And they didn't smell like fishermen either."

Tobias scowled as he searched for a striker. "Even if they are from Sykor that doesn't say that's where they'll be takin' Darstan. They could be at the docks now, preparin' to leave on a ship. I say we search there first."

"I agree with Tobias," Rhaven said. "We search the docks first. If we find nothing, then we pick up their trail in the woods. It will still be there."

～

*T*he noise of the woods at night never bothered Darstan before, but now it did. Escape plans rambled through his mind, but so too, did the futility of them. Darstan had followed each conceived plan through to its inevitable outcome—his recapture, and likely with injuries that brought him close to death. Fear also seeped into Darstan's mind, trickled in unnoticed.

He put on a good act, but he was scared and the uncertainty of what lay ahead proved to be the most unnerving. Now light shined through a pale-gray cloud signaling the arrival of morning. *Blood of rats! I haven't even slept yet.* Darstan laughed at his silent expression. *I've been spending too much time with Wisp. I'm even beginning to curse like him.*

Evin, the younger guard, came to wake him. "Get up."

Couldn't scare a rabbit with that voice, thought Darstan, but he was glad it was Evin and not Caen. Darstan looked up at Evin. Seeing him from this angle reinforced his earlier impression of familiarity, yet he still could not recall where he had seen him.

Darstan attempted to make conversation while he stumbled toward the woods. "Are you from Sykor?" Darstan continued even when he received no response. "Why are you taking me back to Sykor?" He listened for an answer but got none. Pushing branches aside, he stepped into a small clearing inside a tightly knit group of trees laced thick with vines.

"If you are from Sykor," Darstan said, as he ducked under some thorns, "you could all be in grave trouble." He paused. "Force Commander Ludar is my cousin." Darstan spun to see if it drew any reaction, and thought he saw a look of surprise in Evin's eyes, but he couldn't be sure. Darstan reemerged, fastening the clasp on his britches as he tried to elicit some guilt in the young guard. "Why don't you talk with me?" he pleaded with an innocent voice.

Evin's posture relaxed and his expression softened. "I have orders... Darstan. It is Darstan, isn't it?"

Darstan nodded.

"But I would welcome the company and the talk as long as it's not against orders."

Darstan smiled. "Good. At least we'll have conversation." He saw Evin smile, and was sure he could see the tension leave the guard's face.

There were no discussions of significance during the morning meal, nothing that Darstan could gather information from anyway. The khaffe was bad, worse even than the bitter-strong drink served in Genda, but he drank it nonetheless; it helped to take the sleep from his eyes and clear his foggy mind.

He bit into a piece of stale bread and wondered if the guards' bread was any fresher. The meat he also found wanting; it had been salted too generously, but despite all that, it was nourishment, and he needed that to stay strong.

Caen did most of the talking, though his contributions consisted primarily of complaints. The strike leader sat without speaking until the meal ended.

"Time to mount. I want to reach the river by nightfall. There's an abandoned fort we can use for shelter just before reaching the swamps."

Darstan swung up onto the horse's back; they had not given him a saddle with stirrups. Probably to make it more difficult to escape. Stirrups didn't matter to Darstan though, he had ridden Timor and Lanna since he was barely old enough to walk. He needed no stirrups to help him ride. "Is that the Cypress Swamps that we'll be comin' to?"

Strike Leader Wehr barked orders to them but never answered Darstan's question. "Evin, take the rear, and keep a good eye on him. Caen, you scout ahead; I want no surprises. Sergeant, the rear guard. Keep me informed."

Evin steered his mount close to Darstan's, close enough so he could speak and not be heard by the strike leader. "Darstan, I wanted to tell you but I haven't had the chance. The other night in Genda, I..I didn't hurt the girl. I only pretended so they wouldn't bother me, but I would never do that to a girl."

Darstan stared at the young guard. He noted the embarrassed and apologetic look in his eyes, not the look of a cruel man.

Evin spoke again, trying to ease Darstan's pain. "And Wehr didn't either. He's tough, but he'd not do that."

Darstan sneered, and though he kept his voice low, he knew the contempt showed. "He did nothing to stop them. That's just as bad."

"I'm glad they'll get the disease for doin' what they did."

Darstan frowned and a troubled look came to his face. "They won't," he muttered sadly. "Can I trust you with a secret?" Darstan said.

When Evin nodded, Darstan continued. "I lied about her being sick. I was just so angry, I made up that story."

Evin laughed. "Have no fear, they'll not hear the news from me. At the very least they deserve to worry."

Darstan knew he had just taken the first step toward planting discord among his captors. Evin accepted his trust without betraying him. That, he knew, was key. Before long he would find other wedges to drive between these men.

SEPARATIONS

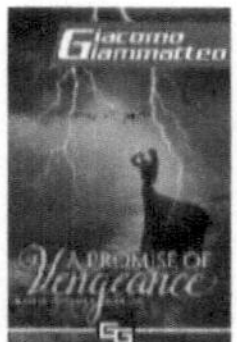

The mountains that served as the backdrop for Genda faded quickly, giving way to open plains, then forests, as the terrain smoothed out. The heat got worse too, even though the morning was only half gone. Rahg pounded his fist against his leg, spilling water from the jug. "Where could he be?" he hollered to no one.

"The clues indicate Sykor," Wisp said. "Two people saw them heading east."

Tobias scratched the white stubble on his chin. "They could be going to another port, take a ship from there, but that means east, too. Either way we're goin' in the right direction."

A league outside of Genda they picked up the trail. "I see six tracks here," Tobias said, "and one is carryin' a heavy load."

Gregor dismounted. "The deep tracks, that would be the one with the two dead bodies?"

"That'd be them. Though I can't understand why they'd still be carryin' them." Tobias said.

Rhaven knelt next to Gregor. "They're half a day ahead of us at least. We'll never catch them in time."

"In time for what?" Rahg asked.

"We sail tomorrow."

Rahg started to say something, but movement near the edge of the woods caught his eye. "Kella's here!"

The big beast bounded toward them. A smile lit Rhaven's face. "She always waits."

Rahg jumped from his horse. "It's good to see you, girl. Perhaps you can help us find Darstan."

"There won't be time. Remember, I said we sail tomorrow."

"We can't leave without Darstan! I'm not leaving my brother."

"You can. And we will," Rhaven said. "We have passage booked with the only man willing to take us. We sail before dawn."

"I'm not leaving without Darstan. I don't care where we have to go."

Wisp grabbed hold of Rahg's shoulder. "I'll track them down. If Darstan's alive we'll bring him back. On that, you have my word."

Anger and denial glowed in Rahg's eyes. "You can't take them alone. Besides, he's my brother. I'm the one who needs to go."

Wisp smiled. "I'm sure that the bounty man will be eager to accompany me. He's not fond of letting his reward get so far away." The thief's laughter relieved the group, if only for a moment. "Besides, if it's Sykor we're going to, Gregor and I will be going home. I'd rather fight a whole patrol of guards than risk my precious life on the high seas."

"We can track them," Gregor said.

"I don't know, Wisp. I'd feel better going with you."

"Take the vargel," Rhaven said. "I doubt she would come on the ship anyway."

Wisp shook his head. "I'm not that fond of the beast."

"She'll be the best tracker we have," Gregor said, then looked to Rahg, "Do you have anything that belonged to Darstan; anything we can use to let her catch the scent?"

Rahg nodded, struggling with his decision, though he soon resolved what to do. "I'm coming with you."

Wisp shook his head. "We can find him. We—"

"No!" Rahg set his jaw like a stonemason's mall. "I'm going with you."

Rhaven came alongside of Marchall and yanked Rahg off the saddle. When he hit the ground, Rhaven slammed the pommel of his sai onto Rahg's head, stunning him but leaving him conscious.

"Rhaven!" Camissa jumped off of Ranger and ran to Rahg, but Rhaven was already lifting him to lay across the saddle.

"He's not hurt," Rhaven said.

"Why did you hit him?" Camissa shouted and reached to tend to Rahg.

~

Rhaven pulled Gregor and Wisp aside. "When you catch them, kill them all, so long as Darstan's safety is not at risk."

"What about the young one?" Wisp asked. "the one Nirida said had no part in anything."

"He was there. Kill him."

Tobias nodded. "If you fall into a wagger's nest you don't ask which one did the bitin'."

Rhaven climbed on Argus' back, turned him toward Genda. "We'll meet again when this is over."

Wisp shook his head and mumbled. "I guess we kill them all."

Camissa bid Kender farewell then directed her mount in behind Tobias's. "Do you have any idea what we'll face when we reach the Sea of the Lost?"

A sarcastic laugh answered her. "Oh I do, lass. I'm quite afraid that I do. But don't worry, we'll get through it all. The gods will see to that, I'm certain."

She sensed the lies he told and saw the images in his mind—unwanted memories flashed to life; nightmares of horrible storms, violent lightning, wrecked ships, and visions of men washed overboard.

Tobias shook his head and called to Rhaven. "Better hurry. We'll have long days at sea, so we need rest."

More than long days, thought Camissa.

~

Darstan wiped the sweat from his brow; it seemed like he had to do that too often of late. The heat was stifling and the dampness made it unbearable. Evin rode behind Darstan, close enough to hold a conversation though far enough back to use his bow if necessary.

"Did it bother you, killing those two?" Evin asked.

Darstan turned and stared at Evin. "Why, were they close to you?"

Evin thought for a moment before answering. "No, I suppose not. Fact is, I don't think I even liked them. It's just that... well..." Evin shifted on his horse and his boyish face turned red. "I've never killed a man before. And... and I was just wondering how it felt. If it bothered you, I mean."

He's green as a shoot of spring grass. Good, that's one I'll not have to worry about shooting me in the back. Darstan hid his smile. "It did, Evin. It bothered me very much."

Evin seemed relieved, like a boy caught in the act and having the comfort of a friend caught with him. "I don't know how you did it, Darstan."

Darstan shrugged. "It's not as difficult as you might think when you believe your life's in danger. It's just that... I thought they'd kill me." Darstan glanced sideways at Evin, and saw the look of sympathy. He knew there would be no arrow shot at him from Evin's bow. Least-wise, none that would find their mark.

Darstan's stomach moaned. They had not eaten since morning except for a few pieces of dried meat while riding, and the outlook for supper appeared bleak. He could smell the soup and the aroma proved to be anything but enticing. But at least there was something to eat.

~

Wehr sat silent while Darstan and Bartel ate. He would finish his meal later. Evin had watch, and the sergeant —Bartel was his na— had drawn the duty of keeping guard on Darstan. It was dark when they finished eating and Darstan said he would lay down to sleep.

The strike leader sat away from Darstan at the edge of the camp. Caen approached him wearing a smirk. "Good eve, Wehr. I'll share your company if it's no bother."

The strike leader twisted inside. In Sykor he would have lashed Caen for not addressing him by rank. On this assignment, he could only grin and count time until he arrived back in the city. "Sit where you will, Caen."

"I hope he turns that boy loose," Caen said. "I'll have my revenge on him then."

Wehr put another piece of dried meat to his lips, tore a hunk off and chewed slowly. "When I was but a lad I asked for a baby mountain-cat. On Wish Day, my pa gave me what I wanted and by that night I ached so bad from scratches and bites that I begged my pa to take him back." Wehr grinned. "That was a long time ago but I still remember."

Caen's face flushed red. "He killed Gerrald. Or did you forget."

"No, I didn't forget. But you be careful what you wish for. He's a dangerous one for being so young. Killed Gerrald and Nord when it was three against one. Have no doubt, he'd have taken out Bartel if we hadn't come. No, Caen, you might not wish him set free. Just might be the death of you."

Wehr took another bite of meat and chewed while he spoke. "I've seen that look before in men's eyes. Have you stared at his eyes? That one'll not die easy. And he doesn't even know he's dangerous—yet. Once he finds out though, you can bet good gold he'll be trouble."

"We could end it here," Caen said.

The strike leader smiled when he recognized the fear in Caen's tone. "Even without our orders I'd not give him up to the slaughter. He deserves a soldier's death."

Wehr smiled. He never liked Caen, always thought him to be a coward and a bully, a brave man only when facing helpless people. That thought brought a frown with it. Ludar seemed to be surrounding himself with those types of late, and it caused Wehr to wonder anew about the force commander.

Why did he want this lad? And why did he go to so much trouble, having them traipse halfway across two countries to bring back someone who had done no wrong, so far as Wehr could determine.

Darstan didn't have powers. They'd all be dead by now if he did. Wehr had not minded tracking down those with powers. Bloody creatures. They all deserved to die anyway. The odd thing was that most went without a fight. If this one had powers he wouldn't have, of that, the strike leader felt certain. This one had fire in his eyes, and if he had fire in his hands, he would have used it.

Once again, the strike leader focused on Caen. "Perhaps you're right, Caen. Perhaps I should allow you to fight the lad." Wehr smiled to himself. He enjoyed watching Caen squirm.

"No, we better deliver him to Ludar like we're supposed to. Though I sure would have liked the chance," Caen half-mumbled.

"I'm sure," Wehr said, and spat.

"Kender," Gregor tugged the reins of his horse. "We have been on their trail for a full day and more. By the looks of these tracks I can't see that we are making headway. We—"

"Why don't you just call me Wisp, Gregor? Or does it bring back too many memories of failing to catch me?"

"You are an arrogant man, Kender Darnell."

"Aye, that I am," Wisp replied in his best Gendan accent. "Now then, what was it that you wanted to say to me?"

"We will have to push harder," Gregor said, then laughed. "How is it that you can find humor under these circumstances?"

"I can find nothing but humor, Gregor. Think of our situation: The most celebrated bounty man in Sykor accompanied by the most sought after thief, and both of us trying to kill a Sykoran guard patrol." Wisp laughed. "If you think long enough on it you'll turn back."

Gregor enjoyed the respite. "You neglected to mention the vargel."

"I try not to." Wisp sneered, and looked down at Kella. She stared up at him and growled. "Mother of rats, but that beast makes me uncomfortable."

"Did you ever think that we could work together, Wisp? You must admit, it's an unusual alliance."

"I never thought I'd be on the same side of an argument with you, Gregor, let alone fighting against common foes." Wisp sighed. "A lot has changed since we met Rahg. I would still be roaming the rooftops if not for Rhaven."

"Was that regret I detected in your voice, thief? Do you miss the game so much, or has there not been enough action with your present group of friends?"

"Too much action," Wisp said. "Too much danger. I never wanted to get this involved. Now there's no backing out. I promised to bring Darstan back, and I will. With your help, of course." Wisp smiled as he looked at the bounty man.

"If nothing else, thief, you have given me laughter. Since leaving Sykor I have met more happiness than at any other time in my life. But I dread the outcome of this journey with Rahg. Who are we to stand against the Evil One, if that is who pursues him? Who are we to fight against immortals? I fear that this may be my last journey, and the saddest thing about that, is that this is my first one."

Wisp turned toward Gregor staring wide-eyed with brows raised. "I have no intention of meeting the Lady Death, Gregor. And since thieves are much smarter than bounty-men, I'll do my best to keep you alive. Now let's eat supper. I'm hungry."

∼

*R*ats blood! It's been two full days. Where's Rahg?

Darstan looked up at the two moons shining above; Ranal and Ranalla provided enough light for a man to see, even in the forest. Perhaps Rhaven was out there now, lying in wait behind a thick grove of trees. Or they could even have circled around to prepare an ambush. Darstan smiled. That would make sense. Rhaven wouldn't attack with the forest lit so bright. They must be out there, waiting for the right opportunity. Darstan smiled again, a vicious, vengeful smile.

I hope they don't kill Caen. I want him myself.

Bartel sat rigid against a large oak tree. To Darstan's dismay the guard was wide awake. Darstan tucked himself into a bedroll and curled up.

The dreams started at once, and they proved to be as familiar as they were strange. Darstan had an awareness of the dream, but he never remembered anything once he woke. Regardless, he knew the dream was the same. Each time it had been identical, but with every dream something more occurred. *The sea.* He recalled a violent, smashing sea that tossed a ship about like a twig caught in a maelstrom. Lightning cracked white across a sky blacker than black. The blinding flash illuminated the horrors that lay in the ship's path. The sea smelled like death.

Another bolt cracked and the sea-sky whitened long enough to see what awaited them: rocks the size of taverns, their jagged–edged points protruding through the violence of the murderous waves. The sea swayed, boulders lurking underneath the surface, spears poised to pierce the trembling shell of the ship. Darstan shivered. Nothing could survive that.

The dream took him away again, swept him to another place, another time. The images were vague and a heavy fog hid the truth from him. He could make out certain things, but the only one clear enough was three people walking up a hill with a determined gait.

Darstan felt the danger, a sensation like death's cold touch. Atop the hill stood a man with a faint glow surrounding him. *A Banished One!* The realization jarred Darstan. How he knew he couldn't say, but he felt positive of the identification. *How did he escape?*

For a moment the visions faded before returning with renewed clarity. The fog no longer concealed them; no haze or mist hid the truth, yet he still couldn't identify the three who were about to be attacked by the Banished One. To the side an army rushed to join the battle, clashing with allies of the Evil One. Just when Darstan felt sure that they would be killed, a man with one hand entered the fray shooting flames from a stump at the end of his arm. At that point everything blacked out.

He wiped pouring sweat from his hair when he woke, cold sweat, though the night was steamy hot and horribly humid. Darstan looked to the tree where the guard had been posted. Bartel rested against the trunk. It had not been as long as he imagined. Bartel's watch lasted half the night, and half of that he had served before Darstan fell asleep. He wiped his brow on his shirt sleeve as he sat up. Bartel looked over to him but said nothing, just stared. "How long before dawn?" Darstan asked.

"I'll be wakin' Caen for his watch in a moment," Bartel answered. "I'd be thinkin' about sleep if I were you. Caen's not friendly like me." Bartel laughed as he rose from his position. "I'm goin' to wake him now. If you can't sleep, leastwise, pretend." Darstan knew Bartel's advice to be wise, so he closed his eyes and prayed for sleep—sleep without dreams.

DEPARTURES

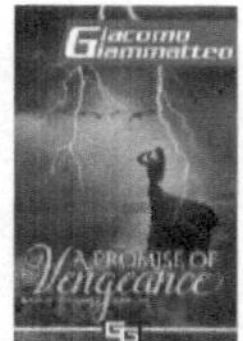

*R*ahg sat alone, sipping on a mug of hot khaffe. He was tired, and his head hurt where Rhaven hit him. *I can't believe I let them go after Darstan without me.*

Rhaven pulled out a chair and ordered breakfast.

"I don't like what you did, Rhaven. That's my brother! If he dies—"

"If he dies it won't be because you're not there."

Tobias sat to Rhaven's left. Smoke leaked from his pipe, mixing with the aromas of sausage and khaffe wafting in from the kitchen. "Can't say I don't agree with him, lad. If those men want Darstan dead, he's already dead. If not, Wisp will rescue him." He puffed a few times, rekindling a dying ember. "Rhaven, I don't say much to question a man's lead, but you had no right hittin' that lad yesterday."

A long silence followed and no response from Rhaven.

Tobias nodded. "Well, I said what I had to say. But I'm tellin' you, don't hit the lad again."

Camissa grabbed the seat next to Rahg. Pink tinged her cheeks and her eyes danced with every smile. "Good morning, Rahg."

She had a voice like the song of a thrush. "Good morning, Camissa. Te or khaffe?"

"You know I always have te, but you could use more khaffe. Your eyes make you look like you're still asleep."

Rahg stared at those dancing eyes without saying a word. *She is beautiful.* It was her smile and warmth and caring that made her pretty.

"Rahg, stop staring. You are embarrassing me."

"I'm sorry, Camissa. It's just..."

"No need to explain." Camissa smiled back at him. "Sometimes we just stare at things without even knowing why. I do that often."

"Don't eat too much," Tobias said. "The first day at sea will probably bring up whatever you put down." Tobias looked around the room until he spotted the serving girl. "Narrie, bring more khaffe, and send someone to fetch some sickness root."

Rahg was prepared to ask what *sickness root* was, when Tobias explained. "You'll need the root, lad. If not the first day, the next. If you chew on it all day, it might help. You just might be able to keep food in your stomach instead of all over the deck."

"I've never been to sea," Rahg said.

"That's why you'll be chewin' on this root, lad. It's a terrible thing to be sick at sea. You'll wish for many things in your life, but none will you wish for as hard as dry land if you get the sickness. That, I promise you."

Rahg nodded his head and took another sip of khaffe. Tobias had spoiled his appetite. Besides, it had been a long time since Rahg had been up this early; it wasn't even light yet.

Narrie set the drinks on the table. "Sedgie went to get the root, Tobias. He'll be back soon. Is anyone ordering a meal?"

"Just biscuits for me," Rahg said.

Rhaven finished quickly then stood to leave. "I'll settle the debt for our rooms and get Argus. You and Rahg get the other horses." Rhaven handed Tobias some money. "Pay for Darstan's mount. Tell him to hold it until we get back, or until the gold runs out."

Camissa stood. "I'll meet you at the docks, need to get more herbs first."

Tobias finished the last of his khaffe. "Guess we best get goin' ourselves, lad. Sennar will be bitin' our ears if we hold him up for long."

Rahg wore a long frown.

"I know you're worried about him, lad, but they'll find Darstan. Much as I might not care for the thief's ways, he's one I'd trust more than my money to. I've not seen anyone faster with a knife than that thief, and the bounty man handles the staff like a master. You won't find two together that are much more talented. Those two know the city like fish know water. And my guess is that's where they'll catch up to them, either in Sykor or in Khatara, whichever place they're headed." Tobias patted Rahg on the shoulder. "No, lad. I wouldn't be worryin' over Darstan. Soon enough, he'll be safe."

Rahg and Tobias arrived at the docks to a scene bustling with activity. It was a strange thing to think about, hauling horses aboard a ship, but Rhaven wanted to bring Argus. They passed a large building with a yard that had barrels stacked high atop each other, a horrendous odor leeching from them. "What is that smell?"

Tobias laughed. "That's where they process the ambergis, lad. They make it into lamp oil, and some of it into the perfume the ladies use."

"But it smells so bad."

"It does when it's like this," Tobias said, "but once it's separated and placed into a little container... well, the ladies like it."

They passed by a building full of nets, and another shop where women made sails for the ships, giant sails sewn in sections, each about a length long. On the next block carpenters were laboring on giant hardwood trees.

"They'll carve a keel out of that one," Tobias said. "The keel's the spine of the ship, lad. That's why they use only good, hard wood. But nothin' will go to waste. They'll use the rest to make masts and planks and anything else that needs makin'. Even the tiniest of scraps will be used for plugs, dowels, or timber to cook with. A seaman is not one to waste things. But you'll see that once we put to sea."

"I can't wait."

"You'll wish you had in a few days," Tobias mumbled. "Look, there's the ship, lad."

Camissa paced the deck near the ship as she waited. "It took you long enough. I suppose you stopped to gaze at everything on the way."

Rahg gritted his teeth. It irked him when she did that, especially when she was right. "I stared, Camissa, but I didn't stop. We had horses to bring, remember."

Camissa smiled as if she had already won the battle. "Are the horses so much slower in walking than you?"

"Help with these horses, lad, they'll not want to go aboard. Horses are funny like that."

Rahg was glad for the distraction from Camissa. He could have spent all morning trying to figure out why she was upset and probably never would arrive at the right conclusion. He dodged several seamen herding pigs before them amidst continual grunting and an occasional squeal that pierced the inner ear.

"Ho!"

Sennar's gravelly voice carried above the noise. "What of those horses? I'll not have horses aboard my ship."

Sennar glared at them from the top deck of the ship. The Sea Skate it was named.

"The horses go, or I find another captain." Rhaven's glare was more threatening than Sennar's, but the gnarled old man shouted a rebuke.

"Your payin', so I'll be considerate, but I'll have no horses aboard. Mind me, I'm the captain of this vessel, and my word is law at sea. I'll tolerate no arguin'. If I can't have your word on that, ya can hire another captain."

Rhaven continued glaring at Sennar. "I'm no seaman, so you'll receive no advice from me on running this ship. I said what I needed to. If the horses are loaded, I have no argument."

Sennar growled. "There'll be no horses aboard my ship. No animals that won't be used for food. ya can look for another captain, but none will take ya."

Rhaven said nothing, but Sennar must have seen his dilemma. "There's a man I know like my own son. Owns a stable. Good man. Takes good care of his animals. Ya can keep your horses there, but ya can't bring 'em aboard. Don't fret none, though. Those horses will be good as ya left 'em."

Rhaven thought for a moment, then nodded. "Where is the stable?"

Sennar seemed satisfied. "I've got men to take 'em."

Two of Sennar's men attempted to grab the reins, but Argus stomped wildly and bit savagely at them. Fear drove them back. Rhaven whispered to Argus, patting his neck. "Have one of your men lead the way. I'll take Argus and we'll get Darstan's horse as well. Rahg, bring Marchall and the others."

"Don't be wastin' any time. We need to be movin'."

They returned before long, and no sooner had they stepped on deck than Sennar bellowed the orders.

"Make sail!" The words reverberated throughout the ship's decks, a catalyst for a series of activity that sent men scurrying up ropes and all about the deck.

~

From inside a cabin near the captain's quarters, two men watched Rahg. "That's the one."

"Why are we watching? Why don't we just kill 'im?"

"That's a thing that might come later, but for now we just watch."

"Make sail." The order from Sennar echoed through the room.

"Come, 'fore 'old crazy' gets nervous." The two men departed, leaving the door ajar.

~

Aentarra strolled through the little cabin picking up trinkets and instruments used for measurements. *So, these men have an interest in Rahg?* She rubbed her chin, deep in thought. *I may have to kill them before this is over. I may have to kill them all.*

AT SEA

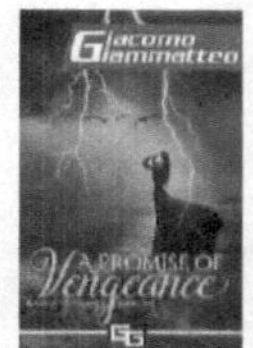

A steady wind blew west, and kept them on course. Rahg's stomach rolled with the sea, a horrible reminder of the first two days when he would have gone back to Genda even if it meant riding on a shark. He couldn't remember how many times he'd been sick, only that it had been a lot, and it proved embarrassing. Things soon got better though, and now, with six days of trouble-free sailing, Rahg felt at ease yet riddled with guilt.

Camissa took his hand in hers. "Kender and Gregor will do everything they can. They'll get Darstan back."

Rahg nodded, then wandered about the ship, his curiosity taking hold. Tobias was leaning against the outside rail, staring into the horizon with a haunted gaze. Rahg walked up beside him. "What's wrong?"

"Storms," Tobias mumbled, then spoke louder. "Storms, lad."

Sea of Lost

Rahg stared at the clear sky and the tranquil sea. "I don't see any storms. It's been calm for days. And Sennar mentioned nothing of a storm. I'm sure he'd say something."

Slowly, Tobias's old, yet still firm hands, uncurled from the rail. His face was a sickly gray. "Worst storms always come after the longest lull."

Rahg took Tobias's place at the railing, his mood reflective. Row after row of swells rolled toward them from some distant, mysterious spot on the horizon. He laughed to himself. *Horizon.* It was one of the new words he learned. He knew what it meant, in a way. He knew it to be that farthest point he could see when staring out into the sea, but if someone were to ask him to explain it he doubted that he could.

For the longest time he stood transfixed. A few stray clouds lingered, marring an otherwise perfect blue sky.

Camissa came out of her cabin and headed toward Rahg. She was dressed much like the men—a top garment with the mid-section uncovered.

Sennar met her in the passageway. "I'll be askin' ya to stay out of sight as much as possible, lass."

Camissa shot a glare at him.

"It's not your doin'. It's the nature of seamen. Not that my men are different than others," he said, "but men at sea are apt to get lonely, and that leads to desperate acts. It would be better for all if you'd not show yourself. And if ya must leave the cabin, cover yourself well, lass. Soft skin's not for a seaman to gaze upon, leastwise not while he's at sea."

Sennar shifted weight from his bad leg to the other then back again. "I don't have any wish to be brash, and I never intend to insult a woman, but, lass, your skin's as soft as any I've ever laid eyes on. I don't want to have to kill my own men for disobeyin'. Not that they're likely to, just that... well, the sight of a soft woman can do that to some men, and I'd rather not kill 'em if I don't have to."

Camissa blushed. "I'll stay close, Captain. I do enjoy the fresh air, but if I find the need I'll be dressed warmly."

Sennar tipped his hat. "You have my thanks, lass. I'll do what I can to make your trip comfortable. If ya find yourself needin' anything, just call. Old Sennar will take good care of ya."

Sennar scanned the sea ahead with his eyeglass, curses slipping out of his mouth like pipe smoke. Fog! A wall of fog thick as the cliffs bracing Genda's back stared at him. He kicked at a splinter of wood, and vowed to punish the seaman responsible.

Rhaven prowled the deck under Sennar's watchful gaze. His every step resembled a mountain cat stalking prey. Sennar eyed him. If he were to have trouble, it would be with him. And yet, if he needed to quell trouble from his own men, Rhaven was the one he'd need to call on. Either way, the black-cloaked man would fall square in the midst of danger. The man's whole life had probably been that way.

Trouble always rode on a shark's fin. The old saying came to Sennar's mind. *Shark indeed.*

Rhaven had that look about him. Might as well approach him now. He would more than likely have need of Rhaven's sword tomorrow; tomorrow, they would see the fog. Tomorrow, they would enter the Sea of the Lost.

The discord began soon after dawn. The eastern sun again shone brilliantly, casting blazing beams across the mirrored surface of the calmed sea, but the western horizon appeared quite different—like the beginning of a huge storm brewing. Some of the seamen grumbled, demanding to know their destination. Sennar wouldn't say. The smarter ones already suspected, but no sense in gettin' them riled up prematurely; that would come soon enough.

By noon, the view to the west left little doubt as to what they would encounter before nightfall; nothing but gray loomed ahead. The men talked among themselves, forming into groups. Sennar had his two mates round up men they knew to be loyal. As the ship drew closer to the fog with no orders to turn about, they came; men scrambled down ropes and climbed topside. Sennar stared into the group of potential mutineers—over half his men. He had ten that would stay the course with him. Another fifteen or so wouldn't fight for or against. With one mind they came, demanding the ship be turned about.

Sennar shouted with all the voice he could muster. "ya signed on for a dead-man's run. Every one of ya knew it. I told ya of the dangers."

One of the men on the front line shouted back. "Danger, I'll face. But no reason to die. Not for gold, not for you." He glared at Sennar. The men behind him muttered approval.

"Some of us will die," Sennar said. "I'm sure of that. But I have no mind to lose a good portion of this crew, and I have no mind of dying myself."

"How do you know you'll not lose us all, and the ship and yourself besides? How do you know, Sennar? No captain's ever sailed here before, not and come back."

Sennar stared gravely at each of them through squinted eyes. "I'll tell ya what I do know, then. I'll tell ya that if ya don't get back to sailin' this ship, a good many of ya will be dead on this deck; not from a storm; not from sea monsters; and not from crashin' into rocks. You'll be dead from your own mates' blades."

He shouted louder. "And we'll have dead ones, too. No doubt of that. I might even die myself. And for what? Because you're afraid to sail into some fog? I picked you men for bein' brave."

Sennar paused again. It was time to call them out. "Well, if it's fightin' ya wish, then let's get on with it. But before we do, think on this. No ship has ever come back, legends say, so we all assume they died. But what if they found the ancient cities, the ones full of gold and beautiful women. The places that all of us heard about when we were barefooted-lads with a head full of dreams?" Sennar thought he might have struck a note with them. He saw them softening—then Turrel spoke up.

"We can't listen to this old man. You know his name—'Old Crazy'. We shouldn't have listened to him to begin with. I say we take this ship and sail it ourselves. I say we—"

Before Turrel had a chance to finish, Rhaven worked his way to the space in front of him, daring him with a challenging stance. Turrel stopped in mid-sentence.

"We have no quarrel with you, stranger. We mean but—"

Rhaven drew his sword, stopping it as it kissed the man's throat. Turrel gasped, and tilted backward, shying from the blade's dangerous touch. Blood dripped onto Rhaven's steel. Pulsations in Turrel's throat shot blood out in squirts.

Sennar looked at the blade, blinked, and looked again. "Gorphon's blood!" *Had the sword drank the blood? It was there, then gone.* He rubbed his eyes and stared. A blinding glare from the sun made the sword appear to glow. Blood stained the blade.

Turrell reached for his knife. Within a heartbeat Turrel's head rolled on the deck. Before his head stopped rolling, the men on each side of him crumpled to the deck, their throats slashed.

The other mutineers looked on wide-eyed. Sennar seized the moment "We've had enough killin'. Let's give these up to the sea—may she be merciful—and go on with our voyage. We still have a mission to complete. Who's with me?" Sennar's voice was not the rousing call it normally was, but to a man, they all signed on with a cheer, if not enthusiasm.

One of the mates looked to Rhaven, and then to the carnage on the deck. Sennar saw a question begin to form on his lips, but Rhaven's black demeanor must have dissuaded him.

"It had to be done," Sennar said. "If he hadn't killed Turrel, we'd have many more dead." Sennar hoped his mate wouldn't ask why the others had to die, because he had no answers. He looked again at the black-cloaked one and stayed silent. He had seen a barracuda strike once; had been close enough to see the death in those murderous eyes. He saw that same look again now.

Rhaven's gaze swept the crowd of dissenters, then he whirled around and descended a ladder to the deck below. As he faded into darkness, Sennar wondered what he had gotten himself into. And, he worried.

CYPRESS SWAMPS

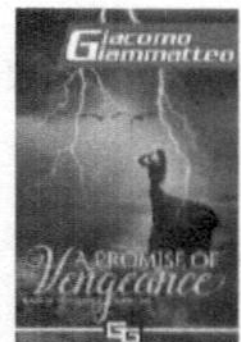

The morning sun rode in against the hoarse cry of a black-crested heron, finished with the night's work. Darstan stretched, shaking off the sleep that lingered. He had lived through another night; that, at least, was something.

Caen sat the guard duty, alert, as always. They veered off in a north-eastern direction late the previous day. Darstan assumed they were heading to Sykor, now he wondered. It was possible to reach Sykor this way, but only by crossing the Cypress Swamps or by going far north and crossing the river.

"Where are we headed, Caen?"

Malice tainted Caen's glare.

"I noticed we changed course," Darstan said. "Are we still going to Sykor?"

Branches stirred behind Darstan. The strike leader emerged from a thick copse of trees.

"We're going to Sykor," Wehr said. "It doesn't matter if you know where we're going." Wehr poured a mug of hot khaffe. "And you can quit leaving marks on the trail. It will do you no good."

Wehr took another sip of khaffe. "I did nothing to conceal your clues; in truth, I wanted them found. As long as your friends are trailing us by your marks, they won't get ahead of us."

"Why tell me now?"

A frown replaced the smile on the strike leader's weathered face. A wrinkle over his right eye turned out to be a deep scar, and the back of his neck showed signs of old wounds. "Because we'll soon enter the Cypress Swamps, and if you wish to live, you'll need to be attentive. One mistake could be your death. We need to watch for each other."

Wehr stared at Darstan. "Your friends will not be able to follow us in the swamps, so there's no need leaving tracks. If you give me your word you'll attempt no escape, I'll return your sword."

Darstan eyed him with suspicion.

"If we meet up with Krovs, you might need the blade."

Darstan had heard stories about the Krovs, about the tortures they inflicted upon captives. Even Caen would be better than them. "You have my word, Wehr, but only while we travel in the swamps. Fair?"

"Give him his blade, Caen."

Darstan took the blade and swung it through the air a few times. It felt familiar, like sitting in his own saddle. It felt good. He envisioned scenarios in which he killed the guards one by one, and the slaying of Caen he relished most.

After riding for a short distance they broke through a thick copse of swamp oaks riddled with dark green yaupons boasting plump red berries. The sound of splashing captured Darstan's attention. Up ahead were a pair of guards astride horses pawing ankle-deep water. Next to the mounts, canoes shifted on the ripples in murky water.

Wehr wasted no time addressing the two soldiers. "Take our mounts and load each one with weight equal to the rider it carried; don't bring your own from the water, I'll see to them." The strike leader leaned forward in the saddle, staring at them. "When you leave, ride north along the river. Don't make camp. Don't dismount. At the first bridge turn west toward Pomanda. Sell the horses when you get there and take the route I gave you back to Sykor."

"What of our mounts?" one of the guards asked.

Wehr appeared angry that he should have to answer a question again. "I said I'll see to them! Worry about your own fate. If this ruse works and the trackers follow you..." Wehr sat erect on his mount and a smile lightened his face.

Darstan got the distinct feeling that Wehr did not care much about the other guards, yet he had no doubt of Wehr's loyalties. *He'd kill me in the blink of an eye.*

"If they catch you, you'll wish you had walked the swamps alone," Wehr said. "Gregor, the bounty man, is one of them. There's a thin man I don't know... and there's another who could kill our Force Commander before he drew his sword."

The strike leader nudged his mount onward, steering it through the reedy grass at the swamp's edge toward a clear patch of water nearly three spans inward. The horses required prodding to move through the mushy swamp. Soon they all gathered in a spot clear of grass and reeds, yet the water remained dark and murky. Wehr dismounted into the knee-deep bog, pulled one of the canoes alongside his horse and climbed into the boat. "Caen, you and Evin take the other one. Bartel, you and Darstan climb in with me."

"Why only two canoes?" Darstan asked.

"You mean, what if you hadn't killed my men?" Wehr glared at him. "It was thought out, don't worry." The strike leader looked to the other two guards. "Take our mounts. Stay this far from shore for half a league then follow the river north. And hurry." Wehr turned to Evin. "Keep their mounts with you. Don't allow them to break free; they'll be frightened when we enter deeper waters so keep a strong hold."

Evin nodded, grabbing the reins of the horses as soon as the other men dismounted. Wehr handed an oar to Darstan and one to Bartel. "Row," he said. "We have a long way to go."

～

Wisp and Gregor took a brief respite then resumed tracking. Gregor led them south, only to have Kella's persistent barking convince him to try an easterly path. They soon discovered the marks Darstan left.

"Better let the vargel make decisions from now on, bounty man."

They followed the trail until darkness prevented further progress, then dismounted to make camp near a fallen moss-covered tree. Kella moved in and sniffed it continually, causing Gregor to inspect.

moss-covered tree

"Looks like someone was here, leaning against the tree," he said. "I can see the wear marks."

"Then we must be on the right trail," Wisp said. "And since we are, let's take advantage of our good fortune and sleep."

"Might as well," Gregor said. "I'm tired anyway."

Wisp slouched against a tree to rest while Gregor built a fire. He ached for hot khaffe and a pleasant meal.

Gregor stirred coals and added more wood. "When we get Darstan back, I plan on resting for a fortnight. We have pushed hard ever since we left the Lorns."

Wisp nodded. "Tired as I am, I wouldn't cross an alley to steal a necklace."

Gregor laughed as he brewed the khaffe. Kella returned to camp, two rabbits dangling from her massive jaws. "They look succulent," Wisp said. "I might change my mind about that beast if she keeps feeding me."

Kella swaggered toward the fire, dropped the rabbits on the ground then departed. Wisp and Gregor wasted no time making a meal out of her gift. "If they go into the swamps, we'll not be able to follow."

"Why would they go into the swamps?"

Gregor frowned. "We should see tomorrow."

Wisp mumbled agreement with a mouth full of food.

Gregor stared into the woods. "I wonder where Kella goes at night?"

"I don't know," Wisp said, "but I'm glad she brought these rabbits."

"If they go to the swamps, do we follow?"

Wisp took two big swallows from his mug of khaffe. "We'll worry about that if the trail leads us there. Until then, let's get some sleep."

*I*n the morning Kella was waiting at the edge of the campsite. As always, she appeared eager to be on the trail. "I wish that I felt as rested as the vargel." Wisp placed his bedroll in the saddlebags and mounted the horse. "If we make good time today we might catch them."

Gregor examined a broken tree limb that once stretched nearly to the path they traveled. "If they enter the swamps, we may never catch them." His monotonous tone was as dry as ever. "But at least we know Darstan's alive. These marks are his, I'm certain of that." The bounty man spurred the horse forward at a gallop. "Come, thief. Now who lags behind."

Wisp kept his mount at a favorable pace so as not to tire it. "No need in rushing, boy. There are swamps up ahead. I can smell them."

~

*H*orrible images of everything he'd ever heard about the Cypress Swamps raced through Darstan's mind: insects that drove men mad; venomous snakes that lurked in the water waiting to ambush anyone who passed by; and sangra—ferocious, insatiable sangra. Darstan shivered. His clothes were wet from the ordeal of climbing into the canoe but the hot, moist air should have warmed him.

"Hold," Wehr ordered, and pulled the boat next to a large cypress tree rising from the chocolate-colored water.

Evin and Caen rowed in next to them. "What is it, Wehr?"

Caen's familiar use of the strike leader's name caused Darstan to wonder. Sykoran guards normally kept to protocol, odd that Wehr allowed Caen the privilege.

The horses stood in water to their bellies. Darstan racked his brain trying to understand why the strike leader kept them instead of letting them go with the others.

Wehr drew his sword and rammed it into the chest of the biggest horse. It screamed, flailing in the sludgy bog. Its front legs flew into the air and lashed out. Evin delivered the fatal blow.

"Not too wise of me," Wehr said. "Use arrows on the other."

"Why are you killing them?" Darstan shouted.

The strike leader backhanded him. Darstan lost balance, tumbling from the canoe. "Pull him up before he dies in there," Wehr said.

Darstan shook like a dog shedding water, part from anger at the strike leader, but also to rid himself of the swamp water. Blood got on his clothes and on his skin, even in his hair. He tore off his shirt to scrub himself.

sangra

Wehr's expression remained grim. "There are dangers in the swamps. Keep alert. A snake bite will kill you, and the sangras will eat you.

We'll use the horses to distract the sangra. They'll smell the blood in the water for half a league or more. Should keep them away from us."

Wehr looked at each of them with a cold stare. "There are even bugs that can cause your death, or so I'm told. And worst of all, there are the Krovs. If you see one, even if one appears ready to attack, make no move against him. Our only chance of getting through is to do it peacefully."

"If we remain quiet they might not even know we're here," Bartel said.

Wehr chuckled. "They already know we're here, Bartel. Probably knew before we got the horses' feet wet. Nothing goes into the Cypress Swamps that the Krovs don't know about. We had them outnumbered three to one in the war, and they still nearly beat us. Left many mothers weeping for a long time."

Caen spat into the muddy water, stains of blood swirling and clinging to vines and reeds. "Why won't they just attack us?"

"They just might, Caen. Then again, I don't think even the Krovs wish another war, and seeing that we are Sykoran guards, they might refrain. Might."

Darstan remembered Rhaven's tales of their tortures.

I don't care what Wehr says, if a Krov comes after me I'm going to kill him. The Evil One can take my soul, but I'll be a blasted fool if I'll let the Krovs have me—not alive.

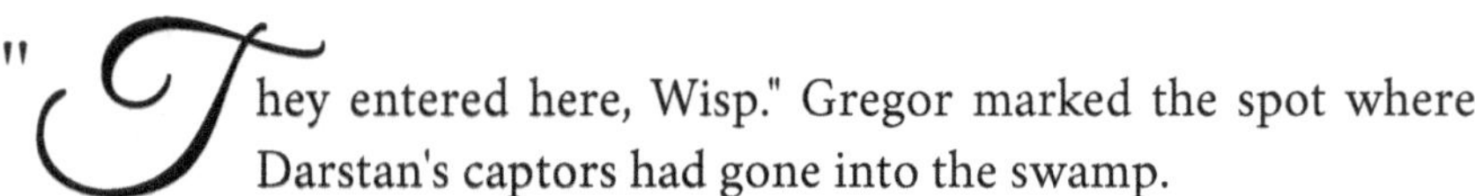

"They entered here, Wisp." Gregor marked the spot where Darstan's captors had gone into the swamp.

"I don't see anything."

"Look at the way these grasses are bent. And see the—"

"Gregor, I can tell you how small a hole a rat can squeeze through, or how fast it can climb a wall, but don't ask me to tell you a wolf track from a mountain-cat."

"Not far ahead of us now. And definitely heading east, into the swamp."

Wisp shook his head and looked to the east—swamp as far as he could see. Reeds, trees, small islands of refuge, and a vast mix of plants and flowers, all thrown together in a turbid brown sea. "We can't follow them. Not through there."

Gregor looked solemn. "They might have wanted us to think they went there. Let's follow the trail north for a ways. If they meant to fool us, sooner or later they'll emerge from the swamp."

Kella sniffed furiously at the water as she ventured deeper into the swampland.

"Kella, come back, girl."

The vargel turned her head but kept moving.

"Gregor, the vargel thinks they went in the swamps."

The bounty man nodded. "So do I, but for now we go north. We can hope to pick up a trail. In the swamps, we would have nothing."

❧

*B*y mid morning the sun transformed the swamp into a veritable hot house. Sweat trickled down Darstan's cheeks. The heat he could withstand; it got hot in Kamnor. The insects, however, were a different matter. Darstan swatted as a barrage of mosquitoes swarmed his face. He slapped the side of his head, where one of them buzzed in his ear.

"Keep the oars moving," came the order from Wehr. "We've got worse enemies than bugs to fret over. Keep your eyes peeled for the sangra and the Krovs; they're the ones to worry over." Darstan gritted his teeth and shook his head, a desperate attempt to chase away the remnants of the most recent mosquito raid. They seemed to know when he was busy.

"Continue to follow the stream, Darstan. Soon we'll all get relief. There's a root that grows in these swamps. The juice repels the bugs."

"There may not be much left of me if we don't find it soon."

"Don't worry, before long we'll be into the real Cypress Swamps, then we'll all need the root."

"The real swamps? What's this?"

Wehr laughed. "This is the outlands, least that's what the Krovs named the area. When the river overflows, this all becomes swampland. When we get to the heart of them the vegetation is so thick it grows while you watch it. It floats on the water, and vines lay in wait to tangle boats in a web they can't break free of. And the bugs are thick as the morning fog in Sandora. During the war that's what hurt the most, the bugs." The look on Wehr's face made the recollection seem painful.

Darstan grimaced. Sangra were one thing, at least with them he could use a sword and fight. But the bugs... He squirmed. "When do we reach it?"

"Not far. Stay alert."

Darstan held the front position in the boat. Wehr sat behind him while Bartel rowed from the rear. Wehr guided them to a small island thick with vegetation. Darstan let the canoe ease into the silty soil at the edge.

"Stretch your legs," Wehr said. "Don't touch anything. Some of the thorns are poisonous. And remember, be careful of snakes."

Darstan shivered. He hated snakes even worse than spiders. He helped Wehr cut the roots, then they rubbed the milky fluid on their skin.

"This will keep the bugs away," Wehr said.

Soon after leaving they entered a tree-covered, shadowy section of swamp where insects congregated in hordes—moving black clouds that buzzed incessantly. Darstan prayed for the repellant to work and, surprisingly, it did.

Soon the channel narrowed. Thick branches blocked out most of the sunlight, making Darstan wonder if they went off course. He looked around for markers, but everything looked the same. The sides of the inlet were rife with reeds, water spiders, vines with small lizards clinging to them, and floating patches of plants that hid gods only knew what creatures. He crashed right into a huge spider web, and spat, the webs sticking to his tongue. By the time he cleaned them off, he had lost the oar.

Wehr reached to get the oar, as a large black snake swam by. Darstan held his breath. *God, I hate snakes.*

Darstan took the oar from Wehr and began rowing.

They continued for hours until Wehr spotted a patch of dry ground with two large cypress trees. "We'll make camp here," Wehr said.

"What about snakes?" Bartel asked.

"And sangra?" Evin asked, looking over his shoulder.

"Snakes we can keep away with fire," Wehr said.

"How about a rope?" Evin asked. "I've heard a snake won't cross a rope."

Wehr scoffed. "You sleep with a rope, I'll sleep by a fire. As for sangra, we'll post a watch. Sangra are patient hunters and usually wait for prey to come to them, but just in case, we'll stand watch. Caen, take first duty. Evin, you're next, then Darstan. Bartel will wake me for last watch."

Evin woke Darstan, then sat with him while he did his watch. "It got lonely by myself. Never been in the swamps at night."

"Scary enough during the day," Darstan said.

Evin nodded. "One time I thought I heard sheep out there and got scared it might have been Krovs."

"Probably sheep frogs," Darstan said. "They're not much bigger than your thumb, but they've got a big voice. Sound just like sheep from far away. They're dark brown, with a thin yellow stripe down their back. Skittish as all get out, though. Makes them hard to catch."

Evin threw a stick at Darstan. "Go on, Darstan. I'm not that green."

Darstan laughed. "That's no lie. I'll wager I can catch a sheep frog out here before you catch a sheep. Then we'll see who's lying."

The eerie hoot of an owl startled both of them, bringing Darstan to his feet, hand on the hilt of his sword. "Guess I'm a little nervous myself. I've heard a hundred owls before, but this one made me jump."

A series of croaking sounds started on the west side of camp, then the chorus came from all sides, surrounding them. "They're the kind of frogs I know," Evin said.

Darstan listened, tilting his head. "Bullfrogs. Couple of big ones too. Wouldn't mind getting a few of those for dinner." He turned his sword over in his hand a few times, then practiced thrusting and feints while Evin sat still against a tree.

"Be time to get Bartel soon," he said.

"Might as well get him now," Darstan said and sheathed his blade. "I'm tired anyway."

*G*regor and Wisp followed the shoreline of the swamp. It had been half a league since the tracks led into the swamps, and now, they were reemerging. "Did they do it to lose us?" Wisp asked.

"Haven't you ever tracked anyone, thief?"

"I've followed a few merchants on cobblestone streets," he said. "What have you tracked besides thieves, bounty man? The more I think about it the more convinced I am that Kella is whispering in your ear and telling you what to say."

Gregor dismounted and studied the marks on the side of the bank. He followed them upriver for a dozen spans or more, stooping frequently to analyze the prints left by the horses' hooves. "Identical," he said, his face mystified. "No doubt these are the same horses. And they each have a rider, otherwise their tracks would be lighter."

"Then we haven't lost the trail."

"Perhaps they thought to lose us in the swamps," Gregor said.

As they rode off, Kella stayed behind, casting her bark into the swamps.

"Kella thinks they're still in there."

"I know," Gregor said, "but the tracks lead north, the same tracks we followed since Genda. If Rhaven were here he could make sense of it, but I say we head north."

"I'm no tracker, Gregor. I follow you."

The tracks continued to parallel the river for several leagues before veering off toward a small copse of trees atop a nearby hill. The river cut a wide swath in the landscape, its western bank a shale-rock escarpment that rose to a height of several spans above the water. The eastern side stayed level with the river and spread into the swamp-lands and, when it flooded, it created a vast sea of smoky-brown water enveloping a forest of green. "They might have gone over there to make camp," Wisp said.

Gregor nodded. "We're not too far behind them. I believe we could catch them in a day."

Gregor walked the perimeter of the campsite again. "I see only two sets of tracks, Wisp. Why would the others remain mounted, unless...the others were not here. They must have taken Darstan through the swamps and sent these two north to lead a false trail." Gregor cursed himself for misreading the tracks. "No matter the risks, we have to get Darstan."

"I'm convinced they're going to Sykor. We can get there faster by taking the lower bridge. There's a road that leads straight to the southern entrance to the city. It would be faster than trying to find our way through the swamps, not to mention safer. Besides, if we hurry we'll reach Sykor before them. If we do, we can arrange a fitting surprise."

"So be it, thief. We ride for Sykor."

∽

The sharp prodding on his back rousted Darstan. He spun and rose in a fluid motion, prepared to lash out at Caen, but he stared down into the black eyes of a man whose head came only to his own chest. *Krovs!* Darstan went for his sword just as Wehr reached for his arm.

"Leave it be, Darstan!"

The short Cergalan sword cleared leather before the Krov with the spear reacted. Darstan spun, striking him on the upper arm with a vicious slash. The Krov stumbled to the side. Darstan followed with a stab, catching his leg instead of his gut. Before Darstan finished him off, Wehr grabbed him from behind. He spun, fury in his eyes. It was then he saw the rest of the Krovs, at least twenty of them. And their spears looked sharp. Darstan slowly moved his hands away from the hilt of the sword.

Where is Rhaven now?

ISLES OF MIST

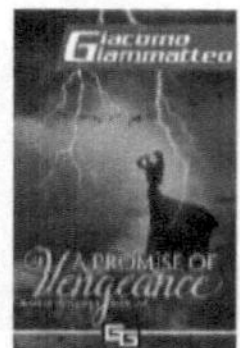

The fog was thick, thicker than any Sennar had ever seen, and something about it was unnatural, the way it hung like a curtain over the sea. The men were afraid. Not that Sennar could blame them. Fear had tugged at his pant legs every waking moment since they first sailed from Genda. Each time a hint of a doubt crept into his mind he reached inside his shirt and felt the smoothness of the healed skin. It reminded him why he accepted the mission. He did wonder though, what drove his four passengers to seek the Sea of the Lost.

They must have heard the tales, and even if they didn't believe the stories, legends were built on truth. Should have been warning enough. Sennar shook his head. They looked too smart to risk their lives over gold. Seemed like good people—*all except that one.*

fog at sea

The fog thickened. Sennar had not thought that possible, but thicken it did. Now he couldn't see the mast or the sails; he couldn't see the bow or the stern. It was as if he'd gone blind. "Half–speed," he called. "Lower the sails."

Sennar called the order to cut speed three times, until they barely moved, yet it seemed as if they were racing. The old captain recalled the bluff on the road to Penova Cove, and how dangerous it was. One rock in their path could mean a cracked hull. "Full stop," Sennar shouted. "Lower the anchor." He didn't want to stop, but he had no choice. The fog showed no signs of abating. They could hear the water, hear the waves lapping at the hull, but that was the only thing to indicate they were still afloat. "We'll wait until it burns off," Sennar said, while he stared into the gray night.

"And if it don't?" his mate asked.

"Then we'll wait some more." The old sea captain barked like a seal. "I'll not be havin' my ship go down for being impatient." Sennar glared at him.

The mate lowered his eyes and moved aside. "Lower anchor!" He shouted the order to the deckhands and had it repeated throughout the ship. "Lower anchor."

~

For two days the fog lay on them, a blanket of eeriness that encircled the ship, permeated every section. It was unmoving, but it was everywhere, haunting even the lower decks where men tried to sleep between nightmares.

"Fog don't linger like this," a crewman said.

"The sun should have burned it off," said another.

From morning till night—if anyone could tell when one started and the other began—Sennar paced the ship, his cane thumping the deck like heartbeats. Rahg leaned against the rail, listening. Between bouts of fear he wondered if Darstan was all right.

Sennar's distinguishable limp came closer. When he got within a few paces Rahg saw him. "How can you tell where to go?"

Sennar continued to stare into the nothingness of the fog. "Can't."

Rahg worried, staring at the captain he once considered verbose. "Then how will we get there?"

"Some say that once ya cross through the fog, the skies are clear and the sun shines all the time... Some say."

"And what do others say?" Rhaven's voice cut through the vapors that hung in the air.

Sennar turned toward him. "Others? Others say that the fog is only the beginning. Legend says that there'll be a brief respite—a place called the Isles of Mist." The captain stopped, a somber mood had taken hold of him.

"And then?" Rahg asked.

"And then," Sennar said, "Then it's raging storms—the Breath of the Gods." Something seemed to give Sennar an extra measure of fortitude. "But we'll make it through." The captain's voice raised. "Blood and sharks be cursed, we'll be the first ship to do it. We'll cut the fog and ride right over the rocks on the Breath of the Gods. We will, or I'll be dead first."

Rhaven nodded. "Then I suggest we begin moving, Captain. I have no intention of commanding this vessel, but we make no headway while sitting still." Rhaven spun and departed.

Sennar stared after him. The fog was thick, but Rhaven vanished quicker than he should have been able to. For the first time Rahg thought he saw fear in Sennar's eyes.

"You travel with an odd lot," Sennar said.

Rahg nodded. "Yes, Sir," then walked toward the cabins. Echoes of Sennar's voice could be heard throughout the ship as he shouted new commands.

"On the top deck, seamen. Topside, or I'll cast ya out with the great beasts of the sea."

Deckhands scrambled from all corners of the ship to topside and stood prepared to hear the captain's orders. "Fetch the small boats," Sennar said. "We'll be riggin' up a tow line and fightin' our way free of this demon fog." The old captain paced before his crew. "I know most are wonderin' where we're headed. I know most worry about gettin' back to Genda, but I'm tellin' ya there's gold to be had out here. Gold enough to keep ya till your dyin' day. That's worth a few risks, I say."

Sennar shored up their spines a little. He hoped he had, anyway. "I need two small ships with strong oarsmen. Take lanterns with ya and sail due west. Due west," Sennar yelled. "We'll be breakin' our next day's fast in the Isles of the Mist. If ya can row like men we will. That, I promise."

The small ships touched the water with little more than a soft splash.

It seemed as if the fog absorbed the sound as well as the sight. They lowered the lanterns, their bright light dimming as they descended into the abyss of grayness. Then Sennar shouted orders again.

"Due west, men. Row hard. Row with your hearts, men."

Rahg wasn't sure if the Isles of Mist awaited them, in fact, he felt pretty sure the captain had no more idea of where they were than anyone else. Rahg approached a young seaman who just finished lending a hand with the small boats. He stood at the rail looking overboard.

"Good eve," Rahg said. "Or good morn', or night. Hard to tell with the fog."

The seaman shivered. "It's eve. I been keepin' track... so I know when to watch."

"Watch for what?"

The lad looked around, as if checking to see if anyone listened. "Mist Dwellers," he whispered, lips trembling. "The Wraiths of the Sea." After he mentioned their name, he looked about in all directions, as if one might be lurking nearby.

mist dweller

A tinge of fear ran the course of Rahg's spine. He had never heard of Mist Dwellers, but the name itself inspired dread, and the young seaman's reaction hadn't helped. Rahg felt something lurking in the darkness. "What do they look like?" he asked. "And what's your name? Mine's Rahg."

"Mason," the lad said. His eyes continued to shift. "They only appear at night, or so it's told. And they look just like the fog, tendrils of smoke with eyes that glow. Somtimes they're ed eyes and sometimes they're blue. They say that just before they attack, you can see their whole form—eyes and all. And the eyes can see right through you. They see everything. That's why there's no hiding from a Mist Dweller."

Mason kept one hand clenched about the hilt of his knife. Rahg wondered whether a knife would be any weapon against something that looked like fog or wisps of smoke. "What can they do to you?"

Mason trembled, and his voice quavered. "They crawl inside of you and eat your soul. That's what they do." He said it as if he were stating the obvious then, staring blankly into the gray, he repeated himself. "They eat your soul."

A tingling sensation ran up Rahg's back. His knees buckled. "How do you kill them? What could kill something like that?" Rahg didn't know if he believed any of this yet, but to be safe, he wanted to know how to kill them.

"Don't know that you can kill one," Mason said. "But I heard that light would do it. Blinding light." Mason laughed. "But how you'd get blinding light in the midst of this fog is a mystery to me."

Rahg felt sorry for Mason. He had not meant to stir up trouble. "Perhaps we won't come close to them. The sea is so vast, more than likely we won't even come near them."

Mason stared at Rahg with the look of a defeated man. "We're sailin' to the Isles of Mist; that's what the captain said." Mason never blinked. "That's where the Mist Dwellers live."

For a long time after Mason left, Rahg stood topside staring into the fog. A sea of gray with no end in sight. He stared, and he wondered, and he searched for red or blue eyes. *Nothing's going to eat my soul.*

Two more days passed with no relief from the fog. The small boats made steady progress and encountered no obstacles: no rocks, monsters, or Mist Dwellers. And, though no one spoke openly about the legendary wraiths, Rahg heard the stories whispered by other seamen since Mason told him of them. If anything was certain on this voyage, it was the crew's belief in the Mist Dwellers. Now Rahg went to sleep dreaming of fog, and storms, and red eyes. No matter what, he could not get rid of the red eyes. They appeared in every dream and followed him wherever he went.

On the morning of the fifth day since entering the fog, one of the men from the boat on the port side called out. "Clear skies!"

"Clear skies!" The entire crew echoed the call. "The fog has lifted, Captain."

Enthusiasm infected the men like laughter, though none more so than Sennar. A smile even appeared on that warped and crooked face.

"Make sail!" Sennar ordered.

As the sails were hoisted and tied aloft, they broke through the barrier of gray that had imprisoned them.

Rahg turned to look at it as they sailed through. "Thick as potato soup," he muttered, "I'm glad to bid that farewell."

Mason came up beside Rahg, laughing. "We escaped 'em, Rahg. I don't know if we outran 'em, or if they let us pass, but whichever it is, I'm bein' thankful."

Sennar's biting voice cut through the noise. "You men on that rope need to be haulin' line. ya got no time to be tellin' lies and flappin' those lips in the breeze." He turned to Rahg and Mason. "If you lads need something to keep busy, we got decks that need scrubbing."

"I'll help," Rahg said. For the rest of the day he worked alongside Mason scrubbing decks.

Sennar was obsessed with cleaning: the masts, the pilot's wheel, decks, blocks and pulleys, and anything else he could see or touch. Sennar had them pay particular attention to the joints.

"The salt of the sea's bad enough," he said, "but the gods only know what poison crept in there when we passed through the fog. Clean 'em good. I'll put the whip to the first one I catch leavin' dirt behind."

"I think he means it," Rahg whispered to Mason.

"Aye, that he does," Mason answered. "I seen 'im toss a man to the sea for not following orders."

"Tossed him into the sea? God's blood, that's cruel."

"That's Sennar," Mason said.

The weather remained calm all afternoon. Just before evening, Rahg went to get Camissa. As they walked the deck, a cry from aloft came.

"Captain, ships in the distance. On the starboard."

Sennar rushed to the side rail, his cane thumping furiously to keep pace with his one good leg. "Give me the glass, lad," he screamed at the mate. "Bring the glass!"

"What's wrong?" Rahg asked.

Sennar peered through his long looking glass. After a moment Sennar put the glass down and stared at him like he just asked if water was wet. "Wrong!" he shouted. "Lad, there be ships ahead. Ships! When we don't even know where we are, and us bein' probably the first Gendans to be here." Sennar smashed his cane to the deck. "Likely pirates from some people we never heard of." Sennar turned toward the main deck. "Arm yourselves, men. Be prepared to bring her about; we'll be needin' to do some fast sailin'."

The captain turned back to Rahg. "Ya better see to gettin' the lass back under, lad. Then come about and keep your hand on the hilt of that sword ya carry. I have a feelin' you'll be needin' it."

Rahg grabbed Camissa's arm and hurried toward her cabin. He could hear Sennar bellowing in the distance.

~

Sennar placed the glass up to his eyes again. *Ships. Out here. Where did they come from? And whose could they be?*

Three enemy ships lay less than half a league from them, spreading out to encircle Sennar's ship. He could turn about and run for the fog, but what would he do in there. More'n likely the men would stage a mutiny at the mere thought of goin' back. The mist had scared 'em good. Sennar decided to pull up and see what these people had in mind. If it appeared to be trouble... then, they could fight. He had a good, fighting crew. *And there's always that black-cloaked demon.* "Half-speed," he ordered. "Lower the sails."

The two biggest ships flanked the Sea Skate. Each carried a crew of fifty or more and they appeared to be heavily armed. The seamen aloft

513

had arrows, and the crew topside held a cutlass in each hand or a cutlass and knife. When within shouting range, a man from the vessel on the port side called out.

"What's your business out here, Captain? Name yourself and the port you sail from."

Sennar shouted back. "I might ask who's askin', and what port you're sailin' from, mate. I'm mindin' my own nets, causin' no harm to no one."

"You might ask, Captain," the man replied, "and I might tell you while I cut your throat. I'm not one that favors patience. I'll be needing an answer—now."

Sennar thought it over, but only for a heartbeat. If trouble awaited them, he'd figure some way to escape. "You're talkin' to the captain of the Sea Skate, mate—Captain Jacopo Sennaro, sailin' from Genda on a voyage that had nothin' to do with you when we started. I reason it's still that way." Sennar paused, then did his best to raise his voice and sound threatening without being insulting. "Now, mate, state your own affairs. Like, why would ya be stoppin' a free ship unless ya be pirates. Are ya pirates, mate? I'm demandin' an answer."

"Would you be known as 'Old Crazy' by some of the sea's best men, Captain Jacopo Sennaro? And if that's right, then would you take my word as an invitation to join us for food and drink. We've got vidda enough for ten seasons of dry weather and ale to last till we die."

Everyone on board must have heard the exchange between the ships, and none appeared more surprised than Sennar. "I'll be raisin' the sails and climbin' up your backside. And if I knew the destination, I'd be spittin' back at ya and hollerin' for ya to catch up. But as it is I'll be satisfied to follow. Just tell me who I'm owin' gratitude. Who be our host?"

The laughter rang through the seas, echoing off the hulls of the ships. It seemed that the wind carried the words round and round adding a mysterious touch to the man's response. "Why, the host be Captain Ardrahan Malakai—the Sword of the Sea."

The smile disappeared from Sennar's face, a scowl and somber mood replacing it. The rest of the crew went mute. Malakai sailed with a bad reputation and ships laden with stolen goods and miscreants. Malakai suffered harsh treatment under Sennar's tutelage on more than one occasion. That was a long time ago, but Gendans were notorious for bearing grudges.

Sennar hobbled to the rail, issuing orders to the crew. "Lead on, mate," he cried. "I'll be eager to show the Sword of the Sea how to drink vidda. You young sea pups might not know it, but it was crazy Sennar that taught your captain how to sail. And it was Sennar who gave him his first drink of vidda. Lead on, mates. Lead on."

A QUAINT LITTLE TOWN

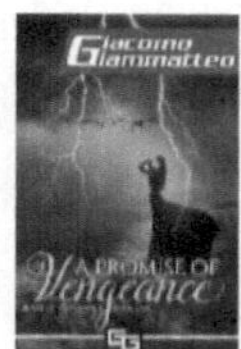

The Sea Skate followed close behind the pirate ships, sailing in a southwesterly direction.

Rahg approached Sennar as he peered through his long glass into the horizon. "See anything, Captain?"

"If your eyes are open, ya always see something, lad. Unless you're blind, or starin' into the black of night. Since the sun's still shinin' and ya know me not to be blind, I'd say ya asked a foolish question. That either makes ya a fool, or worse, a man who speaks before he thinks. Some might call them one and the same. I'd much rather be caught talkin' to a fool." Sennar continued to stare into the long glass as intent as ever, a smile on the good side of his face.

Too embarrassed to ask any more questions, Rahg drifted off to find someone else to talk to. He searched for Tobias, but found Rhaven instead. "Do you know Malakai?"

Rhaven nodded. "I know him. And he knows me."

Before Rahg could ask anything else he heard one of the seamen yell. "Land ho."

Sennar limped across the deck and put the glass to his eye.

"Lower sails, prepare to come to dock."

There were three islands, all protected by high cliffs facing the sea. Two narrow channels curved inland on either side of a large rock formation that rose from the floor of the sea. Once inside that, smaller islands covered by trees guarded the main island, and each one had cannon on it for protection. It would not be an easy place to raid if that's what someone had in mind. The captain from the lead ship barked a warning.

"Follow closely, Sennar."

rock formation

Sennar steered the Sea Skate in behind the lead ship like it was a shadow, veering to port and starboard, duplicating every movement. They sailed through a maze of narrow inlets, high rock walls bordering each side, then between the high rock formation and one of the islands. Outposts sat atop the cliffs at strategic points. In the event of an attack they would be formidable defenses. Enough to render the isle impenetrable.

last guardians of the isles

The pathways opened into a cove with water as smooth as a still pond, guarded by small islands that were armed with cannon. They passed two ships that were just sailing out, and before long came to a quaint little town with rows of houses stacked upon a hillside that over-looked the harbor.

A quaint little town

A group of pirates awaited them at the dock. Sennar announced himself to a short seaman with a scarred face and a gold earring in the shape of an anchor dangling from his left lobe.

The seaman's voice proved to be as gruff and coarse as his looks. "What ill winds blew your ship here, Captain Jacopo Sennaro? I know ya couldn't have come on your own."

"Listen well, lad. I'm not a man of patience, so ya better be informin' your wily captain just who be here to visit."

The short seaman stared at Sennar like he was crazy, then whispered in the ear of another, who hurried off, scurrying up the hill. "So, you've come to see our captain, have ya? Well, ya better pray to whatever gods ya worship that his mood is favorable, cause he can be a bit nasty at times." The other pirates laughed so hard one doubled over.

One of the pirates reached toward Sennar. "Surrender your blade. You'll be taken to Malakai soon."

Sennar's one good hand moved toward his knife. "I'll gut you and half a dozen more if ya try, mate. And I got a man on board who would cost ya a small crew to disarm. Tell Malakai to come see us if he doesn't care for arms in his city."

"I doubt he'll come here just for you, Sennar."

"Then tell him to come for me," a voice called from the ship. "Tell him Tobias Marek, who was once the 'First of Genda' is here. Tell him that; he'll come."

There was a lot of mumbling on the dock, confusion setting in. The pirate in charge looked up, bowing when he spied Tobias.

"I'll tell 'im myself, Tobias. Been too long since we met, but you're welcome to our isle."

A commotion announced the arrival of Ardrahan Malakai rumbling down the hill, straight toward the Sea Skate. He carried two swords in his belt, curved cutlasses, positioned so that the hilts crossed each other and faced inward. Knives peeked out of sheaths attached to his boots. He was a giant of a man, much larger than Takar, and his bright-red hair hung loose over the sides of his ears.

Malakai scowled at Sennar through huge blue eyes over a nose that was too big for his face, big as it was. Quick as a thought, Malakai thrust his arm forward and seized Sennar's blade.

"When my men order a surrender of arms, 'old teacher', I expect it to be obeyed. I would have thought you, of all men, would understand. Order your crew to disarm."

Sennar glared at his old apprentice.

"They'll come to no harm, Sennar. You have my word."

Sennar issued the orders. Knives and swords dropped all about Rahg, but he waited. He didn't plan on disarming unless Rhaven did. As the last few blades dropped to the deck an eerie silence spread. Men moved away from the center of the ship. After they parted, Rhaven stood alone. His death-black cloak shifted and swirled, and his glare aimed straight at Malakai.

Malakai shoved men aside and let his long strides whisk him up the planking from dock to topside. Not ten paces apart, they stared at each other like two wolves vying for leadership of the pack.

"You shouldn't have come to my isle, Rhaven."

The silence seemed ominous; even the waves seemed to stop. Rhaven, as always, was poised to strike. "I thought you dead, Ardrahan. And this isle was not our destination."

Malakai squinted his eyes. "What destination could draw you past the Guardian Mist? Tell me true or die."

Rhaven's hand move toward the sword. Rahg knew there would be bloodshed. He moved his own hand toward his sword. *If Rhaven's going to die fighting, so am I.*

Tobias burst through the crowd and got between Rhaven and Malakai. "No blood needs to be shed. You know me, Ardrahan. I vouch for the lot of 'em, Rhaven included. None of us knew you were here." Tobias laughed. "Fact is, we were lookin' for you in

Genda. Everyone told us ya died, so we ended up hirin' old Sennar."

Suspicion filled Malakai's glare. "I know you, Tobias, but it's been a long while. Do I know you can be trusted? There's a lot of gold offered for my head. Gold can change a man."

Tobias scowled and spat. "A fish don't shed its scales. Only serpents do that. If it's that kind of trust you're extendin' to us, then fit me with a blade and let me join Rhaven. We'll take out half your whole blasted isle before we're taken down."

Rahg pushed through the front line of men and did his best imitation of a confident strut. With a wary eye on Malakai and a fierce determination not to shake, he joined Rhaven, praying that his voice wouldn't falter. "It will be three you need to kill."

Malakai stared for a long time before he smiled. "Where's your destination, Tobias Marek. And don't bother to lie or tell me any of your famous tales. If it's not me you're after, then who is it?"

"Well, it's about time, ya old pirate. I didn't want to be forced to gut ya." Tobias walked to Malakai and they clasped hands like old friends.

Malakai continued to glare at Rhaven then walked over to him. "It has been a long time. Since you've come with no ill will, I'll not be the one to ignite an old fire."

Rhaven's gaze lingered, then he stretched out his own hand, and they joined in greetings.

"Come to my house. I offer food and ale in exchange for stories of my homeland. And you must tell me more of this young shark who is so eager to die." Malakai slapped Rahg on the back.

As they walked up the hill, Malakai hollered to one of his men. "Entertain our guests. They have free run of our isle."

∾

*A*s they walked through town, Tobias questioned Malakai. "What have ya made here, Malakai? It looks as if you've built a pirate city. No one could get in here, that's certain."

"The truth, Tobias, is we've built a home here. A home for all the men who can abide by our laws, men who gave up pirating long ago. We have a good town. We've built a whole city, a whole country if you care to call it that, and we live in peace. No one bothers us, and we make no trouble for anyone else. We govern ourselves and have laws, good men's laws."

"There's no leaving the isles, so if anyone does wrong and, at first, some did, they're banished to one of the small islands you see offshore. It takes only one time for someone to learn a lesson; isolation is a horrible punishment no matter the surroundings. Most men prefer a dingy brig with companions as opposed to being isolated in luxury."

"How many men does an isle hold, Ardrahan? What do ya do if one gets full?"

Malakai's laugh was a bellow. "Tobias, we have seventeen isles, though only a few large ones. In all the years since we built this town, only three were used." Malakai stopped walking while he looked Tobias in the eyes. "I have given up my ways, Tobias. I've taken a wife and expect a child soon. I'm not the man you once knew." Malakai stared at Tobias. "I'll not give this up for anybody. I'd die first. We all feel that way." Malakai smiled. "Now, come. Visit my home, and eat."

His house was small with several windows in the front, each adorned by curtains and with flowers in the sill; gardens decorated the front lawn, and large flowering trees embraced above a walk built from finely carved stone. A delicate looking doorway centered the forward wall. It was small, and Malakai needed to duck to gain entry.

"I have a fine young wife, Tobias. A sassy little thing, she is. And that's the reason for the doorway. She said I needed a reminder every day of how small a man I really am; said I was only meant to be as big as that doorway, but my body just happened to grow bigger, and if I learned to stoop low just to enter a door, then I could stoop to accommodate other things as well. Like my pride." Malakai laughed, a roar that filled the small cottage. "She must have been right, too, 'cause on those days when I forget and hit my head, I'm not a very proud man."

Tobias howled. "Marriage is not the hangman's noose some people claim it to be, but it'll hold ya just as tight."

Rhaven jumped to his feet and bowed. Before Rahg realized why, Malakai's wife entered the room and introduced herself. Rahg offered apologies for his delay, but, Madelin brushed it aside as if it were nothing.

"We don't hold to formalities here, young lad. I only work hard each day to remind my brute husband of his own mortality. If I can do that, I consider everything else a blessing."

Rahg stared at her. She had fine, delicate features—a direct contrast to Malakai's—and her voice was light as air. The same red hair dangled to her shoulders, complemented by lovely green eyes. "My name is Rahg."

Madelin frowned. "Rahg...That's a hard name for a fine young lad like you. What does it mean?"

"I...I don't know that it means anything. It's just a name my father gave me."

Madelin straightened her apron then brushed her hands, looking as if she didn't believe a word of what Rahg said. "Bosh, lad. Every name means something. If you don't know what it means you ought to change it. It's too hard a name for you." She grabbed Rahg's chin and twisted his face. "Strong chin. Good straight nose." Madelin shook her head. "Well, come into the eatin' room, Rahg, if you insist on bein' called such a name. I guess you're all hungry. I don't think I ever laid eyes on a seaman come home from a voyage that wasn't hungry. Come on then, food is waitin'."

Rahg shook his head as he followed her into the kitchen. He didn't know if Madelin was like this all the time, but feisty as she was, he could understand how she tamed Malakai.

"Let me help with things," Camissa said.

Madelin wasted no time, grabbing Camissa's sleeve and tugging her toward the kitchen. "Come with me, girl. Men require a lot of tendin', so I'll not refuse a good woman's help."

Malakai pulled up a chair and lit his pipe, rigorously puffing ringlets of smoke to get it burning. "Now that we have privacy, perhaps you can be free with details, Sennar. What brings a man through the Guardian Mist?"

Sennar leaned on the table, causing it to shift toward him. "I thought I taught ya better, Ardrahan. Poor manners to be askin' anyone their business, and even worse manners to be askin' guests at your home to explain themselves. I expect ya ought to withdraw your questions 'fore that whip of a wife hears what you said. I'm guessin' only, but I'd wager my best pipe she'd knock ya down to her size if she knew." Sennar laughed as he lit his pipe.

Rhaven took a sip of ale from his mug and looked at Malakai. "We need information. You know these seas. Sennar doesn't." Rhaven swallowed the ale with a noticeable gulp. "If I need to ask it as a favor, so be it. I'm indebted to you."

"Tell me where you're going."

"Entiria," Rhaven said.

"Entiria?" Malakai stared at them, fixing his gaze last on Sennar. He let that gaze linger. "You'll die if you try it."

"Why?" Rhaven asked.

"Tell me about it," Sennar said. "I contracted with these folks to take them to Entiria. I aim to take them there if I have to swim the seas myself, and carryin' each one on my back. Ya know me, Malakai. I've cheated men out of gold, and gutted 'em for less, but I give my word to few." Sennar glared at Malakai. "And ya know I've never dishonored my word."

"Why?" Malakai asked, looking at Tobias.

Sennar leapt from his chair. "That's their affair. Not yours. Not mine. I asked your advice. Will ya tell me? Or do I sail off to my grave without even that from my old pupil."

Malakai's face grew stern. "I have no wish to send you off to die. I won't weep for you, and I won't miss a meal, but I still don't like the doin' of it. But if you're dead set on goin', and dead you'll be, then I'll share with you what I know."

Sennar sat as Malakai began his story. "We came seeking the lost land of Entiria. Legends claimed it to lay beyond the Guardian Mist, in the Sea of the Lost. The men were certain that a lost land would be covered with gold and other riches. I never believed there'd be any treasure, but I sought the solitude. When we found these isles, I thought we discovered Entiria. It turned out to be as much a paradise as we hoped for. If there had been gold I have no doubt there would have been fights, and greed would have caused killings. We were happy with the life, and everyone voted to stay on the isles.

"Then, one day, a ship returned with a wild tale. Most of the fishing we had done to the south; the sea stayed calmer, and the catch always good. But one of the men decided to go north and west; that's when he saw the mist. He came back with a tale of fog and mist thicker than the Guardian Mist we came through to get here. He told of the seas ceasing movement and the winds standing still—the doldrums."

doldrums

Malakai gulped the last of the ale from his mug and wiped his beard dry with the back of his oversized hand. "Madelin, I'll be in your debt if you'd fill this mug again. I've a lot of story to tell, and my mouth runs dry."

Madelin returned with a mug filled to the brim. Malakai took a long swig, belched, then continued with his tale.

"He only peeked inside the fog, he said, then returned to report his find. I assumed it to be the real Guardian Mist, figured the one we crossed was just a lure. We sent out an expedition of twenty men on a good, stable ship, not the best, but a good one. She never returned. We waited a month. When they didn't come back, we risked another. This time we committed our best ship, and a full crew. Fifty of the most experienced seamen. I went aboard as captain."

Tobias interrupted. "Then you have a log of your journey, and coordinates for us to chart our course."

"I have nothing. All of it lost. Barely survived myself."

"I know ya to have a memory for numbers, and such, Malakai. What can ya tell me that will help?"

Malakai frowned. "I can recite the coordinates, Sennar. That'd be easy enough. But that will only take you to the point where I entered, and that's where the problems began. Your compass won't work, nor any other instrument; something in the fog must interfere with it. So once you enter the mist, you need to hold to a due westerly course and do it without a guide. And you'll need to use the small boats; there'll be no wind."

Sennar tapped the heel of his pipe against the table, knocking the spent ashes loose. "Just what was it that near caused the death of you, Ardrahan? Doldrums and fog won't do it." There remained a degree of suspicion in Sennar's tone.

"It was after the fog when the trouble started. For two days nary a breeze stirred. We rowed night and day in shifts 'cause everyone wanted to get out of the mist." Madelin placed another mug in front of Malakai. He took a long, hearty swig. "Was the wind, Sennar. When we came out of the fog, the wind was waitin', ready to pounce on us like it had a mind of its own. Layin' in ambush, it was."

The smoke from Malakai's pipe curled upward, then drifted toward the window.

"Nearly tore the ship apart. Wasn't the wind alone, mind you, but the wind stirred up the sea until the waves crashed the ship against the rocks, near breaking it to pieces." Malakai paused for yet another sip of ale, and several puffs on his pipe. "Still don't know how I survived. Everything blanked out, and next I recalled I was floatin' in the sea on the other side of the fog. Madelin found me. She got worried, and set out with a small crew to look for me. Would have died for certain if not for the good lady."

"That's all you can tell us?" Tobias asked.

Malakai frowned. "I can tell you not to go. That's the best advice I'll offer. As to any other help, I'll promise that a ship will wait on this side of the fog for half a month. That way, if any of your crew survives the wreck, there's a chance they'll make it out like I did. I can do no more."

Sennar stood with alarming suddenness. "That'll do, Ardrahan. I'd not ask a man to risk his neck for no reason. Though if you station the ship for a month I'd be more grateful. A man might last that long if he's got water, and I'd hate for some deckhand to be tossed asea and hopin' for rescue and not find ya there waitin'."

Malakai nodded. "A full cycle it'll be then. You can rely on that."

Madelin brought the food, which everyone devoured quickly, then Tobias peppered Malakai with more questions. "Where'd the women come from? I know they couldn't have been with you during your pirating ways."

Malakai laughed. "True enough, Tobias. The truth is when we found this place, we figured it to be a good place to call home. I sent two ships to fetch some women and workers to build houses. I also had them spread the tale of me dying so people wouldn't be lookin' for me. It's as simple as that."

"I'll be," Tobias said. "Never would have figured."

Sennar and Tobias continued to question Malakai about the journey, but they learned nothing new. Soon it was time to leave. Malakai stood and clasped hands with Sennar, then Tobias.

"May the blessings of the gods accompany you and guard your sails. You'll need the assistance." Malakai hesitated, then extended his hand to Rhaven. "The past is gone. May your quest end in peace." Rhaven accepted the gesture of friendship, if reluctantly.

The walk back to the Sea Skate seemed much longer even though it was downhill. "Make ready the sail, men." Sennar shouted loud enough for all the men to hear, but then he whispered, "It may be your last journey."

CAPTURED AGAIN

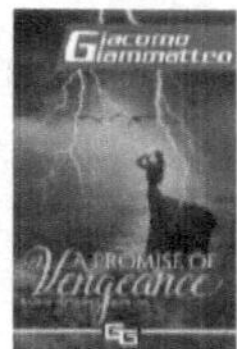

The tip of the spear jabbed Darstan. He swore, but moved quickly to a spot where the Krovs had them lined up to get in the boats. They ordered Evin into the canoe with Darstan.

"What do you think they'll do with us?" Evin's tone stayed level. He showed no fear, even though Darstan knew him to be afraid.

"I don't know, but we shouldn't let them see our fear."

"I don't think they speak our language, Darstan. They don't show any signs of recognition, even when something is said about them."

"They don't need to understand our words to determine our feelings." Darstan listened to the Krovs talk. They spoke in short, terse sentences, with clipped words, unlike any of the dialects he knew.

The Krov in charge uttered a series of commands to the others. Two small boats led the way. Darstan rowed from the front of the canoe. Half the morning passed with small talk, the gaps filled by fear. The Krov in front steered into a narrow channel choked by vines, reeds, and deadwood. At times, the current of the river tugged at them; at other times the channel seemed still, and stagnant, with muck floating atop the water. Evin broke the silence with a whisper.

"What do you think they'll do with us, Darstan?"

"I'm trying not to think of it."

The Krov leader took several more turns through the maze of inlets, stopping at a large island a few feet above the water. It was covered with cypress trees and thick vegetation. Huts lined the edge of the forest, constructed on large wooden supports to raise them above the ground.

"I think we should try to escape once we get to land, Darstan."

"We'd never get out of these swamps. Even if we could find our way, they'd catch us before we got half a league."

Their canoe slid up onto the bank behind the Krov boat, Darstan and Evin disembarking once it sat upon the shore. Four Krovs stood guard with spears pointed at them. In a matter of moments, the thick brush opened to produce more of the warriors. The boat that carried Wehr and the other two guards came ashore, followed by the remainder of the Krov boats. Soon, they were shuffled down a narrow path toward a spot where the concentration of huts seemed thickest.

In the center of a large clearing stood a pole almost a span high. A Krov dressed in ceremonial garb approached them. He had a thick accent, but he spoke the language of Sykor with enough mastery for Darstan to understand.

"You have violated the treaty by coming on our lands. Punishment is death."

"We should have tried to escape," Evin said.

Wehr stepped forward. "We are envoys of Sykor. We come—"

The Krov leader struck Wehr with a stick before he got a chance to finish. Wehr offered no further explanations. The Krovs bound them and tied them to the pole. Krov soldiers stripped them of their shirts, then another Krov poured a sticky substance over their heads, chest, and back. Darstan tried to shake it off, but it stuck to him. He wrinkled his nose at the odor, like sour milk with honey added. Swarms of insects buzzed about their heads and feasted on their bodies.

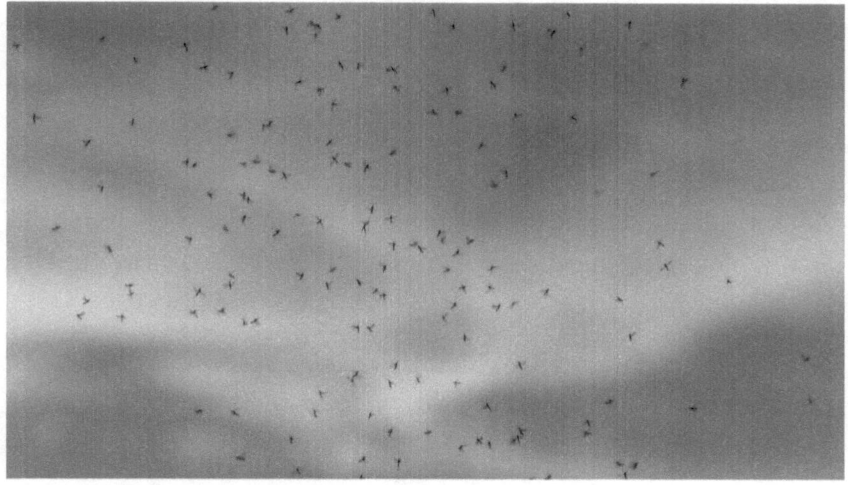

insects

Darstan tried running the short distance that the rope allowed, but the bugs followed, intent on their prey. He shook his head and rubbed against his arms, but they smothered him. Several got into his ears. He screamed.

Then bugs got in his mouth. Several bit the roof of his mouth and more stung his tongue. He felt as if he'd go insane, but he managed to wrangle his tongue and push them into a position where he could catch them with his teeth. Darstan chewed vehemently then spat them out.

The Krovs were laughing. Odd that he thought of it at this time, but laughing was the same in any language, laughing and crying.

What seemed like an entire swarm of insects tunneled up Darstan's nostrils, driving him into a feverish struggle. All the while, he found himself contorting his body in a frantic effort to rid his back and stomach of the armies of insects that fed upon his flesh. The suffering remained the only constant, the stings like thousands of pricks from a pin in a never ending succession. When Darstan felt he could stand no more, a ray of hope appeared.

He smelled smoke, an acrid, unpleasant odor. Within moments billows of thick smoke drove the insects away, though it left Darstan and the others choking and gasping for air.

Someone untied his hands. Darstan collapsed, instinctively clawing at his body. The bites had swollen his lips so much that he couldn't talk, and his eyelids seemed to be fused shut. He scratched inside his mouth, shoved a finger up his nose, and raked his face until he drew blood.

Intense anxiety shot through him. He crawled as close as he could to the fire. It was hot, burning his face, but he would have done anything short of throwing himself in, if he could just get rid of the itching.

Two pair of Krov hands wrestled him to the ground, then they poured liquid over him that felt chilling, then stung. In less than a moment it alleviated his pain.

The Krovs allowed them to rest then provided a hearty meal of strange meat and a soup made from various grasses. Afterward, they gave them berries that Darstan found delicious despite his anguish. Their ecstasy was short lived, however, for following the meal, the Krov leader ordered the torture to begin anew.

"No!" Darstan lashed out, kicking one in the gut. Two Krovs seized him and held him secure amid a stream of curses and thrashing.

Darstan's mind raced. He didn't know if he could withstand another session of torture.

Wehr shouted at the Krov leader. "I speak for the force commander of Sykor."

One of the Krovs struck Wehr with his stick. The strike leader winced, but continued.

"You can see we mean no harm. There are only five of us. We did—"

Again, Wehr felt the lash of punishment, this time, by several of the Krovs with their whipping sticks. Blood oozed from the long gashes, but Wehr proved to be relentless. "We did not come to hunt, or to disturb you; this was urgent business for the force commander." They were about to strike him again when the Krov leader intervened.

"And why does the force commander of Sykor send men to my lands?"

"The force commander did not know we would come this way. In fact, he instructed us to avoid your lands, but the mission was important, and we were followed. I decided it would be wiser to try and lose our enemies in the swamps in order to reach Sykor safely."

The Krov leader grunted his apparent disapproval. "My men saw the tracks of those who follow you. There were only two. If five Sykoran guards are fearful of two men, perhaps we settled the war too soon."

Wehr spoke quickly. "The man without a uniform," he pointed to Darstan, "He is the blood of our force commander. He was taken from Sykor by strangers. We were sent to bring him back." Wehr shot a warning glance to Darstan.

"Why not kill the two who followed you?" The Krov leader asked.

"I didn't fear for my own safety, but for the life of the force commander's blood. One of the men who trails us is a great warrior; he might have slain us all."

"Who is this warrior?"

"His name is Rhaven," Wehr said.

The Krov's eyes nearly exploded. He shouted something which stirred the rest of the warriors. They screamed and ran about brandishing weapons. Finally, the leader settled down. "'Death With Two Swords' is our enemy. He has killed many of our people. If he enters our lands, we will kill him."

Wehr refrained from speaking. After a brief pause, the Krov spoke again.

"You were wise not to fight him. He would kill you. I will set you free, but tell your force commander that a life is owed. And send no more men into my lands."

"You have our thanks and our gratitude." The strike leader was animated in his speech, paying reverence to the Krov leader, who provided them with a guide and boats to leave the swamps.

As they climbed into the boats to depart, Darstan smiled. They would be leaving the swamps alive after all. Now all he had to do was figure a way to escape from the guards. *Then I can seek revenge.*

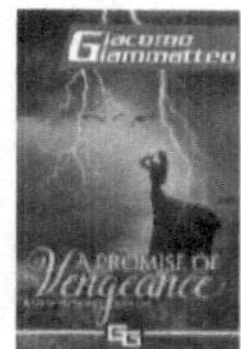

An impatient rapping on the door brought Tirzinitzia through the courtyard, her long legs taking the tiles two at a time. She noticed the coarse hair and pointed ears through the portal on the door—a Wolfen. *Probably a messenger from Ghruehne.*

Her slender fingers slid around an ornate handle carved from desert juniper. The door opened without a sound.

"I bear a message for Lady Melissara," the Wolfen said, failing to address her properly.

The hair on the back of Tirzinitzia 's neck bristled. For a moment, a brief one, she almost allowed instinct to punish the insolent beast, but she now belonged to Melissara, and the thought of repercussions held her temper. "I assumed Ghruehne would have taught you better."

The Wolfen groveled. "My Lady, I beg your forgiveness." His head lowered as he knelt.

Tirzinitzia let him stay on his knees while she decided what to do. Melissara had disappeared before dawn. Where she had gone at such an early hour piqued her curiosity, but duty did not include questioning her new mistress. She remembered the adage about curiosity and the fabled cat.

"It is early, messenger of Ghruehne. At this time, my mistress is most always asleep and I do not intend to awaken her; the last to do so lies in the ravine to the south. You may wake her, though. Come with me."

She started toward a massive arched doorway carved from a single slab of black granite. Her boots clicked on the tiled floor, letting noisy echoes announce their arrival. Before they had traveled halfway across the room, the Wolfen begged an ear.

"Please, mistress? Is there no other way?"

Tirzinitzia stopped, turning to face him. "If you wish, I might accept the message for my mistress."

The Wolfen breathed a heavy sigh. "I am indebted to you, mistress." He handed her a roll of parchment then bowed and departed. Tirzinitzia laughed, then wondered anew where Melissara had gone.

~

*A*t the northern rim of the great desert, a rift opened near the waters of a sparkling oasis. Mikkellana stepped through, bringing a blast of cold into the oppressive heat. Sensing no trap, she released her shield, then scanned the landscape with eyes trained by falcons.

oasis

Around a crystal-clear pond, a ring of rocks mounted a valiant defense against the encroaching dunes. The few trees the oasis supported stood to the right and soaked sustenance from the precious liquid oozing from the dry sands.

oasis with trees

Desert moonflowers hugged one of the shorelines—shining white trumpets with purple throats just now closing to hide from the searing sun. Leopard frogs croaked in the reeds, ignoring Mikkellana's presence, while bumblebee fish danced under the ripples from an arid breeze.

Her sweeping gaze stopped when she saw Melissara perched comfortably on a boulder near the pond, blonde hair hanging to her waist, and her feet splashing playfully in the cool water.

A long-forgotten laugh erupted when one of the fish nibbled on her toes. She cupped her hands, scooped a mouthful of water and drank, a sigh of pleasure escaping moistened lips.

"You could taste the cool waters of freedom every day if you wish."

Melissara jumped, startled. She lifted her feet from the water to let them dry on the rock that served as a seat. Her eyes matched the blue of the pond, but her skin, once as pale as the moon, had darkened under the Sethian sun. "It has been long, Mikkellana. Come and sit so that we may converse." Her voice flowed like a soft wind over a field of Runellan wheat.

Cynical laughter slipped through Mikkellana's lips. She constructed a wall of Shield in front of her, advancing toward the spot where Melissara sat. The shield would alert her to the real boundary, a troublesome effort, but she dare not risk the consequences in the event that Illusion had been used to deceive her and lure her inside the boundaries of Sethia. The small shield jarred with a sudden impact. "This is as far as I go, dear sister. If you wish to speak in hushed tones, it is you who must come closer."

Honey hair bounced against firm breasts as Melissara rose and walked toward her, stopping less than two paces away.

Mikkellana stared. It had been so long. She closed her eyes, took a deep breath and absorbed the scents of desert sage and jasmine. It triggered memories of cuddling in their mother's bed, brushing each other's hair, dressing for a ball.

The chitter of a ground squirrel brought her back, and she turned, checking the surroundings. In another place, at another time, she would not dare expose her back to Melissara, but with the shield between them she had nothing to fear.

"I see that you left your trust behind. But you have no reason to fret over an ambush. I came to listen."

"It has been long, Melissara. Too long."

"Perhaps." Melissara's mystifying eyes stayed icy blue. "We shall see whether the time is wasted or well spent."

"You fare well, I see."

"Fare well? Of course, sister. I have lived so long in luxury that I know nothing else."

A snicker slipped along the path laughter had traced moments ago. "I see that sarcasm has not abandoned you during your ordeal; it clings faithfully to your sharp tongue."

"I tire of the bickering, so be on with it. Your message surprised me to say the least. I assume someone died and you feel a need to share it with me. Who is it? Xanthes? Aentarra? I might even grieve if it is Aentarra."

A disapproving grunt from Mikkellana. "And Xanthes? You never cared for him?"

"So it is Xanthes. I should have known. He's the only one you ever cared for. As for me, I have loved many. He meant no more to me than any other—not since Tarmon."

A fierce look appeared on her face, then disappeared. "But tell me, how does it feel to be forced to accept other women's leftovers? I abandoned Xanthes, so too, did Alithea, and rumor tells me that even our little sister captured his attentions for a while. Are you so devoid of charm that only the men who have been cast out by others are drawn to you?"

"A dog may chew many bones before he finds the sweetest meat, dear sister. I believe Xanthes tired of the sour tastes. I did not represent his last option, more simply, his final choice."

Mikkellana smiled. "Now that we have traded our barbed responses perhaps we will be able to discuss matters in a more civilized fashion?"

When Melissara nodded, she continued. "Our sister, Aentarra, is mad, or at the very least, going mad. It is part of the reason I came. I always suspected she had a touch of it, like father, and the fact that she wants to go back into the Forbidden Lands is proof enough for me."

Melissara stared to the side though her eyes never seemed to focus, as if she were lost in thought. "She always did have an unbridled curiosity about that morbid place, though I have no clue why she would want to go there."

"No one would want to go there," Melissara said. "No one sane. It is the Oath. That Oath is pulling her back to Nelstar, as the moons on Asolo pull the tides. I check the seal often, but I fear she might find a way to break it. None of us can afford to have her unleash powers we can't control."

Deep furrows formed on Melissara's brow as her eyebrows raised. "At last we agree on something," she said, then her smile vanished, replaced by a frown. "But enough of this idle chatter. Since it was not a death that brought you, and certainly not this news of Aentarra, why have you come?"

"The world is changing. Since you have been in Sethia, it has seen much change, and more recently, great change."

Melissara smiled. "When we are free there will be even more change, though none to suit your pleasure."

"You want another conflict? I shall let you think on that, sister."

~

*A*long pause followed as Melissara strolled the edges of the pond, hot sands sifting between her toes. She feigned disinterest but sneaked a glance at Mikkellana when the opportunity arose.

Why is she asking this? What possible good could come from theorizing about the outcome of a war that cannot be? Unless. Yes, that's it. A flood of ecstasy rushed a smile onto her face. Her legs grew weak, then strong. Exuberant. Elated. Calming took a moment, but she soon had control. No sign showed on Mikkellana's face, not a trace, but Melissara knew her sister; a rock exhibited more expression than her. "The shield grows weak. I can feel it. I can sense it."

"A poor attempt at a bluff. You have no ability to sense the shield. None beyond the mere fact of its existence."

Melissara let her canny smile show. "I'll bow to your cleverness. But given enough time, inquisitive minds will find solutions to everything, and as you know, no one is more curious than Tirzinitzia. Did you know that for years Lukaan has been capturing people with any small hint of powers?"

Melissara looked straight at Mikkellana. "No, I thought not. You had no inkling, or you and the others would have made an effort to stop it. Regardless, it doesn't matter. Lukaan hoped to find someone with powers of shielding so that we might see the construction of your shield. If we could but see the way it was made, we reasoned, we could dismantle it. But nobody could even see the first layer of the shield."

Melissara continued to stare at Mikkellana. A sinister little chuckle let Mikkellana know she had postulated a correct theory. "Yes, it does have layers, doesn't it? You see, sister, Tirzinitzia and I used logic to tackle the dilemma.

"Why, we wondered, could mortals without powers go through the shield when we could not? What prevented us from going through?

"In the early period we tried often to escape. It must have been comical to see us blasting away futilely at the shield. I never had an opportunity to test the theory until I got hold of the mortals with powers. I tested them using the utmost in scientific parameters so that I knew which ones were the strongest."

Melissara laughed again. "You would have been proud of me, sister, conducting experiments in such a fashion. You always accused me of being rash, impatient. But I rated them and categorized them down to the minutest detail. At times, it must have been excruciatingly painful for them to withstand the infliction of pain and torture... but they lived, and I was able to test them." Melissara paused and stepped back to drink from the pond.

"Go on with your gruesome explanations, Melissara. But be quick, it sickens me."

Melissara smiled, enjoying every moment of the discourse. "I took them out close to the shield, and set the strongest free first, a male from Khatara. I told him if he could get through the shield he could go free. Believe me, the poor man put forth a valiant effort. I soon determined he would not be successful, but to be certain I sent a rolling wall of fire creeping toward him from all sides. His options were simple: escape through the shield, or die in flames. I felt certain he would have chosen escape if he could. He—"

"Enough! I don't want to hear of your barbarism."

"No. You never wanted to hear about anything if it didn't interest you."

"Do you intend to raise old graves?"

The shaking started in Melissara's chest, pulsing through her body like angry heartbeats. "Don't you dare!"

"I would have thought you over that by now, after so long in the Forbidden Lands, and now in Sethia."

"The desert is lonely at night, but not silent. When the mournful cries of the coyotes ride the cool winds... I can hear Tarmon. Each time a rotting carcass stings my nose, I smell his flesh burning, see his smoldering skin. At night..." Tears flowed, and Melissara found herself trembling. "At night, when I should be feeling his lips, I feel the stubs that were his hands, pawing at my legs as he tried to raise himself." She straightened herself, head erect, firm posture. "And you dare to ask *me* if I intend to raise old graves?"

More tears came and Melissara's face wrinkled into an angry snarl. "You disgust me, pretending as if you have done no wrong. You and the rest of them, all with falsehoods and lies to wear every day. Have you forgotten so soon? Or have you somehow erased the memories?"

Melissara's eyes felt as if they burned. "Perhaps, sister, you do not wish to recall because it was not your child who left the house laughing, a smile on his face, a light in his eyes. It was a bright and sunny day, but soon the sky rained fire." Melissara wept. "Have you ever seen a child look to the sky and wonder why it caused him pain? Have you heard the screams when his he goes blind and his hair bursts into flames? Can you picture him, blind and helpless, and running aimlessly through streets wreaking of death until his body erupted in flames?"

Melissara jumped at the shield, pounding with her fists. "Have you ever looked into a child's eyes that had been hollowed out by fire?" She heaved, dry retching, then memories haunted her again. "No, you cannot imagine, Mikkellana... because you never loved. Everything to you was always black or white. You never understood how people could feel differently about a subject, or wish to worship a different god. None of you could."

"You call her a God!" Mikkellana shook, stepping forward as if she might come through the shield after her. "And whose memory is selective now? Have you forgotten it was Lukaan who killed our own mother?"

A long pause served to settle her down. "Perhaps I could share some of the blame, Melissara. A small part, to be sure. But Lukaan started the turmoil. Lukaan shattered the peace accord. And Lukaan destroyed the Holy Temple of Worship." She paused again. "I have long agonized over your sufferings, sister, but there is no going back. The vengeance Lukaan wrought was well deserved; there is nothing to be done."

Melissara lifted her head. "Do not pretend to have forgotten with me. It was not Lukaan who started the war and you are more aware of it than anyone. Don't be so afraid to admit it. Say it. Speak the name."

Melissara awaited her response. "Very well then, I shall. Antar du Savarra. Antar du Savarra. Shall I say it again? Antar du Savarra!" Melissara screamed. "Does it hurt to hear the name after so long? Does it pain you to admit our father started the war?" Melissara's scowl reflected her emotions. "The Light of Lights, the Eternal Flame, the Seventh One. How many other titles did he lay claim to? How many lands did he rule?" Melissara shook her head as tears carved a path on her cheeks. "And how many millions did he kill? How many billions?"

Mikkellana's face tightened, hands clenched. For a moment, Melissara thought she might actually come through the shield after her, but at the last moment she found her control. "He was mad. You cannot hold a madman accountable."

"I hold *you* accountable."

"There was madness on both sides. During war, madness seems to somehow take control and all the worst emotions surface. All the worst traits govern actions. I tried, Melissara. I made every effort to wage a controlled war, but when horrors were wrought on our people by Lukaan, they screamed for retribution."

Melissara spat upon the ground. "What is it that you wish? Why have you come? It was not to see me. And it was not to tell me of Aentarra's inevitable madness; that doesn't concern me, regardless of what you think. Tell me your reasons and let us be done with this farce."

"I came to offer peace. Peace to you, and Tirzinitzia, perhaps others. But not Ghruehne or Iazzo, and most assuredly not Lukaan. I foresee a world where you and I could once again be sisters in more than name."

Melissara glared, fighting to restrain herself. "There can be no reconciliation. Not ever. Not with Lukaan. Not with the others. And until you can bring my child back, until I can once again hold Canno and Tarmon in my arms—there can never be forgiveness from me—never! So leave, Mikkellana. Be gone. And when we meet again—be prepared."

RETURN TO SYKOR

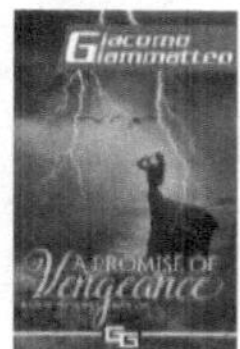

Ranalla had shone bright, waned, and come round again since Wisp and Gregor left Genda, and still they rode hard. "I didn't think I would be excited about coming back," Wisp said, "and yet, as we draw near, I find myself looking forward to the excitement of the crowds. I even yearn for the dull wit of the guards."

"If Takar catches sight of you it may change your mind, thief."

"Never mind about Takar, bounty man. Let's just hope we got here in time. Do you remember the details of our plan, or do I have to explain it to you again?"

"Don't worry about my end of the bargain. I'll gather more men than we need. And when we're done, you need pray I don't change my mind and collect the reward for you. Ten thousand gold can be an irresistible lure."

"You gave your word, Gregor. Break it and I'll slit your throat before you spend one gold crown."

The smile vanished from Gregor's face. "I take exception to threats.

Besides, that much gold tends to make a man reconsider his word, especially when the law of the king demands your capture."

Wisp spat. "Don't try to disguise your shame by hiding behind the law of the king. I didn't think friendship had a price."

"I have spent my life chasing thieves. I have found no honor."

Wisp scoffed. "No honor? What has kept me through this journey? No chains or ropes bound me. I chose to remain based on honor. My word is worth more than gold, Gregor. I value it even over life."

"Then you are a fool."

Wisp laughed despite the tension that clung to the air. "A fool? Am I? At what point does a man become a fool, Gregor? And how does that speak of you; you took the word of a man you thought to be a fool and knew was a thief? And if you believe bounty-men will support you, you're mistaken. Not without gold they won't. It's how they live. The shame of it is, you're a bounty man and you don't even know it."

Gregor's face wrinkled into a sour expression. He made several noises Wisp had never heard before, then prodded his horse with an urgent kick to the flanks. "We'll discuss this in Sykor."

Peals of laughter chased Gregor as he rode off. "You can't outrun it, Gregor. Honor will not hide. Face it, bounty man—with honor, you could be a fool like me." Wisp continued laughing even when he knew Gregor was too far gone to hear it.

～

Wisp found it easy to sneak into Sykor. The guards looked for approaching armies, not one man. Within moments he scaled the wall then quickly descended, blending with the crowds already forming for the day's business. Being back in the city brought a smile to Wisp's face.

No muddy trails, or sleeping in bedrolls, or fighting Black Rose. It's good to be home again.

"Fruit! Farley's fresh fruit..."

The vendor's sing-song tune caught Wisp's attention. He looked up just in time to see two little thieves swipe some apples. Wisp wasn't certain that Farley didn't allow them to steal; he recalled having been poor himself at one time, and he felt certain Farley had let him.

No one hawked their goods like Farley. His tunes proclaiming his fruits to be near virtuous were known throughout Sykor, and there wasn't a vendor in the city whose goods escaped the inevitable comparison to Farley's. *And not by coincidence.*

The two thieves strutted down a side street squeezed between old brick homes, the taller one tugging on the brim of a ragged-edged cap. They tried to remain inconspicuous, their stolen goods tucked into their shirts. Wisp plotted a course to intercept them.

"I beg to speak with you, lads," he said, looming over them like a menacing guard.

They looked up, then to each other, then back to Wisp. "What is it you want?"

"We done nothin' wrong," said the other.

Wisp fought back a smile that childhood memories tried to force out. "I mentioned nothing of wrongdoing. Why would you raise the issue? Have you really done something wrong?"

Denial was vigorous, and though Wisp struggled to contain the smile, a smirk emerged. "If I were to think of wrongdoing, though, I'd likely point to the fruit stuffed in your shirts."

Before the thieves could spirit themselves away, he seized hold of their shirts, unwashed and smelly.

"Don't turn us in, master," the smallest one pleaded.

"We'll split it with you," the one with the cap said, all the while struggling to break free.

Wisp leaned down to stare into their eyes. "I don't need any of your goods, and I won't turn you in." He saw the look of relief in their eyes. "But I need a small favor," he said. "I need a message delivered to the Trader's Inn." When they nodded acknowledgment he continued. "Tell Brock Larnigin that Kender, his sweep-up man, has returned. Tell him to have a room prepared for me, and that I'll be by tonight."

"Is that all you want?" the younger one asked.

The other lad seemed unimpressed. "You mean to say you're just a sweep-up? We don't—"

Wisp pulled the lad aside with a jerk. He was skinny as a stick bug but looked fat next to the little one. A knife appeared from nowhere and pressed against the lad's throat. The boy gulped, but he had fire in keen blue eyes. Stringy hair hung from under his cap like a mop, tempting Wisp to use it to wipe the smudges from his sallow face.

With a keen eye on the people walking by, Wisp continued. "Listen, boy. I can find you no matter where you go in this city. If you don't deliver my message, I'll hunt you down and use this blade. Clear enough?"

"We'll do it, sir."

Wisp grabbed the little one by the face and twisted him side to side. "Don't go to High Town, boy, the wind might take you away." He got a laugh from the tall one, but then they both returned to sulking. "Tell Brock Larnigin I said to give you work. You might earn enough to get shoes."

"Don't need no shoes," stick bug said.

Wisp laughed and flipped a copper coin to each of them. "I don't need to pay, and I shouldn't, but consider it a gift from a man in good spirits. And I'll offer advice—don't take too often from Farley.

He sees you steal and only allows it on occasion, probably because you two look as if you need the food. Next time he may not feel so gracious, or you may not look so starving. Either way, he'll catch you and put you to work, and you can wager that copper it will be hard work. Now be off with you and deliver my message." Wisp booted them in the backside and watched them hustle down the street, being careful not to release his laughter until they were gone from earshot.

Wisp stopped at Farley's stand, the scent of fresh fruit too much to pass up. Temptation challenged him to steal, but instead he bought a few items then made his way toward the nobles' section of town.

near High Town

'High Town' rose out of the merchant district as steep as the peak on Mount Sarro. Stone walls and iron fences guarded mansions that grew in size and grandeur as the elevation increased. Gatekeepers manned each entrance, stiff with duty and wearing faces that looked as if they'd crack at the first hint of a smile.

A uniform with a man inside it served as the sentinel to Lord Talanvar's estate. Wisp gave his best smile and a nod of his head.

"Your business?" the man demanded.

"Inform your master that a messenger has arrived with news from the fish market." The guard scowled. *It must be taught,* Wisp thought, *the art of scowling.*

"Tell me and I will deliver the message myself," the gatekeeper snapped.

Wisp remained firm in his demand. "I have orders to only pass the message on to Lord Talanvar. It is of grave importance. I wouldn't tarry if I were in his employ; news of this nature could be disastrous if withheld."

The guard ran his discerning eyes up and down Wisp's attire with a look he might give a stray dog. He must have harbored suspicions, but he also must have known that his master had many interests. And if one of them faced jeopardy, his decision would be required. "I will tell him. Wait here."

Wisp knew that particular message would bring Lord Talanvar in a hurry; the fish market was his primary means of smuggling stolen goods in and out of Sykor. A perfect arrangement as no one cared much for detailed inspections of fish.

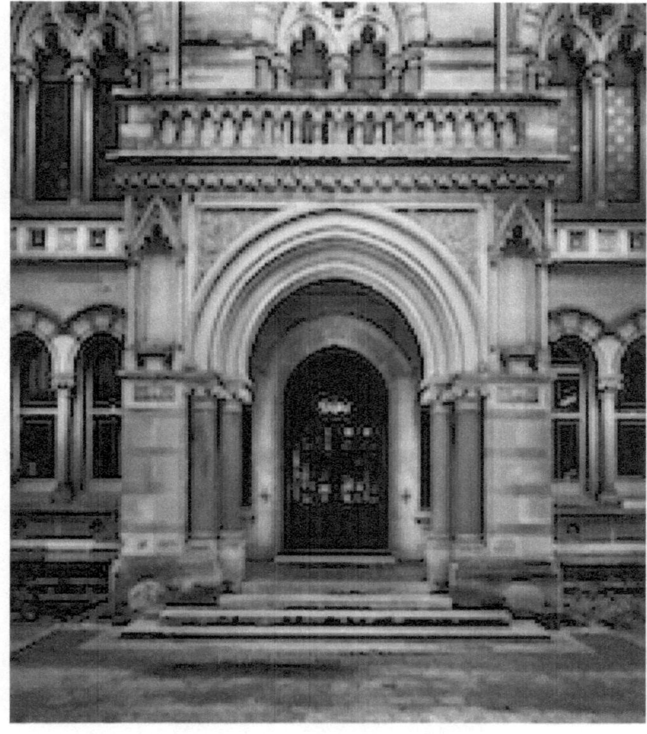

entrance to Talanvar's estate

He smiled as he scanned Talanvar's estate, an impressive home constructed of granite situated atop a hill with an elevation surpassed by only five others. Elevation was the key in Sykor, the higher the elevation the higher the status, and nobles took great pains to establish their claims. Wisp laughed as he thought of how Talanvar had embarrassed the nobles.

Lineage determined a noble's position in the city, and where they might build their home. Though not a drop of nobility ran in Talanvar's blood, he had amassed a fortune as a merchant. The king had granted him privilege to build on a site that served as the tenth highest elevation, but Talanvar had dug his foundations deep and used the excess dirt to elevate his home to the sixth highest. Other nobles objected, accusing him of ignoring the king's edict. Only Wisp knew that the reason he built his house so high was to hide the dirt he removed from the tunnels he had dug under his estate, tunnels that connected him to a vast underground network of passageways that ran throughout the city.

Appalled by Talanvar's audacity, the king was also intrigued by the man's ingenuity, so he granted a reprieve. The brazen move had won Talanvar recognition as a man to be cautious of among the nobles, but more importantly, it had earned him favor with the common man in Sykor. In one bold act, he had earned the king's respect and the support of the populace.

The footsteps on the stone walkway caught Wisp's attention. He looked up to see the gatekeeper and Talanvar. Wisp smiled. It had been a while since he had seen Carmine. There was surprise in Carmine's green eyes, though he feigned no recognition.

"You bring news of my fish market?"

"The message is lengthy and I bear orders that it is to be relayed in private."

Talanvar nodded. "Come with me. I can offer you khaffe and food while we talk."

Once situated in a room secure from eavesdroppers, Carmine's crusty voice rose. "Mother of rats! Where have you been? I thought you were dead."

"It's too long a story to tell all in one night. Suffice it to say I have friends that require the kind of help only you can offer."

"And what do your friends have that I might use?"

"Plenty of gold," Wisp replied, "but I know that wouldn't interest you. Yet they might also be able to offer favors that even you could use at some time."

"Is it your gold or theirs?"

"Gold is gold," Wisp said. "I could never distinguish between one man's and another's."

Coarse laughter filled the room. "So it is your gold. These must be good friends, so I will accept nothing for the deed. Tell me what you require then consider it done."

Wisp sat down to explain his plan. He talked through three mugs of khaffe, a plate of soft cheese, and a hearty meal before excusing himself. "You know where to locate me if necessary, Lord Talanvar." Wisp clasped his hand in farewell.

A servant escorted him to the door, and within moments he found himself strolling along a familiar street, listening to vendors hawk their goods. *It is good to be home.*

Wisp stopped at Farley's fruit stand once again. He began to reach for a coin, but something in his blood would not allow him to pay for fruit twice in one day. He stole two fresh pears then turned left and headed toward the Trader's Inn.

~

Gregor fidgeted, thumping his staff as he stood in the line to enter Sykor. He had been waiting for half the morning when his patience reached the limit. He broke rank and rounded the line, heading toward the main gate.

"You," the guard called out.

"Name's Gregor," he replied, but he never stopped walking or even slowed his pace.

"Stop! Answer in the name of the king. When did you leave?" the guard asked.

"Look at the log if you want to know, but be quick, gate–man. I have no patience for your questions."

The guard stared up at the tall frame of the bounty man holding his quarterstaff firmly. "Be on your way," he ordered. "Make certain you cause no trouble."

Gregor went straightaway to a tavern frequented by bounty-men, looking for their support. To a man, all wanted payment in gold for their efforts. Two more stops brought the same responses.

A long face accompanied him out of the last tavern. When he departed Sykor, a few moons ago, he assumed he had friends; now he was forced to acknowledge he had none—save a thief, and that rankled him more than anything.

He took his mount to the stables then headed toward home. As he walked the streets, passing dozens of people, he realized what Wisp had meant about being alone. No one greeted him, and there would be no one waiting when he arrived home. The words of the thief echoed in Gregor's head, pounding a message into his thick skull. 'They'll not support you, or anyone else, not without gold. It is how they live, Gregor. They live for gold.' *Perhaps the thief was right.*

Gregor turned down the street leading to his house, the echoes of his heels rattling in the alley like an empty drum. Dim light leaked from a few windows, casting shadows on the old brick walls. Gregor had always kept it clean when he was here, now moss grew on the weeping mortar joints, adding its musty smell to the damp air.

He stood below the window to his second floor, observing the few people who passed by. He recalled how well-liked Wisp was in Pomanda, and how Pelle and Rinck lost their lives trying to help Rahg, all because Wisp asked them to. Gregor started up the steps to his home. They seemed longer than he remembered.

The door opened with a slight creak and stiff movement. Stale air filled his lungs. Lonely air. A bare table huddled with three empty chairs, bordered by blank walls. And all clean. Stark and clean. Even the dirt sought company elsewhere. Gregor's staff tapped hollow on the hardwood floor as he made his way to the chair at the end of the table.

A smile crossed his face as he recalled his last day here, when they had interrogated the Black Rose. How happy he had been that day. So many people... in his house. Rhaven, Tobias, Rahg, Darstan, Camissa, and the laughter of the thief. It may have been the first time his walls had heard laughter, and he wondered now why they hadn't cracked.

The bounty man let his gaze sweep the room, searching... but for what he didn't know. After a few moments he pressed his staff against the floor, raised himself and departed. *There is nothing for me here.*

The staff banged in unison with the pounding of his boots on the cobblestone street, Wisp's laughter ringing in his mind. In one day, he was being forced to reconsider all that his life was built on, the very foundation of his existence. *Did thieves have honor?* Unfortunately, he knew for certain that at least one did. It was a truth he could not deny.

Gregor walked briskly, turned two corners, went up a slight hill, then entered the Trader's Inn. *Perhaps it is better to be a thief,* he thought, and made his way to a remote table away from the light. A pleasant serving girl greeted him as he seated himself at the corner table.

"Food, or ale, good sir?"

Gregor grinned. "I wish both. And plenty of each. I have an appetite tonight that I intend to satisfy."

~

*K*ender Darnell quickened his pace as he entered the Trader's Inn, slipping in among a small group of patrons from the merchant district. He wore a cap atop his head and clothes that marked him no different than any other citizen of Sykor. A vacant table near the kitchen door served his purpose; it was not as dark as a corner table, but the area bustled with activity and no one paid much attention to a man seated alone.

Smoke swirled around thick candles, hung in corners, and crept through the air, pulled by the draw of the fireplace. The counter on the bar still shone like it had just been waxed, and the big center post —though it might have gotten a new nick or two—held fresh signs of oil and loving care.

Brock is a good man.

Wisp turned when the kitchen door swung open, sweet potatoes and carrots floating on the aroma of roasted beef. He loved to hear that door swing; it meant business was good.

When the serving girl, Louise, arrived to take his order he placed a copper coin in her hand then gently closed her fist around it. "This is for you, and all you need to do is deliver a message to Brock Larnigin."

Louise's voice carried the distinct tone of suspicion. "He stands not ten paces from here. Why not deliver it yourself?"

"I once worked here," Kender said, "and I don't want to be embarrassed. If you do this quietly, I'll add an extra copper."

Louise peeled Wisp's hand away and unfolded her fingers to inspect the coin. "I still don't know why you just don't see him yourself, but I'll do it. What message shall I deliver, and tell me now what you want for a meal? It will do my aching feet no good to make two trips."

Kender cringed; Louise seemed a bit short of friendly to him. "Tell Brock that Kender Darnell wishes to see him." Louise stared at him like he had lost his senses. "He'll understand," Wisp said. "And bring me khaffe with the food. No ale."

Brock Larnigin brought the khaffe to Kender's table, looming over it like a mountain over a valley. The mug hit the table with a thud, spilling a portion in the process. "And where might you say you've been for so long, laddie? I never even known you to be gone till you wasn't here one day. You and that Camissa."

Brock's tone hinted at anger, though beneath it Wisp detected hurt. "The guards were after us, Brock. I had no time to tell you."

The burly barkeep looked about the room as if checking for guards then pulled a chair to the table seating himself next to Kender. Wisp could hear concern in his voice.

"What did you do, lad? Is it done? I'll help if I can."

Kender smiled and grabbed the barkeep's huge hand. "I need a room that is quiet and safe; the one on the second floor with the back entrance would do. And I need to know if anyone comes asking questions."

Brock nodded.

"There may be others with me. Some you may not be fond of. There will be thieves and perhaps bounty-men, but I can vouch for them all."

Brock wasted no time in agreeing, a trait Kender always admired about him.

"There's a merchant in that room tonight, Kender, but he'll not be there after this day. You have my word." Brock's eyes softened. "How's the girl?" he whispered.

"Camissa is fine. You know I'd not let anyone harm her."

Brock's smile was warm. He reached his large hand out for Wisp to grasp, shaking it vigorously when he did. "Take care of her, lad, and of yourself. May the luck of the gods be with you."

Louise brought the food after Brock had taken his leave. "There's a man across the room that wishes to speak with you," she said. "Keeps calling you a thief."

Kender stared across the common room at the slumping figure of Gregor. "I might have known," he muttered as he rose from the table, the hot food left untouched. No mask hid his anger.

When he got to the table where Gregor sat, he found the bounty man muttering nonsense and talking to anyone who would listen. "What has overcome you, bounty man?"

Gregor looked up, bleary eyes straining for recognition of the face that owned the voice. "Wis—" he started to say, but Kender covered Gregor's mouth.

"Kender Darnell, bounty man. My name is Kender Darnell, or have you forgotten so soon?" Before Gregor could respond, Kender pulled him to his feet. Gregor started to call Wisp by name; this time, Kender clubbed him over the back of the head with the butt end of a blade, then half-dragged him to the bar. "Have you any room for tonight?" he asked Brock.

"Not with all these merchants in the city, but the stable has room to sleep six."

"I only need room for two," he said. "If someone could lend a hand carrying this one, I'll pay for the quarters in the stable." Brock stepped from behind the counter and slung Gregor's limp body over his massive shoulders.

"Rest easy, lad. I'll have none of your coin, you worked hard for many a year for our landlord. Though I'll not go so far as to let you room at the inn for naught, he can well afford to let you room in the stable."

Kender smiled while reflecting on Brock's generosity. "My thanks, Brock. I shall return the favor one day. You may be certain of that."

It was about fifty paces to the stables. "Drop him anywhere, Brock."

The barkeep unloaded Gregor onto a shallow pile of straw. The bounty man's body met the ground with a resounding thud.

Morning wasn't long arriving. Gregor stirred, moaning at the first movement of his back. He pulled himself up using the gate of a stall then arched his back, the pain obvious from his twisted expressions. "Where are we, thief?"

"I'll say it only once more, Gregor. Don't call me thief. My name is

Kender Darnell while we are in Sykor and you would be wise to remember that."

"Then, where are we, Kender Darnell?"

"In the stable behind the Trader's Inn. Brock allowed us to stay here until a room comes available." Wisp reached down to offer Gregor a hand. He looked as if he'd be forced to stay there all day if he didn't get help. "Hurry, Gregor. We have men we must meet."

Wisp led them to the front door of the inn, entered, and claimed a table near the entrance. "You look as if a meal might help you. I know some khaffe would."

"Bring two mugs of khaffe for me," Gregor said, shielding his eyes from the sunshine as the door opened to let in another patron.

The inn filled up quickly; the morning fare had a reputation for being tasty. More and more came in and Gregor seemed to grow more irritated with each creaky sound of the door.

"Why did you sit here? The noise is bothersome."

Wisp laughed. "I imagine everything is bothersome this morning. But I chose for a reason." Wisp nodded his head to the right of Gregor. "Those men are thieves. They have come to assist us."

Gregor looked over at them. "You know them?"

"No. The meeting was arranged for here, and I left word that I would be seated at the first table. As each one entered they gave a signal that identified them. Five have already arrived, we wait for one more. With six more men we'll have enough to post a watch on both the north and south gates, day and night."

"How much gold will it cost? I am willing to pay for it."

Gregor had finished his first mug of khaffe, and could almost see the bottom of the second mug. The effect of the khaffe seemed to be healing him as much as any herb. "No gold. I asked a favor of a friend and in response he sent these men."

"How can we trust them?"

Wisp let out a mock laugh. "Because they don't come for gold, Gregor. That is precisely why we *can* trust them. These are not bounty-men." Wisp detected lingering doubt in the bounty man. "I don't see any of your acquaintances here."

After a long silence Gregor spoke. The hurt showed even though he tried to disguise it. "They are bounty-men. They work for gold."

A pang of pity gnawed at Wisp. "It's the same with thieves, Gregor. I taunt you a lot and like to boast about them, but most of them are selfish and can't be trusted. Some have honor, some not." He reached a hand to pat Gregor's arm. "No different than bounty-men. You, my friend, have honor, no matter what I said about you before. Some of your associates, however, do not."

Gregor nodded.

Wisp spun the handle of his mug around two times, a signal. "Come," Wisp said, "the last of our friends has arrived. It's time we set the watch." Gregor still appeared sullen. "Fret not, Gregor. You could always make a good thief."

Gregor stood, his blackthorn staff banging brusquely on the wooden floor. "Once I would have struck a man for saying such to me."

"And now?" Wisp asked.

Gregor smiled. "Let's go, Kender Darnell. As you are so fond of repeating, 'we have much to do.'"

DISCOVERY

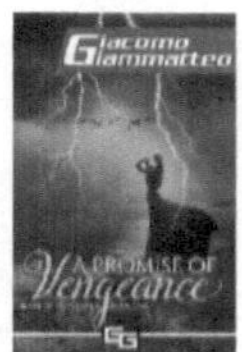

For three days Wisp's men kept watch on both entrances to Sykor, but no one saw the guards enter. "Do you think they're still coming?" one man asked.

southern gate of Sykor

"If their trail went through the swamps they're likely dead," said another.

One of the thieves was an older man, rail-thin, with a long pipe stuffed in his mouth. "It could be, my friends, they arrived before you and even now have your friend in the dungeons." He puffed on his tobacco. "I suggest you check the prison."

Wisp knew it was possible. He thought about asking Takar for help, but wouldn't announce his plan in front of the other thieves.

Tonight I'll find him.

~

Gregor scoffed at Wisp's idea. "Takar? He might take you to prison and let you look for yourself. Did you forget he told you never to come back?"

"I forget nothing. But Takar was friends with Tobias and Rhaven. He might be willing to help."

"I doubt it," Gregor said.

"We'll see. I'll send one of the lads with a message in the morning."

~

Wisp and Gregor waited for Takar. "The message instructed him to meet me at noon. Stay hidden, Gregor. If Takar decides to take me in, he may haul you along with me."

"Why would you care?"

"I see your good humor has returned, bounty man. Is it Sykor's air that provokes you or something else?" Wisp smiled, then nodded toward a square full with merchants hawking wares. "Stay out of sight until we finish talking or until Takar takes me away.

Wisp sat on one of the benches away from the crowd, his feet planted on the ground, hands braced to push himself off and get a good running start. Despite his intuitive trust of Takar, he liked to have an alternate plan. If he smelled a trap, he'd be off in a heartbeat, and as long as he got a start, the guards would never catch him. Running was like anything else—practice improved it. Whispers of a silver crown as a prize for anyone who could beat him in a race circulated throughout the poor neighborhoods, and though all of the street urchins had tried him, only one had even come close.

The aroma of mincemeat pie tugged at him, tempting as a maiden's voice on a cold night, but he maintained composure, taking in each movement in the square. A short distance from where he sat, a merchant haggled over cloth prices with a mother toting two little girls. Across from him a candlemaker displayed his goods to a short plump man with a shining bald spot.

A young lad approached, his face covered in soot. "If you're waiting to meet someone, you might do better if you wait by the king's palace. Not as many people there." He then walked away.

Wisp watched the lad leave, then searched for signs of a trap, but saw nothing. He made his way to the plaza by the king's palace and found a bench to sit on. The lad was right; it was much quieter here, with fewer people.

palace square

Before long, a few guards approached. Wisp stood, alerted to a potential trap. Three guards marched into the square behind him, and then he noticed Takar inspecting leather goods at a vendor's stand not thirty paces away. Soon the guards passed him by, exiting down a side street. Takar headed in his direction.

"I didn't expect to see you back in Sykor this soon, though I always assumed you couldn't stay away forever." Takar had a commanding voice, different from Rhaven's but it had the same effect on people.

Wisp's first glance went to Takar's face and the jagged scar that ran from chin to ear. It was a deep scar, and it was old. Wisp extended his hand in a greeting of friendship, realizing only too late what a mistake it was. Always conscious of his cherished hands, he winced and pulled back from the grip. "I prefer you stab me next time we meet, Takar."

"The next time you may be wearing shackles. Now, to the heart of it; what do you want?"

Wisp told him what happened in Genda, culminating with the capture of Darstan. "We feel certain they were from Sykor," Wisp said, "but we're only half convinced we arrived before them. We've been watching the gates, but nothing yet. If you could check the prison—"

"No need. By chance, I inspected the prison yesterday. I would have noticed Darstan."

"He might have arrived since then."

"I thought you had the gates watched?"

"I'm the only one who saw the men in Genda. Along with that, only Gregor and I have ever laid eyes on Darstan, so we have a lot of room for error. They could slip through, especially at night."

"Tomorrow, I'll search the prison. Position yourself outside the guards' barracks. If you see any of them, send for me. And be careful! This is now my life we involve."

Wisp smiled. "You have my gratitude, Sergeant. Any favor you wish, you only need ask. I have set up room at the Trader's Inn. You are familiar with it, I know."

Takar nodded. "And if you should need me, I—"

"I know where you live. I couldn't count myself a good thief if I didn't know where the most notorious guard in Sykor spent his nights." Wisp broadened his contagious smile.

Takar maintained his scowl for only a moment before his facade broke and a grin appeared. "So it is done. For a time we'll be allies." Takar's smile left him. "But remember, I make no exceptions, Kender Darnell." He extended his hand to seal the pact.

Wisp shunned Takar's offer of a clasped hand with mock exaggeration of pain. "I value the bones in my hand, Sergeant. If you accept my word in lieu of my hand, we can both be on our way."

Takar laughed. "I might learn to like you, thief, if you were not a thief."

"I make no such distinction based on a man's occupation; as proof, I have even grown to think highly of you." Wisp bowed low.

The big sergeant laughed again. "Meet here in two day's time at noon. If you have news before that, send word to my house but use a ruse. I'll do the same."

~

isp wasted no time in scouting the area around the soldiers' barracks. With the assistance of some acquaintances, he located someone willing to let him stay in their home. The sleeping area offered a perfect view of the front gate to the guards' quarters.

The Sykoran guards, if nothing else, were predictable. They organized their watches and duties with meticulous care and nothing short of a great civil disturbance, or war, disrupted their schedule. Wisp soon determined the times when patrols departed and arrived, and calculated the various units assigned to palace guard duty. Knowing the times allowed him to keep continuous vigil, by taking short periods for sleep when there was no action at the gate. He entrusted the duty of waking him to the two lads he had befriended on his return to Sykor at Farley's fruit stand. They were more than eager to earn some coin.

On the morning of the second day, Wisp recognized one of the guards. "Lad, come quick," Wisp hollered to the smallest of the two lads. "Go to the Trader's Inn and tell Gregor that I'm on the hunt. He'll know my meaning. Tell him he must go to the noon meeting. Hurry!"

The lad scurried out the door down the street. Wisp turned to the older one. "Dirk, can you lift a purse from a man without getting caught?" The youngster looked at him with a pained expression. "I have no time, Dirk."

"I can do it," he boasted. "Better'n most, I am."

Wisp leaned down to be eye to eye with the little fellow. "I want you to hit him, but let him know you did. Let him chase after you. Can you elude him long enough to lure him to the Sparrow's Inn?"

Dirk nodded.

"Don't go straight to the inn. Take several detours so I can get there before you. There's an alleyway a half street away to the south side. Lead the guard into the alley. I'll be waiting."

The little thief laughed. "It'll be easy."

~

Bartel's apparent sluggishness bode well for Dirk. The guard had served night duty and his languid stride indicated a man almost spent. Dirk approached from the rear until he came alongside him. With great care, the little thief picked the guard's purse cleanly then tapped him to ensure he was noticed, speeding off down a side street even as awareness must have struck Bartel.

The purse was heavy with coin. More than a guard should have. A quick glance to the rear found Bartel closing ground on Dirk, his face a contorted mass of fury.

"I'll break your skull, thief!" the guard yelled, his arms pumping and his long legs pushing his massive frame toward Dirk.

Dirk traversed the open-air market, crowded with vendors and merchants from Khatara, Pomanda, Genda, and numerous smaller cities. It would be a simple feat to lose the guard among the throng of people. Dirk twisted his head to be certain the guard trailed him. Despite his confidence, or perhaps because of it, Dirk stumbled and fell. Bartel came after him, a grin on his face.

The little thief cursed himself for falling. Fear seized him as the guard closed in. Many years of eluding vendors and merchants made Dirk swift as a stray cat. Instinct helped him dodge the grasp of the guard.

Bartel grabbed again with the other hand, but Dirk bent backward to avoid it. Twice more, he barely escaped the clutches of the guard and, like a roach evading a stomping foot, he seemed to move at just the last moment. Dirk saw an opening and bolted through it. A quick glance confirmed that Bartel stayed close behind him.

alleys

Dirk thought at times that he could feel Bartel's panting breaths on the back of his neck. The fear helped him to run. Through several more twisting streets, he led the guard then made his way to the arranged rendezvous. He had mapped out a longer course to allow ample time for Kender Darnell to arrive at the destination, but he opted to cut that short. *I only hope he's there.*

Worry tore at him and fear clawed his gut. A smile popped on and off his face when he saw the street to the Sparrow's Inn, and he prayed to the gods that Kender was waiting. He passed the inn as instructed, went south for half a street and saw the alleyway. Dirk had committed himself to this course when he noticed that the alley dead-ended a short way ahead. For the second time today he knew fear, but he never slowed.

～

*B*artel raced into the alleyway a step or two behind Dirk, out of breath, panting, and spent. As he neared the end of the alley, a smile appeared on the guard's face, despite his labored breathing. Bartel slowed, resting his hands on his knees as he bent, catching breath. "Was about to give it up, boy. Guess you turned down the wrong alley." His smile grew when he straightened, walking toward Dirk.

Wisp leaped out from a concealed spot midway down the dirty street, emerging just behind the guard. He plunged his knife deep into the underside of Bartel's sword-arm precisely at the joint with the shoulder. A cry of anguish echoed from wall to wall, and the guard's arm fell limp, blood shooting out. Wisp dragged him to the side of the alley, shoving him against the bricks with a resounding thud.

The wound rendered Bartel's arm useless. *Just like Rhaven said.* He placed the blade to Bartel's throat, blood brushing against the guard's collar. Bartel whimpered.

"No more noise or I'll cut."

Fear filled Bartel's eyes. He looked from Wisp to Dirk, holding the wound with his good arm.

"You all right?" Wisp asked Dirk.

He nodded, but never looked at Wisp, just stared at the blood running from Bartel's armpit.

"You can keep the purse," Bartel said, his voice in broken tones.

"I don't want your purse." Wisp tugged at the guard's good arm and directed him to a boarded-up doorway. Wisp removed a few slats of wood and ordered Bartel through the small opening. He told Dirk to bring the Takar and the bounty man.

~

Takar and Gregor arrived soon afterward. When Bartel saw Takar, he shook though he tried to feign innocence.

"Sergeant Takar, thank the gods you're here. This thief robbed me of my purse."

Wisp tossed it to Takar. "Nothing is missing. Though I suspect you'll want to question him on how a Sykoran guard comes by so much gold."

"Is he one of them?" Takar asked.

"There's no doubt."

Takar looked to Dirk, tucked into a corner, then back to Wisp. "Take him outside."

"He's in this far," Wisp said. "We can trust him."

Takar stared at Dirk. "You know who I am, boy?"

A nod confirmed it.

"No matter what happens, keep your mouth shut."

After another nod, Takar turned to Bartel. Wisp had bandaged the wound enough to stop the bleeding, but it would take a full healer to return the use of the arm.

Takar was not a man to mince words, nor one to tarry about business. "Where is Darstan?"

"Who is Darstan?"

Takar reared his arm back and smashed his huge fist into Bartel's nose. The guard's scream deafened the cracking sound of bone.

Wisp winced, recalling the sound, and the feeling, all too well from when his own nose had been broken long ago. Takar drew in closer to Bartel. Blood ran over his lips, around the corner of his mouth, and down his neck. The crookedness of his nose left no doubt as to the status of it.

"Where is he, Bartel? It will go easier if you tell me."

"Told you. I don't know."

Takar's fist slammed his jaw, jarring the guard's head into the plaster wall behind him. A muffled gasp of pain, then Bartel spat blood, using his good arm to wipe his face.

"Where, Bartel?" Takar loomed over him like a bear, a menacing sight with his scarred face and a massive bloodied fist. Bartel, however, remained arrogant.

Wisp counted to ten in the silence, then Takar threw his knee between Bartel's legs, doubling the guard over. Takar shoved his head into the wall, then pounded him again.

"All right!" Bartel held up his hand to stop the beating. Within moments, Takar got all the information Bartel had. He now knew where Darstan was being held.

Bartel tried to spit, but his lip was cracked open so much it dribbled out in little rivulets. "You don't know what trouble you bought, Takar. Ludar is the one who ordered the boy be taken. When he finds out what you've done, you and yours will be facing the same fate." Bartel spat again. More blood, and a tooth, emerged. "I'll ask him to consider your punishment lightly if you set me loose."

"You shouldn't have said that, Bartel. It's a mistake to threaten a man with something he can't escape from, leastwise, you should never do it while you are the captive. Think, Bartel. If a man can't control what will happen, he feels helpless; feeling helpless makes a man afraid. Men do not like being afraid."

Takar moved closer. "It will be quick, Bartel. None have ever accused me of being unmerciful." Before Bartel could react, Takar plunged his blade up through the ribs and into his heart. As he slumped to the floor, Takar murmured a few words. "May the gods forgive him," he said. "And may they forgive me."

"What should we do with the body?" Gregor asked.

"Leave it. The rats will find it before the guards."

"We at least know where he's being kept," Wisp said. "Though other than that, we're not much better off than before."

"Not so," Takar said. "Now, I know Ludar is involved. And I know there is no one save Vlad, my sister's son, that I can trust in the guard."

Takar appeared puzzled. "I don't know why Ludar is keeping him in the old dungeon though. It's not been used for years, and it's underground, outside the king's castle. Only a few people even know of its existence. If this is where he has Darstan, there's more to this than any of us are aware."

"If we know where he is, we can get him out," Wisp said.

Takar shook his head. "Won't be so easy. And we'll probably have to fight guards to get to him." Silence claimed the big sergeant for a moment. "Never thought I'd see the day when I fought against my own guard."

For once, Wisp didn't laugh. "I can get us in, but we'll need some of the

Lady's luck to help with the rest." Wisp grabbed hold of Dirk and tousled his brown hair. "Anyway, we need to get out of here and get a plan. Bartel will be missed soon, and we don't know what Ludar's got planned for Darstan. Let's meet at the Trader's Inn."

Takar nodded. "Meet there after supper. By dark, I want to be on our way."

THE GUARDIAN MIST

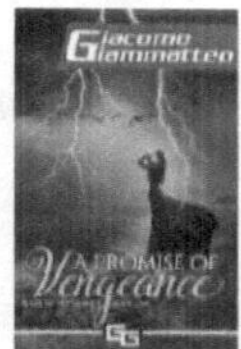

obias stared into the wall of fog, an endless gray curtain undulating in a rhythmic, hypnotic fashion. Many of the crew drifted toward the rear of the ship. Even the ship seemed to slow, as if it had a will of its own. Tobias braced himself, but the ship cut through the mist without so much as a whimper or a moan. Once again he was fog blind.

"Lower sails," Sennar shouted.

"Lower sails." The first mate echoed the command.

Reluctant deckhands responded, feeling their way around, caution accompanying every step. Sennar puffed furiously on a long-stemmed pipe, smoke rising from the bowl in billows. He nudged Tobias, a gesture to share tobacco, but Tobias refused and plucked some out of his own pouch.

"What now, Sennar?"

"Accordin' to Malakai, there'll be no wind, not while we're in this fog. Though not bein' able to see makes it dangerous enough." The old sea captain took a long draw on his pipe. "It'd be best if your men stayed below. I'll not have the time to worry over them. From Malakai's description, we'll be fortunate to even get through the storms. If the storms are really there."

"You sound as if you don't believe him."

"I don't trust any man. 'Specially when gold's involved."

Tobias scowled. "No one's made mention of gold."

A cynical chuckle escaped the old sea captain's lips. "There's real gold and there are legends of gold. Men die seekin' both."

"I've heard the tales, Sennar. All the warnings that go along with those tales too. How do you plan to deal with the winds? I know you haven't forgotten."

"The men'll be positioned. The winds won't take us by surprise like they did Malakai. Just might be enough to gain the upper hand."

Tobias grunted. "I'll keep my men below, but if you need me I'll come topside. It's not been so long that I don't know what to do." Tobias paused before leaving. "Malakai said it would be a few days to get through the fog; the men might get fearful if it takes any longer. If they do, call us."

"Malakai said a few days. I imagine it'll be so. We'll be ready though. Ready as a ship can be."

~

For two days Rahg kept below, listening to the rhythmic sound of the oars tugging at the calm sea. Anxiety about their destination smothered his appetite and churned his stomach. When he lay down to try and sleep, the nightmare came soon after his eyes closed. It started with a violent eddy, an enormous maelstrom that swept him up and swallowed him. Familiar experiences raced past him, until he found himself once again in the mysterious cavern, face to face with the gigantic beast—the one he now knew to be a dragon.

So, you have returned. The beast's bellow shook the cavern.

Rahg trembled. Despite his dread, he managed a steady voice. "So I have."

This dream was different, not obeying the same set of unusual laws. He had been to the cave before. Faced the dragon before, and been past the beast. He should not have lingered at this spot; instead, he should have been whisked past the dragon to the entrance to the four tunnels. This awareness encouraged him to be brave. "Move aside, beast. I wish to pass." It felt good to have spoken his mind.

Plated scales turned into a menacing snarl, teeth bared, and fire danced in its red eyes. Rahg shook as he reached to draw his sword, but instinct made him leap to the side.

The column of fire shot past him, catching his left leg and burning it. "Gods blood!" He rolled, sprung to his feet and attacked, brandishing the sword in his right hand. He swung again, bringing the blade crashing into the beast's leg. It met the scales with a heavy thud, stopping so abruptly it jarred the blade loose.

Rahg stared at the spot where his sword struck. Nothing. Not even a nick in the scales of the beast. Grabbing the sword, he prepared to strike again.

Will you turn back now?

A faint glimmer of hope rode on the dragon's words. Even the suggestion of egress lifted his spirits. "What choice do I have?" He waited. The silence bothered him even more than the dragon's taunting laugh.

Abandon your friends and return safely or proceed on your current path and face my wrath.

Rahg's glimmer of hope vanished with the dragon's ultimatum. The pain in his leg shouted a warning against proceeding, but his mind lay wracked in confusion. The daunting task of escaping loomed as the impossible quest of a legend, yet he could not convince himself to betray his friends. Not Darstan, who had pulled him from an icy river when they were lads of ten and twelve; not Tobias, who had braved the dread of the Victas at Twin Forks. How could he suspect Rhaven, who had slain the gods only knew how many men in Rahg's defense already. And most of all not Camissa.

Rahg's hand tightened around the hilt of the sword. The muscles in his arm tensed and his body shook. The anger that had built inside him uncoiled in a rage, vaulting him forward. Rahg struck twice, a chop and a thrust, but when he registered no damage he retreated. "I'll not abandon my friends," he swore with a vengeance. He raised the blade, rushing to meet the impenetrable scales, but at the moment the steel should have made impact, the dragon vanished.

The momentum from the swing caused Rahg to lose his balance. He stumbled and fell, dumbfounded by the strange outcome of his conflict. Rahg cast a wary glance in all directions as he struggled to his feet. The walls of the cavern still held an eerie glow, but the dragon was gone. Relief settled on him like a heady wine and he laughed. When he looked again, the tunnels awaited.

Rahg stared blindly down the dark corridors, each one identical. "One's as good as the other," he said, and began down the first one, slowly feeling his way using his sword as a guide, like a blind man uses a walking stick.

~

"Storm sails!" Sennar bellowed. He'd tasted the first hint of a salty wind and had no plans to be caught unaware. "Get out that storm gear and lash everything that doesn't move to the deck."

waves

Men scurried about, donning jackets that came down to their knees, covering oilskin pants and boots tarred to keep them dry. Large floppy hats sat on each man's head, pulled snug.

A black cloud rose from the southern sea like a mountain, growing until it covered the sun, nudging its way to set in the west. Sennar could feel the change, as if the air grew heavier. He'd ridden out storms before, climbed aboard them and broken their backs, but this sea had an ominous feel about it. He thought he heard the swells whispering to each other—low moaning sounds. Soon they slapped impatiently against the hull. "Furl those rags on the foremast, men. Top sails, too. Storm rigging on the mizzen. I'll not be caught in this blow with full sails."

"We could outrun this, Captain. Let me give her full sails," the first mate said.

"Sennar sniffed the air, nose quavering and hands gripping the rail at midship. "I've raced a storm or two, lad, but this smells like a demon wind. It's out to sink us. Take our ship and tear it apart peg by peg."

"Captain–"

"Look at it, lad! See how it comes for us, as if we were rocks sittin' still in the water."

Fine salty mist swept across the ship from port side, pelting Sennar's face and clinging to his hair. The storm fed the swells, growing them bigger by the moment. All the while the Sea Skate thundered ahead, dipping high and low, as if it were a wild horse bucking its rider. At times the rest of the sea disappeared as the bow dived into the breach between roaring waves, foam riding their crests like snow-capped peaks.

Cries from the manger echoed throughout the ship: the plaintive bleating of sheep, the piercing shriek of the pigs, and fear in the lowing of the cows. "Do ya hear that, men?" Sennar yelled. "That's no wolf they're cryin' over. It's the storm. Get ready to ride it out. Jacopo Sennaro still has a trick or two up his sleeve."

waves with faces

A wave crashed over the bow, spraying the deckhands and sweeping the first mate off his feet. Sennar limped toward him and fell. His head cracked against the bilge pump, blood gushing out from under his hat. As two deckhands helped him to his feet, Sennar bellowed. "All hands topside!" The orders carried from man to man, down into the crew quarters, even as far as the hold.

"Black wave rollin' in, Captain! And it looks as if it's carrying somethin' with it."

Sennar gripped one of the rat lines with both hands. He turned his head to see a wave half as high as the fore mast looming just off port side.

~

"Wake up, Rahg. Wake up!"

At first Rahg thought the voice was part of his dream, but he opened his eyes to see Camissa standing over him, unsteady, swaying to and fro. "What's wrong, Camissa?"

"The storm!" she said.

The remnants of his dream vanished at the new threat. Camissa fell against the wall. Rahg rolled out of bed and across the cabin floor. After two failed attempts, he scrambled to his feet and made his way to the doorway where Camissa clung to a rail fastened to the wall.

"I thought I'd come and sit out the storm with you. Storms frighten me. At sea they seem so much worse." She shivered.

Rahg jumped when she leaned against his leg. "Ow!" He looked down to see scorched pants and a burn underneath.

"What's wrong?"

"My leg... It's burnt! Gods blood, it was real!"

"Rahg, what are you talking about? How did you burn it?"

The boat rocked but Rahg shook from a different fear. "The dream! It's real... I got burnt in a dream right where this is."

Camissa stooped to examine the wound. "It can't be real. Dreams aren't real."

"Then how did this happen? You tell–" Rahg fell forward with a jolt, grabbing hold of the bedpost to maintain balance. "We'll talk later," he said.

He stumbled across the room to Camissa, wrapping his arms around her. "Sennar will get us through this." He could feel her trembling, and as he listened to the wind howl and felt the raging sea smash against the hull of the ship, he too, trembled. "Sennar will get us through," he whispered.

~

*A*entarra tarried about the Great Library longer than she had wished, but many secrets remained hidden, secrets she yearned to discover. Tired eyes suggested she leave and succumb to a much needed rest, but three old tomes spread among a series of charred scrolls held her captive with promises her curiosity could not refuse. It proved to be a lengthy process. She first had to weave a shield around each tattered page, then turn it gently so as not to destroy the ancient text.

Aentarra learned to be meticulous regarding these old volumes. When she first encountered them her enthusiasm and carelessness caused her to lose several precious pages, a mistake she dare not risk again.

She rubbed her eyes as the morning sun showered its rays through the stained-glass windows. *It will be another perfect day in Vallah,* she thought, then remembered the Sea Skate. *They should be nearing the Isles. I had better go.*

She closed her eyes, concentrating on the spot below deck. In an instant, Aentarra appeared in the hold, materializing in a corner behind barrels of ale.

Immediately she sensed danger. The ship rolled to the side, wood groaning as if it were about to be ripped apart. Aentarra rushed topside and hurried toward the main mast, where howling winds promised to crush the ship beneath huge waves. She doubted the ship would last until dawn.

Row upon row of towering black waves came at them in endless succession. One gigantic wave, double the size of the others, crashed against them, sending the Sea Skate reeling. The ship rolled to the starboard side, dipping into the sea at the other end before uprighting itself. Aentarra held firmly to the mast and uttered a calming mantra. There were times when she needed to remind herself that she was not truly immortal.

Sennar stared at Aentarra then fought his way to where she stood. "Lass, who are ya and what are ya doin' topside?" Anger mixed with his words. "Get below, lass. Get below now, or I'll take a switch to your backside like ya was some ugly cur." The fierce wind howled and the rain pelted them, each drop a stone.

Sennar's jaw dropped open when she glowed.

Aentarra wove a shield around him and squeezed, forcing his breath to come in small measures. "Be thankful I know you to be the captain, insolent mortal; otherwise, those short breaths would be your final ones."

Once she released the shield, Sennar gasped for air, bringing part of the sea in with it. He coughed. "I didn't know—"

"Quiet, old fool, before this wreck of a ship becomes undone."

Sennar bowed.

"What are the priorities, Captain?"

Sennar stared. Amidst the fury of the storm, Aentarra remained undisturbed, her silky hair blowing with the wind like a banner in a gale. "The hull, My Lady. I fear the hull will crack. If it does, we're done for. She can't take much more of this."

Aentarra looked about, then closed her eyes. Like a master metal-smith, she wove a fine layer of shield then fitted it to the ship's hull as if she were a seamstress. The entire process only took moments. Once she completed the task, Aentarra opened her eyes to stare at the captain. "The hull is protected."

Even as she spoke, however, ferocious winds whipped up moun-tainous waves, flinging the Sea Skate sideways toward the rocky isle. The ship bowed so low to starboard the yardarms looked as if they brushed the sea caps. Masts bent like willows and the storm sails trembled. Aentarra fell, sliding toward the edge of the ship. Sennar grabbed hold of a rope and, seizing her arm, pulled her to her feet.

"Never touch me again, mortal."

Sennar curled up like a dog waiting to be beaten. "Was only tryin' to help, My Lady."

"We must stop these winds," she said, and made her way to stand by the mast.

"Anything I can do?"

Aentarra focused her attention on the old captain. "What lies ahead?"

"There are cliffs ahead. And a strait that looks too narrow for my liking, but we've got no choice." He raised a hand to protect his face from the thrashing of the sea. "Not enough room to tack in there. And..."

"What else, Captain?" Aentarra didn't shout, yet her voice carried through the deafening noise.

Sennar hollered, but the wind stole his words and whisked them away. He cupped his hands around his mouth and leaned closer to Aentarra, though he shied from any contact. "If my guess is good, we'll be racing through there like a barrel rollin' down a hill."

A wave broke on the deck near the bow, then another near midship, the spray carrying across to the starboard side. "Another thing, My

Lady. Legends say there are rocks that move in these straits. If we hit a big one, it'll crush our hull like a pig crunching acorns."

"You get us into the straits, Captain. Let me worry about the rocks."

~

They entered the Swan's Neck, as legends claimed the name, with the wind threatening to smash them against the cliffs. Aentarra maintained the shield about the hull, but the effort was draining her. Something was wrong about this. She should not be tiring so soon. "Keep this ship in the center, Captain."

Once they got farther into the straits, the cliffs protected them from the side, but the winds now chased them from the rear, pushing a raging sea into the channel. "I'll do it, My Lady. I'll give ya the center of that channel if I have to get in and guide this ship myself."

A crewman hollered from the bow. "We're losin' it, Captain!"

Sennar turned away, screaming orders. At least they could hear each other now. "Toss that sea anchor astern, men. Get some arms round it and get her over."

"Your men seem reluctant, Captain."

"My Lady, every seaman wonders if his captain is giving the right orders, especially in a storm, but they'll do what they're told. Besides, we need drag to keep us straight. Got no room in here."

Men scrambled to follow orders, stumbling across the swaying deck, and holding onto lines for support and safety. Once they got the anchor over, it helped to stabilize the ship.

Sennar kept a keen watch on the rock walls. "It's not enough, My Lady," he said. "Current's still too strong."

Aentarra struggled to control the winds then decided to fight a different battle. She erected a shield bridging the span between the cliffs that guarded the entrance to the Swan's Neck, fighting until the shield settled in place. The wind beat at it, buckling the center until Aentarra felt it would break. To strengthen the barrier she removed the protective covering from the hull, leaving the ship vulnerable. The force of the wind beat mercilessly against the shield, and even with the additional strength she garnered from removing the covering on the hull, Aentarra found it increasingly difficult to maintain the barrier. "Captain, I require several of your men."

Sennar ordered four of his deckhands to go to her side. Once in place, Aentarra instructed each of them to take hold of her arm.

A glow lit Aentarra's body, faint at first, then brighter. The deckhands slumped as if exhausted, and at the pinnacle of illumination they collapsed while Aentarra grew brighter still. Coinciding with this event the winds slowed, then stopped.

~

*T*obias, Rahg, and Camissa came topside. Camissa stopped cold at the sight of Aentarra.

Rahg hollered over the roar of the wind. "Come on, Camissa."

She followed, but kept her gaze on Aentarra. "Rahg, she's an immortal. I can tell."

"What?"

"Just go, Rahg. Hurry!"

Camissa stood with a curious look on her face. "I'm going to try to sense her feelings."

Aentarra felt the pin-prick and spun about, letting her eyes glow with the fury that burned inside her. *How dare that little bitch!* She focused on Camissa, hurtling her across the deck and smashing her against the cabin door. A loud thud sounded, then she fell to the floor in a crumpled heap.

Rahg raced to her side. "Camissa, are you all right? What happened?"

"She'll be fine," Aentarra said. "Just a lesson learned." As she spoke, Camissa opened her eyes and looked up, awe showing on her face. Aentarra gazed into her eyes, probing her mind. "Careful, little girl, of where you play. The mind is not a plane to play on. Not for you. It is the most dangerous of all."

Rahg glared at Aentarra. "What have you done to her?" He started to rise but Camissa seized his shirt sleeve and pulled him back.

Aentarra's smile was as thin as her lips. "Be warned, lad. I will not be so gentle with your insolence. I advise you to heed your friend's advice." Aentarra returned to her position at the main mast. There was much work yet to be done if they hoped to survive.

Sennar knelt over the men he had sent to assist Aentarra. All of them lay dead on the deck. When she arrived, Sennar shot a fiery glance at the immortal. "You never said you'd be killin' my men."

"They weren't supposed to die. But would it have made a difference? Would you have selected different ones if I had mentioned their fate beforehand?" Her sardonic smile meant to irritate. "Worry not, I won't be needing any more of them unless something unforeseen arises." Aentarra stared at Sennar. "It was no more than a battlefield decision, Captain, one that you might make at any time. Sacrifice the four or lose the entire crew. So you see, there really was no decision."

The captain nodded. "We're nearly through the Swan's Neck, but the rocks await us, and there's no possible way to navigate through them —not from what the legends say. The strait is too narrow, and rocks appear everywhere."

"But the legends didn't count on me."

rocks in strait

Sennar nodded. "No, My Lady, they'd not have counted on that." The old man's voice shook more than it should have, but Aentarra knew she frightened him almost as much as the storm.

"Place men as spotters at the fore of the ship. Once we navigate the remainder of these narrows, I will need them to point out the dangers." Sennar looked at her as if questions went unanswered, but Aentarra saw through his worries. "Fear not, Captain, these men will come to no harm through me." Sennar limped away.

Aentarra made her way to the forward position of the ship, preparing for the task to come. She appeared confident in all her movements, poised, yet beneath the surface lay doubt and worry. The winds at the rear relentlessly pursued a breach in the shield she constructed, and the battering had drained her powers faster than she thought it should have; that, in itself, was cause enough for concern. She struggled to hold the winds at bay, so how could she muster enough energy to get through the rocks. Unless I use more men. But even that, she knew, was not an inexhaustible supply.

The wild currents carried the Sea Skate through the Swan's Neck at a dangerous pace. Aentarra peered into the roiling sea scanning for dangers before they sprung up. Legends told tales that the rocks actually moved. Aentarra did not believe that, but the way that the sea funneled into the narrow opening, it produced a tidal effect that raised and lowered the depths significantly with each ebb and flow, giving the appearance that the rocks moved. With each surge, rocks that had loomed as giant obstacles disappeared under the rising tide then, when the tide receded, the rocks were waiting like immense spears ready to pierce the ship's hull.

Aentarra studied the straits and made her decision, opting for a strategy that relied on the most delicate timing, and all of her strength. "I will need all available hands to post watch," Aentarra told Sennar. "If we miss once, make one error, then all is lost."

"I've got the best, My Lady. These are the men who spot for the whales. Their eyes can spy the wiggle of a fish's tail half a league away. They'll see the rocks while they're still submerged."

"They will need to, Captain. I need to remove the shield behind us, and when I do the currents will swamp us again."

The first boulder came into sight, a large, rounded one that protruded a half-span out of the water. Aentarra focused her energy, releasing the shield to their rear. The winds rushed forward, all the fury of a raging storm at the forefront. She placed a massive ball of light ahead of the ship, hovering over the water, then she reached skyward with her hands, thrusting them into the night. The powers reached upward and sought lightning from the heart of the storm, then it channeled the destructive force through the night into her hands and from there to the rock that blocked the ship's path. With a thunderous crack, it split like a log on a woodcutter's anvil, allowing safe passage for the Sea Skate.

Onward they went, the storm racing to catch them. The ship's front reared up and threatened to crash upon a spear-like boulder just beneath the water's surface. Again, Aentarra raised her hands. The lightning came, splintering the rock into a thousand shards of stone. More danger loomed ahead, but each time it appeared as if they faced certain doom, a blast from Aentarra splintered the rocks.

Sennar gaped at Aentarra. "To port!" he screamed.

"Off the starboard bow!" another shouted.

Two large rocks lay just below the water, and too close together to allow the Sea Skate to slip through. A flash in the darkness revealed another shaft of lightning, and as it funneled through the chasm, it split into two bolts, blasting each target out of the water. Sennar's smile vanished when Aentarra called for more seamen. In a faltering voice, he issued the orders.

The sea boiled in places, steam rising as if it were a giant cookpot. Throughout the night Aentarra continued her mastery over the pitfalls they encountered. Twice she had been forced to replenish her energy, though none of the seamen died. And with the sunrise came the realization they survived; the last of the rocks eliminated.

Sennar lowered his long glass, shaking his head. "My Lady, there's a sheer wall of rock ahead, with only one way out of here. We need to turn hard to port, but these currents are too strong. They'll push us past and into that cliff."

"What can be done?" she asked.

"I think I can cut the anchor and use the currents to steer us into that alley, but the problem is we might take a bump or two..." Sennar stumbled before taking a firmer grip on the rail at midship. "Is there any way you can use that magic to protect us while we get straightened out? Might also need some help guiding us into that alley."

The wind and spray seemed not to bother Aentarra. She stood as still as if it were a soft spring day. "It will have to be quick, Captain. My powers are not without end."

"I understand, My Lady. How much time will you need?"

"A moment. No more."

"I'll signal when I need you." Sennar smiled for the first time since the storm began. "Here's to the sea then, My Lady. That she don't swallow us up today."

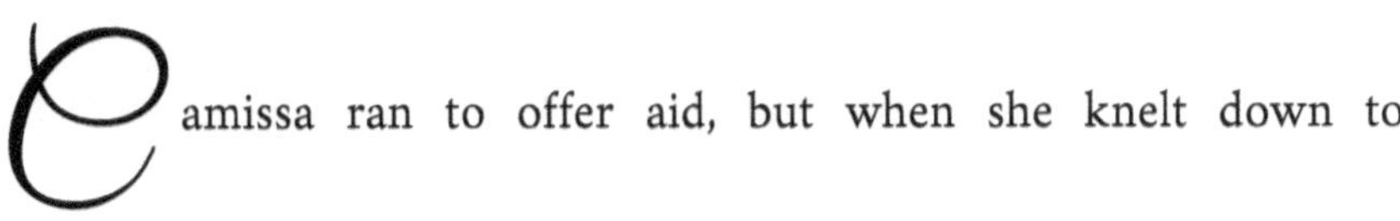

*S*ennar stared ahead at the wall of rock, while keeping a close eye on the channel to port. Timing was crucial. He waited, then waited some more. Currents carried the Sea Skate forward at breakneck speed. It was just about right. "Ready, men. We'll need to come hard to port. Bring her round, man!" he hollered to the steersman.

The Sea Skate nudged toward port side, but the currents pushed them forward faster. Too fast. "Not enough! Chop off that sea anchor! Let the sea run us there."

"But, Captain—"

"Do it now! mate, or I'll toss ya into the sea and use ya for a rudder."

When they severed the sea anchor, the currents pushed the stern hard to starboard, bringing the bow in line with the narrow alley they needed to sail through.

The Sea Skate scudded into the channel, protected on both sides by Aentarra's shields. Their pace slowed as the storm waters subsided. Soon, they sailed into a cove, calm and serene. Aentarra released the shields, then collapsed.

*C*amissa ran to offer aid, but when she knelt down to

administer healing, she discovered a shield surrounded the immortal. Even in her subconscious, she had prepared for danger.

"It would seem she leaves nothing to chance," Rhaven said.

Rahg stood above the body of Aentarra, curiosity rippling through his mind. "At least we're safe."

"Don't celebrate yet, lad. Unless I'm mistaken, this is the Cove of Captivity, and the legends say there's no way out."

DUNGEONS

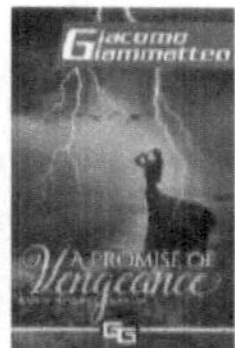

akar eased through the door of the Trader's Inn. The sweet aroma of braised rabbit mingled with onions and carrots as it worked its way through the bustling crowd of patrons. His nephew, Vlad, trailed one step behind him, blue eyes alert for trouble. He wore the dull gray uniform of the Sykoran Guard with the leather-wrapped hilt of a sword peeking over his shoulder. When they reached the bar, Vlad planted his back against the big center column then scanned the room again, hand poised to draw steel at the hint of provocation.

Takar slapped his big hand on the bar, a thick slice of hickory that once had been a giant in the forests of Kamnor. "Here to see Kender Darnell."

Brock nodded, then led them to a secluded room on the second floor. Wisp and Gregor stood to greet the sergeant. Two other men remained seated at the table, eyeing Takar and Vlad apprehensively, guilt etched on gaunt faces.

"I agreed to work with a bounty man, Kender, but not with no guards." Perl and his accomplice both got up from their chairs, ready to depart.

"Sit," Kender ordered. "This is Takar and Vlad, though I'm certain you already knew. Have no fears, Takar knows who you are. He probably knew you'd be a thief before you knew yourself." Neither man moved toward a chair.

"Sit!" Takar said. "For the first time since I took oath I conspire against the crown. It doesn't rest well in my stomach, and I lose patience with the likes of you."

Perl's blue eyes narrowed. "Now you know our faces."

Takar sat. He motioned for Vlad to do the same. "When we go, only Kender and the bounty man go with me. I can't be seen with thieves. Be bad enough if I'm caught where I shouldn't be with a bounty man."

"There's plenty they can do, Sergeant. Perl and Nat can arrange for a commotion to distract the guards. As for me, I'd rather we travel in a small group so we don't attract attention. "

Takar nodded. "Vlad and I won't be questioned, and with a minor disturbance you and Gregor can get in. You're sure you know where to meet? There won't be other opportunities."

"I've been in the castle before."

"Then it's set. Once the second watch is out of earshot, Perl begins his part."

"Done," Perl said.

"Done," they all agreed.

~

*P*erl waited until the watch reached the southern end of the merchant district. Another thief was stationed in a stable close to the main gate of the palace, where visiting merchants kept their horses. When it was time, Perl set the fire. The hay caught ablaze and the flames soon roared, climbing the walls and darting out of windows.

"Fire!" Perl screamed, his voice rife with desperation. "Fire in the stable!"

The other thief ran to the palace gate. "Guard! Fire at the stable. Help!"

The guard looked at his companions, then down to the fire. "Can't leave."

"You must help! I'll lose everything. Please?"

Fire already lit the night sky. The guard looked about as if he hoped to see some other means to aid the man. Finally he ceded. "I'll send two men."

~

Takar and Vlad approached the gate at a run. "Patrol Leader! Report."

"The merchant's stable is afire, Sergeant. I sent two men to assist."

Takar noticed the man's nervousness. "Open the gate. I'll inform the king's guard. Maintain the watch."

Vlad looked back over his shoulder as they made their way into the palace.

Takar slapped him on the back. "Don't worry, they won't follow. Now all we have to do is tell the king's guard so that it will draw them to the front as well. The more confusion we can arouse, the better it will be." Takar stared at Vlad as they walked into the palace. His young face showed nothing but his rapid breathing and short breaths indicated the intensity of his anxiety. "Have no fear, Vlad. Should anything go wrong I'll swear you followed my orders."

"I answer for my own misdeeds, Sergeant. You never thought to treat me as your sister's son in the past. Don't do it now."

Takar almost smiled, only the urgency of their mission kept it from his face. "I'll not mention it again." His pace increased to a running gait, the leather boots slamming on the palace floor and alerting everyone that something was amiss. "King's guard!" he called. "Fire in the merchant's stable!" A bustle of activity filled the inside of the palace; guards and servants ran along the corridors and no one paid heed to the comings or goings of anyone. Amidst all the confusion, Wisp and Gregor made their way to the meeting place.

~

Two flights of stairs led down to a small room with a single wooden door. "The dungeons await through that door," Takar said. "Once we enter we can no longer explain our presence here."

Wisp didn't take long to think. "We get him out tonight," he said. There was iron in his voice.

Gregor nodded approval, as did Vlad.

"So be it," Takar said. "From here on, no torches. And if we see any torches it means there are probably guards, so be careful."

Takar opened the door and they entered into the dark.

"The steps are steep," Gregor whispered.

Wisp shivered from the damp air. He pulled his cloak about him. They moved slowly, very slowly. "At this pace it will take us past dawn to even find Darstan."

"I can't see," Takar said. "We may need to light a torch despite the risks."

"No!" Wisp snapped. "Give me the lead. I'll strike the course. You assume the rear position in case of guards." Wisp moved to the front of the group, squeezing past Gregor, Vlad, and Takar.

"How can you see if I can't?"

"My occupation has provided me with much practice, Sergeant.

Scaling walls at night and sneaking through tunnels in the dark have allowed my eyes to adapt. I'm now like the owl and the rat." Wisp laughed to himself and walked ahead. *Let them wonder about that,* he thought, as he disappeared into the shadows.

Wisp saw everything now: the path ahead glowed as if it were day and the darkness hid nothing. Takar and Gregor both knew he was Wisp, and Vlad knew he was a thief, but none of them knew the rest.

The dampness increased as they progressed into the dungeon. Several times Wisp's hand brushed against the wall, filled with slime and layers of moss. The sound of tiny feet on wet ground echoed in the darkness as something scurried by.

"What was that?" Vlad asked.

"A rat. And if that's all we meet, consider us fortunate."

Vlad winced, and tiptoed for a while. "I hate rats."

"Takar, there are corridors ahead that lead to both sides, and this path continues. Which way?"

"You be the judge."

"Fair enough," Wisp said, and led them straight ahead. "The floor slopes, Takar, and there's water. Be warned, there may be rats that are hungry. If they're desperate enough they might chance a nibble or two of flesh."

A gasp escaped Vlad's lips. "I'd rather face a patrol of guards."

Wisp led them through the tunnel until the water approached ankle depth. When they arrived at an apparent dead end he steered them to the left. The dampness and the water made it seem colder than it was. As he navigated another turn, the slope of the floor rose again and the tunnel narrowed. *Darstan better appreciate this.* "The way leads left."

He cursed the darkness, and the dampness. Only the noise of rats scurrying across the stone gave him comfort. The steady dripping of water sounded throughout the tunnels, offering no promise of relief.

Gregor grunted. "Why I've chosen now to engage in such foolishness is beyond me. Risking my life for someone I didn't know a few moons ago."

"You're doing it because it's the right thing to do, bounty man."

"If we get caught, I'll never forgive any of you."

Wisp smiled. The bounty man was coming around. "You all right, Vlad?"

"Just thinking about Lynna, my girlfriend. I didn't get to tell her anything."

"She'll wait for you. Don't worry."

The pitter-patter of a rat brought Vlad's head around, his hand racing to the hilt of his sword. "I hate rats."

"Anything behind us, Sergeant?" Wisp asked.

"I didn't join the guard yesterday, thief."

Wisp kept a keen eye on everything, but his focus remained on Ludar: *why would the force commander worry so much about Darstan? Why would he send guards all the way to Genda to capture him? And why would he put him in the old dungeons instead of the regular prison? None of it made sense. Perhaps Darstan will have answers.*

The tunnel narrowed with the turn and the headroom grew smaller as well. "I see light ahead. Tread softly." As they turned the next bend, the sound of voices could be heard ahead. Two knives fitted the palms of his hands as he planned the confrontation.

Takar came forward from his position in the rear. "Let Vlad and I to go first, Kender. They won't question me."

"Lead the way, good sergeant."

"Hold," called a voice from ahead. "Who advances?"

"Sergeant Takar. Come to see the prisoner."

Takar and Vlad entered the lighted area of the tunnel. As well as being bright, it also opened to full height allowing Takar to stand erect without stooping.

"Forgive my asking," the sentry said, "but whose orders do you bear, Sergeant?"

"The force commander issued my orders," Takar said. "I have them here." He reached into his shirt and withdrew a rolled-up piece of parchment, handing it to the guard nearest him. Vlad slipped in next to the other guard then he and Takar drew knives and dispatched the guards. They barely had time to gasp.

Takar bent down, wiping the blade off on the dead man's uniform. "I know you probably feel bad, Vlad, and my telling you different won't help but if we left them alive Ludar would kill us." Takar stood and looked through the small, barred opening in the cell. "Darstan, are you okay?"

"I am, Takar, and never so glad to hear a familiar voice. But I'm chained, and a guard named Wehr holds the key."

"You worry over chains and locks? It was a thief that invented locks so merchants would feel safe and leave their goods unprotected."

"Kender Darnell, is that you?"

Wisp laughed as he extracted a thin piece of wire from the inside lining of his cloak. Long ago he had secured the services of an expert seamstress to alter his clothing so that he might secrete the special tools he required for his trade. "It is none other" Wisp said as he worked the lock on the cell door. "I'll have you free soon, Darstan. Fear not."

"How did you find me? Where's Rahg? Is Rhaven with you?"

"Only the bounty man," Wisp said, "and Sergeant Takar, along with his brave nephew, Vlad." The lock clicked open and the cell door swung ajar, its rusty hinges creaking with each jerky movement. Holding a torch, Vlad led them into the dungeon chamber. Darstan lay upon the cold stone floor, both feet shackled to an iron ring set in the foundation of the stones.

"Thank the gods, you're here," Darstan said, "but where's Rahg?"

Wisp went to work on the shackles, inserting the slender strand of wire into the mechanism that bound his friend.

Gregor grasped Darstan by the shoulders as if to examine him. "Have they hurt you, lad? We all worried."

"I'm fine. But where's Rahg? Why didn't he come? Is he hurt?"

"He set sail for Entiria," Gregor said.

"Without me? He went without waiting for me? Without even waiting to see if I lived?"

Takar grabbed hold of Gregor's shoulder. "Entiria! Who's going to Entiria? Does Rhaven have anything to do with this?"

Vlad held the torch, dumbfounded.

"Place no blame on your brother, Darstan. He stayed the night searching for you and refused to quit even when Rhaven issued the command. You know the importance of him reaching Entiria. Rhaven forced him to go, and Tobias and Camissa went with him. Kender and I came to find you."

Darstan nodded, though his face showed disappointment. "What about Kella?"

"She came with us, though as usual, abandoned the cause once we reached Sykor."

The first of the shackles popped open, allowing Darstan's leg to wriggle free. He stood, stretching it while lifting it in the air. "God, that feels good." He walked about the cell stiffly on one leg. "I can't wait to get the ones who did this to me."

Wisp worked feverishly on the other leg iron. "Takar killed Bartel. That's how we found you."

Takar pressed his question again. "What of Entiria?"

Wisp turned to the sergeant. "Takar, we'll explain what we can once we find safety. For now, let's concentrate on getting out of here. I grow nervous inside a prison."

Gregor laughed. "It's where you belong, thief."

Takar sighed. "The dungeon will be home to all of us if we don't get out of here soon."

"We have to escape," Darstan said. "I must have my vengeance. Not just for me, but for a girl also."

"If you mean Nirida," Gregor said, "she's fine. She suffered no physical harm, though some say what she did suffer is worse."

Darstan's eyebrows rose, and his eyes opened wide. "You saw her?"

"We saw her. And Rhaven gave her enough gold to keep even a woman content for many a day." Gregor sighed. "She worried for you," he said with a softer tone. "It seemed that she cared for you."

Darstan's mouth twisted down and the skin bunched under his eyes. "I'll kill them," he swore. "I'll kill them all before I leave the city. I swear."

Wisp soon sprung the catch on the other ankle chain. "Let's go," he said. "I'll lead the way. Darstan, get a sword from one of the dead guards. Vlad, give me the torch. There's no reason not to use it now."

Darstan stooped to recover the sword. "He'll have no need of these either," Darstan said, and took their knives. "I want the others myself," he said. "No one kill them but me. And besides, Caen has my sword."

~

*S*trike Leader Wehr waited his turn before entering the room where Ludar waited. Wehr glanced at the force commander, his large frame crowding the throne-like chair. Ludar had commissioned a craftsman to construct the chair in the likeness of the king's own throne, a mocking gesture to the ineffective leadership provided by Favian.

Wehr struck his chest with his right hand three times in succession, the traditional Sykoran salute to a superior. He did not stare, not wishing to risk offending the force commander by any action, or inaction. The strike leader looked tired; he had only slept once in the past three days, but Ludar's impatience, and his reputation for punishment, kept Wehr alert. The strike leader delivered his report with precision, articulating every word and making certain to account for all time during the day.

"What else, Strike Leader? Now that I know who killed two of my men, what report on the others?"

Wehr quivered. The force commander had an obsession for accurate reporting; Wehr dare not be found in error. Ludar knew every man in his command, so there was no need for monotonous explanations involving titles. The strike leader composed himself before speaking.

"Evin performed well. No mistakes. Recommendation is for promotion, even considering the brief time served." Wehr paused, but only momentarily. "Bartel—satisfactory. Caen..." The strike leader paused again. He considered telling all then thought better. "I would ask only to be relieved of ever having Caen in my command."

Wehr never smiled throughout the report. It would have been dangerous to smile, but the glint in his eyes must have betrayed him.

"That request leaves much unsaid, Strike Leader. Is there more I should know? Need I remind you of my penchant for details—full details."

Wehr need not hide the smile this time, there was none to disguise. "He raped a girl, and on several occasions I was forced to caution restraint on the prisoner."

Ludar's expression never altered. "The incident with the girl, it took place prior to the capture of the boy or after?"

Wehr knew without saying there was no concern for the girl, only the assignment. "She was with the lad, Force Commander. It happened after we subdued him." Wehr lowered his head. He had no desire to stare into Ludar's eyes, not now. They would be aglow with the fires of anger. And when Ludar's eyes glowed, it was a harbinger of death.

"Where is Caen now, Strike Leader?"

"He was assigned to guard the prisoner tonight, Force Commander. He and one other. They should be reporting to the palace guard soon."

"Order his relief, Strike Leader. Have him report to me, instead."

"Yes, Force Commander." Wehr's rigid stance remained as he spun on his heels and prepared to depart.

"Strike Leader Wehr."

Wehr spun, once again facing Ludar.

"You will need to reschedule the watch. Caen will no longer be with us."

Fear formed a frown on the strike leader's face. "Yes, Force Commander." Wehr whirled about, marching toward the exit for what he hoped was the final departure. Too much time in the presence of Ludar grated on his nerves. Even now, he shook, grinding his teeth together.

Wehr experienced a pang of pity for Caen. Though he considered him a bad soldier and a coward, he still felt a strange sense of pity for him. No man wants to die by Ludar's hand. Wehr shivered. It would not be an easy death.

The strike leader exited into the yard, where a patrol of eight guards just returned from the night's duty. He recognized Evin. "Evin, who is your leader?"

Evin pounded fist to chest in salute. "Mennar. He comes even now, Strike Leader."

Mennar once served under Wehr as a recruit, and it was Wehr who promoted him to patrol leader. "Mennar, your patrol will come with me."

Mennar struck his salute fiercely in recognition of his old strike leader. "It will be an honor, Strike Leader Wehr." The guards fell in behind the strike leader, his long strides closing the distance to the castle gates in heartbeats.

~

*W*isp retraced their steps out of the dungeon without a hitch. He had an uncanny memory for detail and direction. Darstan knew of Wisp's recall and he had heard the tales of his exploits through the tunnels under the city. Still, he marveled at his ability to navigate this maze in the dark.

As they ascended the stairs to re-emerge in the palace, Takar again assumed the lead position in the event they encountered a patrol or the palace guard. All being clear in the passageway, he signaled them onward, and the five of them crept along the corridor.

"Where to?" Darstan asked.

Ahead, two guards rounded the corner. "Stay the course," Takar ordered, "they'll think you with me." The sergeant resumed a normal stride and everyone followed his lead.

As they approached, Darstan saw that one of the guards was Caen. A slight bit of fear ran through his veins at first, then vengeance overshadowed it, filling his mind with the thoughts of retribution he dreamed of. He never let on, not until they were about to pass one another in the hall.

Caen's eyes widened just as Darstan drew his sword. He looked as if he searched for an escape. Darstan's sword sang as he whisked it out of its sheath. "Now let's see who's the better man, coward."

"Alert the guard!" Caen shouted the alarm then drew his sword.

Takar's reaction came too late. He spun around just as Darstan's blade landed the first, and fatal, blow to the guard, a crushing chop to the man's neck which nearly decapitated him.

The second guard drew his own blade then backed himself into an alcove—a position that provided good defense from multiple attacks. Vlad moved in, but a knife from Wisp found its mark, humming past the young guard and into the other man's throat.

"Retrieve the weapon," Wisp said. "I can't afford to lose a good blade."

Takar seized hold of Darstan, who shook with the fires of vengeance. He still swung the sword, hacking at the dead body, though his own face and arms were soaked with the man's blood.

"Need to get out of here," Takar said.

Darstan heard the footsteps rushing toward them. Probably a patrol of eight or ten, he calculated, and looked about for an escape route. They couldn't retreat unless they went back to the dungeons, and Darstan had already made up his mind about that. He wasn't going there. Darstan drew a knife for his left hand, while holding the sword in his right.

"Looks like we'll have to fight," Takar said, and drew his own sword.

"Search behind the tapestries," Wisp said. "Look for a secret passage." Wisp pulled aside the one nearest him, but found nothing but stone. 'Hurry!"

As Gregor and Takar rushed to the next one—a representation of

Lassic and his vargel—Vlad hollered from the other side of the corridor. "I found it."

A small opening in the stone wall led to steps rising in a steep circular fashion. "The guards will round that corner at any moment," Wisp said. "Let's go!"

Takar led the way, followed by Vlad, Gregor, Wisp and Darstan. Darstan closed the tapestry just as the patrol rushed around the corner. "I think they saw us," he said, and took the stairs two at a time.

"The Palace Guard will be called out now," Takar said. "It's going to be impossible to escape."

"There's an exit here," Darstan said as they reached the second level.

"Keep going," Wisp said.

~

Wehr negotiated the turn into the corridor running at full speed; the alarm had been raised, and this being the king's palace, their effectiveness, or lack of it, would be judged harshly. He noticed the tapestry fall closed against the wall, and thought he saw someone disappear behind it. Sprawled across the marble floor, were the bodies of Caen and his partner lying in an ever-spreading pool of blood. Caen's face was almost unrecognizable.

"Mennar, follow through the tapestry. Take everyone but Evin with you."

Once Mennar departed, Wehr continued his examination of the dead bodies; Caen had been hacked almost beyond recognition but the other guard sustained just one wound, blood gurgling from his throat even now. The guard whispered a name.

"Takar," he said.

"Are you saying that Sergeant Takar did this to you?"

"Takar did... this." He managed to force the words out before he expired.

Wehr slowly regained erect posture, though he felt sluggish. "This doesn't bode well, Evin. I assume that Darstan escaped, and by the looks of Caen's body, I would say he's bent on revenge. For some reason, Takar is helping him, and if that's true, my young friend, we may well be in danger."

Evin kept silent a moment then spoke. "I can't believe Darstan would do this. He might kill him, but not like this."

"I don't have any trouble believing it," Wehr said. "I expected it. Now let's go, we need to alert the remainder of the guard. And Ludar must know. It will require an order from him to persuade most men to pursue Takar. I know I'd not be eager to be the one cursed enough to catch him."

"Strike Leader Wehr, why would Takar risk himself to help a prisoner escape?"

Wehr deferred his answer, electing to walk along the corridor in silence.

Takar once held the position, didn't he, Strike Leader? Perhaps Takar doesn't like the way Ludar is running the guard." The young guard paused for a moment while they walked then uttered another comment. "Can't say that I wouldn't agree with Takar."

The strike leader spun to face the younger man. "It's dangerous to speak with such irreverence, Evin. Should the wrong person be within earshot you could be hanged for treason. Feel fortunate that I had been distracted and couldn't swear to what I heard. Be careful, though, on most days my hearing is remarkable." Wehr turned about and resumed his course through the corridors.

Evin smiled. "And how is your sense of direction, Strike Leader? I only ask because we're headed in the wrong direction if we plan to warn the palace guard."

Another abrupt stop as Wehr turned to face the young guard. "Do you know how to get there faster?"

"No, Strike Leader. I couldn't say for certain."

The strike leader smiled. "Neither can I, Evin. Neither can I. We shall, however, continue to seek them out. I feel confident we will locate them soon enough."

Wehr delayed as long as he could. The least he could grant an old friend like Takar was the courtesy of a few moments delay in the reporting. "All right, Evin. Time now to report to Ludar. I suggest you get some rest. I feel you'll be needing it."

~

They reached the third level of the palace and emerged from the passageway into a corridor that looked identical to the two floors below. "Hurry," Wisp said, "the guards will be coming soon."

Gregor showed reluctance. "I say we fight them."

"I know you're eager to use that new staff, bounty man, but I have no new weapons, only old knives, so I say we make our escape without a confrontation. I only know of one man who ever died running, and he fell from a roof."

"No one wants to fight them more than I do, Gregor, but I agree with Kender. There are too many guards, and more will be coming at any time."

"There's no way out that I can see," Takar said.

Vlad grabbed Takar's arm. "If something happens, don't blame yourself. I would have come without you."

Takar smiled. "Thank you, Vlad."

Wisp laughed. "No one need bury us yet, my friends. Follow me."

"Where are you taking us?" Takar asked.

"To visit Princess Cynemar. She'll provide the means for us to escape. There are secret tunnels that lead out of here to various points in the city. Her room is just ahead."

Takar laughed. "So, the stories are true. You *did* steal a kiss from her."

Vlad looked as if he would fall over. "Are you the Wisp?" he asked, but his tone implied he almost didn't want to hear.

Wisp shot Takar a scalding glare. "Just because I'm acquainted with the princess, doesn't make me Wisp."

A series of coded raps upon Cynemar's door soon brought it open to reveal the princess standing before them. Cynemar appeared alarmed, though a smile soon followed. She hurried them inside, giving Wisp a quick kiss on the cheek.

"What are you doing here?" Her eyes flashed to Takar then the rest of them, and her voice took on her haughty princess tone. "Sergeant Takar, what is the meaning of this?"

Takar looked to Wisp, then back to the princess. "I—"

"Blame me," Wisp said. "I brought them here because it's our only way out. Ludar's men are after us. If they catch us it will be our necks. We need to get out of the palace."

"Ludar? Why would he be... What does Takar have to do with this?"

"I don't have time to explain. Just trust me. Can you get us into the tunnels?"

She nodded, more somber now.

"Good. The rest can wait."

Cynamar led them through her chambers to a secret doorway behind some bookshelves. This will take you to the house near the old fortress."

As they started down the steps, Wisp turned to the princess. "No matter what happens, do not trust Ludar."

"Why? What—"

"Don't trust him," Wisp said. "If you need a friend, seek out Talanvar and use my name."

"Lord Talanvar?" Cynamar's face showed puzzlement. She grabbed him, planting a kiss on his face. "I love you."

"Keep that thought in your head," Wisp said and kissed her back.

~

Wehr awaited a signal to speak. Silence and patience were the only options when in the presence of the force commander—until he called for a report. Upon receiving the sign, the strike leader began. "He is gone, Force Commander. Caen and the guard that accompanied him are dead, as are the two sentries at the dungeon."

Ludar's eyes glowed, an angry fury about to erupt. "You have more to report, Strike Leader?"

Wehr thought of Takar, of the friendship they once shared, and of the vengeance Ludar would exact in retribution for Takar aiding Darstan. Loyalty weighed on his conscience as he considered not revealing the dying confession of the guard on the palace floor. He weighed against that, what would happen should Ludar discover his own treachery. Wehr lowered his head.

"There is more, Force Commander." He said it meekly, like a boy caught stealing for the first time and forced to apologize.

"Speak then," Ludar barked, his hands already red from squeezing the arms of his throne.

Wehr's head remained bowed. "Bartel is dead, and Caen's body lays hacked to death on the palace floor. Caen's demise might well be attributed to the escape of the prisoner; however, I believe they both carry the signature of Darstan's accomplices. I am sure the force commander already knows, but Darstan travels in the company of dangerous men—one seems especially dangerous, and he—"

"I know him," Ludar said, his voice shaking. "I am acquainted with all of them."

Wehr dared not raise his head for fear of betraying himself. Dared not, for he dreaded he might inform on Takar in a moment of weakness. If nothing else, this had set one thing clear in his mind. He would not be true to the force commander. Not now. Not evermore. Wehr pounded his chest three times in salute. He pounded as hard as he could so that his hands hurt. He never wanted to do this again and wished a strong reminder. "Yes, Force Commander, of course you are."

"Find them! Rouse all watches and find them. Don't let them leave my city."

Wehr found Mennar's patrol awaiting him in the courtyard. He held a brief, but informative discussion with them until no one had further questions, then he bade them all leave. "Remember, Mennar. Tonight, at the north gate." As the patrol departed, Wehr walked briskly toward the barracks.

~

"Are you certain of where this leads?" Gregor asked again.

"You asked the same question several times, Gregor. Do you expect my answer to change?" Wisp maintained an attitude that kept spirits high despite the situation they faced. "It won't be long, the tunnel comes out near the old fortress. We're close."

They exited the tunnel through a locked door that Wisp picked, and entered into a basement room of a vacant house at the bottom of the hill leading to the fort. The walls in the basement were stone, but not the musty, dirt-encrusted stone found in most cellars; these walls had been scrubbed clean on a regular basis. Wisp stepped lightly on the stairs, a finger to his lips cautioning the rest of them to keep quiet. He opened the door at the top then moved ahead, his footsteps soft as a cat stalking a mouse. Before long he returned and motioned for them to come up.

The doorway led into a small room with a table for dining and a few extra seats against the wall. Two pictures depicting floral scenes adorned the white walls, and a small cabinet sat at the far end of the room.

Darstan flopped on the floor, resting his back against the wall. "I can't believe we made it out."

"We're not free yet," Gregor said. "I imagine Ludar has guards looking for us."

"There's nothing keeping you here, bounty man. I doubt they even know you were involved. They know about Darstan, and perhaps suspect Takar and Vlad."

"I said I'd help, thief. I'll not run out on you now."

Wisp nodded. "I've got some messengers we can use. In a moment I'll go fetch some to scout for us. Before long we'll know where every guard in the city is. But for now, I suggest we get some sleep. The sun will rudely remind us of another day soon."

Vlad's eyes popped open wide. "Have we been gone all night?"

"Nearly," Wisp said. "Now get some sleep, I'll be back soon." Wisp left through a door he first picked the lock on, then hustled down the street of merchants. It was a street he knew from memory, and in no time he located Dirk and enlisted the services of several other young thieves, "gutter rats," as Wisp liked to call them.

At this age most were only good for getting information, but they were good for that. A youngster of eight or ten, even twelve years old, could pass unnoticed among most conversations. They were ideal for spying on the guard or on merchants. Satisfied that he'd soon have his information, he went back to the house. He couldn't wait to close his eyes.

~

*V*lad returned with food and drink. Gregor accompanied him, though he stayed his distance to ensure he had not been followed. "I noticed more guards than I ever have," Gregor said. "We passed a patrol on this street and two others before we reached the tavern."

"Why is Ludar so intent on finding you, Darstan?"

"I don't know, Takar. I only met Ludar one time. He asked if Rahg and I wanted to join the guard. You know the rest better than me."

Takar nodded. "Just odd that he'd go to so much trouble to catch you. Very odd."

The room went quiet at the sound of a series of raps on the door, a code that Wisp responded to by bringing it slightly ajar to ensure it was Dirk, then opened it to let him in. "That was quick," Wisp said. "Almost too quick. Did you take all the precautions I suggested? Did anyone follow?" Wisp scanned the street from a slit he made in the window shade.

"No one trailed me," Dirk said.

The reply did nothing to convince Wisp, but he relented and left the surveillance at the window. "Go on," Wisp said. "Report."

"He's got guards everywhere," Dirk said. "They're settin' a trap at the Trader's Inn, so they must know you'll come back there. And they have a whole patrol takin' turns at the bounty man's house." Dirk's face reddened. "Beggin' pardon, sir," he said to Gregor.

Gregor's nod hid the smile, and the little fellow got right back into the frenzy of reporting.

Another rap on the door interrupted them. Everyone froze. It was not the coded tap Dirk had used.

Takar got there before anyone, without a sound being made. Wisp peered out the slit he made moments ago from the window. "It's a guard," he whispered to Takar, then shot a glare at Dirk that froze the boy in his place. "Just one, Takar, and I can't see any others on the street."

Takar yanked the door open and seized the guard by the collar. He dragged him inside, then slammed him against the inside wall of the house as the door shut. Takar's eyes went wide as he saw who he held.

The Sykoran guard stepped away from the wall with impunity. "I'm surprised at you, Takar. The recruits you use grow smaller each year, and they are so untrained. I always thought you a good trainer."

Wehr drew his sword just in time to block Gregor's staff, but the impact jarred, causing Wehr to lose balance. "Hold," he cried, "I've not come for trouble."

Darstan stood less than five paces away. As soon as Wehr started talking, he moved to strike. Takar caught his arm at the last moment, directing the blow away from Wehr. "Stop! Darstan. We'll hear what he has to say."

Darstan's eyes never lost their intensity, nor their conviction. "He's the one who took me, Takar. He was their strike leader."

Takar grabbed Dirk by the scruff of the neck. He had remained perfectly still since Wehr entered, as if Kender might kill him for failing in his duty. None of the lads knew who Kender was, but stories in the streets told of harsh punishment for failing to do a job properly.

"Chase the lad away, Kender. If we need him we can call him back."

Once Wisp ushered Dirk out the door, Takar turned to Darstan. "I know that Wehr led them, lad. Bartel told me just before I killed him."

Takar looked to Wehr just in time to catch a slight sense of surprise, though it was far from shock.

"You killed Bartel, Sergeant? That's unlike you."

Takar spat. "The fool threatened to tell Ludar what I meant to do. I couldn't let him do that."

Wehr nodded as if it were an inevitable fate that Bartel finally met. "He was a fool, but I didn't come here to speak of Bartel. Ludar is scouring the city for Darstan. And you, Gregor," Wehr said, turning to the bounty man. "And you," he indicated to Kender, "but he has only a description of you and where to find you."

Wehr once again turned about to face Takar. "You know Ludar. He won't stop. The guard at the exit gates has been trebled and sentries have been posted along all the walls. He means to keep you inside the city, where he can take his time finding you."

"I plan to kill you, Wehr." Darstan's candor was chilling. Fire burned in his eyes, and his sword trembled under his tight grip.

Wehr stared at Darstan and held his gaze. His voice, when he finally spoke remained cool. "I knew you would. I told Caen you'd kill him, though I didn't imagine it would be so soon. If you want to kill me, fine. But first allow me to help you escape from Sykor. It's the least I can do after bringing you here."

Darstan opened his mouth to reply but Takar stopped him. "Why would you help us?"

"Let's say that I have reason to believe I might disappear like so many others once this mission is completed. If that will suffice, Takar, then I have Mennar's entire patrol set to follow my lead. We intend to leave Sykor."

Wehr looked around the room, taking note of Gregor, Wisp, and Vlad.

"I'm convinced that you and the young guard could blend in with us. And I feel certain that Darstan might as well, providing we suited him in a Sykoran uniform. The other two might prove too much though. The guards at the gates will be questioning everyone."

Wisp spoke up. "Don't worry over my friend and me, nor for Darstan. I'll see that we get out."

"I won't regret leaving Sykor," Vlad said. "Perhaps one day Ludar will be gone and things will be as before." A sad look came to Vlad's eyes. "Guess I'll miss Lynna though. I wish she could come."

Takar slapped the lad's back. "You've spoken for me as well, Vlad. Wehr, we'll join you whenever you're ready. And as for Lynna, you can send for her later, Vlad."

"There's no time to waste," Wehr said. "The longer we delay, the more chance Ludar will catch us." Wehr stared at Darstan for a brief moment, then reached to draw a sword from a scabbard at his side. "I thought you would want this back, Darstan. Though if you intend to use it against me..." Wehr smiled as he handed him the sword. Darstan didn't return the smile.

"Provide me with a few moments to speak with the lad, Wehr."

Wehr gave the salute due an officer of higher rank, even though Takar only held the position of sergeant. "We have all agreed, Takar, when we leave the city you'll assume command. Once you were my force commander; to this day I still consider that true. All the men agreed." Wehr bowed. "It will be dark soon; we'll meet at the north gate." Wehr pounded his chest three times then departed.

Takar studied the room. Everyone maintained a somber expression. "Can we trust that lad outside to carry messages for us?" he asked Wisp.

"After that fine example he showed us today I'd not trust him to clean the floor."

Gregor came to the lad's defense. "He's done a good bit of fine work, Takar. I'd not say the lad's a full-bonded message runner, but he'll get the gist of what needs saying."

"That'll do with the little time we have. Vlad, if you have any words for your mother get them ready. Kender, bring that lad back in here so he can deliver these messages. But don't set him free until long after we're gone, just in case."

Vlad looked to Kender. "I have nothing for my mother," Vlad said, "but I need to get word to a girl named Lynna."

Takar laughed. "Well then, the lad has grown up, to be thinking of his girl instead of his mother." Takar turned to Kender. "Take care of Darstan, and see that you stay clear of the road once out of Sykor. As for meeting, there is an old stone marker five leagues north on the road to Kamnor. Do you know it?"

"I do," Darstan said. "We passed it riding to Sykor with Tobias and Rahg."

"Good. Meet us there as soon as you can. If you ride hard, you might reach it by daylight." Takar started to leave, then as if he had forgotten something, turned back again. "And Darstan, forget your vengeance on Wehr. He followed orders from Ludar so if you wish to exact revenge do it on the force commander. Besides," Takar warned, "Wehr would kill you. I know, Darstan. I trained him."

"See you soon, Sergeant," Wisp said.

Takar nodded and departed with Vlad.

~

Wisp gave Dirk his final instructions then sent him on his way.

Gregor seemed busy sanding the slightest nick out of his blackthorn staff, and Darstan sat on the floor sharpening his reacquired sword. "I thought I wanted to kill Wehr. Now I don't know."

The bottom of Wisp's boots were caked with mud. He picked at them with one of his blades. "My advice is never set out to kill a man. Only kill someone if you have to."

"And you're telling me that you wouldn't look for revenge?"

"I didn't say that. Your vengeance is just misguided. Ludar is the one you should kill. Not Wehr and Evin."

Darstan stood, adjusting the sheath then replacing his sword. "Are we ready?"

"Don't be so impatient," Gregor said. "I'm not so eager to test the whims of fate. Destiny is too fickle to embrace so fondly."

Wisp laughed. "You worry me, Gregor. You're beginning to sound like a bard. But don't worry over fate. I create my own fate."

"When do we leave?" Darstan asked again.

"Not until dark. By then everything will be ready."

"Then wake me at dark," Darstan said as he covered his head with a cloak. "And not before.

Gregor put the staff down. "What do you intend to do about Wehr? Have you forgotten what you promised Rhaven?"

A wry smile formed on Wisp's lips. "I haven't forgotten, bounty man, but I didn't swear to kill them the moment I saw them either. I see no logic in killing a man who is trying to help us. Besides, we need to concentrate on getting out of Sykor before Ludar casts his net too wide." Wisp stared at Gregor, his smile now gone. "Remember, bounty man, I have never broken a vow."

PURSUED

*D*irk tugged at the corner of his cap until it cast a shadow over the top of his left eye. Kender Darnell had given him some odd instructions, strangest of all being the one to deliver a message to one of the lords. Apprehension infused his body as he approached a noble's house. *I'll probably get put to the whip just for asking about a great lord like Talanvar.*

He wondered again how Kender knew a noble, and it filled Dirk's mind with wild thoughts. A hoax would be apt punishment for letting the guard follow him back to the house. That puzzled Dirk also. Why would one of the guards, a strike leader, want to help Kender and his friends? And why would Takar be helping them? There was much more to Kender Darnell than he yet realized, but he need not worry about that, his only duty was to deliver a message, and he had no intention of botching this assignment.

He finished climbing the hill to Talanvar's home taking the few remaining steps to the front entrance two at a time. A black metal gate with carvings of ferocious fish blocked the way. Rumor said that Lord Talanvar got all his money dealing in fish. *Guess he honors 'em that way,* Dirk thought. He still wondered why a great lord like Talanvar would trouble to hear from a man like Kender Darnell, but he had sworn to deliver this message, and whip or no, he intended to do it.

Stern discipline kept the gatekeeper's posture as stiff as a stone pillar. Dirk had kept a wary eye on him ever since he breached the hilltop and had yet to see the man even twitch. His demeanor shook Dirk's confidence, though he managed to muster enough courage to present a calm appearance.

"Go away," the gatekeeper warned. Lord Talanvar's not giving food to beggars." A look crossed his face as if he reconsidered… but if your belly's empty enough and you've a mind to work he might find need for you at the fish market."

"It's not food or work I'm lookin' for," Dirk replied as haughtily as he could. "I've been paid good coin to deliver a message to Lord Talanvar." He reached into the pouch tied to his britches and produced a silver coin, waving it in front of the gatekeeper's face. A twisted smile framed the corner of his mouth, certain the man now envied his wealth.

The gatekeeper bowed then extended his hand through the gate to receive the message. "I will deliver it to my lord immediately."

Dirk stared at him, worry crowding his young face. His thoughts had been set on meeting a real lord. He pushed his own hand forward, one jerky motion at a time.

The gatekeeper seemed to notice Dirk's reluctance, then his gaze fell to the nearly undetectable scribbling on the bottom corner of the sealed letter. "It will be delivered right away," he promised. "If someone paid you a silver crown then this message must indeed be important, and my master demands immediate notice of urgent news."

His words comforted Dirk but when he took the letter Dirk almost pulled back. Only the gatekeeper's warm and friendly eyes stopped him. "You're sure your master will get it right away?"

The gatekeeper reached into his own pouch and extracted two copper dirnars, flipping them to him through an opening in the gate. "Rest easy, lad, and be on your way. My master will be reading this letter before you reach the merchant district."

Dirk hustled down the long hill. He had delivered his message safely and earned two extra dirnars. It had already been a good day. The wind tugged at the corner of his hat, nearly stripping his head bare, but Dirk yanked it down tight. He ran down the steep roadway until he was out of control, unable to stop himself. It was a dangerous and wonderful feeling. *How did he know I was going to the merchant district,* Dirk wondered, but then pushed the thought from his mind. He was having too much fun to worry about things like that.

~

A series of taps upon the door brought Darstan, Gregor, and Wisp to their feet. Wisp walked over and undid the latch with no hesitation. Long ago Talanvar and Wisp developed a secret code that only the two of them knew. They also had a backup plan in the event either one was taken prisoner and tortured for information. Under the conditions of that unlikely scenario, they agreed to reveal a code that would gain entry; however, they had it structured so that the other knew it to be a false code.

Under threat of torture they could state without qualms that the code they told would gain a person admittance. It was an important subtlety but necessary, as some say there are certain people that possess the ability to determine if someone is telling the truth or not; this code would allow Wisp or Carmine to use the alternate code, and when phrased properly, still be saying nothing but truth.

Darstan marveled at the complexities of Wisp's arrangements and dealings. In some ways, he envied Wisp, and at other times felt a strange sense of pity for the amiable thief. Nonetheless, Wisp's mind contained a storehouse of information when it came to subterfuge, cleverness, and stealth, and Darstan vowed to learn everything he could from him.

Talanvar cast worried glances at Darstan and Gregor. Many people knew him by sight as Lord Talanvar, and they might wonder why a lord would be visiting a commoner like Kender Darnell. If it had not been for the urgency of Wisp's coded message, Talanvar would have departed upon seeing the thief's companions. The lord kept his head held low. Perhaps they wouldn't recognize him. Not many commoners travel in circles that brought them in contact with nobles.

"We need to leave Sykor," Wisp said.

Talanvar paused, strolling the perimeter of the empty room with his head bowed low. "The force commander seeks someone desperately. Orders have been issued to apprehend this unknown person with haste and the gates and walls have been secured against even the most auspicious adventurer. I do not believe that even the notorious Wisp could effect an escape with the number of guards that Ludar has posted."

The man's raspy voice did not fit his manner of speaking, but his message remained unmistakably clear; it would be difficult, if not impossible, to escape from Sykor.

"Allow me to bear the uneasy burden of how to elude the guards," Wisp said. "All I need are a few services."

Talanvar nodded his consent, allowing Wisp to continue. It all was done so fast it almost seemed like he had only paused for breath. "I have sent instructions to have Gregor's horse, and mine, taken to the stable nearest the north gate. If you could see that another mount with necessities are provided for Darstan, my man will have them prepared to depart just after dark.

We also need a wagon laden with perishable items, anything to provide reason for leaving Sykor at night. Three men must accompany the wagon, and they are to tie our three horses behind them. If the guards ask about the mounts tell the men to say that they are to deliver the goods and the wagon then use the extra horses to return home."

"All well and good, but how will you escape? They have guards at the gates, and they have dogs. I fail to see what good the wagon will do."

"Leave that to me. Just provide what I ask—"

Talanvar responded before Wisp finished his statement. "Consider it done. Shortly after the sun sets the wagon and men will pick up the horses at the stable. And I will purchase the best mount available for your friend. May the goddess herself smile upon your journey."

Talanvar's departure did nothing to alleviate the tension in the room. If anything, the questions he posed to Wisp increased the apprehension of Darstan and Gregor. "How will we get past the guards, Wisp?"

Wisp ignored Darstan's question, instead addressing the bounty man. "Gregor, did you never wonder why no one ever reported seeing the Wisp?"

A scowl came to Gregor's face. "What has that to do with anything? Darstan asked a more important question. How do you intend on eluding the guards, not to mention the dogs?"

"Watch," Wisp said, and stared at the wall as if he were in a trance.

Darstan and Gregor kept their eyes on him. Suddenly, his form distorted, like heat waves rising from the ground on a scorching summer afternoon.

"What's happening, Wisp?" Darstan's voice nearly broke. By the time he finished the question, Wisp disappeared. "Gods blood!" Darstan said. "Wisp! Where are you?"

Gregor stood silent, locked in an amazed stupor. "So this is how you did it."

More suddenly than he disappeared, Wisp blinked back into view, his figure solidifying almost instantaneously. He wore no smile, no smirk. "That's how we'll escape," he said, then awaited their reaction.

"What? How?" Darstan's composure soon returned. "How will that help *us*?"

Gregor shook his head as if his vision needed clearing. "It's no wonder that I couldn't catch you, thief."

Wisp beckoned each of them closer. "You asked how it would help, Darstan. I'll show you." He grabbed hold of each of their arms. "Stand still," he said, "and watch one another."

Gregor instinctively pulled back but then stayed himself, and let Wisp demonstrate his point. Darstan's eyes went agape as the transition began. This time, not only Wisp disappeared, but Gregor as well. The bounty man staggered, his own eyes wide. When he looked down at himself, he gasped.

Panic seemed to set upon both Darstan and Gregor. "What sort of magic is this?" Darstan screamed. "Wisp, answer me."

Gregor's reaction was to pull away, and Wisp let him go. Once the hold was severed the bounty man became visible. Then Wisp let go his hold on Darstan, and he regained his form. Though both remained shaken, their curiosity and wonderment overwhelmed their fear. Darstan had been worried about escaping, but this newly revealed secret of Wisp's settled his mind.

"With this, we have nothing to fear," he said. "We can walk right out the gate and the guards will never see us." Darstan laughed.

Gregor saw the pitfalls. "What exactly does it do? Will we still leave imprints on the ground? I already know that others can still hear us because I heard Darstan; what else do we need to be wary of."

Wisp smiled. "I'm glad you're more concerned with how to use the powers than you are worried over the fact that I have them. As to escape, it will not be as easy as you think, Darstan. Gregor has the right of it. Though I can render us unseen with the power, any noise we make will give away our position; our tracks will still be seen; and most troublesome of all, the dogs will still be able to detect our scent."

"Not so promising," Gregor said. "What do you propose?"

"If it were only guards it would be simple," Wisp said, "but with the dogs we must be more careful. First, we need to get to the stable next to the north gate, and do it without using my powers."

Wisp must have noticed Darstan's confused look and elaborated. "It's a strain for me to hide us all; I'll need all the strength for the task of escaping, but don't fret, Darstan, it should be no trouble for the three of us to reach the north gate stable."

Gregor nodded his approval as Wisp continued. "Once we reach the stable, we await the wagon and men that my friend is sending."

"How do we know we can count on your friend?" The bounty man's query carried a sarcastic tone with it, almost as if he wished the man to fail.

Wisp shot him a scornful glare. "You needn't worry about that, bounty–man. Both wagon and men will be there on time, as will a mount for Darstan."

Wisp's confidence seemed to irk Gregor all the more, but he kept silent while the thief detailed the plan for their departure. "Our mounts will be tied to the back of the cart, though we will be astride the horses pulling the wagon. They will be rubbed down with the grease merchants use to repel insects while on caravan."

Darstan balked, recalling the scent from the wagons he smelled in Pomanda. "It's a horrible odor."

"That it is," Wisp said. "But it's a scent that will draw the dogs. When the guards see nothing but horses they will keep the dogs away from us, especially since the smell will be offensive."

Darstan smiled, as usual Wisp seemed to have things worked out in his head. He relaxed a little and listened to the rest of the plan. "The wagon will make enough noise to cover up any inadvertent sound we might make; and there will be no tracks to bother with as we'll be on the horses the whole time.

Darstan, you'll have to ride with me. Gregor will be on the horse next to us. I must be able to touch each of you the entire time. And no matter what happens, keep a firm grip on me. If we break contact, you'll be visible. I only hope that my ability holds out long enough to pass through the gate, though the guards shouldn't keep us long. The horses will be empty and the wagon can be easily checked."

"Why is he helping us?" Gregor asked. "Who was he? He looked like one of the nobles."

"He is."

"Then why would he help you?"

"Not for me to say, Gregor. Let's just leave it that he owed me some favors. Now that slate is cleared." Wisp's response appeared to have satisfied Gregor, even if he still exhibited a sour mood.

"It's dark now," the bounty man said, "time we got to the stable."

~

*W*ehr led the patrol down the hillside street, the heavy clomping of hooves against stone echoing in the narrow lane. Not often did a full patrol of the Sykoran guard prepare to leave the city at night, most departed during daylight to make better use of their time. The strike leader signaled a halt at the sight of the sentries posted along the north gate wall.

"Wehr," a guard called from the shadows.

Wehr wondered about a guard calling him by name. Not many would be so insolent as to call a superior by his first name, then he saw who had spoken—Strike Leader Margan. They had been recruits together. Even though he knew how much Ludar wanted Darstan caught, it shocked Wehr that the force commander bothered posting a strike leader on guard duty.

"Margan." Wehr returned the casual salutation effecting a surprise in his voice that could be taken for the greeting of an old acquaintance. "I see that the force commander has you busy. I drew extra duty too, forced to lead a search that any competent patrol leader could do. What have these men done to warrant such attention?"

"My orders cite no crime, only to apprehend them." Strike leader Margan glanced about in a manner that hinted at suspicion. "Wehr, I thought all patrols were to remain in the city tonight?"

No surprise showed on Wehr's face, only a frustrated frown. "Margan, I will gladly trade duties. There is a young serving girl at the Cobbler's Inn that I direly wish to see, and leading this patrol will take me through the night."

Wehr knew Margan had no reason to suspect him, yet the patrol must have struck him as odd.

"I see Mennar, and since it's his patrol, I understand him being assigned, but why is Takar with you?"

Takar spat toward Margan, the wad of spit splattering on the strike leader's boots.

"Because he's the best tracker in Sykor," Wehr said. "If the men that Ludar seeks have already escaped, Takar will find them; on that you can rely."

Margan nodded. No one would deny Takar's ability when it came to tracking. "Be on your way, Strike Leader. If fortune is with you that serving girl may still be waiting when you return. Open the gates, men," Margan said, as he reached over and slapped Wehr's horse on the flanks.

Wehr looked on with worry at the hounds that Margan kept at the gate. They probably had Darstan's scent from the prison. *I hope the lads can get out without trouble.* When the patrol came to the fork in the road, they took the one that headed north toward Kamnor and Nyauran. Sykor could no longer be seen, and the heavily wooded terrain provided excellent cover.

"Wehr," Takar called, "I think I'll stay and wait on them; there could be trouble."

Wehr halted the advance, bringing his mount to a stop with a light tug on the reins. Like all Sykoran guard mounts, his was well trained. "If you feel the need to wait on them, Takar, then we all wait." Wehr could almost feel the grumbling from his men, but he forestalled it before it even began.

"Remember, we took a call, men. All agreed that once we departed the city Takar would command." Wehr waited for the looks of acceptance before he continued, then pounded his fist in salute to his former force commander. The remainder of the patrol did likewise.

The sergeant acknowledged his newfound role as leader showing no hesitation about assuming command. "Divide the force in two. Wehr, take half, Mennar, the others. Take up a position on either side of the road and each post a guard. It should not prove a long wait."

~

*W*isp, Gregor, and Darstan sat huddled in a darkened corner of the stable by the north gate. Wisp kept busy slitting individual pieces of hay into slivers with one of his knives. No worry showed on his face yet he reconfirmed every last detail. "Have you both put your cloaks away? We can't afford to risk the sound of a cloak flapping in the wind."

"I doubt they'll show," Gregor said.

"They'll come as promised. And once they arrive I'll conceal us. After they check the horses and hitch them to the wagon, we'll mount them. Make no noise, and be careful to follow my lead. Remember, once we reach the gate don't move, even if the dogs approach."

"Listen." Darstan heard them coming before anyone. "They're here, Wisp."

Wisp sheathed his blade then extended his arms. "Take hold," he ordered, and used his powers.

While the three men labored with tying the extra mounts to the back of the wagon, Wisp, Darstan, and Gregor mounted the horses in the front. Soon they were approaching the north gate of Sykor.

"Halt," the guard called.

The men brought the wagon to a stop. A tired-looking guard shuffled over to inspect the wagon. Behind him, came two more guards, each with a dog on leash. "Where are you headed, merchant? And why leave at night?"

The driver appeared as tired as the guard. "Pomanda. We have orders to deliver these goods quickly."

The guard poked his head into the back of the cart, pushing a few crates aside and peering down to the floorboards. "What are you hauling that is so important?"

The other two guards had now reached the cart, tugging repeatedly at the leashes to keep the dogs from inspecting the horses up front.

"Back here," the guard commanded a dog. "Can't get this hound to stop sniffing them horses," he complained.

"Guess they must smell good to the dogs," his partner said.

"Don't smell good to me." The first one yanked hard on the leash. "The dog yelped but followed orders.

"What are you hauling that's so important?" the guard asked again.

"Don't know," the driver said. "We hired out to haul this load to Pomanda as quick as it can be got there, then return here even quicker. That's what we have for instructions. We're gettin' paid good coin; that's hard to come by these days so I'm not one to ask what's in the cart."

The guard nodded his understanding but continued his search, moving more things around in the back and checking under the wagon. He tapped on the sides and bottom a few times to see if there were any hollows carved into it, then finding nothing wrong, allowed them passage through the gate. "Go on then, may the gods speed your journey." The two dogs tugged at their restraints in an attempt to get to the horses in front.

"Come now," the guards yelled. "There's nothin' for ya there."

The wagon veered at the fork in the road that indicated Pomanda, slowing down only enough to negotiate the turn. At Wisp's signal, Gregor and Darstan both jumped, landing in the heavy brush that bordered the roadway.

"What was that?" the man seated in the middle yelled.

"Whoa." The driver yanked on the reins, bringing the wagon to a stop. "Something fell from the back."

Gregor and Darstan quietly made their way back up the road and awaited the second stage of the plan. As the three men stepped down to inspect the cart, walking back toward the spot where the noise was heard, Wisp clubbed the driver over the head with the hilt of his knife, knocking him unconscious. At the sound, the other two spun to face Wisp, who still could not be seen, and when they did, Darstan and Gregor fell upon them. Gregor cracked one with his staff, and

Darstan used the hilt of his sword. It was over in an instant. "I wish all fights could be so easy," Wisp said.

"Hurry, get our horses and let's leave," Gregor said.

Darstan was on his mount and preparing to head toward Pomanda when a shrill whistle from Wisp brought his attention back. "This way, Darstan," Wisp said.

"Why? Rahg's still in Genda."

Wisp adopted a tone not to be argued with. "And half the Sykoran guard will be searching the roads from here to Pomanda and Genda. I don't intend to let them find me. And did you forget that we were to meet Takar at the stone marker? Besides," Wisp said, "they left Genda long ago."

"We have no time for this," Gregor said, spurring his horse. "Let's go."

Darstan wore a frown, but he followed them as they sped along the north road leading toward Kamnor. "Won't those men tell Ludar what happened?"

"They were paid good gold to deliver something to Pomanda. Just because they were attacked, they won't quit."

They met Takar and the patrol a short distance away on the trail, Wehr and Evin in the front to greet them. "I'm happy you escaped, Darstan." A smile lit Evin's face as he extended his hand in friendship. Darstan accepted his greeting with no hesitation then turned to Takar. "Where are we going, Sergeant?"

"Nyauran territory, and we need to move, so let's be on our way." Takar prodded his horse forward at a fast walk.

"Shouldn't we be covering our tracks?" Darstan asked.

"There are only two roads to take out of Sykor. Knowing that, they'll find signs of our passing no matter how much time we spend trying to hide them. Our best shot is them not knowing we're gone for a few days.

Darstan rode alongside him. "What if that doesn't happen? Then, how do we elude them?"

Takar leaned out from his mount and spat a wad of tobacco. "We'll wait until we cross the Tasla River and get to the Great Plains."

"The Plains. I need to get to Genda and find Rahg."

"I already told you, Darstan. They set sail long ago. Even if we could make it to Genda without being caught we'd never find anyone else crazy enough to go after them."

Takar issued the final order. "Darstan, when we reach Khatara you can hire out on a ship bound for Genda. Sykor's too dangerous for us, and since Wehr and this patrol are bound for Khatara, we'll stay with them. A group this size will be left alone."

Darstan nodded. "All right, but I'm finding a ship when we get to Khatara.

～

The dampness of the stone floor chilled the reception room. Force Leader Bragh shivered, drawing his woolen cloak tighter; it was not just the temperature of the room that caused his discomfort, but waiting for Ludar. The force commander's chamber lay behind a pair of large oaken doors that even now creaked open to admit Bragh. That he wished not to go did not matter, Ludar had sent for him, and the command had been marked urgent. Bragh couldn't recall any orders that weren't marked urgent.

The force leader's long strides carried him across the room in quick fashion with his head hung low. Bragh struck his chest three times in salute. "Force Commander, I bring your report."

"Then report."

Bragh hesitated, seeking the courage to continue. "We didn't find Wehr, Force Commander. I didn't think it odd until I discovered Mennar and his patrol missing as well. After investigating I learned that they left the city by the north gate claiming to be on a mission for you." Bragh looked up at Ludar. Rage filled the force commander's eyes. Bragh swallowed hard. There was more he had to tell Ludar. "Takar was also with them."

"What of the village boy?"

Bragh frowned. "Margan stood duty at the gate, and though he knows many of the men, he cannot be certain if the lad was with them, Force Commander. There was a full patrol."

Ludar stared straight ahead, shaking. "I do not believe in coincidences, Force Leader. Occurrences of chance are for those who gamble. Find them. Bring them back to me. Darstan, the village boy, must be unharmed. All the rest may die, though I'd prefer it if Wehr and Takar survive to meet death at my hand. In fact, Force Leader, I relish the thought; let it be so. Take a full strike force and hunt them down. Remember, Takar is a great tracker and fine strategist, and Wehr only slightly less so."

Silence chilled Bragh while he waited. "You will need to overwhelm them with force. Do not account yourself brilliant enough to succeed without such an advantage."

"Shall I divide the force?" Bragh asked.

"Take your men north until you find the tracks. Takar would not go west."

"But Strike Leader Wehr will be in command, sir, and he—"

"He will cede command to Takar. Of that, I am certain. Takar taught Wehr everything he knows as a soldier. Even if he doesn't give him the title, Takar will be issuing the orders. I'll send birds to the west to alert them just in case, but they won't be needed."

"And if they should cross into Nyauran?" Bragh asked.

"Ludar leaned forward. "I don't care if they cross into Sethia itself, Force Leader. I want them found."

"Your will, Force Commander." Bragh saluted and prepared to depart.

"Have you forgotten anything?" Ludar's question caught him by surprise. Bragh spun around to face him again. "I have received word that you questioned a citizen who knew something of the ones we sought."

A surprised look came to Bragh's face. "But, sir, he—"

"Bring him to me," Ludar commanded.

"But, sir—"

"Now! Once you have delivered the boy, gather your force and find Takar and Darstan."

"Yes, Force Commander." Bragh obeyed, but he felt cowardly doing so. He wondered if the boy would be safe.

~

*T*he Tasla River proved to be an easy crossing. The bridge was always kept in good repair to enable caravans from Khatara to pass, and they made frequent use of it. Soon after entering Nyauran, the landscape changed; steep hills and mounds gave way to a gently rolling plain grown high with wild grasses. The heavily wooded sections that populated Sykor and Kamnor were nowhere to be found, only sparse copses of trees that loomed like oases at the edge of their vision.

grasslands

"Stay alert," Takar warned them. "A full strike force could hide in these fields and you'd never know until their arrows dug into your flesh."

"Nobody could have gotten here before us," Vlad said.

"Not Sykoran patrols," Takar said, "but there could be Wolfen or Victas, even Gnakas."

Wehr laughed. "Even Nyaurans. They are not so fond of Sykoran guards."

Darstan kept alert after hearing of the dangers that might await them, but couldn't help allowing his eyes to wander to the vast stretches that lay before him. For two days they traveled nonstop through monotonous fields of grass; the plains seemed endless. The grasses grew tall, nearly to the bottom of his saddle, and it felt strange riding through it.

He recalled some of the stories he had heard about Nyaurans; how they were such expert horsemen, and how they traveled with their herds. He recalled hearing stories of their skill with the short bow, and the ability to shoot accurately while riding at full gallop. "Have you ever been to Nyauran, Evin?" Darstan asked.

"I've never been anywhere except where we followed you. This is all new to me. Seems strange, doesn't it, to be so open, with no trees?"

"Back in Kamnor we had mountains. Big mountains. And on clear days you could see all the way to the Great Whites. Rahg and I always dreamt of going there someday, though with our luck rock dragons would have probably killed us."

"I wonder if they sent anyone after us?" Evin asked.

Darstan heard him, and it brought to mind something he had wondered about. "Takar, how do we hide our trail out here? Anyone with eyes could follow the tracks. They have no need of dogs."

"Be patient, Darstan. Soon we will have what we need." Takar stopped, scanning the terrain ahead, finally settling on what appeared to be a small copse of trees off to the northeast. "We'll make camp in that grove, Wehr. Send someone to scout it."

copse of trees

They reached the grove by nightfall; it had been much farther away than it appeared. Darstan dismounted and took care of his horse, giving him water and food. *I wish I had Grayson again.*

~

*V*lad built a nice fire and two of Mennar's men carved the deer they shot.

"Game's plenty good here," Mennar said. "Had our pick of a whole herd. Saw signs of 'em though. They'll be here soon enough now that they know we're huntin' their herds. The Nyaurans don't take kindly to that."

"You can't call deer *their herds*," Evin said.

"If it's on their ground, so they claim the herds," the other guard explained.

Darstan listened to them argue for a few moments before leaving to wander about the large grove, taking time to enjoy the cool evening while waiting for the meat to be cooked and prepared. When ready, he got the food then joined Wisp and Gregor. The bounty man had been in a dour mood for days. *I've never seen Gregor like this. I wonder what's bothering him?* "So, bounty man, tell me if you ever decided what to do with your life."

"I have given it no thought, Darstan, but perhaps I should. It seems like thieves have more friends than bounty-men. Nothing is what I thought it to be."

"I wonder where Kella is," Darstan muttered.

"I don't know," Wisp said, "but I'd like to have her with us before we cross the Empty Lands."

Evin had arrived at the tail end to the conversation. "What are the Empty Lands?"

Wisp gave a suspicious look to Evin, a look like he was not welcome, and though he did nothing to deter Evin from sitting with them, neither did he answer the young guard's question.

Gregor shot a disapproving look to Wisp. "The Empty Lands were once part of Sethia, and though they still belong to Sethia they are supposed to be outside the shield. It is the route that the caravans from Khatara travel, and though it occasionally draws attacks from Wolfen and Victas, it is generally safe with a large enough force."

"Are we a large enough force?" Evin asked.

"Let's hope so," Gregor said.

Darstan heard a horse galloping toward camp and stood to go hear the report. It was the advance sentry coming in.

The guard dismounted, saluting Takar in ritual fashion. "Nyaurans approaching, Sergeant."

"How many?"

"Too many to count, sir, and they're riding fast."

Takar steadied the man before he addressed the rest of them. "They'll be friendly for now, so don't get edgy with your weapons. Besides, their leader will likely have a dozen or more bows aimed at us the whole time. Act normal. I'll negotiate with them. I'm sure they'll want satisfaction for the meat."

Wisp waited until Takar finished. "I have gold if that's what they want, Sergeant."

Takar laughed. "No. Won't be that. But the offer is appreciated."

The thunder of hooves pounding the ground roared through the night. Darstan listened as the echo permeated the air until it became impossible to distinguish from which direction it originated. The earth rumbled and vibrated under his feet. There are hundreds of them. The night came alive in the form of a sea of mounted soldiers.

Wisp sidled next to Darstan and Gregor, whispering in a secretive tone. "If they attack, hold fast to me and I'll conceal us. There are too many to fight."

Gregor nodded, though Darstan saw him fidgeting with the blackthorn staff like he was eager to use it. "I will," Darstan said, though he never took his eyes from the advancing forces.

Takar stood in front of them, his own massive frame looming like a statue in the square. He didn't flinch, even when the horses raced toward him, giving no indication they would stop. Darstan's hand found the hilt of his blade, certain that any moment they would be engaged in battle.

The Nyaurans swerved at the last moment, narrowly avoiding Takar. Two of them brought their mounts to an abrupt halt on either side of him. Charging in behind them came a warrior astride a wild, but beautiful looking horse that looked to be as big as Argus. With but a slight tug on the reins, he stayed the mount, halting a length or two short of trampling the sergeant. As the giant beast snorted in protest, Darstan breathed a sigh of relief.

Takar stood silent until the man on the stallion spoke. "I will know why you come to my land, Takar."

"We have need of your friendship, Ictar, and we have come to offer trades as well as gold."

Ictar's gaze focused on the deer. "You seek friendship in a strange way. For days you have trampled our crops; now you steal our meat. If you trained your horses properly our crops would yet stand tall. And if your men could eat the grasses instead of the meat, the herds would have had plenty of time to grow fat for the winter. You have done all this, and now you wish friendship. What have you to trade in return?"

"Our friendship *and* our swords. Swords which once served Sykor."

"You have shed a lot of blood for Sykor with that sword."

Ictar stared over the heads of the other Sykorans. "Does Takar speak for all of you?"

As one, they shouted their approval.

Ictar smiled. "Come then, friend Takar. Join me in the camp of my father, which is the camp of his father. You have earned the protection of Ictar, First-son to Melos, chief of all Nyaurans. You are all well come to my land."

~

"We have brought him, Force Commander."

"Bring him in," Ludar barked from his throne-like chair.

The two guards led a frightened lad across the large room, not stopping until they reached the foot of the steps leading to Ludar's immense seat. The boy stared at the floor.

"Look at me, boy."

The boy raised his head slow, twisting the corner of his cap in defiance. "I didn't do nothin' you black-hearted son of a cur."

Ludar laughed. "I see your tongue has been sharpened on our finer streets. You are braver than most of my guard." Ludar descended from his lofty seat taking the steps slowly and letting his boots pound noisily on each one as he did. "But you have no respect for the guard, little one." Ludar's last step brought him close to the lad, and he struck him across the face with the back of his hand. Blood ran from the boy's lip in a small stream that trickled down his chin.

"Mother of Rats!" he screamed and recoiled, knives of hatred forming in his eyes. Before he could fully recover Ludar struck him again, this time across the side of the head. The lad reeled, falling to the ground amid curses aimed at the force commander.

"Are you a thief?" Ludar posed the question but awaited no response. "They say thieves need good hands in order to make a fair living. They say a thief without a thumb is like a guard without a sword. We shall see."

Ludar grabbed one of the guards and shoved him toward the boy. "Hold him on the floor." The lad watched as Ludar took out a knife. Screams filled the chamber and echoed down the corridors when Ludar cut off his thumb. Terrible wailing and crying and begging for mercy.

"Are you prepared to answer my questions?" Amidst uncontrollable sobbing, the lad nodded vigorously that he would.

"What is your name?" Ludar demanded.

"Dirk!" the suffering lad yelled. "Gods, let me go."

For a long time Ludar questioned the lad, never having to resort to further torture after severing the thumb. When he had extracted all the information he felt he could get, he pulled Dirk to his feet.

"Stand like a soldier, boy. Don't slump like a drunken fool."

Dirk did his best imitation of a guard at attention, holding his pain-wracked body as erect as he could, fearing further punishment. He fought to restrain sobs that lay just under the surface, cursing when a few tears rolled from his reddened eyes.

"What will you do now, little thief? A thief cannot steal without a thumb."

Mustering all his composure, he struggled to answer with dignity, no crying, no sobbing. "I will find work... sir."

"I know of no one who will hire a one-handed man," Ludar said. "But I do know one job you could do. Would you care for me to assist you? Make you better suited for this job?"

"Whatever you think best, Force Commander."

The sinister smile that formed on Ludar's face terrified Dirk. It frightened him more when he noticed the chilled expression of the guards, and the way they shook with fear. "Cut off his other thumb," Ludar ordered. "He will make a better beggar with no thumbs. People will pity him all the more."

One guard's mouth fell open, but before he could talk, if he had been inclined to, Ludar lashed out at him.

"Cut it off, or I'll remove both of yours."

Ludar's boots rang noisily on the floor but the heavy sound was drowned by the horrific screaming of Dirk as the guards held him down.

"Please?" he wailed. "I pray to the goddess herself, please don't do this? Haven't you any children? Any boys? Don't—"

One guard cried as he turned his head, holding the boy; the other begged the gods for forgiveness and prayed for mercy for Dirk. In between excruciatingly painful outcries from Dirk, the guards could hear the diabolic laughter of Ludar.

NOBLES, GUARDS, AND BEGGAR BOYS

Darstan let tired eyes wander as Ictar led them across leagues of terrain almost identical to what they had traversed for days. "This is getting old, Kender. I long for the mountains of Kamnor."

"It will change soon enough. Even the Great Plains don't go on forever."

One of Ictar's scouts rode in to report. "A vargel comes this way."

"Kella!" Darstan turned in his saddle. "Don't kill her!" he shouted to Ictar.

The First-Son of the Nyaruans stared at Darstan with a perplexed look in his eyes. "Kill her? Vargels are good omens."

As Kella loped in toward them, Darstan dismounted and rushed to greet her. "It's good to see you, girl." He leaned down and wrapped his arms around her. It felt better just to be near her again.

grassland of the Nyaruans

Two more days of traveling saw the number of men and horses diminish, dwindling to the size of two patrols. Ictar kept seven men with him, having sent a large force back the way they had come and the remainder north. The terrain had even changed somewhat, with gently rolling hills the predominant feature. They veered off to the east, following a large road that had been kept in good repair. Soon Darstan spied the fringes of a city the likes of which he had never seen. Made up of tents, it stretched for more than a league along a shallow valley bordering a river.

Takar stood up in his saddle. "City of Tents. This is where the goods from Khatara arrive. Make sure no one causes trouble."

~

The Sykoran patrol came to a halt in front of Lord Talanvar's mansion. While the gatekeeper watched, Ludar dismounted and approached the entrance to Talanvar's home. "Tell him I am here," Ludar ordered.

The gatekeeper raised his eyebrows. "I will inform my lord that you are here."

A strong breeze ripped the top of the hill, blowing Ludar's cloak wildly about his massive frame. He paced with his hands clasped behind him, his head darting about. "Did you inform your master that it is the force commander calling on him?" Ludar lurched so far forward he came close to pushing his face between the gate.

"I did, but Lord Talanvar is frequently occupied. He shall come soon though, I am certain."

"He had better," Ludar growled. "He had better."

Within a few moments Talanvar strutted to the front gate of his home, pride and nobility pronounced in his deportment. "What a marvelous occasion," Talanvar shouted from twenty paces away. "Force Commander Ludar, you are so generous to pay me a visit, unannounced though it may be."

The sarcastic implication of impropriety did not escape Ludar's notice though he didn't worry over protocol. "There has been an escape from the prison. I have reason to believe you know something of it."

Talanvar's eyebrows raised in mock indignation. "I would do no such thing. A conspirator to such a bold plan? I thank you for the compliment, Force Commander, but I have partaken of no such wondrous feat."

"Open the gate so that we may speak privately."

The gatekeeper started to speak but a wagging finger from Talanvar stayed his tongue. "Do not allow this contemptible man to upset you," Talanvar said. "He disdains all nobility and, I suspect, all men with the exception of himself. Open the gate. I will converse with the lout."

"As my lord wishes," he said, and let loose the latch that held the gates secure.

Talanvar pushed through the gate. "What is it you want, Force Commander?"

"There was a young beggar lad that delivered a message here yesterday."

Talanvar laughed. "There were no less than a dozen beggars at my gate yesterday."

Ludar spoke through gritted teeth. "This one's name was Dirk, and he carried a message from a thief. Why would a thief be sending messages to you, Talanvar?"

Talanvar never blinked. "I receive messages from many people. The story behind this one is not so strange. This thief once robbed one of my markets only to be apprehended by my personal guards. He came before me for judgment bearing a sad story of sickness heaped on top of poverty, though he displayed a sufficient amount of remorse to impress me. I forgave the man and set him free with no punishment. Until yesterday, I never heard from him. It seems that trouble has once again found him, but this time I could offer no assistance."

"I don't believe you, Talanvar."

"And I don't care, Ludar. Now if you are finished, I have business that I must attend to."

"I urge you to be careful. Even those of noble blood have been known to fall prey to accidents, especially while traveling at night."

Talanvar's attitude changed abruptly; his voice altered, adopting a raspy, coarse tone—like a file scraping wood, and his eyes betrayed a dangerous look. "Do you threaten me, Force Commander?"

Talanvar's green eyes met Ludar's glare for glare. "The city is in turmoil. The streets are dangerous, as you say. And considering the opinion of many I know, there is much ill feeling toward the guards. If I were the force commander, I would be careful myself. Very careful. I have known of occurrences in other cities where the leader of the guard was set upon by unhappy citizens. Why you, yourself, cannot forget that our own force commander died unexpectedly such a short while ago. It was his death that provided you with your job, was it not? And if memory serves me well, did not your previous promotion come after the untimely demise of yet another of your superiors?"

Talanvar leaned in close, coming face to face with the force commander. "Do not mistake me for a trusting superior with a large ego. And do not think me some weakling noble with more money than sense. If you wish to cross swords with me, force commander, we will do it on *my* terms. I shall put such a price on your head that your own mother would stand in line to slay you. I will have every thief, beggar, rat, and dog, watching you from every blind alley and darkened corner. And each one of them will be an assassin." Talanvar shook his head. "No, Force Commander, you'll not do well to cross swords with me. I am not quite the man that you think I am."

Ludar was stunned to silence. Never before had he encountered a noble with so much gall and courage. As Talanvar disappeared behind the gates to his house, Ludar called out a final warning. "Mark me well, Talanvar. I will uncover this mystery. And I'll come for you again."

Talanvar waited for Ludar to depart then turned to his gatekeeper and issued the command. "Find that messenger and bring him here. He needs a lesson in how to keep his tongue still."

The gatekeeper nodded. "Shall I wait for a replacement at the gate, My Lord?"

"Now," Talanvar said. "I will send someone else to tend the gate."

~

"I could have retired in just one year had I plied my trade here." A slight hint of envy tinged Wisp's voice.

Darstan laughed, but a look of concern soon crossed his face. "You haven't done anything, have you? We are Ictar's guests.

Wisp's look of indignation even brought a smile to Gregor's sour face. "You surprise me with your lack of trust, Darstan."

Darstan warmed his hands by the fire inside their tent; it had suddenly turned cold. "I was just concerned, Wisp. That's all. We have enough trouble without offending allies."

"This has only heightened my interest in reaching Khatara. A large number of these merchants hail from there. And if their security is any indication of how they monitor goods in Khatara, then the pickings should be rewarding."

"One thing I enjoy about traveling with you, thief," Gregor said. "You always make me laugh."

Takar entered to the three of them laughing. "I'm glad to find you in such good spirits, but we must leave."

"We just got here," Darstan said.

Takar glared at him. "And now we must leave. Pack up."

~

Ictar rode alongside of Takar as they prepared to depart. "We will delay them as long as possible, Takar, but I won't start a war."

Takar nodded his thanks, "Your friendship is valued, Ictar. Remember my warning; Ludar cannot be trusted and he is the one in charge of Sykor, at least the guard."

"Be careful, Takar. The Empty Lands hide many dangers."

Takar bid Ictar farewell and led the men across the bridge spanning the river Daureia into what was once called Sethia. The southern part was now known as the Empty Lands.

Darstan rode alongside of Takar. "What was that about, Sergeant? Ictar said he would delay someone. Who?"

"His men spotted Sykoran guards following our trail. An entire strike force, maybe more. That's why we hurry, Darstan. They'll not be able to pick up our tracks, being mixed in with all the Nyauran horses and the travelers, but they'll eventually determine where we're going; it won't take them long."

Darstan let his mount fall back until Wisp and Gregor caught up to him. "Takar said there's an entire strike force behind us. And we have the Empty Lands in front. Things couldn't get much worse."

"Just stay alert, Darstan," Gregor warned. "They say the Empty Lands are rife with the minions of the Evil One."

The wooden bridge groaned under the weight of so many horses, creaking loud protests to the excessive burden. "I only thought they couldn't get worse."

~

The two guards escorted Dirk out of Ludar's chamber room. He sobbed uncontrollably and his hands yet bled; the rags they had wrapped around them were soaked red. Twice he collapsed, then one of the guards picked him up and carried him.

"What are you doing, Kurt? Let the boy go."

Kurt turned to face his fellow guard. "Look what we've done to this lad. I'm through with it. I'll not see him suffer any more." Kurt turned about once more to finish carrying him out.

"If Ludar sees us helping him we're liable to get the same," his companion shouted and yanked at Kurt's arm.

Dirk fell from his arms, crying-out when he hit the floor. Kurt drew his knife and rammed it deep into his partner's stomach. "I've done enough for Ludar," he swore. "Fact is, I've done far too much." He replaced the knife in its sheath and reached down for Dirk again. A tear had formed in the corner of his eye. "I'm sorry, lad. I know sorry won't mean nothin' to you now. But sorry I am, and I'll do what I can to take care of you."

Kurt hurried to get him out and into the streets of Sykor. "Have you any place to go to?"

Dirk shook his head.

"None?" Kurt said. "Then you don't have a home?" Kurt wiped a tear from his eye. "That's all right, boy. You can come home with me. But we'll need to leave the city fast. Ludar will soon be after me."

They stayed at Kurt's house that night. Dirk tried eating but it all came back up in moments. Kurt encouraged the lad to drink some wine. It eased some of the pain, allowing him to sleep. In the morning he was hungry enough to eat without becoming sick. "We must go quickly, boy," Kurt said. "I feel Ludar will not be long in coming."

Dirk gulped down the remainder of the meal. Kurt felt the anguish all over again as he watched him try and don his cap. The lad had insisted on retrieving his cap even with both thumbs cut off. Seeing that it was so important to him, Kurt carried it for him. Now he watched in anguish as Dirk pitifully tried to tug it down over his forehead using only his fingers.

Kurt had changed the bandages, dressing the wound the best he could with clean cloth and a salve he heard about from a healer woman. Still, the lad looked a pitiful sight. His hands appeared more like stubs than fingers, wrapped as they were. "Come on, lad. We'll go and find you a place to stay with someone who can care for you." Kurt led him out the door and onto the streets of Sykor.

They had not been gone for long, when a Sykoran patrol of six men spotted them.

"Halt, Kurt."

He didn't bother to turn to see who it was. "Run, boy! Find shelter. I'll hold them off." Kurt pulled three coppers from his pocket and placed them in a purse that he handed to Dirk. This is all I have. Go quickly."

Tears ran freely from Kurt's eyes now. "I'm sorry, lad," he said and rushed to challenge the guards.

Dirk ran for what seemed like leagues. He still cried occasionally, and the pain seemed never-ending, but at least he was alive—more than he could have hoped for after yesterday. It had proved much more difficult than he imagined getting accustomed to doing things without thumbs but he was learning fast. "I'll learn," he swore. "And I'll get that black-hearted Ludar if I have to wait twenty years."

A voice came from the shadows of a nearby building. "You may not have to wait so long as that, young friend."

It startled Dirk. His first reaction was to take flight.

"Don't run, lad. I have come from Lord Talanvar."

Dirk recognized the voice of the gatekeeper even before the name of the lord. He stopped and turned to see him, relieved that it was not the guard.

The gatekeeper stared at his mangled hands for a moment before he spoke. "Come with me, lad. We will go see my master. He will feed and protect you."

~

"And you say Ludar did this to you, just to learn what message you delivered to my house?" Talanvar paced the floor like a cat caught from the wild.

Dirk cried, not from anything Talanvar did, simply reliving the memories of his torture in Ludar's chambers. "I didn't tell him nothin', Lord. Didn't tell him nothin', till he cut off my thumb. Then... then, I told him all. I tried not to but I couldn't help it." Dirk sobbed. "Then, after he swore he'd let me go... he cut off my other thumb. I swear, I'm gonna get him good someday."

"Dirk, are you willing to toil hard for your day's bread? If so, I may find work for you."

A scowl had formed on Dirk's face thinking about Ludar; Talanvar's offer caused it to vanish. "What work can I do?" He held up his hands as proof.

Talanvar remained pensive a moment then addressed the gatekeeper. "Birol, you have a new assignment. You are to instruct young Dirk in everything that is proper to become a master gatekeeper."

"But there are no positions for the lad."

"He will replace you, Birol. Your duty will be to teach him well. I will have other things for you to do. Now, I will."

Birol nodded. "Yes, My Lord."

Talanvar looked once again to Dirk. "Lad, can you become a gatekeeper? Not just someone to watch the gate, mind you, but an honorable and respected member of my household. You'll be required to learn your speech so that you are able to address nobles without offending them, and you must be able to maintain a fair disposition, as there will be people who will rile you. Well, lad?"

Dirk stared at Talanvar as if Ludar had cut out his tongue too. No one had ever treated him so well. "My Lord," he said through tear-stained eyes. "I am your servant forever. Thank you."

Talanvar smiled at him and tousled his scruffy hair. "You will do fine, lad. I am certain that Birol will transform you into the finest master gatekeeper ever."

As Talanvar turned to Birol, he replaced his smile with a scornful sneer. "Now, Birol. It is time we prepared. Send messages to all my contacts—all of them. And have meetings arranged before the next seventh day."

As Birol departed, Talanvar spoke to Dirk. "Do not fret, lad, the force commander has committed a grievous error. He has begun a war that he cannot win. To be effective, Dirk, the successful force commander must know everything about his opposition. And Ludar knows nothing of me. He does not even know who I am."

A slightly sinister laugh escaped Talanvar's lips and for the first time in days Dirk had something to laugh about. He couldn't wait to plunge a knife into Ludar's heart.

IAZZO

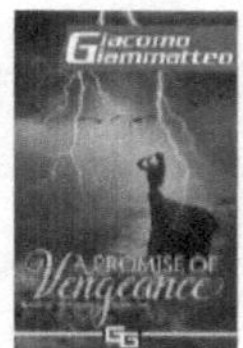

$\mathcal{I}$azzo crouched behind a desert willow riddled with demon claws, thorns pricking his arms drawing droplets of blood. Instinct forced a smile at the sweet coppery smell. The pain proved to be more of an inconvenience than anything.

He recalled times when he visited the Jimora district on his home world of Nagasha, so crowded, so loud and noxious. How many times had the people brushed against him, lesions on their skin and God knows what in their hair. The thorns were far more agreeable.

He focused on a cottonwood less than ten paces away, giving thanks that its tall canopy spread enough shade to cover his spot.

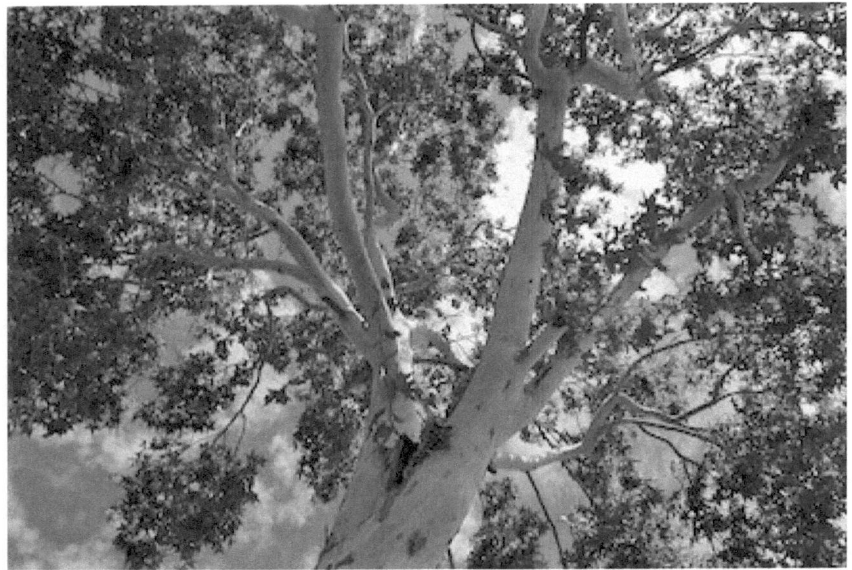

cottonwood

He avoided the sun at all costs, not wanting his soft skin to darken or lose its suppleness. The lesser heat of the morning passed, giving way to temperatures that could cook a man if standing still long enough, yet, despite it all, Iazzo remained still, silent. During the Wars of Light, he had insinuated himself into an enemy camp and tucked between rocks and shrub that a serpent would abandon. He hadn't moved for two days, using sheer willpower to overcome the cramps and fatigue, and a contrivance he designed and built to hold water so he could sip from it without stirring.

Movement behind the cottonwood caught his eye. Long ears, strong hind legs, a black-striped tail. *Yes, I see you, my sweet.* Iazzo fired a narrow stream of Fire at the rabbit, hitting the mark on its back leg. It screamed, piercing the solitude of the afternoon, then tried to escape. Iazzo jumped to his feet and pursued, racing hard with short, quick strides. Even on three legs, the rabbit could elude him if he gave it enough lead.

After running a short distance, Iazzo scooped the creature up in his hands, its back leg thrashing about as it cried. The fur was soft and warm. He grabbed the good back foot and twisted, snapping the bone. Another shriek tore the silence of the desert. Iazzo smiled then pressed his finger into its eye while he squeezed its face with his other hand to forestall any bites. Blood oozed from the socket. The screams grew louder and longer, if less frequent. It gasped for breath.

A flash of light hit the corner of his left eye and caused him to flinch. He turned, but nothing was there. Further examination brought no clues, until... Iazzo dropped the rabbit, a dull thud sounding as it hit a rock at his feet. He stared, eyes wide, body limp, then rushed toward the shield with arms outstretched. He almost cried for joy when his hand went through the shield, but then he came to a jarring stop as if he had hit a wall. Many times he tried with no more success. *I better report this.* He focused his mind on a Shift point then vanished, reappearing in the Sethian Palace.

*ukaan's chambers were always cold. Dark and cold. And fear claimed a permanent base, lurking in corners, living in the floor and walls and columns. Vaporous clouds hovered at varying heights, some clinging to marble pillars, others floating like silent guards.

What is it, Iazzo?

Iazzo bowed until he felt the blood rush to his head. A smile dissected his face as he rose. "I have found a spot, Great Lord. My hand went through the shield."

The darkness surrounding Lukaan throbbed, pulsing with power. His eyes filled with fire.

Take me there. I will summon the others.

A rift opened near the eastern border with Khatara. Lukaan and Iazzo stepped through, a tendril of mist from Lukaan's chambers following behind. Soon rifts opened around them, admitting Melissara and Tirzinitzia, then Ghruehne. Sendra and Zorn came last.

"How did you do it?" Tirzinitzia asked, almost before her feet touched ground.

"Have you tried again?" This from Melissara.

Ghruehne poked and prodded at the shield. "I don't believe you. Nothing has changed that I can see."

"It was right here," Iazzo said, pointing to the spot where it happened.

Ghruehne and Zorn blasted away with Fire and Lightning, though the shield seemed to absorb it.

"What did you see, Iazzo? What made you put your hand through to begin with?" Tirzinitzia asked.

A slight curl of his lip was as far as Iazzo got before Lukaan's command struck him.

Answer her.

He bowed to Lukaan then faced Tirzinitzia. "I saw the shield in layers. I turned to see a bright light and saw layers in the shield. That's when I tried to get through."

She nodded then approached Lukaan, head bowed. The fiery suns that had been burned in her cheeks glowed in the afternoon sun. "I have an idea, Great Lord."

A slight nod of his head was all Tirzinitzia needed.

"Close your eyes, Iazzo, then walk toward the shield. Don't—"

"What lunacy is this? If we—"

Lukaan's glare cowed Ghruehne. *Tirzinitzia has insights you can only dream about, Ghruehne. One more interruption and you will get another scar to match the one you have.*

If Lukaan hadn't stopped Ghruehne, Tirzinitzia's glare would have, and she kept it focused on Ghruehne as she addressed Iazzo. "As I was saying, don't do anything but walk. Don't stop no matter what happens."

Iazzo cleared his mind, focused, then closed his eyes and moved ahead. Each step was careful, calculated. Twice he thought he had gone far enough to be through the shield, heart fluttering, a slight trembling in his limbs.

The hair on his arms and neck bristled, just before violent shuddering swept through his body. Iazzo felt as if he should stop, but fear of Lukaan gave him courage. Skin prickled. He pulled his arms in tight against his body. Iazzo clenched his teeth. It felt as if something tried to force its way under his skin. A sharp intake of breath brought musty air. Damp air. Just as he set his mind to wonder about that, he heard the shouts behind him.

"He's through!"

"The shield is gone!"

Iazzo turned and opened his eyes, afraid to believe he was free, though he could sense it with every breath, every feeling. Even the air felt different.

Ghruehne and Zorn rushed the shield but they were thwarted as always.

Lukaan moved forward, touched the shield. *What can you tell me, Tirzinitzia?*

"Through my studies I concluded that the shield was constructed based on the order of strength, built as a barrier only to powers. This was easily proven by the fact that mortals may come and go as they please; only we were imprisoned.

"The answer didn't come to me, however, until Melissara and I found a mortal with just a hint of powers. It was a woman from Nyauran. She was weak, but she did have powers. When we released her, she stepped through the shield like any other mortal. Sometime later, another mortal with stronger abilities could not."

"Then how can Iazzo get out and we can't?" Ghruehne asked.

"The shield must be faltering. Iazzo is the weakest of us. If it continues to deteriorate, it won't be long before the next of us can leave. Probably you, Zorn. Unfortunately, Great Lord, if this theory is correct you will be the last to go free."

Then it shall be soon. The Awakening will soon be here.

Careful not to step back through the shield, Iazzo addressed Lukaan. He struggled not to smile, not wanting to risk the appearance of gloating. "What would you have me do, Lord?"

I want the boy.

Iazzo bowed low. "Yes, Lord... But suppose—"

Suppose what?

He backed up and bowed lower still. "How will I find him? And suppose Mikkellana is with him?"

Are you so afraid of Mikkellana? You would be wiser to fear me.

Lukaan turned to Zorn. *Gather a small force of Sethians, Victas, and Wolfen. One thousand should do. Enough to crush the boy and his allies, but not so many as to stir the nations to arms against our cowardly friend.*

Melissara stepped forward. "Perhaps we should give the Slicer to Iazzo, the one we found in Kardel's ashes."

Lukaan sent the Slicer through the shield to Iazzo. *Use it well, Iazzo. If you return without the boy...*

INTO THE COVE

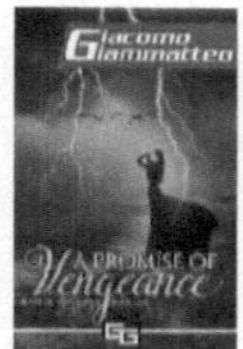

With half the sails down, and the remainder shredded and torn, the Sea Skate roared into the protection of the horseshoe-shaped cove, the might of the sea funneling it through the narrow opening. At first glance the cove appeared inviting—calm waters prevailed and steep walls of sheer rock sheltered it from the wind. Remnants of the storm hovered over the spot they had just passed though it remained outside the cove.

Odd. I've never seen a storm behave in such a way, Rahg thought.

Sennar issued commands to anyone able to work. "No sittin' on your thumbs, men. There are sails to repair and leaks to tar." Through it all, he stared back at the storm they had left behind as he steered the ship toward the port side of the isle.

cove with rocks

Rahg wondered about the decision as he looked around at cliffs, and he worried about where they might land. Sennar had them lower all sails, using oars to power the ship through the cove, but fortune wasn't smiling on them; the cliffs offered no point to disembark.

Tobias was squinting, as if he had been studying the situation intently. "There's no way to scale those rocks, even if there was a place to dock."

Sennar looked back to the entrance of the cove; the sea boiled with fever and the winds of the storm still brewed waves big enough to topple a ship—there was no going back.

"Looks to be a place to land over there," Tobias said, and pointed to a sandy spot with a beach.

"Look closer," Sennar said. "Nothing behind it but sheer cliffs."

beach area

"What'll we do, Captain?" a deckhand asked.

"We'll go 'round this cove again and find a way to scale these walls," Sennar said. "There's got to be a way to leave this cove."

The first mate issued the orders and the Sea Skate once again began the tedious journey around the cove, rolling on gentle waters in search of an escape route. By nightfall they had found no egress and the men grumbled openly, some even talked of trying to steer back through the Straits of Death.

"There are no rocks now. May be we could find another route out of here," one said.

Sennar would hear nothing of it. "I'm tellin' ya for all to hear. There's a way out of this cove and I aim to discover it. And I'll cut the throat of the first man who raises a voice against me."

The crew had come to believe Sennar had earned the name of "Old Crazy" justly. None of them had the desire to challenge his command. They muttered offhanded remarks and complained, but in the end they accepted his orders. Sennar knew their loyalty would be short-lived; he had better find a way out, and quickly.

The following day brought no relief, and by supper the men were showing fear. "Men filled with fear are the most dangerous," Rahg remembered Rhaven saying.

Just before the day gave way to darkness, Tobias spotted something unusual and called Sennar to investigate. "If you look closely, Sennar, the water appears to be a different shade in that one spot, right past where it breaks on the rocks."

"It's a cave," Sennar said, "And it just could be a way out of here." Sennar turned to the first mate. "Send three men. We need to know if it leads to dry ground."

cove with opening

Rahg paced the deck with Camissa, eager for the men to return, anxious about the news they would bring. Darkness soon settled on the cove, bringing silence with it. Most of the crew now paced the deck, or sat in groups gaming with dice, but even they were quiet.

The sound of splashing interrupted the calm, stirring seamen to their feet in a mad rush to the starboard side. Sennar rushed over and pushed Rahg aside, grabbing a lantern from one of the deckhands.

"Eduard, is that you? Have you found a way out, lad?"

Eduard paused, catching his breath while treading water. "It's a long cavern, Captain, but Marro says to tell you it's safe. He said to bring a full party and meet him at the entrance tomorrow morn."

Sennar's cackle bounced off the walls of the cove. "And you all thought old Sennar was crazy, did you? Well, I got us here, and now it seems like I got us out." Another round of laughter rolled across the ship. "Sleep well, men. We'll likely be dancin' with pretty maidens in the morn."

~

*S*ennar's bellow roused everyone for morning fare, and after breakfast he selected a crew of six to accompany Rhaven, Tobias, Camissa, and Rahg. Camissa insisted on taking Aentarra along with them, even in her unconscious form.

"We shouldn't take her," Tobias said.

"The least we can do is to try and find someone to heal her," Camissa said.

Sennar consented, though it was apparent he didn't care for the idea, and his men seemed to like it even less.

"It'll take a full breath to get through," Eduard said, "so fill your lungs before you go under." Eduard went first, followed by Camissa and Tobias; Rahg and Rhaven brought Aentarra through. Rahg worried that they might drown Aentarra, but Camissa insisted that whatever means she had used to shield herself would keep the water out.

Rhaven grabbed hold of Aentarra's arm. "Ready, Rahg?"

He nodded and took her other arm, then they filled their lungs and dived. Eduard and Camissa went under an arched opening, with Tobias close behind. Sennar and the other crewmen trailed. Rahg paddled hard with his left hand and kicked to generate speed, but dragging Aentarra proved to be more difficult than he imagined; his lungs were aching already. His heart beat furiously and panic set in. They hadn't even gone under the arch yet.

Rahg let go of Aentarra and began to use both hands, then caught hold of himself. Using all the willpower he could muster, he reached back, took Aentarra's arm and regained his form and rhythm.

Though it seemed like forever, within heartbeats after going under the arch, they surfaced. Rahg breathed deeply. Nothing had felt so good as that first taste of air. Several more times he stretched his lungs as they made their way to land. "I thought I'd drown," he said, and looked at Rhaven.

"You did well, boy."

Rahg smiled, then looked about the cavern. It was smaller than he expected—perhaps two spans at the widest, and it seemed no more in length. At the end of the cave a series of boulders formed a natural set of steps which led to a path leading inland. As Rahg studied it, he heard Marro's voice from further down the trail.

"We've found a way out, Captain."

Sennar's smile lit his eyes and his good leg twitched. The message was received with a round of cheering and exultation. "Where does it go, lad? What have ya seen?"

"Leads to the bottom of a big hole, Captain. Looks like a mountain turned inside out."

"Cyclone Stairs," Tobias said. "That's what the legends call it." All the men looked first to Tobias and then to Sennar.

Sennar was quick to respond. "Doesn't mean anythin', men. Just a name in a legend, nothin' else." The crew nodded in agreement. "No need to waste any time," Sennar said, and off he went, leading the way down the narrow path.

~

*I*t seemed as if they traveled half the morning through the cave. At times it became so narrow Rahg had to turn sideways to squeeze through. At one of the spots, Minnoso, who was nearly as round as he was tall, became stuck and had to be pried loose and sent back.

"Go tell the men what we're doin', Minnoso. Tell 'em to anchor the ship and follow us, but you'll need to bring mallet and chisel to carve an opening for yourself." Rahg and the rest of the crew laughed, even Minnoso found it humorous.

"How much longer?" Rahg called out to Marro, who shared the lead with Sennar.

"Few hundred paces, perhaps less. The path opens wide a short distance ahead. It's soon after that."

Rahg's heart quickened. Soon they would be exploring a new land, and if Shera Kevon had been right, it was a land only heard of in legends—Entiria.

After the trail widened, light burst into the cave. Rahg rushed to reach the front, knowing the exit couldn't be far.

*T*hey emerged in the bottom of a depression that reached as deep as some of Kamnor's mountains. Marro hadn't exaggerated when he called it a mountain turned inside out. The pit easily measured fifty spans across in each direction, and a trail had been carved into the sides of the walls, spiraling toward the top around the circumference of the inside of the pit. It wouldn't be an easy journey.

Rhaven assumed the lead position, with Tobias and Rahg behind him. Sennar's men came next, while the rear consisted of Camissa and the men carrying Aentarra.

Night had fallen by the time they reached the top and climbed onto level ground. Rhaven found a site to make camp in an enclave of large boulders, and before long Rahg gathered enough wood for a fire. After a strenuous day of climbing, the evening proved restful. Sennar and some of the others told stories of the sea; they proved to be entertaining even though Rahg assumed most of them to be exaggerated. As he lay down preparing for sleep, he stared up at the two moons, Ranal and Ranalla. They were both shining bright. *A good omen*, he thought, and smiled.

~

Rahg began to rise, then heard Rhaven's calm voice call for them to be on alert.

"Keep your weapons sheathed," he said.

The warning alone was enough to make Rahg want to draw his sword. Sennar rose immediately and, in hushed tones, he ordered his men to follow Rhaven's commands.

"We're not at sea now, lads, and while on land I'll cede my position to him."

Camissa rolled over and pulled the light blanket off of her, careful not to make a sudden move. Her eyes flickered from one hillside to another, wondering what the danger could be, glancing about while strolling toward the fire where Tobias cooked the morning meal.

Rhaven stood in the recesses of two large boulders, whittling on a stick. "Did you see someone, Rhaven, or just signs?" Rahg's voice was a whisper.

"You've ridden with me long enough to know."

Rahg felt foolish. "How many were there?"

"Still are," Rhaven said, letting his eyes point out their location to the north, and more to the east.

Rahg didn't look right away, but when he did he saw nothing but rocks.

Rhaven stopped carving on the stick, slipping his knife back into its sheath. "They're there. Look back to the north."

Rahg turned to see a band of men emerging from behind the shelter of the rocky cliffs where the narrow trail turned upward.

"Who are they?" Camissa asked.

"Just be careful," Rahg said, and drew his blade, stepping in front of her.

"Sheath the sword!"

Rhaven's harsh tone struck Rahg, and he once again looked to the strangers descending toward them. He obeyed, though he kept his hand close to the hilt of his sword and his eyes fixed upon the strangers.

Almost all of them stood as tall as Rhaven, and some a full hand taller. They numbered about twenty and, to a man, were clad in loose-fitting brown clothing that blended well with the surroundings. Their skin was dark, and they carried no weapons.

Suddenly they stopped. The one Rahg presumed to be the leader continued toward them alone, hands outstretched, palms facing upward. When Rhaven signaled in return, the leader of the group bowed his head to them. As he raised it again, his intense gaze met Rahg's.

His hair was cropped as close as moss on a rock, and his face was clean shaven and gaunt. The man's almond-shaped eyes seemed to peer right through Rahg.

Camissa leaned close to Rahg. "I can sense their feelings. They mean no harm. Perhaps they have a healer who can help Aentarra."

"I'm not concerned with Aentarra," Rahg said, "Or did you forget that she killed those men?"

Camissa spun Rahg around. "I didn't forget, but you seem to have forgotten that it was Aentarra who saved us and got us through the storm."

"You agree with her?" He shook his head, mumbling while he turned away, "... all alike."

Camissa seized him again, and this time she tugged him back violently. "Who is all alike? Who are you comparing me to now?"

"Nothing, Camissa."

"No! You said it. Tell me what you meant."

Rahg sighed. "I didn't mean you. I meant the immortals." He could see she was still fuming, but just then the leader of the Entirians spoke, stunning Rahg.

"They speak the Old Tongue," Camissa said.

When no one responded, the Entirian spoke to them in their own language. "You are well come to the land of Entiria. We offer food, shelter, and friendship."

Camissa placed a warm hand on Rahg's shoulder, offering comfort for the apprehension apparent in him. "This is what we came for, Rahg. The shera said the Entirians could help you. They may be the only ones with the answers we seek."

Rahg tensed. "It's those answers I'm afraid of, Camissa."

The Entirian suggested they follow him, so the men broke camp and packed the few goods they had brought along. Rahg and Camissa fell in behind Tobias and Rhaven as they ascended the narrow trail twisting through the rocky terrain. It reminded Rahg of the mountains in Kamnor. "Their village must be near, Camissa. I see no horses or pack animals and I don't think they'd have walked very far on foot. Not in this terrain."

Sennar squeezed in between Rahg and Camissa. "I don't trust 'em," he muttered through a twisted mouth.

"Why?" Camissa asked.

"I don't trust people that talk so softly. If they can't speak up, they must have somethin' to hide."

Camissa laughed. "Trust me, Captain Sennar, these are good people."

It had been early morning when they began what Rahg imagined would be a short journey; now supper ran long overdue and night threatened to drape them in darkness.

After achieving the summit, Rahg smelled cooking, though it still seemed to be a good distance away. They ate a late dinner, slept, and began again in the morning. By noon they were cresting the mountain the Entirians said led to their home. Rahg stood numb, and speechless. Rising from the center of a vast plain was an enormous plateau; rising from it was a city unsurpassed in beauty or size. "I've never seen the likes of it," Rahg muttered. "Never imagined...."

He struggled to take in a thousand sights, but his eyes, and his attention, were repeatedly drawn to the center of the city; inevitably all focused their gaze there—to the center of Entirian civilization—the center of their very life.

Rahg lost his voice, even his breath. Towering above even the tallest buildings stood an obelisk of immense proportions, its spire piercing the sky. It looked like black granite, but he could tell it wasn't. It shone like glass. Even the rays of the sun seemed drawn to it.

The leader of the Entirians bowed. "You are well come to our village. It is called Sunnara—City of the Sun."

Rahg laughed. "That is a very big village."

The leader bowed again. "We shall arrive soon. I will send a runner to alert them."

They arrived at the city in a parade down the center street; it was wide and straight, providing an appearance of order and organization. The buildings dwarfed any in Pomanda or Sykor.

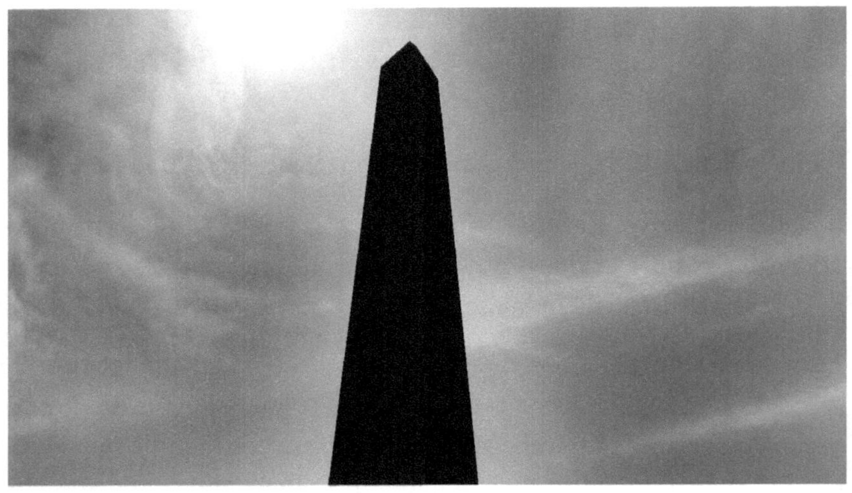

black obelisk

Rahg stopped, staring in awe at the obelisk, a monolith that loomed over everything. All streets either led to the square surrounding the obelisk or to the two main streets that intersected it. In more than name it was the center of attention; everything the Entirians did had something to do with the obelisk.

Joyous citizens lined the street to make them feel welcome, as if they were a victorious army returning home.

Although it seemed impossible, the closer they got to the mysterious black tower, the larger it seemed. The tower was surrounded by huge, rectangular buildings constructed of a similar material, though it was different. He could tell even from afar.

The buildings resembled palaces, with massive columns and a vast array of statues adorning the perimeter of a flat roof. The street led to a square and from the square rose a series of steps carved from white stone. Rahg was close enough now to count; there were twenty-one steps to reach the first level of the palace. The others appeared to be identical.

"What are those buildings?" Rahg asked the leader of the Entirians. He received no response. In fact, ever since they had entered the boundaries of the city the Entirians had been silent.

They entered the first of the palace-like structures, each being assigned a room that a king would envy. The same white stone that adorned the steps tiled every floor, and works of art that would have shamed some of the masters graced each wall. Baskets of fruit lay upon a table beside an immense bed, and velvet curtains draped stained-glass windows that stretched from floor to ceiling. As Rahg marveled at the magnificence of the surroundings, a servant arrived bearing a silver tray filled with wine and cheese. Soon after, a beautiful woman entered and instructed Rahg to follow her.

She led him to a room containing a large tub filled with hot, scented water where another servant stood ready to bathe him. He refused, at first, but upon their insistence, he accepted the offering, nearly falling asleep in the relaxing waters while she washed him and massaged his sore body. The bath left him with a sense of pleasure that he hadn't felt in a long time. It also left him tired. The servant informed Rahg that there was ample time for him to rest prior to supper, so rest he did, falling fast asleep on the most comfortable bed he had ever slept in.

When Rahg awoke, his body was charged with an abundance of energy. The only thing keeping him from bounding through the corridors was the lack of knowledge regarding their destination, and he noticed his escort seemed reluctant to provide him with that information. Regardless, Rahg was happy. On the way to the dining hall he met Camissa and told her of his experiences, detailing everything save the servant girl and the bath.

Camissa smiled throughout his tale but when he had finished she stared at him with a questioning glance. "Have you forgotten to tell me something, Rahg?"

Rahg sensed trouble brewing but he couldn't bring himself to tell her about the servant girl. "Oh, yes, and there was the bath. I suppose you had the same, a servant who gave a bath."

"Oh, yes, I had a bath as well," Camissa said. "Though, my servant was not a young girl, but a handsome young man." Camissa increased her pace to move slightly ahead of Rahg.

"A man!" Rahg shouted, and ran to catch up to her.

"Shush! Some guests may yet be resting."

"You allowed a man to bathe you?"

Camissa turned to face him, but slowly. "And you, Rahgnar Fal-Thera, allowed a woman to bathe you?" She sounded like a princess who had been called a commoner, just the kind of indignation she had hoped for in her voice. Rahg fell silent.

Halfway through dinner one of the Entirians approached Rahg. "We will begin tomorrow, early in the morning."

"Begin what?"

"Begin the questioning. Long have we waited your arrival, but I fear there is little time left. We must begin at once."

"What do you mean, you have waited for me? For what? Begin what?"

Camissa's eyes welled with tears. She knew it was coming soon though she had hoped it would wait until at least the end of the night. Rahg had been enjoying himself so much. *Couldn't they have waited until morning.*

Rahg gulped the last of the wine from his cup, excusing himself. "I'm going to bed," he said.

As he dressed for bed a noise from the next room alerted him. It was where they kept Aentarra. He opened the doors slowly, apprehension about what he might find helped contain his excitement. Lamps lit the interior of her room, illuminating the area around her bed. She was alive! Moving, waking. "By the gods!" he swore, "You healed yourself." Rahg's own exhilaration proved the impetus for his lack of caution as he raced to her side. "My Lady," he called in a consoling manner. "Are you all right?"

Aentarra searched Rahg's face for recognition; she rose abruptly, in a panic. "Where am I?"

"In Entiria, My Lady."

"Entiria! How long have I been unconscious?"

"I don't know, My—"

Aentarra seized him and shook. "How long? I must know exactly how long." Aentarra's eyes glowed.

Rahg thought he might die at any moment. "Four days."

"Four days!" Aentarra screamed curses Rahg had never heard, in languages he had not known existed. "Four days. They could all be out by now." Barely had she finished her last statement than she Shifted, vanishing before his eyes.

Rahg was left to stare at an empty bed, and wonder. *What is she so concerned about? Who might get out?* Suddenly it struck him.

By all the gods, please don't let it be them. She can't mean them.

THE HUNT BEGINS

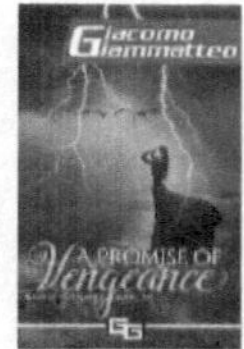

In a crevice along a narrow trail close to the Sethian border, the air shimmered, then glowed, revealing the form of Aentarra. This was the safest place she could imagine to Shift to—one of only two oases in Sethia—and under the circumstances Aentarra took no risks. Ordinarily she held no reservations about where she appeared when traveling to Sethia; today, she approached uneasily.

During the time she lay unconscious the shield had weakened. If any of the Banished Ones happened to test it, they may have escaped. Aentarra came to verify her suspicions and to repair any damage.

She moved toward the shield, tense and battle-ready, casting a wary eye to ensure no trap awaited; caution ruled this day. Slowly, she extended her hand until it almost touched the shield. A curse rang through the steep mountain pass. "By the Blood! One has escaped." She focused on priorities. *The shield. Must strengthen the shield first.*

Aentarra once again moved her hands toward the shield, letting her fingertips, just the tips, touch the outer layer. An eerie glow emanated from her and seemed to be absorbed into the air itself. Aentarra tensed, then quavered, and the glow grew brighter. At length she rested, removing her hand from the shield.

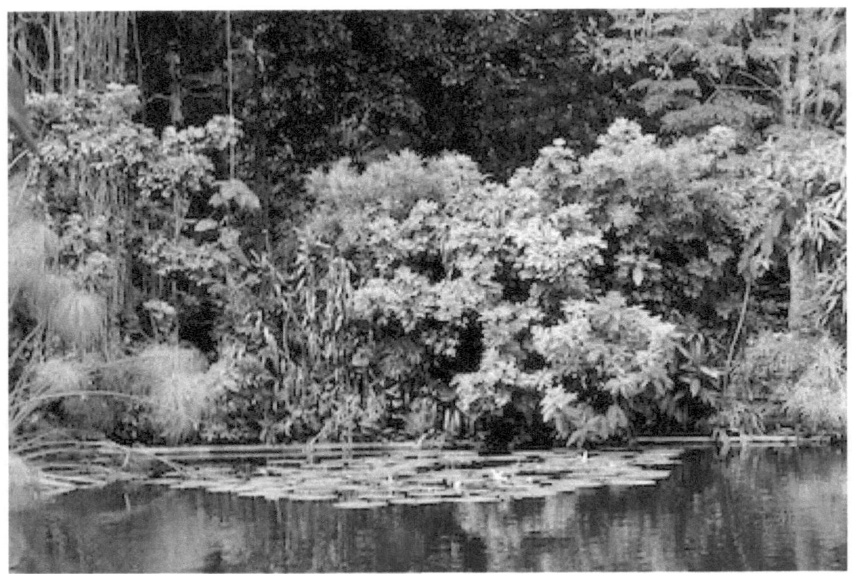

oasis with trees

Where was Mikkellana when she needed her? Only Mikkellana knew the secrets of the shield. Aentarra stood, brushing her hands on the gown as if they had been soiled. *I wonder which one it is. Probably Iazzo. Yes, unless something drastic has changed, it would be Iazzo that escaped.*

That presented unique problems though, and she no longer had the luxury of waiting. No longer able to work on her timetable. *The lad must be taught. Prepared quickly.* No sooner had she concluded the last thought, then Aentarra Shifted.

~

*A*wake and dressed when the Entirians arrived, Rahg took a cup of khaffe then followed them down the corridor. "Where are we going?"

"To the temple," a guard said, "the shera awaits us."

The walked for a while down the hall, across a promenade, up a wide span of marble steps, then through large bronze doors with intricate carvings on them.

The guards stopped at the doors. "Only those invited are permitted access to the sacred temple."

The chamber was huge, and an eerie light from the glow of a thousand candles filled the emptiness by reflecting off of the strange black glass. Three Entirian priests stood in the center of the room—exactly in the middle of three circular designs that were part of the floor.

Rahg made his way across the chamber, heels clicking noisily as his boots met the cold stone. The priest in the center wore a long black robe, while the others wore red, but all of them were long and dusted the floor with every movement. Like all Entirians their hair was cut close to the head, and like all Entirians they were thin. They bowed in unison when Rahg got near. Rahg returned the gesture, mimicking their own graceful stoop.

He decided to take an aggressive approach. "I am Rahgnar Fal-Thera. What is it you wish of me?" If Rahg had hoped to make an impression on them or catch them unaware, he had erred in judgment; the two priests let only a slight twitch show. The shera even less.

Rahg waited in silence. It was the shera who spoke, his voice as soft as any of the Entirians. "We are acutely aware of who you are. Please sit, we have many questions."

The stone felt cold, uncomfortable, not accommodating for a long session. No sooner had Rahg worked into position than the shera began.

"We would like to examine the letter."

Stunned, Rahg could only stare from one priest to the other. "Who told you of the letter?"

"Is that of consequence?"

Rahg bristled, but what did it matter who told them. They would need to see it sooner or later. He reached into his shirt and retrieved the scroll, just as it had been delivered to him. Rahg's hand quavered as he gave it to the shera.

The shera smiled. "Do not be afraid. We are friends."

Something in his words comforted Rahg. Perhaps it was his soft voice, or his gentle mannerisms. Whatever it was, Rahg felt more relaxed. He even managed a smile. "I'm afraid, Shera. Afraid to discover the meaning of this letter."

The priest to the right of the shera suppressed a laugh; even the shera smiled. "You are not alone. All of Entiria has awaited your coming."

Rahg's eyes went wide but he remained silent to allow the shera to continue. "For countless generations we have studied the prophecy. Each son of each father certain that the time would come during their lifespan. We, too, have lost much sleep. But now the time has finally come. You are here."

"But... how..."

The shera held his hand up. "Allow me to read the letter. We will talk later." The shera read the letter, then reread the letter. Each of the priests also read it twice, careful to examine each phrase, each word, for hidden meanings. When they were done they talked, each asking numerous questions and poring over the answers in excruciating detail. Rahg's fear had given way to excitement. They worked straight past the midday meal, even well past supper before they had concluded. The shera finally stood.

"We must nourish ourselves, Rahg. We shall meet again tomorrow."

Rahg agreed to arrive early then bade them farewell. It wasn't until he had walked a long way that he realized how hungry he was.

∾

"*I* haven't seen him all day," Camissa said to Rhaven. "Where do you think he is?"

Rhaven maintained his quick pace down the long corridor, forcing Camissa to adjust her own to a near run simply to keep up. "He's with the priests," Rhaven said. "I imagine they'll question him for days— knowing priests."

Camissa was about to speak when, without warning, Rhaven spun about. He released his hold on the blade when he identified one of the Entirians as the leader who had led them to the city. Another stood with him, and Rhaven assumed him to be of some importance for even though he dressed plainly, a tiara studded with diamonds adorned his head, and emerald rings decorated each finger.

The newcomer bowed, then spoke in the soft voice that so unnerved old Sennar. "There are many questions that we must ask," he explained, "but first allow me to honor you as our guest. I am J'en Kar, Keeper of the Keys, Guardian of the First Ones, and Shulan of Entiria." He bowed lower this time, as a servant would in obeisance to his master. J'en Kar held the position for a long moment before rising. "You are well come to our land."

Rhaven had grown adept at understanding the nuances of individual customs. He bowed low, even lower than J'en Kar, letting his gaze fall to the floor below. He held it for slightly longer a period of time than J'en Kar. When Rhaven rose to face J'en Kar he found a smiling face. "We are pleased to receive your gratitude, Shulan Kar. I am called Rhaven."

The smile remained on J'en Kar's face. "You learn with expedience, my friend Rhaven. Now, I must seek answers."

Rhaven took a seat on the bench that J'en Kar indicated. Camissa joined him.

"Our shera has spent much time speaking with your friend. They are convinced he is the one that has been spoken of in the prophecies. For thousands of years have we waited, have we watched. And now he has come. It has been foretold."

J'en Kar sighed. "That is why I have come to you, his friends. Rahg refuses to accept his responsibility. He insists that events will proceed without him. Our shera is the one who is upset. He feels shame that he could not convince him to see the truth."

Camissa looked to Rhaven, then to Shulan Kar. "Why would you want him to accept responsibility? Isn't it the duty of the Messenger to free the Evil One? Why should he accept that?"

Shulan Kar remained silent a moment while he listened to a whispered comment from his assistant, then he smiled. "My friends, I suspect there has been a grave misunderstanding. Rahg is not the Messenger—he is the one prophesied to deliver us from the fate of the Messenger. He is the Fate Sealer. The destiny of the world will be decided by him. He is the only one who can stop the Messenger."

Camissa almost shouted with glee. "Please go on, Shulan Kar. Tell me all." The shulan ordered meals to be prepared and brought to them while he informed Camissa and Rhaven of everything he knew. Every bit of news seemed to light her face.

Shortly after darkness fell, they concluded their business and the shulan excused himself. Camissa wasted no time, heading off in the direction of Rahg's room.

~

*I*nside Rahg's chambers the air shimmered, bringing a glow that briefly lit the room. Aentarra appeared at the foot of the bed, staring at Rahg, his slumber undisturbed by her silent entrance.

Aentarra sighed, then whispered. "Alas, my dear boy, I can no longer afford you the privilege of remaining a lad. You must mature quickly now." She concentrated, and from deep inside Rahg's head a Slicer stirred for the first time in many years—a Slicer that growth had secreted long ago. As it struggled to break free, Aentarra sensed the battle and issued a command for the Slicer to emerge. With a final burst of energy it uprooted itself, launching free of Rahg's mind but tearing through flesh and bone as it hurtled out of his head.

~

*R*ahg screamed. He thought it was part of his dream, another nightmare. His head felt as if it were being torn apart from the inside. He screamed again. Violent thoughts poured into his mind. He wanted to kill someone—anyone. Jealousy entered. He pictured Camissa in someone else's embrace, gritting teeth at the image and already plotting the murder of the one she held. Then for the third time Rahg's cries broke the night air.

Aentarra watched it all, occasionally grimacing at Rahg's pain. She heard footsteps in the corridor—someone coming fast—and cloaked herself just as Camissa entered.

Camissa grabbed Rahg in her hands, holding him close to her breasts. "It will be all right. It's just another dream."

Rahg awoke but the pain lingered. Camissa gasped when she looked down at him—blood covered everything. His hands were soaked in blood, as were the bedsheets and pillows.

"Dreams don't make you bleed," Rahg said.

Camissa sat on the edge of Rahg's bed, her back turned while he dressed. "How does your head feel?"

"Awful. I don't remember ever having a headache this bad. It's far worse than the other times." Rahg moved slowly to lessen the throbbing.

"This is something else. There was blood everywhere, yet I saw no wound. Can't you remember anything else? Something had to cause that bleeding."

From outside came a rap on the chamber door. "If that's the Entirian guard tell him I'll not be going to see the shera today. Tell him why if you want."

Camissa responded to the knock, relaying Rahg's instructions. "He did not seem pleased." She reseated herself carefully so as not to disturb Rahg's fragile head.

Rahg frowned. "I expect the shera will come himself. But this is a discussion that concerns us all. Go get Rhaven and Tobias. Everyone should be present for this. We all have a say in it."

~

The shera did come and so did the two priests, arriving soon after Camissa returned with Tobias and Rhaven. The priests sat on the floor and Rahg offered a chair to Tobias, who plopped contentedly into the thick cushions. Camissa sat beside Rahg on the bed, gently massaging his throbbing head. Rahg sat silent, watching Rhaven pace the room like a hungry predator. The shera was the first to speak, quietly, as always. "We have come for your response. Many lives rest on your words."

Rahg stared at the shera. "The decision is not mine alone. I told you that yesterday."

"But it is," the shera argued. "Only you can decide what course you will take. And the world awaits your decision."

"Enough of that," Rahg shouted. He started to rise but the pain from his head seated him.

Tobias sat up in his chair. "Lad, you'd better tell us what's takin' place.

What decisions are they talkin' about and what do we have to do with any of it?"

Rahg felt their eyes focus on him. "They claim the prophecies have foretold my coming; they claim I am to—"

The shera stood up in a swift, fluid motion that succeeded in drawing attention to him. "Perhaps I should explain the prophecies. There is much to tell, and your friends should know all."

He spoke so softly that Rahg wondered if his voice had carried across the room, but a glance to Tobias and Rhaven told him that they had heard. Rahg nodded his consent. "Tell your tale, priest. I'll not be the one to interrupt."

The prophecy is one of the oldest. It is titled 'The Coming of the Messenger' and can be found in the 'Book of Legends'." The shera recited the prophecy from memory, clearly enunciating each word and pausing frequently to stare at Tobias and Rhaven.

'*A*nd the seed of the one who is, and is not, shall bring forth a message—a message of death.

And all who stand in fear of the one who is to be feared shall cry out to their gods.

And they shall beg to be remembered by the ones they have forsaken.

They shall beg for forgiveness and they shall once more pledge adulation and fealty to the Great Lords.

But they will not be forgiven, nor accepted, and Darkness shall shatter the Truth.'

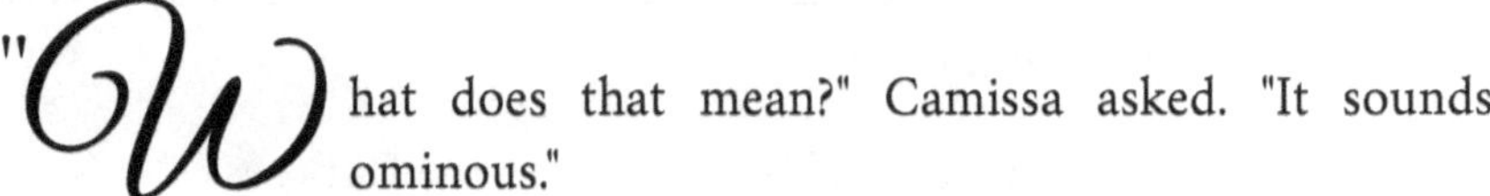

"*W*hat does that mean?" Camissa asked. "It sounds ominous."

The shera bowed to her. "It is. More dark and ominous than you can imagine. This prophecy foretells the Messenger setting the Evil One free. This is what will occur if Rahg refuses his destiny."

Rahg jumped from the bed, even the pounding in his head could not prevent him this time. "If the prophecy says the Messenger will set him free, then why am I besieged with this nonsense about stopping him. I don't even know who this Messenger is, or what I can do about it. It doesn't sound like it will matter anyway."

The sheer will of the shera's forceful stare quieted Rahg. He sat down once more. "There are more prophecies, Rahg. Some predict that evil prevails, while others foretell the crushing of the Evil One and his minions."

"Who is the Messenger?" Rahg asked, impatient as ever. "Do any of these prophecies name him, or her, or provide any information at all?"

"Only one," the shera explained, and proceeded to unravel an ancient scroll.

'*B*eware the Dark. Beware the Light.

They both embrace the Dark.

And the one who is the spawn of the Dark

Is the seed of the Light.

And he will embrace the Light.

And the Endless Sea shall bring forth a Messenger

A seeker of Truth. A bane of Darkness.

And he will come bearing the knowledge of 'Those Who Always Were' in the caverns of his mind.

And he shall seek the Truth, and the Light, and the Darkness.

'From the lands of 'Those Who Always Were', From the lands of mighty Arangar, he shall come.

And on the last day the Truth shall come to bear,

And the evils of the world will Awaken

And come forth to banish the Light, under the sign of the Light.

And Darkness will reign and blacken the world And the people will scream for their savior,

But death shall grip the world.

Only the Fate Sealer can stop the carnage.

Only the Fate Sealer can cease the doom.

Only 'He Who Is Foretold' may weave a prison about the Messenger and keep him in mighty Arangar.

For should he leave the shores of that ancient land, all the world is doomed.

'Beware the Light. Beware the Dark. Beware the coming of the Messenger.'

Once he finished, the shera gazed intently at each person in the room. "If the Messenger is not stopped, if he is allowed the freedom to see this part of the prophecy through—then all the world is doomed. The Evil One will be set loose upon the world and we all will succumb." The shera turned to face Rahg again. For the first time ever, his voice rose to a feverish pitch. "Rahg, you must destroy the Messenger. You must seek him in the lands of Arangar. And once he is identified you must destroy him. No hesitation. No doubts. It is something that must be done. No one save you can—"

While the shera talked, the air in the corridor outside rippled and shook. Aentarra made her appearance quietly, listening through the keyhole in the door. When the shera dispatched one of the priests to the library for more scrolls, Aentarra Cloaked, and stepped into the room unnoticed. In a fully Cloaked state, she could not be seen, nor heard; she could not be scented, or sensed; and if she stood on terrain subject to impressions, no tracks would remain from her feet. Fully Cloaked, she was immune to detection.

The conversation soon evolved into a debate, then erupted into an argument. Rahg argued vehemently. "Prophecies can be wrong, Shera. You said that yourself."

The shera nodded.

"So, how can one prophecy say that this Messenger will set the Evil One free and another say I will kill the Messenger? Which is right? Suppose there are other prophecies that are just as confusing. When I talked to Shera Kevon he assured me that I was the Messenger and all this time I've nearly gone mad worrying over it. Now I find out that I'm not the Messenger, but I'm supposed to kill him." Rahg cursed and threw his arms up in disgust. "All I plan on doing, Shera, is finding my brother, Darstan. He and I will go off somewhere and settle down. We'll find a place where no one will ever look for us. Besides, Lukaan has no wish to bother me."

An eerie glow brought more light to a room already illuminated by the bright rays of the sun. Aentarra's unexpected appearance startled them all.

"Aentarra!" Rahg shouted, shock registering on his face.

Aentarra glanced at each person. She had taken the precaution of shielding herself, though it would likely prove unnecessary. She strolled about the room like a shadow—cat until she stood in front of Rahg. Camissa held onto him with a fierce, protective grip.

"So, you don't believe that Lukaan wishes you any ill will?" Aentarra stared into Rahg's eyes. He remained silent, numbed by her presence so close to him. "Then perhaps you will find some clever response to give to Iazzo when he arrives."

"Iazzo? Who is Iazzo?"

Aentarra's laugh was taunting. "It's no wonder you aren't familiar with him. It almost escaped my memory, but he has lived in Sethia for centuries—trapped." Aentarra moved closer.

Rahg felt her sweet breath on his face and her presence, so close, made him feel strange, uncomfortable. He found he could not stare into her eyes.

"Iazzo is a Banished One. He has another name as well. Long ago, during the Wars of Light, he earned the name of 'Persecutor'—a designation that suited him well."

Rahg's face turned to horror. "He has escaped from Sethia, Rahg. Even now, he seeks your name in taverns across the lands. It won't be long before he finds you. And when he does—when, not if. How will you answer his call?"

Rahg sat on the bed, stupefied, but Aentarra had no intention of letting him off so easily.

"How will you defend yourself when Iazzo hurls fire at you?" Without warning, Aentarra released two, small balls of fire, though she kept them moving very slowly. Shock held him paralyzed until the first one struck him, burning his arm. The pain served as a reminder that she had dispatched two, and his reflexes took charge; he leaped to the side, barely avoiding the second attack.

Rhaven jumped, sword drawn but Aentarra spun a shield about him, holding him fast. Rahg scrambled to his feet in time to see two more assaults coming, these in the form of small lightning bolts. He started to draw his sword but realized he had no time, pivoting to narrowly miss being struck by the first one. His quick action was clumsy, however, and he found himself off balance, unable to avoid the second bolt. It caught him on the leg, near the upper thigh. Rahg howled. Aentarra smiled even as he cried out and fell toward the wall.

"Why are you doing this?"

Camissa cringed, focusing for an attack but Aentarra must have sensed her intent and issued a dangerous glare that stayed her hand.

Rahg sat crumpled against the wall with one arm limp and a leg burnt badly. Tobias rushed to lend him assistance, then a third attack came. It was a ball of white-hot flame, aimed straight for Tobias. Rahg screamed and leapt in front of Tobias into the path of the fireball, but when it struck—nothing. Nothing happened. It stopped dead, less than a hand's-length away from Rahg and Tobias. *I have woven a shield!*

"I wove a shield," he said aloud, all the while not even knowing what weaving a shield meant.

Aentarra moved to the center of the room. She released Rhaven from his protective shield. "Yes, Rahg, you have indeed woven a shield. And a good one, too, by the looks of it."

"But—"

Aentarra's interruption stifled Rahg. "The only way I could make you find your powers was to attack. When you wouldn't defend yourself, I attacked your friend. You'll have no trouble now in recalling the process for later use; however, I fear there is precious little time for practice. Iazzo will be coming soon, so you must learn quickly. You must develop strength by creating larger and more complex shields. Practice. Experiment. Stretch your limits and your imagination. The shield can be a wondrous weapon if your imagination is strong. Have your friends test your constructions; have them use sword, arrow and other weapons against it. The more danger and the more urgency there is to the test the quicker you will learn. Be warned though, when you feel the shield weaken it is time to be cautious, for it can disappear at once. It might not fade; it might simply cease to exist. It could withstand an attack and suddenly collapse. You will have ample warning if you learn to listen to it." Aentarra turned to the shera, her tone altered to one of command. "It has begun, priest-man. Warn your people and arm them. There will be a lot of blood. Iazzo will not come alone."

Aentarra stepped away, looking first to Rhaven. "That sword." She nodded toward Mikkellana's sword. "It has more qualities than you might suspect. If you haven't yet discovered, it will never lose its edge. What you might not know, however, is that it will deflect the powers of fire and lightning." Aentarra flung a small lightning bolt at Rhaven. He held his sword up and blocked it, causing it to disappear.

After glancing at Aentarra, he brought the blade up for a closer inspection, discovering no nicks, nor marks of any kind. "Then this was truly a gift of the gods."

Aentarra emitted a slight chuckle. "Not the gods, my friend, though I am working on that; however, it was a gift from my sister, Mikkellana, and giving her the credit she deserves, she makes the best weapons of all. You must use that to help protect Rahg. He will need your skills and knowledge and much more before this is over." Aentarra stepped back. "Now I must depart. I need to find some others who can help us. We will need everyone." She began to depart then turned back to Rahg. "There is one more thing, young Fal-Thera. If ever you find yourself slipping into a different realm, a vast emptiness where the merest thought can conjure up the wildest dreams—leave immediately. Do not tarry. Do not delay. It is not a place to play. To linger could spell death." With that said, she Shifted.

A FRIENDLY VISIT

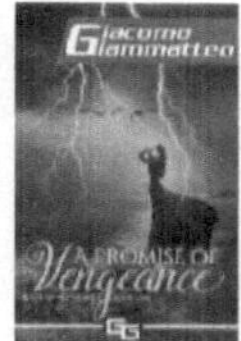

*I*n the alley behind the Trader's Inn, the cool night air cracked, and for the briefest moment the darkness disappeared, replaced by an eerie, luminous glow. Aentarra appeared in full splendor. She thought briefly of assuming a different form, different face, but quickly dismissed the idea. Her vanity seldom allowed her to adopt a less gracious form. She looked herself up and down, nodding approval. It was the body of a woman that could drive men mad.

She waited until the door closed behind the last patron before entering, silently, in her own fashion. Brock Larnigin locked the door and turned toward the bar, preparing to clean up after the long night. Aentarra's form at the bar startled him.

"By the gods, woman. I thought everyone had gone." Brock looked her over good, his eyes widening at the sight of so much flesh. The barkeep wiped his big hands on the apron that always hung from his neck and reached out as if to lend assistance. "Come now, lass. I'll help ya out. Help ya home if need be. A pretty one like you shouldn't walk alone, too many men might try and have their way with ya."

A smirk came to her face. Her eloquent voice had a way of putting men in their place. "I need no assistance of the type you think; however, I do need assistance. I seek a man you know as Kender Darnell."

Brock laughed. "You're a bold one, lass. I'll say that for ya. As to Kender Darnell, I'd not tell ya his whereabouts if I did know. Now leave on your own or I'll help ya out myself. And I won't be gentlemanly about it."

The smirk vanished from Aentarra's face and her thin lips formed a dangerous frown. Fire exploded from her hands setting chairs and tables aflame. Brock gawked in astonishment. "Be thankful I'm in a generous mood this eve," Aentarra warned. "Otherwise, the flames would have engulfed you." Brock rushed to put out the fire but Aentarra formed a shield and squelched the flames before he got to them. "Before I lose control, tell me where I might find Kender Darnell."

Brock overcame his instinctive fear and faced Aentarra. "I don't know what you are, but I'll not be turnin' Kender Darnell over to someone who means him harm."

"I shall forgive your lack of manners, ponderous one, and not interpret that as an insult. As to your concerns, I mean no harm to your friend. You have my word."

Brock's expression showed the release of tension. "I'm thankin' ya, lady. But I still say I don't know his whereabouts. He was bein' sought by the guard, though. Why don't ya try Force Commander Ludar. He'll know where he is if anyone does. He's the one that wants him caught."

The wily smirk returned to Aentarra's beautiful face, accenting her features. "Have no fear for your friend, barkeep. If the force commander has harmed him he will pay my price of vengeance."

Something in her voice made Brock believe her. He headed for the door. "Come, lass. I'll let ya out."

"No need," Aentarra said, and disappeared.

~

Brock stared at the spot where she had been for a long time. Occasionally, he looked from side to side; twice, he peered under the table nearby. Finally he rose, walked to the bar, and for the first time in many a year, poured himself a tall mug of ale. There was a time when Brock would have downed many a mug each night, but it had been ten years now without even a nip. He swallowed the contents of the mug in a single, long gulp, staring again at the vacant spot where Aentarra had stood. "May the gods bless Kender," he said aloud. "I pray she means him well."

~

Curses echoed off the walls of Force Commander Ludar's interrogation chamber as the back of his gloved fist struck the guard's bloodied face. "How could you have lost the prisoner?" Ludar demanded, striking the guard harder. He reeled, falling to the cold, stone floor. "Take him away," Ludar ordered. "And if the prisoner isn't found by tomorrow eve have this one serve the sentence for him." The door clanged shut, leaving Ludar alone.

The surprise of a female voice caused him to jump. "You were harsh in your treatment of that man, Force Commander. Are you always so cruel?"

Ludar spun to face her, only the feminine tone kept his sword sheathed. Ludar smiled lecherously when his eyes beheld the silky skin of Aentarra's body. "It is a cool evening to be clothed so, my lady. Before I ask how you came to be here, let me inquire as to how I may be of service to you."

Aentarra bowed, mocking him with the gesture. "I am pleased to see you so willing, Force Commander. I was led to believe you might not be so cooperative." Aentarra smiled her thin, wry smile. "I seek the whereabouts of a man who travels with one named Kender Darnell. I understand that you sought him as well."

The smile remained on Ludar's face, but it was a forced smile, not natural, and no longer lecherous. His hand tightened around the hilt of the sword. Slowly he unsheathed it. "I will tell you what I know of him, lady, and after I have my way with you, I'll let my guards have their pleasures before you die."

He let his eyes take in the richness of her body, caressing her luscious frame, drinking her loveliness. "Though I must admit, if you please me as much as you please my eyes, I might opt to keep you for a while." Ludar's smile widened and he felt his body stiffen in anticipation.

She wove a shield and spun it around his sword arm, paralyzing it. Then she rendered him immobile with a wrapping of shield about the remainder of his body save from the neck up.

The force commander struggled in vain. "What evil is this?"

"Evil?" Aentarra mocked him. "You ask of evil? From one who follows the Sun, I find that humorous."

Ludar's eyes went wide as her shield squeezed his private parts until he fell down in pain.

"Do not appear so shocked, foolish mortal. I am Aentarra. And if you thought you had reason to fear Lukaan—know well that you have more reason to fear me. Lukaan is imprisoned in Sethia, and will be until I decide otherwise. I, on the other hand, am here."

Ludar stared, still in disbelief, but now tinged with dread. He recalled the oath he swore in the Great Hall in the Sethian Palace. He remembered the words he spoke, and the sense of dread he felt, dread that emanated from the very walls. He never saw the Great One, but he felt him, felt his presence. Ludar shivered at the memory of the chill that racked his body. No, no matter who this woman was, he could not betray Lukaan, not Him. "I'll tell you nothing."

A Slicer roared from the pouch she kept attached to her sash and slammed into Ludar's head, swiftly penetrating the outer layer of skull. Ludar screamed, reeling from the pain. Soon he told everything he knew, everything Aentarra wanted. When she finished, she removed the Slicer, slowly strolling in a circle around the immobile force commander.

"You are fortunate, my mortal friend, that I am in rare humor. You are the second to escape the throes of death this eve. I shall keep you breathing for one purpose only—to deliver a message. Tell your master that I will be setting him free—soon. And when he is free, he can come and kneel at the feet of Aentarra—or, he can die. The choice is his."

IAZZO THE PERSECUTOR

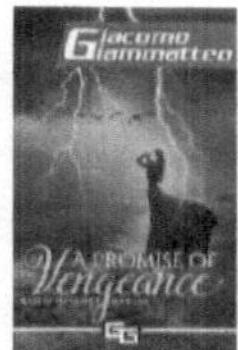

$\mathcal{L}$udar entered through the front door to his chamber. Sleep had been elusive for days, and his patience diminished in proportion to his fatigue. Hard leather heels stomped angrily on the stone floor, resounding off the drab walls. He stormed toward the throne preoccupied with thoughts of grandeur. Someday the throne would be real. Sykor would have a strong king.

Ludar took the steps one at a time, spinning upon reaching the third step and drawing his sword. Beads of sweat formed on his head and he sheathed the sword for fear of punishment. "Master?" His voice was weak, pleading, not the confident tone of the force commander.

Iazzo stepped from the shadows beside a pillar, his appearance forcing Ludar's bow lower. Ludar crawled off the steps and onto the floor. To stand above a Banished One would mean death, or worse. "I am at your service, Master."

Iazzo strolled, his eyes wandering over...... and holding Ludar fixed in the subjugated position much longer than necessary. Ludar perspired, shook uncontrollably.

Iazzo smiled. "He has sent me."

Ludar trembled at the mention of 'Him'.

"You are to tell me all concerning the village boy. Where is he? Who is watching him?"

The Force Commander fought with his emotions, finally gaining some semblance of control. "He sailed from Genda on a ship named the Sea Skate. We have two men aboard who will watch him."

Iazzo paced in front of Ludar coming closer to him with each passing. "What are their names?" A pause followed, not long, but for one such as Iazzo the slightest hesitation was deemed too long. "Their names," Iazzo demanded.

Ludar almost wept. "I do not know. I only know the name of the agent in Genda—Talen Marek." Ludar kept his head lowered. He dare not look up at Iazzo.

"Expect no further contact from Genda, Force Commander. I shall see to it myself." Iazzo's voice was like the wind on a harsh winter night.

Ludar's mind raced. Should he tell him about Aentarra? "Master," Ludar begged. "Master, I had another visitor two days past."

"Why should I care about your visitors?"

"She claimed to be an immortal."

"Who?"

Ludar shook. "She claimed to be Aentarra, and she sought the other village boy."

Iazzo straightened to a perfectly erect posture while he marched about the room. He seemed more alert than before.

"Aentarra," he muttered. "I care nothing of the other village boy, but Aentarra is another matter." Silence followed again. Ludar wondered whether to speak or wait.

"She is unpredictable, Force Commander. Some say she is touched with genius; others name her mad." Iazzo stared at Ludar for a long time. "Get up you morigerous fool. Do not fail us again."

"Yes, Master," Ludar said, and when he looked up to acknowledge Iazzo, he found him gone.

Ludar stood slowly. His knees ached from kneeling on the stone floor and his pride hurt even more. Sleep no longer a consideration, he called for his private guard. They entered with haste, closed fist pounding chest three times in succession.

"Yes, Force Commander. Your orders?"

Ludar came face to face and struck each in turn, screaming his commands. "Find that little thief who escaped from me and bring him here. I want him now."

∼

Talen Marek gulped the last of the two drinks on the table in front of him, the final obstacles to winning a wager on a challenge from Benuto. "More, Fharlo," Talen called to the barkeep. "Another mug of ale."

The fat barkeep waddled over to the table, belly bouncing with each strained step. "No more until you settle your account."

Talen looked at him with one eye partially closed. "I told ya, Fharlo. I'll be gettin' gold, soon. A lot of gold."

Fharlo snatched the bottle from the table. "I've heard enough of your tales about gold comin' from Sykor. Seems like the whole town has heard that tale for over a fortnight, and unless it's enough to fill a ship to sinkin', I doubt you'll have enough to pay everyone. You'll be gettin' no more credit here, Talen, so find another to listen to your tales."

Talen stayed only long enough to save pride, what little he had left. Tobias had seen to it that their family had been shamed and ridiculed.

707

He could go nowhere without feeling like people watched him, and talked about him. At least Fharlo hadn't taken the mug; there were a few sips yet left in there.

Talen took longer than he should have to swallow that little bit, then he mustered all his composure and walked out as gracefully as he could, careful not to miss a step as he descended the stairs to the street. A warm bed lay only a few blocks away, he suddenly recalled. Surely he could make it that far.

He tilted and swayed, but managed to cover the distance to the inn, well known in Genda for the quality of its ladies. Talen grasped the railing firmly and climbed the stairs.

"Talen Marek," a voice called to him from the darkness of the alley.

Talen leaned forward, straining his eyes in an attempt to make sense of the vague form he saw. "Who is it?"

"Talen Marek, come. I have something for you."

The voice proved to be as nondescript as the image. Again, he strained his eyes, but only succeeded in seeing shadows that seemed to move. The lure of the ladies called to his weakened mind, and he was about ready to give up on the stranger in the alley when a thought shook him with excitement. "Are ya the one from Sykor? Have ya brought my gold?" Without waiting, Talen turned, nearly fell backward, then straightened himself and stumbled in the direction of the stranger's voice.

When he got closer, Talen could see the man, and his gaze darted from the man's eyes to the pouch he held in his hand. It was difficult to tear his eyes away from that pouch, knowing how much gold it contained. Talen urged his muscles to function properly, wishing to appear as sober as possible.

"Beginnin' to worry when I didn't hear from ya. Made me out to be a liar with all the folks in town, me tellin' 'em I'm gettin' gold and all." For a moment, Talen thought he saw something in the man's eyes he didn't like. "But nobody's the worse for it. They'll be happy once I pay 'em." Talen held his hand out to receive the pouch. "Anytime ya need things done, don't forget me."

Iazzo smiled. The coldness of it chilled Talen though it was a warm night. "I will not forget you, friend, but tell me, what are the names of your associates, the ones who set sail on the Sea Skate?"

Talen cast suspicious eyes at the stranger in the alley. He couldn't quite see his face; a foggy mist hung about him. "They're just men I use on occasion. I can get those kind anytime I want."

"Their names."

Talen shuddered. Even though the stranger had whispered, it shook him. Talen fought to get his tongue to work, then sputtered the names out, "Eduard and Marro," Talen said, then heard the man repeat it.

"Eduard and Marro, and they sailed on the Sea Skate."

The man reached inside his cloak and extracted something long and thin—so thin that at first Talen hadn't noticed it, but then the light caught it and reflected off of it like a piece of crystal. Talen looked about, even though the alley was dark, the little bit of light that did shine managed to seek out this object. It glowed.

He noticed the man stared at it for a while, like he was talking to it, but his lips never moved. Then it just disappeared. He could have sworn he saw it leave. Things like that couldn't fly, Talen thought, and nothing could have moved so fast. Nothing. "What was that?'

Iazzo stared for a long time. "I believe you came for this," Iazzo said, and dangled the heavy pouch in front of him. Slobber formed on Talen's lips when he heard the coins jingling.

"Hold out your hands, Talen Marek. Payment awaits you."

Talen's breathing grew heavier. Hands shaking with anticipation, he grabbed for the pouch. It wasn't until he saw the glow emanating from Iazzo that Talen realized he faced someone with powers. He stopped himself in time, or what he thought was time, and held his hands outstretched, cupped together. "It's been long," Talen muttered. "So very long."

He trembled when Iazzo lifted the pouch and untied the string that held it closed. He laughed as Iazzo tilted the pouch forward. Abruptly, the laughter ceased and the smile vanished from Talen's face. As the coins fell from the pouch, they melted. Talen tried to pull his hands away in time, but he was too slow; the molten gold filled his waiting hands. His body shook from the pain, and his scream shattered the night air.

"What is wrong, my friend? Do you find the coins uncomfortable?"

Iazzo looked on with an unnatural interest as the melted gold burnt through Talen's skin. It ran through Talen's fingertips and coated him like a statue, forming one unit where before there were two hands. Talen screamed until he had no breath remaining; no words to shout. "Why are you shouting?" Iazzo asked. "Perhaps you cannot see that what I give you is gold. Stop squirming and I will remedy that."

Talen writhed about on the ground, still howling, though no sound escaped his lips. Iazzo knelt beside him and held him still. Then, when Talen realized what the man was going to do, he tried to move, tried to scream, but he could do neither. Talen watched as Iazzo brought the two gold pieces closer and placed them in his eyes. "You see," Iazzo said, "it is gold I give you." Then, they too, began to melt. Iazzo stood and watched for a few moments, taking pleasure in the agony and pain. Soon, however, Talen stopped moving.

~

*I*azzo returned to his army near the Sethian border. J'ag Tem approached with an honorary bow. "We have nourishment to break your fast, Lord."

"I have made contact with our men," Iazzo said. "The enemy numbers are many but they are ill prepared, and few possess weapons."

The Sethian leader nodded approval even if he felt doubt. "Weapons or not, they will be formidable foes. Has your contact selected a site for arrival, Lord?"

Iazzo smiled. "Marro claims there is a ritual site of worship atop a steep rise west of the city. It is surrounded by high walls of rock with only one point of entry, a passage of two or three spans. It will be perfect."

"Could they not simply wait us out? It is they who have the city with food, and we who are besieging them."

Iazzo quickly lost his smile; he had no patience for foolish questions. "I think not, J'ag Tem. I shall provide the motivation, and the Entirians will attack our position. Trust me. And if he is not a coward, the village boy will accompany them."

J'ag Tem stared at Iazzo. "Yes, Lord. Your will is mine."

"Prepare your men, J'ag Tem. Marro will soon be in position. Do they know the procedure? And where to stand for the Shifting?"

J'ag Tem issued the order for all to join hands, and at the end, he reluctantly reached out to touch Iazzo's. "They stand at the ready, Lord. We only await your command."

THE EMPTY LANDS

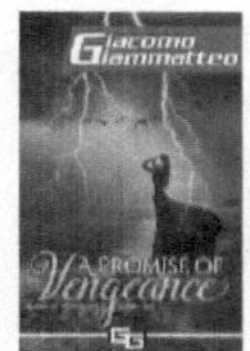

*D*arstan lay awake, restless. He wondered how long Ictar could detain a whole strike force, or if he'd even try. And he wondered how far the Sykorans would follow them. Everyone seemed nervous. Even Takar looked worried. That bothered Darstan the most. He curled his shoulder and tugged the bedroll over himself. The nights in the hills were cold, reminding him of autumn nights in Kamnor.

Two more days passed with an anxious eye to the rear during the day and wool cloaks wrapped about them at night. When he wasn't standing guard, he huddled by the fire trading stories with the others to fend off deep-rooted fears. This was the Empty Lands, and somewhere out there lurked Lukaan and the Banished Ones.

Empty Lands

Darstan rubbed his hands together and kicked dirt at Wisp. "What's the matter, Kender? You've worn that same face since we crossed the Daureian River."

A false smile crossed Wisp's face. "Nothing that a night with a Qorami wouldn't cure."

One of the guards turned his head and spat. "I've heard one night with a Qorami can make a man jump off a cliff. Heard of men that did it."

Heads nodded around the fire. "Had a cousin that saved up all his money for one night with one of them witches. After that he went stir crazy. Followed her around like a trail dog until one of the emperor's soldiers killed him." The guard's bright teeth shone in the firelight. "Still want to find one of them, Kender?"

"I'll take my chances. For those of you who don't know me, I have quite an effect on the ladies myself. In fact, it's more than likely that half of that strike force following us is made up of the wives of Sykoran nobles."

The guards erupted in raucous laughter as Wisp effected a gracious bow. Darstan grabbed Wisp's cloak and tugged. "Come on, we better get some sleep."

Wisp walked slowly, eyes catching every glint of moonglow on stone. "That shield is here somewhere, Darstan."

"We don't have to worry about the shield."

"Don't we? I'm not so sure. And that's the problem. At least in Sykor I knew what I faced. Out here..."

"We'll be all right as soon as we get to Khatara."

Wisp nodded. "You're right. Let's get some sleep."

~

Darstan entered the dream almost before his eyelids closed. He was dreaming, yet he knew it was a dream. He recognized the terrain and everything about it—that much he was cognizant of—and the memories were vivid: the roiling sea; the strange land full of strange people; and most important of all, the fog-shrouded mass of warriors atop the rise. He felt as if he were an observer of history.

Three people advanced toward the armies from the crest of the hill. They were just now appearing on the summit, and the hordes of enemies they approached stood silently awaiting a signal from a man in their midst who glowed, reflecting the sun's rays like mirrored glass. As always the mysterious ones stood to the side: a beautiful woman, another person whose face Darstan had not seen, and the man with one hand—the one who had the powers.

The woman was beautiful. Her honey-colored hair danced in a gentle breeze, a graceful magnificence like he'd never seen, and her emerald-green eyes enchanted him, sparkling in the sun like priceless jewels. He would have let his gaze linger longer, forever perhaps, but he was drawn to the other image, the man with no hand. When he thought he might finally see the man's face, a bestial roar awakened him. Darstan was halfway to his feet before he truly woke. "Wisp! Wake up. Alert the camp."

~

*P*ack Leader Kadir crept closer to the top edge of the mound, his yellow eyes piercing the black night as if both moons shone brilliantly. Slowly, like the setting of the sun, he raised his head and sniffed the night air, his sensitive nose quivering at every trace of scent. With an almost imperceptible movement of his arm he signaled for the others to advance.

Empty Lands

Within moments the entire pack lay upon the crest of the hill—a dozen Wolfen prepared to strike. "We only seek to capture them." Kadir repeated the orders for the third time tonight. Ordinarily, he would not have done so; however, the eyes of the Master watched this mission. "Be swift," he cautioned, then gave the signal to proceed with the plan. There was no need to tell a Wolfen to be silent.

Less than fifty paces away, Gregor and Wehr stood guard; it would not take the Wolfen long to cover that much ground, so they let the other half of the pack move out first; they had farther to travel. Once the first six had crept out of sight, Kadir led the others toward the camp of the guards.

"Let the voices of the guards mask your movement," he reminded them, and timed his steps to coincide with the conversation between Gregor and Wehr. The pads of their fur-covered feet trod softly over the rocky terrain—silent as the passing of a cloud—and the darkness concealed the figures furtively creeping from rock to rock, their dark gray fur blending perfectly with the dull tones that made up the landscape of the Empty Lands.

~

"That's a fine looking staff, bounty man. I've never seen better. How did you come by the blackthorn?"

Gregor smiled. Despite his morose disposition, he loved to discuss his quarterstaff. Most bounty-men wielded fine quarterstaffs, but none could boast of owning a staff made from blackthorn. "Our travels took us through the Blackthorn Forest. The leader of the Lorns claimed friendship to one of us and his son bequeathed it to me. It's my greatest treasure."

"How does the blackthorn compare to hickory? Or did you use emerald?"

Gregor's smile broadened. Finally, someone he could converse with who knew something of staffs. "Emerald was my finest. Hickory makes a fine staff but I prefer emerald, even rock maple, over hickory. Every bounty man owns many staffs, Wehr. Much, I'm sure, as you have more than one blade. Staffs are different though. More than any other weapon—with the possible exception of a thief's throwing knife —mastering the staff requires adopting a feel for the weapon. That's why bounty-men constantly experiment with new designs, new woods, and exotic oils to rub into them."

"I wouldn't think there was so much to making a good staff."

Gregor laughed. "A good staff and a perfect staff are two different things, my friend. The weight must be right. Too heavy and a man is spent before a fight is half over." Gregor paused to strike fire to his pipe, a habit he picked up from Tobias. He had grown to enjoy the occasional smoke, especially when accompanied with good conversation or a hot mug of khaffe. "It must be hard wood, but not brittle. The structure of the wood must be able to withstand a good whacking from a sword blade or bear the brunt of a collision with a man's thick skull, or a stone wall in the event of a miss.

"Also, the end of the staff must be crafted to perfection. It is one of the most important aspects. Some bounty-men, most in fact, prefer to have the shaft taper to a slightly thinner end. I have mine trimmed, then I cure it with special oils and fire-harden the tip. After several treatments, I wrap a thin metal band down the shaft about a hand's length; it provides strong support and, driven by the proper jab, it can pierce a man's gut with the ease of a pike. I also test the staffs rigorously. I don't want to be surprised by the wood splitting down the center the first time I ram it into a coat of mail or hit the hilt of a hidden blade."

Gregor caressed the blackthorn staff like the wife he never had. "If I could only convince the Lorns to let me sell these staffs... I could become a wealthy man." Gregor had talked more this night than he had the entire time since leaving Sykor. He placed the center of his staff on one outstretched finger and balanced it perfectly. "Do you see, Wehr? The staff is flawless."

Wehr nodded. "I've seen what the Lorns can do with arrows. They fly true to the mark and never split. Once, during a mission with Takar

—" Wehr stopped, jumping to an erect posture, sword in hand. As one, he and Gregor both yelled, "Alert the camp," then turned to run toward the rear.

~

*V*lad and Tomas peered into the blackness of the Empty Lands. The veil of clouds prevented any moonlight shining through and cast a pall of impending disaster over a night already laden with tension. The jagged peaks of the rocky terrain appeared as shadows, looming over the camp like predators. The sound of a falling rock grabbed their attention. Both focused their eyes on the trail ahead, straining in the darkness to determine the origin of the disturbance. As they reached for their swords the Wolfen attacked.

Kella stirred, then leapt up from under Darstan's arm which had been draped over her body, and darted toward the perimeter of the camp where Tomas and Vlad stood watch, her roar splitting the night. In only a few tremendous bounds she arrived. The Wolfen were carrying away the two guards when Kella leaped on them. Another roar split the night.

Kella dispatched two of the Wolfen almost before they could scream. She tore the throat out of one, and crushed the head of the second. Two of the other Wolfen drew blades and killed Vlad and Tomas. Kella roared again, louder and more ferocious than before. She managed to disarm another one and had secured a death-lock on the fourth victim when Takar and Mennar arrived. Takar stabbed the Wolfen with his first thrust then proceeded to scout the area, calling for everyone while he did.

"Alert the camp. Go to the north watch to check on Gregor and Wehr. Post two sentries on the horses; everyone else protect the perimeters." Four of the six Wolfen lay dead. Kella had taken off in hot pursuit of the remaining two just as Darstan and Wisp arrived brandishing their weapons.

"What happened?" Darstan asked, panting.

"Wolfen," Takar said. "Check on Wehr and Gregor." They ran to the north side.

Takar knew the Wolfen had gotten them when he saw Gregor's black-thorn staff on the ground next to Wehr's sword. He wasted no time in searching for tracks. If it had just been Wolfen it might have been impossible, but they had dragged the two captives, leaving plenty of marks. "Mennar, Darstan, Kender, come with me. Evin, you and the rest of the men guard the camp." Takar started off at a run, almost before he issued his last order.

"I don't know how you can run and follow tracks at the same time," Darstan said, straining to keep pace.

～

Kadir chanced a quick glance behind them and saw the guards gaining ground. "Maggi, Rendl, stay and delay them. We must have the time we need or the Master will see to all of us." The two Wolfen ducked behind the cover of some freestanding rocks, waiting for Takar and the other guards to arrive.

"It won't be long," Maggi said, and positioned himself for the ambush. Meanwhile, Kadir and the other Wolfen hauled Gregor and Wehr closer to Sethia.

～

The Wolfen set upon Takar just as he bolted over a small mound, but they must not have expected such instinctive reactions from a man; Takar fended the attack from his left with the sword, thrusting forward viciously with his knife to catch Rendl just

720

below the ribs. Rendl snarled and lunged to attack. Maggi pressed aggressively but before he had the advantage Wisp threw two knives, one hit the mark in the chest, the other missed.

Before the Wolfen could remove the first blade, Wisp held two more and was now upon them. He stabbed low with one, catching Maggi in the leg and when the Wolfen involuntarily reached for the wound, Wisp jabbed upward with the other, puncturing his throat. By now Rendl must have realized his fate, and he fought like a maddened animal. Takar succeeded in holding him at bay until Darstan arrived, then dispatched him with no trouble.

Takar never paused even to catch breath. Mennar was already in hot pursuit. "We might be able to catch them on that rise ahead," Takar yelled. Mennar was in the lead. There was no need for tracking, they could see the Wolfen in the distance.

Wisp began to show signs of worry. They were heading toward Sethia, that much he knew. And legends told of a shield that contained the Banished Ones, kept them inside of these forsaken lands. He didn't know if any of it was true, but he had heard the tale often enough to give pause to rushing blindly into the heart of Sethia. He knew that most legends, no matter how ludicrous they sounded, had some basis in truth.

He tried his best to concentrate and become aware of the surroundings, though it was difficult while giving chase. Wisp trailed the others but only by a few steps. The two Wolfen who carried Gregor maintained about a fifty pace lead, but the two who held Wehr were now within reach of Takar and Darstan; Mennar had gone ahead to try and catch Gregor.

Just as they breached the pinnacle of the rise, a woman appeared out of nowhere.

"Halt!" Her scream pierced the desert night air like the screech from a hawk.

Wisp stopped dead, being wise enough to sense danger. Takar stopped. So had the Wolfen who held Wehr. "Go no farther," the woman commanded. Darstan bolted forward, reaching out with his left hand to try and seize hold of the Wolfen, now only three paces away.

"We have to catch them."

"Halt!" This time, her voice shook the very air. She stood next to Takar who remained frozen in place. Wisp stepped backward a pace. Darstan obeyed this time. He froze in mid-stride with his left hand extended, but when he tried to pull his arm back it wouldn't move. He yanked again, struggling, yet something kept it away.

The Wolfen holding Wehr was escaping. Darstan pulled harder then started to move forward but the lady seized him from behind. Mennar quit the pursuit and returned to stand by Takar. Wisp made his way to the top of the rise and stared at Darstan then at the lady. Darstan tugged and yanked, all to no avail. Panic set in.

"Do not move," she said. "You are trapped inside the Sethian Shield. If you go forward you will be lost altogether."

Wisp stepped back. The thing he dreaded most—the Sethian shield— was real, and he stood right before it.

Takar regained his composure and had hold of Darstan. "I see nothing holding him?"

Darstan's face burned crimson from struggling with the shield. He wouldn't believe the fate that this strange woman pronounced on him.

"I am Mikkellana," she said. "I designed this shield that is holding your friend."

～

A horde of Gnakas rushed toward them. Panic set in anew as Darstan fought to free himself. His shoulder felt dislocated, and his hand felt as if it had been crushed in a vise. He gaped wide-eyed at the onrushing Gnakas, their battle cries piercing the chilled night air.

"Cut it off," Mikkellana ordered.

Takar stared blankly at her, disbelief showing on his face.

"Cut it off! Now!"

At first, it didn't register with Darstan what she meant, not until Wisp looked so horrified at her. "No!" Darstan screamed just as Takar swung the sword. "Noooo!" he screamed again as his hand fell to the ground, blood spurting out like a broken vessel.

The Gnakas were almost upon them when Darstan's last scream erupted. With it came an outpouring of pain—and a rush of fire. Yellow flames leapt from the stub that still spouted blood and shot at the Gnakas in a cylindrical tube of death. "Noooo!" he screamed again. Red flames poured forth, searing the wound. The bleeding stopped but the pain and suffering didn't.

With a final howl the stub emitted white flames that engulfed the night's coldness and drank the air itself. The flames roared outward from Darstan, encompassing everything. The air exploded, producing a deafening, thunderous roar.

When the fire died out, everything was gone. There hadn't been much alive beforehand; now there was nothing.

Empty Lands

The Wolfen who had sought escape with Wehr looked back in horror. They must have assumed their escape made good, now they could only stare as oblivion came down on them like a tidal wave of fury. Wehr seemed to explode when the flames struck. It was brief and he died quickly. The Gnakas screamed, their shouts engulfed by the roar of the flames that raced across the once-cool desert night.

Wisp looked on, afraid. It appeared as if the air itself had become flammable and burst into a liquid death. Fire still spewed forth, but it was changing again. Now what emerged was a blue flame covered with ice.

"Coldfire," Mikkellana muttered, almost imperceptibly. "I have not seen its like since..." She stopped and looked about. Darstan collapsed shortly after the final outburst and with his unconsciousness the fire ended.

Takar stared into the wasteland of Sethia—certainly now it was a wasteland. All the Gnakas lay dead, hundreds of them. The few not burned to a crisp were frozen in place, some with terror still painted on their faces.

Wisp knelt to look after Darstan though he had no idea what he could do for him, if anything. "Is it safe, now?" He looked to Mikkellana who hovered above him, all aglow.

"If you mean are you safe from the shield, Kender Darnell? Yes, as long as you don't cross the boundary." Mikkellana eyed him with a smile. "Or should I call you Wisp?"

How does she know who I am? And how does she know I have powers?

Mikkellana knelt down to inspect Darstan, looking at the severed limb. "He has no need of Healing. The fire seared it and protected it from infection." Mikkellana checked him thoroughly, fixed his shoulder, then turned to Wisp and Takar and Mennar. "Mark me well, Takar. You also, Wisp."

Wisp was still stunned that she knew him, especially that she knew him as the Wisp.

"This one is strong. Very strong. Take care of him. Nurse him. And above all, ensure that he remains on this side of the shield." Mikkellana turned to stare at Mennar. "And you will speak nothing of this to anyone." Mennar nodded unconsciously. "And you will tell no one of Wisp."

They were all too stunned to speak. "Now you must hurry. They have surely heard this in Sethia and that means Lukaan will soon be here. I'm afraid that even though he can't escape the shield, he would find some way to get you inside, and if that happened you would be lost beyond all hope."

That was enough to convince Wisp and Takar. They scrambled to pull Darstan to his feet, then Takar threw him over his shoulder. Mennar was almost in tears from fear.

"What about Gregor?" Wisp asked.

"He's gone."

"I didn't see him burned."

Mikkellana frowned. "I didn't mean to imply that he died, though he will wish he did soon enough." She reached her hands out. "Take hold, quickly. Lukaan will be here any moment; he will have detected the powers." Mikkellana grabbed hold of them as they prepared to depart. "I'll take you as far as your camp, but you must make haste for Khatara. Don't stop for anything, and above all else, keep Darstan away from this shield."

"I feel certain Darstan won't want any part of this shield ever again," Wisp said.

Mikkellana glared at him. "You don't know Lukaan. He will do anything—anything, to get hold of Darstan now that he knows he has powers like this. And believe me, if he gets hold of him, we are all doomed. So keep him safe, but most of all keep him out of their hands. Kill him before you let him go beyond this shield."

Wisp gulped a large ball of fear. "What's wrong with the shield? Isn't—"

"The shield is weakening... and I think I know why. I'll need help to fix it and keep them in. Find as many people as you can with powers. We will need all the help we can get."

Mikkellana grabbed them tightly and they all disappeared, instantly reappearing on the outskirts of the campground they had recently left. Within the blink of an eye, she was gone again.

REPERCUSSIONS

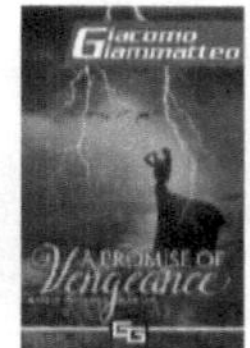

Melissara leapt from her bed, surrounded by energy, eyes scanning all sides. Someone had used a massive amount of power and it had been nearby. This was not some simple demonstration of temper by Ghruehne.

With no imminent threat she relaxed, but kept herself at the ready. Her doors opened and when she stepped into the corridor Tirzinitzia was already there, as was Sendra and Zorn. Ghruehne appeared soon after.

"What was it?" Tirzinitzia asked. The red suns in her face almost glowed.

"Something powerful," Sendra said. "I haven't felt that since—"

Just then a summons rang in their minds and they headed for Lukaan's chambers.

"I see everyone has felt it. It happened near the Caravan Trail. Come."

~

*G*regor peeked out of the ravine. When the fire came, he and the Wolfen jumped to safety on a ledge below the surface, then scaled the rock walls to descend farther into the canyon. During the final stage of the descent, he seized upon an opportunity to free himself by wresting a sword from the Wolfen on the ground while the other maneuvered for positioning to come down.

By the gods, what a nightmare.

He recalled the horrors as he had seen them from below. The sky illuminated with yellow light, a glow that equaled the early dawn of a new morning. Then abruptly it altered. A red-hot angry sky roiled overhead, even from below he could feel the heat, and as he peered upward the sky loomed like an angry god about to punish his subjects. He heard the screams then the explosion, and he felt the trembling of the ground. It was then he saw, though only briefly, the explosive, white-hot blast that roared viciously through the desert sky, washing all the previous night scapes away like a ritual cleansing.

He hid his eyes, and when the heat grew too intense, he found shelter under an outcropping along the ledge where he had stationed himself. He rubbed the festering sores on his face and arm as he recalled the fiery night. So many had screamed that he could not determine if that is what had caused the noise, or if that merely added to the destructiveness above.

Empty Lands

Gregor scanned the scorched-earth landscape, charred masses of flesh heaped atop each other told of stampeding bodies that were too slow to escape the flames. Using a small crevasse in the rock, he attempted to pull himself up, but jerked back, a reaction to the still-burning boulders above. He could barely see over the top, but he could discern some things.

Who had done this? he wondered. *What had transpired?*

He had many questions, but all he really wished to do was make his way back to camp, and safety. I'll down ten mugs of water when I get there. His mouth was parched, partly from the heat, but mostly from fear.

About to take another try at scaling the final hurdle to leave the ravine, this time, with hands wrapped in rags taken from the bodies of the dead Wolfen, he saw a group of figures appear in the distance to the south, toward camp. He nearly shouted, assuming them to be Takar's men, but wisely studied the group more. Though they were a hundred paces away and he could not discern features nor claim recognition, he knew instinctively that he must hide. Must seek shelter, quickly. Cautious to avoid a sound, he crept back down and tucked himself into the deepest, darkest recesses under the overhang.

~

Alone Gnaka crawled on the ground dragging himself over bodies of his brethren.

"What happened?"

The Gnaka struggled to speak, lips charred, almost seared shut.

"No need to speak, soldier. I will hear your thoughts."

"It was an immortal, Master. He—"

"He?" Lukaan moved closer to the shield, touching it, smelling it. He turned to Captain Jernan, a Sethian Guard who stood with him. "Go outside the shield and gather me dirt from those footprints. And there, that blood on the ground. That too."

Lukaan cupped the dirt in his hands, smelled it, tasted it. "She was here," he said. "Mikkellana was here, but this was not her work. Someone else did this—the boy."

"Impossible," shouted Ghruehne.

Lukaan glared at him. It was all that was necessary. "Call Iazzo, and bring him to me."

Once Iazzo arrived, standing outside the shield, Lukaan spoke. "Your assignment will be more difficult now. The boy must be captured alive. Alive! I do not care if a hundred die in the process, or even a thousand, or ten times that. I want the boy alive." Lukaan dismissed Iazzo, then Shifted to his chamber in the Sethian Palace. "Captain Jernan, send for the Sethian priests. Instruct them to bring all the writings that deal with the Prophecies."

So, he has found his powers. The prophecies may yet be fulfilled as they were written, with no need for my interference. Still, I can help matters along. Even from here I can affect the future of this world. Soon they will regret having constructed this shield. Soon they will pay for having imprisoned Lukaan.

KHATARA

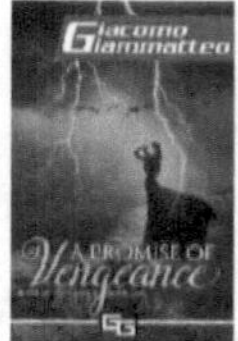

*D*arstan slipped in and out of delirium, a constant battle to regain his sanity—to once again become lucid. The memories flooded his mind every time he surfaced near reality; he recalled the shield, and losing his hand. After that there was too much he didn't care to remember. He struggled to lift his head and stared down at the stump tucked away inside the sleeve of his shirt. *Good. Let it stay hidden.*

He hated Mikkellana for creating the shield that trapped him, and he hated her more for giving the order. *What right had she to do that?* And he hated Lukaan. If not for him, the shield wouldn't have been necessary; and he hated the Wolfen for taking Gregor and Wehr captive; and he especially hated Takar.

Most of all though, he hated himself. A cripple, an aberration, a curiosity—and he only had himself to blame. *Why did I have to have powers? Why not Rahg, or someone else?* He tossed fitfully on the litter, falling in and out of restless sleep. "I'll kill them all," he mumbled, tossing his head from side to side.

Evin had ridden faithfully by Darstan's side since breaking camp. "He's sweating badly, Sergeant. Can we stop for a bit?"

Takar fell back to check on the lad, calling for a rest period while dismounting to examine him. He had taken care of many soldiers in the field and knew more than most about keeping wounded men alive. "Fetch another blanket. And some rope to bind him."

"Bind him! He's sick."

"Fever's high. Never felt a man so hot. More'n likely he'll be going into fits."

Takar wrapped Darstan in another blanket then grabbed hold of Evin's shoulder as he secured the final cinch. "If he begins babbling, warn me. And listen well to any lucid requests. When he wakes he'll need water."

Fading in and out of consciousness, Darstan saw Evin several times. *Evin. If not for him, I'd never have gone through the shield. If not for him and Wehr, I'd still be with Rahg.* Suddenly, his twisted frame of mind remembered Wehr—captured by the Wolfen. Caught by the flames. *My flames. I killed Wehr.* "He deserved to die." The words rode out on peals of laughter.

Darstan looked at Evin, staring at him as if he was a man gone mad. His brow poured sweat profusely, and his eyes felt as if they had been pried open. Evin deserved to die too. Darstan tried to get up, struggled for a moment, then fell into a slumber.

~

While the men ate supper, Kella returned, the first time they had seen her since the attack. There had been conjecture that she must have perished when she failed to return after giving chase to the other two Wolfen, but Wisp always maintained that she would return.

"I'm not even certain you can kill a vargel," he said. For all of his complaining about the beast, Wisp had grown to trust and even enjoy Kella. The journey from Genda to Sykor had been a long and arduous one, and Kella had been good company for he and Gregor. The wiry thief greeted her warmly although he shunned her sloppy kisses, uttering a gagging curse when she sneaked one in on him.

Kella soon sought out Darstan and stood by him the whole time they rested, licking his sweaty face and brow, and jealousy guarding him from the attention of others. A slight twitch of a snarl is all that it took to deter a potential intruder.

"She apparently has decided to nurse Darstan back to health," Wisp said to Takar.

The big sergeant sipped slowly on his khaffe. "She can do no worse than me," he said. "I've seen animals do wonders for sick lads, perhaps she can help Darstan. There's nothing I can do for him, not with a fever that high."

By the fifth day, Darstan improved enough to be able to sit astride his mount, though for only half the time. The remainder of the day he spent on the litter so that he could preserve energy and rebuild his strength.

When they stopped to make camp that night, Kella stayed right next to him. Takar swore that the vargel healed him, but Wisp suggested that the sudden onset of powers caused Darstan's illness, that it simply took time for his body to adapt.

By the next morning Darstan felt so good that he insisted on riding the entire day. They had begun the ascent into the mountain range that separated Khatara from the Empty Lands and the air had turned much colder. Snow sat atop the highest peaks and flowed down the sides. Darstan put on his woolen cloak. Even though the sun still shone bright, he found he needed the warmth.

"We'll likely run into some Khataran patrols before long," Takar said.

"Tell them straightaway who we are. No sense in telling stories that hide the truth. We're deserters. Nothing else describes it. We've got good reason, mind you. I'm not claiming we acted hastily, but when it comes down to it, deserters are what we are.

Those of you who want mercenary work, speak up when asked. You'll find work fast. And if you want caravan duty let that be known, but until this mess in Sykor is fixed, I'd not accept a job on the caravan trail—too much chance of Ludar's men recognizing you and taking you back."

Wisp listened to Takar, all the while entertaining thoughts of grand escapades leading him through the streets and over the rooftops of Khatara. He had never been to the great desert-city, but he had heard the tales and he had witnessed the prizes that the merchants brought with them to Sykor and Pomanda.

Khatara still loomed as the premier trading city in all the lands and, where such commerce existed, opportunities for a thief were to be found in abundance. *It would almost be too easy,* Wisp thought.

The full day of riding seemed to be wearing on Darstan. "You should try and rest," Evin said. "I'll join Takar while you get some sleep. Barnett said tomorrow will be worse. Said the high passes might even have snow in them."

Darstan made no attempt to convince Evin to stay. He thought of whittling on a stick, a habit he had gotten accustomed to, but the half-empty sleeve rudely reminded him of his newly–acquired handicap.

I can't even whittle. Can't do anything.

He recalled the way others treated people with defects. *Freaks like me.* He remembered Maria, who had a club foot, and Brandon, who had lost an eye. Darstan cringed as he recalled the comments others made about them when they weren't around to hear. He had not partaken of the cruelties, but he had not stopped them either. Now he wondered if that was any less a sin. *Perhaps it's worse.*

As he lay down, he thought of dreaming, and that caused him to start with a jump.

The one-handed man! The one in my dream is me!

And as he replayed the dream over in his mind, he once again saw the person who, so far, had remained a stranger. Now though, when Darstan looked to the man, there was a face attached to him—his face. What did it mean? And who were the others? As he struggled with identification he continued to review the dream over and over in his head.

He saw the three people coming over the hill; saw the fog that covered their faces, but try as he might, he could not see through to determine who they were. Then it struck him. That swagger. It had to be Rhaven. And if that was Rhaven the others must be Rahg and Tobias. "Rahg's in trouble! I've got to get there."

First light brought new worries for Darstan. How could he find Rahg? How could he even get to Genda, let alone find him after that?

Wisp sat across from Darstan, close to the morning fire. Darstan had told him of the dream and subsequent revelation. "Do you have any ideas?" Darstan asked.

"I've told you. Getting to Genda will be easy, but getting someone to take us to the Sea of the Lost will probably be impossible, and even if we could, how would we find them? But don't worry, I'll go with you. I know what ship they sailed on."

Darstan nodded. "We need to hurry, Wisp. I told you of the dream."

"I don't believe in dreams, Darstan. I prefer to place my faith in what I can see with my own eyes, and I don't entirely trust that."

Darstan looked up at the narrow pass, snow piled deep all around it. The wind tore at the woolen cloak he wore. He reached for the clasp to fasten the cloak and was harshly reminded of his missing limb, but this time he didn't allow the frustration to overcome him.

hataran soldiers guarded the pass, inured to the cold, even comfortable, wearing hats and other garments made from the heavy fur of the mountain animals: sheep, bear, and some Darstan didn't recognize. They stood erect, alert, lances at the ready. Takar ordered the men to halt. Darstan hated to stop; it was cold up here and colder still when they weren't moving.

Khataran mountain pass, Jattan-Kir

The Khataran in command approached Takar. "Why do Sykoran guards come to Jattan-Kir? I see no caravan." The Khataran soldiers behind the man slipped their hands to better grip their lances.

"I'm Sergeant Takar, and these are what remain of my men. We are all deserters from the guard in Sykor."

The Khataran guard examined them with an experienced glance. Darstan felt certain that he could ascertain what each had in their saddlebags from that look alone.

"I am called Pasha, the Haffir-rond of the mountain tribes. The charge of guarding the pass falls to us. My family has been blessed by the All-Knowing One with eyes that can see good or evil." Pasha waited a brief moment, then smiled. "I am happy to see we will not be forced to kill you." Pasha bowed low to the ground, so low, that Darstan thought his head might scrape his boots.

"Forgive me if I detained you too long. You are welcome to the lands of Jattan-Kir, home to the First Ones and the great city of Khatara. If you seek a new life in Khatara, be warned of the laws. Make them known to you at first opportunity. Punishment for some crimes can be severe, not what a Sykoran might be accustomed to."

Pasha smiled. "I have spoken even more than I wished to though I am not often afforded the opportunity to speak at length. Most who pass through are eager to arrive at their destination. May the light of the All-Knowing One be ever with you." He bowed as he delivered his blessing for their travels.

Darstan looked to the sky. There was half a day yet to travel before Takar would call a halt to make camp. Several of the guards who had already been to Khatara were talking about how the weather would be warm and sunny when they arrived. "Always was," they said. Right now, Darstan could not imagine that, with snow whirling about his head, and him struggling constantly to maintain a firm hold on his cloak. They would reach Khatara in about six days, Takar said. Darstan was anxious about what they would find.

The descent from the mountains proved easy, traveling a well-worn trail that led to a flat desert surrounding Khatara on all sides. Darstan continually turned around to check the rear, the worry of the Sykoran force catching them ever on his mind. Takar must have noticed, for he told him it was unlikely that they would even attempt to cross into Jattan-Kir, and even less likely that Pasha would allow them to enter.

Darstan felt relieved. Now all he needed to worry about was getting to Genda. It was not until the latter part of the day that Darstan first caught sight of Khatara.

Khatara

It's the biggest city I've ever seen. Bigger than Pomanda.

"We should be there by nightfall," Takar said.

Three rivers coursed into Khatara, rushing down from the mountains to the west and north. The melting snows kept them flowing with fresh water, creating abundant strips of fertile land along each life-giving source. It presented quite a different circumstance than the one they faced on their journey to get here. There was even enough water to bathe if you didn't mind the cold.

The only thing keeping Darstan awake by the time they entered Khatara was the excitement of being there. The road they came in on led into the poorest section of the city. Dirty houses made from sun-dried mud and straw stood as a greeting to newcomers who arrived. Slits in the walls served for ventilation and remained open during most of the winter season, at other times a veil of coarse cloth was draped over them to help keep out the dust that blew in from the arid lands surrounding Khatara. The houses, once whitewashed to conform with the rest of the city, had long ago turned brown from too many dustings of the desert sands.

"Dismount," Takar said. "These horses are as tired as we are, and these streets are narrow."

Darstan nearly choked from the foulness. The streets were thick with the stench of urine and animal droppings. He glanced around and noticed that the women hid their faces as they passed by, avoiding eye contact at all costs. Most carried babies in their arms, though their frail bodies looked so thin he did not see how they could carry them for any distance. The babies, too, were thin, and trailing behind the mothers small children clung to their robes. For the most part, the women appeared somber, although he did see one smile and noticed that her teeth had already begun to rot.

At the juncture of two crowded streets, throngs of people waited to move through the intersection, some hauling children, some herding animals, and others maneuvering carts laden with goods. All seemed to be patiently abiding the wait, a thing that Darstan dreaded.

A small group of people burst through the street junction at the same time, heading down the street toward them. The women gathered their children close and turned sideways to squeeze by, offering sincere apologies for their unforgivable behavior.

A herder drove some animals down the street, a haggard old man with wrinkled skin. Surprisingly, he was able to keep the animals to one side with amazing discipline. When they passed by, the old man smiled. Darstan noticed he had no teeth and his gums were stained black and brown. A skinny dog whose skin looked to be drawn over protruding bones followed the old herder's commands religiously, nipping at any beast who feigned an attempt to move astray.

And darting right through the middle of this came an eager young boy with dirty-brown britches and a torn, ragged-edged garment that served as a shirt. In his haste to rush past he bumped into Darstan, but hurriedly acknowledged his error, begging pardon in a thousand different ways. The lad came across with such charm he brought laughter to Darstan's bitter frame of mind. Bowing one last time, he made his excuses, and departed—or would have departed, if Wisp had not seized him by the collar.

"Don't be so eager to leave, my friend. We have only just made your acquaintance." Wisp's cunning smile unsettled the lad.

His hazel eyes darted from side to side. "I must deliver a message to my sister," he explained in a tone that indicated a certain urgency.

Wisp would not be misled. "Before you go to your sister, perhaps you should return the purse you stole from my companion."

Darstan reached for his purse, instinctively, with his left hand, and though he had no hand to feel with, he could also determine he no longer possessed a purse. He seized the little thief with his right hand and yanked him forward. "Give me back my coin, scoundrel."

Takar grabbed the boy's shoulder and dragged him to the side. "Just get the coin, Darstan, then the Khataran guards can have him. He's old enough to have known better."

"Please, good Master? I am just a boy. I must feed two brothers, my sister, and my mother." His eyes pleaded for mercy.

"You should have considered that before you took my purse," Darstan said. "Take your punishment."

"You do not understand. They will cut off my finger. I will be maimed. You cannot do this, Master. Please?"

The smile slowly left Darstan's face. He lifted his left hand to display it in front of the little thief, and when he did the sleeve dropped to reveal the burnt stub of an arm. "Maimed like this?"

A ruckus from down the street diverted Darstan's attention to where a group of men wearing dark brown uniforms approached wielding staffs and blades, jostling their way through the crowds. Wisp cringed when they knocked down an elderly woman toting a small child, and not one of the bystanders cast even a second glance. Darstan looked as if he would start after them before Takar grabbed his good arm and held him back.

"This affair is not our concern, Darstan. Remember, the laws here are strange, and those men know the laws."

Darstan directed his attention back to the little thief once the mercenaries had passed. Difficult as it was, he had controlled his temper even when some of them had issued challenging stares. "Why should I allow you to go free, thief? You stole my coin."

The little rascal displayed an indomitable spirit, and, a tremendous talent for lying. "It is the very first time, Master. My family goes hungry, and I needed food." He held his head low, shame contorting his face.

Wisp smiled. "Since this is for your brothers and mother, lead us to them and we'll give them the food they need." Wisp shifted his grasp to a shock of the lad's hair and spun him around to face him, pulling back to put pressure on the boy and causing him to stare up at Wisp.

"You probably don't even have a mother," Wisp chided the lad. "And we know you are a thief, boy. And this is not your first time, or your second, or third. You lifted my friend's purse much too smoothly to be the novice you proclaim. No more lies. Tell the truth or I'll give you to the guard."

Smiling, Adju held up both hands, displaying all ten fingers. "One could not reach so many years without losing even one finger." His warm smile served him well; he thought he had convinced everyone, but Wisp's smile told the lad he had met his better. He thought briefly, then opted to divulge the truth, at least in part.

"My name is Adju. And until now, I was known as the best thief in the Hajaran." Adju saw the confused look on their faces. "Hajaran is this section of Khatara. No one here is wealthy, as you can see, but I manage to feed my family on goods taken from travelers." He looked at Wisp with a smile in his eyes. "And I do have a mother, and two brothers," he added.

"Adju." Wisp stated the name like he was saying it just to hear it himself. "And are you a good thief, Adju?"

The lad bowed low. "Not so good as I thought, Master, or you would not have caught me." Adju had fallen back into his charming habits again, instinctively using flattery to lure Wisp off guard.

Darstan laughed aloud. "Don't judge yourself so harshly, Adju. You stood no chance of deceiving him." Takar laughed along with Darstan.

Adju gleaned more from the disguised comment than Darstan imagined he might. "So, a student sought to teach the instructor. Is this so?"

In reply, Wisp dangled several items in front of Adju's face; Darstan's purse, and a knife and lock pick that he had removed from Adju's pocket.

Adju grabbed for them like a hungry dog scrambles for a bone. "Those are mine. Give them back."

"I'm certain the former owners of these goods would argue that. But, if you help us for two days, I'll let you go free."

Adju considered his predicament, though there really was not much choice; he would do what they asked, at least for a while. After all, this stranger might be able to teach him some things. "I would be most delighted to help you, Master."

Wisp smiled. "We will need someone who knows the city well, Adju. Someone who knows the merchants, and the mercenaries, and of course, some women who might take pleasure in meeting us."

Adju grinned from ear to ear. "I know everyone in Khatara. If you paid in gold no one could be a better guide."

Wisp laughed and returned the items that were his. "First, we need an inn. A good one, where we can have a hot bath, and good food."

Adju lightened his expression after receiving his goods back. "I know the best inn, Master—the Tracks in the Sand. It is where all the fine merchants go, and though I have never been inside, I have stolen glances through the windows. I can tell you, Master, that the serving girls there are the best in Khatara." Adju beamed. He knew he had done well on his first assignment. They would enjoy the Tracks in the Sand. *Someday, I will stay one night there,* he vowed.

Darstan tied his purse tightly about his sash. "There'll be no thief take it this time."

Adju smiled. "No, Master. No one will get it now."

"Stop calling everyone 'Master.' My name is Darstan, and he is Kender, though he is called many names; and the big, mean one is Sergeant Takar." Takar sneered at the introduction, but extended his hand to greet the lad.

Adju grimaced from the painful experience. "By the light of Ranalla," he swore. "He tried to crush my hand."

Darstan and Wisp laughed, and the guards roared; Takar's handshakes were well known, and avoided, by most of the men in Sykor. "He's just a burly old bear," Darstan said, and introduced Adju to the rest of the men. "This is Evin, and ...."

Wisp interrupted. "Adju, we want a good inn, but not one so nice as the Tracks in the Sand. We don't want to be noticed, and if this many newcomers to the city were to stay at the Tracks in the Sand it would attract attention. Especially Sykoran guards."

Adju's face lit up. "I have told you, Master Kender, Adju knows all. There is a small, but clean harjana only two streets from the Tracks in the Sand. Many of the lesser merchants from Jarana-Kalla stay there. It will serve you well. Come, I will show the way."

Adju started to go, but Wisp stopped him. "Adju, if you escape, I will find you. If it takes me two years, I will do it then turn you in."

The little thief smiled. "I would be hurt, Master, if I had known you longer. As it is I forgive you for not trusting me. But, come. We will go and meet the master of the harjana. His name is Mufed."

"Do you know him?"

"Know him?" Adju replied indignantly. "I have met him. I have talked with his wife and sat with his daughter. Someday, Khalina will be my wife. When I am a wealthy merchant, we will wed."

"What is a harjana?" Darstan asked.

"That is but a small inn," Adju explained. "It is where one family works all. It is especially good for people who do not wish to be seen, or noticed."

Wisp maintained a suspicion of the boy, and would, until he proved beyond doubt that he could be trusted. "Do you truly have a mother, Adju? Or was that a lie as well?"

A belly full of laughter erupted from the skinny boy. "I see that I cannot fool you even once, Master Kender. You are my family now. I have no one else."

Mother of rats! He was affected by Adju's contagious charm even more than the others, though he tried his best not to be. "I thought so, you blasted thief. Take us somewhere to get you clothes. I'll not have you looking like a beggar if you are to travel with me. And besides, if you ever plan to marry this Khalina, you'll need to impress her father."

Adju spun around so fast Darstan thought he would fall. "New clothes for me." He bowed low, and kissed Wisp's hand. "Thank you, Master Kender. My life is fulfilled."

Wisp blushed. "Just lead the way, Adju."

⌇

*T*he advance lookout approached riding hard, dismounting just as Pasha stepped out of the hut to greet him. "A great number of riders, Haffir-rond. Perhaps one hundred." Pasha stared into the distance toward the Sethian border. "How far?" he asked. "One league. Not much farther."

When the force of Sykoran soldiers arrived, Pasha greeted them alone. "Why do Sykoran guards come to Jattan-Kir? I see no caravan."

Force Leader Bragh bowed slightly in recognition of the Khataran leader. "We have been in pursuit of a band of deserters, following their tracks all the way from Sykor. I seek permission to enter your land so that we may capture them."

Pasha let his eyes search the force leader and the men surrounding him. He could sense no evil, and yet, he had not detected any with the others either. "I know those you speak of; they are but one day ahead of you." Pasha stared up into Bragh's eyes. "I do not see why so many chase so few. Are these men so dangerous? What acts have they committed that were so barbarous?"

Bragh allowed Pasha to finish, though his patience had been tried to the limits in Nyauran; Ictar had delayed him purposely, he knew, and he had no desire to have his patience tested again by further delays. But Ludar had issued explicit instructions regarding interference with the other regions, and he was not about to disobey Ludar's orders. "There are men dead because of them," Bragh told Pasha. "Again, I seek permission to enter your land. I do not wish to be forceful, but..." Bragh realized he might be insulting Pasha and stopped in mid-sentence.

Before he could offer apologies, Pasha delivered a threatening reply. "I am Pasha, Haffir-rond of the mountain tribes." Pasha rotated slowly, letting his arms indicate the mountain peaks surrounding them. "Look about you, Force Leader. See the archers whose arms strain from holding their bow strings taut."

Bragh didn't bother to look. He knew that he had erred in speaking so, and knew that if he made a threatening move toward the Haffir-rond, his body would be riddled with arrows in an instant. "I beg the Haffir-rond his forgiveness," Bragh pleaded. "No harm was intended. We come only to apprehend the offenders of our laws. I know that laws are important and respected in Jattan-Kir. I should trust that you understand."

Pasha remained tense but he recognized the argument of the force leader from Sykor; laws must be obeyed. "I will allow you to pursue them, but you may take only thirty men. No more."

Bragh started to protest, then thought better of it. "I congratulate you on your wisdom, Haffir-rond. We will go at once." Bragh turned to his strike leader and issued the commands. "Select three patrols of ten; the best three. Order the remainder of them back to Sykor with an explanation to the force commander. Hurry. We are one day behind."

As they prepared to depart, Pasha bade them enter the lands with the customary blessing. "Forgive me if I detained you too long. You are well come to the lands of Jattan-Kir, home to the First Ones, and the great city of Khatara."

TRACKS IN THE SAND

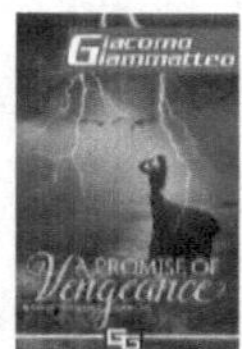

*A*dju led them from one side street to another, always rushing, and constantly on the alert for an unsuspecting traveler he might ply his craft on. Wisp caught him lifting the purse from a merchant just arriving from Pomanda. Adju had been so good that no one else even noticed.

"I only did it to test you, Master Kender."

"Consider the testing over with," Wisp said. "If I catch you again, you go to the guards. When I said no thieving, I meant from anyone, not just us."

Adju bowed low. "I am filled with shame, Master Kender, it will not happen again."

"What is the name of this place, Adju?" Darstan felt tired and his patience grew short.

"Mufed's," Adju said. "There, see that man?" He pointed ahead to a merchant entering a tavern. "That is Mufed."

The inn was small, much smaller than the Trader's Inn, or even Hardy's. "I doubt they'll have room," Darstan said.

"They will make room for me. I have met Mufed and sat with his daughter, Khalina. Mufed will make room for me."

Darstan laughed. "All right, Adju. We're relying on you."

Mufed met them at the door.

Adju beamed. "I have brought you business. Many rooms and meals. Let me introduce my friends. This is Master Kender."

A scowl covered Wisp's face. "It had better be a good inn, boy. After I let you talk me into staying here."

Mufed rushed to greet them. "May the blessings of the First Ones be upon you."

The innkeeper stood shorter than Darstan by almost a head, and he owned a round belly that draped over his britches in the front. He had chipmunk cheeks and his hair was thinning from the back of his head.

"I told them you had the best inn in Khatara. And the best food. Except the Tracks in the Sand, of course."

Darstan almost laughed. *The little rascal would lie about anything.*

"Master Mufed, would you like for me to stable their horses?"

"Please attend them, Adju. And when you are finished, come inside for a hot meal..." Mufed paused briefly, "and a room in the upstairs."

Adju darted out the door, calling back to Wisp as he rushed past. "I shall not be long, Master Kender."

Mufed and his wife seated them and had hot meals prepared quickly. Soon after they all retired for the evening.

∽

*D*arstan and Wisp sat in the room talking while waiting for Adju. He helped Khalina clean up after the meal. "No doubt, he's happy now," Darstan said. "He talked about that girl enough on the way over here."

Wisp pulled out one of his many knives to fiddle with while he talked, something he only did when he was bored or nervous. "I miss the bounty–man, Darstan. Even though we didn't always agree, I grew accustomed to his company." Wisp carved shavings off of his finger-nails to trim them while he spoke. "Darstan, do you remember the night we chased after Gregor?" Wisp paused briefly. "Do you remember what Mikkellana said to us?"

A scowl formed on Darstan's face. "The only thing I remember is Mikkellana saying 'cut it off.'" Darstan spat the words. "I don't want to discuss it. It's over, and I'll always have this as a reminder." He held up his left arm. The scowl on his face had turned to hatred.

"It had to be done or you'd have died." Wisp stopped carving and stared at Darstan. "Takar wasn't to blame, and neither was Mikkellana."

"All I'm thinking about now is how to get to Genda. Rahg is in danger and I've got to be there when it happens. I saw it in the dream."

"What you saw wasn't in Genda," Wisp said. "Not from how you described it."

"Genda is the last place I saw him, so I guess I'll have to start looking there."

"What else did you see?"

"Kella was there, and you. And there was a beautiful woman. I didn't know her, but she was one of the most beautiful women I've ever seen."

"I'm beginning to wonder if you're not mixing up dreams. My dreams are always about beautiful women; seldom do I dream about ugly ones."

Darstan laughed. "So how do we get to Genda?"

"Tomorrow, I'll make inquiries. There will be some seamen willing to risk taking us, despite the dangers with the pirates that Pasha told us of. Whenever there is gold to be made there are those who will risk all to earn it. And I'm guessing Adju will know where to find them."

Darstan nodded then rubbed his eyes. "I'm too tired to think any more tonight. I'll see you in the morning."

"Until the morrow then, Darstan. I intend to see what the great city of Khatara has to offer. Rest well, I'll not rouse you when I return. And I'll tell little Adju to sleep in the room Mufed offered so that he doesn't bother you."

~

*D*arstan awoke early, but it was the first good rest since leaving Sethia. He stepped quietly so as not to awaken Wisp, then looked and realized the bed lay empty. Darstan went to check with Mufed. When he stepped into the corridor he nearly tripped over Adju, asleep in the hall. "By the gods, Adju, what are you doing here?"

The little thief leapt to his feet. "I am sorry, Master. Did I disturb you?" Adju always seemed repentant, even when he did no wrong.

"Why were you sleeping on the floor?"

The little thief bowed low. "So you could rest. Master Kender told me not to disturb you. I stayed here to prevent anyone from waking you."

"Come inside, Adju. Get some sleep on the bed." Darstan turned about and entered the room, only to discover Wisp seated in a chair. "What are you doing here?"

Wisp nodded to the open window. "I would have returned sooner but there was much to learn. Adju, shut the door. We have business to discuss."

The little thief started to leave, but Wisp halted him. "No, don't go. Shut the door and come in; I'm counting on you to provide much of the input to this conversation."

Wisp settled comfortably into the chair. "Darstan, take Adju and see if you can find out which of the larger merchants have made successful voyages to Genda." Wisp then faced the little thief. "Can you get this information, Adju?"

Adju smiled broadly. "Whatever you need to know is on someone's lips in the street, Master Kender, and the right color coin will pry open the tightest lips. But there is no need to pay for that information; the one you seek is the richest merchant in Khatara—Harun Bulta. At night, men in dark alleys whisper that Harun Bulta will kill his own passengers to get their gold."

Harun Bulta. Wisp frowned. "I have no doubt about that. He has a brother in Sykor who is much the same."

"And one in Kamnor," Darstan said. "Arn Bulta. He may have been the most hated man in Kamnor."

Wisp thought for a moment. "Adju, there must be other merchants who have made the voyage safely. Find out who they are and where we can talk to them. We'll want to book passage quickly." Wisp turned to face Darstan. "Last night I saw some of the guards discussing mercenary opportunities with merchants at the Tracks in the Sand. Perhaps they uncovered some information that we could use. You should check with them before you leave the inn."

Adju cast his gaze to the floor. "You are leaving Khatara, Master Kender?"

Wisp heaved a frustrated sigh. "Not to worry, Adju. If we ever get to leave, you may join us."

Adju's ever-broadening smile cracked new skin. "You will not be sorry, Master. I can do anything to help." The little thief was so excited he could barely speak. "Master Darstan, I will prepare to travel the city. It is best we not take horses; it is vendor day and the streets will be crowded." Adju darted through the door, his bare feet making almost no noise as he ran swiftly down the corridor.

Wisp stood, shaking his head. "You better buy some more new clothes for that dirty lad, Darstan."

"You like him, don't you?"

"Just leave me be," Wisp said. "I plan on sleeping the whole day."

Darstan joined Takar at the table, setting aside his differences with him for now. "What have you planned for the day, Sergeant?"

"Right now, waiting on Evin." Takar sipped noisily at his mug of hot khaffe. "Some guards got positions with caravans, and some as mercenaries with a few of the larger merchants; two of them even joined the guards of Jattan-Kir, the emperor's unit stationed in Khatara. Only Evin and myself need find work now. And you."

Takar turned the question to Darstan. "What have you planned, lad? Have you given it thought yet? I don't wish to raise tempers, but there's not much you can do with just the one hand." Takar set the mug down and looked at Darstan. "I haven't had time to talk to you about this yet, but I feel badly about what happened. And though I don't think I would have done things differently if I had to repeat the scene...well, I still feel badly."

Darstan restrained himself. "I haven't forgotten the incident, Takar, but that's for another day's worry. Today, I plan to book passage on a ship bound for Genda. Wisp and I are going. And Adju."

Takar took two more cautious sips of the hot khaffe, steam rising from the mug. "I'll be joining you, too." Takar spoke as if he had just that moment resigned himself to the decision, and wasn't entirely satisfied with it. "I was there when Mikkellana spoke to us, and if I tell you I understood it I'd be lying bigger than Tobias, but I do believe there's great danger behind that shield. I saw what it did to you." The sergeant sat pondering his choice of words. "And I saw what you did." Again, Takar hesitated. "Only thing we need to discuss is Evin."

"What does Evin have to do with anything?"

Takar nodded to Evin just now descending the stairs. "He'll want to come with us," Takar said, "and if he does, it's only fair we tell him everything. I don't like taking men on missions where they don't know what the dangers are. Vlad knew—may the gods accept him— and he took the risks anyway. Which reminds me, have you told Adju?"

Darstan watched Evin as he walked toward their table. He was young for a guard, but no younger than Darstan. *I don't imagine he's any greener than I was last planting season,* Darstan thought. He gave quick consideration to telling Adju, but reserved that decision for Wisp. "I'll tell Evin, and I'll have Wisp tell the little thief."

"I don't know how I've become acquainted with so many thieves," Takar said. "Me, catching thieves all my life, and now I'm traveling with two of them. Surely the gods will not forgive this."

Darstan laughed.

"What's so funny?" Evin pulled a chair up to the table.

Darstan noticed Adju standing near the entrance to the inn; he appeared apprehensive about joining them. "Look at him. He can look so innocent when he wants to."

Evin sat down. "He reminds me of a little brother I have back in Sykor. No one ever thought he did wrong, but he was the worst of the lot."

Darstan motioned for Adju to sit with them, but no sooner had he seated himself, than Takar barked orders to leave.

"Hurry," Takar said. "We have a lot to do today."

"I only just sat down," Evin said.

Adju shot up like he had sat on a needle. "I am ready, Sergeant."

"But you haven't eaten, Adju."

"I do not need to eat, Master Darstan. There are many times I don't eat all day." Adju stood almost like a soldier at attention.

"You might make a good soldier yet," Takar joked. "If you manage to keep all your fingers."

"With Master Kender's help, I will always have them."

Takar couldn't help but laugh. "Well then, lead the way. But mind you, none of that when you're with me. I'll not condone it, even if I *am* forced to travel with you."

"Sergeant, I would not risk your good reputation in such a manner. Do you believe me to be without honor?"

"Just lead the way, Adju."

The sun had barely had time to heat the air when Darstan, Takar, and Evin followed Adju through the streets of Khatara toward the market. Darstan wondered why the streets had been constructed with such narrow space between buildings. More than six people abreast would be forced to squeeze together in order to pass by in the more narrow ones, but even the widest of them would only compare with a good-sized alley in Sykor. Now, Darstan understood why Adju had suggested they start early; the crowds already gathering made navigating the streets difficult.

Twice Adju flashed hand signals to people they passed—a small lad leaning against a vacant building, and then a crusty-looking older man dressed in rags who mimicked the sign then disappeared into a crowd of beggars. Darstan made a mental note to inquire about it later. For now, his curiosity was aroused by Adju's expression as he came running back toward them from the intersection ahead. "Guards on the next street."

Takar grabbed hold of Adju and spun him about until the little thief was staring into the sergeant's scarred face. "Are they any of the men who came in with us?"

"They wear the same uniforms, Master, but I did not recognize any of them, and I always remember faces."

Takar spat, and cursed. "It's the force Ludar sent after us. Must be." He scanned the narrow street for means to escape.

Darstan turned back in the direction they had come. A full patrol of guards marched straight for them. When he spun to ask Takar what to do, he saw the others, only fifty paces away.

"Darstan, go with Adju. They might not recognize you, especially with a local lad." Darstan began to speak, but Takar shoved him onward. "Go, lad. Now." Takar quickly analyzed their position and decided to turn back toward the guards approaching from the rear. "Come, Evin. It will give us more time if we go this way."

Darstan allowed Adju to lead the way while he trailed closely, head hung low in an attempt to avoid eye contact. *Come on, Adju,* Darstan prayed. *Just a little bit more and we'll be safe.*

The patrol leader cast Darstan a sidelong glance but passed him without confrontation. Darstan kept his eyes glued to the ground, walking slowly and following Adju's footsteps. He dared not risk a look at any of the guards and could not help but breathe a sigh of relief when he passed the last of them. The smile remained but briefly, as he heard a guard in the patrol call out.

"Force Leader, look ahead. It's Takar?"

A thousand thoughts ran through Darstan's mind, the predominant one being to run away and not return, but he couldn't leave Takar. Not after failing Gregor and Wehr. He slowed his pace, and mechanically turned about to face the guards who seized Takar and Evin, and held them captive with drawn blades. Adju slid inconspicuously to the other side of the street, positioning himself next to some baskets being offered for sale by an old woman.

"Stay out of it, Adju."

Darstan stood less than ten paces from the patrol, which had now been joined by the other group. They numbered nearly two full units. The force leader stepped up to Takar, his voice cold but not menacing.

"Sergeant Takar, where's the one who escaped from the prison?"

So, it is me they're after, Darstan thought. When he heard Takar laugh, he nearly laughed himself. The force leader must not know Takar if he believed to frighten information out of him.

"We left him with the Nyaurans, Bragh. Ictar hid him for us." Takar clenched his teeth and leaned forward. Several of the guards closest to him shied away. Darstan hoped Takar could make an escape by bluffing, though he knew it was a wish in vain. If Ludar's men had trailed them this far, they'd not give up so easily.

Force Leader Bragh nodded. "Very well, Takar. I know you won't break, but your young friend is another matter." Bragh looked at the soldier who held his blade on Evin. "Kill him."

Darstan had no time to debate. He must act now or allow another friend to die for him.

"Halt!" he screamed in his loudest, most-commanding voice.

Adju shrank into the recess between the basket and the wall, becoming all but invisible, leaving himself only enough room to observe the spectacle.

"Force Leader, it's the one who escaped," a guard said.

Bragh turned to stare at Darstan but did not lose concentration. "Keep guard on the sergeant and the other. Do not allow them to escape." Bragh stepped to the front of the line until he stood only a few paces away from Darstan. "Force Commander Ludar wants you to return with me." His voice retained the coolness that Darstan heard moments ago when he ordered the guard to kill Evin.

"Let Takar and Evin free and I'll go with you."

Bragh laughed. "You are in no position to dictate terms. Come with me and we'll not be forced to hurt you or your friends." Bragh stared into Darstan's eyes.

"Set them free!"

For a moment it set Bragh back.

Before he could react to Darstan's demand, Takar shouted a warning.

"Darstan, no! Don't do it, lad." He said it like a man commanding an unleashed dog not to attack.

Bragh raised his hand. "Archers. Aim for the legs and arms. Ludar doesn't want him killed."

Darstan's body began to vibrate, internally at first, then he visibly trembled.

"Darstan, no!" Takar screamed his last warning, then turned to Evin. "Fall to the ground when it starts, lad."

Evin stared at Takar as if the sergeant had lost his mind. "When what starts?" He had time for no further questions, being distracted by a shout from the front—Bragh had issued the ultimatum.

"Cede now or I order them to shoot."

Darstan felt it coming on, the burning sensation like a fever run wild, and the trembling. He knew it was happening, yet he couldn't stop it, or, wouldn't stop it.

"Then, die!" Darstan shouted. YellowFire spewed forth from the severed arm in a cylindrical shape and sped toward the Sykoran patrol, flaring out as it neared them to a width that covered the whole of the narrow street. The flames struck Bragh with full intensity and, as he screamed, the cylinder of fire burnt a hole through him. The archers had begun to draw back on the bowstrings, but when the fire rushed toward them, they dropped their bows and scrambled to escape.

Adju's big eyes nearly bulged out of his head. "By the Hand of the Lady!"

The men who had held Takar and Evin fled. Evin lost his composure and tried to flee as well. Takar leapt forward, seized the young guard by the back of his uniform and tossed him to the ground. Fire caught Takar's uniform and burst into flames.

Adju raced up to Darstan, yanking on his arm. "Master Darstan. Stop, Master Darstan. You are hurting Takar."

The little thief's words sparked Darstan into regaining control; he ceased the fire, slumping to the ground. Adju wasted no time. He rushed to Takar with a blanket taken from the baskets where he hid, and then smothered the flames. Evin managed to escape with only a few blisters. They soon quelled the flames and stooped to inspect the sergeant.

"He's bad," Evin said. "We need to find a healer."

Adju surveyed the scene of disaster: six Sykoran guards lay dead, burnt to a mass of smoldering ash, or with holes bored through their bodies, and five or six others wandered the street moaning and screaming about powers and the Evil One. On the side of the narrow street, two Khataran merchants lay on the ground, both burnt badly.

"We need to hide," Adju said. "The emperor's troops will come. They will search everywhere, even in houses. Hurry, I know of a stable we can hide in for a while. Hurry." He helped Evin raise Takar to his feet, but it took both of them to support him.

"Hold him," Adju said. "I will see if Master Darstan is able to walk."

Adju ran to Darstan and knelt by his side. "Master Darstan. Master Darstan, can you get up?"

Darstan shook his head, still in a blur. "What happened? Are they dead?"

"Some are," Adju said, "but Takar is hurt, and we must leave before more guards come. This time there will be too many, Master. Hurry." Darstan leapt to his feet. "Gods, not again. Don't let this happen to me again." Darstan rushed to help Evin support Takar. "Adju, we need to find a healer."

Adju scanned the street to the front and rear. "I know he needs a healer, Master Darstan, but first, we must hide somewhere. At least until I can talk to the healer. There is only one I know of who might be able to heal such wounds, but it is forbidden to bring someone to her unannounced. Follow me and I will take you to the stable."

~

*W*isp heard the scratching sound of someone scaling the wall beneath his bedroom window, a sound he was quite familiar with, having been careful not to make it himself for so many years. Without so much as a whisper, he rose from the bed and positioned himself in the shadows of the wall near the open window. A head poked through first. Wisp seized it and placed his blade to the throat of the intruder. "Adju? What are you doing coming through the window?"

"Master Kender. You must come. Sykorans tried to capture them, and Master Darstan attacked." Adju's eyes went wide. "Master Kender, he..he attacked with fire!..from his hands! He has killed many, and now I am afraid that the emperor's guards will find him. I have them hidden in the stable of a friend but if he discovers what they did he will not keep them safe. He is not a brave man."

"You did well, Adju." Thoughts raced through Wisp's mind. "Help me gather our things; we'll leave right away." As the two of them packed weapons and other necessary items, Wisp plotted their course of action. "Adju, you now know what kind of trouble we represent. You should not feel obligated to travel with us. I will still think highly of you. Most men, even brave ones, would have fled after the scene you witnessed, yet you stayed and helped my friends."

Adju stopped Wisp short. "I will go with you, Master Kender. Word will soon spread that I helped you, after that I could not remain anyway."

Wisp smiled, and clapped the lad on the back. "Lead the way to the stable. If what you say about the guards is true they will probably be scouring the streets even now." Adju began toward the door, but Wisp hailed him. "Adju, this way." Even as Adju turned to face Wisp he saw him climbing out through the window. "No sense in letting Mufed, or anyone else know we've gone. We need every advantage we can get."

Adju smiled. There was much to learn from Master Kender.

"Leave the horses," Wisp said. "If anyone figured out who we are, they'll have a watch on the horses, assuming we'd not leave the city without them. But we can always buy new horses."

Adju agreed. "There is no need to be secretive yet, Master Kender. No one will recognize us, at least, not until we join with the others."

"Don't forget the clothes, Adju. We must stop somewhere to purchase garments for Takar and Evin; if the fire burned them like you said they will need new clothes." Adju nodded. "It is just around the next corner."

Wisp bought a set of clothes for the two guards; Evin was easy, being about the same size as Wisp; as for Takar, he took the largest size they had available. Some of the emperor's guards had come into the shop while they were there. As Adju indicated, they had already begun the search. Wisp hustled them out of the merchant's shop. "Hurry, Adju."

The little thief scanned the streets as they walked, constantly checking the rear and side alleys for signs of being trailed.

"I've been checking also, Adju. I think we're safe."

After three more streets lined with small houses, they arrived at a slightly wider avenue filled with shops of lesser merchants and vendors who hawked their wares from tables placed right in the middle of the street. "Just ahead," Adju said, "the stable at the end of the street."

Wisp and Adju entered cautiously, their eyes darting about from side to side looking for trouble. When they detected nothing out of place, they walked toward the rear of the stable. Darstan was the first to see them.

"By the gods, Kender, I thought I'd not see you again."

"How is Takar?" Wisp asked. "Can he travel?"

A gloomy look shadowed Darstan's face. "He's bad. I don't know if he'll even live. He definitely can't travel."

"The emperor's guards are searching for you, Darstan. And Adju assures me they will be absolutely thorough. We must find a safe place to hide, and a healer for Takar." Wisp turned about. "Adju, you said you knew a healer?"

He pondered long on the answer. "She has forbidden us to come to her without permission. If she is caught, she will be put to death by the emperor's men. It is law."

Darstan's anger rose with his impatience. "What do you mean by this nonsense? There are healers in every city."

Wisp grabbed hold of Darstan's good arm and spun him about. "Don't be so foolish. The best healers are the ones who possess powers; I assumed everyone knew that. Nonetheless, we need her assistance."

"In Khatara," Adju explained, "only the emperor's physicians are permitted to heal. For someone to practice without the emperor's permission means death."

"Adju, I understand your concern, but you must take us to her."

"Yes, Master Kender, but, I do not know if we can make it during daylight. The guards will be searching everywhere. Perhaps we should go under cover of the dark."

"We have no time, Adju, so listen closely. You tell me how to get to the healer; Darstan and I will bring Takar." Wisp noticed Adju was about to protest, but he forestalled him. "Don't fret, Adju. We will arrive safely. You take Evin and a few of our items with you. With Evin in new clothes it should present no problem."

"All right," Adju muttered. "But you must hurry, or wait until dark. The longer you wait, the more guards there will be." The little thief grabbed Evin by the sleeve of his new garment. "Come, Evin, but try not to walk like a guard, and keep your head hung down."

Wisp laughed at Adju's observation; Evin did walk like a guard.

Once they left Darstan looked at Wisp. "You know Takar can't walk. Are you planning to do like we did in Sykor?"

Wisp nodded. "It might be the only way; we have no time for anything else. Adju said it's only a short walk from here; I can do that if we move quickly." They helped Takar to his feet and, once standing, Wisp invoked his power of Concealment.

Wisp avoided the crowded streets so that people would not inadvertently bump into them. Once, they were forced to remain perfectly still in the midst of traversing a courtyard to allow a patrol of the emperor's guard to pass. Darstan's heart was beating so fast he felt certain they could hear him. Takar remained semi-conscious, occasionally mumbling something incoherent about Vlad, or someone else from the guard in Sykor.

"We are almost there," Wisp said.

Two more streets led them to a narrow street packed tightly with small, but clean, homes. At the second house on the left, Wisp stopped and knocked, simultaneously removing his cover of Concealment. Almost at once, the door swung open. Adju frantically signaled them inside.

"We are very fortunate," he said. "The kind mistress agreed to look at our friend, Takar." It did not escape Wisp's notice that Adju was staring at him with a strange look upon his face, like he wished to tell him something privately. "I have already told the good mistress how the sergeant got burnt by that stranger with the fire in his hands." Now, Wisp understood.

Just then, the healer woman rushed over. "Hurry. Close the door lest someone see you."

Wisp had not even had a chance to admire her beauty when he was stricken numb by Darstan's words. "It's her, Wisp! She's the one in the dream. It's her."

Wisp stared at Darstan. *How could he have called me by my real name.*

Evin's mouth fell open. "You're Wisp?"

Adju's eyes nearly exploded. "No wonder you caught me!"

The healer eyed each of them with calculating eyes. "Enough of that," she ordered. "Bring that man over here, and lay him on this blanket. I can already see that he is badly hurt." She examined Takar, then rose and addressed them. "There are no herbs or lotions that can heal these burns. I only know of one medicinal remedy that is able to heal so severe a burn, though the price for such a healing is steep. How good a friend is he?"

"We have gold," Darstan said. "I am certain—"

"Who are you to offer me gold?"

"My name is Darstan; he's my friend."

Her lips had not cracked any smile. "Listen to me, Darstan, it will be my price, or nothing. You can take your friend elsewhere."

"What is your price?" Wisp asked, always eager to negotiate.

"I will tell you my price when I have completed the task. I can assure you, however, that it will be within your means to pay. You may not wish to, but you will be able to; that, is the important aspect."

Her eyes scoured both of them like a jeweler would a gem, but even so Wisp nodded agreement. "It is done, My Lady."

"It's her," Darstan said.

"I don't care who it is," Wisp said. "Let's get Takar taken care of, then you can discuss your dream with the healer." As they put Takar down the healer took charge. "You must leave while I work. It is the only way I will do this."

Adju appeared worried. "But, Mistress. the..the.."

Wisp interrupted. "Pardon, madam, but it is impossible for us to leave at this moment. Can't we stay until darkness has set in?"

"What are you hiding?"

She ambled over to Darstan; her walk mesmerized Wisp. If this was the woman from Darstan's dream, he had been right—she was beautiful, perhaps the most beautiful woman he'd ever seen.

"Very well," she said. "You may remain; however, when I have finished with your friend, you will answer my questions. *All* of them."

Her emphasis on that final statement made Wisp nervous. *She suspects something.* "You have my word," Wisp said.

The healer stared at Wisp and then, Darstan. "For what that is worth, I will accept it. Move your friend to the back room. I work alone and cannot be disrupted. Trust me, your friend's life hangs in the balance." Wisp and Evin moved Takar, then returned to the outer room to wait.

Adju struck fire to the lamps hanging in the front room, their light casting eerie shadows on the walls. Darstan paced the wooden floor; it was now halfway to midnight, and still the healer had not reappeared. Several times during the long wait they had heard Takar moan, and Darstan swore he could hear a humming noise of some kind emanating from behind the door, though no one else supported his claim.

"She has never taken so long," Adju said. "I have brought others here and I have spoken to many who have come themselves, but never has it taken this long."

The squeak of the hinges on the door made Darstan pivot to face the healer. Her face and eyes looked as if she hadn't slept in days.

"He will be fine," she said. "By tomorrow, he will be safely recovered, though not able to move much."

Darstan rushed past her, brushing aside the arm meant to restrain him. Wisp and Evin jumped up to stay Darstan, but the healer bade them stop.

"He needs to see for himself," she said.

A moment later Darstan reappeared wearing a look of amazement. "He is healed. I mean, there are no burns on him. None." He spun to face the woman. "How did you do this?"

"I believe I am in position to demand answers, my friend. You agreed not only to answer all my questions, but also to pay my price. You were in the room. Do you deny my work?"

Darstan held her mesmerizing gaze for a long time, finally bowing to the piercing emerald-green eyes she had. "You are the one in my dream," he said. "I need to know why."

She laughed. "I'm certain that I am in the dreams of many young men, though I cannot say I relish the thought. But that is something we can discuss at a later time." She lifted up his left arm and examined the severed limb.

"There is nothing you can do for me," Darstan said.

"I know that. But tell me—when did your powers develop? And how did you lose your hand? I have been blessed with the power of Healing; I can also sense powers around me. When you entered, I knew one of you possessed powers though I couldn't tell which."

Darstan didn't know what to say. Here was someone else with powers, and she was a Healer. Not the kind who used lotions and herbs, but a true Healer, the kind told of in stories. True Healers could cure almost like the gods themselves. That served to confirm his theory regarding her being the girl in his dream. "You must come with me to Genda and help my friend."

An aura of patience seemed to settle over the healer. "What is your name?"

"Darstan. But we have no time for niceties. My brother, Rahg, is in trouble, and I have to help him."

She spoke to Darstan in a voice drenched in sweetness. "Darstan, perhaps you have misunderstood the agreement. It is I who will issue the orders regarding who will help whom. And you, my friend, will be going nowhere. I have plans for you, and none of them involve your presence in Genda."

"No! I'm not ungrateful, My Lady, but I *must* get to Genda. I'll come back and fulfill my end of the bargain, assuming I'm able, but I must go. I must. And if you can't come with me, I'll go myself." Darstan shook his head. "You don't understand. He's my brother!"

The look in her eyes changed from sweet innocence to consummate danger. Now, the sweetness was gone, no more the dulcet sounding princess, but the cool detachment of a battle-tested force commander. "You will accompany me wherever I say, Darstan. You *will* keep to your promise."

Darstan laughed. "What will you do if I refuse—heal me to death? I'm going to help my brother, but have no fear, I'll come back when I finish." Darstan turned to leave, but with his first step pain gripped his head. Fear seized his heart, and he reached for his chest, pressing against it in a vain attempt to alleviate the pain. He felt his heart being squeezed, could feel his blood racing faster as the pain increased. "Let me go! Stop it."

Wisp and Evin looked on in a stupor. Nothing apparent was happening, and it was obvious that no one had a hold on Darstan, yet here he was screaming about someone holding him, and about pain with no visible source. Adju knelt on the floor and began offering prayers to his god.

"You will come with me," the healer said again, but when Darstan did not respond, the torture continued.

Darstan bolted for the door, but to his horror his legs were paralyzed. The pain increased to an unbearable level; if something was not done soon, he would die.

Fire. I must use the fire. Deep in his mind he didn't want to, feared more of his friends getting hurt, but he had to, had to, or he'd die. Darstan searched the depths of his mind for the fire, struggled to locate it. *It's gone!* He searched deeper into his soul, tried to force it out of his hands like before. Nothing. It was gone. He had no power left, and he was dying. Then, as suddenly as it had started, it ceased.

Darstan collapsed to the floor in a heap. He found it difficult to open his eyes, he tried several times but his lids seemed to weigh a hundred stone. When he tried yet again, the pain wracked his brain until he began to lose consciousness. To his surprise he discovered his lips still worked. "What happened?"

The healer loomed overtop of him like an enemy soldier on a field of battle. Her voice had now lost all traces of innocence, and sweetness; it chilled Darstan clear to the bone.

"I stopped you. I couldn't let you leave until your commitment was honored." She knelt alongside Darstan, gently placing her hands upon his head. "I will remove the lingering pain. I know it is uncomfortable."

Darstan felt a coolness rush through him, causing an involuntary shiver. But then the pain was relieved and he found himself not only able to open his eyes, but to sit up without discomfort. Immediately, he began to plan his course of action.

The healer woman seized Darstan's face with both hands and stared into his eyes with her own chilling emerald-green glare. "I saw a foolish look in your eyes, Darstan. A look I did not like."

She came ever closer to him, until Darstan could feel the warmth of her breath on his face. "Know this. What I did to you, I can do again. The pain you experienced can be increased ten fold without causing death. And also know this: in the time it takes you to move your lips, to blink an eye, or to think a thought—I can kill you. Long before your Fires rage inside your body, long before the first flames dance from your fingertips, before your body even glows with warmth—I can, and will, extinguish your young life. I will snuff you out like a candle if you ever dare attempt that with me. You will come with me, and you will heed me."

Wisp recognized this moment as a good time to shed new light on their position. "My Lady, we seem to be at a disadvantage by not revealing to you our mission."

She turned slowly to stare at Wisp, and for the first time since entering her house, he took the time to look at her, to really look at her. He had, of course, noticed her eyes before; who could not, their emerald-green sparkling like lamps of light in a room full of shadows. And he had taken note of her honey-colored hair—the way it bounced off of her slender hips when she walked, and the aroma—something had endowed her hair with the redolence of a heady wine, or a field bustling with the fragrance of fresh blooms. And her walk. She had completely enthralled him with her lithe legs, sinuous body, and tantalizing grace.

A whimsical thought blinked in Wisp's mind, just for a moment, then he tried to banish it to a lost recess of forgetfulness; however, he did not succeed, and the errant notion rushed to the forefront of his consciousness.

He had heard tales of the Khataran women called Qorami—women trained since birth for one thing only, to bring pleasure to men. They were raised in an isolated environment consisting solely of others such as they, and were taught by the older Qorami. Their bodies were bathed in milk taken daily from a special breed of mountain goat whose location remained a closely guarded secret. And their lips...

Wisp shook his head clear of such ludicrous ideas, the logical portion of his brain finally wresting control from this fantasy he enjoyed momentarily. She could not be one of the Qorami, he told himself, yet the possibility, no matter how remote, so piqued his interest he could not help but to dream.

He knew he dared not insult her and fought a valiant battle within himself to control his choice of words. "What is your name, madam?" Wisp breathed a sigh of relief; somehow, he had managed to remain sensible and not embarrass them.

She smiled benevolently, like she knew the struggle he had been through. "Aenaila."

The name floated on the currents of air, carrying to Wisp like it was meant for him alone to hear. "Aenaila," he repeated affectionately.

"What is it you wish?" Aenaila asked.

Wisp managed to break free of his fascination for her long enough to speak. "Aenaila, we have no desire to act in a dishonorable fashion, but we face a dilemma that holds possible interest for even you." The look in her eyes told Wisp she was intrigued and he motioned for Evin and Adju to leave the room.

"Continue," Aenaila said.

Wisp explained how Darstan lost his hand in Sethia, and he told Aenaila about Mikkellana saving them. He informed her about Mikkellana's message regarding the weakening of the shield, and the eventual release of the Evil One if something was not done soon to prevent the shield from deteriorating.

"How does all this affect me?"

"Though you probably paid no attention to him earlier, Darstan mentioned that you were the one in his dream."

She nodded.

"He has foreseen everything correctly, so far. Even the loss of his hand was foretold by his dreams." Wisp waited for a sign from her but she sat silently listening. "I would propose that you accompany us to help save our friends, and afterward we will return to keep our vow to you." He anxiously awaited her reply.

"So, you too, would cast honor aside and go with him."

Wisp did not hesitate. "Honor will have no meaning if the Evil One breaks free of the shield. I believe that this has much to do with it, and I believe that you also have much to contribute, else you would not have been in the dream. You must go."

"And how do you intend to locate your friends?" It was a logical question she posed.

"We will sail to Genda and secure a ship to sail us to Entiria—"

"Entiria! You are brave fools if nothing else, but still fools, and bravery will not make you successful. You will never reach Entiria."

"We will," Darstan said.

Aenaila considered their unusual request; something inside tugged at her conscience, telling her to accept the proposal. "How familiar are you with Genda? Did you live there? Do you know a spot in Genda so well that you can describe it to me perfectly, with no errors, with your life at stake on one flawed description?" She stared first at Darstan and then Wisp, allowing her piercing gaze to burn into their souls.

"Why do you want to know?" asked Darstan.

Aenaila's curt response stung. "It is nothing unless you know it."

Wisp suddenly recalled the night in Sethia when Mikkellana had transported them from the shield to the camp, whisking them across the distance in the blink of an eye. It struck him that she might be probing for the same reasons. "Can you travel like Mikkellana?" His excitement showed, an unusual event in itself.

Aenaila scrutinized Wisp, reflecting pensively on his last statement. "So, you really did meet her. What do you know of it?" Curiosity had stimulated a burning desire to know more of these interesting strangers.

Wisp related the particulars of their transportation that night to Aenaila in excruciating detail, culminating with the actual traveling process and their reappearance in the camp. Halfway through the explanation, Aenaila's expression turned sour. "It does not matter," she explained when Wisp had finished. "It requires complete knowledge of the area. Nothing can be out of place. Even for one who possesses the power, the training is long and arduous."

"Wisp remembers everything," Darstan boasted. "He can tell you."

Aenaila sighed. "It is more than a telling," she explained. "I must be able to actually 'see' the site in my mind. If an error is made we could be forever lost; we could even die."

The three of them mulled over their circumstances; failure loomed imminent until Wisp's active imagination originated an idea. "Aenaila, are you able to 'look' into my mind? Actually see for yourself what images I possess?"

Her initial reaction was to laugh, but then, she understood what he asked and considered the question seriously. "Yes, I could. But still, I would only be able to extract what images you retained in conscious memory; it could not be something from the recesses of your mind."

Darstan realized what they were talking about. "I told you, Aenaila. He remembers everything. Test him." He saw Aenaila smile, obviously she liked his suggestion.

"Turn and look at the fireplace, but only briefly, and then we will conduct our experiment."

"There is no need for me to turn, Aenaila. Do your test now." Wisp stated it without bragging, though Darstan managed to let slip a chuckle.

Aenaila appeared stunned, the first time Darstan had seen that particular expression on her face. "No need?" she asked incredulously. "You have a complete recollection of it even without knowing it would be of import?"

Wisp laughed this time. "Everything is important to me, Aenaila. It is second nature for me to commit to memory all the people I encounter, and the rooms I enter, even if it is for only a short time. I never know when I may need the information."

Still doubtful, Aenaila sought permission to probe his mind. "It will not be harmful, but it may instill a strange sensation throughout your body. Remain steady. Do not move and you will be fine."

With that as the sole explanation, Aenaila cupped her hands about his head to begin her search. Darstan observed closely. He saw Wisp's eyes go wide, noticed his teeth clench tightly. Other than that, there were no exclamations of pain and no sudden movements. It was over in a matter of moments. "Now we shall truly test it," Aenaila said.

Darstan watched as she stood up and closed her eyes, obviously in a state of heavy concentration. Suddenly, she vanished, only to reappear on the other side of the room by the fireplace. Her face beamed with joy and excitement. "You have an incredible memory, Wisp. I have never seen anyone with a comparable one."

A brief pause occurred while she struggled with her own decision. "It will be dangerous," she cautioned them. "Traveling to Genda is much more difficult than skipping across the room. More can go wrong when covering a distance so great, much more; however, I am satisfied that we can make use of his memory as a suitable site. It must be somewhere where there will be no people, or, at a time when no people should be present. Once in Genda, we will find some way to reach Entiria."

Darstan nearly jumped out of his skin with excitement. "Wisp, did you ever see the boat?"

The skin on Wisp's forehead wrinkled from confusion. "What boat?"

Darstan grabbed him by the shoulders and shook him. "The boat that Rahg and Rhaven hired to take them to Entiria. Did you see it?"

Suddenly, Wisp understood. "Brilliant, Darstan. Yes, I did. And I specifically recall the masthead, and the area surrounding it." Wisp turned to Aenaila and hugged her. The excitement had become infectious. "We can go right to them, Aenaila. We have no need to go to Genda."

"Wonderful," Aenaila muttered, but with no enthusiasm. The prospect of rushing across the world to do battle with a Banished One did not seem promising to her. In fact, it appeared rather daunting. "You will inform your friends of what we face? If they are of sound mind, they will not wish to go."

"Takar already knows," Darstan said.

"He can't go," Aenaila explained, interrupting. "He's not well enough yet. I will make arrangements for him to remain here. He will be safe."

"Then I'll tell Evin and Adju, if they wish to stay with him it's fine by me." Darstan lowered his head like a little child as he asked the next question of Aenaila. "There is one more who must go. She was in the dreams also."

Aenaila frowned. "I should have guessed that a woman would be not far from one with your looks, Darstan. Who is it, and where is she?"

"Her name is Kella," Darstan said. "She's a vargel that travels with us. The last we saw of her was just before we entered Khatara from the mountain trail."

Darstan thought he heard Aenaila curse and the look on her face would have supported that supposition. "If Mikkellana had not been involved with this, I would never have agreed. Even now, I feel certain we are wrong."

She sighed aloud, a frustrated sound. "Hurry. Tell the others, and make whatever preparations are necessary. I know of a spot outside the city I can Shift to. If we can locate the vargel, we will depart from there. Wisp, have you got a good picture of that ship in your mind?" Her tone indicated that his answer had better be affirmative.

"I do," Wisp said. "And don't worry about Kella, we can always find her."

Doubts continued to creep into Aenaila's mind. "I worry about much more than finding your vargel. I don't even know how far this Entiria is. We should stop first in Genda; I know I can make it there."

"We can do that," Darstan said, "Wisp knows plenty of places in Genda." Darstan rushed toward the other room. "I'll tell Evin and Adju to prepare." It didn't even occur to him that they might not want to go.

Aenaila left briefly to give her friend instructions regarding the care of Takar, and what to do and say if any guards came. She finished quickly then returned to her house, wasting no time with unnecessary words. "Grab hold of me," she said, "and do not let loose your hold. We will find the vargel then depart for Genda from there. Wisp, you had better be prepared, and for all of our sakes I pray you are accurate with your description."

"My name is Kender, not Wisp. In some places, it would not be wise to call me Wisp. And have no fear of my part; I will be prepared."

Wisp thought of a spot just outside of Khatara, where Kella had last been seen, and let Aenaila know that he was ready. Once they found the vargel, he then formed the picture of one of the alleys in Genda over and over in his mind until he could recall it immediately. From there, he pictured the masthead on the ship until a perfect image rested in his mind. I've got it, he thought. I only hope the ship is still afloat. I have no desire to reappear on the bottom of the sea, though it might be better than fighting a Banished One. At least I might swim to safety from the sea, if it's not too deep. "What will it take to kill a Banished One?" Wisp hoped for a favorable response.

"Your friends had better be strong," she said. "Very strong. And someone had better be a master strategist, because no Banished One has ever been slain by mortals."

IMMINENT DOOM

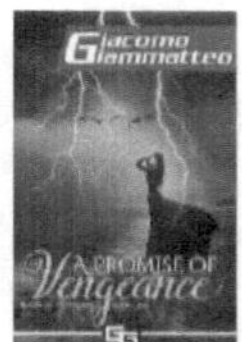

*A*board the Sea Skate the men gathered about topside, listening as Minnoso told the story about getting caught in the cavern between the narrow passages. "Must not have any people over ten stone in this land. I'm glad there are no women so large, but it strands me on the ship; I won't even be able to see what they look like." Minnoso laughed at his own misfortunes along with the other seamen.

"Easiest I've ever had it while asea," one seaman mentioned.

"Aye." echoed from the lips of many others.

"Just wait. When old Sennar gets back, he'll find work. Even if it's diggin' a hole in the floor of the sea." Minnoso's belly shook with his laugh. "By a shark's own eyes, he can't bear to see a man idle."

Another seaman lifted a mug of ale in salutary fashion. "Then here's to his not returnin'; leastwise, not soon." While the men drank their toast and laughed, the air in their midst crackled and glowed.

"Blood and salt. What's happenin'?" Minnoso dropped his mug and stumbled over backward.

In the middle of the ship, out of nothing, appeared a small group of strangers—and one humongous dog-like creature.

❧

Once they fully materialized, Aenaila collapsed. Wisp supported her while Darstan glanced at the terrified seamen, fixing them with his gaze. "I seek Rahgnar Fal–Thera," he said. "He boarded this ship with three others. Where is he?"

"Not here," Minnoso said. "Went with the captain to see who claims rights to this land."

"We need cabins for the night," Darstan said, and no sooner than he said it than Minnoso offered to lead the way, a frightened look in his eyes.

They retired to cabins on the deck below, gathering together for a discussion of strategy. Adju and Evin had not uttered a word since appearing aboard the ship. "How long before you can leave, Aenaila?" Darstan asked, his impatience already showing.

Aenaila sat up straight on the bed and stared at him with entrancing, emerald-green eyes. "I know you are anxious about your brother, Darstan, but Shifting tires me. I need rest before we can leave. If we met trouble now..."

"I can protect us."

Aenaila managed a weak laugh. "And do you recall, Darstan, that with little effort I held you powerless? The power of a Banished One is mine a hundred fold. That is why we must rest. We need to enter this fray prepared, for all the good it will do."

"I'll tell them we're leaving in the morning. Sleep well, Aenaila." The door shut quickly behind him.

"Sleep well, Darstan," Aenaila whispered.

Adju and Evin made way for the door. Wisp, too, began to leave. "Well, Aenaila. I shall bid you a good night, unless you have need of company." His brown eyes sparkled at her.

"You are a bold one, lad." *And I like bold men.* She looked at Wisp only to see the expression of indignation that so readily came to the thief's face. "Don't attempt that with me, lad. And yes, you are but a lad."

"I didn't realize you felt so old. Perhaps I could help you regain some of your youth."

She signaled for him to leave, but she couldn't restrain a smile.

"I only offered to stand guard."

"Then you have my gratitude and I accept your kind offer. You may stand guard outside my door."

Kella joined Wisp in the corridor to stand watch. Kella wasn't Wisp's favorite companion but at least her company allowed him to get sleep. No one would dare try to enter the room with that beast blocking the way.

~

*D*arstan rose before the sun. He found Wisp asleep, but Kella fully alert. "At least someone kept guard," he said. "I'm going topside to get guides."

Wisp yawned and stretched. "There was no sense in both of us staying up all night. I'll wake Aenaila and the others."

None of the seamen volunteered to guide them, so Darstan selected three. "I'll kill the first one to lead us astray," he warned, and saw the fear rush back into their eyes.

Aenaila frowned. Threats were not a favorite tool of hers, but she said nothing; Darstan was under extreme pressure. *By the Blood of the*

Blade, we are all under strain—going to face a Banished One. We are all mad.

The guides led them into the cavern, despite the protests from Wisp about going under the water to get there. No one else complained, not even Kella.

"There is nothing to argue about," Aenaila said. "They say there is no other entrance."

Once inside, the lead guard began offering excuses in the event they became lost. "None of us have ever been here," he said. "I can only go on what Minnoso said. But..but. I'll not steer ya wr..wrong. Not me."

Darstan glared at him. "Just lead on. And brighten that lamp."

At midday they stopped briefly to eat then, after a quick meal and a bit more walking, they saw the light from the outside shining into the cavern ahead of them. The seaman in the lead made signs to his gods and closed his eyes in prayer.

"Keep moving," Darstan ordered. They made steady progress up the steep trail leading to the top, arriving at the summit by nightfall. "They made camp here," Darstan said as he stooped to examine the remains of the site. "It's dark, and we all need sleep, might as well make our camp here also."

When they were safely out of hearing, Aenaila spoke. "Tomorrow, I should be able to use my Vision Shifting so we can speed this journey along."

Darstan perked up at the mention of hurrying things up. "What is that?"

"It is the most simple form of Shifting. Similar to what we used to come here from Khatara though easier to command. And much less exhausting."

Darstan nodded. "Good. The sooner we get there the better."

Aenaila yawned. "Let's get some sleep."

~

*H*igh atop a rise on the western part of the City of the Sun, the air split with a noise like thunder. For the briefest instant, the rocky terrain of Sethia could be seen but it quickly blurred as the force of a thousand men stepped out onto the lands of Entiria. At their head stood Iazzo the Persecutor.

A seasoned glance at the terrain provided Iazzo with enough information to begin issuing orders. "Secure the gap. Place a double row of pike-men at the opening and reinforce them with archers. Put archers atop the rock walls and a second line of them in the forefront until ordered to the rear."

Iazzo looked to see that his orders were being carried out even as he spoke. "J'ag Tem. I want a full band of Sethian palace guards about me at all times. You will oversee the battle as it progresses, keeping me informed as necessary." Iazzo laughed. "I will draw the Entirians into battle."

~

J'ag Tem shouted orders at Sethians and Victas and Wolfen. He had chosen his leaders carefully; victory was only a question of time. Sejja, the Wolfen leader, was a big, strong Wolfen with battle intelligence that few possessed. J'ag Tem selected him because he had never been beaten in hand to hand fighting. The other Wolfen would follow him anywhere.

Kraffr ruled the Victas, and he too was a proven leader with the respect of the tribes. J'ag Tem once saw Kraffr stabbed three times, yet stay to finish fighting for half a day. His ferocity alone would provide inspiration to the others. This was the first true battle outside of Sethia since the wars a thousand years past; J'ag Tem felt that leadership was the key to success. "Sejja. Kraffr. Prepare your men for battle."

❦

Rahg and Camissa strolled through a courtyard next to the building that housed their quarters. A myriad of new fragrances exploded from flowers they had never seen. "You're not yourself today, Rahg."

A guard raced toward the temple, and moments later Entirians poured out like ants whose mound had been disturbed. "What are they shouting?" Camissa asked.

"The attack has begun," Rahg said. "A Banished One is here." Before Rahg could react, before he could even think, a huge ball of fire struck at the palace-like structure next to the temple. He yanked Camissa toward him. "Let's go, Camissa. Find Rhaven and Tobias. Tell them I'll meet them at their quarters. I'm going there now."

"I'm coming with you."

Rahg stopped to confront her, his face red with anger and worry. "No!. There's no reason for you to come."

Camissa took his hands in hers and held them gently; her smile comforted him. "No need to worry. No matter what happens we will be together."

From behind, Rahg heard another voice.

"And no matter what happens many of the enemy will die."

Rhaven's smile chilled Rahg. *A man shouldn't smile before a battle,* Rahg thought, but in spite of his feelings he smiled also. "We'll do what we must, Rhaven. And the enemy will die. If we die as well, then the scribes will have a story to tell." Rhaven laughed, a rare occasion, but he laughed heartily.

784

"You know, for nearly thirty years I feared dying in the sea because of the dreams I had. Now it looks like I'll die on dry ground after all. Don't that beat all." Tobias slapped his leg, roaring with laughter.

"It is nothing to be laughing about. We could all die," Camissa said.

Rhaven stopped and pulled her toward him. "You're right. And we probably will die, so those of you who have words to say to your gods had better say them now. There is not always an opportunity to say them when the time actually comes."

Camissa and Tobias bent their heads in reverence and muttered some prayers.

"No words to say, lad?"

Rahg stared at Rhaven. "No gods to say them to. I'll trust in my sword, and now, my shield."

Rhaven nodded understanding. "You haven't had much time to practice the shield; stay close to me during the fighting; we can help protect Camissa as well as each other."

Rahg lifted his eyes. He knew what he meant was stay close so he could protect Rahg as well as the others, but Rhaven knew Rahg wouldn't accept the offer for his own sake. "Thank you. She'll need the help."

"Then let's be off, lad. I hunger to meet the enemy."

Rahg tugged at Camissa and they hurried down the corridor toward the outside entrance that led to the west gate. Rhaven ran ahead, restraining himself to let them keep pace. There was something in the way he smiled when he spoke of killing the enemy that had chilled Rahg. *I'm glad he's with us.*

*A*entarra appeared inside the cover of her favorite enclave of rocks near the Sethian border where Darstan, Wisp, and the others had battled only days before. Carefully, she touched the shield. *Good, it still holds, but something has transpired.* Aentarra sensed the surroundings. A battle. Here. She searched, careful not to go too near the shield. Then she saw the bodies; smelled the scorched earth. She looked to the ground just inside the border of the shield, and she knew at once.

These powers came from the outside. Now I must find him.

~

*T*he Entirians ran about frantically. *They're not accustomed to battle,* Rahg thought, then laughed. *As if I'm some veteran of wars.*

Rhaven was talking to J'en Kar, the Shulan of Entiria. "Your people must fight."

"We have no weapons."

A large ball of fire hissed through the air and landed in the garden next to the temple. Trees and flowers burnt to ashes. Rhaven seized the shulan and shook him. "Do you see what we are fighting? If you do not fight they will kill you anyway. Tell your people to get work tools, shovels, hoes, mallets, anything. But they must hurry, Shulan, or we'll all die."

J'en Kar nodded. "They will come."

At the temple, Rhaven and Tobias discussed strategy with Rahg, Camissa and the leaders of the Entirians. "Surely, they'll have archers," Tobias surmised, "and probably have them up high on those rocks above the clearing."

J'en Kar had gathered over two thousand men already, and, though they were not armed with anything other than farm tools, they seemed willing to fight. "There is no other way to reach them," J'en Kar explained. "The hill is steep and only those two paths lead to the top."

Tobias cursed. "That'd be like killin' sheep. We'd be walkin' right into it."

"What if the sheep were protected?" Camissa suggested.

"You mean by the lad?"

Camissa scowled. "I mean by Rahg. He can weave a shield around three parties of men, sufficient to protect against arrows. It will bring us near enough to engage them hand-to-hand."

"And the Banished One?" Rhaven threw a hitch in the plan. "From what I know of the powers of the Banished Ones, Rahg won't be able to hold his shield."

J'en Kar's interest was aroused. "You could do that?" he asked Rahg. "You could protect us from their archers?"

"I don't know. I don't want to be responsible for all these lives."

Camissa knew it was frustration and concern for the Entirians that sparked his emotions. "In practice you held shields over five positions. No arrow pierced them."

"That was practice, Camissa. Practice. And no lives depended on me holding that shield." Rahg's head dropped and his voice lowered. "And there was no Banished One testing my shield." His voice raised to an angry tone. "Do you think Iazzo will be idle while we advance on his position? Well, I can tell you, he won't."

"You can only do your best, Rahg. We can all only do our best."

Rahg shook his head. "So many lives, Camissa. So many depend on me. I..I only hope I don't fail them. I..."

Camissa placed her fingers against his lips. "Sh." Then she placed her lips against his, and gave a soft, warm kiss. "No matter the consequences, Rahg, I will always be with you."

Her voice was the softest whisper he had ever heard, and the sweetest. Rahg hugged her tightly; the reassurance had been needed.

"Let's go then. No sense in waiting any longer." Rahg walked back to face the shulan. "J'en Kar, I'll shield your people as long as my shield holds. But I must warn you, it might collapse at any time. I can promise that I'll hold it to the very end but that's all I can promise."

"No," J'en Kar shouted. "If you feel any weakening of your powers, release the shields over my people. All who have come here are in agreement; you must save yourself. You must defeat the Banished One, then slay the Messenger. The prophecies have foretold it. It must be done."

"I'll just have to hold the shields as long as I can, J'en Kar. I won't give up one of your people to save myself."

Rhaven resumed control of the meeting. "We have no time for argument. Rahg will do what he must when the time comes. As for the rest of us, this is what we will do." Rhaven instructed each leader in the details of the plan. Much of it depended on Rahg, and on his timing and ability to control the shield.

Rahg prayed that the practice Aentarra had him doing the last few days was sufficient. He also worried about the Banished One. *What will he do? And how will we defeat him?* All these thoughts spun around in Rahg's head like a windmill. Ever-present was the thought of Iazzo the Persecutor. *I wish Aentarra hadn't told me his name.*

"It is time," Rhaven said. Rahg fell in behind Rhaven, worry drenching his face. "There was a time when you told me you planned to kill every Victa in the world. If that is still your intent, then today will present a fine beginning to your quest."

Rahg laughed, remembering that night on the journey to Sykor after the battle at Twin Forks. "I guess we'll have to start here, Rhaven."

"That's right. We will begin here. And don't concern yourself with Camissa, or anyone else. You uphold your part of the plan and we will all be fine."

Rhaven burst through the doors leading to the temple courtyard. Already, several massive balls of fire had scorched the ground black and destroyed all the gardens. Rahg's eyes widened at the extent of the destruction, and, at the number of soldiers who stood at the ready. If they could be called soldiers—men with picks, shovels, hoes, and rakes. And all prepared to die for some prophecy and a man they knew nothing about. Their fervor and courage inspired him.

No matter what happens, I'll protect these men.

J'en Kar wanted to wait for more volunteers to arrive, but Rhaven convinced him that to delay would only serve the purpose of the enemy. "The more destruction he wields on your city, the more frightened your people will be, and less likely to join the fight. But if they know you have already entered the battle, that their countrymen are shedding blood, they will pick up arms and come to your rescue."

They divided the men into three units. Eight hundred went with J'en Kar to attempt a furtive climb from the far west side up a narrow trail that had been all but forgotten. They would be under cover of the sheer cliffs that rose from the sea, and if all went according to plan Rahg would not even have to shield them as they could not be seen from where Iazzo had his men positioned.

One thousand men would attack from the east side, navigating a twisting road of stone that weaved in and out of a heavily covered forest.

The remaining two hundred would accompany Rahg on the southern trail, straight toward the summit. It was open and offered no protection.

Rahg questioned Rhaven's strategy when he first heard it, but after

Rhaven explained it in detail, it did appear sound. The Entirians under J'en Kar would advance unseen until they were almost upon them, and even then, the enemy archers could not fire upon them without exposing their flanks.

That left Rahg with the task of shielding the eastern army and his own group, and the eastern army would require only light shielding, and intermittent at that. The heavy cover of trees would afford them strong protection most of the time. If all went as planned, he could concentrate nearly all his efforts on a shield to protect his frontal assault. Despite the logic of it all, Rahg worried. So much could go wrong.

He glanced at Rhaven, still as a statue. Everyone else walked, or paced, or fidgeted in some way, but Rhaven moved no more than a rock.

I wish I had his courage.

As if reading his mind, Rhaven came over and slapped Rahg's back with a supportive pat. "It is time, Rahg. And don't fret, you will do fine."

Rahg was still smiling from the rare compliment when Rhaven addressed the others, his voice deeper, more gruff; a battlefield commander's tone that reached to all corners of the crowd.

"J'en Kar, it is time. Remember, kill the archers first, and steal weapons; but above all, everyone's goal is to slay the Banished One. If you can steal a bow, shoot at him, if a sword, fight through the ranks and strike him dead. If victory is to be hoped for, the Banished One must die."

J'en Kar turned to face his men. "Death to the Banished One!" he shouted. The voices of two thousand Entirians rang through the valley, raised to a fever pitch. "Death to the Banished One. Death to the Banished One."

Rahg found himself shouting with them, hot blood racing through his veins. "Attack!" Rahg's scream rang through the crowd. "Attack!" Without even realizing it, he had assumed the command.

Rhaven smiled, nodding to J'en Kar, and to Mesla, who would command the eastern army. We'll follow the lad, his silent gesture said. They acknowledged with orders to their men.

Marching up the hill toward certain death, Rhaven repeated the instructions. "At the first sign of arrows, or enemy archers, report to Rahg so he can shield us.

~

The sun had not broken the darkness when Darstan awakened. He prowled the campsite, suspiciously checking the seamen they had taken as guides, as well as the surrounding area. Something had caused him to rouse, yet, he could find nothing.

Darstan looked up at the sky, stars blanketed the pre-dawn of morning and Ranal and Ranalla yet shone, though soon they'd cede to mother sun and the day would come alive. "Wisp, get up." Darstan made no attempt at being quiet. Kella bounded into the enclave from somewhere outside in the forest.

I didn't even see her. Good thing she's not on their side.

"Why did you wake me so early?" We can't leave yet. Aenaila needs light to Shift."

Darstan smiled. Wisp normally slept little so Darstan could not blame him for complaining. "We can eat, clean-up, and pack. By then it should be light."

Wisp sat up, resting his head against drawn-up knees. "Worried over Rahg, or just in a hurry to die?"

Darstan glared at Wisp for an instant, then walked away. "Come right, men. We depart shortly."

Adju had gotten up as soon as Darstan arose; he heard everything, or nearly. "I'm ready, Master Darstan." Pride beamed on his face.

"You're ready for nothing," Wisp said. "They'll be no battle for you, beggar boy." Adju began offering protestations, but Wisp cut him short. "No. There are other things you must do. Needs more important than having you killed, and you surely would be killed."

Wisp walked over and hugged the little beggar. "Look, Adju. I wish I could stay with you. I wish I didn't have to go to this battle." He bent down and pressed close to his face. Adju's tears were just beginning to roll out of the corner of his eyes.

"Adju," Wisp said softly. "I don't want to die. I'd rather stay with you, teach you what I know." Adju's tears flowed faster and Wisp did all he could to restrain his own. "But, I promise this. If I come back alive you will be with me, and I'll teach you all I know."

The little beggar finally looked up; his dirty hand smudged the tears across his cheeks. "Make the promise, Master Kender."

Wisp looked about him, then whispered. "On the honor of Lady Death," he swore.

"We will make a good team," Adju said with renewed confidence. "I will have to teach you some things, but I believe you could learn fast."

Wisp stared indignantly at the brash beggar who now walked over to get some food. "Mother of Rats," he swore, shaking his head, "he's as bad as me."

"Not quite," Aenaila said from behind him.

Wisp jumped. "Not quite, what?"

"He's not quite as bad as you, but given time, under your tutelage I'm certain he could equal, or even surpass, your arrogance and conceit."

Wisp's eyes probed Aenaila's. "Can you read my thoughts?"

"No, they were evident to anyone."

They walked toward the campfire together. Aenaila touched his hand and held him back. "Wisp, I..." She blushed. "You know, I don't even know your full name. What is it?"

"Kender Darnell."

Aenaila smiled, trying to hide the redness in her cheeks. "I like that name. Kender. It is a good, strong name." Wisp noted she became serious again. "Kender, I..."

Wisp reached for her, began to speak, but she pressed a finger to his lips. "Let's talk about this later," she said. "I'm hungry."

Aenaila had no sooner begun eating than Darstan interrupted her. "How much longer?" His impatience grew with each new ray of sunshine.

Aenaila swallowed the last of her food and sipped the khaffe. "As soon as everyone finishes their meal. If we encounter trouble the nourishment will be needed, and by everyone, Darstan, you included."

Darstan tied the final knot on a pack he carried on his back. "I've eaten."

"Then allow us to do the same," Aenaila replied brusquely.

The process of traveling by Shifting was slower than anticipated. At many points, the heavy forest and steep inclines prevented her from obtaining a good enough view of the spot to chance a Shift. Aenaila was forced to travel shorter distances in order to keep it safe. Even so, they were crossing the terrain at an incredible rate of speed.

At the crest of the next hill, Darstan stared out over the canopy of the forest below. In the distance, he could see a city, a great city like he'd never seen before. For a moment Darstan stood numbed by the magnificence and wonder, then abruptly the smile disappeared from his face; terror replaced it. "The battle has begun!" he shouted.

"How do you know?" Wisp asked.

Darstan stared blankly, like he was entranced, his cloak flapping in the breeze a contrast to his motionless body. "I can feel the battle. I can sense the powers being used. The Banished One is there. I can feel his fire."

Darstan's voice raised to a fever pitch. "Aenaila! We must risk it all. Take us to the city. Focus on something, anything, but get me to that city. The battle has begun."

BATTLE OF DEATH

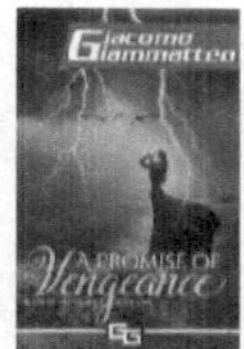

The hill was steep, but Rahg held an erect posture and confident strut as he closed the distance between him and Iazzo. His throat tightened and his stomach sickened, but just as the fear slipped to his chest the first volley of arrows came.

Rahg erected a shield, quickly dispelling the threat. After that, he was bothered no more by fear; there was no time for it. Two additional volleys followed closely behind the first attack, but all were repelled by the shield. Pride showed in every movement. "Stay tight, men. Don't leave the cover of the shield."

Rahg looked west, toward J'en Kar and his men, advancing under cover of the cliffs. Soon they would be within striking distance of the Victas which formed the right flank of Iazzo's army.

cliffs with narrow passage

If they can get through the pass and engage the Victas in the open, it will give us the time we need.

He looked to the eastern army; no shield had been required as yet for them either. Mesla had cleverly led them through the forest using the natural cover of the trees and plants to conceal them. All was proceeding according to plan.

Rhaven had counted on the west or east army being able to reach the enemy safely, then once engaged in hand-to hand combat, where Iazzo could not interfere without killing his own men, the rest of them could race forward and join the fray. *A good strategy.*

Another volley of arrows struck the shield with the same uneventful results. During the lull, Rahg thought back to the short bit of training Aentarra had been able to provide him on shielding.

Focus and concentration are the keys. Focus and concentration. Forget that and you'll die.

~

*R*ahg's attention abruptly returned to the present when he heard Rhaven's warning. "Victas attacking. Prepare for hand-to-hand fighting. All men with picks and axes on the front line, and remember, get weapons from the dead ones. Aim for their throats and heads, Victas are most vulnerable there." Rhaven turned to Rahg. "You know what to do."

Rahg nodded, and swallowed a big lump of nervousness; he prayed he was up to the task.

About two hundred Victas approached, walking slowly. Soon they would make a furious charge to break through the lines and get to him; at least, that's what Rhaven thought. They were better armed, and Victas were known to be among the best open-field fighters. They had two packs of Wolfen with them. Rahg didn't know why, but the Wolfen frightened him more than the Victas. He cringed. A screeching hiss erupted from the army of Victas as they charged.

~

*J*azzo scanned the battle scene from a vantage point high among the rocky ledges. He was safely out of range of arrows, and he wanted to see what forces had been arrayed against him. *Pitiful*, he thought, surveying the opposition. His archers fired. Rahg's shield deflected the arrows. "So, the boy has powers. That makes it more interesting."

J'ag Tem walked briskly over to Iazzo, bowing slightly. "The enemy advances straight at us with the village boy among them, Lord. There are two hundred natives with him. Our arrows do no good, Lord. I do not see why we should continue to waste them."

Iazzo's cruel smile was chilling, even to J'ag Tem. "I know you do not understand. You were not meant to. What else is there to report?"

J'ag Tem bowed in obeisance. "There is a large army on the western side which has almost reached the summit. They cannot be—" J'ag Tem stopped himself short of giving advice, perhaps he had been in time. He prayed so.

Iazzo glared at his Sethian commander, enough of a rebuke for now. If they had not been at war, he might have had fun with him—tore some flesh from his bones and made him eat it perhaps. Iazzo smiled at the thought.

J'ag Tem took the smile to mean all was good and relaxed as he walked with Iazzo toward the army stationed at the entrance to the enclave. Iazzo stopped when he reached Marro. "I have known about that western army ever since the plans were made. Haven't I, Marro?"

Marro appeared nervous; he shook with fear. "Yes, Lord."

Iazzo closed the gap. Sweat poured from Marro's brow. "You have the honor of joining the Victas in doing battle with your former friends. It should prove to be an enjoyable slaughter; the pass is narrow and we have blocked it off. There remains no means of egress for the Entirians unless they place themselves in a position for our archers to have a clear shot at them." Iazzo's laugh rolled around the enclave and down the valley, it was a cruel and unnatural laugh. "Enjoy the feast."

Iazzo turned back to J'ag Tem. "And what of their eastern army?"

It came as no surprise to J'ag Tem that Iazzo already knew of it. He would have been more shocked if he hadn't. J'ag Tem did wonder though, where the other traitor that had accompanied Marro was hiding. *Ah, there he is.* J'ag Tem saw the other seaman, Eduard. He would have preferred to kill them himself, but it would be more fitting to allow their fellow countrymen to have their revenge.

J'ag Tem made a note to be certain and place the traitors at the front of the line once the battle commenced. "The eastern army is being led by an Entirian called Mesla; they approach through the forest. It will be much more difficult to deal with them, Lord. They know the land well and our archers will be able to provide little support due to the heavy canopy."

"Send Sejja." It was all Iazzo need say.

~

J'en Kar led the western army quickly, and silently, along the shadows of sheer rock wall that protected them. It was a small hidden valley between the mountains and the cliffs that led almost to the enclave at the summit where Iazzo's army was positioned. Though Iazzo's men could not see them, Rahg could keep a watch from his vantage point, prepared to use the shield to protect them if necessary. The most dangerous part of the journey was the final section; they would need to escape the valley through a narrow pass, though it was hidden from view and J'en Kar doubted they would have discovered it. Once they entered the pass, Rahg would not be able to offer them any protection.

J'en Kar's heart raced at the thoughts of conquering the Victas, and his blood boiled when he dreamed of doing battle with the Sethian guard. Dreams of victory and glory flashed before him, the glory that would be showered on his family and all to come after them. Of the hundreds of shulans who had waited their life to serve the Fate Sealer, it was to be him, J'en Kar, who was chosen to bear the task. His descendants would bathe in his glory for millennia. They would become the greatest of shulans ever to rule Entiria.

"J'en Kar," his guide called back to him. "The pass is just ahead. Prepare."

J'en Kar gave thought to sending a patrol through first; it would be the safe thing to do, for once they entered the pass half his army would be exposed at any given time, and an ambush could prove deadly. J'en Kar quickly decided against a patrol; their best hope of victory was a complete surprise. He prayed for success as he issued the orders to proceed at an increased pace. "Hurry, the battle awaits us."

The Victa squad leader descended from the hidden crevice at the end of the narrow pass, marching stolidly toward his commander. "They are coming," the squad leader said, and stared at Commander Kraffr, known as 'The Fearless.' Kraffr was tall for a Victa, and brawnier than most. He earned his name with difficulty. Victas were afraid of little, and for one to have earned the name of 'Fearless' required deeds of heroic proportions.

The squad leader focused his attention back on Kraffr. He had not responded to his report though he felt certain he had heard it. "Shall we prepare to attack?"

The sibilance in Kraffr's voice, like steel-on-steel, chilled to the bones; even the other Victas cringed when they heard it. "When as many as possible have entered the pass, then we attack; not until. I will lead the charge."

The squad leader acknowledged the order and conveyed it to the others personally so that no one misunderstood. "Kraffr will lead the charge," he reminded them. "Anyone in his path will die."

~

*M*esla separated his men into groups of twenty–five, each with orders to advance as quickly as possible, but with the primary directive to remain undetected. "Stay off the trails and away from open areas," he warned. "They will surely have spotters searching these woods, and we must make it without being seen."

Halfway to the summit they had encountered no resistance. Mesla remained calm, not allowing his optimism to affect his cautious approach. Swiftly, yet silently, they darted from tree trunk to bush and heavy brush, always shying away from clearings and the main trail. "Stay alert," Mesla whispered. "We will soon—"

Sejja's sharp blade sliced through Mesla's throat drawing a long, thick line of blood. The men with Mesla met a similar fate. "Now that their leader is gone, we can proceed," Sejja whispered to the pack. The Wolfen moved through the forest like snakes, making no noise save a faint rustle of a leaf, and that only at the hint of a breeze. The Entirians proved to be easy prey, their own natural skills dulled from so many generations of peace.

Eight packs of Wolfen warriors had come with Sejja, nearly a hundred in all, but their tactics of silently stalking, then striking, confused the Entirians. When combined with the predatory skills of the Wolfen, the effects had been devastating. With still a long way to go before the summit, the Wolfen had deprived the Entirians of their leader and no less than one hundred men. Sejja had only lost two of his warriors.

The Entirians were close to a panic situation. Nentala assumed command and decided to proceed with a different strategy. "Call all the men. We will stay together and follow the main trail." Several of his followers objected but he overruled their protestations. "They know of our position now; nothing is secret. Our mission is to reach the summit, and we can do that best by following the main path."

Sejja crept backward out from under cover of a thick bush less than a span away from the meeting of the Entirians. He listened to their new strategy, and agreed with them. In fact, it was exactly what he projected they would do when he killed Mesla and the others. Once he rejoined the pack, he issued new orders himself. "Make only minor attacks at the fringes, then run from them as if afraid of their numbers. They will believe they have successfully defended themselves. I return to join J'ag Tem."

~

Fifty Entirians formed the first line of defense. Rhaven stood firmly planted in front of them with both weapons drawn and ready. His black cloak danced in the breeze as he positioned himself for battle, eyes sparkling with admiration of his newest blade. Rhaven's right hand twitched in anticipation, eager to truly test the new sword—the Sword of Mikkellana.

Tobias had come to his side but Rhaven ordered him back. "Guard the girl. She can't defend herself against Victas. Besides, it will ease the lad's mind if you are there with him, and he is the key to it all." Tobias agreed, returning to stand next to Camissa, but close to Rahg.

The force of Victas rushed toward them, their battle cry a blood-curdling, beastly scream. Two hundred Victas and two packs of Wolfen against fifty poorly armed Entirians, backed up by another hundred and fifty armed only with farm implements.

What appeared to be an unruly charge by a maddened mob, began to take shape as the Victas neared their target. They formed into three separate phalanxes meant to break the line of defense. A pack of Wolfen, taking full advantage of the speed they were renowned for, raced to each end for flanking maneuvers, supported by an equal number of Victas.

Once they were within striking distance Rahg formed his shield according to plan. The lead Victas struck the shield with a jarring impact, shocked to disbelief.

"Now, Rahg!"

Rahg heard Rhaven's command, and put the second stage of the plan in effect. He erected a wall out of shield that divided the Victas in the front from those supporting them, leaving an isolated group of about forty to face Rhaven and the Entirians on the front line. Simultaneously, Rahg used another shield to isolate the Wolfen and Victas on their right flank, trapping nearly thirty of them apart from their army.

Once that was accomplished, the rest of the Entirians attacked with a ferocity that Rahg had not imagined they possessed. Their hoes and shovels were transformed into deadly weapons in the hands of the crazed soldiers. Rahg released the front shield separating the enemy from them, but kept the rear shield in place, keeping the Wolfen and

Victas pressed tightly against it and leaving them no room to maneuver; the slaughter took little time.

~

As soon as the front shield dropped, Rhaven jumped in, slaying half a dozen before they regained their composure. His blade swept through the air, whistling, and dripping blood as it danced from one victim to the next. With each victim his fervor increased.

Victas screamed as the deadly blade cut through their scales, severing limbs. Huddled together, like rats trapped in a corner, they shook as Rhaven approached, his eyes as wild as the blood-soaked blade he wielded.

Eight Victas fought for their lives against him, though only a few managed to even lift a sword, so cramped was the space. Rhaven used his left arm, wielding a sai, mostly for defense, dealing death mercilessly with the blade he wielded in his right. But whenever an enemy came near enough, Rhaven's sai struck with deadly accuracy.

A horrible hiss erupted from the surviving Victas as Rhaven's sword sliced through the head of a Victa, severing his skull at the nose.

Rhaven continued his onslaught, never stopping, or even pausing. Rahg released the shield to allow him the opportunity to reach new Victas—the ones inside the shield all lay dead. As he rushed forward into the crowd of Victas outside the shield, they ran.

~

Atop the rise, J'ag Tem brought Iazzo's attention to the setback below. "The Victas are retreating, Lord."

Iazzo glared, and his eyes glowed. "They must understand who they need fear," he said, and unleashed a mass of flame at the retreating

Victas. The howls of agony filled the valley as they burned. The rest of the Victas rejoined the battle, massing to form a new charge.

"The boy shall see power, now," Iazzo shouted, and a huge ball of red flame shot toward Rahg.

"Rahg!" Camissa screamed a warning.

Rahg froze, then his instincts took charge and he constructed a shield to ward off the fire. The collision jarred him; he staggered and swayed, nearly falling to the ground.

Camissa ran to him, supporting his back. "Are you all right?"

"For now. But I don't know how long I can hold a shield against that." Rahg turned his concentration once again to the battle; the Victas, driven by fear of Iazzo had succeeded in driving back the front line. Many of the Entirians lay dead, or wounded. Even Rhaven retreated.

"Shield, Rahg," Rhaven called for support, swinging sword and sai in a sweeping arc to hold the lizards at bay.

Still dizzy and weak, Rahg concentrated and managed to weave a new shield between Rhaven and the blood-crazed lizards. This time there was no shock or surprise as they encountered the shield, instead, they hammered and pounded it with their swords and green-scaled fists. Fear overcame the surviving Entirians who quickly retreated.

Rhaven dropped back near to Rahg. "Can you withstand another attack?"

"I must," Rahg said. "I will."

"Good, we need time to formulate a new strategy. Something they don't expect."

Camissa rushed to Rhaven, examining first his side and then his arms. "You're bleeding. You need bandages."

"I have no time for bandages or healing, Camissa. If we don't do something soon, those Victas will have all my blood. Rahg can't hold this shield forever."

"If you can distract him, lad," Tobias said, "anything to draw his attention from us for a while, perhaps it will give ya time to rebuild your strength, if that's how it works."

"That's what I need, Tobias. Time will bring back strength. The only problem is that even with full command of my powers, it's only a matter of time before he crushes us. He's only toying with us as it is." Rahg saw Tobias staring at him. "He's a Banished One, Tobias. And I'm only..." Rahg seemed lost for a moment, confused. "I don't even know what I am. But I'm not strong enough to hold off Iazzo."

Rahg seized the brief respite to rest his body, and what he could of his mind. At any moment, Iazzo could strike and finish it all—his worries, and his life.

A brilliant flash of light streaked the daytime sky. "J'en Kar's men," Tobias shouted. "Look."

Rahg turned toward the pass where J'en Kar planned to emerge and attack. The entrance to the narrow passage teemed with Victas, hissing their bloodthirsty battle cry, while above, lightning struck the walls of the cliffs, peeling huge sections of rock from the sides that plummeted onto the helpless Entirians trapped in the gorge. Rahg cringed when he heard their screams of agony.

Camissa tried to comfort him, her voice, soft and sympathetic. "There is nothing you could have done."

Rahg's jaw jutted forth as he clenched teeth. "I still can," he said, and closed his eyes to concentrate on forming a shield.

Standing close by, Rhaven saw what he attempted and grabbed his arm. "Don't try, lad. You need to save yourself."

Rahg tore away from Rhaven. "I have to try. They trusted me with their lives."

"Then form a shield so I can attack the Banished One myself. I have—"

Rahg never let him finish. "No." He began to form the shield. It started at the front end of the pass where the debris caused by the lightning piled high above the ground, atop the dead bodies of Entirians. Another flash of lightning came, this time Rahg's shield repelled it.

Iazzo received a jolt from the repercussion, a minor one, but the insult slapped him hard. He cast a vicious glance at Rahg, eyes filled with hatred. Two more bolts crashed against the rear portion of the cliff; more Entirians died in an avalanche of death. Rahg's shield had not stretched so far as that. He grimaced with each painful scream, a reminder that he failed them.

The narrow entrance to the trail had been rendered impassable; J'en Kar's lifeless, bloody hand protruding from between two huge boulders a testament to the carnage that lay beyond. Kraffr ordered a small patrol to remain on guard in the unlikely event any stragglers managed to escape, meanwhile, he led the main body of the Victa army toward the rear, a move intended to finish whatever was left of the Entirian army.

"There's nothing to do but go on, lad," Tobias said. "Make this shield as strong as you can and hope that Mesla gets through to flank them."

It was good advice, Rahg knew, especially considering the amount of pressure the Victas were placing on the barrier he had constructed in front of them. It proved difficult enough keeping them at bay.

If Iazzo attacks again—when he attacks again, Rahg corrected himself, *the shield will likely fail.*

~

J'ag Tem seldom smiled, but the sight of the Entirians being slaughtered at the hands of Kraffr caused a slight crack in his stoic expression. Kraffr was especially brutal. The Entirians would suffer. The Sethian commander waited until he detected a propitious moment to address Iazzo. "Lord, the army in the forest has not yet been disposed of." J'ag Tem stood still as stone, awaiting orders.

Iazzo surveyed the field of battle: the Entirian army of the west was crushed; over half lay dead in the pass, or on the trail behind, and it would not be long before Kraffr slew them or drove them back to the city. Either way, it mattered not to Iazzo; he was here for one reason —the village boy. In the center, a hundred Victas beat at the simple barrier the lad had woven. The boy had an equal number of Entirians behind his shield, and, he had the black-cloaked one.

The only true warrior. He reminds me of Arton. Not as proficient to be sure, but like him.

Iazzo looked about at his own resources. A total of four hundred Victas had been dispatched to the west, two hundred more faced Rahg. Surrounding him as a guard stood one hundred Sethians, an elite force from the palace, and almost twenty packs of Wolfen.

It is time to be rid of the eastern army.

"J'ag Tem, does all stand ready in the forest?"

J'ag Tem cast a frenzied glance to Sejja. "Call your men from the forest, Sejja,"

The Wolfen pack commander emitted a series of howls that cut through the din of the battlefield. The sequence of calls formed a signal that the Wolfen remaining in the forest recognized, and within moments the pack returned. Sejja nodded to J'ag Tem when he saw them emerge from the woods, signaling Iazzo to begin.

A large mass of red flame blazed across the sky, landing behind the army of Entirians. The trees and undergrowth caught fire quickly even though dampness filled their roots. Smoke billowed up from the forest floor creeping along like a hungry fog. Atop the trees, it crawled through the branches and lingered beneath the canopy swallowing what little light had penetrated below.

Nentala ordered an immediate attack on the enemy camp. "We can't wait," he cried. But even as he spoke, another massive wall of fire struck in front of them. Trees burst into flames, engulfing some of the Entirians, and thick deadly smoke surrounded them. The soldiers panicked, choking and coughing as they ran for safety.

Rahg's ears burned with death cries as the Entirians succumbed to the flames. They screamed in the Old Tongue and in his own language, though it sounded the same. His head pounded from the pressure of gnashed teeth and the burden of so many deaths weighed on him.

"Hold, Rahg," Rhaven shouted.

Rahg suspected the reason for the warning to have originated with Iazzo, and when the lightning bolt struck the shield, he knew. Rahg braced himself, bearing the brunt of the impact with no apparent effects, though he ached inside and his mind felt bruised.

Rahg stared at Iazzo, challenged him with the set of his eyes. Even from this distance, somehow he knew the Banished One would know. Iazzo hurled a massive assault; four lightning bolts and a ball of white fire. Rahg saw them coming, and he prepared. Two bolts hit first; Rahg staggered. The fireball enveloped his shield burning at every pore, searching for a path to enter. It exerted great pressure on him.

Rahg fell to one knee, bracing himself by placing his hands on the other. Camissa tried to help him to his feet, so did Tobias, but Rahg was weakening fast.

"Hold fast, Rahg," Rhaven called.

When the final two bolts of lightning struck, Rahg felt the shield crack, only a tiny one initially, but it soon widened to a gap, then a fissure of size enough to allow the Victas to gain entry.

Finally, Rahg's shield collapsed. When it did, he did too. Another bolt from Iazzo came toward Rahg.

Rhaven dashed to intercept it, holding the Sword of Mikkellana high above his head. The lightning cracked against the blade, creating the sound of a hundred thunderclaps, but Rhaven stood.

Aentarra had told no lie, the Sword of Mikkellana withstood the power of the Banished One. Rhaven's smile was demonic.

If I can stop a Banished One's power, I can kill him, he thought, and advanced.

~

Iazzo looked down upon them from his position on the summit. "Mikkellana made another sword! She always managed to make a battle interesting, even when she wasn't present."

Iazzo relished his imminent victory. I'll not spend myself against a mere mortal. "J'ag Tem, keep one hundred Wolfen and half the Sethians here, send the rest to dispatch them. The shield is down now."

J'ag Tem issued the orders.

Ten packs of Wolfen and fifty Sethians advanced. Already, the Victas were streaming through to attack. Rahg was just getting to his feet.

"Can you shield?" Rhaven asked.

Rahg drew his sword as answer, preparing for battle in traditional fashion. "Stand back, Camissa. I can't protect you anymore."

The raw nerve Rahg struck prickled the hair on the back of Camissa's neck. "I've lived many a year without you to hide behind, Master Fal-Thera."

The Entirians rushed to the front of Rahg, willing to sacrifice their lives for him. "You must leave," they said. "Seek protection from the shera; he will know what to do." The Victas poured down onto the Entirians, slashing them with their short swords and axes. Close behind them were the Wolfen and Sethians. Hope seemed a distant thought right now. Rhaven's laughter cut through the air. It was an eerie, almost evil sound.

"This is how battle was meant to be," Rhaven screamed. "Come to me, Victas. Come, Wolfen. It is time we bled. It is time we died."

Rahg shivered, but vowed not to let Rhaven die alone. He screamed his own battle cry and raced to join Rhaven in death.

~

The air cracked and a passage opened near the temple in the city of Sunnara; Aenaila appeared with Darstan and the others. Wisp raced to several Entirian priests who were caring for the wounded.

"Take care of this boy," he said. "We shall return for him." He had no time for any further instructions. Already, Darstan shook with impatience. Once again, they linked together: Aenaila, Darstan, Wisp, Evin, and Kella, and once again, Aenaila Shifted with her vision, carrying them ever closer to the field of battle.

The air shimmered, and cracked loudly, though no one heard, and a passage opened amidst a battlefield strewn with the corpses of hundreds. From the corner of his eye, Darstan saw Rhaven and Rahg fighting gods knew how many Victas and Wolfen.

He remembered Twin Forks, and how the Victas killed Magmar—and he exploded in a rage, a raging inferno. Fire erupted from Darstan's severed limb emitting a column of white-hot flame that shot into the enemy ranks. Several packs of Wolfen burst into flame, fire hopping from one to another like windblown sparks in dry brush. Bestial howls of agony produced a deafening roar, a sound that sent chills through friend and foe alike.

For a moment, the attack paused. The stench of burnt fur and the putrid smell of charred flesh permeated the battlefield. Darstan whirled to face Victas who were almost upon him. Another lethal dose of fire shot from his arm, slaying them in the same gruesome fashion as the Wolfen.

Panic ran rampant in the enemy ranks; Wolfen ran about on fire, howling their death cries, and now, a new danger—a vargel. Kella charged through the still-burning Wolfen, lending an eerie grimness to her growls. Wolfen and Victas scattered, and if the Sethians held their ground, they made no move to attack nor stand in her way.

Kella struck with indeterminate suddenness. Each throat she ripped, each limb she tore, produced three times the number of warriors paralyzed with fear. On several occasions blades struck her, but she always seemed to have just moved aside, or swayed enough to thwart a direct hit.

Blood poured from her sides, and two spots on her massive head, but dark green and red blood also dripped from her dagger-like teeth; the effect of the combination left most awe-stricken. She darted and struck, then moved and struck again, following no path, no definitive course.

Wisp, too, set upon a course of action, not unlike the one Kella had unwittingly undertaken. Using his power of Concealment, he rendered himself invisible, and carefully made his way to the rear ranks of the enemy. At first, his thought was to strike the Banished One himself, but as he came closer, he saw it would be impossible; the Banished One had surrounded himself with nearly fifty Sethians, tightly woven around him.

Wisp chose another tack, and began from the rear. Selecting the largest of the Wolfen and Victas, he approached unseen and plunged a knife in their backs, quickly darting away afterward to avoid the inevitable reflexive reaction.

It soon began to have a devastating effect on them, as they saw fellow soldiers fall to the ground screaming, and bleeding, or in some instances, dead. And all from no apparent cause. Soon, all began warily turning about to check their backs.

A huge Wolfen loomed in front of Wisp, barking commands to his pack to keep them moving forward. Wisp crept up behind him and shoved the knife into the back of his neck, having to leap off the ground to do so.

When the humongous Wolfen fell, his pack fled in terror. Wisp moved on to other targets, striking when he could. He began to worry though, for he knew the effect of his Concealment would not endure, especially under such stress. *If I'm caught here, I'll not be earning any more gold.*

Sejja witnessed the decimation of his pack-brothers; he had seen the newcomer, 'one-arm', strike them ablaze, and he heard their howls of death. Sejja's yellow eyes burned with vengeance as he raced to vent his wrath. "One-arm must die," he howled.

Darstan kept up the attacks upon the Victas and Wolfen, hurling balls of red flame and columns of white fire. He relentlessly attacked until only sparks remained, then nothing; he was spent, replete.

The Victas gained courage when no new assaults came. Aenaila devised a strategy of her own. Darstan needed time to regain his strength. She cast an Illusion, a power rare even among those who possessed powers. In the minds of all the Victas the image of a great wall of fire stood between them and Darstan. So real was the image that they could feel the heat, and in defense, threw their hands up to cover their faces.

~

Sejja approached the wall of fire that towered above the tallest of his pack and threatened them with flames that struck like swords from an enemy's hand. It had been effective at keeping them at bay, but Sejja was suspicious and looked closely at the flames; they seemed different somehow.

He stepped closer and sniffed; there was no smell of smoke. Carefully, the big Wolfen approached. When no heat burnt him, Sejja knew they had been fooled. "Come, pack-brothers," he called, and leapt through the imaginary flames with a war cry meant to instill courage in his pack.

Darstan was taken unaware by Sejja's sudden appearance. He attempted to dodge the Wolfen but Sejja's long knife found Darstan's leg, bringing him down. Darstan howled, rolling to evade another strike. Evin rushed to defend Aenaila as two Wolfen raced toward her. Evin attacked, but the Wolfen were much too quick; the first Wolfen's sword pierced Evin's mail, and the other thrust his blade into his throat.

Aenaila cursed, and concentrated on stopping them, using all her powers. Powers of Healing could be used for other purposes, in fact, there was little difference between healing and killing in most cases. Just a measure too much, or too little, and the patient became a victim.

The first Wolfen howled, grasping his chest to alleviate the pain, a pain that constricted his heart and made it feel as if it would burst through his frail body. Quickly, it spread throughout the Wolfen's chest, then down his arm; the Wolfen fell dead to the ground.

The second Wolfen started toward her, but abruptly began gasping for breath that would not come. His throat tightened, then closed. No more breaths would he take; he joined his pack-brother. But the price for Aenaila was heavy, she had been weakened so much she was forced to drop the Illusion; the wall of fire fell. A cry went up from the Victas gathered less than four spans away as they rushed to slaughter the hapless victims.

Darstan managed to roll, then kick Sejja aside with his good leg, while he tried to reclaim his footing; it proved difficult with a knife in his leg. He stumbled and fell again. Sejja crouched, and sprang for

Darstan. Just prior to reaching Darstan, the Wolfen felt the penetration—a blade pierced his neck from the rear.

A beastly howl emerged, yet he struggled onward, obsessed with Darstan's death. Wisp materialized, still extracting the blade from Sejja's neck. He quickly drew another blade and plunged it into the side of Sejja's head, just above the ear. Wisp felt the crush of bone, and heard the sound of steel penetrating flesh, then brain. Sejja was dead.

Wisp turned to see the horde of Victas advancing rapidly. "Mother of rats!" The Victas were almost upon them when they ran into a wall of flame. Real flame. Thinking it another illusion, many were burned. Darstan had recovered his powers, at least temporarily.

Aenaila knew something had to be done, and quickly. "There, Darstan," she shouted. "Up on the hill. It is the Banished One."

Darstan followed her direction, instantly recognizing the Banished One. Flame spewed out of his severed limb aimed straight at Iazzo. Two Victas in the path of the oncoming column were charred instantly, and it proceeded unencumbered toward the Banished One.

Preoccupied with the destruction of Rahg, Iazzo paid no mind to his unprotected side. J'ag Tem saw at the last moment and jumped, hitting Iazzo and shoving him from harm's way. Simultaneously, three Sethian guards leapt in the path of the fireball.

Iazzo jumped to his feet; embarrassment and anger burned in his eyes and vengeance consumed him. He spun to where the assault originated casting burning eyes at Darstan. Three, huge balls of flame flew from Iazzo's hands on a course marked for Darstan's death. They moved faster than Darstan's creations, and were much larger, and hotter.

Darstan saw them coming. There was no way to avoid the imminent destruction. "Save yourself, Aenaila."

Aenaila heard, but instead of obeying, she seized Darstan's arm; she already held Wisp's. The heat singed their clothes just as they disappeared, but the sphere of death roared through empty space and, ultimately, fell harmlessly to the ground.

~

*I*azzo stood astonished. He stared at the spot where they had been, until suddenly, it struck him what transpired. Someone could Shift. He spun back to where Rahg was fighting the Victas and Wolfen, and there stood Darstan with his two companions.

The village boy fought with unrelenting fury, as did the black-cloaked one. *No doubt with a bit of shielding power restored,* thought Iazzo. The Banished One fumed. *Now that they are together, I shall crush them both.*

Lukaan's orders that Darstan be taken alive flashed in Iazzo's mind, but he quickly discounted it. *I'll not let a lad with powers destroy me. Lukaan will have to be told he died another way.*

Iazzo scanned the field, so many armies were lost. More Entirians were coming to reinforce the village boy and it prompted him into a maddened state. Fire engulfed the new arrivals, diminishing their numbers, and bolts of lightning struck all about Rahg, one striking dangerously close to Rhaven. Iazzo unleashed another salvo, a brutal force of a dozen bolts.

Iazzo staggered with disbelief and shock when they were repelled by a shield. *The boy cannot be so strong.* His pride was injured more than he, and the Banished One prepared for Rahg's final destruction. "Call them aside, J'ag Tem," he roared.

J'ag Tem issued the order, but none had time to respond. A giant wall of fire raced toward Rahg. It was a curtain of flame several spans wide and at least a half a span high. And it was black—BlackFire.

Victas screamed and hissed, and Wolfen howled wildly as the Black-Fire charred their bones. Even those it did not touch directly cried in agony; from a span away it had the power to kill. The black curtain of death raced toward Rahg at a speed that defied escape.

Iazzo laughed as the wall of BlackFire destroyed everything in its path. Suddenly a column of shields arose, wider than his destructive force of fire, and concave to surround it. The shields were constructed of columnar shapes conjoined and stacked in rows. Between the spaces of the first row of columns the ground had been torn away until only a gaping hole remained. The BlackFire smashed into the shields creating a thunderous noise at impact. Nothing.

Impossible, Iazzo thought. *Those shields are strong, stronger than any I've seen save for the one at Sethia.* The BlackFire sunk into the ground, scorching and burning everything it touched, but burning itself out in the process.

The first indication that something was amiss, was when the Black-Fire struck the impenetrable wall of shields. *They cannot shield like that. They cannot stop BlackFire.*

His mind raced to determine a solution, quickly arriving at a logical conclusion, and, as he arrived at that juncture—it struck him. He felt it first near the back of his head, like a tiny pinprick. Then the pain increased and he felt his mind being invaded. "Aentarra!" he shouted. "Protect me, J'ag Tem."

J'ag Tem heard the fear in Iazzo's voice, saw the panic in his eyes. Iazzo stood motionless, as if in a trance, but inside was where the real battle was taking place—in the Planes of the Mind. Iazzo knew the dangers; everything else was put off, nothing else mattered—not now. He must fight this ultimate challenge, this definitive test of power.

Into himself he shrunk until his mind eliminated all other thoughts, all images, all memories. Devoid of all distractions, he crossed the barriers and gained entrance to the Planes of the Mind.

∼

*A*entarra lurked inside the Planes—where power is truly the ability to rule. Here, brawn and size were of no import; one could make themselves larger than mountains, or small as a grain of sand. In this plane of consciousness between the physical world and dreams, only power ruled.

Aentarra smiled. She was prepared, though she harbored no false illusions regarding Iazzo's preparation. He would be ready, she knew, and awaited his entry. Only a few could enter, and once inside, fewer returned. One only entered the Planes of the Mind to do battle and, once inside, battle was to the death. Here, in this world apart from everything real, strategy and cunning prevailed.

PLANES OF THE MIND

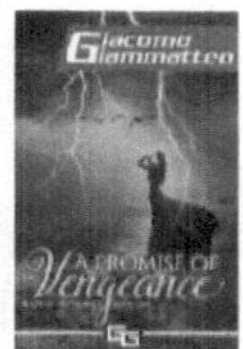

Camissa could not get the tingling out of her head. "The Mind," she muttered.

Aenaila stood close enough to hear. "What?"

Camissa's eyes never strayed; she stared ahead, entranced by something. "The Mind," she repeated. "I can feel them fighting in there."

A look of shocked recognition tore at Aenaila's face. "You can enter?"

Camissa looked at Aenaila. "I have in the past. And you obviously can or you wouldn't know what I'm talking about."

"I can enter," Aenaila said. "But I have no sense of anyone in there. Nor have I ever."

Camissa drifted to a hypnotic state of mind.

"Don't do it," Aenaila screamed, but not in time.

Camissa stood oblivious to all around her. "Protect her," Aenaila said. "She'll not be conscious of this world. Not until she returns." *If she returns.*

Rahg's clothes were covered in blood, a mixture of red and green. "What happened to Camissa?"

Aenaila's grim expression matched her voice, like a healer telling a mother the child will not live. "She has entered the Planes of the Mind."

Tired and confused, Rahg had no patience for riddles. "What are you talking about?"

Aenaila continued to stare at Camissa, but without hope. "It is like another world. And she believes the Banished One is fighting someone in there. Whoever it is, I pray they win."

A flicker of hope crossed Rahg's face. "If it's one of the good immortals, then Camissa—"

Aenaila placed her hand on Rahg's shoulder to steady him. "Perhaps not. It is a dangerous place and in the passion of battle even someone with good intent might kill her."

"Can't you get her out?"

"We both could die if I tried."

"What do you mean," Rahg shouted. "How could you die?"

Aenaila tried to remain patient. "If I go in, the Banished One could kill me with a thought. It is too much risk."

"So, you're afraid. Then teach me to enter."

Before Aenaila could respond the Victas came. "Look out!"

Rahg spun to face two lizards. The battle had worn on him, but it also aged him quickly in battle experience; his sword found the first Victa's throat with the initial thrust. The other Victa leapt, slamming into Rahg with all its weight. As he rolled to the ground, he grabbed his knife and stabbed the Victa's stomach.

The Victa hissed, then Aenaila stabbed it in the neck. Through it all,

Camissa hadn't moved. Rahg had no time to help her. Sennar's men were being set on by a dozen Victas. Rahg still had no power to shield with. As he thought of what to do a large band of Victas approached from the west.

Kraffr had destroyed the Entirians, and now led his army to crush what remained of the resistance. "Protect her," Rahg yelled to Aenaila. "If you won't get her out, at least do that."

~

On the plane of nothingness he stood, bedecked in battle gear the likes of which the world had never seen. The sun was appropriately bright and all else appeared normal. Normal for the world as people knew it. It could just as easily have been blacker than night or any other color, or scene, Aentarra wished.

Aentarra had entered first, so the setting was hers to dictate. Iazzo looked about, his steel helmet glistened, drank in the brightness, then reflected the rays with even more brilliance. It was a defense, a mild one meant only to annoy, but then, any edge could mean victory as opposed to death. Iazzo pulled the ends of his blood-red gauntlets tight around his wrists, each emblazoned with the insignia of his ancestors—the Graffyr, a giant bird of prey.

Smooth, silver mail adorned his chest. It dripped with blood, or appeared to. Iazzo made it seem that way. Black boots rose to just below his knees making it difficult to distinguish where the dark pants began and the boots quit.

Iazzo thought of Aentarra, and how she might be attired today. She was unpredictable, not just in battle and politics, but in everything she did, garb included. He recalled a meeting in Council which she attended naked; only too late did the males realize she wished to sway their vote.

Thinking these thoughts helped Iazzo, helped him to recall how devious she could be. He could not afford to be lured into a false sense of security by her legendary beauty or seemingly endless charm. The Banished One formed a vivid image of her body in his mind, the long, lithe legs, the silken skin and glistening hair.

He fought with his emotions to control them. That is what she would do. She would attempt to allure him, use her wiles to take him off guard. He prepared for the inevitable by subjecting his mind and body to the irresistible enticement of her tantalizing form. As he dwelled on Aentarra, a landscape suddenly arose, complete with a deep forest to hide her whereabouts. It was one she created to suit her needs, no doubt.

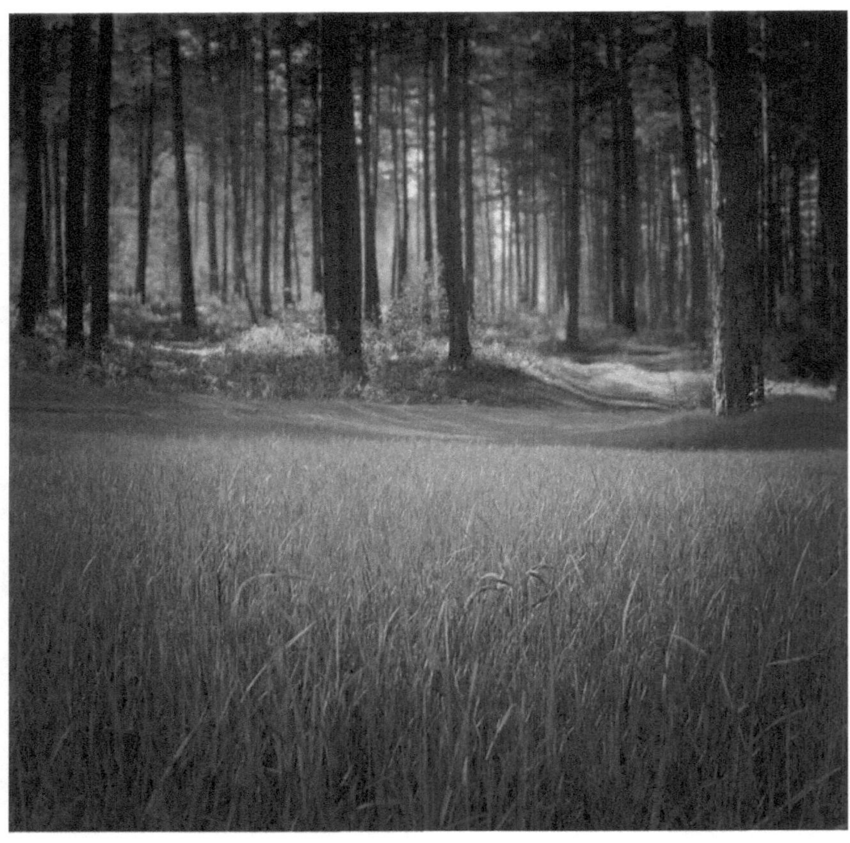

Planes of the Mind landscape

Iazzo's gaze swept the landscape searching for her. *Where is she?* The landscape disappeared, and once again, Iazzo could see forever—for a thousand times a thousand leagues, uninterrupted—and yet, he could not see Aentarra. *How is she hiding?* For the first time since leaving Sethia fear entered his twisted mind. He had known Aentarra before the Wars of Light, before the battles with Lukaan. Even then she had been odd. Some might have called her evil. She was evil, and worse, she was mad.

Iazzo heard a noise and spun quickly—nothing. Again, from behind, a sound teased him, and again he spun. In front of him lay another newly created landscape. *A decoy? Perhaps,* he reasoned. *And just as plausible is that the decoy is the real place she will attack from, she will presume I would think it a decoy.* But then, this line of reasoning could go on forever. Iazzo never relaxed, could not. She could strike at any moment, and he'd only have one chance. He felt like a mouse stuck into a room with a cat.

Iazzo used his mind and searched, sent out probes, slowly. One at a time. She was here, but where he kept asking himself. Immediately, he set probes all about him, on each side, above and below. *Twelve, that should suffice,* he reasoned and concentrated on locating her once again. Searcher probes went out, one at a time. He could not maintain more with so many stationary probes set, but they were the most important, they would alert him to her arrival.

Perspiration rolled off Iazzo's forehead. He never liked doing battle here, not even mock battle. It was far too dangerous, especially with one as mad as Aentarra. She was unpredictable, likely even to kill herself, but that would not be comfort if she took him along.

～

*A*entarra contemplated her attire, then dressed in something plain. She considered an elegant, silky gown that would have barely concealed her flesh; she even thought about appearing naked, it wouldn't be the first time Iazzo had seen her so. But, at length, she opted for this, a dull-green garb that fit loosely about her frame. Iazzo would assume her to come prepared to entice him. She opted for the opposite. Her only consistency was her unpredictability. Aentarra's laughter shook the air and echoed throughout the endless leagues of emptiness.

The first probe exploded, sending its warning of her arrival. Iazzo shook with fear. The battle was about to begin.

~

*R*ahg's shield gave out long ago, and he needed rest to regain any semblance of power. Tobias, and Sennar and his men, fought alongside Rahg. It was amazing how Sennar fought so ably with only one good hand, Rahg thought, recalling how the old tar had charged into the Victa line to get at Marro, the traitor. Sennar moved so quickly that Marro didn't even raise his blade to block the stroke; it took him in the chest. Before he went down Sennar's blade smashed his skull.

"There are more Entirians comin' up from the city," Sennar called to Rahg. "If we can hold out long enough, they'll get here."

Rahg nodded, but Sennar's news gave him no confidence; they were already swamped by Victas, and now Wolfen and Sethians were advancing. *It will all be over soon.*

~

*I*azzo was not caught ill-prepared. He had planted a dozen probes to warn him of attacks from the most likely places; most likely, not most logical. Aentarra was anything but logical. At best, she was unpredictable as the wind—at best. Iazzo sent a sensing probe to measure the force of the attack; it was feeble. Not what he would have presumed her to do.

Iazzo laughed at his own thoughts. 'Presumed' and Aentarra did not belong together in the same phrase. He dispatched a wave of energy to counter the attack, crushing it handily, then searched for her. It disturbed him that she managed to conceal herself so well. Perhaps she had learned some new trick. Suddenly, she appeared as if from nowhere, as if she had only just entered. The Banished One stared, shocked at seeing her dressed like that. Exactly what Aentarra had hoped for; precisely what she had counted on.

In the blink of an eye, a new landscape formed, this one spires of rock interspersed with trees of all kinds. Iazzo searched relentlessly; she could be anywhere.

Aentarra's thought formed a huge boulder out of nothing. No sooner had it appeared than it hurtled toward Iazzo at incredible speed, its thunderous roar filling the air as it accelerated. It stood a full span high and just as wide, a perfect circle.

Iazzo smiled. Aentarra always liked using solid forms. Perhaps not much had changed after all. He dispatched a probe to discover its strength. The probe touched, circled it to uncover any secrets that might lay hidden behind, then transmitted the data to Iazzo who instantly assimilated it.

The wave of energy Iazzo fashioned to counter it was thin, and powerful. Taking up only a hand's width of space, it hovered a half a span above the surface awaiting further instructions. On Iazzo's command, it departed, undulating like a wave of the sea, and rushing headlong into the massive boulder, splitting it in two.

The Banished One's smile was premature, for the two separate pieces continued as if they had a mind of their own, each now back on target and racing toward him. Hurriedly, he constructed a forceful wall of shielded energy and sent it to disrupt the attack. It stood a full span high, like Aentarra's weapon, and when they met, hers was crushed.

A smile again began to form on Iazzo's lips, began, but never finished. The echoes of Aentarra's laughter stopped that; stopped it cold. *She is toying with me,* Iazzo thought, and, he worried.

~

*M*ore Entirians had come to reinforce Rahg but the Victas and Wolfen alone still outnumbered them. The Entirians fought boldly and bravely, and even though most were now armed with swords or axes taken from the dead, they stood at a severe disadvantage in fighting prowess. *Time is what we need,* Rahg thought. *If only we could have time to regain our powers. Powers.* He had seen Darstan shoot fire. *By all the gods, how did it come to be that Darstan possessed powers?*

The thrust of a sword from an enormously tall Wolfen quickly seized Rahg's attention. He slipped to the side but could not avoid the blade, and it slashed deeply into his upper arm. "Gods!" he screamed, and countered with a lunge. The Wolfen parried and once more attacked, wielding his sword in one hand and the Wolfen long-knife in the other.

Rahg jumped backward, sucking in his stomach to barely avoid a gutting. Again, the Wolfen advanced. Rahg stumbled over a stone, falling to the ground. The Wolfen leapt to finish him off. As the blade of his sword came rushing down, Rahg strained, finally managing to weave a shield that deflected it. He could not maintain it though, and now the danger came from the Wolfen's other hand, the long-knife.

Aenaila had no powers remaining. She raised the sword and brought the blade crashing down onto the Wolfen's head; he fell instantly. Rahg nodded his appreciation, but had no time for words; his left arm bled profusely and the Entirians guarding the left flank were being massacred by a giant Victa. With some difficulty, Rahg rose to face the new challenge.

Kraffr cut through the Entirians like a wolf through a flock of lambs, his only thought to get to the village boy; that had been their goal. He wore a shield on his left arm and wielded a Victa short sword in his right. The blade struck an Entirian's left arm, nearly severing it; the thrust to the stomach finished him. Kraffr roared onward, straight for Rahg.

"Guard Camissa," Rahg shouted to Aenaila. "Please?"

Aenaila nodded. "I will try," she said, and when Rahg left, Aenaila entered the Planes of the Mind in search of Camissa.

Rhaven danced and whirled and twisted through the field of battle, slicing and cutting and stabbing. An enormous number of the enemy lay dead. No matter how many they sent against him, he destroyed them. The warriors feared his blade; it glistened bloody-red, and emerald-green, not the color of steel, and fresh blood always replaced whatever dripped from its hungry edge. Rhaven himself looked like something from a nightmare. Blood ran from his neck, and face, and several places on his chest.

A pack of Wolfen ran toward Rhaven. He thought of retreating but opted to stay and kill as many as he could. He whirled his blades through the air, their steel whistling death to come when, suddenly, Kella appeared at the Wolfens' flank. They howled, scurrying toward the cover of the forest to the right with the giant vargel snapping at their backsides. Only three Wolfen remained to face Rhaven.

Rhaven screamed a battle cry and swung the Sword of Mikkellana. It struck the first Wolfen's blade and cut it in two. The Wolfen were more astonished than Rhaven. He seized that advantage, quickly slaying all three with only a few more strokes of the sword. It now felt like nothing in his hand, like he swung only his arm when he fought.

How had it cut through that sword?

More Wolfen and a whole band of Sethians were almost upon him. *It should be over today,* he thought, and only prayed to take as many as he could with him. *I wish Argus were here; he would have loved this battle.*

❧

Inside the Planes of the Mind, Camissa stood trapped, a mute witness to a battle for the ages. She had always used this place as a refuge, a safe haven of retreat when sadness overwhelmed her or confusion pricked her mind. It was a playground, a place to express creative thoughts, and artistic urges. Here, she could paint the world in her own colors, build cities the way she would like to see them, and tear them down again with a moment's notice.

Never before had she encountered anyone else here; Camissa thought it to be a place of her's alone; a place of solitude somewhere in the deepest recesses of her own mind. Now she knew differently. Two immortals were using her world to do battle; all Camissa hoped for was to remain uninvolved. She had created a line of trees with heavy brush to conceal herself, praying to avoid detection by remaining still, and quiet. Camissa jumped, startled at the sound of a voice behind her. It was the girl who had come with Darstan. *What is she doing here?*

Aenaila approached with palms raised upward. Camissa strained to hear her voice, barely a whisper. "My name is Aenaila. I am a friend of Darstan, and have come to help Rahg. Do not be afraid."

Camissa had not realized that her anxiety had become so obvious, though even Aenaila's presence helped to calm her. She felt a noticeable decrease in tension. "I'm trapped," Camissa said. "I can't get out. Do you know this place well? How can we escape?"

Aenaila heard the crashing sound of matter impacting and started with fright. She too, felt nervous about being here with immortals. She had played here often, but only played, never battle. Somewhere in this strange world, the Banished One was doing battle with another immortal and Aenaila wanted nothing to do with it. She grabbed Camissa's hand. "Come, let's leave this place."

Aenaila tried, but failed to gain egress. Anxiety filled her. "Help me, Camissa. Let's both concentrate as one." Aenaila closed her eyes, and together they sought a way out, but to no avail. The exit was closed to them.

"This has never happened to me before," Aenaila said. "Have you ever experienced this?" All Camissa could do was shake her head. As Aenaila gave thought to their predicament, another collision occurred; this one nearby. Aenaila crept through the trees and up to the ridge, poking her head over to catch sight of the source of disturbance. In the valley below stood Iazzo, fire and lightning erupting from his hands, like the eye of a storm.

Camissa slipped in alongside Aenaila and together they watched as the two immortals fought. "That's Aentarra," Camissa whispered.

Aenaila shivered. "If that is true, then we may be lost. With someone else we could have prayed for a victory over the Banished One as a means of gaining safe passage out of here, but with Aentarra—"

Camissa stopped her. "She helped us, saved us from sinking at sea." Camissa's explanation did little to soothe Aenaila's feelings, or convince her of Aentarra's beneficence.

"That one is mad. From all I have ever heard, she cannot be trusted."

~

*I*azzo searched, scanned the false images of mountains and woodlands for any indication of her presence. She lay out there somewhere, waiting to attack. A faint glimmer of light, tucked deep into the recesses of a steep hillside, caught his eye. He unleashed a barrage of power, though careful not to let loose so much as to be dangerous should he succeed in taking her completely unprepared.

Iazzo knew all too well the rules that applied here. Energy he created that remained unchallenged would return to strike him with a vengeance. He would have no recourse; he could do nothing to combat energy created by himself. Iazzo tensed, anticipating the collision. When his force met with resistance, he cringed. Aentarra met the challenge. Iazzo continued his search, patiently scanning every length of ground. He had time; time meant nothing to the ageless, and it especially had no meaning here.

A deafening roar disrupted Iazzo's concentration. One of the sensing probes exploded, then another went off, then a half a dozen erupted. Iazzo spun to face the assault. The equivalent of an entire mountain raced toward him. He dispatched a quantitative probe to measure the true strength of the attack. When he got the report, sweat rolled off his brow. "She is mad!"

When the first shield fell, Iazzo worked feverishly to erect more of them. He built shields in all shapes and sizes, experimenting with radical designs, hoping to slow the advance, but shield after shield fell to the fury of Aentarra's onslaught, like tiles in a children's game. Iazzo howled a death cry as the final shield succumbed to the juggernaut, sweeping over him, eliminating his mind. His body fell limp to the ground, then disappeared.

Aentarra cursed when she saw Iazzo fall. "Fool! Weak, pitiful fool." She had not anticipated such an easy victory, or such a weak defense. Now she worried about the repercussions; her assault yet contained a vast amount of energy. She worried she had made a grievous error.

When Iazzo's body disappeared, Aentarra dropped the images she created; the landscapes and scenery vanished, leaving the Planes of the Mind a vast field of emptiness—empty with the exception of one copse of trees. The colorful dot of greenery drew Aentarra's attention like a beacon in the night. A faint glimmer of hope ran wildly through her veins. She dispersed with Camissa's camouflage without so much as a flicker of exertion leaving them alone in the emptiness.

Camissa and Aenaila stood, hovering in midair, Camissa coyly beginning the conversation. "My thanks once again, Lady Aentarra."

Aentarra never let go of her defenses, keeping her body enveloped in a shield and her eyes fixed on both of them at once. "How is it you came to be here?"

Aentarra's head darted back and forth, as if searching for something. "Never mind. We have no time for pleasantries or explanations. You must create the strongest shields you can muster. There will be a wave of energy coming soon, from there." With a nod of her head, Aentarra gestured to the north. "You must construct the most powerful force you can, and send it against that wave." Aentarra created a small hill at a great distance to the north. "Use that as a benchmark for placing your shields."

Aenaila was distrusting, but Aentarra convinced her to cooperate. She and Camissa used all their energy to produce a formidable wall of shields. "There, it is done," Aenaila said with a sigh, and only a slight degree of suspicion. "Now, tell us how we might leave this place."

"You can't leave."

"What are you saying?" Camissa shrieked.

Aentarra studied the two women. "You really don' know, do you? To be brief, I foolishly overestimated the strength of my foe, the former, Iazzo, and created an excessive amount of energy for my assault."

Aentarra focused on them. "And though you will never need the advice, when battling in the Planes of the Mind one must be very careful of how much energy is expended during battle, for whatever energy is dispatched against a foe must be used or it will come back and strike at its own creator." Aentarra moaned. "Unfortunately, I cannot stop it myself. Oh, and your pitiful shields won't stop it; however, it might slow it down enough so that I will suffer less damage."

"What will become of us?" Aenaila asked suspiciously, though she felt certain she knew the answer.

"You will probably die." With her final words, Aentarra departed.

Kraffr burst through the last of the Entirian defenders. Red blood covered his green-scaled body, and a glaze filmed his black, slitted eyes. The large Victa headed straight toward Camissa. Rahg rushed to intercept him.

Rahg's first blow was a mighty, two-handed assault. Kraffr caught Rahg's sword with the shield he wore on his arm, though the force from the blow caused the Victa to reel slightly to the side. He hissed loudly, viciously returning the attack. Rahg had no shield, only a Wolfen long-knife in his left hand, and with his upper arm cut so badly, it was increasingly difficult to do anything useful with that.

The Victa's blade rushed toward the left side of Rahg's body. He maneuvered to a position that allowed him to intercept the attack with his own sword. Kraffr grunted, then resumed the attack.

Rahg repositioned himself on the upper side of the hill, at the least, a better offensive stance. He and Kraffr traded blows back and forth, each inflicting minor wounds, but succeeding mostly in wearing away at Rahg's stamina.

Kraffr charged ahead, swinging his blade and pushing with his shield to deflect any advance. Rahg stepped back, then back some more. He managed to steal a quick glance behind him and noticed that a line of battle was being fought just a few lengths back.

If he backs me up to there, I'm as good as dead.

Rahg felt for his powers. He had recovered a small portion of them. At the same time, he recalled the lessons Tobias had given him about fighting. 'Be defensive. Let the other person make a mistake, then, take advantage of it.'

Rahg thought about constructing a shield to buy time, but opted instead to weave a small arm-shield like Kraffr's, though the Victa would not be able to see it. Rahg planned quickly in his head. At a propitious moment, Rahg dropped the long-knife, as if by accident, and formed the shield.

Kraffr attacked. When the Victa's blade impacted the shield it stopped with such suddenness that Kraffr nearly lost control of his grip. For the briefest moment, the large Victa stared blankly, taken aback.

Rahg thrust his blade into the Victa's leg, then as Kraffr lowered his shield arm, Rahg thrust again. This time, the thrust went upward into the Victa's neck, driving it through the bone in his skull. Kraffr hissed a death moan that sent panic through his fellow lizards. Inspired by his unexpected victory over the giant lizard, Rahg became invigorated and rushed madly into the fray. The rest of the Victas turned and fled; once again, the momentum in the battle shifted.

~

A crushing, grinding sound demanded Camissa's immediate attention; she turned to see what remained of their shields fall to the wave of power that Aentarra created. The shields proved to be an insignificant defense, and Aentarra's assault pressed onward. Camissa stood awe-struck, but she didn't linger and wait for death. "Aenaila, perhaps we can escape now that our shields are gone. We must try."

The mountain of energy advanced rapidly, destined to crush them. Aenaila seized Camissa's hand. "Now!" she screamed. "Try now." Together, they concentrated on escaping the Planes of the Mind.

Just as the enormous wall of force struck, Aenaila disappeared; Camissa was right behind her, but the edge of the power caught her. She reeled from the impact.

Aenaila looked down at Camissa, prone on the ground; she knelt and rolled her over, staring into a blank expression. Aenaila tried gathering enough power to attempt a healing, but she was spent; nothing would come.

Aentarra heard the crushing and grinding of her force as it struck the shield and she saw the feeble defense fall to her wave of power. She sent a probe to determine the strength remaining in that wave of power. *Pitiful beings. How dare they enter here with so little power?* A sigh escaped Aentarra's lips when the report concluded. She braced herself for the collision. It would be a horrific impact. One she might not survive.

It struck with ferocity. Intent on the destruction of everything in its path the immutable force crashed furiously into Aentarra. She screamed when it struck, using all her will to concentrate on not submitting, not succumbing to its power. Aentarra was swept away, tumbling over and over like a pebble caught in a tidal wave. She began to feel light-headed and distraught; despair toiled diligently to overtake her mind, but she fought it.

She focused her thoughts on stopping the penetration. *I'll not allow it to invade my mind. Not my mind.* The power loomed undeniable, irresistible, yet Aentarra struggled, refused to admit defeat. Through the emptiness it dragged her battered body until it showed signs of weakening.

She felt the first stab of power as it pricked her inner consciousness. Mustering all her wits, she rushed to defend against it, screaming her denial though no one could hear. Again the force struck her, this time from another angle—and again, Aentarra darted to the breach, a fresh array of defenses poised to thwart the invasive force.

The attacks came with more frequency until she could no longer meet the challenge of the assaults. Inevitably, the defenses halted, allowing Aentarra's own destructive power to enter her mind. It faded into nothingness just as it breached her final rebuke.

Aentarra's once-vibrant body lay limp, floating in a void of empty space, leaving her calculating mind to flicker like a distant star.

❧

On the plateau north of Sunnara, the struggle for victory yet ensued. J'ag Tem managed to inspire enough fear into the Victas so that they rejoined the battle. The advantage of victory had shifted back and forth several times this day, and right now fortune favored the Sethians; their troops were fresher, stronger, their foes weakened.

All except the one called 'black death.' Does he never tire?

J'ag Tem issued new orders to his next in command and removed his sword from its sheath; he longed to personally join the fray.

With a sound like heavy thunder, the sky cracked open, rent apart like a piece of tattered cloth. What had been daylight seemed dark. On the field of battle all warriors covered their eyes. The fighting ceased.

Mikkellana's voice demanded attention from everyone. "Your leader is dead," she announced to the Sethians, and Wolfen and Victas. "Iazzo lives no more. Look at him." Her tone grew stronger, more authoritative. They turned to stare at the lifeless form of Iazzo. "You have no hope of victory, no chance to survive. If even one resists, I shall destroy the lot. Or, if you prefer, I could transport you to safety."

Mikkellana hovered in the sky like a great goddess. The Victas cowered. Even the Wolfen and Sethians trembled with uncertainty. J'ag Tem convinced them to accept the terms she offered. "We will forsake the battle, Great Lady. Our fate rests in your hands." Mikkellana alit near the corpse of Iazzo, a shield enveloping her for protection.

J'ag Tem ordered his men to cease fighting and gather about him. They would be traveling as they did with Iazzo. Mikkellana touched J'ag Tem and another Sethian; when the contacts were complete, she Shifted.

Rahg ran to Camissa, but halted when the glow from something on the ground caught his eye, a blinding reflection from an object inside Marro's head, split like a rotten melon. He stooped to pick it up, cautiously. It felt warm to the touch, sent a shiver through his body. Rahg checked to see if anyone was watching, then quickly wiped it clean of blood and placed it inside the hold of his cloak. He quickly raced to Camissa's side. "What's wrong with her?"

Again, the air cracked, and shimmered, opening a passage for Mikkellana. "I am Mikkellana," she said.

The Entirians bowed reverently; no one spoke. Mikkellana glanced at the wounded and the dead. "The battle is over. Take your wounded to the city and tend to them." Mikkellana finished and turned to Aenaila. "Where is Aentarra? I know she was here."

Aenaila felt cowed by her presence. "She fought the Banished One in the Mind. I...I do not think she escaped." Mikkellana's face grew red with fury. She erected a shield about herself for security, and all the while issuing commands. "You!" she shouted to Rhaven.

Rahg almost laughed. If it had not been for his concern over Camissa he would have. No one shouted at Rhaven like that.

"Protect me while I am gone," Mikkellana said.

Blood covered most of Rhaven's body, much of it his own, but he held himself like a warrior fresh for battle. "I will guard you, Lady. None will approach." With that vow, Mikkellana sunk into the Planes of the Mind in search of her sister.

The Planes stood empty, always did unless someone created something there, yet, empty as they were, it could take days, even longer, to locate someone. *I have no time for delays. Aentarra must be found.*

Mikkellana concentrated, dispatching hundreds of probes, their sole purpose to locate Aentarra. Within moments, Mikkellana found her, seeing her body suspended in the void. Mikkellana guided Aentarra safely out, back to her body in Entiria where she reappeared on a remote spot in the far western reaches of the island atop a steep cliff. Instantly, Mikkellana noted the location, then proceeded to her own physical form being guarded by Rhaven.

She Shifted to where Aentarra lay, and then returned with Aentarra in her arms, to stand next to Rhaven and Rahg. "I must have silence while I attempt to heal her. Every moment she remains unconscious the shield in Sethia weakens."

Aenaila moved closer in an attempt to observe so that she might learn some of Mikkellana's techniques. Healing had always interested her.

For long periods of time, Mikkellana worked on Aentarra, constantly doing odd things with her hands. Often, an eerie blue light emanated from Mikkellana's fingertips only to be absorbed by Aentarra's body. They had lost the light of day sometime back, though Mikkellana kept the illumination constant with a strange type of shield that glowed like fire.

"What about Camissa?" Rahg asked.

"I am almost done. I must restore Aentarra first." The finality of Mikkellana's tone silenced Rahg. After a few more moments, Aentarra moved, moaning softly. Mikkellana stood; she had been on her knees for an exceptionally long time with no respite.

Within moments, Aentarra stirred, then stood, though her legs wobbled and her voice quavered. "Sister, I presume a debt of gratitude is owed you, or at the very least that you believe so." Aentarra's words had lost none of their cutting edge from her near-death experience.

"You have made yourself clear, Aentarra. You may take your leave."

"Your tone appeared threatening. Or did I misjudge?" A devious smile lit Aentarra's face. "Yes, I must have miscalculated. You would no more harm me than I would you. If I die, Lukaan goes free."

Aentarra's smile became almost demonic. "But then, you were aware of that, weren't you?" Aentarra's sarcastic laughter bit at Mikkellana. "Yes, you were aware, sister. If not for the shield you would have left me gasping for breath like you did Ronell at the Battle of Grannameer."

Aentarra's tone betrayed the anger inside her. "Do you still remember, sister? Or have you managed to hide those unpleasantries with sweet, veiled memories of your few good deeds?"

"You may leave, Aentarra. Go now, before I choose to scold you in front of others like the child you are."

Aentarra fumed but there was nothing she could do. She was too weak to consider battle and Mikkellana was too strong. "I believe I shall take leave of you. I have much to attend to, though I am certain we will see each other again. And soon, Mikkellana. Soon." Without another word, Aentarra vanished.

Mikkellana sensed the air to be certain Aentarra had gone, then busied herself with the prospect of healing. I shall need to tend to Camissa first—if she can be healed.

"Why didn't you capture her?" Rahg asked.

"If you were hunting and found yourself with no arrows, would you still pursue the bear, or the mountain cat?

Besides, she is much too important to dispose of, Rahg. Just as you are important, so too, is Aentarra. If I killed her, Lukaan and the Banished Ones would be free within the day." Mikkellana stopped to stare at Rahg and the others. "Do you realize what that means? If they escape, the world is doomed. Not possibly, not probably. Doomed."

Mikkellana knelt beside Camissa and placed her hands on Camissa's head. She looked up at Rahg one more time before proceeding. "Iazzo was the weakest of the Banished Ones, a worm under Lukaan's heel. Any of the others would have been much more difficult to stop. Tirzinitzia's battle plans would have proved more deadly than his, and Melissara would have destroyed you without so much as a second thought."

Rahg felt her eyes bore into him. "And Lukaan would make Melissara appear merciful. You would beg to be killed by her. That is why I need Aentarra, at least for now. And that is why you must fulfill the prophecy. The Messenger must be stopped and the shield in Sethia must be strengthened. Now leave me undisturbed while I attempt to cure your friend."

Rahg stepped away from Mikkellana to allow her more room. He didn't want anything to interfere with her healing Camissa.

Camissa lay upon the ground, her breaths coming with difficulty. Mikkellana's hands touched her head, sending probes deep into Camissa's mind to uncover the root of the problems. She moved her hands gently over Camissa's head, a faint blue light penetrating her flesh. Mikkellana worked unceasingly for a long time, examining every part of Camissa's mind. Finally, she stood, looking worn and ragged herself. "It is done," Mikkellana said plainly. "At least, what can be done."

Rahg appeared worried. "What do you mean? Will she be all right?"

Mikkellana reached for Rahg's bloody arm while she formulated a response. "There may be powers she will not be able to use, at least for a while. Some powers she may have lost forever. But physically, she will be fine. She will suffer no repercussions."

Rahg jumped as Mikkellana's powers healed the deep laceration on his upper arm. He felt weakened, sapped of strength, yet the wound had healed. It was an odd sensation.

Mikkellana looked about at those who had gathered. Those wounded the worst would receive the immediate attention. Rhaven was a mass of assorted blood, with several wounds yet dripping.

"You, warrior." Mikkellana called to him. "Come here and be healed." Rhaven started toward her, and collapsed. Mikkellana soon healed his serious wounds, reserving some of her own energy by not healing the minor ones. "They will heal themselves," she explained to Rahg. "Find me any with deadly wounds and bring them here. The others must wait."

Throughout the night Mikkellana worked, healing all those she could, all with wounds of a serious nature. As dawn approached she saw Darstan limping badly from the knife wound in his leg. He could barely walk. "Come here, Darstan. Allow me to heal you."

Darstan looked at her but made no move in her direction. "I will be fine, Lady. I've had worse wounds that have healed on their own." To Rahg's surprise Mikkellana did not press the issue.

Mikkellana turned back to Rhaven; he was awake, though resting. A warm smile lit her face as she stared into his eyes. "Guard him well, my warrior friend. It is why I blessed you with my sword."

Rhaven smiled in return. "I owe you my debt, lady of mystery. You seem to always be about when I require healing." Mikkellana's laughter was light and warm. "Be warned, I may not be at hand the next time. I suggest instead that you practice more and stay clear of danger."

Rahg and Darstan finally found each other, though they had no time to speak privately, and joined the others who had gathered around trading stories of the day's battle. Tobias, as usual, had managed to draw most of the attention with his rendition of the events, holding the audience of Entirians captive with his flavorful speech. Mikkellana approached the group, singling out Sennar. "Come with me, old man."

The old sea captain looked strangely at her as if questioning her choice, but he followed her. Sennar followed her for a short walk until they entered a small grove of trees, one of only a few still standing after the devastating fires. The old sea captain was curious more than anything else. *What does she want with me?*

Once they were completely out of sight of the others, Mikkellana stopped and turned, staring straight into Sennar's eyes. "I once made a promise to you."

Sennar stared back at her, eyebrows raised.

"Perhaps this will help," Mikkellana said, and adopted the guise of the old healer woman that she had used on so many occasions. Recognition came instantly to Sennar's eyes, now wide in astonishment. "You?" he nearly shouted. "You."

Mikkellana nodded. "You upheld your part of the arrangement. I see no reason to wait until your return to Genda to uphold mine."

Sennar's heart raced; shock took control of his body. "You're... you mean to heal me?"

Mikkellana smiled broadly, but her hands were already at work, the strange blue light perforating every pore of the old man's burnt body. He felt like screaming, but he clenched his teeth and restrained himself. His body felt once again like it was on fire, but this time the sensation was ecstasy. Sennar closed his eyes and imagined the transformations taking place. He did not wish to look until it was all over with, but he could feel it happening.

It only took a few moments, then Mikkellana's warm voice pried his eyes open. "It is done," she said. "Our pact is concluded. Perhaps in the future we will have more business."

Sennar's eyes darted first to his hand. Where once there had been only a charred mass of burnt flesh, now a hand was there, a real hand. Quickly, he used his new hand to feel his side and chest; the flesh felt soft, and sensitive, and new.

Sennar smiled. For the first time in many years, he could actually feel the skin move on that one side of his face, and for the first time in as many years, Sennar had reason to smile. Tears swelled in his eyes.

"My Lady," he fell to his knees in adulation, but Mikkellana stopped him. "No. It is not your worship I wish, simply your loyalty." The old sea captain rose at her command, looking straight at her. "My Good Lady, anything you ever wish, it is yours. If it can be done, I'll do it."

Mikkellana smiled. "Remember that, Sennar. I will see you again." With that, Mikkellana departed to return to where Rahg stood. Sennar remained alone for a while, admiring his newfound body.

Mikkellana approached Rahg. "Do you know what you must do?"

Rahg looked at her with trepidation. "If you mean—"

"I mean this." She reached into her sleeve and extracted a scroll, old and worn. "This is the prophecy that the shera read to you. This is your destiny. Prepare to follow it, or prepare to die."

"Why did you let those Wolfen and Sethians go? Why let them live so they could fight us another day?"

She wrapped a shield around his midsection and tightened her hold. Rahg choked, gasping for air. Mikkellana noticed the dangerous look in Darstan's eyes and enveloped him in a shield also, though only a protective one, not one to crush.

She let Rahg struggle until he was almost devoid of air, then released her hold. "Play no child's games with me, boy. Anger me, and you might well regret it. You might well regret your very life." Mikkellana took a breath to calm herself. "As to the Wolfen, you will never fight them again."

Rahg could barely speak. "What do you mean?"

"I had to conserve energy so I could heal. I put them on an island that is not much more than a rock, though there is water. Before long they will be eating each other. Not pleasant, but it had to be done."

Rahg gulped, fear stuck in his throat. He recalled what Aentarra said about Mikkellana leaving someone to die, gasping for breath.

If these are the good ones, Mikkellana and Aentarra? Then what are the others like? And what, by all the gods, is Lukaan like, to instill such fear in Mikkellana and Aentarra?

Mikkellana caught Rahg looking at her from the corner of his eye. "And don't think you can hide from me, boy. I know where you go, and even where you think about going. And remember—you are oath-sworn to me."

When she said that Rahg nearly collapsed.

Mikkellana's thin smile taunted him. "Yes, oath-sworn. Or did you think I would forget? It was in Pomanda, do you recall?" Mikkellana didn't wait for an answer; she could see it in his eyes. "Yes, I see that you do. I will call the debt in some day. Some day soon, I suspect." Rahg raised his head to ask her a question, but Mikkellana vanished.

RETURNING HOME

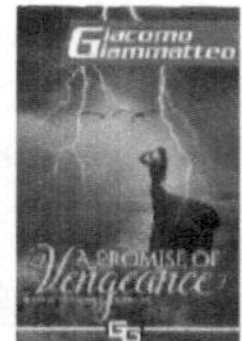

"Hurry, Darstan," Aenaila called. "Everyone needs to rest. And I need help getting Camissa back to the city. She is still not well, and that worries me. She should have healed like everyone else."

"I'll only be a moment." Darstan shouted back to her. "I just want to see Rahg."

"Go on," Wisp said. "I'll help with Camissa."

Darstan limped over to Rahg, blood stained his clothes at the arms, leg and chest. Bandages had been applied, and Mikkellana had tried to convince him to accept a healing, but he refused, opting to limp instead. Rahg fared no better; his left arm had been burned and he had received a deep slash on the upper part. Mikkellana had healed the cut, but the rest yet ached. He felt certain she had left the pain on purpose.

"When I saw your arm, Rahg, I thought you would lose it. Luckily, Mikkellana was able to heal it." Darstan frowned, staring down at his own missing limb.

Rahg tried to ease the stress. "At least we survived. Before the battle I wouldn't have bet on it."

"It did seem daunting, Rahg. Even when we got here." They embraced, laughing to relieve the tension.

"By the gods, there's so much to tell you, Dar. And so much to ask. What happened? How did you escape? Where's Gregor? And what happened to—"

"It happened in Sethia. I guess we both have a lot to tell each other. The last time we were together neither one of us had powers; now, I shoot fire from a stump where my hand was, and you make shields from nothing but air."

"It's called weaving, Darstan. When you make a shield you weave it." Rahg paused. "But is it for the good, Dar? Or is it evil? Sometimes I just don't know." They both stood in silence for a moment, then Rahg spoke again. "There's something I want to do. If you agree."

"You don't need my consent to do anything."

"For this I do. Come, I'll tell you." Rahg took Darstan by the arm, and as they walked toward Sunnara, he explained his intentions.

"Aenaila can help us, Rahg. She can get us there and back by the time you eat a meal. That's how we got here. I came here from Khatara."

Rahg appeared astonished. "She's that strong?"

Darstan laughed, thinking back to Khatara when he first met Aenaila. "She nearly killed me the first time we met. She's much stronger than we are. Much stronger."

Rahg's excitement was building. "She can travel then, like the immortals?"

Darstan nodded. "They call it Shifting, but yes, she can do that. All we need do is be able to form a perfect picture for her. A place where we know every blade of grass, and each bump in the ground."

"The tree stump," Rahg shouted, "where we practiced arrows."

Darstan thought for a moment, picturing the spot in his mind. *A perfect recollection,* he thought. *The image is clear.* "That should do. I'll ask Aenaila. Even though she doesn't like to do this, I think she will for you, just this once."

~

*A*enaila held both their hands and concentrated, focusing on the images she received from the two beside her. Once clear in her own mind, she Shifted, reappearing atop a rocky knoll outside the village of Twin Forks. Her legs faltered, but Darstan was there to support her.

"Lean on my shoulder," Darstan said, offering himself to her.

Momentarily, Aenaila's head cleared and she stared out over the village. She noticed the tear in Darstan's eye, but pretended not to. *No need in embarrassing him,* she thought, and held her gaze in the opposite direction. Rahg, she observed, had no tears, but the grim expression and firm set of his jaw did nothing to hide the anger, and hurt.

Slowly they descended from the knoll, walking toward a small frame house nestled between trees at the end of the valley. Rahg stopped to look into the barn, then marched to the front stoop. A large supply of wood lay under the eaves; good, seasoned wood that Rahg had split not so long ago. The front door stood open, and a shutter banged noisily against the bedroom window. The wind whistled through the house from front to back. It made it seem cold. Rahg's memories were always of a warm house, with a hot fire burning and the aroma of something good cooking in the kitchen. Darstan started up the steps to go inside. Rahg grabbed his arm, holding him back, his voice harsh. "Just do it, Darstan. Burn it."

Aenaila grabbed hold of Darstan. "Why?"

Rahg never flinched. "It's something we must do, Aenaila. Darstan and

I discussed it, and we both agreed. Our old life is over." Rahg stared one last time at the house he shared with Darstan, and Magmar. He pictured Magmar standing on the porch, calling them for supper, or chores; he pictured Darstan and he running off to join Eru and Tomas in the town; and he pictured Timor and Lanna grazing in the lush green pasture beyond. "Burn it, Darstan. Now."

The flames roared out of Darstan's missing limb and raced through the empty home. Instantly, the house became an inferno, fire erupted from every room; from every window flames leaped high into the air, and figures made of flames danced on the roof, spreading the fiery destruction. Rahg watched unemotionally until the final collapse, when nothing stood. Nothing but smoke, and ash, and burning timber.

Darstan's eyes were red with the pain of past memories, memories now seemingly lost. Aenaila comforted him. It felt good to have her here, Darstan realized, and at the same time it occurred to him that Rahg had no one. He went to his brother to console, to help him forget.

Rahg stood motionless, still staring at the ashes where once his house had been. He turned to face Darstan as he approached. There was no redness in his eyes; he had not cried. Rahg shed no tears.

"Let's go, Darstan. We're finished here."

ACKNOWLEDGMENTS

Many thanks to my wonderful long-time friends, Elizabeth Hull, Jeanne Haskin, and May-Lin Iverson for being true in their feedback. And to Brian Johnson, my cousin, my sister, Rose, and my daughter-in-law Missy. You have helped me make the book better.

ABOUT THE AUTHOR

Giacomo Giammatteo is the author of gritty crime dramas about murder, mystery, and family. He also writes non-fiction books including the No Mistakes Careers series, No Mistakes Publishing, No Mistakes Grammar, and No Mistakes Writing.

When Giacomo isn't writing, he's helping his wife take care of the animals on their sanctuary. At last count they had forty-five animals—eleven dogs, a horse, six cats, and twenty-six pigs.

Oh, and one crazy—and very large—wild boar, who takes walks with Giacomo every day and happens to also be his best buddy.

nomistakespublishing.com
gg@giacomog.com

You can see all of my books here.

And you can buy them on the platform of your choice here.

Nonfiction :

No Mistakes Resumes, Book I of No Mistakes Careers

No Mistakes Interviews, Book II of No Mistakes Careers

Misused Words, No Mistakes Grammar, Volume I

Misused Words for Business, No Mistakes Grammar, Volume II

More Misused Words, No Mistakes Grammar, Volume III

No Mistakes Writing, Volume I—Writing Shortcuts

How to Publish an eBook, No Mistakes Publishing, Volume I

How to Format an eBook, No Mistakes Publishing, Volume II

eBook Distribution, No Mistakes Publishing, Volume III

Uneducated

Whiskers and Bear—Volume I of the Life on the Farm Series (sent to editor)

Fiction:

Friendship & Honor Series:

Murder Takes Time

Murder Has Consequences

Murder Takes Patience

Murder Is Invisible

Blood Flows South Series:

A Bullet For Carlos: A Connie Gianelli Mystery

Finding Family, a Novella

A Bullet From Dominic

A Promise of Vengeance (Fantasy)

Redemption Series:

Necessary Decisions: A Gino Cataldi Mystery

Old Wounds

Promises Kept, the Story of Number Two

Premeditated

OTHER BOOKS COMING SOON:

You can always see the current and coming-soon books on my website.

Fiction:

My first fantasy, and the first book in a four-book series—the Rules of Vengeance. (Three are already written and the fourth is being outlined.)

Memories for Sale (mystery/sf)

The Joshua Citadel (SF novella)

Nonfiction:

No Mistakes Writing, How to Write a Bestseller

Children's Books:

No Mistakes Grammar for Kids, Volume I—Much and Many (sent to editor)

No Mistakes Grammar for Kids, Volume II—Lie and Lay (sent to editor)

No Mistakes Grammar for Kids, Volume III—Then and Than (sent to editor)

Shinobi Goes to School—Life on the Farm for kids. (working on illustrations)

Get on the mailing list and you'll be sure to be notified of release dates and sales.

Mailing list

And don't forget to leave a review!

By the way, if you're an author and you liked the formatting in this book, you might consider us for your next book. Information can be obtained here.

www.ingramcontent.com/pod-product-compliance
Lightning Source LLC
Chambersburg PA
CBHW032151180726
48284CB00001B/6